I Saw You
First

Cindy Blake is an American writer living in London with her husband and children.

Also by Cindy Blake

I Saw You First

CINDY BLAKE

POCKET
BOOKS

LONDON · SYDNEY · NEW YORK · TOKYO · SINGAPORE · TORONTO

First published in Great Britain by Simon & Schuster UK Ltd, 1998
This edition first published by Pocket Books, 1999
An Imprint of Simon & Schuster UK Ltd
A Viacom Company

Simon & Schuster UK Ltd
Africa House
64-78 Kingsway
WC2B 6AH

Simon & Schuster Australia
Sydney

A CIP catalogue record for this book is available
from the British Library

ISBN 0-671-01600-8

1 3 5 7 9 10 8 6 4 2

Typeset in Goudy by
Palimpsest Book Production Limited, Polmont, Stirlingshire
Printed and bound in Great Britain by
Caledonian International Book Manufacturing Ltd, Glasgow

This is dedicated, with much love, to my brother, Francis S. Blake, who must be tired of saving my sanity, my sense of humour and my bacon.

Thanks for everything, Fathead. You've got gold.

And I'd also like to thank my agent, Jo Frank, my editor, Clare Ledingham and the Shearer and Sheringham team – intelligent, industrious, creative, wild and crazy party animals.

Chapter 1

'It's a pleasure to have you here, Lisa.'

'It's my pleasure to be here, Mike.'

'Your bestselling book, *I Saw You First*, has made you famous, as we all know. *Newsweek* magazine has called you "The Relationship Guru". You've been on *Oprah*, you've been on *Ricki Lake*, you've helped millions of couples in this country with their problems. What I think the public wants to know, Lisa, is what made you write *I Saw You First*? What inspired you?'

'Well, Mike, I believe that what inspires any book is personal experience. How can anyone write from ignorance? Perhaps someone with an incredible imagination can write a novel about what it's like to be an ant, but that's a rare person, isn't it? I couldn't do it myself. I'm not an ant. I have no idea what an ant's life is like. I know they're very busy little creatures, of course. I know they have those colonies or farms or whatever, but I couldn't possibly get inside an ant's mind. I'm a human – '

Declan Lewis leaned over and whispered in Alison Austin's ear: 'Is she absolutely sure she's not an ant?'

'Shhh,' Alison whispered back. 'You're supposed to be paying attention.'

' – and Mike, what I know about is human emotion. I know what

1

it's like to be in a relationship. I know what it's like to be in a marriage. I know the problems, the difficulties – I've lived them myself. So I feel qualified to write about them, to help other people come to terms with relationships, to help those people make those relationships *work*.'

'And you *have* helped people, haven't you, Lisa?'

'I have, Mike. Yes. You wouldn't believe the response I've received. I get hundreds of letters a day. Telephone calls. Faxes. All of them saying: "Lisa, thank you. What you've written has changed my life for the better." In fact, just today, on the way to the studio to speak to you, a woman stopped me on the street. She said: "Lisa, I listen to the audio tape of your book every day on my way to work and I can't bear to get out of the car. I sit in my parking space and I listen, and what you have to say makes so much sense, I keep listening and I get to work late every morning. If I don't finish your book soon, I'll end up losing my job."'

And your mind, Declan said to himself.

'That's a lovely story, Lisa. I hear even Oprah Winfrey was impressed with the advice you give.'

'She was, Mike. She said: "Lisa, what you say in your book is so simple, but so true". And that's the point. I'm not saying anything revolutionary. You don't have to have a high IQ to understand it. It's common sense. But you know something? These days common sense just isn't common. We get all tangled up in complicated theories. We tie ourselves up in knots trying to figure things out because we don't believe anything can be simple any more. I'm here to tell you it *can* be simple. You know, one of my readers wrote to tell me that he'd been reading the book as he was walking around his house and he'd been so stunned by the obvious sense of what I'd written, he'd walked straight into a wall. Can you · believe it?'

'I believe it,' Mike nodded. 'Could you share some of that common sense with us now?'

2

'Of course. But the best way for me to do that is to ask *you* a question, Mike. You're married, I know. Tell me – what's your wife's name?'

'Linda.'

'What do you see, Mike, when you look at Linda now?'

'Well, Lisa, what I see is a fabulous wife and a terrific mother.'

'That's a wonderful response. But Mike, do you really see *her*? Do you see her in the same way you saw her when you two first met?'

'Not exactly. I mean, we've been together for twelve years now. We have two children. Obviously our lives have changed; *we've* changed. It's not as if we were on our first date.'

'There you go. That's exactly my point. What happens between couples, what can eat away at relationships is exactly that kind of thinking. The days, the weeks, the months, the years go by . . . and you lose sight of the person you first saw. You forget, Mike. Day-to-day life wears you down and you forget. What's that wonderful expression? "Today is the first day of the rest of your life." Well, every day with your partner should be the first date of the rest of your relationship.'

Declan put his hand over his mouth to smother a laugh. Alison elbowed him in the ribs. 'Ouch!' he mouthed to her. 'Shut up!' she mouthed back.

'Instead of getting into stultifying patterns of behavior, instead of taking each other for granted, you should concentrate on what you first saw in each other, the reasons you had for falling in love. All those first impulses. You say when you look at Linda that you see a fabulous wife and a wonderful mother. But is that the way she wants to be defined? As wife and mother? What happened to that *woman* who made your heart stall every time you looked at her? The one who made you want to conquer the world?

'Tell me something, Mike – if Linda were to describe you to me, which statement would you prefer? "Mike's a fantastic husband and a great father"? Or: "Mike is the man who makes my heart skip a beat, the man of my dreams"?'

'You've got me there, Lisa. I'd prefer to be called the man of her dreams. But isn't that impossibly romantic after a certain time together?'

How long was this going to go on? Declan wondered. It was supposed to be an advertisement for Lisa's book, but it was already far longer than any advert he'd ever seen on television. And the format was crazy. This man was interviewing Lisa Thomas about what was, after all, only another self-help book with the serious air of a Jeremy Paxman quizzing Tony Blair about his intentions towards the homeless.

The Americans might listen to this endless talk about relationships, but did Lisa really believe the Brits would, too? Was she really so set on making the same kind of commercial – what she called an 'infomercial' – for the British market? It would never work. It just wasn't possible.

'Mike, sustained romance *is* possible. Can you remember when you and Linda first met?'

'Yes. We were at a party. I saw her standing in a corner, talking to a friend of mine. I couldn't take my eyes off her.'

'That's right,' Lisa said, clapping her hands in delight. 'You couldn't take your eyes off her because you saw *her*. And that's what the title of my book is all about. You know when that mountaineer was asked why he climbed Everest and he answered: "Because it was there"? Well, people have never understood where the emphasis goes in that sentence. The emphasis should be on the word "it". "It" is the spiritual feeling he had when he reached the summit. "It" was the essence, the awe-inspiring essence of nature. "Because IT was there." That's why he climbed that mountain. And the emphasis in the title of my book is on the "you". I saw *you* first – the real you, the essence of you.'

*　　*　　*

4

Christina Billings closed her eyes. She couldn't believe what she was seeing and hearing. Were there people in the world who took this psychobabble seriously? The real you? The essence of you? As opposed to what? The fake you? The non-essence of you?

'Any person in love will know what I mean, Mike. It's almost childlike, that first vision you have of your partner. It's uncomplicated, pure. Then, as the relationship develops, the pressures of the world set in and those pressures can blur that picture, can put that vision out of focus. You forget what you first saw, you forget the person and concentrate instead on what role that person plays in your life.'

The lights were off in the huge living room – only the television screen cast its glow. Declan could just make out the woman sitting across from him, the phenomenally long-legged one with the dark hair and the pale face who had closed her eyes: the actor named Toby Something's girlfriend. Christina – that was her name. She and Toby were an unlikely couple on the face of it, Declan decided. Toby looked like the kind of man who would have a blonde sex goddess on his arm. He was wearing a Hugo Boss jacket over a carefully pressed T-shirt and his wavy hair had a professionally tousled appearance. Declan was always suspicious of men who cared about their hair – he didn't know why. It went along with his mistrust of women who wore heavy scent. And anyone who couldn't shake hands with a firm grip.

Toby's girlfriend seemed to be having as much difficulty watching this advert as Declan himself was. Why else would she have closed her eyes? Her hair was messy in an unconsidered, natural way. She'd pulled it back, but stray bits had escaped, bits which framed her thin face. Toby, sitting beside her, was staring at the television, eyes wide open, looking rapt. He had to, Declan supposed. Toby was up for the part of 'Mike' in the British version of this advert. He couldn't afford to

5

laugh out loud or smirk. But then neither, Declan realized, could he.

He was the Marketing and Sales Director of Lisa Thomas' British publisher. It was his job to sell *I Saw You First* in Britain, to make it as successful here as it had been in America. This was the part of his job he most disliked: selling something he didn't believe in himself. Lately he'd found it easier not to read any of the books he was responsible for. He'd trust the editors' judgments and not make his own. Declan felt far more comfortable trying to hype a book he hadn't read than one he had read and hated.

He certainly hadn't read *I Saw You First*, knowing that he would immediately react badly to it. How could anyone tell couples what makes a relationship work? The idea seemed ludicrous to him, despite the fact that these books sold so well. Why should someone else, a total stranger, have any special insight into what makes two people tick? America was full of self-help gurus like Lisa – people who set themselves up as authorities on human behaviour. Declan wished they would stay on their side of the Pond.

Lisa Thomas was convinced her 'infomercial' should be done for the British audience. It had been wildly successful in the States, she'd informed him. 'You must come see it, Declan,' she'd said. 'You won't understand the power of infomercials until you've seen it. You and that girlfriend of yours should come to dinner – we'll play it for you beforehand. Then you'll understand what I'm talking about.'

Well, he'd been polite and accepted her invitation, bringing Alison along with him. And now he was beginning to understand what Lisa Thomas had been talking about. All too well.

'Take my own life, for example, Mike. My husband Skip and I have been married for twelve years. But about two and a half years ago, I have to tell you, we had a crisis. Our marriage was in trouble, big trouble. Why? Because Skip was then working so hard in the corporate world, he didn't have any free time to spend at home. He was a slave to his job, a slave to money.

'He was thirty-four and I was thirty-three and we were acting like a couple of old folks who had lived together for centuries and were taking each other for granted. We didn't talk to each other any more, so we didn't understand what was happening. Skip thought *I* wanted that money he was killing himself to make. He was doing it all for *me*. And *I* thought he was doing it for himself, for his ego. I'd forgotten, you see. I'd forgotten the man I'd first met, the idealistic student who cared about people; the Skip Thomas who, on our second date, stopped by the side of the road to help some poor woman who had a flat tyre.'

Christina Billings opened her eyes and glanced quickly over at Skip Thomas who was perched on the end of the sofa, watching his wife's advert intently. If he had been thirty-four two and a half years ago, he must be thirty-six or thirty-seven now. He had a boyish face for his age. But he looked tense and a little worn down. His shoulders were hunched and he kept reaching up to scratch his short, dark hair. When Lisa mentioned the woman with the flat tyre, Christina noticed that he suddenly smiled. 'What did that woman with the flat tyre look like, Skip?' Christina wanted to ask. 'Was she a babe?'

'And Skip had forgotten who *I* was,' Lisa continued. 'He saw me wearing designer dresses and hosting elegant dinner parties. He'd forgotten the girl he met who wore blue jeans and loved picnics in the park. We had to rediscover each other, Mike. Skip ended up by downshifting; in fact, Skip quit working entirely. We moved to a much smaller house, we concentrated on our relationship, we put the time into each other, so to speak. We saved our marriage. Not everyone can quit work, of course. But everyone *can* seek out a way to re-establish the connection which first brought them together. Now – and I mean this – every day with Skip is like a first date.'

'Lisa, those are inspirational words. And now I think we should hear from some of the couples those words have helped. First we have Jan and Bobby. Their relationship was on the brink of collapse, but Jan picked up a copy of *I Saw You First* and it all turned around. I interviewed them in their house yesterday and I'd like to show you what they had to say . . .'

'That's it, folks,' Lisa Thomas said brightly, switching off the television set with a remote control and switching on the lights in the living room. 'The rest is people giving testimonials. Of course, if you want to watch them—'

'No, no,' Declan Lewis said quickly. 'You must have seen it so many times yourself, you don't need to go through to the end just for our sakes, Lisa. I'm sure we can imagine what the testimonials are like. Thank you so much for showing it to us. It was truly an experience.'

'Well, I thought it would be fun to invite you four Brits along to see it in a relaxed atmosphere – almost as if you were at home. And I said to Skip: "Why don't we have a little dinner party – nothing fancy – and ask Declan and his partner and Toby and his partner?" I hate it when people don't include partners. It's so wrong. An occasion like this is a good opportunity to get to know people.' Lisa, as she was talking, moved toward the television set.

'I wanted you to see this, Toby, because you'll be taking the part of Mike, I hope.' Lisa stopped and focused on Toby Goodyear. 'I wanted you to see how crucial a role it is, and I wanted to meet you, so you'll get a feel of what I'm all about. So of course I want to meet your partner, too.' Her eyes took a brief trip to Christina's face, then to Declan, across the room. 'And I've only met you once, Declan, so of course I wanted to meet you again, outside of the office, and meet your lovely partner Alison as well. They say you should never combine work with pleasure. Well, I say: Nuts to those old crabs!

'Anyway, it's time to eat now.' Lisa reached out to eject the video cassette from the television, but then stopped. 'Are you sure you don't want to see the end? That's where I offer my book, and an audio cassette of my book, *and* a video cassette of this infomercial. Everyone thought I was crazy when I suggested that, you know. "Why would anyone buy a video of an infomercial?" my public relations woman asked. But you'd be amazed, Declan. People don't see it as a commercial, that's the point. They think of it as an interview. A kind of documentary, really. And they send off for it in droves.'

'That's fantastic,' Declan commented, standing up and stretching discreetly. 'That's truly clever marketing. You probably don't need me for your book. You could do the whole job yourself.'

'Oh, I'd never pretend to be a professional,' Lisa smiled at him. 'That's your job. I'm a writer. Full stop.'

'You're fantastic on camera, Lisa,' Toby Goodyear commented, standing up as well. 'You're a natural.'

Why has she chosen *me* for this part? Toby asked himself. Do I look like the kind of actor who would play someone as silly as Mike? And am I *that* desperate to take it? Yes, I'm that desperate. No doubt about it. The last job coming my way was an advert for toothpaste, and I didn't even get that. Some jumped-up little twenty-year-old twat with glasses got it. 'We want someone believable,' the advertising executive had said. 'You're too old and too smooth for toothpaste, Toby.'

What the hell did *that* mean? Did thirty-three-year-olds stop using toothpaste all of a sudden because they were so ancient? And how could he be 'too smooth' for toothpaste? Was he supposed to have turned up for the audition looking like a *Big Issue* seller?

'Thank you for that compliment, Toby,' Lisa said brightly. 'That's sweet of you. I'm nothing like you, of course. I mean, I still feel like fainting every time I hear that voice of yours, that accent. I can't believe you only had those few lines in the *Northanger Abbey* adaptation. I said to Skip right off the bat – he's the one. He's the one to interview me in England.'

'She did.' Skip Thomas nodded in assent. 'Do *you* feel like fainting every time you hear his voice?' he asked, turning to Christina Billings who was sitting on the end of the sofa.

'Yes. Absolutely. Every day with Toby is like a first date, after all.'

Christina couldn't believe she'd said that in such a sarcastic tone. Lisa and Skip Thomas would probably chuck her out of the house – chuck her and Toby both, and then Toby would be apoplectic. These two had asked them to their house for dinner and she'd returned the compliment by smirking at their advertisement. Fantastic, Christina, she said to herself. Bloody brilliant.

'That's just wonderful, Christina.' Lisa clapped her hands together. 'See? I'm right. Romantic bliss *can* last. How long have you two been going out?'

'Almost a year. Nine or ten months,' Toby answered. He didn't dare look over at Christina, in case everyone saw the rage in his eyes. What did she think she was doing? How could she jeopardize this part for him with that sarky comment when she knew how badly he needed the money? Christina kept banging on about how he should believe in himself and wait for the right part to come along, but she had no clue exactly what that meant. Days sitting beside the telephone like some lovestruck teenage girl waiting for the object of her affection to ring. Nights spent watching films or television knowing that someone else had been chosen for those roles, not him. Christina didn't understand rejection. She wasn't a particularly creative person, so she didn't know what it meant to have to put yourself on the line continually. She couldn't comprehend that sometimes it was absolutely necessary to grovel.

Toby Goodyear concentrated on his hostess, his future employer, his interviewee – the irrepressibly bubbly Lisa Thomas.

She had remained standing in front of the tube, as if she were still on it, addressing her audience. She was a bundle, a tiny little blonde dynamo dressed in jeans, a plaid cotton shirt and trainers. Toby could picture her setting off with a group of lumberjacks, heaving the axe over her shoulder and whistling cheerfully. Who was the leader of the Seven Dwarfs? Was it Doc? Yes. Well, Lisa was the female Doc, mixed with the female Happy. She had an omnipresent grin, a truly disconcerting cheerfulness. What actress would play Lisa in a film? The answer to that one was too easy – the young Doris Day.

Toby found it almost impossible to visualize her in a designer suit, presiding over elegant dinner parties. At the same time, he realized she was immensely successful and also immensely rich. This house she and her husband had rented in Pimlico was huge. It came complete with marble floors and antique French furniture. He knew about houses like this; he'd lived in them himself when he was a child, before the river of Goodyear money had trickled into a sea of debt. When he had first sat down in the Thomas' living-room chair, he remembered breaking a chair just like it in his grandfather's drawing room. 'You have to treat furniture with respect, Toby,' his grandfather had chastised him. Lisa Thomas looked as if she were about to jump on top of the chair nearest her and start in on a cheerleader routine.

'And you two?' Lisa swung around to address Alison Austin and Declan Lewis. 'How long have you two been together?'

'Two years,' Alison answered. 'Declan and I met two years ago today, as it happens.'

'An anniversary! How fabulous! Skip – let's get some champagne out. We should be celebrating.' Lisa finally moved away from the television set and grabbed her husband's arm. 'Come on everybody. This room is so stuffy, it depresses me. The kitchen is much cosier. Follow us.'

As Declan fell in behind Lisa and Skip, he recalled the first time he and Alison had met. It was at a funeral; the funeral of a friend of his who had died, at an absurdly young age, in a boating accident. Alison was his friend's first cousin and Declan remembered being struck by the sight of this young woman coming into the church wearing a snow-white fake fur coat. She had looked like a polar bear, he thought. A stunning arctic animal in a sea of black. Her face had a strong set to it which he'd immediately admired, a 'don't bullshit me' appearance. That's what I would like to

11

look like if I'd been born a woman, he'd found himself thinking. Attractive, self-confident, ballsy.

The funeral was in January, a few days after New Year's Day. It was now a hot day in July. Either Alison had forgotten their first meeting or had deftly, purposefully, switched the date to please Lisa. Declan was positive it was the latter.

She's much better at this than I am, he thought. Alison shouldn't be stuck in the lower echelons of the pop video world, she should be in charge of sales and marketing for some huge multinational corporation. She could sell microwaves in Hell. Whereas I am becoming increasingly hopeless at selling anything. I try to concentrate on my work, but end up looking at people's hairstyles or wondering why I'm doing what I'm doing. Something has gone wrong with me. I want to have a successful career, but then I suddenly start to think selling is a con game and I should find a job in a dry-cleaning company or some equally practical industry. Wouldn't that be a better option than trying to convince people to part with their hard-earned money in order to buy books like *I Saw You First*?

'Sit down, everyone,' Lisa commanded as Declan, Alison, Christina and Toby entered the kitchen. 'I hope you weren't expecting anything special for dinner. I've got some smoked salmon, some caviare and lots of salads. It's so hot, I didn't think you'd want roast beef and Yorkshire pudding. Besides,' she gestured at the stove, 'I can't get a grip on these Aga things. I know people who swear by them. In the old days, in Connecticut, when Skip was climbing the corporate ladder at AT&T, I had at least three girlfriends who had Agas specially installed in their houses. They drove Range Rovers too. It was all part of the game. The corporate game Skip and I actually despised. One-upmanship the whole fucking time.'

Christina Billings blinked. She would never have expected the woman she'd been watching in the infomercial to say 'fuck'.

'It was a nightmare,' Skip Thomas added, pulling out a bottle of Moët et Chandon from the refrigerator. 'You had to have the right car, the right stereo system, the right clothes, the right mobile phone. It was a rat race for sure, but we rats were *rich* rats. Rich rats who never had time to drive those cars or listen to the stereo sytems or do anything which might give us an iota of pleasure.' He paused for a moment to uncork the bottle of champagne.

'At first it goes to your head,' he continued, as he poured the liquid into the six fluted glasses Lisa had set out on the counter. 'I used to love it when we'd go on vacation and I'd get phone calls and faxes from the office the whole time. I'd think – wow – this means I'm important. I was so into it, you wouldn't believe. And I justified it all by saying to myself that I was doing it for Lisa. In fact, I was on a mammoth ego trip. I mean, my ego was Supersonic. It could have flown from here to New Zealand in two seconds.'

'The word "relax" was not in Skip's vocabulary,' Lisa commented, handing the glasses out to her guests two by two.

And it isn't in it now either, Christina thought. His shoulders are still hunched, his whole body is tense, wired. All his hand gestures are staccato and clipped. Skip Thomas' body is in a mess, no matter how wide the smile on his face might be. I'd like to get him to lie down right now and then I'd mix some bergamot with some camomile oil and massage that tension out of him. A sustained course of aromatherapy would sort him out. But I'm not here to drum up clients. I'm here as Toby's girlfriend. Still, I'd quite like to see everyone's expression if I told Skip Thomas I'd take care of him later, on the bed of his choice.

'So, guys,' Lisa lifted her glass, 'it's time to drink a toast. But don't stand up – we can do this sitting down, it's more comfortable. Here's to the six of us. I hope we'll all become great friends during our stay in this lovely country. And here's to Declan and Alison especially, on their second anniversary. Remember – loving well is the best revenge.'

'Hear, hear,' Toby Goodyear said with enthusiasm. The rest of the group then echoed his words and clinked glasses.

'Dig in, folks!' Lisa pointed to the food arranged haphazardly on plates and in bowls on the centre of the marble-topped table. 'Enjoy.'

'Tell me, Declan. What did you think of Lisa's infomercial? As a selling tool, I mean.' Skip leant back in his chair, one arm draped over the top.

Declan, as he took a large sip of champagne, studied his host for a moment before answering. Skip was decidedly casual, dressed in jeans, like his wife, with a white Gap T-shirt. He looked like a typical preppy American male, but his light brown eyes had a sharp, appraising gleam not normally associated with men who were born into a privileged world. While Lisa was all ebullience and exuberance, Skip exuded a slightly battered air, as if he weren't quite sure whether to smile or frown and was tired of making the decision every few seconds. Was that why he kept scratching his head, Declan wondered. Because he couldn't make up his mind whether to be pleased or annoyed by life? Skip and Lisa were another couple who didn't seem to fit together. But then, Declan asked himself, would anyone think he and Alison were perfectly matched? Probably not. Perhaps that was the joy of relationships. Odd people pairing up.

Skip's tone was jovial, he sounded as if he wanted an honest answer to his 'infomercial' question, but Declan sensed an underlying nervousness. Neither of the Thomases would like Declan's honest opinion. They didn't want to hear that the advert was unadulterated, embarrassing crap, but Declan couldn't bring himself to rave about it either.

'I thought it was interesting,' he finally responded. 'And obviously just the thing for an American audience. But I'm not sure it would work in the UK. To be blunt, advertisements here are more sophisticated than American ones. The consumers here like subtlety, they—'

'They would love it,' Alison Austin interrupted. 'I'm afraid Declan is a little behind the times as far as television goes, Skip. He knows everything about books and bookstores and all that, but he doesn't know about television. I try to tell him, but he doesn't listen. I don't know if he mentioned it, Lisa, but I work in television – on pop videos, so I have access to popular taste. And I thought your infomercial was brilliant.'

'Really?' Lisa's high-wattage smile lit up even further.

'Absolutely,' Alison said with fervour.

She had sussed this little gathering out within ten minutes of arriving. The actor, Toby Goodyear, was dead handsome, certainly. Tall and dark, with appealingly symmetrical, straight features which would send most women into orbit. But she'd seen his kind often enough before and wasn't particularly impressed. Men like Toby had pointless good looks. She could tell from his lazy blue eyes that he lacked both drive and self-confidence. No wonder he was here, queueing up for the lame part of Mike.

Toby's girlfriend, Christina Billings, was actually frighteningly tall, but clearly not a participant in the evening. She was probably a nurse or a social worker; in some sort of caring profession, anyway. She had that pale look of someone who wanted desperately to help people.

No – Lisa and Skip were the players, Alison knew. They were the ones worth concentrating on. If Declan wasn't going to make an effort this evening, then she would. Sometimes she wondered how Declan could keep his job. He wasn't a natural salesman, he didn't seem to know how to stroke other people's egos. He was far too watchful and wary. Alison knew she had a choice. She had control over this situation. Either she could stand by while Declan floundered with these Americans or she could wade in herself, help him out and possibly help herself at the same time. It was an easy decision to make.

'When Declan first told me we were going to come here tonight to watch your infomercial,' she addressed Lisa, 'I did some research. We have a few infomercials here, on the cable and satellite channels, but they're nothing compared to yours. We're at the starting point, whereas you Americans have obviously taken the concept and run with it. Infomercials are the future. Extraterrestrial channels are expanding exponentially, they're multiplying like rabbits and they need infomercials to fill all that air-time. What you are delivering is what the public wants – information and help. Products that will make our lives better, easier.'

All eyes at the table, Toby Goodyear noticed, had focused intently on Alison Austin. What a piece of work, he thought. She'd saved her boyfriend Declan's ass *and* she'd taken off like a rocket, delivering this spiel as if she'd rehearsed it for weeks. There was an air of natural authority to her, although she couldn't be more than thirty, if that. She had on a baby-blue lowcut dress, which would have been far too revealing if she hadn't been wearing a white, thin-strapped top underneath it, creating the perfect layered look set off against the perfect tan. Her dark hair was cut short, curling just beneath her ears, making her appear both competent and sexy at the same time.

The only imperfection he could spot was a bump on the bridge of her nose. Had she been in a fight once? Toby found himself wondering. If so, he would have bet on her to be the winner. Who would be the perfect actress to play Alison? Sharon Stone – no doubt about it.

Alison would have been a good actress herself, he decided. For a moment he felt the familiar surge of jealousy invade him. Then he remembered that they weren't in competition. It wasn't as if Lisa Thomas would hire Alison for the part of Mike, was it?

Still – why hadn't *he* bothered to do some 'research' on these infomercial things? He'd never even heard of the word until a few days before, when Lisa had contacted him through his agent, and he hadn't made any effort to find out about them afterwards. All he wanted was a job, a little money. He could play Mike or he could play one of those people who gave testimonials at the end; at the moment he'd do anything to make a tiny impact on his overdraft.

Declan Lewis was openly helping himself to another glass of champagne, Toby saw. Which is what any bloke would do when he'd been so comprehensively shown up by his ladyfriend. *Extraterrestrial channels are expanding exponentially*? The girl deserved a

Best Bullshit award. She'd pushed her way up from somewhere, he reckoned. Somewhere like Slough or Watford or Basingstoke. No Sloane Ranger, she, anyway. In fact, she reminded him of the girls from town with whom he and his fellow Harrovians used to fraternize. What she was doing with Declan, he couldn't fathom. Alison Austin was a wolf; Declan Lewis was a turtle. Toby had a brief moment of private hilarity as he pictured a wolf and turtle mating.

'I had a friend in New York Fed-Ex me a few infomercials,' Alison continued. 'And I was amazed. That one about the pillow – that was incredible.'

'The pillow?' Christina asked Alison. Her legs were scrunched up underneath the table, making her sit up even straighter than she usually did. There was never enough room for her legs at dinner parties, which was one of the reasons she always felt uncomfortable going out.

'Yes, it's fabulous. This pillow is made out of barleybean husks or wheatgrain husks – some sort of husks. And it's guaranteed to give you a fanatastic night's sleep. What happens is this: the camera is underneath a glass table top, shooting upwards, if you can imagine it. And an egg is placed on top of the table. A normal pillow is put on top of the egg and someone drops a facsimile of a human head on top of the pillow. The egg underneath the pillow breaks. But then they get a new egg and substitute the barleybean pillow for the normal pillow and they drop the head on top of it and the egg doesn't break.'

'A *facsimile* of a human head? What's it made out of?' Christina queried. She was surprised by how infectious Alison's enthusiasm was. As Alison had been describing the infomercial, Christina had been visualizing it. She could see the splattered egg. And she could imagine that even she would be impressed when the next egg didn't break.

'I don't know what it's made out of, exactly,' Alison replied. 'But it certainly looks like an authentic human head.'

'I've seen that pillow infomercial too,' Skip said. 'It's famous in the States.'

'And there's another one which stunned me. The one which tells you how to lose weight without dieting or exercising. That is totally brilliant.'

'Excuse me?' Declan looked wildly around the table. 'Did I hear you correctly, Alison? *How to lose weight without dieting or exercising?*'

'And then there's the infomercial where they freeze the engine of a car – you literally see this car engine sitting in a block of ice. And the car still starts.' Skip grinned. 'Now *that* is impressive.' He helped himself to a slice of smoked salmon.

'The one for the Psychic Friends Network is the most popular, though.' Lisa was looking directly at Alison. 'You see, there are a lot of lonely people out there watching television. People alone or people in lonely relationships. Those people need help. The kind of help my book can give.'

'Lisa,' Declan said in a firm voice. 'Your book has been a huge success in America. You've made my job easy. I'm sure we can market and sell it here with no problems whatsoever. We're already getting masses of publicity. My point is that you don't *need* an infomercial. As Alison said, infomercials aren't the same here as they are in the States. Ads running for fifteen or thirty minutes just aren't on. BBC1 and BBC2 don't have *any* ads, so you have to understand that the whole attitude to commercials is different in this country. Informercials haven't taken off here. Maybe they will, maybe they won't. But why spend money you don't have to? I mean, I'm assuming you don't expect *us* to pay for it, Lisa. TV ads are expensive. I'm afraid Green & Wilson aren't going to pay for publicity when we don't have to.'

'No, Declan,' Lisa replied. 'I don't expect you to pay for it. I can take care of the costs. I'll set up a fufilment house, then buy my books from you at a discount. This is good business for both of us.'

'Well, we'd have to talk about the percentage of discount on that, obviously. But what I'm trying to say is that I honestly don't believe you have to pay for air-time – which is expensive. Satellite channels have lower rates, I'm sure. But then they have lower viewing figures. I'm not sure it's worth your while, that's all.'

'Why not be more successful if you can be?' Skip Thomas barked. He took his arm away from behind the chair and placed his elbows on the table. 'We're talking about a gap in the market, Declan. One which I believe I can fill. You know, I came to this country fifteen years ago on a short trip after I'd graduated from the University of Colorado, before I went on to Harvard Business School, and I noticed something. You all had electric kettles here. We didn't have those in America. At the time I thought: whoa, some smart bastard is going to make a lot of money. And that smart bastard is the person who first markets electric kettles in the States. Every household wants one, right? And now every American household has one. A gap in the market was plugged.

'At the moment it is you folks over here who have a gap. And I intend to be the one who plugs it. You say that the viewing figures for satellite channels are lower – sure, I believe that. But don't tell me they're not rising all the time. The computer revolution means more time spent at home. We don't have to move from the comfort of our own house to fax, to e-mail, to do anything we damn well want to. And when people stay at home more, they watch more television. It's a simple equation. And here's another simple equation. The more television people watch, the more choice they want. Then the law of supply and demand kicks in. People want more channels, they get them. Which brings us right back to the beginning. All this air-time needs filling. What can fill it? Infomercials; infomercials which run for fifteen or thirty minutes. I plan to bring them over here. I'll be the king of infomercials in this country. I'll start with Lisa's. And I'll go on from there.'

'You're going to freeze car engines and drop fake heads on bar-leycorn husk pillows?' Declan stared at Skip in evident disbelief.

'You bet.'

'And tell people how they can lose weight by eating as much as they want without lifting even a finger in exercise?'

'Sure.'

'What about the Psychic Friends Network?' Declan grimaced.

'What about it? As Lisa said, it helps lonely people. What's wrong with that? You identify what people want and you give it to them. It's as simple as that.'

'And not one little secret part of your soul says to you that you're conning these people?'

'Declan—' Alison put her hand on his shoulder.

'Don't worry, Alison,' Skip said, raising his chin. 'I don't mind answering that question. The car starts, Declan.' He smiled. 'The engine is in a block of ice and the car still starts. I don't call that a con.'

'And the pillow works,' Lisa put in. 'A friend of mine has one. She says it's heaven and she'd be willing to give a testimonial on an infomercial herself. You should see the one for the Psychic Friends Network,' She turned to Christina. 'Toby told me when I called him about this dinner that you're an aromatherapist, so I know you'd appreciate it. Dionne Warwick fronts it. It's wonderful. Think of all those people who live in the sticks and can't get to a psychic. All they have to do is make a telephone call.'

'Aromatherapy is a kind of science, Lisa,' Christina said as kindly as she could. 'It's not about mysticism of any sort.'

'Whatever – you know what I mean. Dionne's just lovely. I thought of asking her to go on my infomercial, but then I decided it would be better to have ordinary people give testimonials, not stars. Real people, with real problems. My book,' she turned from Christina to Declan, 'is not a con.'

'I didn't say it was.' Declan lifted his head and stared at Lisa. 'I'm beginning to think they're a very clever concept, these infomercials. We could have one for the Psychic Friends Network and get Fergie to front it, with Madame Vasso sitting in a pyramid tent in the background.'

'That's an *excellent* idea, Declan.' Lisa clapped. 'Do you think Fergie would do it?'

'Depends on what she'd be paid, I'd guess. Still, I'm beginning to see all sorts of possibilities for these things. I mean, let's say I have an irrational fear that my house will be burned to the ground by a random arsonist. If I saw an infomercial which sold a product that protected me from that possibility, I'm sure I'd buy it. Ideally, I'd watch a thuggish-looking lout spread petrol all over the carpets and toss a burning flamethrower on to them then marvel when the flames never took hold. I see it now – all the possibilities. It's staggering, actually.'

'Flameproof carpets – not a bad idea.' Skip nodded. 'Do they have those over here?'

'Or a specially designed aerobic rocking chair.' Declan took on the voice of a used-car salesman. 'Tired of going to the gym? Now you can get in shape in the privacy of your own home, watching television. Rock till you drop those pounds. No strain, no pain. Sit back and let the chair do the work.'

'Sounds great,' Skip said. 'You're getting the hang of it, aren't you? The fantastic thing about them is that they can sell a number of products at the same time. So, for example, if you get the special pillow, you also get a cassette of relaxing music and a book on the interpretation of dreams.'

'Would that be a Jungian interpretation or a Freudian one?' Toby asked.

'I don't know.' Lisa screwed her face up into a puzzled expression. 'Maybe it's both.'

'Wow!' Declan exclaimed. 'Do you get the block of ice if you buy whatever that car engine infomercial is peddling?'

'Declan, sweetheart. I think it's time we thought about getting home. Tomorrow's a work day. I have an early shoot with a rap group.'

'No, no – Alison, please. As Skip said, I'm just getting the hang of this. I see it now. A new infomercial combining the best of all of them. We watch as a frozen car is dropped on a pillow and the

21

egg *still* doesn't break. And after the frozen car has been dropped – from a great height – on to the pillow, the car *still* starts. And then the camera pans to a person asleep in the back of the car, using the barleyhusk pillow which is in a block of ice itself but *still* produces heavenly sleep. How about that?'

'Wait, wait!' Toby put his hands up in the air. 'Then you wake the sleeping person up and ask him what he dreamed about when he was in the back of the car and you get a hologram figure of Jung or Freud, or a combination of Jung and Freud to interpret that dream.'

'Maybe you should get Dionne Warwick to interpret the dream,' Christina put in.

'No, no, no.' Declan put *his* hands in the air. 'Hold on. You get a psychic friend to interpret the dream by telephone.'

'To die, to sleep,' Toby suddenly intoned, sitting back in his chair, his eyes raised to the ceiling. 'To sleep; perchance to dream; ay, there's the rub; for in that sleep of death what dreams may come when we have shuffled off this mortal coil, must give us pause.' He inhaled dramatically, then brought his eyes back to the table and smiled. 'You have a hologram Hamlet whispering that into the sleeping person's ear, then he grabs the barleycorn pillow and says: "Guaranteed to give you *great* dreams, guaranteed *never* to give you pause." Or you have someone off camera screaming "Sleep no more! Glamis does murder sleep." Then another person holds up the pillow saying: "Not even Macbeth can murder sleep when you use this fabulous pillow!"'

'What's Shakespeare got to do with this?' Skip stared at Toby. 'People watching infomercials probably don't know who the hell Macbeth is.'

'What? Do you think they'd think Macbeth was Ronald McDonald's first cousin? Not in this country, Skip.' Toby narrowed his eyes. 'We have at least a modicum of cultural intelligence here. Though I have to agree, it's getting thinner and thinner on the ground. When I played Hamlet, for example, I was in a production in a tiny theatre in Tooting and the audience there didn't really understand it. They thought it was too long, for one. And—'

'Well, Christ, come on, it *is* long,' Skip interrupted. 'People can only take so much. We're too busy these days, that's the problem. We don't have the time to sit down and read books cover-to-cover or watch a play for three and a half hours.'

'But people should know the classics.' Toby felt passion rising in his voice. 'They *should* be well-read, they *should* have a stake in culture.'

'Then you have to cut the thing,' Skip said, chopping the air with his hand. 'Cut, cut, cut. A lot of *Hamlet* is boring, anyway. All that gravedigger junk. We worship it because we know we're supposed to worship it. You could take huge chunks out of the classics and nothing much would be lost. Be honest.'

'That's absurd,' Toby was about to say, but then checked himself. What did he care about Skip Thomas' views on culture? All he cared about was Lisa Thomas' chequebook. He was suddenly tired of this dinner party and wanted to leave. It was fun for a while, getting going on the infomercial riff with Declan, but the idea that Skip Thomas could think he knew the first thing about *Hamlet* was offensive. And Lisa was still sitting there with a stupid cheerleader's grin on her face. Americans were idiots. That's all there was to it. Idiots with money.

'People want information, yes,' Skip continued. 'But they want it quickly. They don't want to have to read hundreds of pages describing Napoleon's tactics in his advance on Moscow, for example. Cut that whole bit out of *War and Peace* and you're getting somewhere.'

Declan banged his knife against his glass and the entire table turned to look at him.

'That's it! That's the answer! You've got your next infomercial, Skip. What you have to do is to summarize all the plots of all the best literature on to a thirty-minute cassette tape. So everyone who doesn't have a clue will know what happened in *Ulysses* and *Anna Karenina* without having to turn all those boring pages. All they need to do is to listen – for a very short time-span. You do an infomercial on the tape, market it, and call it . . .' He paused, seemingly searching for inspiration and weaving slightly as he did so. 'Call the tape *Plots in a Box*.'

'Declan.' Alison closed her eyes and sighed. He'd gone one step too far, she thought. She'd tried to stop him, but failed. He'd crossed the border from playful teasing into rudeness.

'Declan.' Skip Thomas stood up.

Here it comes, Declan thought. He's going to boot me out. But there's nothing I can do about it now. The deed is done.

'Declan, that's pure genius.'

Toby Goodyear stifled a laugh. Now this was becoming fun again. Now he could really start to act.

'You should offer something along with the *Plots in a Box* cassette,' he commented, using his most sincere voice. 'Something useful. Something of everyday value. Something like – ' he paused, looking down at his plate – 'china. A set of dinnerware. With a picture of an author in the middle and a quote from one of his or her most famous works around the rim. This could *help* people. "Take a bite of your steak and see more of Tolstoy. Don't finish your food because there are starving people in India, finish it so you can see the face of a genius like Charles Dickens staring out at you." Culinary culture.'

'What did you say?' Skip swung round to Toby.

'I said "Culinary Culture. Eat Your Way to Intelligence".'

'From Microwave to Brainwave,' Christina found herself adding.

'Brilliant! This is just way too brilliant. I don't believe you guys. You're so sharp.'

'But,' Declan thumped both hands on the table, 'You have to put the *right* quote around the rim. With Tolstoy, for example, you put that "all happy families" one. Nothing to do with boring war tactics – right, Skip? Everything to do with family values, so it will appeal to everyone.'

'Exactly.' Toby frowned. 'You have to be very careful what quote you use. I mean, we wouldn't want "Lolita, light of my

24

life, fire of my loins", would we? That might upset the digestive system.'

'Right,' Skip said, nodding.

'And you wouldn't want "Call me Ishmael" from *Moby Dick* decorating the plate, either.' Declan rubbed his chin thoughtfully. 'It sounds too much like an advertisement for porridge.'

'You're so right,' Skip nodded again.

Alison Austin knew she had to think fast. She wasn't going to be left out of this conversation, not if Skip Thomas was taking it seriously. As soon as he had said he wanted to be the infomercial king of Britain, she pictured herself as the Queen. Why not? At the moment she was in a dead-end job she'd had for far too long. Being a production assistant for pop videos involved a mind-boggling array of dogsbody tasks: checking on continuity, timing shots, making a shot list of roll number, take number etc – all necessary but mindless work. *And* she made coffee *and* she drove people around. She was, effectively, a few steps up from a runner and as time went by, she despaired of making the leap to director or producer. She was stuck. Twenty-nine was too old to be in this job. If she could make a break and team up with Skip Thomas on the infomercial front, she might just be getting somewhere. There was money to be made out of infomercials, she was sure of it. Declan and Toby were taking the mickey out of the Thomases, but that was only because they didn't understand where public taste was heading. Public taste always headed in one direction: from America to Britain. That was the way of the world.

'After you've done one on literature, you could do one on philosophy,' she said, her brain racing. 'All the great philosophers no one ever has the time to read. You could start with—'

'Plato,' Declan interrupted. 'Plato on a Plate.'

'Declan,' Toby sat back in his chair. 'Declan, I'm in awe.'

'*You're* in awe, Toby? *I'm* mesmerized. This boy has it.' Skip came around to the back of Declan's chair and put his hands on his shoulders. 'I want you to do it for me, Declan. Start with *Plots in a Box*. Put it together. You and Toby. He can be the front man, the one talking to camera. He has the voice, he has the looks. He's the Shakespearian actor, goddamn it. What a combination. Perfecto. Absolutely perfecto.'

'Hang on a second, Skip.' For the first time that evening, Lisa's voice had an edge to it and her smile had vanished. 'Declan already has a job. And part of his job is to market *I Saw You First*. Besides, Toby is supposed to be working on *that* infomercial, not some other one about literature or philosophy.'

'Lisa, honey, Declan is not, as I understand it, your personal PR man, he's a *Director* of Sales and Marketing. Your book is one tiny bit of his domain. He's been very nice to come here tonight and pay you special attention. I'm sure he knows your value to his company. But he's not the one accompanying you on promotional tours. They have a PR person for that. What I am talking about is a completely different deal, something he could work on, if he wants, during after-office hours. And you won't be ready to shoot the infomercial of *I Saw You First* right away. You have to find the right people in commercials here to do that first. So Toby doing some extra work for me is not a problem.'

Christina looked at Skip Thomas, who was suddenly exhibiting all the signs of the business person he had once been. For the first time in the evening, he appeared relaxed. Beside him, Declan's face was a picture of bewilderment. He obviously couldn't believe Skip was taking him seriously. This evening had turned out to be even odder than she could have imagined at the beginning. *Plato on a Plate*? She realized she was smiling with childish pleasure. The heady ridiculousness of it all had infected her as well.

'You could,' Christina offered, still smiling, 'sell a book on relationships in literature as well, along with the *Plots in a Box* tape and the plates. An advice book. What made Anna Karenina fall for Vronsky? How can all women avoid that sort of disaster? What do you do if you're a Jane Eyre in love with a man like Rochester? Is there a Heathcliff in every woman's life?'

'I don't think that would work,' Lisa said firmly.

'Why not?' Skip dug his hands into Declan's shoulders. 'I think it's brilliant, Christina. A tape, an advice book, a dinnerware set. What a package. Perfecto! So – will you do it, Declan? Put a proposal together?'

'Of course,' Declan answered.

Now he was smiling too, Christina saw. And that smile transformed his face. He was an average-looking man in his early thirties, she guessed, with a thin face, dark blond hair and pale blue eyes, but when he smiled he radiated warmth and humour. If she were playing Toby's game and choosing which actor would be cast as Declan in a film, who would it be? She couldn't think of one who was physically similar or who had the same smile. He'd have to play himself, she thought. And that was unusual. Most of the time Toby's game was a simple one and the choice was obvious.

'It would be tremendous fun, Skip,' Declan continued. 'Absolutely perfecto. No problem.'

'Great – and you, Toby? I think it would be a good idea if you worked with Declan as he goes along, give him your input. All of this will be well paid, of course.You two work on it together, I'll give you, say, a hundred pounds an hour for your time. Does that work for you?'

'It works for me,' Toby echoed, thinking: A hundred pounds an hour and I'd do an infomercial for loo-paper. Now, finally, we're getting somewhere.

'I love it,' Skip said, kissing the top of Declan's head with a loud smack. 'I love you guys. You Brits. You're something else, you know that?'

Chapter 2

All people are products of both nature and nurture. Our genetic legacy and our upbringing shape us. It is important, in order to truly 'see' your partner, to understand what makes him tick, that you find out as much as possible about his relationship with his parents and siblings, if he has any. Otherwise, you are seeing him with blinkers on. People, as a rule, form the same kind of romantic relationships as they do familial ones. Does your partner have a combative relationship with his mother? His father? His sister? If so, how does that reflect itself in his attitude toward you?

Think back. When you first saw him, did you do your job correctly? Did you focus on him or were you blinded by his looks, his manner, his charm? You must take responsibility for your own vision or lack of it. If you didn't see him properly, you should do so now. Study his background, his childhood. Investigate it as if you were a psychiatrist or a private detective. Until you know where he is coming from, his roots, you can never hope to know who he really is.

Of course he should be doing exactly the same with you. You are not only each other's lovers, but also each other's confidants. If you cannot open up with your partner, you must ask yourself why you are involved with this person.

Don't just go back to your beginning as a couple. Go back to the very beginning of each other's lives.

Dig deep and you will find depth.

Stay in the shallows and you will founder.
              I Saw You First, *Chapter Two, p. 21*

'You are *so* lucky,' Alison said, as she put down the clutch and shifted into third gear. 'You weren't just sailing close to the wind, you were heading straight for a fucking hurricane.'

Declan shrugged and looked out of the window.

'You took it too far, Declan. There was no need to be rude.'

'I wasn't rude, Alison. Skip loved *Plots in a Box*.'

'I know he did, but you were pulling his leg the whole time. Are you really going to work on this project? Because if you don't he *will* think you're rude and I'm seriously considering the idea of working on these infomercials with him. I don't want you to ruin that possibility for me.'

'I wouldn't do that,' Declan protested. 'I know you need to get out of your job, but do you honestly believe all that stuff you were spouting about infomercials?'

'Stuff? Spouting? That's a dismissive way of putting it.'

'I'm sorry.' Declan rubbed his forehead. 'I didn't mean to be dismissive. It's just that the whole concept of infomercials seems so bizarre to me.'

'So you're *not* going to work on *Plots in a Box*. You *are* going to let Skip down. That's wonderful.'

'I don't know.'

'You don't know what?'

Declan slouched in his seat. He didn't want to have this conversation. He'd had far too much champagne and now all he wanted was to go home to bed. But Alison wasn't someone who would let a topic drop if she wanted to discuss it. She would keep on and on until *she* had decided she'd had enough. Sometimes she was so tenacious it frightened him.

'I don't know whether I'll work on *Plots in a Box* or not,' he told her wearily. 'On one hand, the whole idea appals me and on the other . . .' He paused.

'On the other?' Alison pressed.

'Well, I know this may sound idiotic, but for a while back there at dinner, I felt creative. I mean, I was getting more and more outlandish, sparking off with Toby, but that was actually fun. It got my imagination going. I could almost see this silly advertisement, hear Toby hyping *Plots in a Box*. And I felt like a combination of a comedy writer and a producer – someone who could make something happen. Still, it's such a ridiculous thing to make happen.'

'It *could* be commercial, you know. It *could* make money.'

'Jesus Al, you're obsessed with money.'

'Jesus, Declan, you sound like your brother. Or your father.'

'That's unfair.'

'Is it? They both hate money, don't they, and all that it stands for? I'm sure they'd hate infomercials, they'd hate *Plots in a Box*, they'd hate the Thomases.'

'No.' Declan turned to face Alison's profile. 'My father doesn't hate anyone. You don't understand him. If he'd been at dinner, he would have asked Lisa and Skip Thomas approximately two thousand questions. By the end of the evening he would have been able to write a doctoral thesis on *I Saw You First*, not to mention infomercials in general.'

'That's hardly the point, you know.'

'What *is* the point? I know we're having a row, but I have no idea what we're rowing about.'

'I think you should have more initiative, that's all. Everything turned out fine tonight, but it could have been a disaster. Lisa Thomas is obviously a successful author – you shouldn't take the risk of offending her.'

'Alison, why didn't you tell me you'd done all that research work on infomercials?'

'Because I know you by now, don't I? You'd think they were worthless and if I'd told you about them you would have tried to get out of this dinner with the Thomases so you wouldn't have to watch Lisa's. Am I right?'

'I suppose so.'

'See? I'm always right.' Alison laughed. 'You're such a baby sometimes.'

Declan closed his eyes. 'Is that so bad?' he asked.

'Well,' Alison switched the left-hand indicator on. 'I suppose not. Not when you have me to look out for you. You know, I was thinking of that when I was watching Lisa's infomercial. I was thinking of the first time I saw you, how I thought: There's a man who needs to be rescued.'

'Rescued?' Declan frowned. 'Rescued from what?'

'From yourself, sweetheart,' Alison replied. Pulling up in front of their house on Henning Street, she turned off the engine and unbuckled her seat belt. 'You're all over the shop.'

'How do you mean? How am I all over the shop?'

Standing behind her as she opened the front door, Declan considered kissing the back of her neck. Instead he followed her inside and watched as she punched in the code for the alarm system.

'You don't know what you want from life. You had that completely off-the-wall upbringing, so I don't blame you. But you're thirty-two years old now. You have to work out where you're going and how you're going to get there.'

Declan scratched his head, then recalled Skip Thomas doing exactly the same thing all night.

'I have *some* clue, Alison,' he murmured. 'I'm not entirely helpless.'

'Oh, I know. Or I wouldn't be here, would I? Listen, I'm knackered and I have to be up at the crack of dawn. I'm going to bed now.'

'Right. I'm going to have a couple of glasses of water and then I'll come upstairs, too.'

'Fine.' She started up the stairs, then stopped, reached over the bannister and rubbed the top of his head. 'You really are a jammy bastard. *Plots in a Box.* I thought he was going to go ballistic. Instead he ends up kissing you.' She continued up a few more steps before leaning over the bannister again. 'Have you ever seen a woman that tall? I mean, apart from on the catwalk?'

'I haven't seen many women on a catwalk,' he answered from the kitchen. 'But no, I don't think I have.'

'She must have been over six foot. Lucky that actor was even taller. She has to have problems finding blokes she can kiss without providing them with a ladder first. Come up soon or I'll be asleep.'

'Right.'

Declan grabbed a bottle of Evian water from the fridge, and marvelled, as he often did, at the gleaming neatness and order of the kitchen. Alison was close to obsessive in her tidiness, one of the many qualities that endeared her to him. At times, after they had moved in together, he would walk around the house in a state of wonder. When is this going to end? he'd ask himself. She can't possibly be as anal-retentive as I am. It has to come apart soon. But it hadn't. Not yet. They were perfectly suited in their compulsion for order.

She'd inherited that gene, he suspected, from her mother. When Declan had first visited Alison's mother's house, he'd been shown the family albums. In every picture Alison was dressed immaculately in perfectly pressed clothes. Any indoor photographs showed equally immaculate rooms. There were no toys strewn on the floor, no cushions out of place, and always beautifully arranged flowers on table tops. Declan was seriously impressed. When he'd taken Alison to visit his parents for the first time, he wasn't in the least surprised by her reaction.

'How does she stand it?' Alison had asked in horror on the way back to London. 'How can your mother cope? It's havoc, Declan. I'd go berserk.'

Havoc is putting it mildly, Declan thought. It is havoc, mayhem, and entropy all rolled into one. Everything in his father's house tended toward chaos. And it was definitely his father's not his mother's house. His mother, if she'd had her way, would have had an entirely different atmosphere. She would have . . .

Declan poured the water into a tall glass and took a long drink, preparing to go over yet again the list he had composed when he was fifteen. She would have: 1) locks on the doors 2) some decent furniture 3) a dishwasher 4) a television set. She would have: 5) banned the invasion of goats and chickens into the so-called living room 6) banned neighbourhood children treating the house as if it were their own.

No wonder Alison thought he was all over the shop. He *had* had an off-the-wall upbringing, one that he was unlikely to recover from in a long, long time.

Declan poured himself another glass of water. Were there only six points? There must be more. He knew there were plenty more. Oh, yes: 7) His mother wouldn't have, if she'd had the strength to cross his father, allowed all those university students to come every weekend and monopolize his time. All those students who also treated the house as if it was their own and who acted like little children at Disneyland.

Every weekend a horde of students would spend hours in the garden swinging on the rope swing his father had made, acting like Tarzans and Janes, jumping on it from the roof and yelling wildly, beating their chests. When they weren't jumping off the roof of the house on to the rope-swing, they were jumping off the roof of the garage on to the mattresses his father had strategically piled on the ground underneath. It was a playpen, their house, one giant playpen. Sometimes he wished one of those students would break a leg and file a lawsuit; that was the only way he could think of to make it all stop.

'But we had fun, Declan,' his brother Michael kept trying to tell him. 'Why are you so upset about what was a perfect, ideal childhood? I don't understand.'

Of course Michael didn't understand. Michael loved every minute of it. Michael didn't mind if some student of their father's barged in on him when he was on the loo because of course there were no locks anywhere in the house. In the Lewis household the concept of privacy did not exist. Michael laughed about it. And

Michael had no desire to watch television anyway, so why would he mind that there wasn't one? Michael was a carbon copy of their father, Owen. He had the same principles and beliefs and had had them, it seemed, from the cradle.

'What's wrong with Dad's students coming over at the weekend?' he would ask. 'They're fun and they have interesting discussions. You should listen to them sometime.'

Declan had listened, endlessly it seemed. Aristotle, Plato, Marx, Hegel, Proudhon. Communism, anarchism, the dialectical imperative, 'to each according to his means/from each according to his ability' . . . blah blah blah. Every single student wanted world peace and equality and Platonic perfection, and seemed to think if he/she talked about it for five hundred hours, he/she would achieve it. They would sit at Owen's feet, although not literally at his feet because there were no chairs, only pillows scattered around the living room, the bulk of which was taken up by a ping-pong table.

How was he expected to be a normal human being when the living room of his house consisted of a ping-pong table? That wasn't normal. It was mad.

The students would sit and talk and talk and talk. Owen would listen extremely carefully. He'd nod a lot. And ask questions occasionally, but for the most part he let them bang on about how they could save the world. And how disgusting capitalism was.

Only once in his life had Declan heard one of his father's students give a dissenting view. Declan had been sixteen at the time and was rushing to get out of the house and down to the pub for an illegal drink. Owen was sitting on the floor with a glass of goat's milk in his hand. Five students were splayed out on pillows around him.

'I think it's all about conspicuous consumption,' one of the females said. 'When I leave University, I want to have no possessions whatsoever. I want to be free from the tyranny of commerce.'

Declan gritted his teeth and calculated that it would take him only ten seconds before he'd be out the door.

'I don't know about that,' another, lower female voice announced. Declan couldn't stop himself from looking over at her. She was beautiful, dressed in tight jeans and an electric-blue jumper. 'When I leave University, I want to make enough money to afford a maid. A maid and satin sheets.'

Declan Lewis fell in love.

'Why satin?' his father asked, but before she could answer the other students had rounded on her.

'Elizabeth, that's disgusting!' the girl who didn't want to be tyrannized by commerce shrieked. 'That's *so* shallow.'

'How could you think of employing someone to clean up after you, to do something you're perfectly capable of doing yourself? Do you really want to exploit people? Is that your goal in life?' a male student asked, jabbing his finger in her direction.

'I don't know.' Elizabeth paused and looked around the group, then suddenly, magically, up at Declan standing dumbstruck at the end of the ping-pong table. She winked at him. 'Yes,' she giggled. 'If having a maid means exploiting people, then yes, I suppose I do. And ' she turned to Owen ' – I think satin must be fabulous for sex.'

Owen laughed.

'Elizabeth, you're hopeless,' another male student said, sighing. 'You shouldn't be here. You have no grasp of political principles.'

'Stop!' Declan wanted to shout. 'Don't drive her away. She's wonderful, you stupid bugger. Shut up.'

'The point about tyranny,' the student continued, 'is that it is not only commercial, it is spiritual. When you buy something, it's not actually buying something that you're doing, it's the opposite. You're giving away a part of your soul. You know, I learned something fascinating the other day. In certain primitive societies, a tribesman believes that a part of his soul is stolen if a Westerner takes a photograph of him.'

Crikey. What a discovery! No one has ever heard that one

before, have they, shit for brains? Declan rolled his eyes; he was the best person he knew at rolling his eyes in exasperation. But no one was watching him.

'Him? What about *her*, you sexist pig?' the third girl in the group spat out.

Declan stared at Elizabeth. She had a blank expression on her face and was concentrating on the floor. He willed her to look up at him again, but she didn't. Hesitating for a moment, he was finally forced to move away and out the door when he heard the word 'antithetical'. For at least six weekends afterwards, he hoped Elizabeth might reappear. She never did. She was, he reckoned, rolling around blissfully with some man savvy enough to own satin sheets.

Which was why, Declan reflected, placing his glass in the Zanussi dishwasher, he had, since the time he moved out of his father's house, slept in satin sheets. At this very moment, Alison was ensconced in satin. In a bedroom with a lock on the door. And a television set.

He turned off the lights and headed upstairs.

'You know,' Alison murmured from the bed as he took off his shirt and trousers and folded them, 'you should take Skip Thomas seriously. He was obviously a successful businessman at one point in his life. If he takes you seriously, you ought to return the compliment.'

'How can I take a man seriously when his first name is a verb?' Declan climbed into bed beside her.

'But there's no harm in doing it, developing the *Plots in a Box* idea. It couldn't possibly hurt.'

When Declan didn't respond, Alison turned her back to him.

'I'm shattered and I have to be up at six. Goodnight, sweetheart,' she whispered.

And on our two-year anniversary, too, Declan sighed. *'Dear Lisa, my girlfriend turned her back on me on the night she pretended was our anniversary. Without so much as a kiss. What should I do? How can I make her see the real me again? The person she first saw?'*

36

And who is that person? Declan asked himself. Some basket-case who needs rescuing. If that's what she *really* sees, then it's time I did something. High time I took some initiative.

He smiled into the darkness, remembering *Plato on a Plate*. I had fun tonight, he thought. My brother would hate *Plots in a Box*, Alison is right. My father would most probably be horrified. But so what? They're disappointed in me anyway. It was my idea and I'm going to go ahead with it. Fuck them if they can't take a joke.

'Did you see the way Lisa Thomas looked at you when we first came in?' Toby Goodyear sat back in his chair and lit a cigarette. 'I thought she was going to keel over. You must make her feel like a midget.'

'I make almost every woman I meet feel like a midget,' Christina replied.

'She couldn't be more than five three.'

'She's five three and a half.'

Toby crossed his legs and stared at Christina, doing her exercises on the floor.

'You should stop doing that.'

'I need to stretch, especially after an evening sitting in those uncomfortable kitchen chairs.'

'No. I mean stop measuring people like that. It's spooky, you know. How precise you are.'

'I've always done it,' Christina mumbled.

'You're too self-conscious about height.'

'I'm self-conscious because people bring the subject up all the time. You did just then. You said I made Lisa feel like a midget. And Skip turned to me tonight and said: "Whoa – you are some tall lady!"' Christina felt her voice start to shake, and her neck start to ache. She very carefully rolled her head in a circle, trying to calm down.

Height. She hated the word. Height had turned her from a coordinated, gymnastic little girl into a gawky, gangling woman. There had been times, as a child, when Christina had been

37

desperate to grow up, to leapfrog the years and turn into an adult. But she hadn't known then. She hadn't known that she would grow and grow and grow. Grow so much that she'd actually hit her head against walls to try to slow the process down, to stop it in its tracks.

When the head-bashing hadn't worked, she'd become more scientific. She found out all about growth hormones, how children could take drugs to make them taller. But there were none on the market to stop the inches accumulating, at least none that she could locate in her research. Still, she wanted to go to a growth clinic. She wanted to talk to doctors. 'Don't be silly,' her mother had told her. 'You can't fight nature. Besides, it's not as if you were a giant.' 'Oh no?' she wanted to cry. 'Look at me. I'm sixteen years old and I'm six feet tall. You don't call that a giant?' But she didn't say this because there was no point. Her mother wouldn't listen. And it was too late anyway. When it all finally stopped, she was six feet two and a half inches tall. It was not enough to classify her as a freak, she knew. She wouldn't get a job in the circus. *The Guinness Book of Records* wouldn't be interested. But the day-to-day living of it, the looks, the comments, the *fear* she sometimes saw in people's eyes when confronted by her, made her often actually envy midgets.

'So – what did you think of our American host, Mr Skip Thomas?'

'He was nervous,' Christina replied. 'I could see how tense his neck was – his muscles were all knotted up.'

'You take this aromatherapy business too far. He didn't look nervous to me; he looked rich. Both of them did. They can spend their life in jeans but did you see all that marble? The rent on that house must be astronomical.'

'Are you going to do Lisa's infomercial?' Christina stopped rolling her head and stared at Toby.

'Why wouldn't I?'

'Toby. It's beneath you.'

'Christina. My overdraft is above me. Hanging like the Sword of Damocles.'

'But we're managing.'

'We're managing because of your salary. I'm managing because I moved into your flat. The point is – who is going to see this? No one – only sad people who watch infomercials on satellite channels. No one important will know. No one aside from my bank manager, that is. If Lisa wants me to play Mike, I'll play him.'

'And *Plots In a Box*? Are you going to do that one as well?'

'Why not?'

'It was fun, I know, talking about it. But do you really think Declan was serious?'

'Declan probably wouldn't mind the extra cash, either.'

'Well, in a weird way, it makes more sense to me for you to do that than Lisa's infomercial. I just can't picture you playing Mike.'

'I can. It's not as if I were talking to Hitler about the meaning of *Mein Kampf*, for chrissakes. It's a simple self-help book which God knows, may even help some couples out there in television land.'

'Do you believe every day should be like the first date, then?' Christina smiled.

'Well, it has to be better than believing every day should be like the last date. In my experience, the beginning of a relationship has always been better than the end.'

'So tell me, Mike,' Christina adopted an American accent. 'What did you see when you first looked at your lover?'

'I saw a giant, Lisa.' Toby grinned. 'A female giant I wanted to conquer.'

Christina looked away from Toby.

'Oh, come on, lighten up. I was joking.'

'Were you?' she mumbled.

'Yes – I mean, obviously I noticed how tall you are – it's impossible not to, Christina. You should have got to grips with this a long time ago. It's nothing to be ashamed of.'

'But that's the first thing you noticed? My height?'

'Yes – so what? What's the first thing you noticed about me?'

'I noticed that you were talking to a little boy on the set, and I thought it was incredibly sweet that you were paying attention to him.'

'You mean Freddie? Gavin's son?'

'Is that who he was?'

'Yes. Gavin brought him on location to watch him direct. Father-son bonding, you know. It never hurts to chummy up to the director's family. If he does another Jane Austen adaptation, he might hire me again. For a bigger part.'

'Because you talked to his son?'

'No, because I'm a good actor. But as I said, it doesn't hurt to make some extra effort. It can pay off.'

'Right.' Christina felt as if her head weighed ten stone.

'What does it matter, how we saw each other to begin with? We're together now and I'm doing Lisa's infomercial. It's as simple as that.' Toby stubbed out his cigarette. 'I don't need a lecture. I don't tell you what to do in your job. I don't give you shit about all those oils which have supposedly magical properties. People believe in them so they undoubtedly work. There is nothing either good or bad but thinking makes it so. If people want to believe in what Lisa Thomas has to say, why shouldn't I help her say it?'

'I wasn't trying to lecture you, I was only saying I couldn't imagine you playing Mike. That's all.'

'If I play Iago, do you think I *am* Iago?'

'No, that's not what—'

'I'm an actor, Christina. I can play anyone. If I choose to play the idiot Mike, that's a part I take. Now I'm going to bed. Are you coming?'

The way he looked at her frightened Christina. She couldn't afford to prolong this discussion, she knew. It was too close to an argument. As far as she was concerned, her relationship with Toby was precarious and always had been. If she pushed him too far, he might push back, and his method of pushing back would be to bugger off. At which point she'd be left alone. Again. No one to come home to after work, nobody to talk to, no one to share her bed. Most of her female friends were either ensconced in relationships or married. The two closest friends she had were still unattached, but they had moved to different countries. If Toby left, she'd be spending her evenings watching television on her own. She could do it, she knew. She'd done it before. She could even go through the awful process of being set up with dates by well-meaning friends. Dates which invariably ended up with no interest on either side. But she didn't want to. Toby had chosen her, had pursued her, had – yes – conquered her. Why should she mind that he'd put it in those terms? He'd stayed with her, he'd moved in with her – what else could she ask for?

She didn't want to row with him; she didn't honestly mind if he played Mike. She wanted him to stay, that was the point. She *needed* him to stay.

'Let me just check the machine,' Toby said, heading off to the kitchen where the telephone was. 'I might be offered a part which would make this entire conversation redundant,' he called over his shoulder.

Christina turned into their bedroom on the left-hand side of the hallway, while Toby continued into the kitchen. She heard the *You have one message* announcement from the machine and wondered who had that job. Who auditioned to be the voice on an answering machine? Were they embarrassed to put that on their CV? Or thrilled to be the unknown person infiltrating countless houses? Once she had gone on a blind date with a man who told her he made a habit out of intruding into other people's holiday photographs because it was his way of travelling the world. 'I'm in homes in Japan,' he said proudly. 'In India. In Alaska.' 'That's fantastic,' she'd replied, 'but wouldn't it be more fun to save up some money and go travelling yourself?' They were both relieved when the evening ended early.

Sitting down on the end of the bed, she took her top off and threw it on to the chair beside the dressing table.

41

'It was your step-sister,' Toby announced, when he came in. 'She wants to know when she's going to meet me. So – when *is* she going to meet me?'

'Which step-sister, Lucy or Chloë?'

'Lucy.'

'I'll ring her tomorrow.'

'But you won't set up a meeting, will you?' He sat down beside her on the bed. 'You know, normally I hate meeting girlfriends' families; I avoid it at all costs. The mothers pull out pictures of her when she was a little girl and expect me to ooh and ahhh and say how cute she was in her nappies and the fathers try especially hard not to ask me about my work prospects because they've been primed not to and I have to pretend I'm enjoying it all. I have to keep acting. But you, you won't let me near your relatives. I'm beginning to wonder. Are you ashamed of me?'

'No, of course not. But you wouldn't just be meeting Lucy. You'd have to meet her husband and two children and then Chloë and her husband and one tiny child and my mother and step-father. You'd die of claustrophobia.'

'You make it sound gruesome. I could charm them, you know. I'm good with kids. For short periods of time.'

'I know you would charm them. All of them. And you will meet them sometime.'

'Are you sure about that?' He sat back a bit and stared at her.

'I'm sure,' she said, smiling.

When is he going to notice? she asked herself. When is he going to realize that I always smile when I lie? Probably not for quite a while, given that I hardly ever lie to him. Or to anyone, for that matter. Only on the subject of my family. That's the only thing I've ever had to lie about.

Christina closed her eyes as Toby put out his cigarette and then leant in to kiss her. She put her arms around his neck and held on tight. She'd keep him away from them, one way or another, for as long as she could possibly manage. The meeting, if it were ever to happen, would be successful. Everyone would be thrilled, including her mother and step-father.

'He's fabulous, Christina,' she could hear Lucy and Chloë say. 'Just fantastic. We never understood what went wrong with Richard, but we always knew you'd find someone again.'

And that would be the phrase that would make her want to weep. The 'we always knew . . .' the mantra she'd heard throughout her teenage years. 'Don't worry, Chris, you'll find someone. We know you will.'

'It's difficult for you now, Chris, but when you're older it will be easier. We know it will.' All these statements leading to one conclusion: 'You'll get your man, Christina. You'll catch that fish and haul him in. You'll be one of us, one of these days.'

One of us. One of the women who know how to deal with men. Who know how to keep relationships going. Who know what make-up to wear, what clothes to buy, how to flirt.

She had been thirteen when her father had died, fourteen when her mother re-married a widower with two daughters. And fifteen when she'd had her first period. Her mother and step-sisters had taken her out to celebrate. They'd plied her with beauty products that evening. Eye-shadow and lipstick and blusher and scent. As they'd doled these presents out, they had giggled away happily. 'You're certainly a late developer, Chris, but we always knew it would happen one of these days.'

Christina had tried to giggle with them. They were being nice, she knew. Kind. But she'd looked at them that night, the three co-conspirators, anxious to introduce her to the joys of femininity, and all she had wanted to do was go home and cry. How could it be that her mother was so much more attuned to her step-daughters than to her natural daughter? Lucy and Chloë were her mother's real family, Christina realized that evening. They looked more like her mother than she did. They were interested in the same things her mother was. They were lively and engaging and alluring. Whereas Christina – well, Christina was different.

She wasn't one of them.

She especially wasn't Lucy.

Christina opened her eyes and saw Toby's face. His eyes were closed. He was concentrating on making love to her. He'd *been* making love to her all the time she'd been thinking of her family. How could that have happened? She couldn't even remember him taking her knickers off. It was as if she'd hypnotized herself; her body hadn't recognized what had gone on since Toby first started to kiss her; it had blanked out. Was she turning into some kind of Alien, some *X-Files* creature that could turn physical feeling off and on and travel through time zones?

Suddenly Lisa Thomas' voice invaded her brain and she heard that voice say: 'I'm not an ant.'

Christina Billings burst out laughing.

Toby Goodyear took it as a sign of passion.

'Interesting people,' Skip Thomas commented, clearing away the last of the dishes.

'Interesting people,' Lisa concurred. 'But what did you think of Declan? I mean, what did you think of his abilities? Do you think he'll do a good job on my book?'

'Does it really matter, Lisa?' Skip sighed. 'You're a number one bestseller in America. You're huge in Japan, for chrissakes. Do you have to conquer every damn country? Napoleon met his match at Waterloo. Would it be so bad if the Brits didn't succumb to you either?'

Lisa didn't reply. She couldn't understand why he should be so irritated. All along the line, he'd helped and encouraged her. From the very beginning, when she'd first come up with the idea of writing the book, he'd been supportive. He was helpful while she was writing it, pleased when she'd sold it to a publisher, positively thrilled when it began to sell so well. Why was he sounding so churlish now?

'I'm tired, hon,' he said, his back to her. 'Of course I think Declan will do a good job. He knows this country, he knows how to market books or he wouldn't have the job. He didn't get the infomercial concept at first, but when he caught on, he ran with it.'

'Maybe he's right. Maybe I don't need to do one here.'

'Maybe he's wrong. I do know *some* things. I do know a good business opportunity when I see it. At first he thought the British are too sophisticated for that kind of marketing technique. He'd *like* to think they all watch *Newsnight* and *Panorama*. I've done my research, you know. People like Declan Lewis forget about the mass-market taste. They forget about *Family Fortunes* and—' Skip picked the *Daily Express* off the kitchen counter and scanned the page of television listings.

'And – listen to this – *Vets in Practice*. "Springtime, the birthing season, proves hectic for the vets, as Trude faces her first lambing session." Or – here's another great one: *Emmerdale*. "Chris takes pleasure in telling Kim what it will take to keep his mouth shut." Now don't tell me those people watching these shows wouldn't watch infomercials. All television watchers in the Western world are the same when you scratch the surface. They want time filled in for them. If, during that time, they are offered something which they think might improve their lives without too much effort on their part, they'll buy it. Simple as that.'

'But don't you think they were kind of laughing at us tonight? Didn't you get that impression?'

'So what?'

'I don't know, it was their tone of voice or something, but I got the feeling they think we're stupid.'

'Like I said: so what if they do? That doesn't hurt us in the least. Because Declan Lewis *will* work on *Plots in a Box*. And so will Toby Goodyear. They'll do everything we want them to do and then they'll see how it succeeds and they'll pretend they believed in it all along. Meanwhile we'll be running the show. Us dumb people from the sticks.'

'I'm not talking about *Plots in a Box*. I'm talking about *I Saw You First*. It makes me nervous, that's all. The idea that they somehow feel superior.' Lisa frowned. 'I'm not used to people quoting from

Shakespeare and talking about all this literature. They seem to *know* so much. I mean, who was that guy Anna Karenina fell in love with? I don't know his name. I've never read the book. It makes me feel stupid.'

'Why, Lisa?' she could still hear her mother's livid voice. 'Why did you squander your education? How could you be so stupid? Wellesley's out. Smith's out. Forget Vassar. You'll end up somewhere like Oak Manor Junior College. What happened to you this year? Was your social life so important to you you forgot what you were at school for? You were an intelligent girl. Now you've thrown it all away.'

'Oak Manor isn't so bad,' she remembered answering, not looking her mother in the eye.

'Oh, Oak Manor is fine, if what you want in life is to meet and marry a Harvard man. And never have a career yourself.'

'Like you,' Lisa surprised herself by having the courage to say.

'Exactly. Like me,' her mother had replied before walking out of the room.

She had never seen her mother so angry before. Up until that moment, Lisa had never understood that her mother might have wanted something else from her life aside from a husband and family. People used to say, she knew, that her mother was so organized, so sharp and intelligent that she could have run a company. Friends of her parents were always impressed by Ruth's abilities; the way she entertained, the way she ran her household, how she managed six children without ever seeming to suffer from fatigue, illness, or just plain irritation. She organized car pool schedules, she took all six children to all sorts of different after-school activities, she cooked, she gardened, she played tennis at the club. Her skill at backgammon was close to legendary. Yet she'd never had a job in her life. And she'd died of a stroke the year before Lisa wrote *I Saw You First*.

'Your mother would have been so proud of you' her father telephoned to say after she'd appeared on Oprah Winfrey.

Lisa had wanted to yell, 'Fuck you!' and slam the receiver down on him. What could that statement possibly mean except that her mother *hadn't* been proud of her before! After that single, angry outburst, Ruth had never said another word indicating displeasure. She'd seemed happy enough when Lisa had fulfilled her prediction and married Skip, not a Harvard man, but a Harvard Business School man – practically the same thing. And she'd visited Lisa often in Connecticut without making any remarks about Lisa being simply a 'wife', not even a 'mother'. The fact that Lisa's five brothers were all engaged in various careers with varying degrees of success was never thrown in Lisa's face.

But it was always there, lurking. Once, Lisa had had the nerve to refer to that terrible afternoon. 'Sometimes I think I'm so pathetic,' she'd said as they were walking around a supermarket together, buying food for a dinner party she was giving for Skip's boss that evening. 'I'm one of those pathetic corporate housewives with no job of my own.' She stopped by the fruit section as she was saying this and concentrated on the mangoes. For the second time in her life she found it impossible to look her mother in the eye.

'I could have been a contender. I could have been a lawyer, like Jimmy. Or a computer programmer, like Sam. I'm the runt of the litter, aren't I? The one child who hasn't found a career.' Her mother was silent and Lisa tried but failed to smile. Picking up a mango, she turned it over and over in her hand. 'I always did so well at school and then I blew it. I know it's all my fault for getting such bad board scores. And ending up at Oak Manor.'

Was that, strictly speaking, the truth? Yes, she'd always done well at school, but only when the work involved memorization or research. She was diligent, she did her homework carefully, but as soon as the subjects became more complex – when she had to write creative essays or make judgments of her own, she started to falter. She hadn't done badly on the college boards because of her social life, she'd done badly because by that time she'd realized she wasn't as intelligent as she or the teachers had thought she was. She'd watched as classmates began to overtake her in grades and she'd tried, but failed to keep up. Her academic career had peaked when she was fifteen years old. After that, it had been a huge struggle to keep her head above the water.

'Well, what can I say, Lisa? You made a choice. If you're happy with it, that's all that counts,' her mother had replied. Lisa squeezed the mango so hard her fingers went right through the skin. That comment hadn't been scathing, she knew. But it had hit her hard, at a moment when she was fishing for reassurance and comfort. Her mother could have said: 'Marriage is the most difficult career of all to make a success out of. I'm so proud of you,' or 'Lisa, it's never too late. You can do anything you want to with your life.' But she hadn't and Lisa was left feeling her mother was disappointed in her. It still hurt, that feeling. Sometimes she wondered if it would ever go away.

'Declan won't think you're stupid when he gets the sales figures on your book,' Skip said, placing empty bottles by the side of the garbage bin. 'Boy, he went through the champagne like a demon, didn't he? Do you think he might have a problem?'

'I don't think so. People drink a lot more over here, though. I've noticed that.'

'He should watch it.'

'I don't think Declan's a drunk,' Lisa said, getting up from the kitchen table. 'You're over-sensitive on that subject because of your mother, I know. But one night drinking champagne doesn't make Declan an alcoholic.'

Skip didn't respond. He picked up a J-cloth and began to go over the counter with it.

'Skip, you know you never told me what went on that weekend in Chicago with your mother. That was thirteen years ago. Don't you think you could talk about it now?'

'What? Is your next book going to be about healing the wounds of family life? Do you want to use my past the way you used our marriage to make another bestseller?'

'What are you talking about?' Lisa put her hands on the kitchen table to steady herself.

'You could go on *Oprah* again, except this time, you could wheel on me and my alcoholic mother. Great TV, Lisa. Great publicity. Especially if my mother apologizes for everything she's ever done and she and I hug each other with tears in our eyes.'

'Skip, I don't understand. I thought you were proud of me, of *I Saw You First*. You never said—'

'Oh, forget it.' Skip put both hands up in the air. 'I'm tired. I've got an important meeting with people at a commercial production company tomorrow. The book is great – you know I think that. You're great. Our marriage is great. I just wish you could back off on the subject of my mother.'

'I haven't mentioned it since the night you came back from that visit to her in Chicago, Skip. That's thirteen years.'

'I know, I know. You're right. As always. That's my only question. Why do you always get everything right?' Skip threw the J-cloth into the sink. 'I'm going to bed now.'

Lisa moved towards him, to put her arm around his waist, but he slipped out of her reach and headed for the stairs.

'I think I should sleep in the spare room tonight,' he mumbled. 'I couldn't sleep well last night. If the infomercial idea doesn't work, I'm going to go into the air-conditioning business here. That's a definite gap in the market.'

He kissed her on the forehead lightly, then trudged away, leaving her standing helplessly confused. Why was he so angry? And why had he suddenly decided to go into business again, with the infomercial idea? Tonight was the first she'd heard of it, this plan of his to bring infomercials to Britain. He didn't need to work. They had made more than enough money from her book already. What was this meeting all about, and why hadn't he told her about it before? They were scheduled to be here for three weeks, no longer. She had commitments back in the States after that, he knew. None of it made sense.

Were these secret plans, this burgeoning anger all due to the remark she'd made on the plane over? Was he acting out in this way because she'd said, somewhere halfway across the Atlantic, that she wanted to put back their agreed-upon date to try to have a child? If so, he was being silly. What difference could a year or two make when she was only thirty-six and he was thirty-seven? There was plenty of time for a baby. She was enjoying herself now. They both were. The book had given them each a new life.

Suddenly they were meeting important people, travelling to different countries, having a blast. They were basically footloose and fancy-free, living a life that was even better than the one they'd had back in their student days because they had the cash to go along with it. And it was definitely better than their life during his years at AT&T. He didn't have to get up at six in the morning and work until nine at night, for one thing. They had time with each other, to spend as they liked. There were no bosses to please, no hierarchy to kowtow to. If they had people over for dinner, they could dress in jeans or whatever they damn well wanted to dress in. They had clout; the book had given them clout. What was he doing complaining about *Oprah*? The show had helped make them.

This attitude of his was probably just a blip on the radar screen of their happiness, nothing serious. He wouldn't really go ahead with the infomercial scheme. Yes, he'd help her with *her* infomercial, but he wouldn't branch out into others. What would be the point?

'You are not stupid, Lisa Thomas,' she said to herself as she went up the imposing staircase. 'All right, maybe you shouldn't have asked him about his mother, since it's such a touchy subject, but you are not stupid. You've proved that to yourself now. Skip's tired, that's all. He'll get over it. And life will be back to its perfect state. Soon.'

Chapter 3

I've often thought that every person should give a romantic résumé to their prospective partner, detailing previous relationships – what went right, what went wrong etc. We can learn a lot about people by discovering how they have conducted themselves with other partners in the past and why they were attracted to them in the first place. Are you part of a self-destructive pattern, or a fresh start? Is he looking at you or at the image of his last love? Perhaps he is trying to recreate his last love with you, or to forget the misery of his last relationship by diving headlong into your arms.

Where is he coming from, romantically speaking?

What is he looking for?

WAKE UP AND MAINLINE THE COFFEE! This is information you need to know. If you don't know already, find out.

Too many of us are too threatened to ask about our partners' ex-loves. We fear our own jealousy. But ask yourself this: when you first saw him, was there another lover in his heart? If so, where has that lover gone now? Is she still there? Is she what is coming between you?

Or perhaps he has never had a long relationship before. You are the first. This does not mean you can relax. You may not be the last.

When you first saw him, was he a man looking for a stable, long-term partnership or did you think you could change him *because you were so intent on looking for that stable, long-term relationship yourself? Remember those signals he first gave off. I'm sure they were clear enough at the time. Did you deliberately ignore them? If so, you can't complain now. You closed your eyes and refused to see.*

The truth can only be seen with wide-open eyes.

Throw away those sunglasses – even if they're designer ones (jokey, jokey!).

LOVE IS NOT BLIND!!!!

IGNORANCE IS NOT BLISS!!!!

I Saw You First, *Chapter Two, p. 29*

Declan Lewis was surprised to hear the distinctive voice of Toby Goodyear on his voicemail. It was only nine-thirty, so Toby must have been up early. Declan had assumed actors slept in when they weren't on a film set. He envied them for that. He wouldn't have been able to stand the auditions, he knew, nor would he be able to memorize lines or say them with any kind of conviction, but he did wish he had their sort of lifestyle. No office hours. No bloody sales conferences. No endless meetings discussing book jackets and sales figures.

'Declan. Sorry to bother you so early, but I wanted to talk to you about last night. If Lisa is serious about this infomercial, I'm interested. And if Skip is serious about your admittedly crazy idea, I'm interested in that as well. My number is 0171 731 9798. Ring me anytime. I'm home. Thanks. And I hope you're not suffering too much from the champagne. Oh, this is Toby Goodyear, but I'm sure you know that by now. Goodbye.'

Susan, one of the women who worked in the publicity department, popped her head in and asked if he would like a cup of tea. Declan said, 'Yes, please,' then sighed as he looked around him at the open-plan offices of Green & Wilson. His colleagues were busy on telephones or computers, their desks a mess of papers and books. Why couldn't he work in an office environment where each person had his separate, enclosed, private space? As it was, people wandered in and out of each other's glass-walled sections, trading information, gossip and general chitchat. It was difficult to concentrate.

When he'd first started work here, he had an 'open door' policy himself. People came in to chat, to confide, to grumble – and he'd been more than happy to listen. He *liked* listening, and he enjoyed helping, whenever it was possible. Yet as time went by, he'd found that he was swamped by other people and their needs. Few of these discussions had anything to do with his own work, and bit by bit he began to feel his privacy invaded, yet again. It was like the old days at his parents' house. People barged in on him in the middle of telephone conversations, just as his father's students and neighbourhood children had barged in on his family life when he was a teenager.

In the days when he used to go out to the pub with his co-workers, he'd find himself always the last one to leave. People began to take him for granted. 'Declan will sort it out,' they'd say. 'Tell Declan what's going on; he'll help.' There were times when he felt like an unpaid psychiatrist; one who couldn't stop thinking about his clients' problems at the end of office hours.

'Pull yourself together,' Alison had told him after he'd come home late for the umpteenth time. 'Do you think any of these people would help *you* if you were in trouble? Would they care? You're trying to be like your father except with the people you work with instead of students. You've always told me how much that irritated you – the way he listened and listened and listened to them. If you don't lay down some boundaries in your life, you'll find yourself in huge trouble.'

She was right, of course. He wasn't like his father. He wanted to make money, he wanted to succeed within the system, he didn't want to give himself away to every person in his vicinity. He had to be selective. He had to concentrate on Alison and on himself. So he had purposefully closed his door and stopped socializing. At first the people at work hadn't quite believed him. They'd tried to breach his wall of privacy; they'd continued to ask him along to the pub or attempt to sit down and pour out their woes, but he'd stopped them with uncharacteristic abruptness. Now, he reckoned, they were used to his attitude. They left him alone.

'Declan. We haven't talked in such a long time. Would you and Alison like to come out this weekend? Michael will be here, although Sarah and the kids can't come because she has a pottery workshop. Don't worry – no students. The coast is clear. Please come. And don't work too hard. Bye.'

His father had a deep, mellifluous voice, almost as engaging as Toby's. Declan wrote 'Owen' underneath 'Toby' and waited for the next message.

'Declan. You're a difficult man to get hold of. This is Miranda from Dillons. Call me as soon as you can, please. I'm beginning to think you're avoiding me.'

He was surprised she didn't *know* he was avoiding her. Miranda wanted only one thing: further discounts from Green & Wilson. Well, she'd get them in the end, but he would dodge her calls for as long as possible.

'Declan. It's Lisa. It was great to see you last night and to meet the lovely Alison. She is stunning, isn't she? Anywho, I called to say I've thought about it and I'm going to go ahead with the infomercial. Now, I don't see, the more I think about it, that this overlaps with your work on marketing the book. You go right ahead and do what you think best and I'll go ahead with the infomercial idea. We'll discuss how many books should be printed and what discount I'll get on the books later. But while we're on the subject of infomercials, I honestly think this *Plots in a Box* idea isn't a runner. Skip was all excited, but I'm sure he'll calm down. We're not here for long enough to see that project through, for one. By the way, your publicity people have been very efficient so far. My schedule is hectic, as I'm sure you know. Gotta run now. Be in touch soonest. Bye.'

Lisa.

Declan stared at her name, as he wrote it down, trying to sort out the subtext of her message. She didn't want his 'input' on her infomercial and she didn't want him working with Skip. Why not? he asked himself. Did she think he would sabotage her carefully crafted commercial? Or did she think he wasn't clever enough to understand its potential? Well, perhaps she had a point there. Although Declan had done his share of thinking last night as well, and the more he had thought about it, the more he had seen the wisdom of the infomercial approach for *I Saw You First*. The people who would buy that sort of book were also the people who would want to hear those testimonials and see Lisa on air, talking about her marriage to Skip.

In fact, Declan himself was beginning to be very interested in Lisa's marriage to Skip. Why was Lisa writing off Skip's infomercial plans? Why wasn't she supporting her husband, even in such a harebrained scheme? Declan had met her only twice, but he was starting to think she was a control freak. She'd convinced Skip to quit his job, she'd somehow managed to persuade him to sit back without complaint as she broadcast the ups and downs of their relationship in public, and now she had made a telephone call, presumably without Skip's knowledge, to persuade Declan to give up the *Plots in a Box* idea.

Skip was, effectively, Lisa's sidekick. Mr Lisa. How likely was it that Skip enjoyed that role? Declan, remembering the night before, wondered what lay behind Skip's gung-ho, enthusiastic, 'perfecto' façade.

Susan stood at the doorway, a cup of tea in her hand.

'Here you are,' she said, approaching his desk and cautiously placing it in front of him. 'Milk and two sugars.'

'Thank you, Susan.' He looked up at her and saw a very uncomfortable expression. 'How are you doing?'

'I'm fine,' she said quickly, backing away.

'Hang on a second. Why don't you sit down? Tell me what's going on.'

'Everything's fine,' she answered, without moving toward the chair by his desk.

'No news? No hot gossip?'

'I'm sorry?' Her eyes were wary.

'Never mind. Thanks for the tea.'

'Right,' she said. 'You're welcome.' He watched as she scurried off to Alan's desk in the corner of the room. Alan was a science-fiction editor who was very good at his job but who otherwise appeared to regard life as one huge cosmic joke. Declan watched as Susan lingered by Alan's desk, talking away.

Well, he couldn't go back on himself now, could he? He couldn't turn around and sudenly tell people he wanted to become a part of office life again, after he'd so decisively given up on all that. What would he do? Make a public announcement, saying: 'I've missed you all. Please come and chat with me'?

He had to keep reminding himself that he wasn't like his father and brother and never would be. If they'd been working here, they would have had office love-ins, he supposed. They'd discuss Aristotle at lunchtime and organize five-a-side football matches in the park on summer evenings. Michael and Owen would lead expeditions to the coast and play Frisbee on the beach with the sales reps. But then neither Michael nor Owen would ever work in an office to begin with – that was the crucial distinction. They were both teachers, givers, carers – patient with children, tender with animals, unselfish paragons of virtue. They didn't drink, smoke or eat meat. His father and Michael wouldn't step on a bug if they could help it. Declan remembered the look of pain on Owen's face when he, Declan, at age twelve, had killed a wasp.

He watched as Susan walked back to her office with a smile on her face. The smile reminded him of someone. Who was it? Searching his memory bank, he lit upon a name from the past: Anne Tilney. She was an American girl he'd met at University. In England on a student-exchange programme, she'd captured Declan's heart the first time he'd seen her. He'd managed to manoeuvre a date with her and they had fallen, magically, into bed that same night. Anne was a wonder, in bed and out. She was fresh and exciting and teased the hell out of him. He couldn't remember a moment when she wasn't laughing – except, of course, the final moment, when they'd broken up.

'Jesus, Declan,' she'd said, her voice pained and exasperated. 'What *is* your problem? I went on the fucking rope-swing at your parents' house and you have a shit fit? I mean, get real. You've got some kind of fucked-up relationship with your father, fine. But don't take it out on me.'

'You're too old to go on a rope-swing, Anne,' he'd shouted.

'Well, excuse me for having fun. I don't get it. You're a normal person most of the time. Ninety-nine percent of the time you're a great person. But then you turn into an old, bitter man shaking his stick at young people who are having a good time. You're only twenty-two years old, for fuck's sake. And I'm only twenty-one. I can go on any rope-swing I want to. *You're* too old to act like such a baby. Are you jealous of your father, is that it? Jealous that he knows how to enjoy himself and knows how to make other people enjoy themselves too?'

Declan couldn't remember the rest of the argument; all he could recall was watching Anne's back as she walked out of the room. They'd seen each other a few more times after that, but the whole tenor of their relationship had changed. She'd stopped smiling. They both had.

There had been moments the night before at Skip and Lisa's, Declan realized, when he'd felt the way he used to feel at home. Before all the anger had hit him, all the resentment about the Lewis lifestyle. Those days and nights when he'd been a part of the family, playing ping pong, going on the rope-swing, fitting in easily and happily with the family ethos. The days when he and his brother were friends. This was a strange connection to make, he knew. What did *Plots in a Box* have to do with his chaotic upbringing? Nothing – except he'd felt a wave of uncontrollable excitement as he'd become more and more outrageous on the topic of infomercials, the same kind of excitement he'd experienced once upon a time on that damn rope-swing.

The rope-swing he'd sworn to himself he'd never go on again.

The childish, idiotic rope-swing which represented, for reasons he knew he would never fully understand, everything he couldn't bear about his father's house.

I'm going to do it, he thought, frowning at the well-ordered, colour-coded files on his desk. I'm going to ring Toby Goodyear and tell him I want to go ahead with *Plots in a Box*. I'm going to ring Skip Thomas and tell him I'm starting on the project tonight. And I'll go to my parents' house this weekend, as well. Anne Tilney was wrong. I'm not some prematurely old fogey. And I'm not someone who closes his door on people either.

I've got it all wrong, somehow. I've boxed myself into a corner.

Declan in a Box.

It won't sell.

Alison Austin congratulated herself on thinking ahead. She'd dialled 141 before the Thomases' number, so she had no worries about hanging up when she heard Lisa's perky voice say, 'Hi.' Skip was the person she wanted to talk to, not Lisa. Skip was the man with the vision, while Lisa couldn't see beyond her own ego. That much had been patently obvious the night before. Lisa had started to withdraw from the conversation as soon as it deviated from *I Saw You First*. Even with her bouncy, smiley appearance, Lisa had a negative aura. Not unlike Declan sometimes, Alison thought. Although his job was essentially to sell a product to the public, he often said he was uncomfortable doing it. Declan wasn't particularly ambitious, Alison knew, and she wondered why he had chosen a career in marketing when he had such difficulty selling himself.

'What would you think about going out to dinner with me sometime?' he'd asked when he'd rung her the week after they'd met at the funeral.

At the time, she'd quite liked his tentative approach. And as time went on, she found she quite liked everything about him. If pressed, she would have said she loved him. They got on well, they had reasonable sex, they sometimes laughed together. They were a functioning, healthy couple.

But that was just the problem, she reflected, as she drove along the A40, on her way back to the office from the rap group shoot. The whole couple business was the problem.

'Man, can you imagine having sex with one person *for the rest of your life?*' she'd overheard one of the rap singers ask another member of the group. 'She wants to fucking get married. She laid that on me last night. That's dark. That's so dark it's a nightmare.'

Alison had found herself nodding her head in agreement. It *was* dark. In six months' time she would have been with Declan for two years. They would have been living together for one year. Twelve whole months. Whereas most of her female friends were panicking about the thought of reaching thirty without having a steady man in their lives, Alison increasingly panicked about the opposite. Why had she tied herself down so young? She hated knowing exactly what was going to happen every morning and every night. She didn't like being boxed in, having to function as half of a twosome.

Last night had been a prime example. She was the one who had done the research on infomercials, she was the one who immediately understood what Skip Thomas was talking about, while Declan threatened to alienate both Thomases with his over-the-top remarks. As it turned out, Declan had saved himself with the *Plots in a Box* idea, but that had been pure luck. If he'd had his way, he would have dragged her down with him yesterday evening. They would have been *personae non gratae* in the Thomas household, having made enemies for no good reason whatsoever. And Alison would have had to go along with him because they were a 'couple'.

Declan hadn't set out to undermine her, she knew. He wasn't a liability, exactly. But she wouldn't have described him as an asset either. He was obsessed with his crazy family, he had no plan for the rest of his life and he acted, occasionally, like a complete prat. She didn't mind his tidiness or his compulsion for privacy, quite the reverse, but she was increasingly put off by his childish behaviour. He never seemed to act his age. Unless she was careful and monitored him, he'd behave irresponsibly, spending all his time with co-workers at the pub, trying to sort out problems which he should have known he couldn't solve, or teasing Skip Thomas about infomercials or suggesting crazy expeditions to far-flung and dead boring parts of England. Last weekend he'd actually proposed that they visit Solihull – *for fun*. The man was mad.

She didn't like his childish behaviour, when he exhibited it, but she was prepared to put up with it because she knew it stemmed from his totally bizarre, freakish family who were supposed to be great, deep thinkers but who spent most of the time playing silly games or talking until they were blue in the face about the fate of the universe. Owen Lewis might be a University lecturer and author, but on most of the occasions she had seen him he'd spent as much time as possible playing with Michael's children, rollicking around on the floor like a two year old, giggling like a maniac.

Declan was the one Lewis male who had a chance of growing up, she reckoned. The fact that he hadn't yet worried her. She wished he'd get his act together. He was thirty-three years old. It was about bloody time.

Alison decided to ring Skip again in the early evening. She needed to talk to him about infomercials. If he was planning on bringing them to the UK, she wanted to be involved in their production, on the ground floor. She was too old for the pop world and too old for the job she had in it. Enough was enough. The sight of one more druggy-looking bass player wearing black might push her over the edge. Yesterday morning she'd almost screamed: 'Get a life, get some clothes,' at a Liam Gallagher lookalike who had walked into the production company office, radiating disdain.

Skip Thomas had said how happy he'd once been to have his holidays interrupted by calls and faxes from the office. That kind of happiness appealed to Alison. She could complain about it later, if she wanted to. From her house in the Caribbean.

When she picked up her ringing telephone, she was smiling.

'Al. It's me. I wanted to check something with you. Are you OK with going to my parents' house this weekend?'

'Do we have to?' The picture of a goat wandering through the Lewises' living room made Alison's smile instantly vanish.

'I think we should. We haven't been in ages, you know.'

'Are Mr and Mrs Mia going to be there? Have they found another child yet?'

Mr and Mrs Mia was her nickname for Michael and his wife Sarah. How else could you refer to people who had adopted four children, all under the age of six? Alison was convinced Sarah was in competition with Mia Farrow and would adopt at least one more child than Mia had, in order to win.

'Michael will be. The kids and Sarah won't. She has a pottery workshop, apparently.'

'I love that word – workshop. It's so Woodstock. Are you sure Mrs Mia isn't older than she says she is? She *can't* be only thirty-five. She *has* to have been at least a teenager in the Sixties. She even uses phrases like "far out" and "groovy". I think you should tell Mr Mia he's been deceived. Get him to find her passport.'

'Al, if you don't want to come, just say so.'

'All right – I don't want to come.' She waited for a response from him but wasn't surprised by his silence. 'We're not joined at the hip, you know, Declan. They're your family. I'm sure they won't mind having you to themselves. I can't face it, honestly. That house makes me mental. And I have a lot of work to do over the weekend.'

'That's fine.'

Was he annoyed? He didn't sound it. She'd expected him to put up more of a fight and couldn't decide whether she was relieved or disappointed that he hadn't.

'I'll see you later, then.'

'It will be later than usual. I'm going to the pub after work with a few of the people here.'

61

'Declan! You've stopped going to the pub after work, remember?'

'I feel like going today.'

'I see,' Alison said. 'It's like that again, is it?'

'You sound as if I were an alcoholic telling you I was just going to have one drink.'

'Do I? Could that be because other people and their problems *are* an addiction of yours?'

'I'm not that bad,' he said, his tone defensive. 'I want to see some people, that's all. I won't be late. I want to talk about football, relax. Chill out.'

'Football.'

'Yes. Football.'

'Oh shit. You're not going to try to drag me on to the football terraces again, are you? Listen, football isn't coming home, as far as I'm concerned. It isn't coming to *our* home, anyway.'

'I have to go now, Alison.'

'So do I. I'll see you when you get back from the pub. I'll open the door wearing a Chelsea strip. Au revoir, Monsieur Cantona.'

What was that all about? Alison asked herself, staring at her mobile phone. Why had he suddenly regressed? They'd agreed that he had to stop socializing at work. And football? It was July! Football hadn't even started its torturous reign yet. Why did he have to talk about it now? Who was this man? What was she doing with him?

Alison flashed to a picture of Lisa talking on the television the night before, asking 'Mike' about his wife 'Linda'. 'What happened to the woman who made your heart stall?' Lisa had asked. And then droned on about getting back to those marvellous, consuming feelings of the first date.

'Why do you assume she made his heart stall?' Alison had felt like screaming at the television. Perhaps Mike had simply liked Linda; perhaps she hadn't sent him into paroxysms of romantic bliss. Would that have been so terrible, if Mike hadn't swooned the first time he saw Linda? Swooning was not compulsory for a relationship, was it? Sometimes swooning was a huge mistake. Part of the reason Alison had taken up with Declan in the first place was because she *hadn't* swooned. He hadn't driven her wild with desire. No – what she'd felt more than anything with Declan was relief.

That first night, after their first dinner out, he'd taken her back to his flat for coffee. She hadn't decided yet whether she was going to have sex with him, she was keeping her options open, waiting to see what developed between them. He was reasonable-looking enough, certainly. Pleasant company. An interesting bloke. Yet not to die for. When he'd opened the door of his flat and switched on the lights, she'd seen a vision of cleanliness; a well-lit, well-ordered haven. And that's what had done it for her. He's not Peter, was the thought that had overwhelmed her. He's not anything like Peter. He would never sit around smoking dope all day. He wouldn't leave dirty clothes and dirty dishes everywhere. Chances are he probably doesn't even play a musical instrument.

The disastrous shambles of her relationship with Peter lay behind her, she decided later on in the night, as she settled into Declan's arms.

Peter was history. There were certain compromises you had to make in life and she was fully prepared to make them. She didn't, for example, have to have abandoned sex to be happy. That kind of sex could lead to all-consuming jealousy and self-abasement. At least in her case, it had. She'd made a complete fool of herself with Peter. Making a fool of herself was not part of her game plan.

Declan was safe. He needed her to rescue him, to guide him and help him grow up, yes, but he was, at heart, responsible. She and Declan were adults who were getting on in the world, not lovestruck kids who messed up their lives. Being with Declan would be easy.

That's what she had thought the first night. Now that being with Declan was not so easy, now that she was beginning to wonder whether he ever would really grow up, she had to ask herself what should happen next. They'd pooled their resources to buy the house in Battersea; everything they had was jointly owned. When Peter had left her, he'd simply walked out the door with his fucking guitar. She couldn't do the same with Declan; disengaging would be a difficult process.

Perhaps she was jumping the gun. She needed to slow down and reassess her situation. If she started working with Skip, at a new job in a new field, she might not want to go through all the hassles of breaking up with Declan, moving out and finding a new flat as well.

She had to study her position, think over all the pros and cons before making any decision.

'*Alison Austin asks for extra homework. That's all she does – study. She's a teacher's pet.*'

Alison remembered overhearing this conversation between two girls at school when she was fourteen years old. It should have made her feel like a toffee-nosed swot, she knew. Instead she'd felt proud and pleased. There was nothing wrong with asking for extra homework when you knew you could do it.

EXERCISE NUMBER TEN

Write a description of your partner, emphasizing all his best qualities. Follow that with a description of the best night you two ever spent together, the best night of your life. Where were you? What were you both wearing? What did you talk about? Do you remember laughing together?

Next, write a description of your partner, emphasizing all his worst qualities. And follow that with a written description of the worst night you two have ever spent together. Do not leave anything out, however painful it might be.

Study both sheets of paper carefully.

Set fire to the second and throw the ashes into the trash where they belong.

Then concentrate on what you have left. Those best qualities and that best night.

Unbelievable, Toby Goodyear said to himself, tossing the book Lisa had thrust into his hands the night before on to the floor. Next time out she should write a guide for pyromaniacs. 'Why not set fire to your partner?' he would have liked to write in the margins. 'A much simpler solution.'

Was the best night you've spent with your partner supposed to be the best night of your life as well? Why? Because you'd had the best sex? Or eaten the best food? What was Lisa on about? Christina was lovely and had given him many wonderful evenings indeed, which was why he continued staying with her, but she hadn't given him the best night of his life. Did that mean there was something wrong with their relationship? With her?

No. Christina was fine. She was quiet, funny and intelligent. She never pushed him for a commitment, never acted as if she owned him and had taken in stride his suggestion that he move in with her for a while to save money.

She hadn't screamed: 'You're using me because you're broke', or: 'It's time you got a steady job.' All she had said was: 'That makes sense,' in that calm voice of hers. Nothing seemed to faze her. Plus she had those magic hands.

They had met when she was the aromatherapist tending to the cast of *Northanger Abbey*. He'd wangled his way to the front of the list and spent an hour in heaven as she sorted out all his tensions. During that time he'd decided he had to have this woman. Not only because she could work miracles on his neck, but also because she was so tall. He liked the idea that she'd be too tall to nestle her head against his chest like some stricken bird looking for comfort, the way every other woman in his life had. And he liked the idea of those long, long legs. So he set about getting her and get her he had.

They'd spent some very good nights together since that time, that much was certain; but she certainly wasn't responsible for his best night.

No, the best night in his life had had nothing to do with women, unless he counted Gertrude and Ophelia into the equation. They'd helped him have his best night, certainly. It was more than possible that they could have wrecked his best night if they'd fouled up their lines or knocked down the scenery. But in the end, that night had been his alone. He'd triumphed. He had *been* Hamlet, he had been the best Hamlet ever seen on stage. Only no one except a handful of fellow actors knew about it. The audience didn't have a clue. They had clapped at the end, but they didn't know what they were clapping for.

How could they, a bunch of no-hopers in Tooting? They hadn't seen Olivier, they'd probably never even heard of Olivier. For the most part, he could see, as he secretly studied them during the interval, they were punks with an attitude, young people who had come for God knows what reason, wishing that they were at a rave instead. They'd probably watched him perform, all the while dreaming about who they were going to shag that night. Or replaying some crucial football match, kick by kick.

'It's a shame, Toby,' the actress who had played Gertrude told him in the pub later. 'You were incredible. I've never seen anything like it. And not one critic. No one who can spread the word. I'll do my best, but I don't know how far word-of-mouth can take you. The chances of anyone important trekking to Tooting are minimal.'

The chances were nil, he reckoned. And that thought had insinuated itself into his subsequent performances. He couldn't reproduce the magic when he knew no one who understood that magic would be watching. He *should* have been able to, he knew. What did it matter that his genius wasn't recognized properly? He should have done it for the love of acting. But he wasn't sure what had prompted it in the first place, how he had suddenly taken off with the role and flown to the heavens. He felt as if he had had a perfect one-night stand with a stranger who had disappeared the next morning never to be found again. He searched and searched for her but she had vanished into thin air.

After that night he watched every performance of *Hamlet* he could, both on stage and on video. He studied them all, judging them against his own and always rating himself higher.

Olivier? Brilliant, of course, but in the end too old-fashioned.

Gibson? Not bad, actually, but impossible to forget he's Mel Gibson.

Fiennes? Too fast. He threw the words away, garbled them.

Branagh? One-dimensional and noisy.

Toby had, for one night, on a shitty little stage in a shitty little theatre, out-acted all the greats.

Lighting a cigarette, he went over to the desk in the corner of the living room and searched out the programme from that night. It was a piece of paper, actually, not a proper programme. One sheet of paper with the name of the play, the director and the cast typed out. Not something one would save for two years, he reflected. From a testimonial to brilliance, it had turned into a searing reminder of failure. The best he'd managed since that time was a sad collection of parts in even sadder repertory companies, plus a one-off gig as a diabetic in an episode of *Casualty* and a two-line walk-on in *Northanger Abbey*.

How the not-so-mighty have fallen.

Could he do it again, if given the chance? he asked himself, wandering into the kitchen, clutching the offensive bit of paper. If someone were to offer him the part of Hamlet in an RSC production, could he do what he'd done before? Or had he lost it now? Had the lady vanished *for ever*?

'And that,' he said out loud, putting out his cigarette and picking up the envelope containing, he knew, his overdrawn bank statement, 'is THE question.'

Toby stared at the envelope in his one hand and the programme in his other. Using his hands as scales, he shifted the balance between them, up and down, up and down. When he put the envelope back on to the kitchen table, he pulled out a lighter from his pocket.

'Double, double toil and trouble,' he intoned. He set fire to the flimsy programme, watched it burn and then dumped it in the ashtray.

When the telephone rang, he was emptying the ashtray into the bin. He waited a few rings before picking it up, during which time he found himself hoping it might be Christina's step-sister Lucy. He'd spoken to her once or twice, although he'd never told Christina that. They had laughed about the fact that they'd never met and discussed Christina's strange reluctance to introduce him to her family in conspiratorial tones. He'd like to meet Lucy and find out about Christina's family, her past. He'd quite like to meet Lucy secretly, in fact.

'Toby. It's Declan Lewis.'

'Declan. Hello. Thanks for returning my call.'

'Listen. I don't see why we can't go ahead with this *Plots in a Box* idea. We both know it won't work, but we can be paid for our time, and it might be a hell of a lot of fun.'

'My thoughts exactly.'

'I'll ring Skip, shall I? Tell him we're ready to start work on the project?'

'Fine by me.'

'And let's show how keen we are. Let's tell him we're meeting up tonight.'

'That's fine by me too. Should we *actually* meet tonight? Would you like to come here after work?'

'Why not? Yes, I'd like to.'

'Excellent.' Toby gave him his address. 'What time is convenient for you?'

'Six-thirty?'

'Six-thirty. Declan, is Lisa going ahead with her infomercial as well?'

'Yes. But I'm out of the loop, as the Yanks say, on that one. I'm sure she'll be in touch with you. She's out doing publicity at the moment, I know.'

'Right. I'll see you later, then. Goodbye.'

Toby pulled the bag out of the bin and tied the ends together. He hoisted it over his shoulder, walked outside and put it in the wheelie bin. The rubbish collection wasn't until tomorrow morning, but he needed to get rid of the charred remains of his past, banish them from the flat.

Declan Lewis was a hard person to place, he decided when he returned to the sitting room and lit another cigarette. Public-school boy? No, he didn't think so – unless he'd been on a scholarship. Declan didn't have the arrogant face that went with the monied classes – the face Toby had once had himself, but which had disappeared by the time he was fifteen. Oh, the class bit was still there, Toby knew. He had an aristocratic look; fine, straight, slightly haughty features. But the actual arrogance had gone when the money had.

All that furniture Toby had been told he should respect had been sold, as had the houses containing it. His family hadn't crashed and burned in a Lloyds syndicate, nothing as dramatic or understandable as that. They'd just pissed it all away, confident that there would always somehow, somewhere, be more. In fact, they'd barely managed to pay the school fees, and there had been many moments of crisis when Toby thought he'd have to leave Harrow abruptly because of unpaid bills. That was when he'd first discovered he could act. When all his classmates talked about their summer holidays in the States and their winter holidays in the Alps, he'd listened as if he were still one of them. He didn't stupidly manufacture exotic holidays of his own; he simply sat back and acted unconcerned.

When he was with his family, he pretended he couldn't care less about the financial upheavals. He, Toby Goodyear, was above this petty world. His mother could scream at his father for being so unprepared and so hopeless about money, his father could sit in aggressive silence, his parents could get divorced. All the genteel veneer could be stripped away layer by layer from people he'd once loved and admired. He, Toby Goodyear, could prove that he didn't care. This disruption, this terrible behaviour was beneath him.

He was an actor.

Toby reached down and picked up *I Saw You First* from the

floor. Perhaps he'd never had a best night with a woman because he'd never fallen in love with a woman. He'd been genuinely fond of various women in his life, particularly Christina, but he'd never said 'I love you' to any of them. If they chose to believe he did love them, that was their problem. At the moment, his relationship with Christina was fine, but he knew from past experience that it would eventually peter out. One of these days she'd ask him to make some kind of verbal commitment – that's what all women did; some sooner, some later. And at that point, he'd have to leave. It would be a shame because they got along so well together and he still fancied her, but he'd never promised her anything and he wasn't about to make a promise he couldn't keep.

At least he wasn't shacked up with some nightmare female like Lisa Thomas, he thought, thumbing through the pages of the book.

Relationships are, in the end, what life is all about, he read. *One is a lonely number, as they say. Imagine taking a walk in the woods. Wouldn't you prefer to have someone beside you, holding your hand as you breathe in that fresh air and marvel at the wonders of nature? True joy is always shared joy.*

'Yuck,' Toby said to himself. 'Yuck, yuck, yuck.'

'You folks aren't the people I should be talking to, are you?' Skip finally said after he'd listened to two men waffle on about a beer commercial. 'I'm not talking about those super-clever ads you show before movies in this country – which, by the way, strikes me as a very stupid thing to do because people go to the movies to see movies not commercials – but never mind. I'm talking about *basics*. What appeals to the ordinary housewife sitting at home on a weekday afternoon, the one who channel-surfs extraterrestrially. She's not looking for some glitzy beer ad, she's looking for a *life*.' Skip studied the men's faces and sighed. 'I want to talk to the right people, OK? I thought I made that clear when I set this meeting up.'

'As I said,' one of them stated, his mouth set in disapproval, 'we're already familiar with infomercials. What we're *not* familiar with is your company, or your track record.'

'The few infomercials you have here are rinkydink infomercials. You don't need to be familiar with my company or my track record. What you need to do is to *listen* to me. No, what you need to do is set me up with the people who *should* be listening to me.'

'You have no experience in television,' the other said, with a wry half-smile. 'As I understand it, you're trying to sell American infomercials to British people, having had no experience in the field yourself. You want to bring those sleep-inducing pillows here, those car engines that will start no matter what foul atrocity is committed on them, all these products which have been successfully merchandized in this way in your country. Why should we talk to you when you have, as I said, no experience in the field and seem to be marketing products which the manufacturers themselves could market directly? If they wanted their infomercials here, they would have bought the advertising space themselves, am I right?'

'Listen – I helped produce my wife's infomercial, which has been one of the all-time successful infomercials in America. I was responsible for that. Have you watched the tape I sent you?'

'Absolutely.' The man with the wry smile nodded his head. 'Very interesting. My wife wants to buy the book. She says I don't recognize her for who she is. I told her she should be thankful for that.'

'What is the problem with you people?' Skip stood up. 'This kind of superior attitude may come in handy when you're subjugating nations, but it doesn't help one bit when you're trying to do a deal. I'm not saying you have to sell the same product, but the same concept. People will buy antifreeze if they see a frozen engine start up. I *know* the mindset, the way these things work. I've studied them. I know that infomercials are the future here. I can help make that happen.'

'I think the point is that we're *not* trying to do a deal, Mr

71

Thomas. Frankly, if we want to put car engines in blocks of ice and talk about them for thirty minutes, we can do it ourselves. The concept is not exactly difficult to figure out. We're already doing it on a limited scale. It's not a British concept, however. It won't work here on the scale you seem to think it will. As I said, it's limited. We don't need thirty-minute adverts. We don't *want* them.'

'Yeah, and you don't need *Cheers* or *Melrose Place* or *ER* or *Friends* or *Baywatch* or *Frasier* or *NYPD* or anything American whatsoever on your screens either, do you? They don't do shit for ratings, right? They're not a *British* concept. You know what? You guys will end up being a nation of extremely well-educated butlers.' Skip walked out then, shaking his head.

'I've lost it,' he kept repeating to himself as he hailed a taxi on Brewer Street. I can't function like a businessman any more. They were right. I wasn't making any sense back there. I didn't have any recognizable gameplan. I was desperate and not thinking straight. Lisa has taken over. Like some body-snatcher from outer space, she's taken my drive, my brains and my money-earning ability. And I'm left with what? My old self. The caring, compassionate idealistic Skip Thomas who changes tyres for ladies in distress. Give me a break.

Skip was in no mood, when he arived back in Pimlico, to hear Lisa's message on the answering machine informing him of her hectic schedule doing thousands of radio interviews. He didn't want to know. One more word about *I Saw You First* and he thought she just might never see him again.

Her success, at first, he was forced to admit to himself as he collapsed into one of the uncomfortable kitchen chairs, had pleased him tremendously. Of course it had. There was no money coming in and he was beginning to panic. All their romantic notions of downshifting and leading a life without worrying about finances had been fine to begin with, but had rapidly worn thin.

It may be difficult to make money, Skip reflected, gazing at the high-tech kitchen around him, but it is even more difficult, once you've achieved a certain lifestyle, to give it up.

Lisa had made him choose between his job and his marriage and he'd opted for his marriage. He'd listened to her talking about their old days together, the way they used to feel about each other, their dreams of what life would be like, and what she had said kicked in powerfully. He was tired of his work, exhausted by the demands made on him, the time spent at the office. Their marriage *was* in trouble because they spent so little time together, because he was so preoccupied with work. So he'd quit. Just like that. They'd sold their house, moved into a much smaller one and scaled down drastically, financially speaking. For a while, it had been wonderful. They'd lazed around, acting like the college students they'd once been – except without any term papers to write or exams to take. It had been idyllic.

But it wasn't real. No way was it real. Bills kept coming in; financial demands which were eating away at his savings. He knew he'd have to start work again soon, but he wanted to savour the unaccustomed feeling of freedom for as long as he could make it last.

When Lisa first told him she was going to write a book to help other couples in trouble, he'd figured it was a fun diversion for her. She could type away while he decided exactly what he wanted to do and how he would set about doing it. Eventually, they'd be back to a situation where he earned the money and she, well, she took care of the house and, he hoped, the babies. They would have had a great break from the rat race and rebuilt their marriage all at the same time.

How could he have guessed that Lisa would a) find an agent b) find a good agent who negotiated a mega-advance on the basis of Lisa's synopsis c) become a bestselling author d) turn into a TV personality and e) a quasi guru? It was unthinkable, and for a long, long time, absolutely fantastic. He honestly hadn't minded basking in her reflected glory. 'I'm the wind beneath your wings,' he'd joked. 'I'm what every successful woman needs – a good wife.' He'd helped her prepare for *Oprah*, like a professional sports coach or a personal trainer. He'd suggested the infomercial idea and worked on the script with her. He'd even found the right director. He'd done everything he possibly could, including keeping his mouth set in a smile every time she blabbed about their private life to countless viewers.

I'm not some old-fashioned macho pig, he kept telling himself. So what if she's the one who brings home the bacon? It doesn't matter. I don't give a damn if I'm treated like her chaperone or bodyguard at glitzy media parties. Why should I mind if people ignore me? Or if they, when they are forced to talk to me, spend the whole time asking how my brilliant wife saved me from myself? Where's the problem? We're making huge amounts of money, we're travelling all over the country and we're *hot*, we're celebrities. Or rather, *she's* hot, she's a celebrity. Lisa deserves her time in the sun. She went through a lot of shit with me when I was making a success out of my career, the least I can do is stand by her.

It's great being a wife.

Just great.

He almost didn't pick up the phone when it rang, dreading hearing Lisa's further tales of her day dealing with the media. But not answering the telephone was as unthinkable a concept for him as not opening his mail.

'Skip. It's Declan Lewis.'

Skip waited for Declan to say: 'Is Lisa there?'

'Skip? Are you there?'

'Yes. Sorry – what did you want?'

'I wanted to talk to you about the infomercial.'

'Lisa's in charge of that, Declan. I helped her in America, but she knows how to do it all now. I'm going to bow out. She's the best person to sell her own book, you'll see that as you work with her.'

'I meant the *Plots in a Box* infomercial.'

Right, you asshole, Skip thought. Go ahead and tell me it was a joke. I couldn't give a shit any more.

'I just spoke to Toby. We want to work on it.'

Skip felt the click in his brain so clearly he wondered whether it was audible. OK, sure, the Brits could make their own infomercials if they wanted them. Let them freeze their own engines and devise their own painless weight-loss schemes. But this – this was different. Who else would come up with this idea? It hadn't been done in America. No one had seen anything like it. This wasn't selling pillows or romantic advice, this was selling *culture*. He could sell it to both countries, then translate it and sell it all over the world.

'Declan, that's great. What I need, obviously, is a script. I need to know whether Toby is going to talk straight to camera. I need to know if you think testimonials will work on this one. If they do, we have to get serious people, heavy hitters on board, as well as ordinary types. By that I mean you have to have Joe Shmoe relating how *Plots in a Box* has helped his life, but you also need someone famous, someone you might not expect to need *Plots in a Box* come on and rave about it. Like that Gielgud guy, if he's still alive. Someone like that. See what I mean?'

'Yes.'

'Also, we have to talk to china people.'

'Chinese people?'

'No, the guys who are going to make the dinnerware, you know. We have to have people who can produce it – cheaply. We have to find the guys who market the audio cassettes, too. And then we have to do some consumer research. That girlfriend of yours would be good at that. Plus we need a—'

'Hang on, Skip. Slow down a little. Why don't we start with the script? Toby and I can work on that first. We're meeting tonight, actually.'

'Great. We'll go on the £100 an hour basis while you do that – work on the script. Then, if I like it, we'll hammer out another deal. Does that sound fair?'

'Yes.'

'You deliver me a script – let's see . . . Today is Thursday. Let's say Tuesday. How about that for a deadline?'

'Fine. But Skip – I'm not going to tell Alison about this yet. I don't want to get her involved until further down the line.'

Meaning you don't want to get her involved at all. Now why would that be? Afraid she'll take over from you? Judging from last night, she looks like she could do just that with no problem. I'll see how you do on the script and then *I'll* decide who gets involved and when.

'No sweat. Listen, I'd prefer it if you didn't tell Lisa about this either. Let's keep it between us for the moment, all right?'

'All right.'

'Good. Tell Toby that too. Then it will be a done deal.'

'Skip – are you thinking of this for the American or the British market?'

'Good question. I think we have to start with the American market – it's the biggest one, after all. Plus I know how my fellow countrymen eat up *Masterpiece Theatre* and all that stuff.'

'Are you sure, though, that Americans really want to know about culture? Even in such a shrink-wrapped package?'

'I *could* take that question personally, Declan. But I won't. I'll tell you something off the record. Lisa told me last night she felt you all thought she was dumb, and it bugged the shit out of her.'

'Skip – God, I'm sorry if that's the way we sounded.'

'No matter. She'll get over it. The point is, she doesn't want to feel dumb, she wants to feel as educated and as conversant with the classics as you are. See what I'm getting at here?'

'Yes, I think I do.'

'So Lisa would buy the tape. And Lisa is representative, right? Understand the equation? Lisa sells to the mass market, she has a take on what they want. You sell Lisa *Plots in a Box*, you sell all those people out there who buy Lisa's book *Plots in a Box*. Write this script as if you were selling the idea to Lisa. You're trying to make people who feel dumb feel smart. That's all this is about.'

'I feel awful about last night, Skip. Really. I didn't mean—'

'Save it, Declan. I told you, it doesn't matter. Lisa's fine. Lisa's out right now being interviewed by thousands of radio stations. Don't worry about Lisa.'

'All right. But I *am* sorry.'

'Call Toby – OK? Get working. Everything will be fine.'

'I will. Goodbye, Skip.'

'Yo.'

Skip, when he hung up, opened the refrigerator door and searched out a tin of caviare. Lisa didn't want a baby yet – fine. She didn't understand why he was in a rush, and he wasn't sure why he was either. The desire probably stemmed from his own childhood and a yearning for what he saw as the American Dream. Two kids, a station wagon, a back yard with a basketball net. Parents who didn't get blind drunk or run away from home. He had the pictures all mapped out in his mind; he could even imagine what his son and daughter would look like and how proud they'd be to have him as a father. They wouldn't grow up in an atmosphere of shame and embarrassment as he had.

But when he'd tried to explain this to Lisa, she'd said: 'I thought the American Dream was that any person, no matter how poor or from what humble origins, can become President of the United States.' Maybe she was right. Damned if he knew for certain. At this point in time it seemed more likely that she'd become President than that they'd have his dream nuclear family.

Well, Lisa could do her own thing and he could do his. For now, *Plots in a Box* would be his baby – nothing to do with her.

Nothing whatsoever to do with her.

Chapter 4

You started off this romance like two kids let loose in a candy store. Of course you did. That's what romance is all about. Remember those feelings? Weren't they great! But then what happened? You settled down and day-to-day life took over. You had heard all each other's funny stories. You discovered all each other's irritating little habits. You stopped making an effort to look terrific. As the daily grind of life wore on, you began to take each other for granted. Even your sex-life turned from thrilling to mundane.

That's life, kiddo, you said to yourself. That's just the way things happen.

Oh yeah?

Give me one good reason why.

You're still the same woman, he's still the same man.

You can make those good times happen again.

I'm not saying you have to be at the door dressed up in a French maid's outfit when he comes home. Please! Although that might not be a bad idea (jokey jokey!).

I'm saying put yourself in a hypothetical situation. Imagine what you would feel like if some other woman was there opening the door to him, looking fantastic. If this thought sends you ballistic, then it is time to stop taking him for granted.

(A brief pause before I go further. I have taken the decision to say 'she' rather than 'she/he', thus seemingly addressing these

words to women solely. This is not the case. This book is for men just as much as it is for women. However, to use she/he throughout the text is distracting. It also goes without saying that all I am writing applies to homosexual couples as well.)

Imagine someone else meeting him for the first time. Imagine what she would see. Would you want him telling all those funny stories to her? So you've heard them before. That's not the point.

This man is not from Venus and you are not from Mars. If you think the male attitude is alien to females and vice versa, you have forgotten how in synch you two were to begin with. You were two people bonding, two human beings with the same kinds of experience. As soon as you forget that, you allow someone else to see your partner the way he wants to be seen – not as a boring, aging, alien male, but as an exciting, vibrant, simpatico human being.

Don't follow the trend and concentrate on how different men and women are. See the truth.

We're all in the same boat.

We all want to be recognized as the invaluable, irreplaceable people we are.

Do it now – see your partner for the first time again.

Before it's too late.

I Saw You First, Chapter One, p. 2

'Well, where do we start?' Declan settled into an armchair in the tiny sitting room and tried not to wonder what the hell he was doing in this flat off Fulham Palace Road. Either he should have been at home or out at the pub with his fellow workers, as he had told Alison he'd be. He'd lied to her for no good reason; although he wouldn't call it a blatant lie. He *had* been intending to go along to the pub, but his plans had changed when he'd rung Toby. Nevertheless, he'd entered into a strange contract with Skip – that neither Alison nor Lisa would know about his work on this project – and that contract worried him. He had always been private, but not secretive. Secrecy was for people who had something to hide, not for people who were having some innocent fun. Why hadn't he told Alison he was going to work on *Plots in a Box*? He couldn't answer that question except to say it had been an instinctive decision.

'Would you like a drink?' Toby was standing, cigarette in hand. 'We have some white wine and some lager. Nothing fancy, I'm afraid.'

'A glass of white wine would be fine. Thank you.'

When Toby had gone off to the kitchen, Declan quickly glanced around the room. It was small, but not cluttered. Toby and Christina had obviously worked out that two blue armchairs, one glass table and a standing lamp were all that could fit in without producing instant claustrophobia in their guests. To the right of where he was sitting was a bookshelf, filled with plays. On top of the bookshelf was a photograph of Toby in what Declan guessed was some theatrical role. His eyes were heavily made-up and he was posing like a swaggering pirate. All that was missing was the eye-patch. Was it a joke? He couldn't tell. How seriously did actors take themselves? Clearly, he was about to find out.

'Here you go – ' Toby proffered a glass of wine, and sat down in the other armchair with an identical glass. He had the same studied casual air he'd had the night before, and was wearing blue jeans with a black T-shirt.

I wish someone would mess up that hair, Declan thought.

'Thank you.'

'Do we need a pad of paper, do you think?'

'No, not yet. I think we should throw some ideas around first, before we write anything down.' Declan frowned. 'I feel as if I'm ripping the poor sod off, but then I think – well, maybe he's right, maybe it will work.'

'I don't particularly care whether it works or not.' Toby took a sip of his wine. 'The money isn't bad.'

'If it *did* work, Toby, you might become famous in the States. Have you considered that possibility?'

'I hadn't, no. But now that you bring it up, I suppose that *is* possible. Do people really watch these things?'

'They must.'

'Hmmm.' He picked up his pack of Bensons and tapped one out. 'So we're doing this for the Americans.'

'That's what he wants. It makes sense, when you think about it.'

'I suppose it does.' Toby lit up and inhaled. 'It could be interesting, you know. A lot better for me than playing Mike in Lisa's.'

'You could do both.'

'I probably will do both.'

'Skip wants a script by Tuesday.'

'Tuesday?'

'Yes. And that's a problem because—'

Declan was interrupted by the arrival of Christina. She was suddenly standing in the entrance of the sitting room, looking flushed and slightly bewildered.

'Sorry,' she said immediately. 'Am I barging in on something? I just got back.'

'I didn't hear you come in, but then you're so quiet I never do,' Toby replied, not moving from his chair. 'Declan and I are working on the *Plots in a Box* project.'

Christina, laughing, looked from one to the other. 'You're joking, yes?'

'"Fraid not,' Declan replied. 'Or rather we are and we aren't. Here,' he continued, standing up. 'Would you like to sit down?'

If Toby was willing to tell Christina about *Plots in a Box*, he thought, why had he and Skip decided *not* to tell Lisa and Alison? He'd assumed it was a purely instinctive response, but perhaps the real reason he hadn't told Alison was because he feared her reaction would be *too* enthusiastic and he'd end up having to go through with the project whether he wanted to or not. Alison had a way of urging him on that sometimes came perilously close to bullying. She might do even more research on infomercials and he'd be stuck talking about car engines and weight loss twenty-four hours a day.

'That's nice of you,' Christina brushed her dark hair off her forehead, 'but I'll sit on the floor. I prefer it.'

'Just like a university student,' Declan muttered.

'I suppose so. I was one, once upon a time.' Her laugh had turned into a smile. 'Not a very good one, though.'

He didn't believe it. She had intelligent eyes. She would have been one of the ones discussing Norman Cohn's *The Pursuit of the Millennium* at his father's feet.

Why hadn't Toby offered her a glass of wine, Declan wondered. He seemed to be taking no notice of her at all.

'So what's the problem about Tuesday?' Toby asked him.

'Well, I promised my parents I'd visit them this weekend. And that doesn't leave us much time. I suppose I could cancel. Or else – no.' Declan shook his head. 'That wouldn't work.'

'What wouldn't work?' Toby pressed.

'I was just thinking you two might like to come with me. They live outside Amersham, it's not a long drive. There's no place to work there, though. The house is – well, it's hard to explain. My father is a university lecturer. He has some very strange ideas about how people should live.' But I want them to come, Declan thought. I need a shield from Michael, and Alison won't be there. I could cancel, but I don't want to listen to my father's disappointed voice. Or imagine what Michael will say about me if I don't show up yet again. How long is it that I haven't visited? Eight or nine months. And I've made too many pathetic excuses.

'Your father isn't Owen Lewis, is he?' Christina asked.

'Yes,' Declan sighed. 'Don't tell me you were a student of his.'

'No, but I read one of his books – the one on John Stuart Mill. It was brilliant.'

Mm-hmm, Declan thought, I was right. You would have been one of those ones on the floor, those amazing legs of yours stretching out so far they would have reached under the ping-pong table.

'Isn't there somewhere we could work outside?' Toby asked with what sounded to Declan like irritation. 'I mean, it's so fucking hot at the moment and the weather is supposed to hold through the weekend at least. It would be nice to get out of town, if your parents could put us up. They must have some sort of garden with a tree we could sit under. And you must have a laptop.'

'Yes,' Declan nodded. 'I do have a laptop and they do have a tree – more than one tree, in fact. Although of course they wouldn't say that those trees were *their* trees. No such thing as ownership in Owen's house.'

'Whatever.' Toby waved his hand in the air as if to shoo off a fly. 'It sounds like a good plan to me. Now – Christina, you probably won't want to stay for this. We have to discuss the general concept of *Plots in a Box*. Get some idea of what exactly we're working on.'

Why doesn't he want Christina here? Declan wondered. And why did he accept my invitation on both their behalfs without asking her first? He's a difficult man to get a hold of. I wonder whether he's a halfway decent actor or just a pretty boy who gets the occasional job because of his looks and his voice.

Christina blinked a few times, and then got up to leave.

'Christina, can I ask you something before you disappear?' Declan queried.

'I'm six feet two and a half.'

Her eyes were focused, he noticed, on the photograph of Toby on the bookshelf.

'No. I mean, that wasn't what I was going to ask. I wanted to know where you practise your aromatherapy.'

She switched her gaze and looked at him with suspicion for a short second, suspicion followed by relief.

'At Thames Place, a health club on the Fulham Road. Aromatherapy's becoming increasingly popular, actually. For a long time people were wary – they didn't know what it entailed. If someone asked me what I did for a living, I'd try to make it simple for them and say I was a masseuse, but then they made some unflattering assumptions. Now I don't have to explain.'

'We published a book on aromatherapy last spring.'

'Did it sell well?'

'It did, in fact. We managed to get Tesco's to take it, because they stock their own line of aromatherapy products.'

'Really? I—'

'Christina, we can talk about all this later, when we've finished our work. If I'm going to take this much money from Skip Thomas, I think I should be principled about it. I don't think I should charge him for an hour spent discussing the virtues of lavender and eucalyptus oils.'

'Right,' Christina said quickly. 'I'm off then.'

Declan noticed Toby's use of the first person. Every time he said the word 'I', his voice emphasized it as if it were the most important word in the sentence. Working with him, he decided, might not be so much fun.

When Christina had left the room, Declan leant forward in his chair, put his glass of wine on the floor and said: 'Toby – for some reason Skip doesn't want Lisa to know about all this. I said we wouldn't tell her. Is that all right with you?'

'Fine,' Toby replied. He had settled back into his chair comfortably and was suddenly smiling. Declan could see it then – the charm, the ease with which he turned to the subject at hand. Perhaps he simply dislikes interruptions, he guessed. He must hate it when people cough during one of his monolgues on stage. And can I blame him?

'So – we're doing this for the Americans,' Toby recapped. 'That makes a huge difference to our approach.'

'What sort of difference exactly?' Declan asked.

'Well . . .' Toby began to tap his hand against his knee. 'I would imagine most Americans don't have a clue what these books are about. Some farmer's wife in Kansas would probably think *Tess of the d'Urbervilles* is a story about a dog.'

Declan began to laugh. He was warming to Toby; however large an ego the man had, he also had a sense of humour.

'And *Bleak House*,' Toby continued, still tapping. 'They might guess that was a book on architecture in the Depression.'

'So what an infomercial would have to do,' Declan grinned, 'would be to tell people first of all what the book *isn't*. Proust's *Remembrance of Things Past*, for example, is not a sequel to *Back to the Future*.'

'Exactly.'

'*Mill on the Floss* has nothing to do with oral hygiene.'

'And *Vanity Fair* has nothing to do with magazines.'

'That could put them off, of course,' Declan mused, 'if we told them what the books were actually about. They might pick up *Vanity Fair* if they did think it had something to do with the magazine, and then find themselves liking it.'

'Chances are they'd bin it after the first paragraph.'

'I thought you said last night that people *wanted* to understand culture; great plays and great literature.'

'Some people do. Others don't give a toss. I had an audience once that didn't understand a fucking—' Toby stopped abruptly. 'The point is, this infomercial is designed to sell them a thirty-minute tape so they *don't* have to buy the book – any of the great books. All they have to do is listen to a synopsis to feel intelligent. We tell them what the book isn't, and then we tell them extremely quickly what the book *is*, and we make what it is sound incredibly sexy.'

'So first of all we have to decide what should be on this tape. That's quite a task. Do we put in all of Shakespeare, for example?'

'We don't include plays,' Toby said firmly.

'Why not?'

'I couldn't do it. Imagine: "*Hamlet* is not about a cigar. It is the story of a young man who sees the ghost of his father and goes mad and kills his girlfriend's father by mistake. And then she kills herself and then he kills her brother by mistake because his uncle who is also his step-father and the murderer of *his* father wants to kill him – and then his mother takes some poison meant for him so she dies and then he kills his step-father and then he dies."' Toby paused. 'I don't think so.'

'I see your point. Skip said to me today that what we're trying to do is to make dumb people feel intelligent.'

'Right.'

'He told me Lisa felt stupid last night, when we talked about all this.'

'Really? I didn't think she was clever enough to feel stupid.'

'Well, we *made* her feel stupid, it seems. I feel dreadful about that.'

'Why?'

'She's not a bad person.'

'How do you know? She might be a sadist, she might tie Skip up and beat him to a pulp every night.'

'Toby—'

'All right. But we're getting somewhere with all this. What we have to do is make them feel dumb first, before we tell them we can make them intelligent.'

'That's a little cruel, isn't it?'

'No. You're in the business of selling, Declan. You have to get people to want your product, yes?'

'Yes.'

'So that's exactly what we're doing. We start off with something like – ' Toby paused, put out his cigarette and reached for another. 'Something like: "Have you ever felt uncomfortable in a gathering when people are talking about books you've never read? Do you miss out on some of those questions in *Trivial Pursuit* because you don't know the name of the man Jane Eyre fell in love with?" That sort of thing.'

'All right,' Declan laughed. 'How about: "Do you ever run out of conversation with your friends or your partner? Wouldn't it be wonderful to astound them with the plots of the greatest stories ever written? Tell your friends the plot of *Mansfield Park* and watch as they marvel at your intelligence."'

'OK. That's good. But try this one: "Just because you live in a trailer park and go bowling every night, it doesn't mean that you're not a genius."' Toby grinned. 'Or: "You too can better yourself. You can stun your poverty-stricken Appalachian" – is it Appalachia, by the way?'

'Yes,' Declan nodded.

'Right. "You can stun your poverty-stricken Appalachian friends with tales of epic adventures. Buy *Plots in a Box* and you will take them on an Odyssey they'll never forget."'

'Or . . .' Declan tapped his teeth with his forefinger. 'How about: "Did that lobotomy slow you down? No need to worry, you can keep up with Mensa members if you've listened to *Plots in a Box*."'

'That's brilliant,' Toby laughed. 'I love it.'

'And how about : "Coffee not doing the trick these days? Can't get those synapses firing any more? Have you forgotten who the hell Bill Sykes was, anyway? Do you think Jacob Marley is Bob Marley's brother? Don't worry. You can know everything there is to know about the works of Charles Dickens without having to read even one page of his novels."'

'Yes!' Toby punched the air. 'That's it exactly. The same as losing weight without dieting or exercise. "Do people put you down for being an illiterate? No need to worry any more. You can be well-read without even knowing how to read. Forget all that ABC business. Who needs it?"'

'"Remember when you had to spend hours over complicated maths problems?"' Declan rubbed his hands together. '"Before the calculator came into our lives? Well, *Plots in a Box* is the literary equivalent to a calculator. It does your work for you."'

'As our Führer would say: perfecto!'

'Maximum gain from minimum effort. I suppose that *is* a compelling idea.'

'Well, that's the idea we're supposed to sell, anyway.' Toby picked up his glass of wine and took a large sip.

'We have to tone it down, of course. Leave out the lobotomy and illiteracy jokes.'

'Absolutely, but the gist of it is clear now. We—'

'I'm sorry.' Christina appeared in the doorway with *I Saw You First* in her hand. 'I was reading this in the kitchen and I just had to share this with you. Listen.

EXERCISE FIFTEEN

Did you two have a favorite song? If you did, find it again. And transfer it onto two tapes. Buy two Walkmans if you don't already have them, and sit across from each other, with separate earphones.

Turn the tape on at the same time. And listen – together but separately.

After the song is over, do not speak or discuss anything. Go about your daily routines. But you will both have that song playing in your heart. It will seep into your systems and awaken those memories which need to be brought back to life.

Can you believe it?'

'Don't.' Declan shook his head. 'I'm supposed to be selling that thing, remember.'

'Do you think there are people out there who actually *do* these exercises?'

'There must be. It's a bestseller. The sales of Walkmans must have rocketed.'

'We were in the middle of work,' Toby commented drily.

'Sorry.' Christina backed away. 'I couldn't resist reading that to you.'

'Have you rung Lucy yet?'

'No. I will. Soon – I promise.'

The fear in her voice startled Declan. That and Toby's peremptory manner towards her. What was going on between these two? It wasn't any of his business, but he couldn't stop himself from wondering.

'Before you go again, Christina, tell me. Do you and Toby have a favourite song?'

'I don't know. Do we?' She looked toward Toby for an answer.

'No. We're not into that sort of thing.'

'Come on. I would have thought, being an actor, you'd also be a dyed-in-the-wool romantic.' Declan was aware that he was courting trouble with that statement, but he wanted to see the other man's reaction.

'I'm romantic when the occasion calls for it,' Toby shrugged. 'I don't like silly romantic gestures. Flowers, chocolates, love songs – they're too obvious for me.'

'And how about you?' He switched his gaze from Toby to Christina, but she had vanished.

'So.' Toby waved his cigarette. 'As I was saying . . .'

'So. As I was saying. What's a bright girl like you doing in a city like this? You should be in Manhattan, you know.' Skip put his elbow on the table and his chin in his palm. Alison Austin had called him just after Lisa had. He'd hung up from Lisa feeling pissed off and unappreciated. 'I'm having a drink with this wonderful woman from the *Birmingham Post*,' she'd gushed. These days, Lisa seemed to be gushing the whole damn time. 'She has a terrible relationship with her husband and after the interview was over she asked if she could speak to me off the record. She needs my advice. I hope you don't mind – I'll be back late.'

'No problem,' Skip had replied abruptly. What else could he have said? 'Yes, I *do* mind. Get your ass back here now!' She'd then remind him of all the times *he'd* been back late from work, all those times she'd said 'No problem' herself. Was he supposed to ask *her* to quit her job now?

Skip could envision an endless cycle: Lisa quits working to save our marriage; I have to work in order for us to survive. I then quit *my* job to save our marriage and on and on and on. Of course that scenario wouldn't occur because Lisa had made enough money already to allow them to live for a long, long time without working. The problem was, she was having fun doing what she was doing. He hadn't been having fun when he quit. How could he ask her to give up something she enjoyed so much?

'I'd love to live in New York,' Alison replied. 'I know I'd adore it. I've always wanted to go to the States.'

She had called telling him she was interested in his infomercial scheme. She wanted, she said, to get in on the ground level. As it happened, she had some free time that evening. Would it be possible for them to meet up?

'You bet,' he'd answered. For a moment he wondered why Alison hadn't mentioned Declan, but then he remembered that Declan wasn't going to tell Alison about *Plots in a Box*, either. These two obviously had some secrets from each other. But then that was hardly any of his business. After all, he now had a secret from Lisa too. It didn't mean anything drastic.

He and Alison had arranged to meet at Motcombe's wine bar and now they were sitting opposite each other, both drinking Perrier water with a slice of lime.

'Where are you from, Alison? London?'

'Oh no,' she laughed. Perfect teeth, he noticed. Unusual in a Brit. 'I'm an Essex girl.'

'Where's Essex?'

'It's a county east of London. Essex girls are notorious.'

'What for?'

'Oh, we have dyed blonde hair, wear cheap clothes and scent, fall in love with football players who beat us up, go to discos, get drunk and dance around our handbags.'

'Then you can't be an Essex girl. Your hair isn't blonde, or dyed – at least as far as my expert eye can tell. Your clothes are great, and you don't drink. I noticed that last night. You had one sip of champagne. And now you're on Perrier. Can I ask you why you're off the booze?'

'I don't like the taste.' Alison studied the olives in the dish in front of her. 'No. To be honest, and I don't know why I'm telling you this, but I suppose all Americans eventually get to the bottom of things by asking enough questions. Anyway, the truth is the reason I don't drink is because my father left my mother and me when I was two years old. My mother always told me, when I was growing up, that he was an alcoholic, but I couldn't quite believe it. I think I had a romantic vision of him. A man who drank a lot, but who was appealing anyway, you know? So I found out where he was a while back and I went to visit him and she was right. He was a drunk. A very *unappealing* drunk. I don't like what alcohol can do to people. Or what it might do to me. That's my little tale of human misery.'

'Shit.' Skip sat back in his chair. 'I know that tale myself. Tell me, did Declan make you do it? Find your father?'

'No. I found him long before I met Declan. Why did you ask that?'

'Well, my mother left home when I was twelve. She was a drunk. And Lisa made me go see her when I was twenty-four. Big mistake. Huge mistake.'

'Was it all . . .' Alison paused. 'Was it all incredibly shabby?'

'Every single thing about it was shabby. Shabby and shoddy and sick.'

'I know.' Alison reached out, touched Skip's forearm, then instantly withdrew her hand.

'It was like some movie. A made-for TV one. There she was in this fucking trailer park and of course her trailer has to be the worst fucking trailer in the park. A complete fucking wreck. And she's in it, reeking of booze, with bottles everywhere and when I say everywhere, I *mean* everywhere. It looked like a goddamn liquor store except most of the bottles were empties. And she's wearing this disgusting nylon housecoat and her hair looks like seaweed but the weird part is her make-up is perfect. Not a smudge or a smear. She always let herself go to pot, but she managed to take care of her face. Anyway, she hugs me and calls me "Skipper" which is a name I never want to hear again in my life. Naming me Skip was bad enough. I can just about handle that. Skipper – no way. She's acting as if she's never done anything wrong in her life and I'm maybe five years old. I looked at her and I thought: *This woman can't have anything to do with me. She just can't.*'

Skip put his hands on his forehead and dragged them slowly down over his face. 'It was a nightmare.'

'Had she always been an alcoholic, then?'

'As far as I know. As I said, she left when I was twelve. That's when she burned the house down.'

'She burned your house down?'

'Yup. We were all out so there wasn't a body count. We'd gone to McDonald's, my father and sister and I. She stayed home. She seems to have used the sofa as her ashtray. I guess it was the most convenient place to stub out her cigarette – only it caught fire and instead of trying to put it out, she ricocheted off the walls and outside and watched the flames take hold.'

'That's horrible.'

'Yeah. It was embarrassing, that's for sure. All the neighbours were gathered in the street when we got back, there were three fire engines and there was my Mom, laughing away, a bottle in her hand. "Look how pretty it is on fire" was her truly remorseful comment. That was bad, but it had been a whole lot worse a few weeks before; she'd picked me and a friend up from school and managed to drive us straight through the garage.'

'What?'

'Well, she drove into the garage OK, but she didn't stop. She kept going through the garage wall and into the back garden. My friend and I were screaming "Stop!" in the back but she didn't care. She was laughing. Great sense of humour, my Mom had.'

'My father was bad, but not as bad as that,' Alison said.

'Lisa thought I should make things up with my mother. She has this idealistic, naive attitude – that everything is redeemable, that all life's problems can be worked out if you sit down and talk about them. I couldn't even *begin* to tell her what my mother was like. She wanted me to tell her about my trip to Chicago, but how could I? Christ, Lisa comes from a picture-perfect family – country clubs, tennis on the weekends, smiling happy children all at private schools. She has no concept of what it's like to come home from school when you're eight years old and find a drunken mess of a woman passed out on the sofa. My father was a pilot and was away a lot – my sister and I had to cope. When my mother finally set fire to the house, my father realized how bad things were and tried to get her to AA or in some programme. She'd last about two hours. Finally she ran away. Good riddance to bad rubbish, as they say.'

'Some people don't want to change. They're perfectly happy being useless wankers.'

Skip nodded in agreement. Even if he didn't know what 'wankers' meant, it sounded right. Looking into Alison's green eyes, he saw a like-minded soul.

'Alison, I've got an idea. I know you wanted to talk about infomercials, not my drunk mother. We could do it at dinner. Lisa's busy with some journalist. If you – I mean, if you and Declan would like to come out to dinner with me, I'd really enjoy it.'

'Declan's out at the pub with his office mates. I don't know when he'll be back. Hang on a second.' She reached into her bag and retrieved a mobile phone. 'I'll ring to see if he's home yet.'

He told me he was meeting with Toby, Skip thought. But I suppose he has to say to her he's out at the pub. Why *is* he lying to her? She's a lovely, warm girl. Woman. I'm not telling Lisa because I need to establish my own business again, without any interference from her superstar persona. That's a pretty reasonable motive. But why isn't Declan telling Alison? Is he really frightened that she'd do it better than him, or what? I don't think he's giving her enough credit, that's what. She wouldn't knife him in the back. She's not like that at all.

Skip tried not to look too happy when she announced, after a few moments, that there was no answer.

'There's a fantastic Italian restaurant, Zafferano's, right around the corner from here. What do you say? Shall we go there?'

'Sounds lovely.'

'Perfecto,' Skip said, standing up. 'We're out of here, kiddo.'

Christina could hear the voices in the living room but couldn't make out the words. She didn't want to eavesdrop although she would have liked to know exactly what they were planning. Why had Declan signed up for this? she wondered. Toby needed the money, but did Declan? It was hard to believe he was Owen Lewis' son. Lewis was a wonderful writer and a great thinker, even she knew that and she'd only ever read two or three books on political philosophy. What would Owen think of Declan getting involved with a scheme like *Plots in a Box*? It was fun and all that, but she couldn't picture Declan selling infomercials instead of books.

Families, Christina thought. No one ever knows what goes on in families.

She should pick up the phone and ring Lucy. She should arrange to meet up with Lucy, bringing Toby along. That would, at least, stop her from imagining the worst. Either it would happen or it wouldn't. The point was to stop thinking about it. Get it over and done with.

Yet she couldn't bring herself to. It was too painful, even now. Seeing Lucy only reminded her of bad, sad times. Times Lucy herself had no idea about. Lucy didn't know the secret and never would. Christina would keep it to herself, partly for her own sake, but mostly for Richard's.

Looking at the jacket of *I Saw You First*, Christina concentrated on the title. I didn't see Richard first. Maybe that's why it all went wrong, she thought. Lucy saw Richard first. Richard saw Lucy first. I came in later. Without having any clue of what the real story was.

Richard had been brought along to the house in what seemed to Christina a last-ditch, desperate effort to find her a boyfriend. 'Chris,' Lucy had said, a wide, conspiratorial smile on her face, 'This is Richard, Nigel's brother. He wasn't doing anything tonight so we asked him along to dinner. And guess what? He's at Sussex too. You two have something in common. Do you think you and Mum can set an extra place? Is there enough food?'

Between the ages of fourteen and sixteen, Christina flinched every time Lucy or Chloë called her Chris, and found it hard not to recoil when they referred to their step-mother, her own mother, as 'Mum'. But she had become used to it over the years. Why shouldn't they, if that's what they wanted to do? She could hardly object without sounding over-sensitive or jealous.

'I'm sure we can. There's plenty of food,' she had replied.

One quick look at Richard and she twigged what Lucy was up to. He was tall – by her infallibly dead reckoning, six foot four and a quarter. Lucy must have started planning this as soon as she saw him. How ideal, she must have thought, that my boyfriend's younger brother is so tall. I'll set him up with Chris, poor Chris who hasn't had a bloke for as long as I've known her. I'll give my little step-sister a big treat. I'll bring him along during the Christmas holidays.

She's trying to be nice, Christina kept repeating to herself as she went into the kitchen to tell her mother about the extra guest for dinner. She thinks it is tragic that I haven't had a boyfriend and I'm nineteen years old. If she had a glass slipper, she'd hand it over to Richard and force him to shove it on to my huge foot. If she could, she'd get him to nail it on.

Of course, Lucy and Nigel arranged it so that Christina was sitting beside Richard at dinner. And of course her mother and step-father beamed approvingly at Richard every time he opened his mouth. That was hardly surprising. What did amaze her was how much she liked Richard, how easy it was to talk to him. He loved football, which had been a passion of hers when she was younger, when her father was still alive. She and her father would spend hours discussing Southampton's chances, their tactics, their acquisitions, hours during which her mother would read women's magazines, only looking up occasionally to protest at 'all this sports talk'.

After her father died, Christina stopped following the fortunes of Southampton and stopped talking about football altogether. What with her height, her uneasiness in her own body, the general aura of not belonging she knew she gave off, she was sure Lucy and

Chloë would label her a lesbian if she started banging on about the weekend's matches.

She wasn't a lesbian. She wasn't interested in romance with girls. She liked boys. She had crushes on boys at school, but none of them ever seemed requited. Was it her height? she wondered. Or her looks? Or her manner? What was wrong with her? Lucy and Chloë, respectively two and four years older than she, never had the slightest problem finding admirers. In fact, they made it seem so simple Christina often thought she must be a complete idiot not to understand the technique.

'You tease them a little, then you're nice to them, then you muck around a little and play hard to get and then you decide whether you actually want them or not,' was the advice Lucy had given her one evening. It sounded like a good formula, but Christina didn't know how to tease. She found that she mumbled or laughed too much or tripped over herself at the wrong moment any time she was in close proximity to a member of the male species.

Richard put her at ease. He was a twenty-one-year-old student reading law at Sussex, where she herself was reading history. He had kind, light-blue eyes and a shy smile which made her, whenever she saw it, smile herself. Occasionally, during that first dinner, he'd look over at his older brother Nigel with obvious admiration, verging on awe. Nigel was certainly more attractive, more self-confident and much more at ease with himself. He was already, at age twenty-four, making a large amount of money in the computer sales business. He and Lucy were a beautiful looking couple and, it seemed certain, a couple destined for marriage. How perfect it would have been were Nigel's brother to take up with Lucy's step-sister. Jane Austen would have approved, Christina found herself thinking, as she and Richard cleared the dishes from the table. But should the fact that it was such a patently good result stop it from happening?

No, was the obvious answer and the one Christina chose for herself. If Richard asked her out, she'd accept.

And that was exactly what happened. On his way out with Nigel at the end of the evening, Richard had turned to her and asked if she'd like to go to a film with him. She had said yes. So they went to the cinema and had a lovely time and then, a few days later, they went out for dinner and had another lovely time. They saw each other steadily after that; and, six weeks after they had met, they made love. Christina, who had been warned by Lucy that the first time could often be disappointing, was thrilled to find the opposite was true. She loved every minute of it. She couldn't keep her hands off every part of Richard's body, nor could she believe how wonderful it felt to have him actually inside her. She didn't want it to stop – not ever.

'God, you're like a three-year-old at Christmas,' Richard had remarked. 'And you're indescribably delicious.'

So when was it? she asked herself, her eyes still focused on Lisa's book. When did I work it out? Or did the knowledge creep up on me so slowly I wasn't aware of its presence until it had captured and taken prisoner my entire heart? A poison that seeps into your system so slowly you don't notice the effects until you're dead?

If there'd been love letters lying around, or if she'd overheard Richard talking about it with a friend on the phone, then she would have felt stunned, paralyzed by the shock. But he hadn't done anything egregious. All he had done was to ask: 'So, is Lucy coming over tonight?' in a casual, offhand tone. It was as simple as that. Yet that had been the moment when Christina had finally begun to acknowledge what she instantly realized she'd known for years: Richard loved Lucy. He loved her and he knew he couldn't have her and he knew he never would. So he kept it to himself, this deep, sad secret, and he'd managed to keep it from Lucy and from Nigel and from Christina as well. He and Christina had been living together for three years, to all intents and purposes a happy couple, but underneath it all, that entire time, had been Richard's – unknown to Lucy, unrequited by Lucy – love.

'She'll be over in an hour or two,' Christina had replied, her mind whirring. All those signs, all those thousands of signs over the years, and she'd refused to read them. Richard complaining of a migraine on the night of Nigel and Lucy's engagement party. Richard with a silly, fixed, fake grin on his face during the wedding itself. Richard always, oh so casually, asking what Nigel and Lucy's plans were for the holidays. Richard never, to her recollection, looking at Lucy for more than a few seconds without blinking rapidly. Christina was the one who blinked when she was nervous and smiled when she lied. She would never have expected Richard to share exactly her responses to embarrassment and unease.

She didn't know who had blinked and smiled more that night – she or Richard. Lucy had come, radiantly pregnant, to discuss names of children with Christina. 'What do you think, Chris? What do you think, Rich? How about Harry? Or Samantha, if it is a girl? Or what about another Nigel?'

Of course Lucy was beautiful; Christina had always known that. Lucy was the kind of woman men want to make sacrifices for. But was she, herself, so very different?

'I like them all,' Christina had replied, forcing herself to look at Richard. He was sitting, his back straight, his hands on his knees. He looked like a man about to be executed, although he was smiling away.

It was that bad, was it? Yes. Clearly it was. And she was the only one who knew and Richard would hate her for knowing. They couldn't sit down and discuss it after Lucy had left. Richard would deny it and Christina would have no proof.

'Do you have any bright ideas, Rich? If so, do say. Nigel's hopeless. He says he won't talk about names until the baby is born. So tell me: do you think it would be OK to call the baby Nigel, if it's a boy?'

'I think it would be fab,' Richard said.

What was it, the fact that he'd used a word she'd never heard him use before – *fab*? Was that what made Christina's heart constrict with terror? Or was it that his voice was so strained, so heartbroken? He'd let it slip; for that one sentence, he'd taken the mask off. Immediately he glanced at her, to check – to see if she'd caught the giveaway. She smiled at him. She blinked. She said, 'I bet Nigel would love having a Nigel Junior, Lucy – unless, that is, it's a girl,' and the dangerous moment was over and she could see that Richard thought he'd slipped it by her without her noticing. He believed his secret was safe. If she hadn't already understood, she might *not* have noticed this one lapse. He might easily have got away with it.

As it was, she waited. She stayed with Richard for a few more months. When she broke up with him, she told him it was because she needed 'space' and freedom and wanted to move to London, where she'd finally do what she'd been planning to do for a while – take an aromatherapy course. She had lost interest in history; she was not, at bottom, an academic. What she wanted to do was to help people feel comfortable with themselves and their bodies.

They parted on reasonably amicable terms. Richard didn't put up much of a fight, but then Christina hadn't expected him to. He was, at heart, a good man and must have been tortured by his own feelings. Living with Christina was bound to become increasingly difficult for him. She might have been in some way a salve, the closest he could ever get to Lucy, but she must also have been a painful reminder of what he was missing. Christina felt sorry for Richard, but that didn't stop her feeling equally sorry for herself.

Until Toby had come into the picture and made her fall in love again, albeit in a different way. He had picked her out, pursued her. This handsome actor who could have had his choice of women had settled on her, and that fact in itself had stunned her beyond belief. She didn't have the companionship she'd had with Richard. Toby didn't make her feel at ease. Although they got along well and had, as far as she could tell, a good sex-life, she was always waiting for the bomb to drop, smashing their romance to smithereens. What preoccupied her most of all was the idea that that bomb might have Lucy's name written all over it.

'Christina?' She jumped at the voice.

'Sorry – you looked as if you were lost in space there. I wanted to say goodbye, that's all.' Declan smiled apologetically.

'Sorry – I *was* lost in space. Have you finished, then?'

'Yes. For tonight, anyway. I'll be picking you two up tomorrow evening about six. Is that all right? Toby said you'd be back from work by then. Are you sure you'd like to come too?'

'I'd love to. And six is fine.'

'Was it a good space?'

'Sorry?'

'The space you were lost in. Was it nice? Peopled with friendly aliens who can teach you how to salsa in two seconds flat?'

'Not exactly,' Christina laughed. 'There were a few nasty creatures there.'

'Well, then, I'm glad I brought you back. See you tomorrow.'

'See you tomorrow. And Declan—' she stood up. 'Thanks for bringing me back.'

'My pleasure.'

'So.' Skip finished the last drop of cappuccino in his cup. 'What are you and Declan up to this weekend? Something fun?'

'Declan is going to visit his parents and I'm staying at home.'

'Oh.' Skip replaced his Visa card in his wallet. 'That sounds boring.'

'No, I think it will be nice. It's important to have time on your own, I think. Not to travel everywhere together as if you were a pair of elephants heading for Noah's Ark.'

'Right. I see what you mean. I'm supposed to go to Manchester with Lisa, as it happens. She's signing books there. What's Manchester like?'

Alison frowned.

'That bad?'

'No. I'm sure you'll love it.'

'You don't sound very convincing, Alison. Maybe I won't go. Maybe I'll be a rogue elephant too this weekend. There's so much to do in London. I'd love to go to the theatre, for example.'

'There's a wonderful production of *As You Like It* on at the Barbican, or so I've heard.'

'You haven't been?'

'No. Not yet.'

'If I could get tickets, would you consider going with me? I feel responsible for all this heavy talking we've done about our respective drunken parents. I don't know why we never got down to infomercials. I've never discussed my past like this before. I guess I got carried away.'

'I don't generally talk about my father, either. I suppose it's good to do so occasionally, though. Gets it out of the system. The theatre sounds lovely. But won't Shakespeare be too long for you?'

'When I said that last night, I meant plays like that were too long for people who have no time. I've got a lot of time on my hands, as it happens.'

'All right, then. You're on.'

'Great. Why don't you call me tomorrow, around noon?'

'Fantastic.' Alison smiled.

'Fantastic.' Skip smiled back.

Chapter 5

Often, at the beginning of relationships, we find we're attracted to our partners because of the way they make us feel about ourselves. They listen to us, they laugh with us, they concentrate on us and make us feel special. But are we doing the same for them? Or are we so pleased to have all this attention that we forget to give it back?

Look at couples in restaurants. Isn't it often the case that one person is doing all the talking while the other is doing all the listening? Does one partner take on the role of the caring, compassionate listener while the other gets to be cared for, be empathized with, be listened to?

Many people, when they look at their partner, see only a reflection of themselves in those eyes. Using a lover as a mirror makes seeing that lover impossible.

Ask yourself this question: Are you getting more from your partner than you're giving? Are you looking in the mirror? If so, you must shatter the glass. We all know that truly beautiful people don't have to stand in front of mirrors the whole time. Only egotistical and vain ones want to look at themselves constantly.

Don't you just hate those obnoxious types who can't pass a mirror without checking themselves out and posing? Well, then, don't be one yourself. Get a grip! Start asking what you can do for your partner, not what he can do for you.

And if you're the one giving more than you're receiving, if you're the mirror, ask yourself why you chose this role. Is it because you're frightened to voice your own needs? Are you too afraid to stake a claim for equality in this relationship? Being the caring, compassionate partner allows you to feel good about yourself, yes, but one of these days you'll resent him for not paying enough attention to you. Is that his fault? No. You've allowed him to use you in this way – you've probably encouraged him.

Break out of the pattern.

Start again, from the beginning. On an equal basis.

Remember – today is your first date!!!!

I Saw You First, *Chapter Three, p. 41*

A mammoth thunderstorm erupted when they turned off the M4 on to the M25. The traffic was ensnarled in a Friday evening rush-hour jam, so they sat in the unmoving car, watching the windshield wipers dance furiously in front of them.

At one point the thunder was so loud, Christina jumped in her seat. Toby, behind her, put his hand on her shoulder.

'Should I be Julie Andrews in *The Sound of Music* and sing "These Are a Few of My Favourite Things" to calm you down?' he asked.

'I always hated that song. I hated that film, actually.'

'What? I thought every woman with a heart adored the Nazi youth telegram boy singing "You Are Sixteen Going on Seventeen."'

'I hated it too,' Declan commented. 'I especially hated "Doe, a deer."'

'Doe, a deer, a female deer – ' Toby began, in a falsetto voice.

'Don't,' Christina shuddered. 'Please.'

'Raindrops on roses and – '

'Toby. Stop. We don't think it's funny, all right? It's like fingernails on a blackboard.' Declan drummed his hands against the steering wheel. 'It's almost as dire as a Carpenter's song. Not quite, but almost.'

'You hate them too?' Christina looked over at Declan.

'I do indeed.'

'I thought I was the only person in the world who can't stand "We've Only Just Begun".'

'No. You have company.'

'I quite like that song,' Toby protested. 'I know it's schlocky and I generally hate schlock, but there's something about it that's different.'

'Admit it, Toby. You liked *Forrest Gump.*'

'From an actor's point of view, yes, Declan, I did. Tom Hanks –'

'Tom Hanks is *vile*,' Christina sighed.

'He's *revolting*,' Declan agreed.

'Well, you're both entitled to your opinion, of course. I'm talking from a different perspective.'

'Ah. Thank God. We're moving again.' Declan stared earnestly through the rain. 'I had forgotten how bad Friday nights are.'

'He was good in *Philadelphia*. You can't deny that,' Toby said.

Christina sneaked a sideways look at Declan and saw his quick smile.

'I *can* deny it, but I won't. You're the expert, Toby. I have a visceral reaction to him, I suppose. I hate him and I hate Glenn Close and I hate Andie McDowell.'

'Wasn't she awful in *Four Weddings*?' Christina turned to Toby in the back seat. 'You'd agree with that, wouldn't you? Declan's right. There's something about Andie McDowell that jars.'

'I thought she was perfectly adequate.' Toby's voice was petulant. 'It was a crap film, of course. I'm not talking about the quality of the film, I'm talking about the *acting*. She played her part decently enough.'

'I suppose so,' Christina murmured. 'But I loathe her too.'

'Well, why don't we sit here and trash actors, then.' Toby turned his face away and stared out the back seat window. 'That would be fun.'

'Why don't you tell us more about your father, Declan?' Christina suggested after a long silence. 'Is he still teaching?'

'Yes. He's at Reading. He's still teaching.'

'That's nice.'

'For some,' Declan said. 'The news should be on now. I'll turn on the radio.'

Why was he so prickly on the subject of his father? Christina wondered. He'd been so light-hearted and funny during the drive and he'd suddenly turned sour. Was Owen Lewis some sort of monster? What was awaiting them when they arrrived?

By the time they pulled into the small driveway of Declan's parents' cottage outside of Amersham, Christina was imagining Owen Lewis as an ogre-ish, lecherous university lecturer who seduced his students and ignored his wife. The rain had stopped and the skies had cleared. Within seconds of emerging from Declan's BMW, Christina saw a figure come out of the cottage with a welcoming smile on his face.

'Declan,' the man grinned broadly. 'How was the trip? Did you get caught in that thunderstorm?'

He was six foot exactly, Christina immediately calculated. With broad shoulders, surprisingly thin hips, a round face and bald head. He clutched Declan in a bear hug, then released him and turned to her.

'I'm Owen Lewis,' he said. 'We're so glad you could come.'

'Christina Billings,' she replied, taken aback by the kindness and warmth in his eyes and his voice. 'Thank you for having us.'

'And you're Toby Goodyear, yes?' Owen put out his hand to shake Toby's. 'You look so familiar. And your name is familiar too.'

'You may have seen me on television,' Toby explained as he shook Owen's hand. 'I'm an actor.'

'So Declan said. But I'm afraid we don't have a television, so that can't be the reason. Perhaps there is no reason and I'm imagining things. It happens in old age.' He spread out his arms. 'Come in. You must be exhausted.'

Christina, when she stepped over the threshold of the stone cottage, took a small involuntary pace back in shock. A ping-pong table occupied most of the front room. A rooster sat on top of it. There were no chairs, no sofas, only pillows scattered on the floor. Behind the front room she could see a kitchen where two people stood, one of whom was a man holding a huge dog in his arms. The other, a very thin woman with short, greying hair, approached Declan.

'Hello, darling,' she said.

Thank God, Christina thought. She's tall. Five foot eight and a quarter. She'd make Lisa Thomas feel like a midget too.

'Hello, Mum.' Declan finally smiled and hugged his mother. 'This is Christina Billings and this is Toby Goodyear.' He motioned to them both and the woman shook their hands.

'I'm Jessica,' she said. 'It's wonderful to have you here. And this is our other son, Michael.'

Michael put the dog down on the floor and advanced towards them.

'The prodigal returns,' he said lightly, clapping Declan on the shoulder. 'Good to see you.' He turned to Christina and Toby. 'Nice to meet you both.'

He was the spitting image of Owen, Christina saw at once – only he had hair. But his face was exactly the same shape as Owen's and his eyes were the identical shade of dark brown. Michael appeared to be about five years older than Declan, though possibly a little less. Owen must have been in his late fifties and Jessica probably somewhere roundabout fifty-five. Though Declan looked a little like her, his face having a similar thin bone structure, he wasn't as recognizably his parents' son as Michael was.

'Come in, come in,' Jessica shepherded them through the front room and into the kitchen. 'As you can see, this is the only comfortable place to sit. We actually have a table and chairs here.'

The cottage was almost aggressively chaotic, exuding an atmosphere of 'make yourself at home, anything goes here'. At the back of the kitchen Christina could see a room, a doorless room with a big bed in it. There was a flight of wooden steps facing the front door, missing a few planks on the way up. Not a staircase to climb if you'd had too much to drink, Christina thought. The downstairs walls were covered with ageing, faded posters of Mao, Buddha and Gandhi. Books were piled at various sites along the floor, with newspapers beside them.

'Amazing, isn't it?' Declan commented wrily. 'A table and chairs.'

'Would you like some wine?' Michael asked.

'Love some,' Toby replied as they took seats at the pine table which dominated the kitchen in the same way the ping-pong table dominated the sitting room. Michael had to squeeze around the chairs to get to the fridge.

'Doesn't Toby look familiar?' Owen asked Jessica.

'Yes, he does. You weren't a student of Owen's, were you, Toby?'

'No.'

'He's an actor,' Declan said curtly. 'We're working on a project together. We're going to advertise a tape which is a synopsis of all the great works of literature – a thirty-minute tape called *Plots in a Box*. We're giving away a collection of dinnerware with it as well. Plates with pictures of authors in the middle and quotes from their most famous works around the rims.'

Owen had now picked up the dog, an Irish setter, and held it in his lap.

'Really?' he said, looking from Declan to Toby to Christina. 'That sounds interesting. Tell us more about it.'

'*Plots in a Box*!' Michael exclaimed, pouring wine into glasses he had fetched from a cupboard above the sink. 'Great works of literature summarized in thirty minutes? You can't be serious, Declan.'

'Oh, but I am,' Declan replied.

'We're not exactly serious,' Toby put in quickly. 'It's just an idea we're working on for an American man.'

'How are you going to fit Shakespeare into that?' Michael persisted, handing a glass of wine to Christina. 'Is white all right, by the way?'

'It's fine. Thank you.'

'Yes, white's fine, thank you, Michael. And we're not including Shakespeare,' Toby said, taking the glass Michael passed to him.

'Great works of literature *without* Shakespeare? How do you figure that?'

'Hamlet,' Owen said softly, staring at Toby.

'That's the point.' Toby's voice was nervous now, Christina could tell. 'We couldn't desecrate Shakespeare like that.'

'But you *can* desecrate Proust, for example?' Michael placed a glass of wine in front of Declan's place and Jessica's as well. He took a bottle of milk from the counter and poured himself a glass. 'Want some milk, Dad?' he asked.

'No, no thank you.' Owen shook his head. 'That's where I've seen you before.' He was still regarding Toby intently. 'I saw you play Hamlet.'

'That's right!' Jessica exclaimed. 'We saw you play Hamlet. You were absolutely incredible. We talked about it for days afterwards.'

'In Tooting?' Toby's voice was shaking. Christina looked at him and saw a face she couldn't recognize. His teeth were clenched. His cheekbones were starting to twitch. He seemed as if he were either about to faint or about to murder someone.

'Yes,' Jessica nodded. 'In Tooting, that's right.'

'Do you — can you possibly remember which night of the week it was?'

'It was a Wednesday night,' Owen responded immediately. 'I remember because we couldn't leave for town until after one of my Wednesday lectures and I was worried that we'd be late. We weren't, though. We saw it all. It was remarkable, Toby. You were remarkable.'

'Wednesday. I can't believe this.'

Christina couldn't believe it, either. What was happening? Toby was on the verge of tears.

'I didn't think anyone was there who understood what had happened.'

'So you didn't believe it yourself?' Owen's brown eyes showed instant empathy. 'Does a tree falling in the forest make a sound if no one is there to hear it? Is that how you felt?'

Toby nodded.

'Don't you think everyone there understood, on some level? They might not have appeared to, but I can't help but think that kind of performance infiltrates the soul of all the audience. It has a lasting effect, even if that effect isn't always noticeable at first.'

Owen Lewis leaned forward as he stroked the dog's head. Christina could feel the connection he had made with Toby and knew instantly that this was what Owen could do with everyone he met. Within ten seconds anyone would want to tell Owen the story of his or her life, knowing that Owen would treat him or her as he was treating the dog – with soothing, all-encompassing gentleness. He's a healer, Christina thought. And he doesn't even have to touch a person. What a remarkable man.

'Do you actually believe that?' Toby couldn't take his eyes off Owen. He was leaning forward as well, locked into Owen's gaze.

'Yes,' Owen nodded. 'I do. Everything we do has a ripple effect. We can touch people in ways we never imagine.'

Toby said 'Thank you,' in the tone of someone who had been released from Death Row.

Christina, sitting beside Declan, heard a small, almost inaudible groan. He was sitting in a slumped position, his eyes cast down. He wants to be like his father, she suddenly realized, but he can't be. He wants to be like his father in the same way I want to be like Lucy.

'Jessica and I looked out for you after that. But you seemed to have vanished from the face of the earth.'

'I vanished into the hell of loathsome parts and bad rep companies.'

'Toby – that's terrible.' Owen kept patting the dog's head rhythmically. 'That's truly terrible. Is there anything we can do?'

'Such as what?' Declan stared at his father. 'What could you possibly do? Start a theatre company here and hire Toby as your resident genius? You'd have to take out the ping-pong table then, wouldn't you?'

'Declan.' Jessica put her hand across the table and grabbed her son's. 'Relax. Please.'

'Has Dad taken you out dancing yet, Mum? Has he done anything at all that *you* want to do?'

Declan's tone of voice had switched into anger and aggression, Christina noticed. He wanted to get at Owen, using his mother as his assault weapon. It won't work, Christina wanted to say. You are trying to make your mother side with you against Owen, but she won't do it. If you want to attack your father, you should leave Jessica out of it.

'Mum's going to a line-dancing class,' Michael announced. 'She's having a terrific time. You should see her new cowboy boots.'

'They're fantastic,' Jessica smiled. 'Owen bought them for me.'

'But has he gone *with* you, Mum?'

'I'd be hopeless at line dancing,' Owen said, with a sigh.

'He'd be hopeless,' Jessica agreed.

'That's no excuse,' Declan snapped.

'Well, what's your excuse for this *Plots in a Box* business?' Michael snapped back.

'It's fun.' Declan suddenly sat up straight. 'You're always telling me I should have more fun, Michael. Well, now I'm having it.'

'It sounds like fun,' Owen smiled. 'Tell me more about it.'

'You know you don't really approve, Dad. It's capitalism on the rampage, leaving all culture floating belly-up in its wake.' Declan's expression was desperate, Christina thought. Full of rage and despair.

'I don't see why it's as destructive as you say. Telling people the plots of great books might lead them on to read the books, after all.'

'Exactly. You think they *have* to read them, don't you, Dad? You think everyone has to go into every subject with as much depth as possible.'

'Is that bad?' Owen cocked his head to the side, looking embarrassed. Christina saw him then as a little boy who didn't understand what his parents were arguing about. The fact that he was a parent himself struck her as odd.

'Excuse me, but why did you come to Tooting?' Toby's gaze was fixed on Owen.

'We see as many *Hamlets* as we can,' Owen explained. 'It was listed in *Time Out*, as I remember.'

'And of all the ones you've seen . . .'

'Yours was definitely by far and away the best.'

'I think so too,' Jessica added. 'Oh – the food. I almost forgot. I've reheated some Indian takeaway we had delivered last night. I hope you don't mind. I was going to make something special, but then I got caught up in a book I was reading and before I knew it, it was too late to prepare what I'd wanted to. There's plenty of this to go around, I promise. Hang on a second.' She manoeuvred her way amongst the chairs and went to the oven.

'You had food *delivered*?' Declan asked with exaggerated incredulity. 'Isn't that against your principles, Dad? Isn't that treating the delivery person as a servant?'

'Get a grip, Declan,' Michael said in an amused tone. 'You're not a teenager any more. You don't have to be so stroppy.'

'Which soliloquy did you prefer?'

'Toby – ' Christina put her hand on his arm.

'I'd love to talk to you about it at length, Toby,' Owen said. 'Let's sit down tomorrow sometime and we'll discuss it in detail. A lot more of my memory might have returned by then.'

Owen had a lovely voice, Christina decided, a lovely voice which went along with his lovely, warm manner. He could deal with Toby's one-track mind. He could deal, it appeared, with almost anything. Except his younger son.

'I hope you like curry.' Jessica had the dishes out on the counter and was busy getting knives and forks.

'I'm so sorry, I should have helped.' Christina sprang up from her chair. She'd been so fascinated by what was going on between Declan, his father and his brother, she'd forgotten her manners. 'You're so kind to invite us for the weekend. The least we can do is help.'

'Don't be silly.' Jessica waved her down, back into her seat. 'I wouldn't dream of it. You've had a long drive. Relax. Besides, it's so nice to see Declan again. It's like a party.'

A party with a child who is having a temper tantrum, Christina thought. Yet her heart went out to Declan. He was so miserable in his fury, so vulnerable in his desire to lash out at Michael and Owen. He wouldn't let himself enjoy the occasion, and she understood that. She understood it all too well. Michael, the older brother, had taken after Owen physically and Christina guessed, psychologically. He didn't seem to mind about the lack of chairs, the ping-pong table. He was at ease in this house and at ease with his parents, whereas Declan was at war.

Michael had left Declan no space, no option except *not* to be like Owen. But how could Declan rebel against a father who was so kind and understanding? The only way, Christina reckoned, would be for Declan to become an out-and-out capitalist pig, some Yuppie City man with no scruples. Declan couldn't bring himself to go that far, obviously, but he had the flash car and was wearing the suit and tie. How hard Declan must have worked to be different, Christina thought, and how much pain it must have cost him.

When Jessica put plates and forks and knives out in front of them, saying: 'I hope you don't mind if it's vegetarian,' Declan rolled his eyes in exasperation.

'Have you got a dishwasher yet, Mum? Has the twentieth century deigned to show its face in this house yet?'

'Declan thinks I'm a downtrodden wife and mother,' Jessica said to Christina. 'And to be honest, there was a time when I thought so, too. I lusted after a dishwasher and all the creature comforts.' She glanced then at Owen. 'But now I'm glad we stayed the way we were.'

'Now that is the voice of someone who has been brainwashed,' Declan muttered.

Christina couldn't stop herself. She put her hand out and touched Declan's wrist. He turned to her then and she smiled straight at his eyes. A real smile, not her lying one.

'I'd like you to come and visit my family with me someday, Declan,' she said softly.

'Why's that?' He looked at her with genuine curiosity.

'I'm not sure.' She kept her hand on his pulse. 'I think you might see something important.'

He stared back at her, his eyebrows raised. She shrugged and raised her own eyebrows, then removed her hand. In the general mêlée of the dinner being dished out, no one had noticed this exchange.

It sounded as if there had been a period of time in the Lewis household when Jessica had been unhappy, and that Declan, picking up on this, blamed his father. What he obviously couldn't see now was that they'd come through it and that Jessica was content with her marriage and the environment she lived in. Most women *would* have gone berserk in this kind of atmosphere, Christina reckoned. But it seemed to suit Jessica. She was relaxed, Christina could tell that from her body movements, and she was obviously used to Owen and the fact that he gathered people to him like a latterday Pied Piper. Whatever her struggle had been, she was over it – she'd said that clearly when she announced that she was pleased things had stayed the way they were. If Christina had to choose one adjective to describe Jessica, she would say: 'patient'.

'Declan told me that you work as an aromatherapist, Christina,' Owen addressed her again, with that soft, sincere tone. 'Can you find the oils you use easily or is it difficult to get hold of them?'

She answered his question, aware, as she did so, that she was doing exactly what must irritate Declan the most. She was opening up to Owen, pleased to be asked about herself, pleased to be able to talk to someone who was interested in the subject so close to her heart. As soon as she had explained about the oils, Owen asked about her clients and their problems. Michael became involved in the conversation as well, saying that his wife was also a believer in the healing value of aromatherapy. Christina wanted to stop, to change the subject, but the two men kept pressing her. Toby and Jessica, she could hear, were talking about Olivier's Hamlet. Declan was the only silent member at the table, watching, shovelling food into his mouth mechanically.

He has given up already, Christina thought. He feels lost and abandoned, the way I did when my family would sit around the table discussing who was going out with whom and what would happen with those relationships. 'So who is the lucky fellow tonight?' her step-father would ask Lucy. 'Is it Paul or have you given him the boot?' Lucy would laugh and reply: 'Paul's with Mary now. He and I split up weeks ago, Dad.'

'But I thought Mary was seeing Bob!' her mother would exclaim. 'No, no.' Lucy would then shake her head. 'Mary and Bob are ancient history.'

Why was everyone so interested? Christina would ask herself. Why couldn't they talk about politics or films? Why did her step-father care so much? Because he saw how popular his daughters were, she reckoned. Talking about their romantic conquests was like talking to his sons, had he had any, about their sporting triumphs. And her mother felt exactly the same.

They were all in synch, in tune, and she was the outcast. That's the way Declan must be feeling now. The odd one out.

The topic of conversation finally shifted away from Christina when Michael mentioned that his youngest daughter had an ear infection. Jessica, catching this bit of information during a pause in her discussion of Olivier's Hamlet, zeroed in on Michael and dispensed grandmotherly advice. By this time, however, they had finished their dinner, and Declan had hardly spoken a word.

'So Declan,' Owen finally turned toward his younger son. 'I want to hear more about this project of yours. Have you decided yet which books will be on this tape?'

'Not yet. But we do have a plan for the next tape. After we've done literature, we're going to do philosophy. In the same way. We thought we'd call it *Plato on a Plate*.' Declan said this as if he were throwing down a gauntlet and was waiting for his father to retort with, 'Right, then. Pistols at dawn.'

Instead, Owen burst out in what Christina could only describe as a wild giggle. He laughed with a tee-hee sound, like a child watching a cartoon.

'That's wonderful. I hope you'll let me help.'

'Oh, please.' Declan turned on his father. 'I make fun of the subject closest to your heart – political philosophy – and you laugh? How can you? You spend all your life with students discussing Plato and his caves. Either you take it seriously or you don't – which one is it, Dad? Was all that time with all those students a joke? If it was, why did you do it? Tell me that.'

'It's not a joke,' Owen replied. 'But, Declan – *Plato on a Plate is* funny. It's a relief to be able to laugh at serious subjects. More of my students should laugh. I hope very much that I've never lost my sense of humour, but if that's what you think, I'm sorry.'

At that instant, the rooster suddenly let out a loud crow and everyone at the table jumped.

'He's in a permanent state of jet-lag,' Michael chuckled. 'And he's never even crossed a time zone. Good old Spinoza. He thinks it's dawn. When the sun does come up, he sleeps right through it. He shouldn't have been born a rooster. Maybe in his next life he'll be a nightclub entertainer.'

'That does it,' Declan announced, throwing his napkin on the table. 'I cannot believe that rooster is still here, still squawking on the ping-pong table. Nothing but *nothing* changes in this house. I need some air. I'm going for a walk.' He left abruptly, disappearing with speed out of the front door.

'Do you think he's all right?' Owen asked after the front door had slammed behind Declan.

'He'll be fine, Dad.' Michael waved his hand dismissively. 'You know Declan. He likes to get upset.'

'I think he wanted an argument with you.' Christina turned to Owen. 'He expected you to be angry, to disapprove of *Plato on a Plate*. And he was frustrated when you didn't.'

'But why?' Owen asked. 'I think it sounds like fun. Can't I join in on the fun?'

'Declan doesn't like fun,' Michael commented. 'He was trying to wind you up and he's frustrated he can't, that's all.'

Oh, but you're wrong. Declan *does* like fun, Christina thought. He doesn't know how to express himself here, that's all. The minute he walks through the door, he gets nervous and twitchy and defensive.

'Christina — I'd like to go for a walk as well,' Toby broke in. 'It's been so long since I've been in the country. Let's get some air too.'

Christina wanted to stay and talk to Owen, but Toby had grabbed her arm.

'Go on, you two.' Owen sat back in his chair. 'Enjoy yourselves.'

'The garden stretches down to a little stream,' Jessica said. 'The moon is out tonight so you'll be able to see where you're going.'

'Thanks,' Toby replied. 'Come on, Chris, let's go.'

Chris? He had never called her Chris.

And he had never held her hand, either — which was what he was doing now. They walked, hand-in-hand, through the garden and down to the stream.

'Aren't Owen and Jessica amazing people?' Toby asked.

'Yes,' Christina nodded. 'They are.'

'They're brilliant — both of them. I suppose Michael's all right as well, but I don't understand how Declan fits in. It's as if he were adopted. He's so different.'

'Perhaps he has to be,' she replied. 'It must be difficult being Owen's son.'

'What are you on about? It would be wonderful to be Owen's son. He's an intelligent, kind, discriminating man. The perfect father.'

'Exactly, the perfect father. That puts a huge amount of pressure on Declan to be the perfect son, especially if Michael is already the perfect son.'

'Chris.' Toby stopped, pulled her to him. 'I don't want to talk about Declan. I want to make love. Right here. Right now.'

'Toby. The ground is soaking. We're in their garden. I don't think—'

'Oh, fuck that.' She could see his grin in the moonlight. 'They wouldn't mind. Owen would understand. He understands everything. Come on.'

He started to kiss her then, more passionately than he had ever kissed her before. Within moments, she was lying on the wet grass, Toby on top of her, making love to her like a madman. Her jeans and knickers were down around her ankles, her lower back was on some kind of sharp tree twig, making every movement painful, and her only thought was that this man was as absent from the sexual process as she had been two nights before. Now Toby was the alien; he was lost in a timewarp of his own. I could be the dog, Christina found herself thinking. I could be a tree. I could be Jessica. This act has nothing to do with me. *Who exactly is he fucking here?*

Declan hadn't known where to go when he stormed out of the cottage, and ended up sitting in his car, fuming. Why did they always get to him like this? he asked himself, his brain racing. He was thirty-three years old and he was acting like a screwed-up adolescent. Owen had done nothing wrong – he never did anything wrong. Yes, every single person who walked through the door immediately gravitated to him. But was that a crime? No, of course it wasn't. And neither was Michael a criminal. They were both so unbelievably *good*, that was the problem. Their goodness made Declan feel like an inferior human being.

He didn't care whether the rainforests were destroyed. He didn't particularly care about politics. He was a selfish bastard who wanted to make a decent living and have a normal life with all the modern conveniences, plus a nice car.

Should he feel guilty for drinking wine and eating meat and killing wasps and stepping on spiders and thinking Richard Gere was a wanker for going on and on about Tibet? The only way in which he resembled his brother and father was when he listened to people and helped them with their problems – and now he didn't even do that anymore.

Within seconds Owen had reached Toby on a level Declan hadn't thought possible. The man was practically weeping.

And within minutes Christina was shining as she talked about aromatherapy.

He wished he could be more like his mother. Jessica wasn't a saint, either. She didn't have Owen's or Michael's magic touch with people and animals, but she didn't mind or feel competitive. She didn't get angry, even though he knew she would have liked to have a dishwasher and more privacy and a lot more of Owen's time to herself. Once upon a time she had been angry, yes. They'd been angry together. But that was ages ago, when Declan *was* actually a teenager. These days she'd abandoned him and their common fight; she took everything in her stride. Whereas he bridled and looked for arguments and walked out of rooms in a bate. If he were a good person, he'd be pleased that his mother no longer seemed to mind about Owen's eccentricities, but he wasn't a good person. He saw her willingness to conform as a defection from the cause. It had been he and his mother in league against Owen and Michael. Now he was on his own.

He'd have to go back and apologize – the sulking grump. For a moment, he imagined himself going into the cottage, holding up his hands and saying: 'Please. Let's start again. Something terrible happens to me when I walk in here and I can't control it. I didn't mean this to happen. I came here thinking everything might be reasonable again, but as soon as I walked in I felt the same old fury. You have to help me somehow. I'm not the way I seem.'

But that idea was as implausible as making an announcement to people at work that he was available for friendship again. Actually, it was more implausible. His response to his family was now so hard-wired, he'd never be able to change it.

He shouldn't have come for the weekend. Alison was right: it was far better to cut off and make a separate life for himself. His mother and Owen and Michael were happy campers. They didn't need his negative presence. He'd never fit in again here. It was too late.

When they returned to the cottage, Christina struggled to hide the signs of their bout in the grass. Yet it was too obvious to disguise; her long hair was wet and dishevelled and the back of her T-shirt and jeans were soaking.

'Nice walk?' Declan had returned and was sitting where he had been before. Michael had disappeared. Jessica and Owen were washing up the dishes.

'Let me help,' Christina offered, blushing.

'We're done,' Owen replied, holding a dish he'd just dried up in the air. 'Last one. But thank you.'

'Nice walk?' Declan repeated.

'Fantastic,' Toby said. 'Owen – if you're not going to bed straight away, perhaps we could talk now.'

Christina noticed Jessica's smile. Jessica the Patient, she thought. She knows everyone wants to get a piece of Owen and she doesn't mind. Neither does Michael. It's Declan who minds.

'I think I'll go and read,' Jessica moved toward Declan. 'Goodnight, darling. It's wonderful to have you home.' She kissed him on the cheek and ruffled his dark blond hair. 'We've missed you.'

'Goodnight, Mum.' Declan looked up at her with evident love. 'See you in the morning.'

'Goodnight, everybody.' She gave a little wave toward Toby and Christina and blew a kiss at Owen. 'Christina and Toby – your room is the first one on the left at the top of the stairs. I've put some towels out on the bed.'

'Thank you,' Christina said. 'Thank you for everything.'

This scene would have been perfectly normal were it not for the fact that Jessica then went into the room off the back of the kitchen – the room with no door. Christina stared after her, wondering how she was going to undress in privacy. A part of the back room was not visible, however, which is where Jessica must have changed. After a few minutes she reappeared, lying on the bed in a pair of lightweight pyjamas, a book in her hand. Toby was already involved in a conversation about his Hamlet with Owen, talking away as Owen repeatedly nodded his head. Christina tried to listen and join in but found her gaze constantly going back to Jessica.

'Weird, yes?' Declan nudged her with his elbow.

'Is that their bedroom? Or have they moved in there to make space for us?'

'Come on – let's go and sit around the ping-pong table. I'll tell you all about it. Toby will be hours with my father, I guarantee.'

Christina followed Declan to the front room and they sat down on adjoining pillows.

'Comfortable?'

'I'm fine,' she answered. 'I told you – I prefer sitting on the floor.'

'That's just as well in this house.'

'Where's Michael?'

'He's gone to bed. I think those children of his wear him out.'

'What does he do?'

'He teaches English.'

'No wonder he didn't like the *Plots in a Box* scheme.'

'Exactly.' Declan nodded. 'Anyway, to answer your question,

yes, that is my parents' bedroom. They don't have a door. You'll find there are no doors to the bedrooms upstairs, either. The only doors in this house are the front door and the ones on the two loos. But beware, I warn you. No locks on the loo doors.'

The rooster on top of the ping-pong table had vanished, Christina noticed. The Irish setter was curled up on a pillow across from where they were sitting.

'This house is basically a free-for-all,' Declan continued. 'No privacy. Anyone and everyone welcome. I remember coming back from school one day and listening to a teenage neighbour asking my father what she should do about her pregnancy. The next day another teenager was asking him what he should do about his drug addiction. The whole world is my father's fucking family.'

'And you want him to yourself,' Christina stated softly.

'I didn't say that.' Declan stiffened.

Christina kept silent.

'Why did you say I should come with you to see *your* family?'

'I told you – I thought you might see something important.'

'What?'

'I don't know.'

'Christina – tell me. You can see how crazy this house is, can't you?'

'I wouldn't call it crazy, Declan.'

'You don't think this door business, just to give you one example, is lunatic? You don't think I should complain about that? Fight for privacy?'

'I don't think you have to fight for your father's love.'

'Who said anything about my father's love? This isn't about love. This is about privacy. Sanity. Normal life.'

'It's about love,' Christina repeated.

'Well, go and sit at his feet, then. Join Toby and be another pilgrim at the shrine.'

'I didn't mean—'

'I'm going to bed.' Declan stood up. 'I'm going to bed in my *doorless* room.'

Lisa Thomas' wrist ached from signing so many copies of her book at Dillons. This was a good ache, she knew. One she was more than prepared to put up with. The price of success. She sat down on her hotel bed, a glass of wine in her hand. It was a relief, sometimes, to be able to drink as much as she wanted without the presence of Skip and his watchful eyes. Did he think she might end up like his mother if she had more than one glass a night? Probably. Well, she was three-quarters of the way into a bottle and was enjoying it immensely. Of course she missed him, but a new hotel in a new city excited her. Lisa Thomas the author was having a good time.

Somewhere along the line Lisa Thomas the woman had begun to metamorphose into Lisa Thomas the author, she knew that. The two were fast becoming one inseparable entity. Occasionally this fact surprised her.

This afternoon had been an example. She was talking to the bookstore manager after the signing, discussing the moment when she decided to write *I Saw You First*.

'I was in a park, near where Skip and I lived, watching an elderly couple having an argument on a bench. Suddenly I imagined what they looked like years ago, when they were young and just starting out. In my mind I saw them kissing on that bench, snuggling in each others' arms. And I thought: How can they go back there? How can they get rid of all the baggage they've collected along the way and return to the couple they once were?'

The manager, Fiona, had said: 'You're so right. When I think about how it was at the beginning, with Tom . . .' and launched into the story of how she and Tom had first met.

Lisa, as she listened, suddenly felt as if she were schizophrenic. At least thirty seconds had elapsed before she had recalled that she was telling a lie. Before, whenever she'd told the couple-in-the-park story, she'd always thought: Well, here I go. Lying again.

But this time she had actually seen herself in that park, watching the elderly couple.

In fact, the genesis of *I Saw You First* had nothing to do with parks or old couples. She'd picked up a copy of *Men Are From Mars/Women Are From Venus*, and halfway through reading it, had turned to Skip. 'This is ridiculous,' she'd said. 'I could do better than this. You know how you used to say that half of being a successful businessman was acting authorized? I can *sound* authorized. That's what people want when they read books like this. They want to think the author has all the answers. No one does, of course, but I could bluff. I could persuade people I have the key to making relationships work.'

'You should try it,' he'd suggested. 'Write your own book.'

'I might just do that,' she'd replied.

Of course she had believed in the basic truth of what she wrote, but that hadn't stopped her from laughing at many of her own words and phrases, the ones she had fashioned specifically to sound authoritative. She and Skip had laughed together.

When was it that she'd stopped laughing? When she received the advance from her publisher? After she'd appeared on *Oprah*? When she hit Number One in the bestsellers' list? She couldn't pinpoint the moment, but she knew it had occurred. And ever since it had occurred, she'd taken *I Saw You First* completely seriously. How could she not when so many other people did? There were hundreds and thousands of couples out there her words had helped. *They* weren't laughing.

When Fiona talked about her first meeting with Tom, her eyes shone. Lisa would have bet everything she had that Fiona would go back to Tom tonight in a different mood, ready to love as she had first loved. Lisa was now an authority. She began to believe she always had been.

It was only a matter of time before the transformation became complete, she knew. Soon she would stop remembering that the story of the couple in the park was fiction.

Was that so bad? All she was doing was shedding a skin of false superiority and cynicism. The Lisa Thomas who had lunch with other well-heeled suburban women in Connecticut would have sniggered about self-help books and the kinds of people who read them. But was she such a wonderful woman? No. She was an executive wife who bought the right clothes and gave good parties for men who stabbed each other in the back at work.

And the Lisa Thomas who had opted out of that life wasn't such a terrific creature either. Lolling around doing nothing all day had been fine for a while, but she wasn't expressing any creativity of her own.

The new Lisa Thomas was helping people. The new Lisa Thomas was energetic and optimistic and successful in her own right. If she had to manufacture some stories to prove her point, so be it. Lisa Thomas loved her public. And they loved her. She enjoyed being who they thought she was and giving them what they wanted.

People were desperate to talk to her. They cornered her, told her their life stories, confided in her. Meeting her was their priority. Not one of her fans ever looked bored – and that was just plain miraculous. Because Lisa had a paranoid fear of boring people, dating back, she suspected, to that horrible afternoon when she knew that, unlike her brothers who had all gone to Ivy League universities, she could end up at Oak Manor Junior College. OMJC was an institution renowned for its cute, airhead female students; it also had the dubious distinction of being the butt of family jokes. Located just down the road from where her family lived, it was the source of much hilarity as she was growing up. 'How many Oak Manor girls does it take to screw in a lightbulb? One. She tells her boyfriend she couldn't possibly manage and gets him to do it for her.'

When she was turned down by other colleges like Boston University and Northeastern, she knew she didn't even have a choice, she had no option but to go to Oak Manor. She tried to see the bright side of it, and enter into the spirit of the place. In fact, she joined in with a vengeance. She did everything Oak

Manor girls were famous for doing. She played field hockey. She joined a sorority of preppie, shopaholic, boy-crazy females, she did as little studying as possible. At any family gatherings, her brothers and parents would discuss what was happening in the world and she'd sit there, mute. 'So what does the field hockey team at Oak Manure think about nuclear disarmament?' her oldest brother would ask jeeringly. 'Or don't they have a view on it?'

She felt like a Kennedy child who couldn't play touch football. And the line the Scarecrow sang in *The Wizard of Oz* kept running through her head: 'If I only had a brain'. She knew she should have been able to defend herself, but she couldn't manage it. No one took her seriously. No one listened to her. She began to fear, whenever she opened her mouth, that she was boring and bothersome. As a consequence, she found herself babbling whenever she did open her mouth. In a hurried, rushed desire to get her point across, she'd lose sight of what she was saying, meander aimlessly on subjects and end up feeling a fool.

Skip had rescued her. He listened patiently to whatever she had to say, always looking genuinely interested. He never teased her about Oak Manor. He asked her opinions on every subject. He treated her with respect. She couldn't believe how wonderful it felt to have such concentration focused on her.

After he started at AT&T, however, work became paramount in his life and Lisa took a back seat. She repaid the concentration he'd bestowed on her by focusing on him. Skip *was* her career, she had no doubt about that. And she was willing to accept that role until the demands of his work became so all-encompassing they invaded seemingly every hour of every day. She probably wouldn't have minded even then, had he not been so palpably miserable. Asking him to leave his job had been as much for his sake as for the sake of their marriage.

When they had upped sticks, moved out and downscaled, they'd returned to the beginning again. Paradise had been regained. Yet within six months Lisa could tell Skip was not only worrying about money, which was natural enough, but he was also starting to look bored. Bored with her. Adam wasn't looking at Eve any more, he was searching around the Garden of Eden for trees to prune or a deal to make with one of the snakes. She couldn't keep him interested. His eyes would wander as she talked to him. Often he smothered yawns. Soon she found herself babbling again.

But this time Skip hadn't rescued her; *I Saw You First* had. Nine months into what they called their 'sabbatical' Lisa had sold the synopsis, the first step down the path to becoming Lisa Thomas the Author. Lisa Thomas who had no problem whatsoever in social gatherings – until, that is, the other night with Declan and Toby, when she'd had that familiar sinking feeling of stupidity. Still, she'd managed to shrug it off the next day. It hadn't lingered the way it used to. Within twenty-four hours she was Lisa Thomas the Author again.

Only since they'd come to England had she begun to question whether Skip was comfortable with the new Lisa. He had refused to accompany her to Manchester, saying he was too tired. For the past couple of nights he'd slept in a separate room. Skip, she knew in her heart, was still laughing at bits of *I Saw You First*. The only part of her book he took seriously was the financial dividend it paid.

Perhaps he had never taken *her* seriously. Perhaps he had only pretended to all along. He preferred Lisa Thomas the Oak Manor Girl, Lisa Thomas the Housewife. Well, she'd thrown away her hockey stick ages ago, and she'd moved on. There was no going back now.

Lisa Thomas finished off the bottle of wine.

'That was fantastic,' Skip said, buckling his seat belt. 'You guys really do know how to do Shakespeare.'

'It was wonderful.' Alison started her car and began to find her way out of the Barbican car park. 'I'm glad you could get tickets.'

'No sweat.'

'I'm so relieved not to be at Declan's parents' house. They're all mad there. Animals everywhere. And Declan's father cross-examines everyone the whole time, asks all these questions. It's exhausting.'

'Well, I have to say, I'm relieved not to be in Manchester.' Skip paused as she paid the car-park ticket. 'Alison, are you hungry?'

'I'm famished.'

'Do you know anywhere around here we could eat?'

'There's a place near Smithfield Market. It's not too far, and it's open late.'

'I promise I won't regale you with any more stories about my drunk mother.'

'Ditto. I won't bang on about my father, either.'

'No – I wish you would. I'd like to hear more about your childhood.'

'Really?' Alison turned to Skip for an instant, then focused back on the road. 'It's not particularly interesting, you know.'

'Oh, I bet it is. I bet you were an over-achiever at school.'

'I bet you were, too.'

'Do you think we have a lot in common?' Skip asked.

'We seem to.'

'I still can't believe I told you all that stuff about my mother. I've never told anyone about that weekend in Chicago.'

'Well, it's easy to tell me because we're in the same position. You can only tell the people who understand about those sorts of things. My father paid for this car, by the way. Did I tell you that?'

'No.'

'He was buying me off. For never paying attention to me. For running off.'

'I wish my mother could afford to buy *me* off.'

'Do you think I'm terrible? Should I not have accepted it?'

'Alison, I think you're wonderful.'

'Ditto.'

'I like that,' Skip smiled. 'That ditto business. It's nice.'

'Skip, how did you and Lisa first meet? I can't help wondering.'

'We met at a wedding. A friend of mine was marrying a girl who was a friend of Lisa's – they went to the same college.'

'I met Declan at a funeral.'

'Hey – they could make a movie about us. Except I don't want Hugh Grant playing me.'

'Toby Goodyear could play you.'

They both laughed then and Skip let himself look at Alison again. She was dressed in a short, white, sleeveless linen shift. Her hair was perfect, her legs were perfect. Everything about her was perfect.

'Do you think Toby's devastatingly handsome?'

'Yes, of course he is. But he's not my type. Not that I have a type, actually.'

'Tell me about your first boyfriend. The first guy you kissed.'

Alison giggled. 'We're supposed to be talking business tonight, Skip.'

'I know, I know. We will – but not until you've told me about your first kiss.'

'I'll tell you in the restaurant. On condition that you tell me about your first kiss afterwards.'

'No problem,' Skip replied. 'It's a deal.'

Chapter 6

Do you ever sit around with your girlfriends, trashing men? Come on – be honest. Do you moan about how they can't commit, how they never talk about their feelings, what pains in the butts they are? Do you laugh at their foibles and giggle at their silly ways?

I bet you do. I used to do that myself. It was fun, I admit it. We girls had a great time telling each other how superior we are to the male species.

But think back. Remember those times when you were single and some great girlfriend of yours suddenly found a man? Weren't you jealous when she spent all her time with him? When this great guy was all she could talk about? Where was your guy? you asked yourself. When was your prince going to show up on his white charger? How come she had a man and you didn't?

So – when you finally found that man, didn't you want to spend all your time with him? Talking to him, hanging out with him?

Isn't that what love is all about?

You bet it is.

Until time goes by and you stop talking to him. You run back to your girlfriends and complain about him to them, don't you? He does this, he doesn't do that, blahblahblah.

It's time to talk to him again. The way you did at the beginning. Your lover should be your best friend. If you were sharing an apartment with your best girlfriend and she bugged you because she didn't put the top back on the toothpaste or treated you badly in some way, wouldn't you tell her? Or would you go running to a group of guys and complain about how hopeless females are and laugh your head off? I don't think so.

I hope you wouldn't. That's not friendship, that's not respect. That's not the way you should behave.

I'm not saying you should spend all your time with your partner. You have to have a life of your own too, I know. You have to have those girlfriends. But don't use them as an excuse not to talk to your partner.

Don't keep this ridiculous war between the sexes going.

Believe me. It's a war no one can win.

I Saw You First, *Chapter Five, p. 60*

Declan woke up angry. He didn't want to be back in his old bed, in his old room; he wanted to be in Battersea, with Alison. Alison was the only human being he knew who didn't worship his father. She was the only one who understood how difficult it was for him to be with his family. As Declan sat up in bed, he heard Toby's voice coming up from the floor beneath.

'They divorced when I was sixteen. I stayed out of it. I wasn't about to get involved, and what could I have done, anyway? It was all about money. Money was what had held them together, it seems, and lack of money drove them apart.'

'But that must have been terrible. You must have suffered, Toby. What kind of effect did it have on you?'

Life story number fifty-five thousand, Declan thought. Have Toby and Owen been up all night? Possibly. This is never going to end. Owen is a master of coaxing out personal revelations. Once he starts asking those questions, once he opens them up, they can't stop. They're like serial-killers finally confessing, telling the police about body after body they have hidden over a long career.

Other people take up my father's entire life. That's exactly what Alison saved me from doing – spreading myself out too thin.

'I was miserable, yes. But I wasn't going to show it. They could fuck up their lives, not mine.'

'And is that when you started to act?' Owen asked. 'When reality became so painful?'

Declan listened to a moment of silence then heard the sound of a muffled sob. He swung his legs over the bed and stamped his feet firmly on the floor.

Christina woke up with a start. It took a moment for her to realize where she was and to see that Toby wasn't beside her in bed. He wasn't, normally, an early riser on Saturday mornings, so she was surprised to notice the time on her watch – nine a.m. Looking out from her room, she could see Declan across the hall from her, sitting on his bed with his head in his hands. He was wearing a pair of blue and white striped boxer shorts and a dark blue T-shirt.

This is odd, she thought. I feel as if I were in a school dormitory or a youth hostel.

'Good morning, Declan,' she said, sitting up as well. She had on a massive white cotton shirt that came down to her knees. 'Where's Toby? Where's Michael?'

'I'm here,' Michael called out. 'At the end of the hall. You can come in and give me a massage if you'd like, Christina. On the other hand, that might not be a good idea. Did you sleep well?'

'This is like being in an episode of *The Waltons*,' she laughed. 'We need John Boy, though.'

Declan raised his head and smiled at her. 'I'll be John Boy,' he said. 'I always wanted to be John Boy.'

'Who's John Boy?' Michael asked.

Declan rolled his eyes at Christina. 'See what happens when there's no television in the house? A whole shared culture is lost.'

'You call television culture?' Michael asked. Christina could hear him walking down the landing. 'You are mentally inadequate, Declan.' She saw him appear in front of her room, then watched as he hurled a pillow at Declan's head.

'Michael, you shit.' The pillow came flying back at Michael, who ducked. It landed at Christina's feet. Lifting it up, she stood, then advanced on Michael. 'You shouldn't pick on your younger brother like that,' she laughed, then clobbered him over the head.

'And you shouldn't pick on me,' he responded, grabbing her around the waist and tickling her.

'Unhand her, you fiend,' Declan shouted. He had picked up a glass on his bedside table and threw the water in it at Michael's face.

'You are going to be *so* sorry,' Michael yelled, his face dripping. 'You are going to wish you'd never been born.' He bent down to get the pillow and started toward Declan. Christina grabbed him from behind and did as he had done to her – tickled him ferociously.

'Get off me, you vicious aromatherapy person!' Michael screamed. 'You're killing me.'

'What's going on up there?' They all stopped, frozen, as they heard Owen's voice. 'This is supposed to be a non-violent household.'

'We're just discussing John Stuart Mill,' Christina shouted. 'It's very peaceful, Owen, I promise.'

'Absolutely, Dad,' Michael called out.

'No violence of any kind,' Declan added loudly. 'Although we had a tiny disagreement when I said I'd prefer to talk about Machiavelli.'

Declan was grinning, Michael was laughing and Christina felt as if she would give anything to stop time in its tracks, to freeze-frame this moment and stay forever in this room with these two men.

This is what I never had and always wanted, she thought. A family. People to play with, to laugh with, to feel comfortable with.

'Breakfast is ready,' Jessica called up to them. 'Come down, you naughty children.'

After the room-service waiter had delivered her Continental

breakfast, Lisa poured herself a cup of coffee, stretched and thought: This is the life. I can do whatever I want. Stay in bed. Get up and wander around the city. Watch a film. I don't have to worry about Skip. I don't have to worry about anything at all. Just a very tiny hangover.

How long has it been since I've been alone? Decades. An entire lifetime. I went from a family of six children to a college where I always had roommates, straight to living with Skip. I never had any time to myself, any space entirely my own. I have always, always, shared.

And now Skip wants me to have children. Which means even less possibility of time to myself. If I have children and continue to work, I'll feel guilty. If I have children and stop working, I'll feel frustrated. Every modern woman's dilemma.

Well, nuts to that. Fuck you, Skip Thomas. You're going to have to wait. No way am I giving all this up now – absolutely no way.

'Skip.' Alison shook his shoulder. 'Skip. Wake up.'

He stirred, opened his eyes and swore. 'Oh shit,' he moaned. 'Oh shit. Alison. What have I done?'

'What have *we* done?'

'I'm so sorry, Alison. That shouldn't have happened. Last night. I'm sorry.'

'Well, you weren't entirely responsible, you know.' Alison traced one of Skip's eyebrows with her finger. 'I had a part in it too.'

'What time is it?'

'Nine-thirty.'

'Lisa isn't due back until this afternoon.'

'And Declan's away for the weekend.'

'Alison, do me a favour, will you? Could you please take your body away from my immediate vicinity?'

'Why? Is it so unattractive in the harsh light of day?' She moved her finger from his brow down over his nose and then into his mouth.

'You're incorrigible, you know that?' he murmured.

'Ditto,' she said, before placing her tongue in his ear.

'Your father is amazing. He is so insightful, so full of wisdom.'

Toby Goodyear was lying on the grass, underneath an apple tree in the garden. Declan, his back propped against the tree, had a laptop across his thighs.

'Toby,' Declan sighed. 'We're supposed to be working, remember? Are you too tired?'

'I'm not tired in the slightest,' Toby responded. 'I feel badly about keeping Owen up all night, but I think he really enjoyed talking to me.'

'I'm sure he did.'

'I was thinking. I know this might sound bizarre, but I had an idea, after we finished breakfast and your father went to sleep, I couldn't help but think that anyone in the world who listened to him talking about my Hamlet wouldn't know, wouldn't understand what it had been like in that theatre that night.'

'And?' Declan tried to concentrate on what Toby was saying, but kept gazing over at the house. Christina was with Michael, sitting on the level part of the roof where the rope-swing hung. Would she go on it? And why did it matter to him so much if she did?

'And I thought – wouldn't it be possible to do one of these infomercial things for myself? Make one about me as an actor, with Owen giving a testimonial at the end. Wouldn't that be fantastic?'

'Toby.' Declan put his hand over his face and hung his head. 'You can't be serious. Can you?'

'It was just an idea,' Toby grumbled. 'There's no need to be so dismissive.'

'What?' Declan removed his hand and stared at Toby. 'Would you deliver some soliloquies at the beginning, and then interview my father? Is that the idea? And then sell the tape of yourself to the public so they didn't have to go to the theatre to watch you perform? What is going on here? We don't have to read any books, we don't have to see any plays, we don't have to exercise, we don't have to have normal friends, only psychic ones? Toby, I think we're in danger of going too far.'

'I thought *you* were completely committed now. To infomercials. You certainly seemed to be last night.'

'I was winding Michael up.'

'And trying to wind your father up as well. I don't understand you, Declan. You have this perfect home, perfect parents, and you behave as if—'

Declan tuned out. He could see Christina shaking her head and laughing. Michael grabbed hold of the rope hanging from the tree above the roof and offered it to her. She kept shaking her head.

'You don't understand your father, he has an incredible—'

'Excuse me for a second, Toby.' Declan placed the laptop carefully on the ground beside him. 'I'm going to get a glass of water. Would you like something?'

'No,' Toby said curtly. 'Don't bother about me.'

'I'm not coordinated, Michael.' Declan, coming closer to the house, could hear Christina's words. 'You know how Owen said he would be hopeless at line-dancing. Well, I'd be useless jumping off a roof on to a rope. I'd fall off. I'd bring the whole tree down with me.'

'Christina – come on. You can do it. I promise you'll be fine. You'll love it. It's such an exhilarating feeling, swinging through the air.'

'I'm sure it is.' Declan saw Christina frown. 'And I wish I could, really I do. But I'm too frightened.' She wasn't laughing any more. Declan, as he looked up at her, noticed an expression in her eyes which surprised him. It wasn't just fear, it was a mixture of terrible sadness and loss. When he went into the house, he headed straight up the stairs and climbed out of the top window, on to the roof.

'Declan!' Michael glanced at him, his eyebrows raised. 'You never come out here any more. What are you doing?'

Christina smiled at him. 'Have you come to rescue me from your

evil older brother who wants me to break my neck on this thing?'
She gestured to the rope Michael was holding in his hands. She
was wearing a pair of white trousers and a black, scoop-necked top.
In that one instant, as she smiled, he saw her as a tiny girl. Does
she have a brother? he wondered. Does her brother look after her?
Does her father? Or does everyone think because she's so tall, and
somehow so undemanding that she doesn't need looking after?

'I've come to give you a ride,' he said. 'All you have to do is
hold on to me. It's easier than holding on to the rope. I used to
get rides from Michael myself. It may not be quite as much fun
as doing it on your own, but it's not bad.'

'I should have thought of that.' Michael slapped his forehead.
'I forgot there were times you used to enjoy going on this. I forgot
I used to give you rides.'

'Well, I remember.' Declan stepped to the front of the roof
and took the rope from Michael's hand. 'All right, Christina. All
you have to do is put your arms around my neck, and your legs
around my waist. Wrap yourself around me as if you were going
piggyback.'

'I'm too tall,' Christina said softly.

'Don't be silly. I'm only about an inch shorter than you.'

'One and a half.'

'Whatever. I'm stronger and I have broader shoulders. You can
still go piggyback.'

'Are you sure?'

'I'm sure.'

'Fantastic!' Michael clapped his hands. 'I wish the kids were
here to see this. They'd love it. Toby!' he yelled down. 'Watch
your girlfriend fly through the air. Then come up and join
us.'

There was no response from the supine figure of Toby.

'He's asleep,' Christina commented. 'He must be knackered
from all that talking last night.'

'Dad wears everyone out, that's for certain,' Michael laughed.
'He can talk people to death.'

'He *questions* them to death,' Declan said. 'Come on, Christina, hop on.'

'You're positive about this?'

'I'm positive.'

Christina put her arms around Declan's neck, took a little jump, and fixed her legs around his waist.

'Hold on tight,' he commanded. Taking a big breath, he tightened his grip on the rope. 'Here goes.'

They sailed off the roof, dropping into thin air, before arcing up again and swinging back.

'Oh my God,' Christina whispered into Declan's ear. 'Are we going to crash?'

'Crash and burn,' he replied. The rope hung for a second then descended once more, going less far than it had the first time. Micahel was clapping from the roof. 'Bravo!' he shouted. 'You survived, and so did the tree.'

They swung mildly for a few more arcs before coming to rest in the middle of the garden. Christina climbed off Declan's back.

'That was fantastic,' she said, a little breathless.

'Do you want to do it again?'

'I'd love to.'

'Do you want to go on your own?'

'Yes,' she answered. 'I have the hang of it now, so to speak.'

'Hello, look who's here,' Michael called down from the roof.

Christina turned from Declan and saw a woman standing on the edge of the lawn, holding a young boy's hand. She shaded her eyes and looked up at Michael.

'John has been begging me to bring him over to play on the rope-swing. I said he was too young, but he won't listen. When I rang Jessica she said to come right over, that you wouldn't mind and that he could go on the swing with you. *Would* you mind?'

'Not at all.' Michael grinned down at her. 'We'll give John a swing, won't we, Declan?'

'Of course. It's nice to see you, Joanna,' Declan said as the boy pulled his mother over to them. 'Joanna lives across the road,' he explained to Christina. 'And Joanna, this is Christina, who has just had her very first experience on the rope-swing. You see – she's survived intact.'

Christina shook hands with Joanna and John. John's eyes were fixed on the rope hanging from the tree.

'I want to go now,' he said.

'Please,' his mother added.

'Please,' he repeated. He looked to be around five or six years old and Christina saw his impatience. He wanted to swing *now*; he wanted the grown-ups to stop talking. He took a quick look at Toby under the tree but was uninterested in the strange man asleep on the grass. The rope-swing was all-consuming.

'You're sure you don't mind?' Joanna looked bedraggled and weary. 'Could I leave him with you for a while? I have so much to do—'

'Leave him with us. We'll look after him and bring him back later,' Michael said. 'I've done this thousands of times with my kids. Don't worry. We'll take care of him.'

John grinned with a kind of innocent delight Christina hadn't seen for a very long time.

'Come on then.' Declan swept John up in his arms and carried him to the house as he squealed with pleasure.

'It's so hard sometimes,' Joanna sighed, watching them. 'Being a single mother.'

'It must be,' Christina nodded.

'He needs men in his life. It's wonderful having Owen nearby. He's so helpful, he and Jessica both. I probably rely on them too much, but he needs—' she stopped, then said, 'It was nice to meet you, Christina. Thank you again. I must be going. I have so much to do.'

Joanna turned and walked away.

I wish she had stayed to watch him, Christina thought. But she must not get much time to herself. This must be a very welcome break.

She looked back up to the roof and saw Declan appear with

John. He and Michael argued over who would take John first and settled the question finally by flipping a coin.

'I won.' Declan smiled at John. 'You're mine.'

'Can we do this all day?' John asked as Michael lifted him on to Declan's back.

'I don't see why not,' Michael answered.

Declan took a quick look over at Toby.

'Me neither,' he said. 'If he's not working, why should I be?'

'What about you, Christina? Do you have anything better to do?' Michael stared down at her.

'No.'

'Then get up here. We'll have a competition. Who can swing the furthest and the longest.'

'I'll win,' Declan said.

'Dream on,' Michael replied. 'John and I have this sewn up.'

'Do you want to bet on that?'

'I want to go with her.' John pointed at Christina. 'She's the tallest.'

'John?' Declan sounded offended. 'You don't trust my rope-swinging powers? Get up here, Christina. This is war.'

Lisa Thomas walked into the hairdresser's the hotel concierge had recommended and asked if they could fit her in immediately.

The girl with a dazzling array of earrings and nose studs studied the book in front of her, then said: 'That will be fine. What are you having done?'

'A cut and a blow job, please.'

'Pardon?'

'A cut and a – oh my God.' Lisa began to giggle. She could feel herself blushing. 'I meant a cut and a blow *dry*.'

'All right, then. Jack's available now. Jack?' She called to the back of the salon. 'You have a client.'

A phenomenally thin man with a shaved head and a thin black moustache approached, scowling. He was dressed entirely in black and had black eyeshadow on as well as lower eyelids underlined with kohl. Taking Lisa by the arm, he led her to a chair facing a mirror.

'So. Whaddya want?'

Lisa looked at him in the mirror. 'You sound American.'

'No shit, Sherlock,' he replied.

What was it with trendy places these days? Lisa wondered. Why were waiters often so aggressive at the best restaurants, and hair-stylists at the top salons so rude?

'I'd like a quick cut. Half an inch or so.'

'Okeydokey. Felicity will shampoo you and then I'll do the evil deed.'

For a moment she envisioned him taking a razor to her scalp and shaving her head to match his. She wished she'd been recommended a different salon, but it was too late now.

Felicity took her to the sink and positioned her head for the shampoo. She was in Jack's hands. They have such power, these people, she thought. They can wield their scissors and destroy your appearance in two minutes, if they choose to. If they're in a bad mood and don't care about their job. When she was deposited back in her original chair, her hair combed out by Felicity, she couldn't help but speculate on Jack's romantic life. Who had seen *him* first and what had that person seen? Or was he a loner, living at home, taking care of his ancient mother. Anthony Perkins in *Psycho*?

'What brings you to lovely Manchester?' Jack growled.

'I'm a writer. I was signing copies of my book in Dillons.'

'Uh huh. What do you write? Mystery novels with dyke detectives?'

'Excuse me?'

'They're very popular, those. Or so I've heard. I haven't read any myself.'

'No.' Lisa tried to control her rising irritation. 'I do not write any kind of detective books. I've written a self-help book. On relationships.'

Jack threw his hands in the air. 'Blimey. I left the States to get away from creatures like you.'

'Excuse me?' Lisa felt almost paralysed by his rudeness. She knew she should have been just as rude in return, but she looked at the scissors in his right hand and squirmed in her chair.

'The junk emotion junkies. "My boyfriend won't go down on me. What can I do?" Blah blah blah. "My girlfriend won't go down on me. What can I do?" Yadda yadda yadda. "I'm in love with my pimp. What can I do?" Et cetera, et cetera, et cetera.' He picked up a comb and dug into her head with it.

'I don't think this is such a good idea,' Lisa said, sitting up straighter and bristling. 'I didn't come in here to listen to this kind of talk. You're obviously the sort of person that likes to shock.' How could he be so filthy-minded and continue to keep a job like this, dealing with the public? But then she remembered her 'cut and blow job' mistake and thought he might have overheard her. That was imposssible, wasn't it? He wasn't anywhere near the front of the salon when she'd said it. Could there be some kind of microphone at the receptionist's desk? Maybe every stylist in the place had heard her faux pas. She looked around to see if people were staring at her and was relieved to find that she wasn't the centre of attention.

'Oh right. You going to analyse me now?' Jack kept the comb at the end of her hair, and began to snip. 'You need a cut, I'm giving you a cut. End of story.'

Lisa closed her eyes. This was beginning to be a nightmare. And there was no way out short of bolting like a frightened rabbit. She couldn't picture herself out on the street with wet hair, some of which had already been cut off. He wouldn't actually mangle her haircut? Would he? Had he just broken up with a lover? Was he out for revenge?

'Oh, calm down, lady. Stop shifting around, or I can't be held accountable for the result. I'm not going to do anything you don't want me to do, OK? Although if I had my own way, I'd cut this a lot shorter, give you a Sinead O'Connor look which would suit you.'

'It's already short,' Lisa managed to say firmly.

'Not short enough. Anyway, the point is, the whole point is, just get over it. That's my motto.'

'Get over what?'

'Whatever.' Jack waved his hands in the air again. 'Your boyfriend doesn't go down on you, get over it. Move on, get someone who will. You know what I mean? There is no point in hanging on to the past. Sit around talk, talk, talk. Say – hey man, *why* don't you go down on me? Trouble with your mother? That kind of thing. You know. Waste of time. The thing's broke, throw it away.'

'I don't think—'

'Yeah, well, you wouldn't. You're a Yank. Gotta talk. Gotta analyse, right? People here know better. They don't go in for that shit. Like I said, that's part of the reason I moved here twelve years ago. To get away from all that talk. Although you gotta wonder lately. I mean, they're putting all that Oprah Rickki Lake crap on the television here now. And everyone went apeshit with emotion and talk when Princess Di died. Like we should be like Americans and pour out our hearts all the frigging time. Spare me. Gag me with a shovel.'

'You actually left America so you wouldn't have to discuss your emotions?' Lisa asked. He was such a revolting man, she felt herself becoming transfixed by him.

'Part of it. I mean, that was part of the reason. Freud's dead, right? Get over it. Go to a party or something. Enjoy yourself. Don't sit around and weep about yourself and your parents and what they did or didn't do. It won't help you when the war comes.'

'The war?'

'Yeah. I mean, there has to be another one soon. And who do you want fighting it? Some wimps who've been blabbing on *Oprah*?'

'I admire Oprah. Oprah happens to be a friend of mine.'

'I bet. So tell me, I'm interested. What does this book of yours say about relationships? That you should talk things out, right?'

I could help him, Lisa thought. He needs someone to talk to, that's all. His step-father or his uncle or someone probably abused him as a child. He needs someone sympathetic to talk to.

'Not exactly. I say you should go back to the beginning of your relationship, remember what brought you together. What you first saw in each other.'

'Oh, puleeze. You're supposed to remember how horny that person made you feel, when there's another person walking down the street in front of you who makes you hornier than you can ever remember feeling? And you haven't even *touched* that person yet and you know how great it would be to get that first touch, to discover someone else's body, what turns them on. When you know like the back of your hand what turns this person you've been with for centuries on and you're bored, bored, *bored*.'

Don't get upset, Lisa, she cautioned herself. He doesn't understand the concept yet. He's a little slow. That's not his fault. Explain it to him. Think of it as a challenge.

'I understand that the new can be exciting, of course, Jack. But that's not the point. You can make the old exciting by treating it as if it were new.'

'And people buy this shit?'

Lisa closed her eyes. She had the mirror; but that, for some inexplicable reason, wasn't working. What she needed was some garlic, a cross and a stake.

'What time is it?'

'Three-thirty.'

'When is Lisa coming back?'

'She told me she was catching the five o'clock shuttle.'

'That gives us a few more hours.'

'Jesus, Alison. I don't think I can manage a couple more hours. I'm tapped out here.' Skip stretched and yawned. 'I feel as if I'd played ten sets of tennis.'

How did this happen? How did I get here? he asked himself. We were having dinner like normal people do and now I'm lying in bed beside her but it seems natural, as if it were pre-ordained. Is this what Fate is all about?

'Do you need some food?'

'I need a new body.'

'I wouldn't say that.' Alison bit her lower lip as she looked at him. *I didn't notice how attractive he was to start off with,* she thought. *He looks like a doctor on a TV series. A little worn down by life's anxieties, but someone you can spill your heart out to, someone who will take care of you. American men are easier to be with. They talk and they say what they feel. They're not uptight like most of the sods in this country. And they respect women's ambitions. What a welcome change. I should have gone to the States ages ago. I belong there.*

'You know this is seriously dangerous, Alison, what we're doing here. It's addictive.'

'No. It's a one-off. After this, Declan and Lisa come back and everything is back to normal.'

Tell me I'm wrong, Alison silently begged. *Please tell me I'm wrong. I haven't felt like this in ages. Not since Peter. I need you, Skip – God knows why. You're married and I'm with Declan and I know being with you is wrong, but it feels right. I'm comfortable with you. I want to stay in bed, like John Lennon and Yoko Ono, stay in bed for months, for years. Talking and making love. Don't tell me we have to end this now.*

'You think so? We slide back into the status quo?' Skip looked at her shoulder, wondering whether he'd left teethmarks on it during the course of the night. *There were times when he hadn't been able to control himself, when he'd forgotten there were other people involved in this equation. Hadn't she been as involved as he had? As swept away?*

Boy, is she blasé, he thought. *Any American woman would be playing scenes from* Fatal Attraction *by now. I'd be hiding the pet rabbit, if I had one. Why is she so unconcerned? Didn't this mean anything to her?*

'What's the alternative to the status quo?' Alison edged away from him. She was determined to keep her distance; if he wanted this to stop, then she wasn't going to let him see how upset she was. The idea of Skip feeling sorry for her made her feel ill.

'I guess there is no alternative.' Skip paused and cupped his hands around Alison's face. 'Neither of us expected this to happen.'

'Right. So that's settled. It was a one-off. A fling.'

Fantastic. He's dumping me. I should have known fucking better. American, English – they're no different, not really. Men are men. The pricks.

'I guess so,' Skip mumbled. 'I just feel as if – I don't know – I feel as if we went to school together or something. As if we'd known each other since we were kids.'

'I would have been in nursery school when you were in secondary school,' Alison said curtly.

'That's true, although I don't know what the hell secondary school is. I get the gist. You're a baby and I'm an old codger.'

She wants me out of her life – fine. I'm an old unemployed has-been. English rose? English cactus is more like it. I wish she'd told me how she felt before I'd climbed into bed with her.

Skip turned his head away from Alison but then found himself staring at a photograph of Alison and Declan on the top of the dressing-table.

'I shouldn't be here, in Declan's bed. Especially when he's working for me.'

'Working for you?'

'Yes. He's developing the *Plots in a Box* idea, with Toby. I assume they're working on it this weekend. He promised me a script by Tuesday.'

Alison sat up, pulling the sheets around her. 'He never told me he was doing that.'

'He wanted to keep it a secret from you for the time being.'

'Why? That doesn't make sense. I'm the one who wanted him to do it. I was pushing him to do it.'

'Maybe he thinks you'd take over.'

'He's competing with me?' Alison's eyes widened. 'That is totally outrageous. I can't believe it.'

'To be fair, I don't know if he's competing with you—'

'Why else wouldn't he tell me? Skip – I'm the one who did the research on the infomercials to begin with. I'm the one who believes in them. I had a whole proposition worked out to tell you about. Before this all – before this happened. How can Declan think he can come in and take over?'

'He's not taking over, exactly. He's doing this one project, that's all. I don't know if he has any long-range plans. All I know is he's due to hand me a script on Tuesday.'

'He and I could have worked on it together.'

'I suppose so.' Skip shrugged and sat up as well.

'This sucks. I haven't even discussed my ideas with you.'

'What? Are you more interested in doing a deal with me than being with me like this? Is that why you are with me now? To talk to me about infomercials? I thought something special had happened between us.' He frowned. 'Are you telling me this was all in a day's – or night's – work?'

'Well, I don't think that just because of what's happened you and I can't work together. This is a one-off, remember? A fling.'

'Alison. Are you always this pragmatic?'

When she didn't respond, Skip sighed.

'I don't understand you. You weren't like this last night. You were different. *We* were different.'

'And now that I'm a competent, ambitious woman again, not some mimsy little female looking deeply into your eyes and telling you the story of my life, you don't like me any more? Is that it? You don't want to have anything to do with me professionally? You've used me, haven't you? I should have known bet—'

'Whoa!' Skip reached out and touched her cheek. I've hit a sore spot, somehow. She's not tough, not at all. She's defensive and distrustful of men. Some arrogant, insensitive Brit has probably screwed her over in the past – now why doesn't that surprise me?

'You've been hammered somewhere along the way, haven't you? Some guy really hurt you.'

'That's none of your business.' Alison turned away from him.

'Did you love him that much?'

When she didn't answer, Skip got up from the bed, went around to her side and knelt down, so his face was close to hers.

'He didn't deserve you, whoever he was – you know that.'

'Leave off, Skip. It's time you went home.'

'If that's what you want.'

'That's what I want.'

'You're sure?'

'I'm positive.'

They were both silent for a few minutes.

'How do I get home, by the way?'

'I'll ring a minicab.'

'I feel like a real asshole.'

'Well, there's not a lot I can do about that.' Alison turned away from him again.

Toby got the hang of it straight off. He had always been a good dancer, he knew, not one of those pasty-faced Englishmen who jerk spasmodically on the floor. He had a sense of rhythm and a natural ability to learn steps. Every movement that Jessica made he could copy immediately, all perfectly in synch with the terrible song booming out from the tape player: 'Achey Breaky Heart'.

Christina was struggling to keep up, Declan was flailing and Owen was completely hopeless. Michael managed reasonably enough, but Toby was the star.

'Toby,' Jessica said with wonder, when the song ended. 'You're a natural. You should teach this yourself.'

She was standing barefoot on the grass, dressed in a long flowing skirt and sleeveless top.

'You have an alternative career, if you want one.'

'No, thank you very much,' he replied. 'I've never cared for Stetsons.'

147

'That was *incredibly* difficult,' Owen announced, panting. 'I have no clue how you do that bit where you kick out and then slap your foot and then kick again.'

'I could show you, Owen,' Toby said quickly. 'I'll take you through it very slowly.'

'Oh, no,' Owen protested, falling into a heap on the lawn. 'I surrender. You all go on ahead without me.'

'Owen, please. Let me help.' Toby went over to Owen and offered him his hand to pull him back up. I'll do anything, he thought. Anything at all to help this man. He has changed my life. He has made me believe in myself again. He's a saint.

'Honestly – no. Would anyone like some tea?' Owen allowed Toby to help him up.

'I'd love a cup, Dad,' Michael responded.

'I would too,' Declan and Christina said simultaneously.

'I'll help you,' Toby said, following Owen back into the cottage.

He's like Owen's dog, Christina thought, watching Toby trotting at Owen's heels. He can't leave him alone for one moment. He's acting in a way I've never seen him act before – except he's not acting. This is real. It's almost as if . . . Christina stopped for a moment, amazed by the next thought that had invaded her brain. It's almost as if he has fallen in love.

When Christina had shaken Toby awake after Michael had finally persuaded John that two hours on the rope-swing was enough and it was time to take him home, Toby's first reaction had been to say: 'Where's Owen? Is he up yet?' He had leapt from the grass and gone into the cottage to find his new mentor and then had spent the next hour monopolizing him as Jessica and Christina prepared salads for a late lunch.

After they had finished eating, Jessica suggested line-dancing on the lawn and to Christina's surprise, everyone, including Declan, had agreed. But – she'd noticed – Toby had waited for Owen's approval before he'd gone along as well. And now he was helping Owen make the tea. Toby *never* helped out in the kitchen.

What could he possibly have left to say to Owen? she wondered. He'd been up all night with him; he'd spent all of lunchtime in a virtual huddle with him at the end of the table; he'd talked and talked and talked. She would have thought he'd run out of topics to discuss.

Christina, seeing that Michael and Jessica and Declan were involved in a conversation of their own, headed toward the cottage herself.

'It was so stultifying.' She heard Toby's voice at the same time as she saw him, his back up against the kitchen counter, his face about two inches away from Owen's, who was filling the kettle with water. 'So oppressive. But that was the done thing. Send the brats to boarding school, get rid of them and hope you never have to deal with their messy emotions. I was good at sport, of course, so I got on perfectly reasonably. I had friends and all. But I couldn't express myself – never. Only on stage. Most people want to act because they want to become different people. I wanted to act so I could be myself.'

'I see.' Owen nodded his head. He didn't sound bored, he didn't look bored. 'But how do you become yourself when you play someone else? Isn't that a contradiction? Or is it that truth resides in contradictions?'

'That's it. That's it exactly.' Toby reached out and grabbed Owen's arm. 'Like Hamlet, you see. To be or not to be. Opposites but yet the same. When Hamlet acts, finally, when he has chosen 'to be', he is actually choosing, unbeknownst to him, 'not to be' because the consequence of his actions is his own death. It's all about contradictions.'

'That's fascinating, Toby.' Owen plugged the kettle in. 'The thesis and the antithesis create the synthesis. But do you think that synthesis has to be death?'

Help, Christina said to herself, sneaking out of the cottage before Owen or Toby saw her. This is far too heavy for me. It's lucky Owen isn't the leader of some cult group. I can imagine that, with the sort of power he has to connect with people, he could convince thousands to kill themselves. Yet there is no evil in him. He looked like an eager-to-please kid trying to follow Jessica line-dancing. And that tee-hee giggle of his is innocence incarnate.

But what was Toby saying, exactly? If he has to act to be himself, does that mean he is constantly acting? Where does the actor stop and the man begin? Is he acting when he makes love to me? Is there always an audience in his mind? Am I his partner or his current leading lady?

He has shown a whole new side of himself here, a side I never knew existed. Before last night I could never have imagined Toby baring his soul and discussing his childhood with a stranger. Or is that an act as well? Whenever he has mentioned Harrow to me, he has recalled those days with fondness. Could he be creating this teenage angst in order to feed Owen good lines? It is so tempting to confide in Owen and receive his incredible sympathy in return.

But Toby wouldn't manufacture emotions for Owen's benefit; that's not a fair thought. I don't know him – that's the problem. We don't talk enough. And whose fault is that? It has to be both of ours.

As she approached Declan and Jessica and Michael sitting on the lawn, Christina found herself wishing she had a camera. There they were, in the shade of an oak tree, splayed out in the warmth of the summer sun, seemingly entirely relaxed and happy. Something had changed in Declan, Christina knew. He wasn't fighting any more, at least not for the moment. He had that wonderful smile on his face and a piece of grass in his mouth. Jessica had one hand on his knee, the other on Michael's. Christina wanted to take the picture, and she wanted to keep it for herself.

'Lose weight without dieting or exercise?' Michael was saying. 'What an incredible concept! I'm beginning to understand your fascination with this now. But if you're really going to do it, Declan, you should go all out. Take the *Plots in a Box* idea one step further. Out-informercial the infomercials.'

'What do you mean?' Declan asked.

'Well, I think you should take it to the limit. Not only sell culture, but sell weight loss at the same time.'

'Come again?'

'It would run something like this: "Buy this tape and put weight on your brains, not on your thighs!" Include a low-calorie recipe with each dinner-plate. You know: "George Eliot's pasta primavera, guaranteed to fire your grey cells at the same time as keeping your waist trim. Silas Marner was a miser? Yes, well, you too can save – not pounds, but stones."'

'You're even worse than I am,' Declan grinned at Michael.

'James Joyce, the ultimate – what's that American word? Buttmaster, that's it. The ultimate buttmaster,' Jessica said, smiling. '"Sit down to read *Ulysses* and swear not to eat until you've finished it, and when you reach the end you'll be two sizes smaller."'

'Oh no, Mum,' Michael protested. 'That would mean they'd actually have to read the book. No good.'

'But nice try?' Jessica looked up at Christina. 'Come and sit down with us, Christina. I'm trying very hard to become an infomercial expert.'

'We all are,' Michael added.

What's going on here? Christina asked herself. Why has this magical air descended on everyone in this house? What has happened to reconcile Declan to Michael, and how has Michael become a part of the infomercial joke? Last night the tension was omnipresent – this afternoon it has vanished, replaced by harmony. Toby is discussing metaphysics in the kitchen with Owen, the rest of us are laughing out here and we were all, only minutes ago, dancing barefoot on the grass. It couldn't be that one silly pillowfight has broken a deadlock in this house, could it? One pillowfight and many rides on the rope-swing? Instead of years in family counselling? Is that credible?

Christina glanced back at the cottage and saw a goat wander through the open front door.

Of course. Why didn't I think of it before? It's Midsummer's Night. That explains it. We're all in the grip of supernatural forces.

But what's going to happen when we wake up tomorrow?

* * *

Lisa was amazed to see that Jack's haircut was actually a very good one. She'd had to put up with his incredible rudeness to get it, but it had been worthwhile – almost. She thought if she had heard the phrase 'get over it' one more time, she would have grabbed the scissors from his hand and plunged them into his shining scalp.

The well-dressed older man sitting beside her on the flight back to London had been rude as well.

'Hi there,' Lisa had said politely as she'd put her bag in the overhead locker. 'Looks like I'm sitting next to you here.'

'Please do me the courtesy of not speaking to me during this flight,' he said, his grey eyes glinting with hostility. 'I have yet to recover from a Texas gentleman I had the misfortune to be placed next to haranguing me about his grandchildren on a flight to Rome last year. I have a book in my lap and I very much want to read it. So I would appreciate it if you could refrain from talking.'

Well, excuse me for being friendly, Lisa had muttered under her breath. When the plane landed, this madman had stayed in his seat reading while everyone else disembarked. He looked as if he felt contact with human beings might contaminate him

And the legendary London cabbie hadn't said a word during the trip to Pimlico.

'Nice weather, isn't it?' Lisa had remarked.

He'd grunted and that had been that.

This isn't a country I want to stay in, she'd thought, sitting silently in the back of the taxi. I don't like the atmosphere. As soon as I've finished my publicity, we'll be out of here. Thank God.

But what about her infomercial? How could she get that done in the time allotted – three weeks? And would it work here with such difficult, snobby, rude people? Would they understand what she was getting at? Would they want to see her being interviewed by Toby? The common theme of the day had been that the British didn't like to talk. They especially didn't like being talked to by Americans. Declan had made a big point about the length of American infomercials and the fact that the British wouldn't want to watch such long advertisements. Perhaps he was right. Perhaps she should re-jig hers. But how? If she didn't do an interview format, what should she do?

As the taxi proceeded along Knightsbridge, Lisa had a moment of inspiration.

Cut her interview with Toby entirely and go straight to the testimonials – couples explaining how the book had helped them in their relationships.

British couples, of course.

Yet people loved the personal touches of the book, the story of her marriage to Skip.

Some Brits plus she and Skip – that would do the trick.

Looking for those Brits would be a problem, though, and a time-consuming enterprise. She needed people who wouldn't be frightened by the camera, who were reasonably articulate, whom she could trust to say the right things.

People she already knew.

Toby and Christina and Declan and Alison. The four of them with Skip and her. Discussing the wisdom of I *Saw You First*.

Lisa smiled.

She loved solving problems.

Chapter 7

OK. Let's imagine a scenario. You've just slept with your partner for the first time. He brings you a cup of coffee in bed the next morning. You think: Oh boy, what a fantastic person! So-and-so never brought me coffee in bed. How lucky I am now!'

Now: fast forward the tape of your relationship. Two or three years on and he brings you the cup of coffee in bed and you take it without so much as a thank you or a thought for his kindness. You're used to it. You expect it. In fact, you'd be angry if he didn't bring it.

Ask yourself this: what does he have to do to make you pay attention? Bring coffee with freshly squeezed orange juice? And a warm croissant perhaps? Would that do it for you? Sure. Maybe. But then you'd get used to that too, wouldn't you? Pretty soon he'll have to deliver you coffee, croissants, orange juice, and a diamond necklace on the side.

How we forget. How oblivious we are to the kindness of intimates. A stranger does something nice for us and we get all excited but our partner treats us well and we act like we couldn't care less.

You should be remembering all those so-and-sos who never had the courtesy to bring you coffee; they should be embedded in your mind for eternity.

You CAN NOT expect your partner to keep upping the stakes,

*to do more and more and more for you in order to maintain the
same level of affection. You better start showing your appreciation
or you're in danger of becoming a spoiled brat.*

*You know how they say familiarity breeds contempt? Well, I
say familiarity should breed wonder.*

*Treat your partner like a stranger and you'll end up more of
an intimate. I know this sounds like a conundrum but, you know,
life is a series of conundrums – isn't that what's so fascinating?*

Don't sit back and say: Whatever will be, will be.

Jump up and say: Whatever is, can be better!

I Saw You First, *Chapter Eleven, p. 156*

'Hello, everyone, I hope I'm not intruding.' Alison said this as she
walked across the garden to join the group sitting on two large
blankets. 'Toby – what a surprise. Christina. What are you two
doing here?'

Declan leapt to his feet and rushed to Alison's side.

'I invited Toby and Christina to come for the weekend. Al –
what are you doing here? I thought you said you couldn't come.'

'I changed my mind. Hello Michael, hello Jessica – where's
Owen?'

'He's taken Hercules for a walk. Alison, I'm so glad you could
come,' Jessica said. She stood up as well and gave Alison a hug.
'Sit down. Let me get you some wine. Declan told us you had too
much work to get away this weekend.'

'I finished it early, so decided to drive over on the spur of
the moment. It's fortunate we both have cars – and that I can
remember the best way to get here. I'd love a glass of wine, Jessica.
Thank you.'

Alison sat down on the blanket beside Toby.

In fact, I've done no work whatsoever. I've been in bed with
Skip Thomas and I should feel guilty as sin. Instead I feel irritated
by this cosy little group sitting so cutely on the grass looking as if
they were just about to sing folk songs around a fire.

'We've been talking about Declan's infomercial,' Michael stated. 'At first I protested, but he's won me over now. It's fun, actually. I've been helping him and Toby. We all have.'

'Your infomercial.' Alison turned on Declan who had sat down on the other side of her. 'Which infomercial is this, Declan?'

'The *Plots in a Box* idea,' he mumbled.

'I see,' she nodded. She was trying very hard not to shake. Every bit of her body was in rebellion against her, it seemed. As was every brain cell in her head. She'd been a fool, yet again. She'd opened herself up to Skip Thomas in a manner she would never have anticipated, telling him all about her childhood, her schooldays, her first boyfriends, practically her whole life. She'd ended up in bed with him and made love with a passion she hadn't experienced since her days with Peter. For hours, for an entire night and an entire morning, she'd blotted out the fact that he was married, and revelled in his attentions and affection. She had acted like a stupid, idiotic foolish girl in love. No thought for the future, no control.

Who goes to bed with married men? Women with no self-respect, that's who. Starry-eyed brainless bimbos.

And all the while Skip and Declan were doing a deal behind her back. Skip and Declan and Toby and Christina, from the looks of it. Everyone knew something she didn't know. It was a bloody conspiracy.

'I thought I'd wait and make sure we could do it properly before telling you,' Declan explained in a lame voice.

'I see,' Alison said yet again. She glanced at Michael and Toby and Christina. Michael had his customary glass of milk in hand, Toby and Christina both had glasses of wine. The sun was setting behind them. What a nauseating group photograph this would make, she thought. All we need is the goat to complete the picture. The goat and Owen. And Heidi especially flown in from Switzerland.

'We need your help, Alison,' Christina stated. 'We can't decide.

Do you think Toby should read a passage from a novel to whet people's appetites or not?'

Jessica arrived back with a glass of wine and handed it to Alison.

'Here you are. You look a little flushed, Alison. Are you feeling all right?'

'I'm fine. Thank you. Exactly what financial arrangements have you made with Skip Thomas, Declan?' she asked, ignoring Christina's question.

'He's paying us by the hour, as he suggested the other night.'

'And what happens later, if this goes ahead? What cut do you get?'

'We haven't discussed that yet.'

'He could easily rip you off.'

'I don't think so, Al.' Declan's tone was placating. 'I think he'd be fair.'

'Really? You think he'd be fair? Never doublecross you? Never go behind your back?'

'Skip didn't strike me as particularly sinister,' Toby put in. 'A little naive and definitely uncultured, but not sinister.'

'Besides,' Declan reached for a piece of grass and put it in his mouth, 'at the rate we're going, we may not get this script done on time and he may decide to chuck us. We haven't done a huge amount of work today; in fact we've accomplished almost nothing.'

'Alison!' Owen appeared from the back of the garden. 'How terrific. You made it after all.' He walked over to her, bent down and kissed her. 'I wish you'd been here earlier. Declan and Michael and Christina were going wild on the rope-swing, I've been told. I slept through all the excitement. So did Toby. Then we all tried to line-dance on the lawn. I bet you would have been fantastic at that.'

'Sounds riveting,' Alison replied, pushing away the dog which had bounded up to her. 'So sorry I missed that.'

'I wish you hadn't had to work. How's it going?'

'Terrifically.'

She's incredibly annoyed, Christina thought. She sounds as if she can barely tolerate Owen. She looks stiff and uncomfortable as well, sitting in her cream linen trousers, her legs crossed at an awkward angle.

I know what it's like to walk into a group and feel like an outsider, to be told of all the goings-on and fun that have happened without you. Alison has arrived in the middle of this Midsummer Night party – no wonder she feels out of place and angry.

'Alison, I know this is going to sound strange, but I was wondering if you'd like a massage. I have a few of my oils with me and if you've been working all day, and then drove all this way you might need to de-stress a little.'

Alison stared at Christina, dumbfounded by this offer. Should she take her up on it? Why not? She could use a massage. She needed to calm down. If she stayed sitting on the lawn with these people, she knew she might lose all control over her actions; at the moment she felt a barely controlled desire to smash Owen in the face and wipe that kind, friendly, sincere look off it.

Lisa Thomas must have arrived back home by now. She and Skip were probably having a nice intimate little dinner together. For all she knew, Lisa and Skip might be in bed together as she sat here with this peace-and-love brigade.

What was it about Skip Thomas? she asked herself. How had he made such an impact on her in such a short time? That disgusting, mortifying feeling of jealousy she was all too familiar with was threatening to take her over again every time she thought of Lisa. Finishing her glass in one large gulp, she nodded at Christina. 'Yes,' she said. 'I'd like that.'

'Great.' Christina stood up. 'Come upstairs with me and we'll get started.'

'Can I bring another glass of wine?' Alison asked.

'Al,' Declan protested. 'You never have more than one glass of wine. Are you sure you'd like another?'

'I'm sure,' she said fiercely. 'I'm positive.'

*   *   *

158

'I'm not sure that's such a hot idea,' Skip said, fiddling with the television remote control. 'I mean, I can't see Declan, for example, talking about his relationship with Alison. He's not the type.'

'Will you put that thing down? We're talking, not watching TV.'

'There might be something good on.'

'Skip. Please. Tune in to this conversation. You say Declan wouldn't do it, but I bet he would – it's in his company's commercial interest too, you know.'

'Why can't you find people off the street?'

'I've explained that already,' Lisa frowned. 'Weren't you listening?'

'I'm tired,' Skip yawned. 'Sorry.'

'Toby would do it, I'm sure. And he could persuade Christina. Alison wouldn't mind. She understands infomercials. She'd probably jump at the chance to be on television.'

'I doubt it,' Skip murmured.

'Well, we can ask them, can't we? I'll ring Declan and Toby on Monday.'

'Uh huh. But don't be surprised when they say no.'

'Skip – you haven't noticed my new haircut. Do you like it?'

'Sure. It's very nice.'

'You wouldn't believe the hairdresser I had. He was this terrifying-looking American. And rude beyond belief. I—'

Skip stopped listening. Get me out of here, he thought. Someone please drive me to Heathrow and fly me away from all this mess. What was I doing with Alison? I've never cheated on Lisa. What was I thinking of?

He flashed back to scenes from the night before, the moment he'd first kissed Alison, the way her mouth had opened up to him and her body had melded into his. It hadn't been a conscious decision to kiss her, he hadn't planned or expected it. They'd just left the restaurant and he was helping her on with her jacket and he'd suddenly found himself kissing her.

And that's when the problems began. He'd lost himself in that kiss. He, Skip Thomas, had stopped thinking. His brain had gone on hold and his body had taken over. Nothing like that had ever happened to him before. With women before Lisa, with Lisa, he'd always *thought*, his brain had always functioned in its normal manner. Not that the physical hadn't been enjoyable, not at all, but it had never overtaken the mental. He'd always been aware of what he was doing, aware of where it was leading, ever conscious of himself and the woman he was involved with. Sex had been a mapped-out process, one which required certain steps at certain times for fufilment for both parties.

With Alison, well, he'd *lost it*.

'Skip!'

Lisa was snapping her fingers in front of his face. 'Skip. You're not listening, are you?'

'I'm sorry.' He scratched his head. 'I'm tired. I don't know why I'm so tired. Sorry. What were you saying?'

Men, Lisa thought. They're hopeless.

'Christina. Can I ask you something?' Alison felt Christina's fingers massaging her neck and wished they'd keep massaging for ever. She was lying on her stomach on Christina's bed with only her knickers on. Christina had spread a towel over the lower half of her body and had mixed a few oils together before beginning the massage. For a moment, Alison had felt as if she were taking part in a pagan ritual, but as soon as Christina began to work on her neck, she relaxed.

Women, she thought. That's who you need when you're in trouble. Sympathetic females. I've never had great girlfriends. I was never the type. At school the other girls thought I was smarmy and at work I always gravitated to the men. I was too young for girl power – in fact, I always thought girls rabbiting away to each other were pathetic and silly. If you want to compete in a man's world, you should stay around men and see how they do it.

But where has all that got me? Nowhere. A job with no

foreseeable prospects of advancement. No confidantes to confide in, and a lot of men treating me like dirt.

I wouldn't normally choose someone like Christina to talk to, but what choice do I have now? She's here and she's helping me and I need to talk.

'Of course you can,' Christina replied.

'Have you ever been jealous?'

Christina stopped working on Alison's neck, but only for a second.

'Yes,' she admitted. 'I have.'

'What did you do about it? Your jealousy?'

This seems to be the weekend for personal revelations, Christina thought. I hardly know Alison and I would have thought I'd be the last person she'd talk to in this way. She strikes me as a woman who is more comfortable with men than women. But she's obviously upset and I don't want to be cold to her. If Declan loves her, I'm sure she is much warmer than she appears to be. And jealousy is an emotion I'm horribly familiar with; if she's suffering from it, I should try to help. Is Alison jealous of Declan's family? Or another woman? Could Declan be seeing someone else? He doesn't seem that kind of person. But then you can never tell.

'I ran away from the situation, Alison. I was jealous of someone – a man I was living with – and I ran away. It seemed the only thing to do.'

'Was he sleeping with someone else?'

'Not exactly, no. He was thinking about her the whole time, though. I don't know which is worse. Someone who is being unfaithful to you or someone who wishes he were being unfaithful to you.'

'Someone who is actually cheating on you,' Alison stated. 'That's *definitely* worse. You start to imagine exactly what he's doing with her. It's awful.'

'Alison, I probably shouldn't ask this, but Declan's not—'

'No.' Alison shook her head quickly. 'Not Declan. I'm talking about someone else, a long time ago. When I found out he was with another woman – it turned out he'd been with scores of other women, actually – I went mental. I think I should have been sectioned. I followed him everywhere. I rang him fifty times a day. I opened all his post. I was the stalker from hell.'

'Why do you think you had *such* a strong reaction?' Christina moved her hands from Alison's neck and began to knead her shoulders.

'I don't know. I never analysed it. It might be because my father ran off with another woman when I was a baby. My mother never remarried. She really struggled to bring me up on her own. She managed – incredibly well. But I know how difficult it was for her. Although it would have been difficult if he'd stayed because he was a drunken sot.'

Why am I doing this? Telling the story of my life to a relative stranger for the second time in twenty-four hours? I should go on one of those chat shows.

'That sounds difficult, Alison – growing up without a father. My father died in a car accident when I was thirteen and there are times I still can't bring myself to believe it.'

'Peter – the one I was talking about – he was a guitarist. He wasn't in a famous band or anything, but he'd do gigs in clubs and there were always groupies. Adoring girls all over him, you know? I suppose it was too much to ask, the idea that he might be faithful. The male ego is a black hole. There's no beginning or end to it.'

'Declan doesn't seem to have a huge ego.'

'Well, I would have said that too. And now I find he's doing *Plots in a Box* without telling me. Why? Because he thinks I'd be in competition with him. I'd call that having an ego problem.'

'But he told you he didn't want to say anything until he'd thought it would work.'

'I'm not sure I believe that. Not at all sure. He didn't even tell me you two were coming here this weekend. What's that all about? He's keeping secrets. Hold on – can you do my left shoulder again?'

Keeping secrets, Christina thought. That's what Richard did too. But Toby doesn't. Or does he?

'Oh my God, what was that?'

The noise of squealing brakes and a high-pitched scream echoed through the room and Christina felt panic course through her body – the same kind of panic she'd felt when she'd first been told her father had had an accident.

'Someone's hurt,' she said immediately. 'We have to go and help.' Running out of the room and down the stairs, she almost tripped but regained her balance and rushed outside, to find Declan, Michael, Toby, Jessica and Owen all out on the road in front of the cottage driveway. A car had hit a boy on a tricycle and he was lying on the road, an elderly woman wailing beside him.

'I didn't have a chance to see him. He just appeared. I couldn't see,' she was crying.

'John,' Owen said, heading straight for the boy. 'Jessica, go and get Joanna. It's John.' Jessica dashed over the road and down the short driveway opposite.

John, Christina thought. She could still feel his weight on her back as he rode on the rope-swing with her. They'd won the competition to swing the furthest, though Christina thought Declan and Michael had probably planned it that way. I can't bear this. He can't be hurt, he just can't be.

'I'll phone for an ambulance,' Michael announced, rushing back into the cottage.

'John.' Owen sat down on the road beside John, who was lying prostrate and screaming. 'John. Hold on.' He stroked the little boy's forehead. 'Hold on. We're getting help. Does it hurt very much?'

John was still screaming. His face was contorted in dreadful fear. Like a wounded animal, Christina thought. Like an animal caught in a trap.

'I was going so slowly,' she could hear the old woman sobbing. 'So slowly. I was hardly moving.'

Owen put his hands on either side of John's face. 'You're all right, John,' he said. 'Look at me.'

John stopped screaming. He looked into Owen's face and Christina saw magic happen – all his terrror disappeared. His eyes were soft and yielding and, to her complete astonishment, happy. Almost as happy and joyful as they'd been when he was with them that morning. She couldn't stop staring; she couldn't take her eyes off this little boy and Owen, locked into a tender mutual gaze.

This is mad, she thought. John might be badly hurt. He might be crippled for life and he is now smiling at Owen. And Owen is smiling back, as if they're sharing a joke. Owen *is* a healer. Whenever he meets pain, he takes it all inside himself and transforms it.

'John!' Joanna appeared with Jessica at the end of her drive and raced over to him. Owen looked up and then backed away from John, letting Joanna come and take his place.

'I think he'll be all right, Joanna, but it's probably best if you don't move him,' Owen said. He then went over to the old woman. 'Honestly, I think he'll be fine. He may have hurt his leg, but I don't think it's too serious.'

'The ambulance is on its way,' Michael said, appearing on the scene again, joined by Alison who had re-dressed.

'Is my bike hurt, Mum?' John suddenly said, very loudly.

Joanna laughed a laugh of relief which within seconds turned into a sob.

'I was having a bath.' She looked around at the group wildly. 'I told him not to go out of the house.'

'I wanted another go on the rope-swing,' John said.

Toby lit a cigarette.

Declan, standing with his hands in his pockets, looked over at his father, who had his arm around the old woman. Then he stared at the sky.

What is he thinking? He looks as though he's remembering

something – something important, Christina thought. What is it like to have a father who can take a terrified, hurt child and soothe him within seconds, with only a look? A man who also then goes on to comfort the next suffering person? I would think it might be scary sometimes. Owen has almost supernatural powers.

No one spoke for what seemed like hours; even when they heard the sound of the ambulance siren, they stayed motionless, as if in a still-life tableau.

Why do these things happen so quickly? Christina asked herself. All it takes is a moment and lives can be changed for ever. One morning my father was alive and kissing me good morning, and that night my mother came into my room to tell me he'd had an accident and had died. Good morning became goodbye. The finality of it was beyond me. You think life is eternal when you're a child. You don't understand endings. I'm not sure I understand them even now.

When the ambulance finally arrived, they watched as a man and a woman examined John, then lifted him on to a stretcher.

After they'd put him into the ambulance, where Joanna joined him, Jessica asked if anyone wanted a cup of tea. Michael picked up John's dented tricycle and carried it in with him, putting it under the ping-pong table. Owen remained behind with the old woman, who was dealing with the policemen who had come on the scene just after Jessica had offered tea.

'That was terrifying,' Jessica sighed, filling up the kettle.

'I think, if you don't mind, Mum, I might go home now. I kept looking at John and thinking of our little boys. I need to see them.'

'Of course.' Jessica immediately went over to Michael and hugged him. 'I understand. You'll give our love to Sarah, won't you?'

'Absolutely.'

When Michael went upstairs to get his things, Christina suddenly realized that tears were streaming down her face.

'Christina?' Declan, who was perched on the edge of the kitchen table, stared at her. 'Are you all right?'

'I'm sorry.' She covered her eyes with her hands, but remained standing by the ping-pong table. 'Everything happened so quickly. I thought he might have been killed,' she mumbled.

'Christina's father died in a road accident,' Toby said, as if he were explaining a riddle. He didn't move from his spot, but continued to get teacups out of the cupboard, handing them to Alison as he did so.

'Christina.' Declan got up and went toward her. He took her by the wrist, in the same spot she'd touched his wrist the night before – his fingers on her pulse. 'I'm so sorry. I didn't know.'

'It's all right.' She shook her head. 'I think I might go and lie down for a minute, though.'

Toby. Toby can't be bothered. He wants the tea. How can he be so unaffected? His own pain is worth hours of talk, but mine? Is mine so very unimportant?

Declan let go of her wrist and she stumbled up the stairs, meeting Michael on his way down.

'Christina.' He enveloped her in a hug. 'I'm so sorry I have to go. It was wonderful to meet you.'

She buried her face in his shirt and inhaled deeply, then broke away and ran upstairs.

'Is something wrong?' Michael asked, looking after her fleeing form.

'She'll be fine in a little while,' was Toby's reply. 'Christina's good at looking after herself. There's no point going after her. She's a very private person. She needs some rest, that's all. It's been one hell of a day, hasn't it?'

Skip Thomas closed the door shut behind him, turned right, walked to the end of Elizabeth Street and turned left. When he reached Sloane Square, he passed the Royal Court Theatre and headed for the King's Road.

This is where it had all happened in the Sixties, he knew. This was the groovy place to shop and to be seen. It seemed pretty groovy now, as well, on a summer's Saturday night. Young people everywhere, cafés, clothes shops. The buzz was in the air. Too bad he couldn't be a part of it.

He was born in 1960, so he missed out on being a protestor and/or a flower child. By 1980, when he was in his second year at college, the yuppie work ethos was taking over and now, closing on forty, he was too old to be young and too young to be old. Mr Inbetween. Skip made way for a couple walking hand-in-hand and as he did so, considered turning back.

'Head for home,' he told himself. 'Forget about Alison and go back to Lisa and curl up in bed with her.'

Skip kept walking.

Lisa propped the pillow behind her back and picked up *Hello!* magazine. Something was wrong with Skip. He wasn't concentrating, he wasn't paying attention to her, he'd gone off on his own for a walk.

She'd have to sit him down and get him to talk it all out – whatever 'it' was. She figured it was the baby business and she knew that, given enough time, she could make him understand her point of view. It was simply a question of finding the right time to talk it through, that's all. Time when neither of them were too tired, time when she wasn't preoccupied by work. It would happen. Ignorance wasn't bliss, she knew that. But patience definitely was a virtue.

She flipped through the pages, stopping to study a picture of Camilla Parker-Bowles. What had Prince Charles seen when he'd first met Lady Di? A shy, sweet young thing, Lisa reckoned. He didn't see the complexities, the unbelievable, stunning beauty, the gift she had with suffering people. He must have believed he had a simple package in front of him, all wrapped up and waiting to be delivered to Buckingham Palace. He hadn't bargained for a woman who needed to be loved and adored; he'd seen a teenager.

Well, sadly, it was too late to send him a copy of *I Saw You First*.

Lisa had had one hand-delivered to the White House, knowing that Bill and Hillary might find it useful. She *could* do the same with Tony and Cherie Blair, though they didn't seem to have any glaring problems as a couple. Still, it couldn't hurt. Another one of those old maxims was totally right: Prevention *is* the best cure.

What next? Lisa wondered, gazing idly at a photograph of Jerry Hall. What could she write as a follow-up to *I Saw You First?* Her American publishers were already on her case and she was conscious that she needed to deliver at least a germ of an idea to them soon.

The problem was she didn't have any ideas. None at all. Her agent had suggested *Celebrity Couples and Why They Break Up* as a possibility, but Lisa had nixed that immediately. 'I'm not into invasion of privacy,' she had said firmly. 'I can speculate about what goes wrong in relationships, but I can't say for certain why, for example, Brad Pitt and Gwyneth parted. I'm not about to be a sleaze merchant and go through trash cans.'

And there's nothing I can take from my own life any more, she thought; the thought accompanied by a small twinge of what she knew was inappropriate regret.

Skip and I are fine, when it comes down to the nitty gritty. We might be having a few problems at this particular moment, but basically we're all set. He *does* believe in me. He's *not* bored with me. I wasn't thinking straight in that hotel room yesterday. I'd had too much wine. Skip's just a little restless, that's all. But restlessness is not a major problem.

A problem shared is a problem solved – isn't that what they say? Lisa took a pencil and notebook from her bedside table and wrote that phrase down.

'Maybe it's original. Maybe no one has thought of that before. If someone hasn't said that in print already, I will,' she told herself. 'In my next bestseller.'

'Christina?' Declan stood outside Christina's room, calling her as quietly as he could.

'Yes? I'm awake, Declan – don't worry. I did fall asleep, but I woke up about five minutes ago.'

'I brought you up a cup of tea, in case you'd like one.' Declan moved into the room and stood beside Christina's bed.

She sat up and took the cup he proffered. 'Thank you. That's lovely. Should I turn on the light?'

'No. It's nice in the dark. Do you mind if I sit down on the end of your bed?'

'Not at all. Where are the others?' Christina took a long sip of tea.

'Toby is talking to Owen – which is no surprise. Alison has gone home.'

'Home? Why?'

'I'm not sure. She didn't tell me she was going. I thought she was out taking a walk, but then I went out and her car had gone. And then she rang me from her mobile. I think she's pissed off at me, but she didn't say that. She said she still had some work to do.'

'I'm sorry I couldn't finish giving her a massage. She seemed wound up. I think she was very upset that you hadn't told her you were doing *Plots in a Box*. Why didn't you tell her, Declan?'

'Honestly? I don't know.'

'No one likes secrets.'

'I know.'

'Oh God – I can't believe I haven't asked you yet! Have you heard how John is?'

'He's fine,' Declan smiled. 'Joanna rang from the hospital. He's bruised, and apparently very upset that he won't be able to come tomorrow and go on the rope-swing again, but otherwise he's fine.'

'Declan, what were you thinking out there, after the accident? There was a moment when you looked up at the sky and you seemed so intensely thoughtful, as if you were remembering something important you hadn't thought of for a long time.'

'Are you a psychic?' Declan put up his hands as if in self-defence. 'That's spooky, Christina. I *was* remembering something. I was remembering a time when I was six years old or so. I was barefoot and I managed to step on a rusty nail. My mother was off with Michael somewhere and Owen took care of me. He took me to hospital.'

'And?'

'And he took care of me, that's all. The same way he took care of John today. He has a special way with children.'

'He has a special way with adults, too.'

'I know,' Declan nodded. 'I think . . .' He paused, looked out of the window beside the bed. 'I think I felt excluded from all that. What I'm trying to say is that this house is all about *not* excluding people. That's Owen's way of thinking. But I felt *I* was excluded. The older I got, the more I felt he gave all his time to everyone else. To his students, to anyone who came by. And Michael was a part of all that. He didn't mind, you see. I did. I was selfish, I suppose. And knowing how selfish I was made me feel guilty – which made me angry.' Declan turned from the window to look at Christina. 'I was thinking before, this morning, how different it might have been if there had been three of us. If we'd had a sister – someone like you. Somehow it would have been easier for me. I don't know. Does that make sense?'

'In some ways it does.' Christina leaned forward. She couldn't see his face properly in the dark. 'But three is a difficult number as well. Sometimes two children bond and the third feels left out.'

'I suppose you're right. But when you were with Michael and me, it didn't happen that way, did it?'

'No. But I'm not your sister, Declan. I'm only a guest.'

'What were *you* thinking of when all that went on with John?'

'I was thinking thousands of thoughts. And then, when we came inside, I was upset because I found myself wishing that Owen had been there with my father, when he was in the accident. I've always hated the idea of him being alone.'

'What happened?'

'He was driving home late at night from work and he must have fallen asleep at the wheel. He went off the road and hit a tree. He died on the way to hospital.'

'I'm so sorry.' Declan reached out and put his hand on Christina's ankle.

'I wish he hadn't been alone. I wish so much he hadn't been alone. And then, when we were getting the tea, I had a completely ridiculous thought. I thought that if Owen had been there, my father wouldn't have died. That's absurd, I know, but it hit me so hard I thought for a moment it might be true.'

'You wanted a miracle.'

'I *want* a miracle. I want my father to walk into this room right now.'

'Christina,' Declan squeezed her ankle, 'I wish I could give you a miracle.'

'I'm sorry.' She wiped her eyes. 'I never do this. I never cry in front of people the way I did this afternoon. I don't know what's happened to me today.'

'Why are you apologizing for being human? The accident was terrifying, as Mum said. And what can possibly be wrong with grieving for and missing your father? I'd be devastated if something happened to—' Declan stopped and rubbed the bridge of his nose. 'You know, I'm not sure if Dad's miraculous but I understand what you're saying – he does have a gift. With animals as well as human beings. People used to call him Doctor Doolittle. Although I have to say, I *hated* that film.'

'Me, too.' Christina laughed and sniffled simultaneously. 'I especially loathed that song "Talk to the Animals".'

'It's appalling,' Declan agreed. 'Grotesquely awful. And that "Push Me Pull You" thing. God!' He shuddered.

Christina giggled. 'Thank you, Declan,' she said.

'For what?'

'Cheering me up. I needed to laugh.'

'Tell me, do you have any brothers?'

'No – two step-sisters.'

'Do you get along?'

'Declan, you're sounding like Owen – all these questions.'

'Why *don't* you get along?'

'I never said we didn't.'

'And I never said last night that I wanted my father's love to myself, but you guessed it, didn't you?'

'Christina!' Toby's voice boomed out from the floor below. 'What are you and Declan doing up there? Having wild sex?'

'Absolutely, Toby,' Declan yelled back. 'Give us time to rearrange ourselves and we'll be right down.' He stood up and headed for the landing, but then paused at the doorway. 'So – was it good for you, Christina?'

'The earth moved, Declan.'

'It did, didn't it?' He ran his hand through his hair and walked out of the room.

Skip picked up the telephone receiver, put it to his ear, then quickly replaced it on its hook again. He repeated this action three times before giving up and walking away from the BT call box.

What was the point in calling Alison? None. She didn't want to talk to him any more than he should want to talk to her. What had she said? 'It's a one-off, a fling' – that was it. And she'd been right.

He stood on the pavement, staring at the telephone as people bustled by, occasionally jostling him as they passed.

He was having problems adjusting to Lisa's newfound wealth and fame – it was as simple as that. He didn't know any other male of his acquaintance who was married to or involved with a more successful woman. He, Skip Thomas, was acting like a classic ego-driven idiot, going to bed with the first woman who had showed him some attention and respect. It was pathetic, really it was. He was above all that.

Turning eastwards, Skip set off for the walk back to Pimlico.

I'll go home and I'll be the husband she wants me to be, he decided, quickening his pace. I'll be the Skip in *I Saw You First*. Idealistic, romantic, caring. I'll remember our first date and our favourite song and our best night together. I'll forget things, too. Like the fact that these homespun sayings she spouts are beginning to irritate the hell out of me. And the way she never asks me what I want to do or how *my* day has been. How she assumes I'll go along with her everywhere and treat every word of *I Saw You First* as if it were wisdom incarnate.

I won't think about how easy life has been for her – growing up in a stable, pampered environment, then marrying a man who looked after her pretty damn well for a long time. Lisa never had to struggle. She didn't have to work her way through college or spend hours in an office. All she had to do was shop and cook and take care of the house. Oh – and have lunch with her friends. Tough life. Really damn difficult life.

Don't go there, Skip, he said to himself. This is not where your thoughts should be taking you. You have to remember that you love her and that you aren't exactly perfect either.

The sound of a man's voice screaming: 'You fucking bitch!' stopped Skip's forward movement. The man doing the screaming was standing outside Safeway's, his hands on the woman's shoulders, pinning her to the wall. 'I hate you, you cunt,' he screamed again.

'Fuck you too!' she shouted back.

Should he go over and try to break this up? Skip asked himself. The man was tall, threatening-looking. He could haul off and whack her at any moment. As the man leaned forward, Skip started to go to her rescue. But when he neared the couple, he saw that the man wasn't hurting her, he was kissing her. She had thrown her arms around his neck and was grinding her hips into his.

Whoa, Skip thought. Goes to show you never can tell. I was sure he was going to clobber her. How could the anger I heard in those voices mutate into passion so quickly? Beats me. But then I guess that's why Lisa is so successful. No one, after all these years, after all the advances of technology and science, can figure out what the hell goes on between men and women. And anyone who can shed even the tiniest light on the whole mess is twenty thousand steps ahead of the game.

When he arrived back in front of his house, Skip paused. It was time, he decided, to do something romantic for his wife. But what? What did he used to do, back in the old days? He sent her flowers, on special occasions he brought home a bottle of champagne, and once he'd even serenaded her – outside her room at Oak Manor. He'd sung her favourite song from her favourite movie – *My Fair Lady*. Why not do that again? Their bedroom window looked on to the street. If neighbours heard him, they might think he was silly but they probably wouldn't complain.

As Skip scratched his head, he was assailed by a terrible vision. Alison was lying in bed, her legs entangled with his, her hands in his hair, her tongue licking his neck.

DO NOT GO THERE YOU DIMWIT! he warned himself again. This is not the place you want to visit. There are terrorists there. Evil things will happen to you if you continue along this thoughtpath.

He could remember the first couple of lines of the song, but he wasn't sure about the rest. Never mind. He'd go with the flow and make up words if he had to. No problem.

He sang. As loudly as he could. The first two lines were a piece of cake, but then he started to fumble. Lisa hadn't appeared at the window and he was screwing up badly.

'All at once am I something something high,' he faltered. What came next?

'And oh, that really good feeling! Knowing that maybe you're up there somewhere. That really, really great feeling! Thinking soon you might do something to my ear!'

He felt a tap on his shoulder and turned.

'You've got it wrong, mate,' a burly man said, smiling.

'I know.' Skip hung his head and stared at the pavement.

'I'd leave off if I were you.'

'You're right.'

Skip took the keys out of his pocket, stumbled to the front door and let himself in. All the downstairs lights were off and when he went up to the bedroom, he saw Lisa sitting on the bed, listening to a Sony Walkman. She removed the earphones, smiled at him and said: 'Hi, honey. You've been out a long time.'

'What were you listening to?' he asked.

'The tape of *I Saw You First*,' she answered.

Skip closed his eyes and saw Alison.

Toby lay on his back beside Christina in the narrow bed. She was sleeping, one arm thrown over her eyes, her legs perfectly straight. He thought about waking her up to talk but decided against it. He was too irritated with her to have a rational conversation. She'd ruined his evening. At first, she'd started to talk about the little boy's accident and they'd all had to go over every detail of it – well, that was natural, he supposed, but the boy hadn't been hurt badly, after all, and there was a limit to how many times you could discuss the terrible propensity of children to run out into roads. Toby knew he had to be sympathetic, but he wasn't a parent and he didn't know the kid, so there were times he wanted to say: Enough, basta, the child is fine, let's leave it, shall we?

Then, after that conversation finally wound down, Christina made Owen and Jessica tell stories about Declan and Michael when they were children. Boring, boring, boring. What could be more tedious than tales of two and three year olds and their adorable little ways? He had laughed along with the rest of them, of course, but inwardly he was seething. They'd be leaving tomorrow and he wouldn't have many more chances to converse with Owen. He needed answers from Owen, advice. Instead he'd had to sit back as Declan and his parents reminisced.

Should he, after he'd finished both Lisa's and Skip's infomercials, turn down any offers except ones for serious parts? Should he hold out against the tide and stand firm in his belief in his own abilities? Owen had, from the very first moment, understood him. He now knew more about him than any other human being in the world – and that was after just one night and one day.

How strange people are, Toby thought. I've been with Christina almost a year, but she doesn't know half of what Owen does. She's always told me she believes in my acting ability, but she's never seen me perform at my best, so what does she know? Nothing. And if she doesn't know me, what does she see in me? A good-looking man – is that all it is? How can it be anything else? We've never sat up all night talking about our souls. She won't talk to me about her family; I don't talk to her about mine. We're strangers.

He felt an odd desire to lash out at her and kick her awake. She was like the rest of them – she accepted his surface qualities and never delved deeper. Well, he couldn't have played Hamlet the way he did if he didn't have depth. He wouldn't have stayed up all night talking to Owen if he didn't have a soul to talk about. Christina took him for granted. Not only that, she hid herself from him. It was all very easy for her to giggle and go on rope-swings with Declan or Michael or whoever might happen to be around, but she wasn't paying any attention to *his* needs.

And, now that he thought about it, any normal woman in love would have asked him for some kind of commitment by now. Yes, he would have run away as soon as she did, but she *should* have taken that risk. She was impervious to him, clearly. She didn't really care.

But why? Why didn't she care? Was there someone else in her life, another man he didn't know about?

Toby flashed back to a few months ago, when Christina had received a birthday card in the post. She'd opened it and blushed the colour of a Valentine heart. 'Who's that from?' he'd asked and she'd said, in what he now recognized was a carefully controlled and concealing voice: 'An old friend of mine.'

'Who?' He'd approached her then and playfully grabbed the card from her hand. 'Richard? So who is this Richard?'

'An old friend,' she repeated. 'From University days.'

'An old boyfriend?'

'An old friend.'

He'd left it at that then, foolishly believing her. But now, thinking back on it, he couldn't remember another time when Christina had blushed like that. This Richard person had to be someone important. She *was* hiding something from him. In fact, she was hiding a great deal.

What right did she have to keep him away from her step-sisters and family? What did they know that he didn't? She should be like Owen – open and welcoming and caring. She should sense right now that he couldn't sleep. She should bloody well wake up and ask him what was the matter and comfort him.

As soon as they got back, he would ring Lucy and meet up with her. He'd find out what the hell was going on, why Christina had been so anxious that they shouldn't all get together. For the past year she'd been excluding him from her life. As Owen had said the night before: 'Exclusion is a form of aggression.' Well, he had gone to an exclusive boarding school and grown up in an exclusive environment and he'd seen a shitload of aggression. Then directors and casting agents had had a field day excluding him. Christina doing the same thing wasn't on.

If she was so keen to shut him out, he was going to force open the door himself, by whatever means possible.

Alison paced back and forth in the living room, reading bits of *I Saw You First* out loud to herself.

EXERCISE NUMBER THIRTEEN
Do you have any photographs of you as a couple during those first days? If so, dig them out and study them. Choose the one you like the most. What were you wearing? Do you still have that in your closet? If you do, go put it on. Right now. I don't care if it fits or not any more – that's not the point. Put it on and cast your memory back to the time that picture was taken and exactly how you were feeling at that moment.

You know sometimes how you smell some special smell and it reminds you of a certain time and a certain place? It takes you right back there. Well, clothes can do the same. Live in that feeling for as long as you can – ten minutes at the least.

What if you don't have that same outfit? No problem. Find something that resembles it as closely as possible – the same color is a good start. Go with it. Make it happen.

The memory will become the reality. The past will become the present.

They say every picture tells a thousand stories. Well, there's only one story you're interested in now. Look at that picture and get back to that fairy tale – the one with the happy ending!

Alison hurled the book across the room, narrowly missing a dark green vase on the table by the sofa.

What could Skip possibly see in this woman? She was a walking, talking nightmare. So what could she herself see in a man who fell in love and married a woman like that? He was a nightmare too. At least she'd woken up quickly. She'd make sure it wasn't a recurring nightmare. If she worked with him on the infomercial business, she'd steer well clear emotionally speaking. Let them live their life and get on with it. She'd get on with hers. With Declan. He might not be Mr Perfect. He'd lied to her about working on *Plots in a Box*. But he had one crucial thing going for him: he didn't love somebody else.

Could she work with Skip now?

Yes, but she'd prefer it if he were at a distance. She'd like it better if all their communication was done by phone or fax, from separate continents.

Skip Thomas should change his name, Alison thought. He should fly back to New York and call himself Skip Town.

Chapter 8

When you first met you made a big effort, didn't you? If your partner liked fishing, off you'd go with him, rod in hand, ready to give it a go. Whatever interested him, interested you too. So what went wrong? When did you say: 'Hey, I'm tired of this fishing business, it bores me. Let him go on his own'? You gave up, didn't you? You stopped sharing his interests.

What do you think? Do you think you've done your bit so you can just forget about the side of his life you don't relish? It doesn't work that way, not when you're really in love. When you're in love what works is staying interested.

Remember those nights you could stay up until dawn because you didn't want to miss one minute of being with him? Love gave you almost super-human strength then, didn't it?

Then you turned back into feeble old Clark Kent. You were too tired to do anything. Maybe you had children and they wore you out – whatever; you started going to bed at nine at night and acting like your grandmother. No offense to grandmothers. My point is grandmothers can be as young as springtime; anyone can be as young as springtime – if they make that effort again.

Get a babysitter. Take a day off work. I don't care how you manage it, but get out there with your partner and party!

Remember how you felt when you first fell in love? I bet you felt more powerful than Arnie Schwarzenegger. So don't say, 'Hasta

la vista, baby,' say 'Hi there, darling, I'm back! The me you first knew! And I'm raring to go!!!!'
I Saw You First, *Chapter Nine*, p. 101

'I think we've done well, surprisingly enough. I think the script is quite good.' Declan was tapping the steering wheel as he spoke.

Toby, stretched out in the back seat, coughed.

'I don't know. It occurs to me that I should read a pasage from *Great Expectations* to start off with. Get people in the mood,' he suggested.

'That might be confusing. If we begin with a passage from a novel, people might turn off immediately. They'd be thinking: Who is this Pip person and what a silly name to have.'

'Maybe you're right. Maybe we should stick to what we've done today. But I think we should open the *Plots in a Box* tape itself with the synopsis of *Great Expectations*. It would be fitting. Pip goes up in the world, you can too. The theme fits in well.' Toby yawned.

'Isn't that what everyone wants?' Christina said in a thoughtful tone, staring out of her window.

'What do you mean?' Declan glanced at her, then back at the road.

'Well, all of us want some event to change our lives for the better. That's why we buy lottery tickets or go on diets or try to get a better job. We want to believe that, like Pip, our lives can suddenly be transformed. One thing happens and everything changes. Like falling in love.'

'Excuse me?' Toby queried. 'What does this have to do with falling in love?'

'Maybe men see it differently, I don't know. But women think that if they meet the right man, Mr Perfect, their lives will immediately become perfect too. For women, falling in love is like winning the lottery. At least, that's what they dream about.'

'Do they?' Toby sat up. 'Is that the way you felt when you met me, Chris? All six numbers clicking into place?'

'In a way, I suppose.'

'In a way? You suppose?'

'I mean, I did feel special,' Christina mumbled. 'I felt as if my life had changed – and it did change.'

'What if you only get four of the numbers?' Declan smiled. 'Do you still think you've won the whole lot? Do people confuse three or four numbers with six?'

'What *are* you talking about, Declan?' Toby stared at him in the rearview mirror.

'Well, you never know when you first fall in love, do you? You may think you've hit the jackpot, picked all six numbers. That may be what it feels like at first, but then, as time goes on, you might realize you had only three or four.'

'Christ – you sound like Lisa Thomas.' Toby snorted. 'You should write a book. *I Saw the Wrong Numbers.* That would be a huge seller.'

'But people do get it wrong,' Christina continued. 'There was Pip, thinking he had the money from Miss Haversham when in fact it came from Magwitch. We're all so eager to be rescued, we don't see sometimes who the real rescuer is.'

'Who needs to be rescued?' Toby twisted in his seat and focused on Christina.

'Don't we all?' she asked, turning around as well in order to face him.

'From what?'

'From ourselves,' Declan cut in. 'From our own awful version of ourselves. We want someone to come along and show us how wonderful we actually are.'

'You might have a point there.' Toby sat back, opened the window and lit a cigarette. 'It's important to meet people who have faith in you.'

'It certainly helps.' Declan smiled again. 'Isn't it interesting? We set off on this project laughing about infomercials and people's

181

ridiculous desire to change their lives in one instantaneous rush, by buying a tape or a self-help book or something along those lines, and we end up understanding that we're all in the same boat. We're all looking for someone or something to make us feel comfortable with the person we want to be. Christina's right. Whether it's money or love or career satisfaction – we're all looking to win the lottery.'

'You know, Owen was the only person all weekend who didn't make fun of *Plots in a Box*. And he was right.' Christina rubbed the back of her neck. 'I wouldn't mind buying that tape myself. I may have read some of the books, but I haven't read others and I'd like to hear the synopses. I don't think it's demeaning. And I don't believe it wouldn't work here, actually. I know the plates and all that is a little over the top, but the concept itself is actually a decent one. Owen's right – people might, if they like the sound of the plot, pick up the book itself. We can be all snobby about it, but I'll admit right now I've never read Proust, for example. There are tons of great books I haven't read, ones that intimidate me, too.'

'Of course Owen's right.' Toby nodded. 'By the way, you take the next left, Declan. That's our street.'

'Declan – I keep meaning to ask. Is your family Irish?'

'My father's mother was Irish,' Declan answered Christina. 'That's where the Irish names come from. My grandfather was English – from Surrey, and my grandparents on my mother's side are all English as well.'

'Do you like your name?'

'Yes, I do, in fact. Do you like yours?'

'Yes,' Christina smiled. 'I like Christina. But not—'

'But not?' Declan pressed.

'Here we are,' Toby announced. 'There's no parking space so we'll just hop out. I'll ring you tomorrow, Declan. That was a wonderful weekend. Give our best to Alison.'

'I will.' Declan got out to open the boot and say goodbye but his farewell was cut short by the honking of a car horn behind him.

Christina and Toby grabbed their bags and headed for their flat. Declan waved briefly, climbed back into the BMW and set off for Battersea.

As soon as he entered the house, he smelled it. You couldn't miss it, that odour of marijuana hanging in the air. Sniffing like a dog, he followed the traces of it to the source – the kitchen, where the fag end of a roach lounged in an ashtray. Beside it stood a three-quarters' empty bottle of Sauvignon and one wine glass. Declan called out Alison's name; when there was no reply, he went upstairs and found her asleep on their bed, sprawled over the sheets, snoring.

'Alison?' He shook her gently by the shoulder, but she didn't move.

Had the fact that he hadn't told her about working on *Plots in a Box* upset her so much? he wondered. Enough to make her drink almost an entire bottle of wine on a Sunday afternoon and get stoned as well? It wasn't like her; she'd never behaved like this in all the time he'd known her. Alison didn't like mind-altering substances of any sort, but it was definitely her red lipstick on the glass and there was no sign of anyone else having been in the house. Walking quietly back downstairs, Declan viewed the kitchen again. She hadn't cleaned up after herself, which was also completely out of character. What was going on?

Sitting down, he tried to think things through logically. She'd turned up in Amersham out of the blue, and then had left just as abruptly. Christina had said Alison was tense and hadn't liked the fact that he'd kept a secret from her. It *was* his fault, then. He hadn't paid enough attention to her, and he'd also lied to her. No wonder she'd needed some kind of solace. He should have been the one to give it to her. Instead he'd stayed on in Amersham all Sunday, working on the *Plots in a Box* script and enjoying a hot day in the sun with Toby, Christina and his parents. He'd been thoughtless, uncaring and selfish.

Alison had said that she wanted to rescue him from himself – which was exactly what *he'd* just said everyone in the world was looking for. If she was offering exactly what he was looking for, why had he treated her in such a cavalier fashion? Was it because she'd rescued the wrong person? The Declan Lewis of two years ago who was angry and confused and unhappy?

A great deal of his original attraction to her sprang from the fact that she was in league with him against his family. She thought they were as mad as he did, if not madder. Together they had joked about his strange upbringing and conspired to avoid the Lewis cottage at every possible opportunity. They were in cahoots against his family, and that's exactly what he had liked and responded to. She had justified his sense of himself as entirely different from Michael and Owen. In all sorts of ways she'd encouraged him to leave the past behind and focus on himself and his career.

How could he now turn around to her and tell her he'd changed? That one weekend had made him suddenly revert to the person he'd been before, the Declan Lewis who actually liked the life he'd had as a child? It was as if – Declan suddenly stopped in mid-thought, stunned by the idea that was forming inexorably in his brain. It was as if over the course of this weekend he'd seen his family again the way he'd first seen them – taking Lisa Thomas' advice and going right back to the beginning, rekindling all the old love and affection.

What had he first seen in Alison? A strong, self-confident, attractive, no-nonsense woman. Someone with self-control, that was the main thing. Alison wouldn't leap on his back and jump off a roof; she wouldn't start crying in the middle of a room where other people could see. She wouldn't join in a pillow-fight.

Declan found himself suddenly up and pacing around the kitchen. He didn't like where his thoughts were leading him, not at all. They were speeding toward Christina Billings, and that way, as Toby would say, madness lay. He had to rewind his mental tape and concentrate on Alison. Obviously she wasn't as self-controlled as he'd imagined or she wouldn't have sat alone in their house on a Sunday evening drinking wine and smoking dope. She'd been hurt by him and she'd reacted in a way he wouldn't have expected, so she wasn't an unapproachable tower of strength either.

Perhaps they'd both changed this weekend and they could begin again with each other on a different basis. They'd both seen each other slightly out of focus at first, that was all. So each had made wrong assumptions about the other.

Alison might be secretly dying to have ridiculous, childish fun and all she needed was for him to provide her with the impetus to let go a little. He could rescue her now, the way Christina Billings had unwittingly rescued him. If Christina hadn't been there, he wouldn't have gone on the rope-swing, he wouldn't have relaxed with Michael. The status quo would have prevailed and he would have been as tense and uncomfortable with his family as he had been for years.

'I like the name Christina,' he heard her voice saying again. 'But I don't like—'

You don't like what, Christina? I want to know what you don't like. Am I right in thinking you don't like Toby calling you Chris? Is that it? And what if I am right? What does it matter? It's none of my business. My business is Alison. There are things I don't know about her and things she doesn't know about me. We have to start again, that's all. Beginning tomorrow. Tomorrow will be like the first date.

Lisa Thomas woke up from what was a terrible nightmare. Jack the hairdresser had hacked away at her head, laughing all the while. 'Get over it,' he kept saying as he was shaving her scalp. 'Just get over it.' She reached out for the comfort of Skip's sleeping body, only to find he wasn't there. Again.

All day she'd tried to pin him down and talk to him, but he'd kept avoiding her questions and changing the subject. He'd suggested a Sunday drive to Windsor Castle, or a trip to the Tower of London, all sorts of tourist alternatives to keep her busy. When she'd refused all of them, he'd simply turned on the television, insisting he needed to see what exactly was happening on the satellite channels. And then he'd claimed to be enthralled by some cricket match which went on and on. Lisa couldn't bring herself to watch with him. So she retreated to the kitchen and read cookbooks for hours.

He was exhibiting the signs of classic male behaviour, the sort she had dismissed so easily in her book. 'Don't tell me you can't get him to talk to you if you want to talk,' she had written in Chapter Six. 'Don't fall into that "men don't communicate like women" trap. It's for the birds. Just an easy way to forgive yourself for giving up on establishing communication.'

What *was* his problem? He was antsy and fidgeting, scratching his head continually, shifting around in his chair, and finally and most unusually, not hungry in the least. He had picked at lunch, barely touched his food at dinner and was drinking coffee like a maniac as he watched the cricket. The only time he had spoken more than ten words to her was when he went ballistic about her plan to call Declan, Alison, Toby and Christina in order to ask them to do her new version of the *I Saw You First* infomercial.

'I told you yesterday that was a ridiculous idea,' he huffed. 'Why bring it up again? They won't do it. I won't do it. Forget it. It's just plain dumb.'

Well, he was wrong. It wasn't dumb. And what's more, she now felt she *needed* to do it. If she arranged for the four of them to come over again and have a preliminary talk about appearing on the infomercial, she could start to delve into the subject of relationships; as soon as the two British couples began to talk about their romances, she and Skip would naturally talk about *theirs*.

Lisa turned from her back on to her stomach and tossed her pillow aside. If only she could follow the advice in her book, she thought. Get Skip to do some of the Exercises with her. Unfortunately, however, Skip had always laughed when she would bring one in and read it to him as she was writing. The Dress Exercise – getting back into the clothes you were wearing in your favourite photograph of yourselves – had elicited a horrid response from Skip.

'Lisa – Christ – that dress you were wearing in the photograph of us you like so much? It was *bright pink*. With those puffy sleeves. I couldn't stand the sight of it.'

'You didn't think it was cute?' she remembered asking, feeling defensive and betrayed.

'You looked like an overgrown Shirley Temple,' he laughed. 'I didn't say anything about it then. I mean, how could I? But I'll tell you a secret now. I've always felt a little guilty, in fact. Remember when I spilt that red wine all over it a few weeks later?'

Lisa stared at Skip then, dreading to hear what she knew was coming next.

'I did it on purpose. Red wine on a pink dress. I figured there was no way you'd be able to wear it again.'

'You were so apologetic,' she said, feeling the tears start up at the back of her eyes.

'Sorry,' he shrugged. 'But it was really gross.'

No. She couldn't do any of the Exercises with him – that much was sadly clear. How could any of them work if one of the people involved in the relationship was lying? Skip hadn't told her he hated that dress, and he had acted unbelievably contritely when he'd spilled the wine on it. He'd lied, to spare her feelings. But that wasn't right, was it? A relationship has to be built on honesty, no matter how painful the truth might be. You have to be cruel to be kind. Honesty is the best policy. Ignorance is *not* bliss. He'd treated her like a baby who couldn't take criticism and that was wrong, wrong, wrong.

Lisa turned over on to her back again and stared at the ceiling. What else had he lied about? Had he hated her wedding dress, as well? *That* had had puffy sleeves too. Maybe he hated all her clothes. Maybe he hated all the food she'd cooked for him over the years. Maybe, deep down, he not only found *I Saw You First* funny, but loathed and despised it too.

But did it matter so much any more, what he thought? She didn't have to live or die by his approval. She wasn't some little woman waiting on her master's words, not by a long shot. She paid the bills, she financed their lifestyle, she worked her socks off to take care of them both. When she'd first seen Skip, she'd thought of him as a protector, a man to look after her and provide for their futures. Now the tables had turned and she was the one bringing home the bacon. Far more bacon, as it turned out, than he'd been capable of delivering to the table.

The other day she'd had a terrible moment of panic when she'd phoned Connie Taylor, one of her old friends from Connecticut. Connie and her husband Jim were getting a divorce and Connie was making a big song and dance about how much money she was going to get from Jim. 'It's like that case of the GE wife, Lisa,' Connie had said with great excitement. 'She claimed she deserved half of everything her husband earned because she'd given dinner parties and helped him up the corporate ladder, and she ended up with twenty million. He'd been trying to palm her off with five mill, but she took him to court. I've given dinner parties too, you know. I've wined and dined Jim's bosses. I'm entitled. And I'm going to nail Jim in the same way. He won't know what's hit him.'

Lisa hadn't said anything. She certainly hadn't voiced the feelings she had experienced on hearing all this: What if Skip decided to leave me and wanted half of everything I've earned? Does he have a right to take half of all my hard-earned money just because he's been reasonably supportive? I'm the one who went out there and earned it. He could cook five thousand dinners for publishing people, but it wouldn't be the same as me writing the book which made the money, would it?

Lisa sat up in bed and slapped herself on the cheek.

I'm a nasty person, she thought. How can I have thoughts like this? Love isn't about money; marriage isn't just a question of finances. It's a partnership, it's romance, it's two people who want to spend the rest of their lives together. How can I be so mercenary? What has happened to me?

I have to get back to the beginning again. What I need is a new approach with Skip. Perhaps listening to Toby and Christina and

Declan and Alison talking about their relationships will spark off a new set of wonderful memories for both Skip and me. And maybe tomorrow I should go out and buy some sexy underwear. He'll have to like that, won't he?

But 'gross'? Lisa grabbed the pillow again and hugged it to her. How could he have said that about her dress? The dress wasn't gross. It was cute. It was unbelievably cute.

Toby waited. He waited while Christina took a bath, waited while they had a light dinner of scrambled eggs, waited while she read a book in bed. Once or twice, as he lay beside her, he'd yawn and then wait for her to yawn as well.

'You must be exhausted,' he said after the third yawn. 'How about turning off the light now and getting some sleep?'

'I suppose that's a good idea,' she'd replied, placing her book on the floor beside the bed. 'I *am* tired. I'm not sure why, though. All I did today was sit around in the garden with Jessica and Owen. You and Declan were the ones working.'

'It's the country air,' he said in a voice of wisdom. 'All that healthy atmosphere can wear you down.'

'Did I hear you ask Owen if you could visit them again soon?'

'Yes,' he nodded. 'And Owen said he'd be disappointed if I didn't. That man is incredible. I—' Toby stopped. He didn't want to get into it now, not right this second when Christina was ready to go to sleep. Besides, he didn't feel like confiding in her, not yet. He needed some information first. Until he got it he wasn't about to trust her with his innermost thoughts and feelings. 'I'm too tired to talk,' he told her. 'Let's discuss Owen another time.'

'All right.' She raised herself on an elbow and kissed him. 'Goodnight then.'

'Goodnight.' Toby turned away and switched off the light above the bed.

And then he waited some more.

When he was sure she was well and truly asleep, he got up, crept into the kitchen, and turned on the light. She'd left her handbag hanging over the kitchen chair and he opened it, fished for her address book, found it and quickly flicked to the page with Lucy's number.

Was eleven o'clock too late to ring? he wondered. No. He'd dial 141 first and hang up if some grumpy man answered. Even if he woke Lucy up he didn't expect she'd be annoyed. Not for long, anyway, not if he turned on the charm – which was what he was planning to do.

She answered on the fourth ring. He was sitting on the kitchen floor, his back up against the door, the telephone in his lap.

'Lucy? It's Toby Goodyear here. Sorry to ring you so late on a Sunday.'

'Toby?' She sounded a little sleepy but not as if she'd been jolted awake. 'Is Christina all right?'

'She's fine, Lucy, thank you. I didn't mean to frighten you, I just needed your help with a surprise I'm planning.'

'A surprise?'

'Yes, a surprise for Christina's birthday.'

'Chris' birthday? Sorry, I'm confused. Wasn't that in April?'

'Mmm. Yes, it was. But you see I didn't do anything special for her then and I'd like to make up for it now – when she won't be expecting anything. I was wondering if we could meet, you and I. I was hoping you could help me find the perfect present for her.'

'How sweet you are. That's such a sweet thing to do. But I don't know, Toby. I haven't seen Chris in ages. I'm not sure I'd be much help to you. I adore Chris, but we don't really have the same taste.'

'Still – you know what she'd like, I'm sure. Have lunch with me, Lucy. And let me interrogate you.'

'Interrogate?' Lucy giggled.

'Absolutely. I want to know all about you and your family. How about tomorrow? Can you get away? Where is Esher, anyway?'

'Not that far from London. I could get out, I suppose. My children are in school until four-thirty. It's only about a forty-five-minute drive. And I have to admit, I'm dying to meet you,

Toby. I always say that to Nigel – we keep wondering why Chris has been hiding you for so long. And if I can help you find the perfect present for her, I'd love to. I adore surprise presents.'

'Then we're on.' Toby caught himself before he said 'perfecto'.

'I've heard there's a trendy restaurant in Fulham. A friend of mine went there the other day and spotted Ralph Fiennes. It's Italian. I can't remember the name. La something.'

'La Famiglia?'

'Yes, that's it. What if we go there? My treat.'

'Fantastic. It's on Langton Street. Let's say we meet there at a quarter to one,' Toby suggested. 'Then we'll have plenty of time and you can tell me more about this mysterious woman I'm living with.'

'Has she told you how much she used to like football when she was a child?'

'Football? Good lord! Maybe we should meet at nine in the morning.'

'You're funny,' Lucy remarked. 'I always thought Chris should be with someone who has a good sense of humour. Chloë always said so too. And Mum – but I'd better stop before I tell you everything on the phone. I'll see you at La Famiglia then, at quarter to one. Oh, this is so exciting I almost forgot. We don't know what we look like, do we? I'm blonde, about five foot five and I'll be wearing a light blue dress and silver earrings. That should make it easy for you.'

'Fabulous, Lucy. I'm sure I'll recognize you from that description.' Toby closed his eyes and smiled. 'And I very much look forward to meeting you. Finally.'

Skip couldn't sleep. Every few minutes, he'd think about getting up and going to join Lisa in their bedroom, then discard the idea; at which point he'd feel guilty and ask himself how he could have been so cold to her during the day, then recall the warmth of Alison's body the day before, then feel guilty, then think about going in to join Lisa. The cycle was beginning to drive him crazy.

He'd never in his whole life done anything wrong – not before his night with Alison. On the contrary. He'd behaved almost unbelievably well, even in his teenage days. Friends of his had shoplifted, had sold dope, had cheated in exams, but Skip had always walked a straight line down a straight path. He'd been an honour student at high school, graduated second in his class at college, received a scholarship to Harvard Business School, walked straight into a job at AT&T, married Lisa, moved to a nice house in Connecticut, worked his ass off. All he had wanted was a normal, sane life. With a wife who wasn't a drunk and children who lived in a happy, stable environment.

Then Lisa had changed everything. She'd moved the goalposts. 'You're killing yourself,' she'd told him. 'And you're killing us.' He'd been forced to re-think then, to wonder whether he was as addicted to work as his mother had been to booze. If that addiction threatened to interfere with his vision of a happy family life, he knew he'd have to give it up. The choice, in the end, wasn't as difficult as he would have assumed it might be. The 'happy family' part of his dream was even more compelling than the 'successful businessman' part. For years he'd believed he could have both, but he'd miscalculated.

It would have worked out all right, he was sure. Had Lisa not written *I Saw You First*, they would have had the happy family. He could have found a less stressful job, they would have had those two children he so clearly pictured by now. Life would have been simple. Instead he was marrried to a celebrity who seemed to have traded psyches with him and was as addicted to *her* success as he had once been to his. It wasn't fair, was it? Definitely not.

But then how fair was it for him to have made love to another woman in another man's bed? Which was the more egregious sin? Writing a bestseller or committing adultery?

That question was far too easy to answer.

Skip Thomas had fucked up. Bigtime.

He scratched his head and thought about going in to Lisa. If he didn't go now, he might never go again. He understood, instinctively, that tonight was a turning point. He'd brushed Lisa off all day. All afternoon, as he pretended to watch the stupid cricket game, he'd had wild and crazy and unSkip-like thoughts. He imagined calling Alison and asking her to run away with him. To Tahiti, for chrissakes. That's how crazy he'd been. What the fuck would he and Alison do in Tahiti? Screw their brains out for a few weeks or months or years, sure – but then what? Sell necklaces to tourists on the beach?

Lisa kept saying that he'd been idealistic in the old days – that was one of her big riffs. But where the hell had she come up with that idea? He hadn't ever been dreamy and idealistic. Never. How many idealistic men went to Harvard Business School? Zero. Zilch. She kept telling the story about him helping some woman with a flat tyre, but the only reason he'd done that was to impress her: macho man helps lady in distress. It wasn't a habit of his, that was for sure. He'd never done it before and never done it since, which is why he always smiled when Lisa came to that part in the infomercial. She had fastened on to that one incident and made it into a huge telling point about his personality. She was so far off base, he hadn't known how to set her straight. What was he supposed to say? 'Time out, Lisa. That's some other guy you're talking about. Remember me – Skip? The selfish bastard? The one who would be the father who appoints himself coach of a Little League team and then tells the kids that winning isn't everything, it's the *only* thing?'

He wanted the happy nuclear family, yes. But he also wanted that family to be special and successful. He wanted his kids to be stars, he wanted the '*I'm the Father of Honors Students* bumper-sticker proudly displayed on his car. And he still wanted the good life with the gadgets and the toys and the beautiful house – only he wished he could be the one to provide it, not Lisa. That wasn't idealism, that was pure greed and selfish desire.

And that was what had struck him so much about Alison. She had sensed, he felt, his darker side, but hadn't run away screaming. She understood why he wasn't about to try to reconcile with his mother and she wasn't interested in going on some crusade to make him a kinder, gentler person. Plus sex with her was – well, how would he put it? Earthier. More raw. Much, *much* more powerful. Christ – the first thing Alison had done when they got on top of the bed was to suck his toes. He'd always thought that was some kind of a joke, something depraved Duchesses do when they're bored. But it wasn't – no way. No way whatsoever.

Skip groaned and then made himself sit up.

I can't go on like this, he thought. I'll drive myself crazy. It's not as if any of this is Lisa's fault. I haven't sucked *her* toes, either. It's just life and being attracted to someone different – that's all. I'm the same man I was when I married her. If Lisa thinks I'm a better person than I am, what's the problem? It's a hell of a lot better than her thinking I'm Hannibal Lecter. I'm not about to fly off to Tahiti and I'm not about to break up my marriage on account of some one-night stand. I am about to go next door and curl up beside Lisa. Where I belong.

Alison didn't know how to answer Declan. She sat at the kitchen table, a piece of toast and cup of coffee in front of her and tried to think what to say. How could she explain why she'd had the wine and the joint the night before? Or even why she'd kept a joint one of the blokes in one of the bands had given her a few months ago hidden in her knickers drawer. 'I was pissed off at myself and at Skip Thomas and at Lisa Thomas. I wanted to forget everything for a while.' That would have been the honest response, but there was no point in being truthful.

Declan was sitting across from her with a kind, patient look on his face, as though she were a mental patient he'd been told to be very careful with. 'Why did you feel the need to get drunk and stoned?' he'd asked almost as soon as she'd come downstairs for breakfast. 'Leave me alone,' was what she wanted to say, but her head hurt so much she felt defensive and sad.

'I'm not sure why. I suppose I was feeling lonely,' she finally replied, finding it difficult to look him in the eyes. In another mood, she might have gone into an attack mode. Told him off for lying to her about *Plots in a Box* and the weekend with Christina and Toby. Yelled at him for coming home so late on Sunday. Given him a verbal thrashing which would have changed the whole story and made him focus on his own shortcomings. But not this morning. She was too tired and still far too emotional. During the night she'd had a dream about Skip; one of those dreams that stay with you when you wake up. She and Skip were at her old school, walking hand-in-hand down the corridor. Students and teachers were staring at them, whispering. But she'd felt safe. And ridiculously, absurdly happy.

'Al, I'm sorry – ' Declan began, but he was interrupted by the sound of the telephone.

'Who could be ringing this early?' Alison felt terror set in. Had she forgotten she was supposed to be at some location for a shoot? Had her time with Skip completely unhinged her mind? She went into the living room, picked up the receiver and said, 'Hello.'

'Alison? It's Lisa Thomas.'

Oh shit! Alison's heart began to pound. She's found out. I can't deal with this now. Please not now. It's only eight-thirty in the morning.

'Sorry to call so early, but I wanted to ask you and Declan to come over tonight, for dinner. Again – nothing fancy. You know how we work here. If something's worth doing, it's worth doing casually. Can you make it?'

'I don't know,' Alison faltered. She *didn't* know. Part of her wanted to see Skip again, under any circumstances, despite all her wishes the day before that he'd leave London immediately, and part of her dreaded the prospect of seeing Skip with Lisa. 'I'll ask Declan if we're doing anything. Hang on a second, Lisa.'

Declan appeared in the living room at that moment, his eyebrows raised, mouthing, 'Who is it?'

'It's Lisa.' Alison had put her hand over the mouthpiece. 'She wants us to go over there again – for dinner. Tonight.'

'What do you think?'

The dream re-infiltrated Alison's consciousness. Skip's hand in hers. She saw him reach up with his other hand and scratch his head, then smile. 'We're in this together,' he whispered in her ear.

'I think we should,' she said to Declan.

Find another way to humiliate yourself, why don't you, Alison? Turn up at the Thomas' with a smile and a kiss on the cheek for Skip and sit there inwardly roiling with jealousy and despair. Why not? You make all these perfect plans and you can't follow through on any of them, can you? You pretend to be tough but you're as weak and pathetic as your father. The man with a thousand dreams and schemes and the complete inability to follow through on any of them.

'We'd love to, Lisa,' she spoke into the phone. 'What time do you want us? . . . Fantastic. See you then. Bye.'

Us. Declan and me. The couple who have been together almost two years, who bought a house together. Why? He's staring at me with those soft eyes of his, just like his father always looks at people. Wanting to know what's wrong with me. What's wrong with me is that I don't love him and never have and still I bought a house with him and lived with him and acted as if I did. I'm probably better at acting than Toby Goodyear. And I'm sure I'll be brilliant tonight. Just like I was when I was a little girl, all dressed up neatly, doing my work so bloody diligently no one could believe it, acting the perfect girl. When all along I was waiting to go berserk. All it took was meeting Peter and I became a wild person – mad and bad and dangerous to know. Throwing fits, living in squalor, doing everything in my power to hang on to him. Even finding work in the music world myself so I could try to help him and his rotten band.

And now what am I doing? I'm about to put my head straight into the lion's mouth tonight. 'Hello, Lisa, how nice to see you. And Skip. Wonderful to see you again too.'

'Alison – ' Declan put his hand on her shoulder. 'Are you

all right? You've been standing there since you hung up with a very strange expression on your face. I really am sorry about the weekend and *Plots in a Box*. I know I should have told you.'

'It's not important.' Alison looked at Declan and felt a horrible sense of pity. *He* wasn't important, that was the truth. She'd used him for comfort, as a steadying influence. He was a perfectly nice man and she'd used him horribly. She'd told herself she didn't want to be locked into coupledom, but in fact she didn't want to because she was locked into him – to Declan Lewis whom she didn't love. Right now she'd do anything to be handcuffed to Skip Thomas for the rest of her life. Only that wasn't possible, was it?

Alison sighed and put her hand on Declan's cheek.

'I'm sorry,' she said quietly then walked out of the room, picked up her bag in the hall and left through the front door.

Declan stood, feeling befuddled and bemused. What was going on in that head of hers? Up until yesterday he'd thought of Alison as a predictable person. He could anticipate her reactions and her moods ninety-nine percent of the time. Now he had no clue what she was thinking or why she had apologized to him. Why should *she* be sorry? He was the one who had kept something from her.

What could happen to make a person turn into an enigma overnight? How could he decode the enigma if she wouldn't talk to him? Alison had had a dreamy, otherworldly look in her eyes – the sort she sometimes had after a long session of sex. Yet they hadn't had much sex recently, and that was one of the issues he had told himself it was now time to address.

After this dinner with Skip and Lisa might be the time to sit down and talk through their relationship. Then they could sort out where they stood with each other.

I suppose relationships are like cars, Declan thought. They need servicing, MOT tests and tax discs. You can't allow them to slide or they'll break down on you.

Christ. Didn't Lisa say that in her book? Wasn't that the gist of a sentence I read as I was flicking through the pages? Why *do* I keep thinking about that bloody book? I've only read a few pages of it but it has infiltrated my psyche. I know it's total rubbish, but I can't stop thinking about it. What has my life come to? I'm not only writing scripts for infomercials but I'm also paying attention to an American self-help guru. If I'm not careful, I'll end up on a psychiatrist's couch or else I'll be spending my days on the phone chatting to Psychic Friends.

What type of conversation do you have with a psychic friend anyway? he wondered. Do you talk about each other's future? Or what the weather is going to be like the next day? At least the conversation wouldn't be boring. Instead of saying: 'Hello, how are you?' your psychic friend would say: 'Hello, my vibes tell me you're depressed, but I see that you'll get a salary rise in two months' time, so cheer up!' That might be fun. I wonder if—

Declan shook himself and sighed. The Thomases would be going home soon. At least he hoped they would. They should never have been allowed through immigration controls. Those two were contagious.

Toby jumped when he heard the telephone ring and rushed to the kitchen to answer it. It was probably Lucy, telling him she couldn't make lunch – in which case he didn't want Christina wondering why Lucy would ring at such an early hour. He was too late, though. Christina was standing by the table, the receiver in her hand, her face looking a little out of balance.

'Tonight?' she asked.

'Who is it?' Toby mouthed.

'That's nice of you. Lisa. I'll just ask Toby.' Putting her hand over the receiver, she said: 'Lisa wants us to come for dinner tonight. What do you think?'

'Free food,' Toby smiled. This would mean two free meals in a row.

'Why not?'

'We'd love to,' Christina told Lisa. 'Thank you for asking us. See you at eight.'

'So,' Toby stepped into the jeans he'd brought in with him. 'Is this *un dîner à quatre* or are there going to be other guests?'

'I don't know – she didn't say.'

'I hope they have more of that caviare.'

'That's strange.' Christina had her handbag open on the table. 'I thought I'd put my address book in the side pocket, but it's right here on top of my keys.'

'And some more of that champagne, too.'

'Toby,' Christina grinned. 'You've been in such a good mood this morning. It's lovely to see you so happy.'

'Does that mean you love and adore me and want to have my babies?' Toby did a little barefoot jig on the floor.

Christina couldn't stop herself from staring at him. He had a manic, wild look on his face, an expression of malevolent glee. What did he want her to say? Was he serious? Instinctively, she stepped back from him, and seeing her do this, he approached and grabbed her by the shoulders.

'You can't hide from me,' he said in a theatrical snarl. 'You can run but you can't hide.'

'Toby. Please. I'm not running or hiding. I have to get to work, that's all. My first client is coming in at nine.'

'Ah, mix those potions, Chris. You do that. Anoint those bodies. Be a witch. Fair is foul and foul is fair. Hover through the fog and filthy air.' Toby waved his fingers and said: 'Oooohhhh.'

Christina, nonplussed and a little frightened by this manner of his, started out of the kitchen and toward the front door. Toby was right behind her, dogging her footsteps.

'You're scaring me,' she finally said, turning around to see him face-on.

'"She feared no danger for she knew no sin". How can I scare you if you have nothing to hide?'

'I wish I had a clue what you were talking about.'

'All will be revealed,' he stated. 'It's only a matter of time.'

Christina sighed and walked out of the door. Toby, once she'd closed it, did another jig.

'I love Lucy,' he said out loud, as he hopped. 'Lucy, I love you. You're going to tell me everything. You'll spill the beans on this Richard man, I know. That's why Christina has been hiding you from me – because you know she's still involved with him. And once I have enough information on the enemy, I can defeat him. I will not be vanquished. Christina is mine. *And*, my lovely Lucy, you are paying for lunch. Bravo!'

At ten a.m. Lisa Thomas was sitting in a soundproof room, a pair of earphones on her head, a microphone on the desk in front of her. She was at the BBC in Portland Place, doing a live interview with a radio station in Exeter.

'Lisa,' the voice came through her earphones. 'You'll be on in two minutes. I'll introduce you, ask a few questions about your book and then we'll take phone-ins. All right?'

'Okey dokey.' She should have been used to this set-up by now, she knew, but being all alone in a room, talking to someone she'd never met, whose face she couldn't see, still made her feel a little anxious, as if she were in jail on another planet. Most of the time she tried hard to vary what she said about the book, not to reproduce the same old patter. Today, though, she didn't know whether she could make an effort. Skip had woken her up when he'd come in at three a.m. He'd apologized for being so brusque all day and hugged her as if he were a drowning man and she was the life-raft. Well, that was definitely an improvement on the situation, she knew, but then, within minutes, he'd started in about having babies again.

'We could be such a happy family, Lisa,' he'd crooned.

'We're a happy family now,' she'd replied. 'Skip – I'm all tired out. Let's talk about this later. At least we haven't let the sun go down on our troubles.'

'What?' He'd pulled away from her. 'The sun has fucking sunk, Lisa. It's almost four in the morning. And what are you talking about – "our troubles"? You sound as if you're a politician in Ireland.'

'It's not necessary to use that tone of voice with me,' she retorted, then turned her back on him. 'I'm not your slave.'

'Who said anything about slaves?' He turned his back as well. 'What? You've hopped on a boat in Ireland and ended up in the Deep South in 1860? As I recall, slaves didn't make more money than their masters. Slaves didn't go on television shows or make infomercials. Anyway, forget it. We'll talk about children later. When neither of us is tired.'

After that she'd struggled to get to sleep and now she was wrung out, strung out and tense. As soon as she got the word that she would be on air, she forced herself to concentrate and summon up some real enthusiasm in her voice. For a while, as she talked about *I Saw You First*, she was fine and dandy, humming along, delivering the goods the way she knew only she could deliver them. Then the phone-ins began to come through and she stupidly relaxed. Normally they were a piece of cake, though she knew from experience she had trouble sometimes with the men who called – men were generally more aggressive and difficult than women. Yet she had always managed to handle them. Until ten-fifteen. Until 'Roger' phoned in.

'Lisa, I've got a problem. What if one person in a marriage can remember what they first saw in their partner, but the other can't?'

'I assume you're speaking about your marriage, Roger.'

'I am. The point is, I can remember why I fell in love with my wife Sandra five years ago – I can remember *everything*. I love the way she moves, Lisa. The way she sits in a chair. She has this sort of swan neck which makes her look like Jayne Torville.'

'That's a lovely compliment to give Sandra, Roger.'

Who the hell was Jayne Torville? Lisa thought she'd heard the name before but was having problems remembering who it belonged to. Not that it mattered, really, but it would have been helpful. Suddenly the name clicked.

'Jayne is such a wonderful actress, isn't she?'

'No. She's not an actress. You mean you've never heard of her? She's an ice-skater.'

'Oh, of course. I was thinking of another Jane. That's right. I was thinking of Jane Seymour.' Pull yourself together, Lisa, she cautioned herself. You can't spend all your time on this call talking about famous women named Jane. 'Anyway, Roger, are you saying that Jane – oops, I mean Sandra – can't remember what it was she first saw in you?'

'Well, I'm not so sure she ever saw anything in me, to be honest. She married me because she was pregnant and the bloke did a runner.'

'Mmhhmm. So you're bringing up a child together.'

'You could say that, I suppose – though she's not here much, these days. She's out most of the time.'

'And you're not sure how she feels about you?'

'Well, to be honest, Lisa, I think I fill her with disgust and contempt.'

'I see.' What was this man doing? How perverse could he be? 'I have to say, Roger, maybe you should re-think your marriage. It doesn't sound as if it started off with love on her part, so it's really not a situation my book can help you with. I'm talking about couples who were happy together once and have somehow let that magic slip away.'

'But Sandra is magic, Lisa. I love her. I want her. I need her. She's the light of my life. I know you can help. I know you'll tell me what to do to make her love me.'

I thought British men didn't talk about their emotions, Lisa thought. This guy is spilling his guts like nobody's business.

'Roger, I'm really sorry, but it doesn't sound—'

'I love every single thing about her. Every part of her body. She has a sort of bend in her foot.'

'An arch?'

'Is that what it's called?'

'Yes, Roger, everyone has arches.'

'Is that right? You know everything. Tell me what to do.'

'Just get over it, Roger.'

'Pardon?'

'I said get over it, OK? Get her out of your life. Dump her. Don't let her use you any more.'

'I thought you were supposed to *help* couples.'

'I'm *trying* to help you.'

'It doesn't sound that way to me. You sound like a nasty cow.' Roger hung up.

Lisa put her head in her hands.

I hate this country, she thought. They think Americans are strange? This place is one big island of certifiable loony tunes. The men all seem to like dressing up as women, the policemen don't carry guns, there are topless girls in the newspapers, the phone rings twice instead of once, and the beef is infected with disease.

Then she composed herself and took the next call.

Chapter 9

How many times do you find yourselves having the same old argument? You go around in circles, don't you, like a dog chasing its tail. He says: 'I can't talk now, I'm watching the baseball game.' You say: 'You're always watching the damn baseball game.' He says: 'Why shouldn't I watch it if that's what I want to do' and on and on and on. I don't care if the argument is about money or sports or the children or your friends or food or how long it takes to get to the moon. What I care about is tail-chasing: it has to stop.

Why don't you put a different song on the jukebox? The next time he criticizes you for something, don't get all defensive and bite back at him: try a new tack. Accept that criticism, agree with that criticism. By agreeing with him, you can set a new pace to the old quarrel. Defuse all his anger by riding out his criticism and once you've done that, you'll see you can make any point you want to make and he'll listen.

Think of a little child. You're taking her for a walk in the park and she falls down and starts screaming her head off, saying how much it hurts. Do you whack her one and tell her you're tired and strung out and you don't need to hear all this screaming, or do you kneel down and say: 'Honey, I'm so sorry you're hurt. It must be awful for you. Let me help'? Which one of those approaches do you think will get that child to stop crying?

204

*Your partner comes back and says it's been a godawful day
and all he wants to do is turn on the tube and watch a game and
chill out. You've had a godawful day yourself and you want to tell
him about it and you can't believe how selfish he's being. Well,
think about it. He's waiting for you to complain, as usual. What
happens if you don't? He'll pay attention then. 'What happened
to that nagging partner of mine?' he'll think. 'Maybe she's not
such a nag after all. Maybe she understands.' He'll look at you
differently, then. And he'll start to see the real you again – not
some image he has in his head of a woman out to spoil his fun.
When you become a person rather than a series of predictable
reactions, you'll find he'll become more of a person too. Both of
your visions will begin to clear.*

*Arguments are all about role-playing. Perhaps you were jealous
once, at the beginning of the relationship, and bit by bit you get
labeled as a 'jealous' person in your partner's mind. It doesn't
matter that he may be just as jealous as you – you've taken over
that role, probably because you were the first one in the relationship
to express that emotion. It can all be a matter of timing, the roles
we take on. They may have little to do with our true selves. You
begin to do what is expected of you – whether it be to get jealous,
or to complain about the amount of sport he watches or to irritate
him by spending too much money on clothes. Any little thing can
become an ingrained habit if you're not careful.*

*Surprise your partner! Stop being yourself as he now sees you
and be yourself the way you see you. That's the person he first
fell in love with, get out of that vicious circle you've created over
time. Circles go nowhere.*

*Step off that not so merry-go-round! Walk a straight line. It will
get you where you want to go – back to the beginning.*

I Saw You First, Chapter Twelve, p. 199

Christina was already off-balance when she walked into the
Thomases' drawing room, but she felt her world tilt even further

when she saw Declan and Alison sitting on the sofa.

From the moment she'd come home from work, Toby had been staring at her with the same devilish leer he had worn in the morning. It was still off-putting and frightening and Christina wished she could do something to make him alter his expression. She'd gone to their bedroom to change and he'd followed her, watching her as if she were a prisoner and he was her keeper. Each time she asked him what the matter was he'd leer again, with half-closed eyes, and then smile a terrible, omniscient smile. She felt as if he knew something awful and was waiting for the right moment to tell her – to announce that the world was going to be hit by a huge comet or the Chinese had declared war on Britain. The sense of lurking bad news he was unwilling to divulge kept her jumpy throughout their bus trip to Pimlico and she was relieved when Lisa met them at the door with her open, friendly smile and a big warm hug.

As soon as she caught sight of Declan, however, the relief vanished and she felt besieged by guilt and further fear. Perhaps Toby was a mind-reader and had known she'd been thinking of Declan ever since she'd woken up that morning. Maybe that was why he'd been so strange; he sensed the affection she had for this man – a kind of deep affection which had sneaked up on her over the weekend and then had waged a full frontal attack when she'd woken up this Monday morning. She missed Declan – it was as simple as that. She missed talking to him, she missed his physical presence, she missed his smile. They were safe, she knew, these emotions, because she was with Toby and Declan was with Alison. Declan was like a brother, that was all. The only problem would be trying to explain those feelings to Toby.

'I didn't know you two were coming,' Toby said to Alison and Declan.

'We just arrived,' Alison replied. 'We didn't know you were coming either.'

Alison was wearing a seriously wrinkled white linen shift and deep dark red lipstick. She looked tired, but also determined.

Sitting up very straight, her legs crossed, her hands on her lap, she seemed as if she were modelling for a portrait of a society lady. Christina remembered how knotted her neck had been on Saturday and guessed that it was even worse now.

'Isn't this fun? All of us together again?' Lisa fluttered her hands in the air and motioned for Toby and Christina to sit down in the two chairs flanking the sofa.

'Where's Skip?' Toby asked.

'He's coming down in a sec. He kept changing his mind about what to wear, if you can believe it. As if this were his first date with someone special. Oh – ' Lisa put her hands to her face in a gesture of horror. 'I didn't mean that you all aren't special. Of course you are.'

Declan caught Christina's eyes and smiled.

'Now. I'll get you two a drink, but first I want to explain something. I'm so excited I've just got to get this out right away.' Lisa stood in the middle of the room, in front of the television set, as she had that first night. Christina was dazzled by the pinkness of her blouse; the colour was so bright it threatened to overwhelm the diminutive American.

'I brought you four here not only because Skip and I wanted to see you guys again, obviously, but also because I want to suggest an alternative *I Saw You First* infomercial. As you know, I was planning to do the same one as I'd done in America, basically, with Toby substituting for Mike. But it strikes me that you're right about the British being different from Americans. They may find it hard to identify with me, you know. Unless, that is, they hear other British people talking about what my book has done for their relationships.'

Skip came into the room, then, looking quickly at the four guests before saying: 'Don't let me interrupt, Lisa. You go on. I'll say hello to everyone later.' He went and stood a few feet away from his wife with what Christina thought was a sheepish expression on his face.

'Thanks, honey. So, as I was saying, I want British people to talk about themselves and the book and I thought to myself, well, what British people would be good at that? And immediately I thought of you four, you two couples. Of course Skip and I would join you – there would be six of us, discussing our relationships in the context of the book.'

'What did you say?' Alison said with a note of terror. This was worse than she had imagined. The sight of Lisa had brought a tidal wave of jealousy and seeing Skip, standing with his hands in his pockets, so nervous and yet somehow so adorable, was making her itch to cross the room and put her arms around him. Why had she come? How much worse could this evening get? Lisa wanted them to do an infomercial? The woman was beyond the pale. And that pink blouse was hideous.

'You know.' Lisa put her hands on her hips. 'You guys just talk about how you first met, what you saw in each other, how you can still have those same feelings. Remember,' she turned to Christina, 'you said it the other night. You said every day with Toby was like a first date.'

'I . . .' Christina could feel herself blushing and couldn't think of what to say next.

'Yes, Chris?' Toby glared at Christina from his chair on the other side of the sofa. 'What were you going to say? Were you going to tell Lisa how true that is?'

Christina doesn't love me. Now I know she doesn't love me and she has played me for a fool all along. But she can't get away with it; I won't let her. She is sitting there looking so prim and proper, but she won't be for long. I was going to wait to confront her, but I can't wait any longer. She has made me suffer. Now it's her turn.

'Lisa,' Declan spoke up. 'I don't think we're the people you should be thinking of, actually. None of us – except Toby – have any experience on television, for starters.'

'Oh, that's not a problem,' Toby said quickly. 'I'm sure Lisa wants to go for the natural look, not the stage-managed. I think it's a wonderful idea.'

'Fantastic!' Lisa exclaimed. 'That's one out of four. What do you say, Alison?'

What is Toby doing? Christina could feel all her muscles tense up. Something awful has happened and I don't know what it is. Why is he acting so strangely? Why is he looking at me as if he wants to throttle me? And why is Alison staring at Skip? She can't take her eyes off him. I don't understand what is going on here and I wish I could leave right now.

'Brilliant.' Alison didn't move a muscle. She sat as rigidly as she'd been sitting since Christina walked in. Fuck Lisa, she thought. And fuck Skip too. I don't want to put my arms around him any more. How could he have let me come here knowing what Lisa was going to suggest? He's a bastard. And she's an idiot. 'Why not do an infomercial? We all have these brilliant relationships, don't we? We're all so happy. You and Lisa especially – yes, Skip? You have such an amazing marriage.'

Now Skip blushed visibly and scratched his head.

What's happening here? Christina asked herself. Something is going on between Skip and Alison. But that can't be right. That's impossible! I'm imagining it.

'I told Lisa I didn't think this was such a hot idea,' Skip mumbled, averting his eyes from Alison's stare. Why didn't Lisa tell me she'd invited them to dinner until approximately an hour ago? I'm in deep shit here and I have no idea how to step out of it. Does Alison hate me now? Is that why she is going along with Lisa's idea? 'But if you're so anxious to do it, Alison, then—'

'Fantastic! I'm so glad you're up for this, Alison. Two down, two to go.' Lisa grinned and turned to address Declan. 'Declan – this would be fun. You know it would.'

'I'm afraid I *don't* know that.' Declan shifted on the sofa and crossed his legs. 'I'd be embarrassed, Lisa. I honestly have no desire to discuss my relationship with Alison on a television commercial, or infomercial. It's private.'

Alison is becoming more enigmatic with every passing second,

Declan noted. Why is she staring at Skip like that? What is all this guff about Skip and Lisa's amazing marriage? Could she honestly picture me doing an infomercial about our relationship? Has she gone mad? Her eyes have the tinge of a possessed person at the moment.

And Toby looks wired, like a terrorist on a mission. I wish someone would tell me what was going on.

'What's private about being in love, Declan? You should want to shout it from the rooftops.' Lisa clapped her hands. 'You don't have to talk about intimate details. Only what made you fall in love in the first place and what makes you stay in love now. Why would you be ashamed of having this great romance with Alison and letting people know about it? The whole world loves a lover!'

'God, Lisa – how right you are. Did you make that up, or have you heard it somewhere before?' Alison smiled.

Her smile, Christina thought. It's the smile of the witch in the Gingerbread House as she locks Hansel into the cage.

'The whole world loves a lover? It's an old saying, Alison,' Lisa said brightly. 'But I think the old sayings are the best. Why are clichés clichés? Because they're so, so true.'

Skip let out an audible sigh. Declan closed his eyes. When he opened them, he looked at Christina.

'You know what I'm saying, don't you?' he asked her in a pleading tone. 'I can't picture myself on an infomercial.'

'I know exactly what you're saying. I know I couldn't do it either.' Thank God Declan's here, she said to herself. He seems as puzzled by the atmosphere tonight as I do. Is there something we're both missing?

'Why not?' Toby leaned forward in his chair, his hands on both knees. 'Why couldn't you, Chris? Don't you want to tell the world how much in love with me you are – as Lisa put it so well? Don't you want to say you've never felt love like this before? That there's not some other man in your life who haunts you? Someone you've never got over? Someone you're still in touch with? Someone who sends you birthday cards, for example? Someone who is now a successful barrister? Let's see . . .' Toby stared up at the ceiling. 'Let me guess. Could his name begin with an R? Could it be Robert? No. I don't think so. What else begins with an R?'

'Toby – ' Christina felt as if she'd drunk a bottle of vodka in one go. The room began to dance in front of her and she grabbed on to the side of her chair for support. 'I don't know what – '

'Of course you don't,' he interrupted. 'Because there is no such man, is there? You love *me*, don't you? And you can't wait to tell the world how much. You can't think of anyone whose name begins with an R, can you? I certainly can't. Although, of course, there's always Rory.' His eyes swung over to the centre of the room. 'Christina is aching to do the infomercial, Lisa.'

'I'm not really sure I – ' Lisa stopped mid-sentence, flummoxed. Was this an English game she didn't know? A variation of Charades? Were they supposed to guess names beginning with R? What had Toby been talking about?

'And then there's Roger.' Toby glared at Christina. 'Or Roy. Could that be the name, Chris? Roy? Or Ralph? Is it Ralph, perhaps?'

Declan looked at Christina's face and winced. Toby was inflicting pain and although he didn't understand the context, he knew the intent. Toby had an agenda for this evening, clearly. He reminded Declan of a particularly obnoxious and loathsome older boy from school; one who had tormented the younger ones and taken pleasure in every moment of their discomfort.

'Why are you bullying Christina like this, Toby?' he asked, feeling the anger build in his voice with each word.

'Bullying? I'm not bullying anyone. I'm playing a guessing game. Why are *you* being a pain in the arse?'

'People – people – take it easy. I don't want a fight in my living room,' Lisa exclaimed. 'Whatever you are all talking about can wait, can't it? We're all friends here, remember. We – '

'You should meet Christina's step-sister, Declan,' Toby interrupted, smirking. 'She's a beautiful woman and full of interesting

211

facts. For example, her brother-in-law is a barrister named Richard – Richard Pike. Isn't that fascinating? Richard begins with an R.'

'Lucy,' Christina whispered. Her whole body began to shake. She put her hand to her mouth and tried to stop herself from crying.

'Get a fucking grip, Toby. I have no idea what you're on about but you should stop whatever it is now,' Declan spat out. He rose from the sofa and went over and knelt beside Christina. 'Are you all right?' he asked.

She nodded. 'I'll be OK,' she murmured. 'I'll be all right. Just give me a minute.'

'Even the mention of him has you in a fit, doesn't it?' Toby said with disgust. 'Even the fucking mention of him.'

'Guys!' Lisa protested. 'This isn't – '

'You come to my parents' house to work on *Plots in a Box* and you leech on to my father like a parasite and you don't pay any attention to Christina when she was upset and now you're harassing her in someone else's house? It's not on, you bastard. Christina – would you like to leave? Now? I'll take you out.'

'Declan.' Alison stood up. 'Have you forgotten that I happen to exist?'

'You bloody well aren't taking her anywhere.' Toby stood up as well. 'If she wants to leave, she can leave with me.'

'What do you mean, you were working on *Plots in a Box*?' Lisa stared wild-eyed at Skip. 'Is this something you cooked up? Without telling me?'

'I'd like to go home,' Christina said softly. The last two minutes were a haze. What had Declan said to her? What were the others saying? She couldn't hear properly. Her mind was filled with pictures of Toby and Lucy. *Is it happening again? Has he fallen in love with her? Is that why he's been so strange? Because he met Lucy and fell in love? When? Where? How?* 'I'm not feeling well. Toby – I'd like to go home now.'

'Fine.' Toby strode over to Christina's chair. She got up and he took her arm. 'I'm sorry we couldn't stay for dinner,' he said, glancing from Lisa to Skip. 'But now is the time to make an exit, I believe. And don't – ' he turned back to Declan. 'Do not play the bear pursuing us. Leave us alone. This isn't your affair.'

Christina let Toby shepherd her out of the house and on to the pavement, leaving the rest of the group standing in the drawing room.

'Do you mind if we get a taxi?' she asked. 'I'm really not feeling well. I'll pay.'

Toby didn't respond, but then did hail a cab. When they climbed into it he sat apart from her, his eyes fixed on the back of the driver's head.

'You've got some explaining to do,' he muttered. 'You've taken me for a ride, you know. You're some fucking actress yourself. What? Do you think of Richard every time we have sex? Richard, Richard, Richard and the pots of money he must be making and the life you could have had with him? Instead of some poor, struggling actor? Is that it? Or are you still seeing him, behind my back? You are, aren't you?'

'Toby, I don't know what Lucy told you, but you've got it wrong. I don't love Richard, not any more. I did once, yes – but that was a long time ago. I haven't seen him in years.'

What about Lucy? she thought frantically. Are you in love with Lucy? Using Richard as an excuse to get out of our relationship now that you've seen her? I don't dare ask.

'We'll talk about it at the flat,' he stated. Christina sank back into the seat and stared out of the window.

Toby and Lucy. Toby and Lucy together, talking about me and Richard. What has she said? What does she know? She knows nothing. But they met. Toby and Lucy met. 'She's beautiful,' he said to Declan. Lucy *is* beautiful.

I don't want to think about it. I want to go home and curl up in bed. I want to sleep. That's what saw me through those months before I left Richard – when I knew how he felt about Lucy but couldn't talk to him about it. I slept and slept and slept – so much that he thought I was ill. I *was* ill. Richard was right. I was heartsick. Some people eat. Some people smoke five thousand cigarettes or go out on drunken binges. I sleep.

When they arrived back at the flat, Christina stood in the hallway, unsure of what to do or where to go. Toby lit a cigarette and waved it in the direction of the sitting room.

'Why are you so cross with me?' she found herself asking as she followed him in. 'I haven't done anything wrong. I've never betrayed you, Toby.'

'I'm cross,' Toby sat down, 'because you have kept secrets from me, Chris. You never told me you lived with this bloke for three years. You never told me anything about him. That's why you don't see Lucy any more, isn't it? Because he's Lucy's husband's brother and even if you're not seeing him, which I'm not sure I believe, you can't bear the thought of running into him. You love him madly.'

'No.' She remained standing. 'That's not true. I'm not seeing him, I promise. I don't love him madly.'

'Lucy said she could never understand why you two split up. The only thing she could think was that you'd got pregnant and had an abortion and then run away from him.'

'What?'

'You heard me. Is that what happened?'

'Toby – this is absurd. We split up because Richard was in love with someone else.'

'Lucy didn't say anything about that.'

'Lucy doesn't know.'

'Why not? She's your sister. Why didn't you tell her?'

I should tell him now, Christina thought. But I don't want to. Why not?

'Richard is Lucy's brother-in-law. I didn't want to complicate their relationship. I don't love him any more, Toby. I promise. I didn't tell you because it's ancient history. It's not important. I don't understand why you're so wrought up or what you were doing with Lucy. Why didn't you tell me you were going to see her? *You're* the one who is keeping secrets, Toby. Not me.'

I was inflamed, Toby thought. Possessed by jealousy. The thought of Christina with another man drove me wild. As soon as Lucy told me about him over lunch, I wanted to pluck out his eyes. His and Christina's as well. If I'd had a gun I might have shot them both – a crime of passion. And what astounding passion! I never thought I could feel it in real life and now I have. But she's not in love with him. She's in love with me. I see it now. I see she's telling the truth. She's a goddess. A giant of a goddess, a Greek goddess. Even Declan recognizes that – he was practically worshipping at her feet this evening. But she's mine. And I'm not letting her go. I'm on a roll now and I won't let my emotions stop. Finally I'm expressing myself. It feels like that night in Tooting. The stage is mine and I can do no wrong. All I have to do now is to bring the curtain down with a bang.

Toby got up and approached Christina. She was on the point of backing away from him when he dropped to his knees in front of her.

'Will you marry me?' He grabbed her hand. 'Will you marry me, Chris?'

'Oh Jesus. Oh my God.' Christina stood transfixed. Then the room began to dance again and she could feel herself hyperventilating. 'I think I'm going to faint.' Sinking to the floor, she felt a wave of nausea come and go; as soon as it disappeared she had the visceral sensation of being far, far away – in a different country, in a different century. Strange men suddenly appeared in front of her eyes, wearing battledress and carrying spears.

She could hear a voice saying, 'Breathe!' but she couldn't focus. The men were on horses and they were galloping by her, yelling something in a language she'd never heard before. She was frightened, terrified of the men but even more terrified of the blackness that was now beginning to descend on her, a blank black canvas closing in on her like death.

'Chris! Christ, I didn't know I'd have quite *that* effect when I proposed to a woman.'

Christina looked up into Toby's face and tried to reorientate herself. She was, she slowly realized, lying on the bed in their room, and Toby was flicking water onto her eyes.

'I fainted. Oh God.' She wiped her eyes with the back of her hands. 'I don't know why that happened. I don't know what to say.'

'I could tell you to say the obvious. I could tell you to say yes to my proposal. But that would be like one of Lisa Thomas' clichés, wouldn't it?' He rubbed the top of her head. 'I suppose I surprised you.'

'I don't know.' Christina blinked. 'I know I shouldn't say this, but you've never even told me you love me, Toby. And you've been acting in such a bizarre and hurtful way today. And then you propose. I can't quite take it in.'

'Well,' he shrugged. 'I can't quite take it in either. I meant what I said though, asking you to marry me. I think I didn't realize the extent of my feelings for you until I thought there was someone else in your life. I felt – I felt like Othello. Mad with jealousy. And that made me wake up. That and seeing Owen over the weekend. He reminded me that I can be a better person than I've been. A better actor and a better human being. Talking about my childhood, my parents' divorce and all that, I understood how damaged I've been. I've hidden myself from women because I couldn't bring myself to get involved too deeply and be hurt somehow again.'

It was wonderful, so wonderful that she had fainted. The perfect response. The passion was unstoppable. It was phenomenal. Why had he never seen this side of her before?

'And you love me?' Christina's voice was tenuous.

'Absolutely.'

He's seen Lucy, he's spent time with Lucy but he loves ME.

Christina tried to delve into Toby's eyes and look through them, to the core of the man behind them, straight through to his heart. *Was* he in love with her or was he playing the part of the jealous lover? Becoming Othello as he had told Owen he'd once become Hamlet? Was all this an act?

I am so distrustful, she thought. It's sickening. I'm as mired in the past as Declan was, fighting battles I don't have to fight. It's time to get over what happened with Richard, to stop being so paranoid about Lucy, to look at things squarely and without this terrible, omnipresent feeling of not belonging. Toby wants me to belong, he is offering me love and a future and acceptance of who I am. It's not an act. He knows me, he's lived with me and he wants to marry me. He's casting off his past, too. We both are.

He is as insecure as I am but I never saw that because I couldn't believe someone so handsome and talented could possibly suffer from self-doubt. He does, though, or he wouldn't have been jealous of Richard. We're more alike, more compatible than I ever imagined. That vulnerability and sweetness I was so beguiled by in Declan exists in Toby too, I'd just been blind to it before. Now I see that we can help each other, rescue each other, cherish each other.

He needs me.

I *have* won the lottery. We both have.

'Yes, Toby,' she said. 'Yes, I'll marry you. But I need to ask you a favour. I know this sounds stupid, but I would much prefer it if you stopped calling me "Chris". I can't explain why I don't like it, but it's important to me to be "Christina".'

'You're a funny little thing.' Toby leaned over and kissed her. 'No. That's not entirely correct. You're a funny *big* thing. My tall wife-to-be. My very own giant.'

It doesn't matter, it doesn't matter, it doesn't matter, Christina said to herself. I have to stop obsessing about my height, too. Why can't I? What's stopping me?

'Toby. Sorry to be silly again, but I'd really prefer it if you didn't refer to me as a giant.'

'Christina. We've had this conversation, remember? You have to get over it.'

'But it's important to me. It's not the way I want you to think of me.'

'You're tall. How can I not think that? It's a physical fact.'

'But—' Christina stopped. Was it possible? Could they be

217

having this argument two minutes after becoming an engaged couple? Had nothing actually changed? No. Things *had* changed. Dramatically. Irrevocably.

'Never mind,' she said, blinking. 'It's not important.'

But one thing hadn't changed. She still smiled when she lied.

'Why didn't you tell me you were going ahead with *Plots in a Box*? Either of you?' Lisa looked from Skip to Declan. 'I don't understand.'

'It's no big deal, Lisa,' Skip shrugged. He was sitting in the chair Christina had been in, by the sofa. 'I wanted them to do a preliminary script for it, that's all.' He reached up to loosen his tie, then realized he wasn't wearing one.

Why was Skip so nervous tonight? Declan asked himself. He kept looking around the room as if there were ghosts in all the corners.

'I'm sorry, Lisa. If it makes any difference to you, I didn't tell Alison, either. I think Skip and Toby and I wanted to see how it was going to work out before we told everyone.'

What was going on in that flat off the Fulham Palace Road? he wondered. What was happening between Toby and Christina? Toby had a nasty streak to his character; he looked capable of violence, actually. Was Christina in trouble?

'We're supposed to tell each other everything,' Lisa said in a whining voice, glaring at Skip.

'Is that what married couples do? Tell each other everything? How boring,' Alison snorted.

'Al – ' Declan took her hand in his and forced himself to concentrate on what was going on in this drawing room, not let his thoughts fly off to Fulham. Alison was acting oddly and had been all night. But why shouldn't she be? He'd hurt her by going to Christina's side and suggesting he take her out. He'd been neglectful of Alison's feelings yet again. 'I want to apologize to you again, too. I don't think Skip or I knew how hurtful it would be not to tell you both about it.'

'Oh,' Alison flicked her hair back behind her ear. 'I'm sure there are plenty of other things going on that neither Lisa or I know about, as well. I wouldn't mind knowing why you were grovelling at Christina's side just now, for one. Is there something going on between you two? Did you have a mad night of passion with her over the weekend?'

'Alison – please.' Declan squeezed her hand extremely tightly. 'I felt sorry for her when Toby was having a go at her, that's all.'

'I don't care.' She snorted again. 'I think if you did have a wild night of passion with her, you *should* look after her and think about her feelings now, that's all. Instead of pretending it didn't happen and going along as though it didn't mean a thing. Using her and dumping her like some slapper.'

'I have no idea what you're talking about.' Declan stared at Alison's expressionless face and wondered if she was on some kind of drug. 'I didn't have any night of wild passion, Al. You know I wouldn't do something like that.'

'Of course you wouldn't, Declan,' Lisa chirped up. 'You're not a monster. Alison, honey, there is a section in my book on unfounded jealousy and what it can do to a relationship. It's Chapter Eleven and I don't mean to preach, but jealousy is a very, very destructive emotion.'

'Is there a chapter on people who don't have a clue what's going on in their relationship?' Alison asked.

'No.' Lisa sat back in her chair. 'I'm not sure I understand the point of that question, Alison. Maybe – ' she looked over at Skip. 'Maybe you were right, sweetheart. I think I'll go back to the original scenario for the infomercial. I mean, Toby and Christina clearly have some issues to work on and – ' Lisa shook her head ' – now that I think of it, Declan being on the infomercial might be a conflict of interests.'

'Oh really?' Alison tilted her head and narrowed her eyes.

'I think it's time to eat, isn't it?' Skip asked.

His gaze was still darting around the room, seemingly unable to rest on one person for more than a second. Is he on a drug too? Declan wondered. Is everyone on drugs here except me? The atmosphere in this room is highly charged. It's as if we were all in a Hitchcock movie and there was a bomb hidden under the sofa, ticking away. But who put it there? And why?

'My point,' Alison ignored Skip's question and pulled her hand away from Declan's, 'is that some people in relationships have absolutely no clue as to what's going on, what the other person is thinking, or feeling. My point is that you can think you know someone; even if you've only spent a very short time together, you think you know them. You might even feel as if you'd been to school with them, but then it turns out you don't know anything.'

'Been to school with them?' Lisa looked bewildered.

'That's what I said. Been to school with them. Let's say you feel as if you've been to school with someone and then he or she does something you don't understand at all.'

'I don't think I'm following this.' Lisa turned to Declan. 'Are you?'

Declan shook his head.

'That person does something like ask you to dinner in a situation where you shouldn't be asked to dinner because it's only reminding you of what can't happen. You shouldn't have your face shoved into something, you know?'

'Boy, I don't get this. Alison, I don't mean to be rude, but have you had a lot to drink?' Lisa asked.

'I think I get it,' Skip said quietly. 'I understand what Alison is talking about. It's about people in a relationship who aren't communicating – who are sending the wrong signals out. So, for example, someone may say something was just a one-off event when that's not what they meant at all. So the other person gets the wrong idea entirely. In fact, the other person may not have wanted it to be a one-off event, either.'

Lisa pulled her head back and raised her eyebrows. 'One-off? I still don't get it. What are you talking about, Skip?'

'Oh,' Declan nodded his head slowly. 'I think I see what you're saying Skip. I understand now.'

And I should knock your fucking teeth in. That's why she's been staring at you all night. That's why she said she was sorry and walked out this morning. That's the bomb underneath the sofa. You and Alison. Almost, but not entirely unbelievable. I *should* kick the shit out of you. But I don't want to and I won't. Why not? Because at the same time as feeling betrayed and outraged I also feel an immense sense of relief. If I ranted and raved and screamed and shouted, I'd only be a hypocrite. After all, what do I want to do? I want to do exactly what it seems you and Alison have done – I want to go to Fulham right now and get Christina and take her home to bed. And it sure as hell wouldn't be a one-off either.

But God, why didn't I notice before? It seems so bloody obvious now. Alison and Skip. They must have spent the weekend together somehow. Lisa must have been away and they got together on Friday night. Can that be true? I thought I knew Alison, but then I suppose she's right. Sometimes you can be in a relationship and not have a clue. I thought I was the reason she was acting so uncharacteristically and I was actually pleased with myself for having such an effect – when all along it was Skip Thomas. The infomercial king. Who is now making Alison behave like a teenager. I could never do that with her, I could never reach those places in her heart. We are compatible, yes, on many levels. We thought we had all six numbers there – or at least I did. But we weren't even close. What did I see when I saw her first? A competent, no-nonsense, almost frighteningly strong woman. What did Skip see? My guess is he saw a woman he felt he'd known for ever. What else was all that school business about?

Oh, Al – why didn't you just come out and tell me? We're both in the same situation – it seems to have happened to both of us during the same weekend. How bizarre is that? What are the odds on it? They must be a billion to one. And now you're in as hopeless a position as I now have to admit I'm in. Christina's with Toby. Skip's with Lisa.

We're both involved with people who are already spoken for.

You even more so than me. I have one thing in my favour – Christina's not married to Toby.

At least Skip knows how you feel about him, though. And he obviously has some feelings for you. I don't know where the hell I stand with Christina. I don't think I stand at all. And I adore the woman. I'm completely and utterly smitten.

Declan focused on Lisa's befuddled face.

I can't be the one to tell her, he thought. That's up to Skip, if he decides to. Right now I have to get those two out of the grave they can't stop digging for themselves. If they go much further, Lisa will twig and I don't think this is the time or the place for revelations of marital infidelity.

These thoughts had sped so quickly through Declan's brain, he was able to continue talking with only a few seconds' pause.

'What they're saying, Lisa, if you'll let me try to translate for them, is that there are instances in life when you think you know someone like a book, as you might say, but you then realize you've skipped the relevant chapters. You lose the plot, so to speak.'

'What was all that stuff about dinners?'

'That's part of the plot you miss. You know, a man might ask a woman out for a dinner date and she might say: "Well, yes, but only this once, it's a one-off", when she actually wants to go out with him many times.' Declan was groping for a way to cover Skip and Alison's messy tracks. One thing he knew was that Lisa would respond to some well-worn phrase, if he could come up with one, and then, if he was lucky, she'd go off on a riff about her book. He wished like hell now he'd read the entire thing.

'It's the old story, isn't it?' he began. 'Playing hard to get. You could have a couple, let's say, who were schoolmates, but the bloke doesn't want to put himself out because he's not sure the girl wants to change from being a friend to being a lover, so he plays hard to get, more or less. And then the girl plays hard to get back about the subject of dinner dates.' Was any of this tosh making sense to Lisa? Had he covered all their coded conversation yet? Whatever the case, he'd done as much as he could. 'And then the whole situation goes ballistic and she misunderstands everything and feels hurt. It's all about playing hard to get.'

'Mmhmmm.' Lisa nodded and tapped her mouth with her hand. 'I think I'm beginning to see, too. Hard to get is a tricky one. It works – that's the problem with it. Of course you remember what I said on the subject.'

'Which chapter was that?' Declan asked, deliberately avoiding looking at Alison or Skip, but honing in on Lisa.

'Chapter Seven.'

'Of course.' He smiled reassuringly.

'In that example we were talking about, did the other person *really* not want it to be a one-off?' Alison's eyes were fixed on Skip. 'Is that really true?'

'Oh no,' Declan moaned. 'Oh Jesus. Help.' He pressed his hand to his forehead.

'Declan – what's the matter?' Lisa left her chair and rushed up to him.

'It's a migraine. Oh God. I felt it coming on all day and now – the light – Jesus. Could you turn off the lights, Lisa? Please?'

Lisa scampered over to the far wall and threw the switch that controlled the lights in the room.

'Is that better?' her voice boomed across the darkness.

'Yes, thank you.' Declan leaned over and whispered in Alison's ear: 'We have to leave before this goes any further. You can't do this now.'

'What?' She drew away from him. He leaned in further.

'This isn't the way to do it, Al. I know what's going on. Calm down and come home, we'll talk it through there.'

Alison hung her head. 'All right,' she whispered back.

'Do you get migraines often?' Lisa asked solicitously, tiptoing toward Declan.

'No. Only once in a while, and they come on like that!' He snapped his fingers. 'I'm afraid I'll have to go home and lie down. It's the only thing to do. I know from experience.'

'I'm so sorry,' Lisa sighed.

'So am I,' Skip added.

Are you really? Declan wondered. What exactly are you sorry about, Skip?

He rose to his feet, his hand still pressed to his forehead. 'Alison, can you help me out?'

'Do you want me to turn the lights back on?' Lisa asked.

'No, no, that's all right. We'll manage.' Declan took Alison's arm and together they negotiated their way through the dark room and out into the hallway, where there was a light on.

'Oh dear. My dinner party hasn't worked out so well,' Lisa said, patting Declan on the arm. 'I hope you feel better soon.'

Skip was standing behind her, his eyes glued to the floor. 'Yes, Declan,' he mumbled. 'Get well soon.'

'Thank you,' he replied. 'And I'll get the script to you tomorrow, Skip. You can see what you think.'

'Thanks.'

'I'm sorry?'

'I said "thank you".' Skip raised his voice. 'Thank you for *everything* you've done for me.' His eyes met Declan's then and Declan knew that Skip now understood what had gone on in that drawing room.

'Well,' Declan shrugged. 'To tell you the truth I suspect you're going to need all the help you can get.'

'I *told* you not to go ahead with the *Plots in a Box* scheme.' Lisa stepped back and then put her arm around Skip's waist. 'I knew it would be too hard to do in this amount of time.'

'Doesn't it depend on what he wants to do, Lisa?' Alison asked.

Enough of this, Declan thought. It's not fair on Lisa to have all these conversations which are going right over her head.

'I *must* go now,' he said with force. 'Come on, Al. You have to get me home.'

'Bye, you two.' Lisa waved at them, her arm still locked around Skip. 'Call me tomorrow and tell me how you are, Declan,' she added. 'Otherwise I'll worry about you.'

Not as much as I'm going to be worrying about you, Declan said to himself.

'Wait – can you just wait until I get that phone?' Lisa asked. 'I want to say goodbye to Alison too.'

'I don't think – '

'I'll be right back,' Lisa called over her shoulder. 'Don't go.'

Alison and Declan and Skip stood soundlessly in the hallway. Skip shifted from foot to foot, Alison kept brushing her hair back behind her ears. Declan put his hands in his pockets. He had a fleeting urge to whistle.

'Oh my gosh, that's fabulous! Hold on, I've *got* to tell the others. Don't hang up – I'll be back!' They all started when they heard Lisa shriek these words. Within seconds she was back by Skip's side, panting with evident excitement. 'That was Toby Goodyear. He called to tell us they're getting married – he and Christina. He wanted us to be the first ones to know – isn't that lovely? He said he knew how much I appreciate romance and he wanted to apologize for the scene before, and to let us know it had a happy ending. Isn't that fantastic? I told him to hang on while I told you all. I better get back to the phone now. Goodbye Alison, sweetheart.' Lisa kissed Alison on the cheek. 'And make sure to call me tomorrow, Declan.' She jumped up, fists in the air.

'This is so exciting, isn't it?'

'It certainly is,' Declan replied dully. 'Come on, Al. Or the coach will turn into a pumpkin.'

'So,' he said, after they'd both got into the car. 'Do you want to tell me all about Skip now?'

'Declan,' Alison rested her head against the steering wheel. 'I'm sorry.'

'Listen, Al. You don't have to tell me the details, obviously. But I'd like to know something. I *need* to know something. Are you in love with him?'

'Yes.' She banged her head against the wheel. 'How fucking stupid can I be? I'm sorry,' she glanced at him. 'I should be thinking about what I've done to you, not how I feel myself. Thank you for rescuing me back there. I couldn't control myself. Do you hate me?'

'No.' Declan sighed and put his hand on her shoulder. 'I should, I suppose. Male pride and all that. But . . .'

'But?'

Declan was silent. He could feel Alison's eyes boring into him, but he couldn't bring himself to speak. He could barely bring himself to breathe. Christina and Toby. Within one hour he'd found out his lover had cheated on him and the woman he wanted to be his lover had become engaged.

What else is going to happen tonight? he thought. Is there any possible way it could get worse?

'But? But you don't love me either, do you?' She lifted her head; a startled expression suffused her face. 'Bloody hell. You love Christina, don't you? Jesus Christ. That's why you look as though you've just been told you have a month to live. Not because of me and Skip, but because of Toby and Christina. You *have* been sleeping with her, haven't you?'

'No, Al. I haven't.'

'You wanker. I can't believe this. You are such a fucking wanker!'

'Al – hold on here. I *haven't* been unfaithful to you – *you've* been unfaithful to me. Don't try to turn this around.'

'I should have known it. Everyone does this to me. That's what I'm here on this earth for, you know. To be walked all over, to be humiliated.'

'Alison!' Declan barked. 'Stop this. I have not slept with another woman. Got that?'

'Honestly?'

'Honestly,' Declan sighed. 'And can you please cast your mind back two minutes ago to the point where you told me you are in love with Skip? Can we possibly discuss that for a moment?'

'Oh God, I'm such an arsehole.' Alison banged her head again.

Declan looked at her with wonder. Who was this woman? No one he'd ever seen before, that was for certain.

'Does Skip love you?'

'Oh fuck. I don't know. Oh fuck. Oh shit.'

'Al – get out of the car. And come and sit in the passenger seat. I'll drive.'

'I don't know what to do. I'm such a mess.'

She began to sob. Tears gushed out of her eyes as if they were pumping out of a fire hydrant. Why, in the movies, does women's mascara always run when they cry? Declan found himself wondering. Alison's mascara doesn't run. No one's mascara runs any more. It's all waterproof these days, isn't it? But what the hell am I doing thinking about mascara when Alison is dissolving in front of me?

He opened his door, walked over to the driver's side, took Alison by the shoulders, lifted her out, walked with her to the passenger side and deposited her in the seat he'd just vacated. When he went back to the driver's side, he sat down and started up the engine immediately.

'Let's forget about talking now,' he said. 'We'll talk when we get back home, OK?'

'OK,' she sobbed.

What is it about Skip Thomas? Declan asked himself. How can he have had such a huge effect on her over the course of, what – it can't have been more than two nights, anyway. What does he have that I don't? Mr Perfecto. Is he some kind of Gladiator in bed? If I try, if I set my mind to it, can I win her back? Do I want to?

Only to prove that I can.

How fair is that?

Why should I care about being fair?

What would happen if I *did* get her back, though? I might save her from the clutches of a married man, but I wouldn't be doing her or myself any favours – not when I feel the way I do about Christina.

So what is it about Toby Goodyear? Mr 'I'm the World's Greatest Hamlet'? Is he a Gladiator in bed, too? If I try, if I set my mind to it, can I win Christina's heart? Steal her away from Toby the way Skip seems to have stolen Alison away from me?

Jesus. Declan shook his head. I haven't learned anything from my father, have I? Women aren't men's possessions. You can't steal them. They make choices. Everyone, male and female, makes choices. Alison has chosen to fall in love with someone else and Christina has chosen to marry someone else. There's not anything I can do about either one of them. But I have a responsibility to Alison, anyway. I don't want to see her hurt. Not by Skip Thomas, not by anyone.

As soon as they got back to Henning Street, Alison headed straight for the kitchen, opened a bottle of white wine and poured herself a drink.

'Do you want one?' She waved the bottle at him.

'Yes,' he replied. 'Sit down, Al. You look as though you're about to drop.'

'I don't want to sit down.'

'I think you should.'

'All right.' She pulled out a chair. 'Are you going to lecture me and tell me what a slag I am?'

'No.'

'Are you going to boot me out?'

'Alison – this is your house, too.'

'You say you haven't slept with Christina, but you are in love with her, aren't you? Otherwise you'd be going batshit. I know you would. You're in love with her and she's marrying Toby. You poor sod.' She looked up at him and smiled wanly. 'Maybe we should stay together, you know. That might be the answer to this mess. After all, we've bumped along together reasonably enough these two years.'

Declan looked at her bedraggled face and crumpled dress and thought of how well they had 'bumped' along for those years. They'd had fantastic sex, for one, and he found it painful, now that he was properly processing the information, to imagine her in the arms of Skip. He didn't like the picture, not at all. Perhaps he'd repressed all his jealous and possessive feelings in those first moments, focusing on his feelings for Christina because he'd been so wounded by Alison's betrayal. Was that true? It was so difficult to sort through what was true and what wasn't.

Yet one idea kept knocking on the door of his psyche, demanding attention. If he stayed with Alison he would be leading a reasonable life, but it wouldn't be an extraordinary one. They would work and play and make love and perhaps at some point in time have children. But he had grown up with an extraordinary couple and he wanted to live in that type of atmosphere now. His father and mother still held hands constantly. In his adolescence he'd been deeply embarrassed by this sign of intimacy. He'd thought it was gushy and sentimental and silly. Now he tried to imagine being fifty-something years old and holding hands with Alison. He tried very hard to imagine it, but the image refused to appear. All he could see was a clean and tidy house and a clean and tidy life. When he then thought of the future with Christina, he couldn't see himself ever letting go of her hand.

'I don't think staying together makes sense for either of us,' he finally said. 'I think we're thinking about it only because we're both naturally pissed off about the other one being with someone else. It's more about territorial imperative than love.'

'Oh?' Alison lifted her head and pushed her jaw forward. 'You don't love me any more? Why not? What's wrong with me? Don't you dare tell me you don't fancy me, Declan.'

'I didn't say that. I'm *trying* to be rational. I'm trying not to have a knee-jerk reaction which wouldn't help either of us.'

'I'm not some sad, pale, beanpole of a masseuse – is that it?'

'I don't see the point in being bitchy, Alison. You seem to keep forgetting that you're the one who has a new schoolmate, so to speak.'

'Well, you have a new playmate too, don't you?'

'Hardly.'

'Oh, please. You knelt at the woman's feet. You were practically slavering all over her. How do you think that made me feel?'

'I thought you were too busy staring at Skip to notice.'

'And you would have cared if I did notice?'

'Alison. I refuse to continue this conversation. We can be angry at each other, certainly. But talk like this will lead nowhere.'

'When exactly did you fall in love with her?'

'I can't pinpoint the moment,' Declan sighed.

'You don't want to talk about it, do you? You want me to talk about Skip, but you don't want to talk about the precious Christina.'

'This conversation is becoming surreal.'

'Oh, it's real enough.' Alison gulped her wine. Suddenly her shoulders sagged and she fell back against her chair. 'Do you think Lisa knows?'

'No. But you were doing a good job of enlightening her.'

'That would be the end of her silly book, wouldn't it? *I Saw You First, But You Cheated on Me First*. Maybe that's not true, though. Maybe she's out banging every bloke she meets.'

'I don't think that's the case.'

'No.' Alison shook her head. 'Neither do I. More's the pity.'

'So what happens next, Al? How are you feeling about Skip now?'

'You sound like Owen. Questions, questions. Have you ever noticed that? How he asks questions, but never talks about himself and his feelings. You're both the same, you know. You come on like you're different, you're not typical men, you're oh so sensitive. But you both keep yourselves to yourselves. I'm not allowed to ask you about Christina without you getting all wound up, but you're allowed to ask me about Skip. How the fuck do I know what happens next or how I feel? I feel numb. How's that? Does that answer your question?'

Could I have ever loved her properly? Declan asked himself. If we'd met at a different time in our lives, in different circumstances? With different knowledge of ourselves? Is love a series of exams?

Starting off with GCSEs, then on to A levels then university. Do you learn more each time around until you're qualified for your PhD? At what age do you finally know yourself and what you need and want and respond to in another human being?

'Perhaps you should get some sleep now. We're both done in.'

'This is the end, isn't it?' Alison mumbled. 'You and I. We're finished, aren't we?'

'We can be friends.'

'Oh, Christ. That's the reason it would never have worked in the end, you know. You're so much like your father and brother. So fucking reasonable. So grown up.'

'Alison.' Declan looked at her in blank astonishment. 'I can't count the number of times you've told me I'm not grown up enough and that the reason I'm not grown up is because my family is so childish.'

'You don't understand.' She swatted the air dismissively. 'You really don't have a clue who I am.'

Declan put his elbows on the table, covered his face with his hands and smothered the desire to laugh until he cried.

Chapter 10

I can hear you now. I can hear you saying, 'But Lisa, Freddy (to choose a name at random – don't get all upset, you Freddies out there!) isn't the same man I met all those years ago. Back then he was a great guy with a sense of humor and a knack for fun and then he turned into someone completely different. He's tired all the time. He's boring and irritable. He's gained weight. He's lost his joie de vivre. How can I go back to the beginning, when that person doesn't exist any more?'

Good question. The good questions are always the toughest to answer. All I can say to that is this: Does anyone really change? Aren't we all the same people we were even as children? Think back. Is there anything you really liked as a child that you don't like now? My bet is your answer would be 'no' – in fact, in my experience, the older you become, the more you realize how little you have actually changed.

Circumstances in life may have altered your partner's outlook and some of his characteristics, but unless he is on medication or is a drug-abuser, he hasn't changed fundamentally. What you saw at first is what you've still got, but you have to make allowances for the vicissitudes of life and how they have affected him. The truth is, he hasn't had a personality transplant any more than you have.

You are the life force which can battle against the wear and tear of survival in this tough world.

Freddy has changed? Well, fight to get him back! Don't be a defeatist! Chances are he's worried about work or what kind of contribution he has made to life. He's struggling with the demons of unfulfilled dreams. Show him that your relationship is the dream that can come true!

You and he are tilting against those windmills together.

Remember: you're on the same team! And you can win!

I Saw You First, *Chapter Thirteen, p. 224*

'This is the bit I hate – when you stop. Do you think you could go on for at least another hour? Preferably ten?'

'I wish I could,' Christina smiled.

'It's so calm here, and so peaceful. I'm glad you don't have that music playing – the sound of waves on the beach and seagulls screeching. And it smells so wonderful. Tell me again which oils you've used?'

'Rosemary, geranium and peppermint. The combination is good for your low blood pressure. Take a few minutes to relax and get dressed. I'll see you out at the front.'

Christina left Mrs Halpen alone in the treatment room and waited by Reception until she came out and paid.

'Thank you, Christina. I'll see you next Tuesday.'

'See you then,' Christina waved. She walked back into the room and tidied it up for the next client. Mrs Halpen was one of the ones who didn't speak until the end of the session, while others chatted along throughout. It was hard to guess from looking at them which ones were the talkers and which weren't. Clients almost always made it clear at the outset of the hour, however. Either they immediately began confiding about their lives or else they lay perfectly still and silent. Rarely did a person who started off silent turn talkative halfway through.

The talkers treated her like a shrink or a priest. They told her intimate details of their lives and sometimes even asked for her advice. Christina would always sidestep the temptation to weigh in with her opinion, though. That could create terrible problems later on, and was definitely not part of her job description. She was there to calm, to soothe, to treat and to listen. If she began to tell them what to do, they'd end up resenting her for interfering. Very few people, in her experience, actually wanted honest advice when they asked for it.

The other feature which distinguished clients from each other was their reaction to the potential healing properties of the oils. Every person who came to see her had to fill in a short medical history. That was how, for example, Christina knew Mrs Halpen had low blood pressure. Some people filled in the form but had no interest in the medical side of the aromatherapy experience. All they wanted was a relaxing massage. Others became immediately intrigued and would spend a long time discussing various ailments and the effects the oils could have on them.

Christina always laughed when she recalled one woman who had walked in and said, straight off the bat: 'I'll fill this questionnare out if I have to, but I don't believe in any of this rubbish. Just give me a massage.' That was perfectly fine and Christina didn't mind – she did as requested. The next time the woman came in, however, she looked like death warmed over. 'Listen,' she moaned, 'I know I said before that I didn't believe in this stuff, but I've got a hangover from hell. Is there anything you can do to help?'

Christina soaked a flannel in rosewood and placed it over her temples before starting the massage. When she'd finished the hour, she prepared a mixture of fennel, juniper and rosemary for the hangover victim to take home and put in her bath. She couldn't remember ever having a more grateful client.

'Your next appointment is here,' the receptionist said over the intercom system. 'Should I send him in?'

'Yes, please,' she answered.

Not many men came in, but they were always polite and reasonable when they did. She'd never had any problems; in fact the male masseurs she knew had a lot more trouble with female clients making overtures to them than any female masseuses or aromatherapists of her acquaintance had with men.

'Hello, there,' Declan said as he walked in the door. 'Nice place you've got here.'

'Declan.' Christina stepped back. 'What are you doing here?'

'I wanted to congratulate you on your engagement,' he remarked, and proceeded to sit on the end of the treatment table. 'Lisa told us last night.'

'And you booked an appointment?'

'Yes. It's lunchtime. I had some spare time and thought I'd come here and deliver my congratulations in person.'

'But you'll have to pay for it, I'm afraid. How embarrassing.'

'Do you run to coffee in this health club? Or is that against the principles?'

'I'll get you some,' she said, relieved to have a moment on her own to digest his sudden appearance. She had thought, last night, that she would contrive somehow never to see him again. The weekend at his parents' had been special and she'd had very special feelings for him, but they weren't part of her future with Toby. He and Toby had already clashed last night at the Thomases' and Christina didn't believe they'd turn around and become friends, whatever happened with *Plots in a Box*. How would she feel if Toby had a special woman in his life – one who wasn't a friend of hers? Even if it was perfectly innocent, Christina knew it would be threatening – and if *she* wouldn't be easy with the idea, how could she expect Toby to be? It wasn't logical or fair. She knew, moreover, how jealous Alison could be. So continuing this sibling-like relationship with Declan could threaten Alison as well. However much she had enjoyed Declan's company, she understood that she had to give it up. Still ... as she had struggled to get to sleep, she'd kept remembering those moments when he'd lain at the end of her bed in the Amersham cottage, talking softly in the dark. Perhaps she could recreate that with Toby, she thought, that warmth and the easy intimacy. Now that they were getting married, they *should* be able to, albeit in a different way.

After she'd rustled up two cups of coffee from the staffroom, she went back to Declan, determined to be friendly yet maintain a distance.

'It's like a womb in here,' he said, taking a mug from her hand. 'Thank you. Why is there only that one tiny window? Don't you get claustrophobic?'

'It's supposed to be like a womb. Some of my clients actually fall asleep when I'm treating them. Too much light would spoil the effect.'

'I see,' he nodded. He was wearing a dark blue suit, white shirt and a tie with a pattern of light blue stars. 'So. Congratulations.'

'Thank you.' We're both being so polite, she thought. I suppose that's just as well. But I have a ridiculous urge to reach out and tickle him.

'When's the date?'

'The what?'

'When are you getting married?'

'Oh, I'm not sure exactly. Sometime in the autumn, I should imagine. I think that's what Toby said.'

'You *think*?' Declan laughed. 'Isn't something like the date of your wedding fairly crucial?'

Christina blushed. 'It's September the fifteenth, actually. I don't know why I forgot. Of course it's crucial.'

'You never acted in a school play, did you, Christina?'

'I was a shepherd once in a nativity play,' she said. She had sat down in the wicker chair in the corner of the room and was looking up at him on the massage table. What was he on about? Why had he asked that question?

'You're a rotten liar,' he told her. 'That's why I can't imagine you ever acting. Your face is a dead giveaway. The way you smiled when you said, "September the fifteenth". You have no idea what the date is, do you?'

'I have no idea why you're asking me these questions,' she bridled.

'It's a simple enough question, isn't it? Other people will ask, you know. You should get used to it.'

'Toby and I will talk about it today. We'll set a firm date today. Is that all right with you?'

'It has nothing to do with me. I only asked. Are you going to have a church wedding or go the register office route?'

'We didn't discuss any of the details, Declan. Toby proposed: I accepted. We didn't go into the mechanics of it all or make a guest-list or decide what presents we want from guests or plan the reception.'

'Hey – ' Declan held up his hands. 'Why are you so stressed out?'

'Because I don't like you coming in here and harassing me,' Christina retorted. She refused to look at him and concentrated instead on her cup of coffee. How could she have thought they had a special relationship? He didn't understand anything, not anything at all.

'I didn't mean to harass you, Christina. I'm sorry if I have.' Declan put out his left hand and began to smooth the sea-green towel stretched over the massage table. 'Honestly.'

For a moment they sat in silence, and Christina wondered what she could say next. She'd made a fool of herself, reacting so strongly to his questions, and she knew it. Although she wished he'd leave, she also wanted to part with him on good terms, not in this uncomfortable atmosphere.

'I used to play a lot of football when I was a child,' he suddenly announced in a thoughtful voice.

'Really?' She perked up. This was a subject she could discuss – a safe subject. It seemed a strange one to bring up at this moment, but she was so glad the topic of conversation had shifted away from her and Toby, she didn't take the time to ponder over why he'd introduced it.

'Mmm.' He continued to smooth the towel. 'I was a midfielder.

Not bad, actually. I used to dream about playing professionally, but I suppose most boys do.'

'Some girls do, too.'

'I'm sure,' he smiled. 'I can still remember the worst feeling in the world when you're playing football.'

'What's that? Scoring an own goal?'

'No, I never did that, thank God. No – it's when I would pass to a forward.'

Declan stopped. Christina looked at him, bewildered.

'And?' she prompted.

'And you play with people over a long period of time and you think you know how they move. You pass the ball, thinking your teammate will know what you're doing, will run to the right place at the right moment in order to reach the pass in perfect time. But he doesn't run where he's supposed to, he hasn't read what you're planning, and he doesn't anticipate what you have mapped out in your mind, the way the play is supposed to develop. Then it looks as if you've kicked the ball into nothingness. You look like a complete fool. The spectators think you're a fool. Your other teammates stare at you – they think you've given it away. You can't turn around and say: "He was *supposed* to be there, it was a *perfect* pass. It's not my fault he mucked it up." And then you start to worry that it will happen again, so you don't make the perfect passes any more. You play it safe.'

Declan shook his head and jumped off the table. 'Well, I should be going now,' he said. 'Back to work.'

'But you haven't touched your coffee.'

'I haven't sipped it either,' he grinned. 'Goodbye, Christina.' He came over to her chair, bent down and kissed her on the cheek. 'Maybe we'll meet again sometime. You still owe me a visit to your family's house, remember?'

He was gone before she could say yes or no, or anything at all. He was out the door and out of her life for ever, as far as she knew. Which was exactly what she'd planned to have happen, but now that it seemed to be a fact, it didn't feel right at all.

What was that football story all about? And why had he come here to visit, instead of simply phoning her? It was so frustrating – his sudden arrival and even more sudden departure. She wanted him to come back so she could ask him some questions.

Such as? Such as how he was getting along with Alison, for example. But that would be intrusive and far too personal. No – he was gone and she was doubtless the better for it.

Christina found herself wishing that she and Toby had never gone to that first dinner at Skip and Lisa's house. If they hadn't gone they wouldn't have discussed *Plots in a Box*, and if they hadn't discussed *Plots in a Box*, they never would have gone to Amersham – and if they'd never gone to Amersham, she would never have become so friendly with Declan. And if she hadn't become so friendly with Declan, she wouldn't know that he could read her face and tell when she was lying, and if . . . Christina stopped her thoughts from going further down the 'and if' line, the cadence of which made her try, but fail to remember a child's nursery rhyme with a similar sentence structure. After a moment, she gave up the attempt to recollect it. The nursery rhyme didn't matter. What was important was the fact that they'd met the Thomases in the first place. All the events leading from that meeting had culminated in Toby's proposal.

And yet she still wished that dinner had never happened.

Declan had been back in his office for an hour when Lisa Thomas walked in.

Does she know? was his first jolting thought but it evaporated rapidly. She didn't have the look of a betrayed woman, not in the least. She was dressed in a yellow skirt, a bright blue silk blouse and was wearing a yellow Alice band in her hair. She could be four years old, he thought. On her first day at school or at a little playmate's birthday party.

'Hello Lisa,' he said, standing up. She shooed him down and immediately sat in the chair in front of his desk.

'How are you feeling?' she asked solicitously. It took Declan a second to remember his supposed migraine.

'Oh,' he replied, putting his hand to the back of his neck. 'Much better, thank you.'

'Good. That's wonderful. I could lecture you about not calling me to tell me that, but I won't. I came in here to see Harriet and then I thought I'd pop in to talk to you about something important. I hope I'm not interrupting your work?'

Does she know? he wondered again. If she does, she's being very offhand about it.

'Of course not. I always have time for you, Lisa.' That phrase dripped with false bonhomie, but he actually meant it. Funnily enough, he liked Lisa Thomas. Even more funnily, he liked Skip Thomas. What was the matter with him? How can you like a man who sleeps with your lover when you're away? Was there some male mechanism missing in his psyche?

No – the image of Christina with Toby Goodyear was enough to reassure him that he possessed the normal feelings of rampant desire and jealousy. He had them for an inappropriate person, that was all.

'I was thinking about my next book, what comes after *I Saw You First*,' Lisa began.

'*I Saw You Second*, perhaps?'

'No. My editor in New York suggested that as a title, but—'

'Not seriously?'

'Yes.' Lisa looked startled. 'Of course seriously. We discussed it for a while, but decided it wasn't a good idea. Anywho, I thought I'd run a couple of ideas by you. I trust your judgment, Declan. You're an intelligent man and I like intelligence. What about: *What Comes Next?*'

Declan waited, but when Lisa didn't continue he said: 'I don't know. What comes next is up to you, isn't it? You said you had a few ideas.'

'I mean as a title. *What Comes Next* as a title.'

'Well. . .' Declan drummed his fingers on his desk. 'That sounds fine. What *does* come next?'

'What comes next is how people deal with relationships and careers at the same time. How they juggle them.'

'Doesn't *I Saw You First* cover that ground?'

'Not really. Not in depth. I mean, I said that a career shouldn't threaten a relationship, but then I don't think I explored fully how important it is not to let a relationship threaten a career.'

'Really?' Declan couldn't dampen the surprise in his voice. 'Are you saying careers should come *before* relationships?'

'I'm saying people shouldn't be envious of their partners' careers, that's all. They shouldn't try to sabotage them.'

'Sabotage?'

'Yes. Come off it, Declan – you know what I mean. Someone's working hard, they're doing their best and then their partner can't stand their success and tries to sabotage it.'

'Is that a common phenomenon?'

'Absolutely.'

'Oh. In my case, Alison actually tried to get me to be more serious about my career.'

'That's unusual. To be honest, Declan – and I hope I'm not offending you by saying this – Alison is a teeny bit . . .' Lisa tapped her forefinger on the side of her head. 'I don't mean crazy. A little bit of a weirdball, that's all. Of course that can be very charming, but the way she was talking last night wasn't making much sense. When you explained it, I began to understand, but she wasn't exactly – what's the word? Articulate – that's it.' Lisa leaned forward then. 'Wait a sec – are you saying you're *not* serious about your career?'

'No. I'm only saying I think she's more ambitious than I am.'

'There is nothing wrong with a woman being ambitious.'

Christ, Declan thought. Now Lisa is defending Alison to me. Let's have an irony party. Plenty of people to invite to *that* one.

'Women try to make men stay home more and men try to

make women have babies,' Lisa continued. 'Partners can stifle each other.'

'Lisa.' Declan cocked his head to the right side. 'Let me get this straight. You were the one who told Skip he should leave his job, and now you're saying you were stifling him?'

'No, no, no! Skip wasn't happy – that's the point. I'm talking about people who *are* happy in their jobs.'

'Are there many of those around?'

Lisa straightened her shoulders. 'You obviously don't get it, Declan. You don't understand what I'm talking about. All right, I can accept that. It was just an idea; I have others. How about this. How about *Women Are Necessary*? How does that sound?'

'Fantastic,' Declan replied with as much enthusiasm as he could call up. There was no point in having this discussion, he knew now, because he had little idea of what constituted a 'good' self-help book. He could sell it when it was written, yes, but he couldn't fathom what elements made one better than another. Perhaps *Women Are Necessary* would be a raging successs, and could be followed up by *Men Aren't Necessary*. Come to think of it, he reckoned *that* title would sell in the millions.

'I haven't worked that one out as much as I have *What Comes Next*, but if you think that's a good title, I can explore it further.'

'I think it's a wonderful title, Lisa. But I don't think I'm the one you should be asking. I'd run it by your editor in New York if I were you. It's the American market you're aiming for first and foremost, as you know.'

'Well,' Lisa clapped her hands and stood up. 'It's been great talking to you, Declan. You've helped enormously.'

'Really?'

'Of course.' She came over to his side of the desk and gave him a big kiss on the cheek. 'You're adorable, you know that? Alison is one lucky, lucky girl. Now you get on back to that work of yours. And I'll get on back to mine. Bye bye.' She rushed off in the direction of the publicity office and Declan was left feeling as if the breath had been knocked out of him.

She was a whirlwind, Lisa. What he had to keep reminding himself of was the fact that she was a very successful whirlwind. The amount of energy she had was astonishing. Harriet, the woman who was accompanying her on her publicity schedule, had said to him the day before that Lisa was running her ragged. 'She never stops, Declan. And she's always talking. I've never dealt with an author like her. Usually they get tired after so many interviews, but Lisa thrives on it all. She's nice, though. Sometimes she says the most bizarre things, but she's nice.'

Declan tried to imagine Lisa in Christina's womblike treatment room, having an aromatherapy massage, but all he could picture was her squirming on the table, desperate to get back up and going. What would she do if she found out about Skip and Alison? he wondered. Whatever her reaction, he didn't think it would be calm.

What was *he* going to do about Skip and Alison? That was another question he couldn't give a precise answer to, and it was a question which preoccupied his thoughts. At moments he wished Skip would somehow manage to take Alison off his hands – spirit her off to New York at the same time as buying Alison out of her share of their house. He didn't want to have to sell the house on Henning Street, if he could avoid it, nor did he wish to force Alison to move when she had nowhere to move to. If she wanted, he supposed, she could use the house as a bolthole for a while, until she had decided what exactly she wished to do with her life. They could live as fellow lodgers. But that wasn't particularly satisfactory. Two former lovers co-habiting was not a thrilling prospect. It might have been reasonable if they had been friends as well as lovers, but the more Declan thought of it, the more he understood that wasn't the case. He admired Alison in many ways, even now, despite her affair with Skip, but he didn't see her as a friend, nor, he imagined, did she view him as one.

In fact, when it came down to it, his life was a mess. On a wild whim, he'd visited Christina and although he'd had some satisfaction knowing she and Toby hadn't set a date yet and seeing how discomfited she'd been by his questions about the wedding, he'd also made a bollocks of the whole thing by spouting on about football and then running off. He couldn't bring himself to say: 'Don't marry him, come and be with me' so he'd talked about sport, for chrissakes – as though she'd understand or even care about what he was trying to say. What *had* he been trying to say? That there was someone out there, on your team, who would know instinctively how you functioned and where to be for the perfect pass, and vice versa. That love, when it was right, was like a good combination of footballers. What a ridiculous way to put it. If that were really the case, Dennis Bergkamp and Ian Wright should head for the nearest church.

Christina must have thought he was bonkers.

Declan suddenly noticed Susan standing at the entrance to his office.

'I'm going to get some tea. Would you like a cup?' she asked.

'Susan. Come and sit down. I'll make the tea,' he smiled. 'I need to know what's going on in here these days. I've been out of circulation too long.'

'Sorry?' She tilted her head.

He got up, went over to her, took her by the arm and led her to the chair.

'I'm taking a break,' he stated. 'Take one with me. How would you like your tea?'

When he arrived back with the drinks, Susan looked up at him, her eyes narrowed.

'Can I ask you something personal?'

'Yes,' he nodded.

'Are you back, Declan?'

'Yes,' he grinned. 'I'm back.'

'That's nice.' She took a sip from her mug. 'You've been away for ages. We missed you.'

He didn't have any idea what her number was. During their time together, she'd told him what she did, and explained that she was freelance, often working for the same company but she never actually named it. He didn't know anyone to call to find out who produced pop videos and had already searched in vain through the *Yellow Pages*.

Think logically, he told himself. You're a graduate of the Harvard Business School. You should be able to figure this one out.

After five minutes, he thought he might have found the solution. Call Warner Brothers in the States, find out the name of a big British record company, call it, ask someone there which were the most well-known production companies for videos, call around them and track her down that way.

The whole process took, as it turned out, an hour. Skip listened to countless bits of music as he hung on to be transferred to various people, explained patiently at least two dozen times what he was looking for, and finally, with a profound sense of satisfaction at being a brilliant Sherlock Holmes, hit upon the person who was able to give him Alison's mobile number.

'Hi there,' he said when she answered. 'It's Skip.'

'Oh,' was her less than heartening reply.

'I thought maybe we could see each other again. Talk.'

'About what?'

'About the weather – come on, Alison. Talk about us.'

'Who is us? You and Lisa?'

'No. Look, if you don't want to see me, just say so.'

'Does Lisa know?'

'No.'

'Are you going to tell her?'

'Alison, please. Can we meet first? Can we talk?'

'I suppose so.'

'Good.' Skip sighed. 'What happened with Declan? *He* knows, doesn't he?'

'Yes, and he says he'll kill you if he sees you again.'

Oh shit, Skip said to himself. Oh fuck. What am I doing here? Getting myself shot in the street? If I wanted to do that, I could have stayed in New York and walked around the Bowery at three a.m. wearing a Rolex. I can't wimp out now, though. I have to see her.

'Would you like to meet at Motcombe's again?' he asked. 'At, say, six o'clock?'

'Fine,' Alison said curtly. 'I'll see you there.'

After she'd hung up, Skip sat down and attempted to think through exactly what he was doing. Was he seeing Alison in order to tell her it *had* been only a one-night stand, or that it hadn't? He had no idea, as his moods swung wildly on the subject. Seeing her the night before had been excruciating; he had wanted to jump on top of her but he'd also wanted to get her out of the house and out of his life. The sheer stupidity of his reactions had shocked him: he'd found himself wishing that Lisa hadn't worn the pink blouse, and blaming her for doing so. If she hadn't worn the pink blouse, he would have been able to forget Alison and get back to normal. He wouldn't have responded to Alison's talk about 'schoolfriends'; he would have been perfectly polite, yes, but he wouldn't have allowed himself to be drawn in by her again. It was all Lisa's fault. She knew he hated pink – why had she worn it on that night? Wasn't that tantamount to giving him licence to see Alison again?

And her naivety. Declan had picked up on what was going on. Why hadn't Lisa? Was she that trusting, or did she think no other woman could possibly be attracted to him? Was she so self-absorbed she wouldn't have noticed if he and Alison had had sex on the rug in front of her?

Yeah right, Skip, he said to himself. Why don't you think of some more crazy reasons to justify what you're doing here?

When the doorbell rang, Skip got up to answer it, still absorbed in his thoughts of Alison. A delivery man stood on the step with a package, which he duly signed for and brought back inside. As soon as he noticed the sender's name, he began to panic. It was from Declan Lewis, this package. It was addressed to him and it was from Declan. What the hell was inside? A letter bomb?

Skip placed it gingerly on the kitchen table and stared at it, listening for the sound of ticking.

Declan is an Irish name, isn't it? he thought as he paced. He might have Irish friends who know about these kinds of devices. Alison just told me he wants to kill me. What better way? Kill me or mutilate me. And everyone would think it was an IRA bomb delivered to the wrong address. The perfect crime.

Sure. The perfect crime – except the delivery man would know who sent it. And the Irish aren't blowing Brits up any more, are they? Are they? Is there some Website I can find on my laptop which will tell me the current state of play in Irish politics?

Skip finally sat down and slowly pulled the package toward him. Very carefully, he laid his ear against it. No sounds were emanating from it. He drew his head away and began to poke at it delicately with his fingers.

I'm like a kid at Christmas trying to figure out what the present is, he said to himself. Except this time I'm trying to figure out if the present is going to blow up in my face. And what if it does, anyway? It's not as if my life isn't a complete wreck at the moment. I could be a hero; I could be front-page news. Lisa could write a book and call it: *I Saw Him Last*.

Abandoning all caution, Skip tore into the package and found a sheaf of paper, the first page of which had *Plots in a Box* typed neatly in the centre. He wasn't sure whether he was more relieved or disappointed. He stood up, made himself a cup of coffee and then sat back down again to read.

The camera focuses on Toby Goodyear, sitting at a desk. In the background are shelves of hardcover books, face-out, so the viewer can see titles such as War and Peace, The Odyssey of Homer, Pride and Prejudice. *Toby gestures to the books behind him:*

'Does the sight of all these great books make you nervous?' he says. 'Do you think to yourself: "Hey, I haven't read any of these. What's wrong with me? Am I missing out? I'll go to the library right now and start reading." Or do you think: "I don't

have time for all that reading. I'll never have time. I'm just an ordinary person. The only people who read books like this are those intellectual types who think they're better than everyone else. I remember them from school. They were jerks. I don't need to waste my time reading just so I can be like them."

Let me introduce myself. My name is Toby Goodyear and I'm here to tell you – (Toby leans in to the camera) – that I hated school, too. And I went to one of the best schools in England. I had the chance to be one of those academic people who know everything, but I didn't take it. Why not? Because I hated those kids who read all the time and raised their hands in class and studied their socks off. I said to myself: Who needs it? Who needs to read books all these dead people have written? What's in it for me? I've got more important things to do – like LIVE!

But you know something? (Toby puts his chin in his hand and looks wistful.) Sometimes I wonder. I wonder whether I would have been a more interesting person if I knew what these books were all about. I like to hear a good story when I'm out with my friends, and I envy those people who can spin a good yarn. I'd like to be able to impress others too, once in a while. What if I could say: "Listen, you're talking about date rape. That reminds me of the novel A Passage to India, where an uptight Englishwoman goes to visit some caves in India and you don't know whether she was raped there or whether it was all in her imagination." Now that might make people sit up and take notice.

Perhaps you're like me and you didn't make the most of your education. Or maybe you didn't get to have a great education. Maybe you've had no education at all. Whatever the scenario of your life, you might, like me, be feeling a little less intelligent than other people. You might be saying to yourself: "These people think they're so clever – I can be just as clever as them if I put my mind to it." (Toby pauses, puts both elbows on the desk, leans forward.)

But I don't have the time.

I have a job, I have the kids to look after, I have a demanding, stressful life. How can I go off into a corner and read a pile of books? I'm not some university professor. That's not what I'm about. I can't kid myself. I'm ordinary. Forget these – (he gestures again to the books behind him) *– I don't need to know.*

Well, I want to tell you you don't have to forget these (he gestures yet again). AND YOU DON'T HAVE TO READ THEM EITHER. *All you have to do is listen to a thirty-minute tape – a tape which will sum up all the plots of these books.* (He reaches underneath the desk and brings out a *Plots in a Box* cassette). *Listen to this tape for half an hour and you'll know everything you need to know. You'll dazzle your friends and family, you'll dazzle yourself with your grasp of great literature. After listening to this tape, you too could be a university professor if you wanted to be.*

I can hear you saying: "But what do these books have to do with my life? You talk about some woman in some caves in India – that has nothing to do with me. I've never been out of the country and I don't have conversations about date rape, either. I'm a trucker. Or I'm a housewife. These books have no relevance to me.

Do you want to know what I say to that? (Toby stands up, goes to the front of the desk and sits down on top of it.) *I say, "All right, you're a trucker. All your friends are truckers. You spend a lot of time on the road, don't you? You're out there on the road in your truck and you've left your wife behind, haven't you? She's sitting at home while you're away working and you can't help but wonder sometimes: 'What's she up to when I'm away?' What do these woman do when their husbands have left town?*

I say to you – just tune out of that country and western music channel for a little while and pop in the cassette of Plots in a Box. *Listen to the story of The Odyssey. There's this guy Odysseus, and he's gone off to war and he is taking a long, long time coming home. His wife, Penelope, is waiting for him. All sorts of men are after her, trying to convince her her husband is history and probably dead and she should take up with a new man. Does she fall for someone else? Does she take advantage of the fact that her husband is away? No, sir. She stays true and loyal and she waits for him.*

Isn't that just what you want to hear? It's one of the oldest stories ever written and it will warm your heart as you drive down those long open roads and think of the woman back home.

What if you're a housewife? What, you ask, does Plots in a Box have to do with your life? Let me ask you this. Don't you know some woman who drives you crazy because she is one of those who is dissatisfied with her marriage and who flirts with other men and is generally a no-good tramp with ideas above her station? Well, listen to Plots in a Box and you'll hear the story of Madame Bovary, and next time you run into this woman at the supermarket, you can just casually tell her the plot of this wonderful book and see how her face falls when she hears what happens to Emma Bovary in the end . . .

These great books tell us all about ourselves and our lives. Of course we don't have time to read them – maybe we can't read anyway. It doesn't matter. We can listen and improve ourselves and our minds and our hearts and our lives. After thirty minutes, you can be a different person, who has access to the wisdom of the world.

And you can enrich your life even more. Along with the cassette, you'll receive – at no extra cost – a fabulous set of dinnerware—

Skip stopped at that point. Did it work? Yes, on balance, he thought, it did. Having Toby say that he hadn't read the books himself was a good touch; people would like the fact that this Englishman with the upper class accent was, after all, one of them – an ordinary man with no pretensions to scholarship. They wouldn't have wanted him to lecture or talk down to them, they'd want to be on the same level, and he and Declan had achieved that nicely. He wasn't completely sure about the straight-on talk to truck drivers and housewives; it did have a certain appeal but truck drivers weren't a target group for infomercials. Housewives were, though, and if Toby and Declan could do more along the housewives line, it would have more relevance for their audience.

They had made a big effort, obviously, to sound American. The phrasing and some of the words they used were American, not English and Skip wondered whether that was the right tack to take. Most probably it was, given the fact that people watching this infomercial could get turned off immediately if they didn't understand some of the English vocabulary or saw the whole thing as 'foreign'. The 'date rape' point was questionable, though. Skip would have to talk to Declan about that.

He caught himself, mid-thought. How could he talk to Declan when Declan wanted to murder him? No. he'd have to deal with Toby and keep out of Declan's way. It was a shame, in a way. He liked Declan. The guy had even saved his ass the night before by getting Alison out of the house. During a sleepless night, he had decided Declan was one of those Brits who didn't really have strong feelings and wasn't going to go crazy about Alison and his affair, but evidently that wasn't the case.

What *was* he going to say to Alison this evening? He felt as if he were in one of his recurring nightmares – the one where he was back at Harvard, sitting down to take an exam, looking at the questions and having no idea what any of the answers were. He was unprepared and failure loomed large.

Think of it as a business deal, he told himself. What were the available options?

He could, he supposed, try to continue seeing Alison while he and Lisa remained in England, then end it all when they returned to Connecticut – but that was shabby behaviour, wasn't it? He could end it now. Or he could . . . No, he couldn't. No matter how much he might think he wanted to, he couldn't. There were no other options available. He *had* to end it now.

Skip sighed. He shrugged. He scratched his head.

'Skipper.' His mother's voice invaded his brain. 'Go out and buy me some cigarettes.'

'I can't. I'm not old enough to buy cigarettes.'

'Oh, come off it. You can do anything you want to if you want to enough. Anyone can.'

Had she been right? In her alcoholic haze had she said something which was actually true about human nature?

The odds were against it.

Toby put the phone down and jumped. He then jumped again. When he landed, he told himself to calm down and went in search of his cigarettes, which he found, finally, in the sitting room.

His luck had turned. His life had changed. One telephone call and the future suddenly looked fantastic.

Perhaps he wouldn't get the part. That was always possible. He shouldn't get too excited, not until he had the part for certain. But the whole thing was incredible – simply unbelievable.

'She saw you in that *Hamlet*,' Nick, his agent, had explained. 'You know, the one you're always banging on about. At the time she wasn't in a position to give you work, but times have changed and she's one of the hottest casting agents in town. In fact, she's so hot, she's smoking. When this part came up, she thought of you straight off the bat. It's not Shakespeare, Toby. But it sounds promising.'

She'd seen his *Hamlet*. This wonderful, amazing, smoking woman had seen his *Hamlet*. How wrong he had been! For these two years he'd thought no one had noticed, that nothing would come of that performance, and now – not only had Owen and Jessica recognized his talent, but so had this incredible, fantastic woman. Where had she been in the audience? Why hadn't he spotted her? Or Owen? All he'd seen was a group of loutish kids.

'We're talking television – but not some walk-on in *Casualty* or *The Bill* – a lead role. In a series. The gist is that you're a housemaster in a boarding school – co-educational – and you have to cope with all the problems these rich upper-class kids have. You know – drugs, sex, the lot. They want someone young because they want the character to understand what's going on in these teenagers' minds and be sympathetic. But torn. Torn between being a friend and an authority figure. You might think the upper-class angle won't work any more, but you'd be surprised. People are more rooted in the old class system than New Labour thinks. Of course there will be some egg-headed swots too, so there'll be tension there as well, along the *Upstairs Downstairs* line. When I told her you were an old Harrovian she almost had an orgasm. I'd say now the part is yours, but you have to test for it, of course.'

'Of course,' Toby had replied. 'That's not a problem.'

It's mine, he thought. All mine. I know those housemasters. I had one once who would be a perfect model for this part. *It's mine!*

'So – the test is on Friday.'

'Fantastic.'

'I'll give you the details of where and when and I'll get back to Sally Richmond and tell her you're keen.'

'Tell her I'm in love with her. Tell her I want to marry her.'

'Right.' Nick laughed. 'It's looking good, Toby. Finally.'

Finally, Toby said to himself as he sat down and lit up. Fucking finally. Why is it that everything happens at once? I discover Owen, I propose to Christina, I get this part. I'm on a roll. *Finally.*

Toby recalled his embarrassment at lunch with Lucy the day before when she'd quizzed him about his career. He had tried to make it sound more successful than it had been, but was aware, as he looked at her lovely face, that he was failing. Her smile had faded as he spoke and her eyes had lost interest after he'd admitted he had no upcoming prospects. She had wanted to hear inside gossip about television and movie stars; in fact, it seemed, she knew more about the private lives of various actors and actresses than he did. He'd almost asked her if she worked for the *News of the World*, but had switched the topic of discussion to Christina instead.

'Ah, Chris,' Lucy had sighed. 'We worried about her as a teenager, Chloë and I.'

'Did she take a lot of drugs?'

'Toby!' Lucy laughed. 'Chris take drugs? I don't think so.'

'So what was it that you worried about?'

'The – you know.' Lucy grimaced. 'The height problem. She was so tall and so awkward around boys. She was so alone and she didn't seem quite normal.'

'Not normal?' Toby sat back.

'Not exactly. She was so solitary and quiet. She didn't enjoy anything very much and she never seemed to talk. But of course she had just lost her father – only a year before her mother married our father, so that must have been difficult. She never joined in, that's all. We couldn't understand, really, because Mum – her mother – is so much fun and so easy to be around; Chloë and I both loved her straight away. Anyway, everything was much easier with Chris after Richard came along.'

Richard, Toby had thought savagely. Richard, indeed.

'Tell me about Richard, Lucy,' he'd said. And she'd taken off.

Now that he had overcome his jealousy about this Richard character, he wished he had asked Lucy more about Christina's 'abnormality'. They'd come back to it for a short time at the end, and she'd told him a few stories of Chris' teenage life, but she hadn't told him enough. How strange had she been, exactly? Shouldn't he know if he was going to marry her? He'd proposed in a rush of emotion, in the wake of waves of possessive, jealous feelings. When Christina had told him Richard was in love with someone else, he'd been relieved and exhilarated. Chris was his – not anyone else's – his alone. It didn't matter that he wasn't successful or making money – none of that mattered. Chris didn't care. She loved him; she loved him so much she'd actually fainted. What more could he ask for?

Now, though, he felt oddly deflated. He was going to marry a woman some other man, some ordinary, boring barrister hadn't loved. Why hadn't Richard loved Christina? If Toby loved Christina, Richard certainly should have. He should have been devastated by their break-up. Christina should have broken his heart. His and many others. Lucy had told him, after a few too many glasses of wine, that she had left a trail of wounded males in her youth, old suitors who still rang her.

'But I'd never cheat on Nigel,' she'd confided, blushing.

Want to bet? he thought, as he stubbed out his cigarette. I could make you cheat, Lucy, if I wanted to. I saw it in those beautiful eyes of yours yesterday. I saw it when you blushed. You fancied me. And you'd be in my arms like a shot if you knew I was going to be a television star.

Stop right there, Toby Goodyear, he chided himself. What would Owen think of you if he knew what was going through your brain at this moment? These thoughts are unbecoming to you. The You you rediscovered this weekend with Owen. The pure You. Owen would love the idea of you marrying Christina, wouldn't he? And Owen is the father you wish you'd had. Don't you want to please him? Make him proud of you? Don't you want to ring him right now and tell him about the part?

The part.

How can an actor have a pure soul? Owen wouldn't be able to act if his life depended on it. Is it possible to imagine Owen playing Iago, for example? No. You have to have a deep understanding of human misconduct to act properly. You have to experience all the emotions – rage, hatred, despair, envy, ambition. You can't shut yourself away from the world or close any part of your psyche.

Toby remembered a night he'd experienced a few years ago – one when he'd snorted line upon line of cocaine. Total clarity had ensued, he recalled. For hours he'd had a sense of certainty about life and how he was supposed to live it. The only problem was that after he'd finally gone to sleep and woken up the next afternoon, he'd forgotten what that clarity entailed.

Was the weekend with Owen similar in some way? A sort of

life-altering experience which seemed at the time as if it would last for ever but which, in the light of day and reality, drifted away?

Yes, he had thought he'd like to be like Owen, but when it came down to it, would he really? Would he want roosters on the ping-pong table and goat's milk for breakfast?

Toby lit another cigarette.

I proposed to Christina when I was at a low ebb, he told himself as he inhaled. Well, maybe not a low ebb, but certainly not at the top of the wave, either. Is it fair to myself to limit my options now? Should I tie myself down when I'm just starting to take off?

As he exhaled perfect smoke rings, he thought about Harrow. He thought about housemasters. He thought about *young* housemasters in a co-ed boarding school. He wondered whether any of the scripts would include a storyline where the housemaster fancied a nubile teenage student.

And then he found himself wondering exactly what it would be like to corrupt the beautiful, blushing, faithful Lucy.

Chapter 11

What if you're at the very beginning of a relationship and you're not really sure about your partner? You saw him, you were attracted to him, but there were certain things that put you off right away. You didn't like his shoes, for example. Don't laugh. Shoes are important; how someone dresses is important – it reflects the way he thinks about himself and how he sees the world.

He's a great guy in most other departments, though, so maybe you think you should overlook those awful shoes or that terrible shirt or his unfortunate hairstyle. It's not fair to be turned off by superficial clashes in taste. Or is it?

It is if he cares deeply about the things you object to. If he loves those shoes you think should be thrown in the trash and put out of their misery, you're in trouble. You may say to yourself: 'Oh, give me a little time and I'll get him wearing what I like and looking the way I want him to look.' But if that's what you're thinking, you're cruising for a bruising. You're trying to change him which means you don't love the person you first saw. You'll love him only if he becomes someone else.

But don't jump the gun and ditch him the minute he shows up wearing something you don't like or when he doesn't have proper table manners or tells you he doesn't know how to drive a car – all little things I know can drive people nuts. He may want to change and he may be looking for someone like you who can help him. *Someone who can make him take those driving lessons or tell him nicely he shouldn't talk with his mouth full.*

Find out whether he is passionate about the things that bug you. He may actually enjoy being a slob or he may be wild about his Elvis hairstyle. If he takes the gold lamé suit out of the closet and models it for you proudly, I'd have to advise you to take a hike. (Unless he is Elvis – who, as we all know, is still alive!!!)

Trust those first instincts, but don't let them run away with you. Tread carefully and find out if what you dislike is actually a big part of his character or not. And remember, there may be things about you that irritate or put him off too. Don't change those, either, not unless you want to.

What you see is, more often than not, what you get. Make sure it's what you both want too!!!

I Saw You First, *Chapter Eight, p. 97*

Lisa was deciding what to wear for her appearance on *This Morning* the next day, trying on different outfits and modelling them for Skip, who sat on the edge of the bed, fidgeting.

'I could wear what I wore on *Oprah*,' she said, standing in a skirt and bra, checking through the wardrobe for a blouse. 'But I don't want to be seen in the same dress too many times.'

'You think people would point at their television sets and say: "Oh my God, she's in the same dress she wore last year! What's wrong with her?"' Skip didn't attempt to keep the sarcasm out of his voice.

'What's wrong with you?' Lisa turned from the wardrobe, put her hands on her hips and confronted her husband. 'You used to help me with all this. Now you're acting as if it were a chore.'

'I'm not your fashion consultant, Lisa.'

'I never said you were.'

Skip stole a glance at his watch. 'I'm going out,' he announced.

'Where?'

'I had a call today, while you were out. From a guy I used to know at AT&T who is over here now. We're meeting up.'

'I'll wear that blue dress,' Lisa said, turning back to the clothes. 'Harriet told me Richard and Judy are sweetie pies.'

'Who are Richard and Judy?' Skip stood up.

'The hosts of the show, Skip.' Lisa wheeled around and looked at him with exasperation. 'The ones I've been talking about for the past twenty minutes. You're not paying attention.'

Skip shrugged.

'Goddamn it.' Lisa went over to him and pushed him back down on the bed. 'Do you have any idea how much I used to do for you? I used to call people's secretaries to find out their favourite foods so I'd cook something special for them. I used to find out the important people's birthdays so I could send them a card from you. I used to buy those little presents at Christmas – I did everything I could think of to help and you can't even be bothered to listen to me when I'm talking about something as important as a television appearance.'

'I'm sorry, Lisa.' Skip hung his head. 'You're right.'

Lisa's hands were on his shoulders. Her breasts were at eye-level.

Do it, he thought. Ravage me. Climb on top of me like a pint-sized Amazon and I'll finally submit to the whole damn thing. I'll call Alison and cancel our meeting and never speak to her again. I'll find out what food your publishers like and I'll cook for them. I'll send birthday cards to Oprah. You name it. Just take total control now and close the deal.

Sex, Lisa thought. We could have sex right now. But what time is it? The *This Morning* researcher said he was going to call at five forty-five to ask me a few more questions. She looked over Skip's shoulders to the bedside clock. We can have sex later. Tonight – when he's back from his drink and I have everything under control for tomorrow.

'Honey,' she said, letting go of his shoulders and backing off. 'I'm sorry too. I'm sorry I snapped at you. This country makes me tense. Everyone seems so foreign.'

'Maybe that's because they are,' Skip commented. He felt as if a momentous event had just occurred, as if he'd been unexpectedly released from a long jail sentence.

'I think I'll wear the blue dress.'

'You do that,' Skip nodded. 'Good choice.'

'You're a sweetie pie, too,' Lisa smiled, kissing him on the forehead. 'Later on tonight I'll show you how sweet I think you are.'

'That might not be such a good idea, Lisa. You've got to be up early for the show, don't you?'

'You are *so* thoughtful,' Lisa kissed him on the forehead again. 'You really are. I can't believe I let loose like that before. Forgive me?'

'You're forgiven.' Skip stood up. And thought: But if there *is* a God, I doubt *He'll* forgive a calculating bastard like me.

After Skip had gone to meet his friend and she had talked to the *This Morning* researcher, Lisa sat herself down at the kitchen table with a pad of paper and a pen. She had to do more work on the next book, she knew, but first she had to decide on the title. Should it be *What Comes Next?* or *Women Are Necessary?* As she doodled, trying to make up her mind, she noticed the script for *Plots in a Box* lying a few feet away from where she sat. Picking it up, she leafed through it, then went back over it again, reading it carefully. Declan and Toby had done a good job, she decided when she put it back down. They'd hit the right pitch – especially the part where Toby talked to the truck drivers and housewives. Although, now that she thought about it, she remembered seeing a Ricki Lake programme with a bunch of *female* truck drivers. Declan shouldn't have made the sexist assumption that all truck drivers were men. Women could drive trucks just as well as, probably even better than, men. Women could do just about anything they wanted to do, as long as they weren't brainwashed into thinking they couldn't.

If she'd been born a decade or so earlier, Lisa mused, she could have written a fantastic feminist tract called *You Can Do It, Girlfriend!* She would have concentrated on the two emotions that seemed to cripple women everywhere – low self-esteem and guilt. The minute a woman got rid of her low self-esteem, she was assailed by guilt; guilt for having the nerve to believe in herself. It was as simple as that, Lisa decided. There were times when she felt it too. Only an hour or so ago, she'd felt guilty when she'd delayed having sex with Skip in order to take that call from *This Morning*. Would a man in the same situation have even experienced a flicker of guilt? She doubted it. A man wouldn't have thought twice.

A sales rep in New York had once told her that lines from popular songs made good book titles because they were instantly recognizable and sparked off associations immediately. Perhaps she could call her next book *Don't Think Twice, It's All Right* – a down home feminist tract without all that political malarkey which turned people off. She could encourage women, get them to shed that low self-esteem with tales from her own life. *Anything I Can Do, You Can Do Better* was another possibility. In fact, that was close to brilliant. She'd tell women how she'd made a success of her own life and spur them on to make even greater successes of theirs. Of course, that might be a little impractical – very few women could write bestselling books. But if she could help them define their own individual notion of success, she could still justify that title.

But could she justify excluding men from her reading public? Realistically the answer was probably yes. Women bought more books, and women certainly bought *many* more self-help books than men. Of all the letters and faxes and calls she'd received, only about two per cent came from men. What she could do would be to call *Oprah*'s team and find out the breakdown of viewing figures on a male/female basis. *Oprah*'s public was her public, when it came down to it.

Anything I Can Do, You Can Do Better was a long title, Lisa thought, as she practised writing it down. But then so was *Men Are From Mars, Women Are From Venus*. There was nothing inherently wrong with long titles, not if they were eye-catching ones. The beginning of the book could be like the beginning of the *Plots in a Box* script. She could explain how she hadn't taken advantage of her education and had settled into an unfulfilling life as a corporate wife – Lisa stopped tracing over the words of the title, put the end of the pen in her mouth and grimaced. How could she say that? What would Skip think?

Guilt. She bit down on the pen. Guilt, guilt, guilt. Here we go again. It would be the truth – I'd only be writing the truth. I was unfulfilled. I hadn't worked on bettering myself. Why shouldn't I tell the truth? Skip won't mind if I explain it to him. And if he does mind, he can go jump in a lake. He can go play in traffic. He can take a long walk off a short pier. The truth should set us free. If he doesn't like it, he can lump it.

Alison was late. While he was waiting for her, Skip tried to listen in on the conversation two men at the next table were having, but couldn't understand their accents. He knew they were speaking English of some kind, but he still had no idea what they were saying. This came in handy when Alison finally entered and sat down across from him without so much as a 'hello'. Her face was full of fury and, Skip sensed, resolve. She wanted to end it too, he figured. Just as much as he did. But who was going to start the 'goodbyes' off? And how?

'Can you tell me what those guys next to us are saying?' he asked her. 'And what part of the country they're from? It's gibberish to me.'

She frowned, but listened for a moment. 'They're from Scotland,' she said. 'You wouldn't understand.'

'Ah,' he nodded. 'I guess not.' She had on a bright red T-shirt and blue jeans – a definite change from the white dress. Alison at her most casual, he thought. But she's still ridiculously, unbelievably sexy. Shit.

'I'm not sure you understand anything, actually.' She shook her head as she said this. 'Not anything at all.'

'I know some French.' Skip essayed a lame smile. 'And a little Spanish. Does that help?'

'When are you and Oprah going back to the States? Are you going to renew your vows on television when you get there?'

'Ouch,' Skip said. 'Isn't that below the belt?'

'Most of what we've done together has been below the belt, Skip.' Her mouth was set in the expression of a flagging marathon runner who had one more mile to go.

'Alison, listen.' Skip tried to take her hand but she wouldn't let him. 'Alison. You know neither of us wanted this to be a one-off, whatever we may have said on Saturday. But what choice do we have? I've been trying to work it out and find some alternative, figure out a way we can still see each other, but I can't.' Skip sighed. 'I don't know what to do. It's crazy.'

'You could have rung me.'

'I wanted to. But I didn't know whether Declan was there and I didn't know what to say anyway. I went in and out of a phone box on Saturday night like a jack in the box. I kept thinking of you and I wanted to talk to you, but what was I going to say?'

'You did?' Alison's voice suddenly turned kittenish and her eyes softened.

'Yes. I've been thinking about you all the time. It's horrible.'

'It was horrible for me last night, too.'

'I know. Lisa sprang that dinner-party on me. I had no idea you were coming until about ten minutes before you arrived. I'm sorry.'

'I'm not a cool person, Skip. You should know that. I'd like to be, sometimes I even think I am, but then something like this comes along and I lose it. I'm all over the shop. It's pathetic.'

'I don't think I'm so cool either.'

'Where does Lisa think you are now?'

'With an old friend from work.'

'How much time do you have?'

'I don't know.'

'And this is the last time we see each other, is that right?'

'I guess so,' Skip mumbled.

'I came in here all set to hate you, you know.'

'I know.' Skip took her hand. He tapped his chest with his other hand and said: 'Me – I'm hooked. I'm fucking hooked, Alison. What am I supposed to do?'

'Have you ordered drinks yet?'

'No – I was waiting for you.'

'Let's go then.'

'Where?'

'To my car. It's in a car park around the corner.'

'Alison, do you think that's—'

'Shh,' she put her fingers to his lips. 'It's no use talking. I don't understand American.'

Christina was on the floor of the sitting room giving herself a foot massage with grapefruit oil when Toby came in. At first, as she looked up at him standing in the doorway, she felt a strange sense of embarrassment and she immediately lowered her eyes and head, as if she were a Japanese geisha girl bowing to her master. It was an absurd response, she knew. But she wasn't used to being a fiancée. She didn't know quite how she was supposed to behave.

'Good day at the office?' he asked, striding to the chair and almost throwing himself into it.

'It was all right,' she answered. What are we going to do together for the rest of our lives, Toby? she didn't ask. Please start telling me how wonderful it's going to be right now. Right this instant.

The way he sat made it clear he was waiting for something, something she was supposed to say or do. But what?

'How was *your* day?' she ventured.

That did it. She could see that simple question was exactly what he'd been waiting for and she felt a surge of relief, the kind of relief she used to feel when she got the right answer in a test.

'Oh,' he threw his hands in the air. 'Nothing special. Looks like I'm going to be the new star of a television series, but aside from that, nothing interesting to tell about my day.'

'Toby!' Christina stood, went over to him and hugged him fiercely. 'That's fantastic news! I'm so pleased for you. Tell me all about it.'

'Oh Christ, not that grapefruit shit – that makes me feel ill. Stand back, will you?'

Christina blushed and retreated. 'Sorry. I only put a few drops on my feet. I—'

'Never mind. Forget it. Sit over there where you were and it will be OK.'

She did as she was told, all the while thinking of the bit of Lisa's book she'd read just before she'd begun to give herself a foot rub. *I Saw You First* seemed to be wherever she went in the house; as soon as she'd come back from work and walked into the sitting room, she'd seen it lying on the cushion of the chair where Toby was now sitting. Picking it up, she'd leafed through it quickly, until she found herself stopping at the top of a page where she saw the words *Put on a blindfold*. The section containing that sentence started on the page before, under the heading:

EXERCISE NUMBER TWENTY
I know I said before that love is not blind, but lovers, once in a while, should be blind in order to notice more about each other. We're so used to looking at the same old face, we don't really see it for itself any more. Put on a blindfold. And get your partner to put one on too. Then sit and have a normal conversation together. Talk about what's happened today at work or at home. Talk about your friends, or your family. Talk about the weather. The subject of conversation is not important. But make sure the talk goes on for at least twenty minutes or this exercise won't be effective.

What you'll find as you get used to not seeing is that you'll listen more; you'll hear your partner's voice and he'll hear yours. You'll imagine his face and see in your mind's eye what he looks like all over again. (I bet you anything he's cute!)

Don't take off the blindfolds yet, though! Keep them on, and then, as you're talking, start to try to find each other. This is like

*a game of hide and seek, except you're both seeking. Obviously
you should start off this exercise at a fair distance from each other
in the room of your choice.*

Don't cheat now!! Don't peek!!

*Once you have found your partner, give him a big hug! But
don't take off the blindfolds – go away from each other again,
to where you were originally, or as close as you can get in your
unsighted state.*

*NOW remove the blindfolds. Take a long look at each other.
Don't speak. Then go into separate rooms and be by yourselves
for a while. Think about what you've just experienced and what
it means to you. At this point you will understand a lot more
about your partner – and yourself.*

Christina was almost as amazed by this Exercise as she had been
by the one where you played your favourite song on matching
Walkmen. Looking at Toby now, she tried to imagine the two
of them with blindfolds on, talking about their days at work. All
she could picture was herself bursting out laughing.

'It's the lead role in a series about a co-ed boarding school. I'll
be the housemaster who deals with all these adolescents and their
problems. I'm doing a test on Friday, but Nick says the part is mine.
You won't believe this, but the casting agent saw my *Hamlet*. It's a
miracle, really. I'm on my way now. If I get this, I'm set, I know.
I'd rather do a film, of course, but plenty of very good actors do
television. Think of Helen Mirren, for example.' Toby clapped
his hands on his knees. 'I can't tell you what this means to me,
Christina. I've felt like a teenager myself all day.'

'I wish you'd rung me at work,' Christina said. Was she sounding
petulant because he hadn't rung? And because he kept saying 'I'
instead of 'we'? She rolled her neck in a circle and took a few long,
deep breaths. 'I think it's fantastic, Toby. You'll be brilliant. Do
you think – ' she hesitated, then decided to dive in. 'Do you think
this will change our plans? I mean, I know we haven't set a date
for the wedding yet. Do you think we should?'

'Let's wait for a while on that.' Toby leapt up from the chair. 'I've got some champagne. Let's get pissed and celebrate.'

'What about *Plots in a Box?*'

'What about it?'

'Are you still going ahead with that?'

'The ball's in Skip's court now. He'll have had the script we did. It's up to him.'

'Did you see the way Alison was looking at him last night? It was odd.'

'She's probably bonking him,' Toby said lightly, then headed for the kitchen, leaving Christina sitting on the floor in a state of shock.

Did he mean that? Was that possible? No. It was a throwaway line, a joke. How could Alison and Skip be having an affair? Unless they'd got together over the weekend, which was a seriously unlikely scenario. But how else could Alison's strange behaviour be interpreted? What other reason could she have had for staring at Skip continuously? She hadn't behaved normally; she hadn't looked like her usual self. She'd been acting very strangely, just as she'd acted strangely when she'd been at Amersham. Alison and Skip? No. It wasn't possible. They wouldn't have had the time or the opportunity – Lisa was there. And Lisa wasn't a woman to countenance an 'open' marriage – that wasn't part of the *I Saw You First* ethos.

Christina smiled, thinking of Skip and Lisa putting on blindfolds and Skip sneaking out of the house for a quick rendezvous with Alison as Lisa was left stumbling in the dark, trying to find him to give him a hug.

'Here we are,' Toby announced, coming back with two glasses of champagne. 'Let's have a toast.'

Standing up, Christina took a glass and continued smiling. 'What are we toasting?' she asked.

'The future,' Toby replied.

'The future,' Christina repeated and clinked her glass against Toby's. Why hadn't he bought some champagne yesterday, after he'd proposed? Why weren't they toasting their marriage? Was he more excited about this new role of his than their wedding? Would they ever set a date? Did she *want* him to set a date?

'Now go slowly, Christina,' Toby said, taking a sip. 'Lucy told me all about that time you got pissed on your eighteenth birthday. We don't want a repeat performance of that one.'

'Why?' Christina froze, the glass at her lips. 'Why did she tell you about that?'

'We were talking about your teenage years. I told you that yesterday. She said how sweet it had been to see you trying so hard to be sophisticated and how embarrassed you'd been when you were sick all over the kitchen floor.'

'They gave me shots of tequila, she and Chloë. I had never had shots of anything before. I didn't—'

'You don't have to be so touchy. It's happened to all of us – though I have to say, I've never been sick on the floor. I always managed to make it to the loo.'

Christina took her champagne and went and sat in a chair. She didn't want to remember that night. She had hoped she'd never have to remember that night again in her life. Everyone had laughed at her stumbling, slurring drunken self. Everyone including her own mother. If it had been some sort of rite of passage to adulthood, she'd failed miserably.

'I might use that in my series,' Toby said slowly. 'One of the students gets pissed out of his mind on his birthday. Do I shop him or clean up the mess and cover for him? He could have upchucked all over the Common Room—'

'Toby. Please. Can we change the subject? I don't want to think about that night.'

Toby put his glass down on the table beside Christina's chair, took out his cigarettes from his trouser pocket and lit one. He was standing above her, scrutinizing her as he took his first drag.

'Exactly how out of touch were you when you were a teenager, Chris – sorry, Christina?'

268

'What do you mean by that?'

'I mean, I know now that you didn't fit in with your peer group. I mean how out of it were you?'

'I don't understand the question.'

'Did you have friends?'

'Yes.'

'What were their names?'

'Toby.' Christina looked away from him. 'This is ridiculous.'

'Lucy said you never spent time on the telephone. You never went out. Who were these friends, then? What did you do with them?'

'Why are you bullying me?'

'Why aren't you answering my questions? They're simple enough, Christina. The names of your supposed friends. I can name my friends easily.'

'I'm not playing this game. Whatever this game is. Yes, you're right, I wasn't like most of my peer group. I didn't spend hours on the telephone with my girlfriends. I didn't go out to clubs. I didn't rave. But I *did* have friends. I wasn't particularly happy, Toby. My father died. My mother remarried. I moved into a new house with a new family. I had problems adjusting. Is that a crime of some sort?'

'Of course not,' Toby said, in a soothing tone. He reached over and began to stroke Christina's hair. 'I had an unhappy time too. I want to know the truth, that's all. I want you to feel you can tell me the truth.'

Bad cop turns into good cop? Christina thought. Is he trying to get a confession out of me? Does he think I've been holding back? Well, I suppose he's right. I've never discussed those years with him. I haven't unburdened my psyche. I've always been wary of telling him things, and I shouldn't be – not if I'm going to marry him.

'I told Owen stories about my past I hadn't told anyone else in my life. And it was a wonderful experience; it was cathartic. I want you to have the same experience – with me, Christina. That's all.' He leaned over and kissed her. 'That's all there is to it.'

But you're not Owen. And this is beginning to feel as if it is one of Lisa Thomas' Exercises. And that is an unfair thought, Christina told herself crossly. You're being defensive again, and distrustful. You *have* to talk to him. And you have to start now.

'Could I have one of your cigarettes?' she asked.

'Christina? You don't smoke.'

'I know. But I want one now.'

'Why?' Toby tapped out a cigarette from the pack, handed it to her and lit it. She didn't inhale, but puffed nervously.

'Maybe you should sit down too,' she said to him. 'I have something to tell you. It's about Richard, actually. Richard and Lucy.'

Alison was in the process of unzipping Skip's trousers when her mobile phone rang.

'Don't answer that,' Skip groaned.

'I have to,' she replied. Before he could ask why, she had picked up her handbag and pulled the Nokia out. 'Hello,' she said, sitting back in the driver's seat.

'Lisa?'

Skip, who had honed in on her ear and was kissing the lobe, pulled back instantly. He couldn't believe what he had heard. It couldn't be true. Lisa couldn't be calling Alison. There was some mistake.

'No, no. You're not interrupting anything. I'm on my way home from work.' Alison looked at Skip, her face contorted. 'How did you get this number?' She paused and as she did so, Skip racked his brain. Had he left the slip of paper he'd written it down on somewhere visible? No – he'd committed the number to memory, torn the paper up and thrown it away. Was Lisa suspicious after all? Had she rummaged through the garbage cans and put the shreds back together?

'Oh, Declan gave it to you.' Alison put her hand over the phone and whispered, 'Fuck him, what the fuck is he playing at?'

Has Declan spilled the beans? Skip wondered. Is this his way of murdering me – telling Lisa? It's worse than a letter bomb.

'Is it important?'

Is what important? What's going on here? Skip shifted in the car seat and stared at the gear box. Who the hell drives cars that aren't automatic any more? Who the hell kisses in car parks at my age? What's Lisa going to ask for in the divorce? Will she go on TV and tell the world about my infidelity?

'I suppose so. Lisa, the reception is bad. Can you speak up?'

You suppose *what*, Alison? Turn off that goddamn phone and tell me what the hell is going on.

'All right. I'm not far away, as it happens. I can be there in, say, twenty minutes.'

Skip closed his eyes. That was it. A showdown in Pimlico. Lisa versus Alison. Who would bite whose ear off?

I don't want to see it, he thought. I don't want to be there. I want to disappear. I want to go to Tahiti. How did I get myself into this mess? As my mother used to say when she'd run out of booze: 'What a revolting development this is.'

'Right. Bye, Lisa.' Alison pushed a button and turned to Skip. 'She wants to talk to me. I'm supposed to go over there.'

'What does she want to talk to you about?'

'She didn't say. It must be about us. But she sounded so calm, it was weird. As if nothing were the matter.'

'She couldn't have found out. How could she?'

'You sound positively frightened.' Alison gave him a glance that frightened Skip even more. 'You thought you could wrap this up in a nice little bundle, didn't you? Take what you wanted to take from me and move on as if nothing had happened.'

'It's not like that.' Skip grimaced.

'Oh no? Tell me what it *is* like, Skip. I'd like to know.'

'I don't know what it's like. I'm confused.'

'I thought you were hooked. You *said* you were hooked.'

'I *am*.' Skip scratched his head. 'I think.'

'Oh, brilliant. That's just brilliant. You *think*. Get out of this car. Now.'

'Alison – '

'I mean it. Get out now. I'm going to see your wife. I'm going to tell her every single thing we did in bed. And I'm never going to see you again. Bugger off. I can't stand the sight of you.'

Alison pushed him, so hard that Skip felt the door handle dig into his hip.

'You're a weak, pathetic bastard. You know, that's what I thought when I was first watching that infomercial at your house. I thought, What a weak, pathetic bastard that husband over there must be to sit there like an idiot while his wife bangs on about their marriage and how she pushed him around. Now *I'm* pushing you around. I'm pushing you out of my car.'

'Alison, I thought you *knew* this was our last time together. You agreed—'

'Oh, shut up, will you?' Alison turned the key in the ignition. 'Get out of the car.'

'What are you going to say to Lisa?'

'I said get out, Skip. Or I'll drive you to your house myself and take you in with me.'

Skip opened the door and reluctantly left the car. 'Alison—'

She reached over, slammed his door shut, put the car in reverse and backed out of the parking space, then hared off, out of his sight.

'The parking ticket!' he yelled after her. 'You haven't paid the parking ticket. You have to pay *before* you go.'

She'll probably break down the barrier, he thought, standing disconsolately, focusing on a silver Rolls-Royce sitting three bays away. I'm a dead man. He began to move toward the exit. A dead man walking.

It was a ridiculous thing to do, Declan knew all too well. He was being an idiot. Driving up and down Christina's road was a waste of time and petrol. She was sitting in the flat, ensconced cosily with Toby and he was stalking her like a besotted crazy man. Still, what else was he supposed to do? Al was undoubtedly off somewhere with Skip. He didn't feel like sitting home alone or going off to a pub on his own either. If Alison had told him she wasn't coming home that evening, he could have gone out with people from work and had a decent time. As it was, he'd been pissed off when he'd come home to find the place empty and he'd retaliated by giving Al's mobile number to Lisa when she'd rung. Why should Al get away with having a secret rendezvous with Skip? They'd agreed this morning that they'd have a long talk about the future when he got back from work at six and instead she'd buggered off without even leaving a message. He wasn't going to call her himself and berate her like an angry parent would a delinquent child. He wasn't her father and he was becoming less and less interested in being a decent, kind ex-lover.

Lisa had said she needed to talk to Alison about something important and at that particular point Declan didn't give a shit whether this 'important' topic of discussion was Skip and Alison's affair or something else altogether. He didn't press Lisa to tell him; he simply gave her Al's mobile number and wished her a nice evening. If Alison had been found out, so be it. He wasn't going to cover for her any more. She was on her own.

So now he was going up and down Christina's street like a burglar casing the joint. Declan suddenly smiled, remembering when the cottage at Amersham had been broken into. He and Michael had come downstairs one morning to find the kitchen window jimmied open and a few of the piles of books knocked over.

'Someone should have told them the front door doesn't have a lock,' Michael had said, looking around with a grin. 'They needn't have bothered breaking in.' He rearranged the books. 'Poor buggers. No television, no video player – nothing at all to steal. If they'd woken us up, Dad would have probably offered them something to eat.'

At the time Declan had felt a twinge of humiliation. We have nothing worth stealing, he'd thought. Even burglars must think we're tragic.

Now, though, he was smiling. The dog hadn't barked, the rooster hadn't crowed, the goat hadn't done whatever goats do; no member of the Lewis household was programmed for security.

He might not be able to lead a life like that himself, but he could come closer to it than he now was. Four televisions in the Henning Street house was an excessive number, after all. He could start cutting back on material possessions without going completely cold turkey.

Declan almost didn't bother to look as he passed Christina's flat for the umpteenth time. This mindless driving had become therapeutic rather than purposeful. The chances of seeing Christina, much less seeing her on her own, were minimal. But he took a quick glance anyway and saw what he'd lost hope of seeing – Christina on the pavement. Walking with her head down, at an unnaturally quick pace. His car was pointed in the direction she was going, and as she came closer, he saw her reach up and wipe her eyes with the palms of her hands. He didn't think – he didn't have time to think; she was moving too fast. Before he knew what he was doing, he'd honked the horn.

She stopped, stared at the car and then, as he drew up alongside her, at him. His window was open. She walked over and bent down.

'Declan?'

'Hello, Christina.'

'What are you doing here?'

'I'm not exactly sure. I was taking a drive.' Her face was tear-splattered and achingly unhappy. 'Would you like to get in and drive with me for a little bit?'

'I don't know.'

'Why don't you get in and think about it?'

She opened the door and climbed into the front seat.

'If you want more legroom, the handle is underneath your seat,' he said and then watched as she bent down and slid the seat back. Her face was turned away from him and he couldn't tell whether she was still crying.

Now that he had her in the car, he had no idea what to say or how to start a conversation. The weather? No. The reason for her tears? Definitely not. Racking his brain, all he could think of was to say: 'I should have bought a more practical car. I don't know why I chose a BMW. Michael teases me mercilessly about it. BMW stands for Break My Window, he always says. And of course he's right. You wouldn't believe the number of times I've come out in the morning to find my windshield smashed.'

'It's a nice car, though,' she murmured in a tired voice.

'Yes, but it would have been more intelligent to buy an old banger. One without a radio to steal, too. Car alarms aren't always efficient.' What must I sound like? Declan asked himself. An old fogey worried about car theft. That's wonderfully witty and amusing, Declan. Just the ticket to make an impression. 'Would you like to hear about the time our cottage in Amersham was burgled?'

'Mmm,' she replied half-heartedly.

'Think about it. Think how the burglar or burglars must have felt when they were searching the cottage for valuables.'

He shifted in his seat to see the effect his words were having. There was a glimmer of change in her eyes, a tiny brightening. Keep going, he told himself. It's working.

'What are their choices? The Mao poster? The ping-pong table? Some goat's milk from the fridge?'

She laughed. Declan felt as if he'd scored a hat-trick in a Cup final.

'What do you say? Should we go for a drive?'

Christina hesitated, taking a look behind her at the flat. Some emotion he couldn't identify moved across her face. When it had gone, she nodded yes. Declan stepped on the accelerator with no idea of where he was going to drive to next. All he wanted to do was get out of the road and away from Toby.

'Where are we going?' she asked quietly.

'Windsor,' was the word that suddenly came to his lips.

'To see the Castle?'

'We'll get there just before sunset. I know a way into the gardens beneath the Castle. I had a friend once who went to the choir school there – St George's, I think it's called. I visited him there one Saturday and he showed me the way through a back gate into the Queen's land beneath the Castle. That's where their playing fields were. I think I can remember how to get in. It's a beautiful place – especially on an evening like this.'

They drove in the direction of the M4 in silence, Declan reluctant to push Christina in any way by asking her what had caused the tears. A few minutes after they'd passed Exit Three on the motorway, though, Christina finally spoke.

'What else do you hate, Declan? Aside from *The Sound of Music* and Tom Hanks and Glenn Close and Andie McDowell?'

'Hmm.' Declan drummed his fingers against the steering wheel. 'I hate queue-jumpers. I hate Noel Edmonds. I hate Vinnie Jones. I hate Sainsbury's. How about you? What or whom else do you hate?'

'I hate New Year's Eve. Sometimes I hate Anthea Turner, and sometimes I hate Ulrika Whatshername.'

'The Teletubbies aren't my favourite people.'

'Mine, neither.'

They lapsed into silence again. Declan stopped himself from even glancing at Christina, but kept his eyes set on the road.

'I hate Terminal Three,' he said, after they'd passed the sign for Exit Four.

She didn't respond. Declan heard her begin to cry. He didn't move or say a word, he simply kept on driving and listened to the crying gradually subside.

'Here it is,' he said, fifteen minutes later. 'Here's the entrance to the school. Term's over but I wonder if anyone's here – teachers or staff?' He pulled in, and parked in the courtyard. 'Doesn't look as if there is. If the main door to the place is locked, we won't be able to go any further.' They climbed out of the car at the same time and Christina followed Declan as he went to the entrance to the school and tried the door.

'They're as bad as my parents,' he grinned, when it opened. 'I suppose there's not much to steal here, either. Right – we go down this corridor, if my memory serves me.' He led the way along, past a wall covered with photographs of schoolboys on sports teams. 'Now, we go out of this door and on to this back lawn, past that tennis court and there's another door that leads on to the playing fields and acres and acres of land.'

'How can you remember all this?' Christina asked as they passed though an arched doorway in a stone wall. 'It must have been ages ago, when you came here.'

'It was, but I remember because it seemed almost magical then, as if I were in a fairy tale. Look – ' he took a few steps forward and waved his hand. 'We're right at the foot of the Castle, and this is the Queen's garden. This is where she walks her Corgis when she's in residence.'

'It's beautiful, Declan.'

'There should be more security, but I suppose there aren't many people who know the way in. See – look at the playing fields.'

Christina walked beside him as they headed for the fields, but stopped on a small bridge over a stream. 'Can we sit here for a while?' she asked.

'Absolutely.'

They made their way to a tree and sat down underneath it, facing the Castle.

'Is this the Thames?'

'I'm not sure,' Declan replied. 'It must be, or a tributary. I was never any good at Geography.'

'Why do you think the door to the school was unlocked?'

'They were waiting for us.'

Christina stretched out and touched her toes. 'Will you tell me something, Declan?' she asked, not looking at him.

'Yes.'

'When you first saw me at Lisa's did you think: who is that giant?'

'No.' He shook his head. 'I saw you sitting on the sofa with your eyes closed and I thought, She must be as embarrassed by this infomercial as I am.'

'And then what? What did you think next?'

277

'I thought I liked the way you wear your hair.'

'I was sitting down – that's why you didn't notice.'

'Didn't notice your height, you mean? No. I saw how long your legs are. But funnily enough that didn't make me think you were particularly tall.'

'I told Toby something I shouldn't have told him today.'

Right, he thought. She's backing into it. Let her take it at her own pace, from her own angle. He picked up a blade of grass and put it in his mouth.

'You know how I told you I'd like you to visit my family?'

'Yes.'

'I told you that because I thought I saw some similarities between us. I saw how uncomfortable you were with Michael and Owen.' She stopped speaking.

Declan waited for a moment before he said: 'And you're uncomfortable with your family.'

'Yes,' she nodded. 'I had problems with them. I was jealous of my step-sisters. One of them especially. I think it may have been all right, I might have naturally grown out of it, if my boyfriend hadn't been in love with her, but he was. Not that she knew . . .' Christina's speech quickened. 'She didn't know and nothing ever happened between them. She's married to his brother. He – Richard, that is, my boyfriend – had an unrequited passion for her, for my step-sister, that's all. It's not that big a thing. It shouldn't have bothered me as much as it did.'

'Why not?'

She looked at him then and he could see the surprise this question had elicited.

'You don't think I was silly to take it to heart the way I did?' she asked in a tentative tone.

'I doubt it.'

'Really?'

'Well, if one of my girlfriends were in love with Michael, I think I would have taken it to heart, not to mention a score of other parts of my anatomy.'

'Oh.' Christina began to chew her thumbnail. 'At least you know Alison would never be in love with Michael. That was never a possibility, was it?'

'No.' Declan let out a small laugh. 'No. That wasn't a possibility. Michael was never the object of Alison's affections.'

'Of course not. You were. I mean are.'

'No, Christina. Right the first time. Past tense. In the present tense we have Skip Thomas.'

'Skip?' Declan saw Christina stiffen. But there was something about the way she narrowed her eyes that made him think she had an inkling of this news already.

'Does it come as a total surprise to you?'

'To be honest, no. Not total. I can't quite believe it, though. It seems so unlikely.'

Unlikely, Declan said to himself. That's exactly the word I thought of when I first saw Toby and Christina as a couple.

'Declan, I'm sorry,' Christina said. 'Why am I saying such stupid things? You must be shattered. I'm so sorry.'

'It's not the end of the world,' Declan said lamely. And it certainly isn't the time to declare undying love – not when I've just told her I've been cuckolded. She'd think I was on the rebound. Shit. This is far too complicated. Obviously Toby told her she'd taken her boyfriend and her step-sister's relationship too much to heart and he must have made her feel foolish in some way. That's why she was on her own, that's why she was crying. He had no idea how hurt she must have been or how she felt.

If I seem to be nonchalant about Alison and Skip, she'll think I'm a hard-hearted bastard too, won't she?

Am I?

Who the fuck knows?

Not me, certainly.

'Is that why you came to the Club today? Did you want to talk to me about Alison and Skip?'

'I –'

Declan was interrupted by a stern voice saying: 'What are you doing here?'

He and Christina both started. The owner of the voice appeared from behind them. He was a man who appeared to be in his sixties, with white hair and a menacing look.

'This is Crown property. You're trespassing. How did you get in?'

'We came in via the school,' Declan explained, jumping up and brushing the grass off his jeans. 'I used to be a pupil at St George's. One of the choirboys,' he added, trying to appear angelic as he lied. 'I wanted to show my girlfriend the grounds – the sports fields. You know, a trip down Memory Lane.'

'Well, you'd best be forgetting. You're not allowed here.'

'We're going.' Christina jumped up too. The man looked up at her and Declan noticed his expression – a mixture of curiosity and awe.

God, she must deal with this every day of her life, he thought. No wonder she worries about her height.

'We won't do it again,' Christina said in a little girl's voice. 'We didn't mean to bother anyone.'

'Have you always been that tall?' the man asked, his gaze fixed on Christina. Declan felt like thumping him.

'Ever since I was a baby,' Christina replied, smiling. 'Come on, Declan. We have to get back.'

'Goodbye!' Declan waved, walking off with her. 'Arsehole,' he muttered *sotto voce*.

'He's only doing his job,' Christina said. 'Anyway, we're running out of light. And Toby must be wondering where I've gone.'

'Do you want to ring him?'

'No.' She shook her head. 'I'm going to be spending the rest of my life with him, after all. What's a few hours missing here or there?'

'Exactly,' Declan said, thinking, Oh, fantastic. It's still on. She's still marrying Shit-for-brains. And I'm in so deep I can feel the water closing over my head.

Brilliant.
Fabulous.
Perfecto.

Chapter 12

Sometimes, when you've been in a relationship for a long time, you don't see the flags of unhappiness your partner is waving at you. You ignore them because you are thinking: well, everything seems to be going fine, what does it matter if he's depressed a lot or he's out more than usual, or he's drinking too much? You might say to yourself: 'We've been married for five years, of course there will be a few bumps along the road, but everything is basically fine.'

You think so, do you? Well, you're making a big mistake. You're concentrating on the relationship, not the person. If he's unhappy, it means he's unhappy with you, two. I have to say here that women tend to do this more than men. They're the ones who put out the signals and expect their man to pay attention and ask them what's wrong. When the men ignore them, they begin to rethink the relationship. 'He doesn't care about me,' Susie might say to herself. 'He's selfish and self-obsessed. He can't be bothered to see what's in front of his nose.' You wouldn't believe the number of men who suddenly find themselves being asked for a divorce when they thought things were hunky-dory. That's because they didn't pay attention or notice those flags waving. 'The marriage is fine,' they tell themselves. 'So Susie is acting a little down or crying a lot – she'll pull out of it. Nothing to worry about.'

Be on the lookout for those flags, folks. Your partner is trying *to tell you something. If you don't pay attention, eventually he or she will stop waving those flags and give up hope.*

You may be in a relationship but you're involved with a person. That person is not an automaton. Your partner may be your 'other half' but he or she is also a whole peron who needs individual care and attention.

You know how drowning people are always pictured waving three times before they go down for ever? Don't ignore those calls for help. Or you'll be dead in the water too!

I Saw You First, Chapter Fourteen, p. 286

'Alison – thanks so much for coming.' Lisa hugged her, took her by the arm and led her into the living room. 'I'm so glad you could find the time to drop by.'

What is going on here? Alison asked herself. She sat down on the sofa and crossed her legs. Was Lisa being friendly so she could lure her inside and then bring out the carving knife? Alison calculated how difficult it would be to get up again and run out of the door if Lisa attacked her. Check all the exits, she thought. Like the stewardesses always tell you to do before a plane takes off, in the event of an emergency.

'Would you like something to drink?'

'No, thank you.' If Lisa blocked the way to the front door, I could make a run for the kitchen and find a knife myself. I'm taller than Lisa, and stronger.

'The thing is, Skip's out with a friend and I was sitting here on my ownsome – thinking, thinking, thinking.'

Alison waited for the next sentence, but she felt her body untense a little. As she'd driven over to Pimlico, she'd thought she'd quite enjoy a showdown with Oprah Thomas, but as soon as she rang the front door bell, she'd realized how much she *didn't* want a confrontation – not when she was so clearly in the wrong. She'd slept with Lisa's husband while Lisa was away – what leg did she have to stand on? She'd be lectured or screamed at or worse.

The idea of Lisa having the moral upper hand was loathsome. Yet she was too curious not to turn up. This was the woman whom Skip preferred to her. Why? How could he? She wanted to see her up close, one on one. She needed to understand her rival. With Peter, she'd had so many rivals, she couldn't fight properly. And despite the fact that she'd turfed Skip out of her car and seemingly out of her life, she couldn't bring herself to believe it was over. It had hardly had a chance to begin.

'I needed to talk to a woman, Alison.' Lisa reached over and put her hand on Alison's arm. Alison immediately drew away.

'Oh, sorry. You Englishwomen don't like touching, do you?'

'It depends.' Alison said. Christ, what's she got on tonight? White overalls on top of a checked shirt. She looks as if she's about to start decorating a barn.

'Anywho, I wanted to talk to a woman, you see, and I would have called one of my friends in Connecticut, but one of them is in the middle of a divorce and another is on a yacht somewhere off Mexico, and then there's Julie who has just had a facelift so I don't want to disturb her, so the long and short of it is that I thought of you.'

'What did you want to talk about?'

'Women.'

'Women?'

'Yes. How women hold themselves back. How women don't have enough self-confidence and how guilty they feel if they do make something of themselves. I'm thinking about my next book, what I want to say, how I want to help people. And I was thinking about all this and I thought – well, men sabotage women all the time and then I thought – no, that's not it – women sabotage themselves.'

'How do they do that?' Despite herself, Alison found that she was interested in what Lisa was saying.

'They *look* for guilt.'

'Pardon?'

'Well, let's say a woman is doing well in her career. What

thoughts are running through her head? First of all she has that 'When am I going to get found out?' tape running through her brain. You know, the: 'Who's going to figure out that I'm not as good or as smart as I appear to be?' routine. And if that doesn't feed her feeling of low self-esteem enough, she starts obsessing about how she should be all things to all people – perfect worker, perfect mate, perfect mother. As soon as she figures out she can't be perfect, she starts to feel guilty. It's all about low self-esteem and guilt – the two curses of womankind.'

'I'm not sure about that, actually. I don't feel guilty. Not normally, anyway. And I don't think I have low self-esteem.'

'Then why aren't you running a company?' Lisa's eyes zeroed in on Alison. 'The other night you were the one who had done your homework on the infomercial idea, weren't you? But who ended up writing the script for *Plots in a Box*? Who ended up getting paid? Declan and Toby – two men. You were cut out of the deal, Alison. From the beginning. They took over. Why?'

'I don't know,' Alison mumbled. 'I was going to talk to Skip about infomercials, as it happens. But I never got around to it, for various reasons.' She frowned.

'Exactly. You got sidetracked. You were shunted off the rails. Because you didn't believe in yourself enough to push for what you wanted.'

'It didn't exactly happen like that.' Alison thought of her meeting with Skip. She *had* been sidetracked – by talk of their pasts, by her attraction to Skip, by her emotions.

'Declan told me today that you're more ambitious than he is. Now, that is *not* what I want to hear from a sales director, but then when it comes down to the nitty gritty, *I* sell my book. He doesn't have to do a damn thing, really. I'm in charge. The point is, I can't count on anyone else to help me out here – it's up to me. And it's up to you to do what you know you can do. All of which would be fine and dandy if the guilt bug didn't bite.'

'What do you mean by that?'

'Take me and Skip. I'm more successful than he is. That's a fact.

It shouldn't bother anyone, but it does. It bothers me. I feel guilty. Somewhere lodged in my heart is this idea that I shouldn't be more successful than he is. Boom! The guilt bug bites. And you know why that is?'

Alison, as she waited for Lisa to answer her rhetorical question, looked at her impassioned face and felt oddly excited.

'It's Eve.'

'Eve?'

'Yes. Eve takes the initiative, Eve bites that apple – and what happens? Paradise is wrecked. *Kapoot!* So ever since Eve, women have a free-floating sense of guilt; they have to pin that guilt on to something, so they pin it on themselves. Which is where the self-sabotage comes in.'

'Always?'

'Always,' Lisa nodded. 'Look at me now. Here I am on my own the night before I'm going on television. You know what would be happening if Skip were about to go on television? I'd be here feeding his ego, cooking him dinner, advising him what to wear, supporting, supporting, supporting. I wouldn't be out with one of my old buddies. No way. I'd feel guilty if I were. But men don't have this guilt, do they? Adam is guiltless. So they are too.'

Guilt, Alison thought. I wish she weren't talking to me right now about guilt. Still, she has a point. She's making sense. Have I sabotaged myself? Yes, I do it all the time. I sabotage myself because of men. The wankers.

'Are you sure you wouldn't like something to drink?'

'A glass of water would be nice,' Alison replied.

'Well, I'm going to get myself a glass of wine. Which is another thing that makes me feel guilty. Skip has this thing about drinking. His mother was an alcoholic.'

'Oh?'

'Yes. I guess she *is* an alcoholic – if she's still alive. Skip refuses to see her. It worries me, the way he's abandoned her. But he doesn't seem to feel any guilt about that either. I would if I were him.' Lisa sighed. 'The more I think about this, the more

I'm sure I've got hold of something important here. Be back in a sec.'

Should I tell her? Alison wondered, looking at Lisa's back. Should I tell her she doesn't have to feel guilty about anything – that Skip and I are the guilty parties? No. There's no point any more. Skip and I are finished. I'm going to forget about men, and concentrate on myself and my ambitions. Declan and I can sell Henning Street and I'll buy a little flat and I'll work. I'll work and work some more. But work at what? It doesn't matter. I'll find something. And I won't be sidetracked. Not ever again.

Lisa returned holding a glass of wine in one hand and water in another.

'Here you go,' she said, giving the water to Alison. 'I'm so glad you could come. Tell me about your mother, Alison. Did she have a career?'

'She ran a florist's. After my father left, she had to work very hard *and* take care of me. She's had a difficult time, you know?'

'I'm sure.'

'My father is an alcoholic.' What am I doing? Why am I telling her this? I must be mad.

'You and Skip have something in common. You should talk about it with him sometime. He won't talk to me,' Lisa said regretfully. 'He thinks I wouldn't understand. My parents didn't have problems like that.'

I *do not* want to bond with this woman. I have to get away from her. She's like a snake. She'll wiggle her way into my psyche and I'll end up telling her things I shouldn't.

'I shouldn't tell you this, Alison,' Lisa continued, taking a large sip of her wine. 'But Skip has been acting very strangely lately. I mean, he really should be here with me tonight. He always *used* to help me, to be there for me when I needed him, but now it's almost as if he's—'

'Excuse me, Lisa. I need to go to the loo.'

'Oh,' Lisa said apologetically. 'Of course. It's at the end of the hall, on the right. Do you want me to show you?'

'No. I'll find it. Don't worry.'

Can I do what Declan did last night? Alison thought frantically. Can I say I have a migraine? No – but when I come back I'll look at my watch and say, 'Oh no, I must be going.' Then make some excuse and get out. And then I'll never see her again. Her or Skip. This has all been one huge, dreadful mistake.

I don't understand Americans. I don't *want* to understand them. There's something wrong with all of them. Why is she talking to *me* about all this? Does she actually know what's gone on? Is she laying a trap? Is she being very clever or very stupid? Whatever the case I'm not going to stay to find out. Enough of low self-esteem and the guilt bloody bug and Skip acting strangely. I will never have anything to do with a married man again in my life. It's like buying a ticket for a trip on a boat called the *Titanic Two*.

Skip hesitated outside the door. What was waiting for him when he went in? Would Alison still be there? Had she gone there as she had said she was going to, or had she changed her mind and driven straight home? Would Lisa be in floods of tears? Would Alison? Was it possible that Lisa *didn't* know? No. Why else would she have called Alison? There could be no other reason. And he had to be a man. He had to face the music and try to weather the storm, as Lisa would have put it. The odds were that Lisa would divorce him. Alison had already dumped him. He was on his own from now on. He'd have to start his life again. Alone.

Fucking women, he thought. They use you and then they throw you out like garbage. They set fire to houses and they call you Skipper and they become bestselling authors and they make wild, wanton love to you and then they give you all kinds of shit like making you choose what goddamn dress they should wear or pushing you out of a goddamn car and you're supposed to sit back and take it. What a scam. The weaker sex. What a joke! It's disgraceful. They should all be shot. Fuck them.

Skip squared his shoulders, took out his front-door key and went into the house, in a deeply satisfying mood of righteous fury.

'So,' Lisa greeted him as he walked into the living room, her voice full of petulance. 'You're back.'

'I'm back,' he replied, his tone matching hers. Alison wasn't there. That didn't mean she hadn't been there, but at least she'd gone. That was a plus, anyway.

'I was just saying to Alison how you let me down, Skip. How you would have never done something like this before. Maybe I don't have a right to be upset, but I can't help feeling this way. I can't help but think if the situations were reversed . . .'

Alison had been there. Lisa knew. At least she wasn't screaming or crying or heavily armed.

'It was a mistake, OK? I made a mistake. I'm human. I'm sorry I'm human but I am. There's nothing you can do about it.'

'I wouldn't say it was a mistake, I'd say it was a choice. And you don't even feel guilty – do you?'

'Yes, I feel guilty.' Skip rubbed his forehead and sat down heavily beside Lisa on the sofa.

What happened to my anger? he asked himself. How can it have evaporated so quickly? Now all I feel is exhaustion – overwhelming, paralysing exhaustion.

'Go on.' He put his head in his hands. 'Yell at me. Scream at me. I betrayed you. I fucked up. I made the biggest mistake of my life, OK? Tell me what an asshole I am. Divorce me. Kill me. I don't care any more. Just get it over with – whatever you have to say. Just say it.'

'The biggest mistake of your life?'

Skip looked up and saw Alison at the entrance to the living room at the same time as he heard Lisa say: '*Divorce?*'

'I'm the biggest mistake of your life?' Alison repeated, not moving, standing like a statue called *Rage*.

'What are you talking about?' Lisa looked from Skip to Alison. 'What's going on here?'

'I didn't mean it that way,' Skip sighed. He pinched the bridge of his nose and kept pinching it, his eyes closed.

'Oh,' Lisa said dully, after what seemed to Skip a very long time. 'I get it. Finally.' She sank back against the sofa cushion and held her wine glass against her cheek. 'You two. You two. When? Where? No – ' she shook her head. 'Don't tell me. I don't want to know. Ignorance is bliss. Or it was. Wasn't it? It's always the same old story. Everyone else knows. I'm the dumb one. I'm the dumb one. Always. And there I was thinking everything had changed. As if. As if. I thought . . .' Lisa bit her lip. 'I thought you loved me. And I thought – never mind. I thought wrong.'

'Lisa – '

'No, Skip. Shut up. I don't want to hear. You know something really funny?' Lisa snorted. No one spoke. 'You know what I thought the first time I saw you, Skip? You know what makes my book so funny? I thought, There he is, he's a Harvard Man. That was the sum total of what I thought when I first saw you. I didn't think, Oh my God, he's attractive. Or: He has such a nice smile or anything at all except: He goes to Harvard. And when I found out later that you hadn't gone to college at Harvard, that you were at business school there but you hadn't been there as an undergraduate, I was disappointed. I never told you that, did I?'

'Lisa.' Skip had opened his eyes and was staring at his wife with astonishment. 'What's Harvard got to do with anything?'

'It has to do with *everything*, Skip. I just never wanted to admit it to myself. You weren't who I thought you were and you've never been who I thought you were. I had programmed myself into believing I'd never do anything with my life and that the best thing that could happen to me was to find a Harvard man. I never really saw *you*.'

'Can we please leave the goddamn book out of this?' Skip sat up straight. 'You drive me crazy with that book. I've had it with that book. The book is crap, Lisa.'

'Right.' She kept nodding her head back and forth, the wine glass still against her cheek. '*Now* you tell me the truth.'

'I'm leaving,' Alison announced.

'Take him with you.' Lisa waved her hand in the air. 'He's all yours.'

'What makes you think I want him?'Alison shot back.

'Oh thanks,' Skip mumbled.

'I don't care whether you want him or not. *I* want him out. Now.'

'Do I have a say in any of this?' Skip found his anger had returned. He was yelling.

'No. Get out.' Lisa stood up. 'I'm going to bed. I'm on television tomorrow and I'm not going to screw that up because of you. You can sleep on the street, I don't care. I won't feel guilty – not in the slightest. Reap what you've sown, Skip.'

'Why, Lisa? Because of Alison or because I'm not a Harvard man?'

Lisa strode out of the room without another word. Skip was left sitting, staring at Alison.

'What am I supposed to do now?'

'Am I supposed to care?'

'No, I guess not.'

'I hate you.'

'Join the crew.'

'Oh, fuck it. I'll take pity on you. If you need a place to stay, you can sleep on our floor.'

'While you and Declan share a bed? That would be rich.'

'Why would you mind if I shared a bed with Declan? I'm your biggest mistake, remember?'

'I can't stand the thought of it, all right? I can't stand the thought of you sleeping with someone else, anyone else.'

'That's only because Lisa has booted you out. You wouldn't give a toss if she hadn't.'

'I *would*, Alison. You're so wrong. I know I've been an asshole, I know I've betrayed you tonight: I've betrayed everyone. But that doesn't stop the way I feel about you.'

'I don't believe this.' Alison started toward the hall. 'You're like a bloody yo-yo, you know.'

'I know. But seeing you two together, in the same room, has made me realize that you're the one for me, Alison. Otherwise I'd have followed her upstairs and begged for forgiveness, wouldn't I? I promise I'm not reacting to Lisa; I'm following my heart. I mean, what was all that Harvard bullshit? She's off the wall. That book has turned her into a single-minded, crazy woman. She's not the person I married and she never will be again.'

Alison kept heading toward the door.

'Do you want to know a completely useless piece of information, Alison? Before you disappear from my life for ever? I used to be a wizard with yo-yos. It was one of my talents.'

'It was one of mine, too.' Alison stopped. 'That and skipping rope.'

'I was *fantastic* at that. The other boys thought it was for sissies, but I loved skip-ropes. I spent hours jumping. So everyone gave me shit. You know – "Skip loves to skip", all that crap.'

Alison put her hands over her face to hide a smile she hated having and certainly didn't want Skip to see.

'You know what my father used to do?' Skip asked, standing up and going over to her. 'He used to say, whenever I was upset: "Try not to smile, Skip. Whatever you do, don't smile." It always got me, that one. I'd try so hard not to smile, but I couldn't help myself.' He reached out and took Alison's hand away from her mouth. She struggled to set her expression into a permanent frown.

'It's not working, Alison. I can see that smile hiding behind there. Don't let it out. It would be a catastrophe. It would be cataclysmic if you smiled now.'

Alison smiled. Skip took her hand.

'What do we do next?' he asked.

'I still hate you,' she replied. 'I don't trust you and I hate you.'

'I know. But you might come to a hotel with me, even if you do hate and distrust me.'

'I'm not that silly.'

'Wanna bet?'

'Where have you been?'

'I went for a walk.'

'A three-hour walk?'

'Yes,' Christina smiled.

'You worry me, Christina. You are grotesquely sensitive. I tell you this thing with Lucy and Richard is no big deal and you become hysterical.'

'I wasn't hysterical, Toby. I was upset, that's all.'

She's one straw short of a basket case, Toby thought. Is it up to me to fix her? Do I have the energy for this? Richard fancying Lucy is tantamount to child molestation in her mind. She's made it into some crucial event in her life. The man didn't even *tell* her he fancied her step-sister. Maybe he didn't, after all. And she walks out on him because she *thinks* he did. He had the gall to have a headache at an engagement party. That sounds plausible enough to me. People have headaches. She's paranoid. She can't stand the fact that her step-sister is fanciable. And she's been hiding this kink in her psyche as if it were a buried treasure. Quite right to hide it, though. If she had told me about this before, I would have seen how screwed up she is – I wouldn't have asked her to marry me. Now I'm stuck with it.

Or am I?

'Do you understand what I was saying now? Has your mind cleared on your walk? Do you see how you've over-reacted?'

'I can see why you think I've over-reacted.'

'Well, that's something.' Toby shrugged. 'So you'll understand when I tell you I've rung Lucy and asked her to come here and clear all this up.'

'What?' Christina felt her heart tighten.

'We can't have a proper relationship when you're like this, Christina. You need to confront these fears of yours and vanquish them. I asked Lucy to come here. I said you needed to talk to her about something important and she was gracious enough to say she'd come tonight. Of course I was worried when you went walkabout for so long, but . . .' he looked at his watch. 'She should be here any second now. No harm done.'

293

'Why have you done this to me?' Christina sagged against the chair cushion.

'I'm doing it for your own good.'

'You're not my father, Toby. How dare you say something like that? You're treating me like – like a mental patient or an alcoholic or a junkie.'

'Well, you're hooked on your own jealousy, you know. You're feeding off it, you're having delusions, you're letting it consume your life.'

'That's not true! The fact that I told you about it shows I'm over it – don't you see that? I trusted you.'

'Then you should trust me to know what's best. Talk to Lucy. Get it all out in the open. It will be therapeutic. She's very fond of you.'

Where's Declan? Christina thought. I need him here. I need him to protect me. To understand. She roused herself from the chair and went over to the front window, her back to Toby. Please be there. Please be driving down the street so I can run out and jump into your car and get away from all this.

The only person she saw, however, was Lucy, who was across the street, shutting the door of her car. She didn't slam it, she closed it. Carefully.

Christina felt as if she'd been put into a straitjacket. 'Lucy is here,' she announced and then went and sat back down in the chair and waited. Waited for Lucy to ring the bell, waited for Toby to let her in, waited for her own personal hell to ensue.

When Lucy walked into the room, Christina couldn't bring herself to get up. She smiled, she blinked, she said, 'Hello, Lucy,' and she noticed instantly how beautifully her step-sister was dressed. She was wearing a dark blue cashmere skirt and top. Just looking at that makes you want to touch her, Christina thought. To find out if she's as soft as she looks. I remember when she played the part of Cordelia in a school production of *Lear*. She couldn't act to save her life, but it didn't matter. No one cared. The audience was too busy being beguiled.

'Chris.' Lucy approached her and gave her a quick kiss on both cheeks. 'It's wonderful to see you again.'

'You too,' Christina replied. How confusing this is, she thought. I *am* glad to see her again. I have nothing against her. None of this is her fault. She never set out to hurt me. I'm beguiled by her too. I always have been. 'I'm sorry Toby has brought you all this way for nothing. I don't need to talk to you about anything, actually. He made a mistake.'

She looked to Toby for help. If he doesn't push this now, she decided. I will love him for ever. Read my mind, Toby. Rescue me.

'Let me get us a glass of wine. Would you like white or red, Lucy?' Toby asked.

'White, please.'

Christina felt herself rally a bit. She sat up straighter. He might. He just might let this drop.

'How are Nigel Junior and Sophie?' she asked.

As Lucy was describing the children's latest school reports, Toby returned with the wine, deftly managing to carry three glasses at once.

'Here you are.' He handed them out. 'Now, where shall I sit?' Christina and Lucy occupied the only two chairs. Normally, Christina would have offered to sit on the floor, but she couldn't bring herself to move yet. 'I'll get a chair from the kitchen,' he said, disappearing again. Lucy continued with her account of the school reports.

'Right,' Toby said when he reappeared. 'That's that then.' He swung the chair down, sat on it and lit a cigarette. 'You know Christina actually bummed a fag from me today, Lucy,' he said playfully. 'I thought it was against her religion.'

'Chris!' Lucy exclaimed. 'I can't believe it. You're so pure.'

'I didn't inhale,' she mumbled.

'She was talking about you, Lucy. When she asked for it.'

'Really?'

'Yes. She told me about you and Richard.'

'I don't understand.' Lucy gave Christina a puzzled look. 'What about me and Richard?'

'She thinks Richard was, is, was always, and will always be in love with you. From what she said, I believe she thinks this passion might last beyond the grave. Cathy and Heathcliff are as nothing beside you and Richard.'

'Pu-leeze.' Lucy giggled. 'You're having me on.'

'Not so. Am I right, Christina?'

Christina didn't reply. I'm not here, she said to herself. I'm somewhere else. I'm with my father. He's taking me for a treat. I'm going to get ice cream.

'Chris – you're not serious? *Richard?* Whatever made you think Richard was in love with me?'

'So you never had a hint of this passion, did you?' Toby queried.

'Of course not. Richard? It's preposterous.' Lucy giggled again. 'He might have had a crush on me, I suppose. But some grand passion? Richard's not capable of it. He's sensible. Boring, actually – oh, sorry Chris, I know you loved him, and you two were perfect together, but Richard and me? No *way!* Nigel will adore this. What a hoot. I can't wait to tell him.'

Christina rose then. She stooped, picked up her handbag and walked out of the room and out of the door, and on to the street. After a few steps she heard Toby calling her name but she didn't look back. Nor did he run after her. Taking a left at the end of the Fulham Palace Road, she continued walking down Fulham Road until she reached Thames Place. She had the key to the entrance and as she let herself in she was grateful, for the first time, that the manager of the Club had given it to her 'in case she ever wanted to come in early and open up'. When he'd said this, she guessed he was angling for her to open up occasionally instead of leaving the task to the receptionist whose job it was. The receptionist, Mary, was his girlfriend and was doubtless trying to wangle a few more hours of sleep. Christina did, once in a while, volunteer to take over the early-bird slot before seeing her clients, but she felt as if she were being taken advantage of. Now she wished she could give them both a bottle of champagne and her undying thanks.

When she entered her treatment room, she didn't turn on the lights, but went straight to the table and lay down on her stomach. Pretend you're giving yourself a massage, she thought. With yling ylang oil. Don't let yourself think. You're safe here. They can't get to you. They can't torture you. It's finished. You and Toby are finished. Richard will be able to handle the fall-out. He'll laugh too when Nigel and Lucy tell him about this. They'll all laugh together. 'How crazy is Chris?' they'll say. And somehow or other you'll be able to handle it too when you have to see Lucy and Nigel again. You'll laugh as well. Everything will be fine. If you can just make it through tonight without dying of despair, you'll be fine. You'll be on your own again, but there are worse things in this world. You can't be humiliated like that when you're on your own. You can't be hurt in the same way.

Christina began to sob. The tears exploded out of her and rained down her face. She was crying so much she couldn't believe she would ever stop. But her body began to tire and her eyes began to dry and she finally got up from the table and turned on the light. She found a towel and wiped her face. After throwing it in the hamper, she took a fresh one, flicked off the light, lit a jasmine-scented candle, made the towel into a pillow and lay down on the table again. This time she was on her back and she crossed her right arm over her eyes.

She fell asleep at the exact moment she thought she'd never sleep again.

When Lisa heard the front door slam, she went to the bedroom window and looked out onto the street. There was Skip, all right. Walking away with Alison.

You dog. You skunk. You no-good lying bastard. Lisa began to pace around the room. You think you can walk away from all this without paying a price? You're washed-up. You're nowhere. You're dead. What? You think you can leave me and waltz back into a high-powered job after all these years off? Dream on, Skip. You and Alison will be begging on the streets. You'll be homeless. And you'll pass by windows with televisions on display and I'll be on those televisions. On Oprah Winfrey and Ricki Lake and Montel Williams and Sally Jesse Raphael and David Letterman and Jay Leno and I'll be in the window of every bookstore you pass and I'll be in every magazine and newspaper you wrap yourself up in in the winter. I'll be President of the United States if that's what it takes to rub your nose in the dirt. I'll do it, Skip. Believe me, I'll do it. I'll be seen in Hollywood on the arm of Leonardo DiCaprio or George Clooney or Ben Affleck or whoever is the hottest star of the moment. You will die a thousand deaths. You will wish you'd never been born. You are not only toast, you're burnt toast, sunshine.

Lisa stopped pacing, picked up the telephone by the bed and dialled a number in the States.

'Deborah, honey, it's Lisa here. You're working late, aren't you? What time is it over there? Six?'

'Lisa,' Deborah Parry said happily. 'How's the trip going?'

'Fantastic, truly fantastic. Tons of publicity. I'm on television tomorrow. Some cute couple are interviewing me.'

'I'm jealous – I'd love to be in London.'

'You bet. It's just a fabulous town. Anywho, the thing is, I'm working too. Planning the next book. Thought I'd run it by you. I know you'll love it, Deborah. Editing it will be a breeze. Of course it's always a breeze for you, you're so good at your job.'

'That's nice of you to say, Lisa. So what's the idea?'

'It's great. It's about female guilt. You know how women hold themselves back and have this problem with self-worth, how they sabotage themselves, and it's all because Eve bit the apple and so all of womankind is consumed by guilt and then because of that guilt we get trampled on. *Trampled* on by men who have absolutely no guilt whatsoever and think they can do whatever they want and treat us like dirt. And – wait for it – the title is stupendous. It's going to be called – hold your breath now – *You Can Do Anything I Can Do Better* because it's all about how I managed to succeed despite all these various obstacles and my own problems so any woman can, and all it takes is a brush to wipe away that guilt. Sweep it clean off the boards and *celebrate* Eve instead of dissing her, as they say, and you just take that guilt and brush, brush, brush it off you and—'

'Lisa, could you slow down a second? You sound as if you're on speed.'

'I'm excited, Deborah. Think about it. There you are, for example, editing away, and you are just superb at your work and you *should* be running the company but why aren't you? Because of this guilt bug that sneaks into the sheets at night and bites you and then bites and bites some more, like a parasite, like a—'

'Sorry to interrupt again, but I don't *want* to run a company, Lisa. Not every woman does. Not every man does.'

'I don't care what men want. I care what women want. I'm talking about realizing potential. That's what it's all about. All right, so *you* choose to set your sights low – fine. I'm saying the point is to set those sights and then reach the target. You can't let anything or anyone stand in your way. Men. Children. Whatever.'

'Lisa, is this some kind of feminist tract?'

'No, no, of course not. It's a self-help book. For women, yes. But it's no tract. It's not political in any way. What's political about making something of yourself?'

'Some women might not take to the idea of children as people who stand in their way, you know.'

'Of course.' Lisa sighed and made a face. 'I know you have lovely kids yourself, Deborah. I'd love to meet the sweethearts someday. I'm not talking personally, I'm talking globally.'

'What I had thought,' Deborah said in a slow, deliberate voice, 'was that you would write another book on relationships. Men and women. What goes on between the sexes. This sounds like a call to the marketplace.'

'I don't know what you're talking about.'

'Well, it's not a relationship book *per se*, is it?'

'Yes, it is. Men heap guilt on us too. That's part of the problem. Who wrote the Bible? Men. There you go. I can explore that theme. I can do some research work on the Bible. How women get stepped on in the Bible. Not that it's not a great book, I'm not saying that. I'll be writing about certain parts of the Bible.'

'I have to be honest with you, Lisa. I don't mean to bring you down, but this doesn't sound promising to me. Research work on the *Bible?*'

'This is a visionary concept, Deborah. I'll let you think it over. That's the best plan. You might take a while to understand what an important vein of gold I'm mining here. This is deep. It occurred to me to call it *The Guilt Bug* but that sounds like some Edgar Allan Poe story I think I read when I was a kid. *You Can Do Anything I Can Do Better* is . . . *better*. Think about it today. Mention it to a few friends. I'm sure you'll see what I'm saying.'

'That's a very good idea. Why don't we both sleep on it? Call me again tomorrow, why don't you?'

'Fine. I will.'

'Great. And give my love to Skip.'

'Fuck Skip,' Lisa said and hung up.

'Toby, this is dreadful. You should go after her.'

'She needs to calm down, Lucy. She's very confused. This thing with Richard and you – what she imagined – has clearly affected her ability to think. If I run after her now, it will make matters worse. I thought she might be able to take the truth, but evidently that's not possible. She has manufactured this scenario and she won't admit to herself how deluded she has been.'

'That's so sad,' Lucy replied. 'Chris was always a sensitive little thing – well, not little, but you know what I mean. But to go this far is almost mad. Is that really the reason she split with Richard? Because of this fantasy about me and him?'

'That certainly seems to be the case.' Toby stood up and stretched. 'Let me get you some more wine.'

'I shouldn't, I'm driving.'

'One more glass won't hurt. I wonder . . .' Toby paused on his way out of the room. 'Do you think she needs help?'

'You mean a psychiatrist?' Lucy crossed her legs.

'Yes, to put it bluntly.'

'Maybe. But Toby, are you positive you shouldn't go after her? Where will she go?'

'Oh, she has friends at the Club – other people who work there; she'll stay with one of them. Chris will be fine, I promise. Maybe by tomorrow she will have come to her senses.'

'I hope so,' Lucy sighed.

After Toby left the room, she put her wine glass down on the side table and picked up *I Saw You First* which was lying underneath the lamp. Opening it at random she saw the words EXERCISE NUMBER NINE.

Throw him a party. Decorate the house with balloons and banners and buy him a present. Don't get what you think he should have but what you think he wants. This must be a surprise party – not a birthday party or a Christmas party or an Anniversary party. Do it when he's least expecting it. Make it a party for two. If you can't bake a cake, buy one. (You can always cheat and pretend you baked it – some little white lies are excusable when it comes to romance.) And make those banners meaningful. Have them read: To Pete, the Best Lover In The World or To David: My Guy!!

Toby came in then and saw her ensconced in the book.

'I know the author of that,' he stated, refilling her wine glass from the bottle. 'Lisa Thomas.'

'You do? That's amazing. I've been hearing about this book from friends and I've been dying to read it. I haven't had a chance to get to a bookshop, I'm afraid. How do you know her?'

'She wants me to do an advert with her – to sell the book in this country.'

'That's brilliant, Toby. Why didn't you tell me about that at lunch?'

'I didn't know you were a fan.'

'I'm impressed. I wonder if I should give Nigel a party?'

'What?'

Lucy pointed to the book. 'That's what this exercise here says. Throw a party.'

'Mmmm. Well, Lisa is certainly creative.' He sat back, savouring the moment of triumph he was about to produce. 'It looks as if I'm going to get a part in a television series as well. A leading part.'

'Toby!' Lisa's nose crinkled in excitement. 'How fantastic! Now – what is she like?'

'Who?'

'This woman.' Lucy pointed to the book again. 'Lisa Thomas.'

'Oh. She's very energetic. She's short. She's blonde. Vivacious.'

'I'd love to meet her.'

'I'm sure it can be arranged.' Toby grimaced. Lisa Thomas was more important than a television series? What was happening to this country? Was everyone turning into an American?

Lucy's attraction was fading by the second. He *had* planned to ply her with enough drink to make her stay over for the night. Not that he was necessarily going to seduce her, but he wanted to see how things progressed. Now he was beginning to think she was an airhead, and though he had nothing against airheads when it came to sex, he didn't fancy his chances of walking away scot free afterward. She was soft, she was feminine, she had huge blue eyes and unlined skin which looked as if it had been touched only by the most expensive moisturizers. She was flirtatious and she was doubtless hot in bed.

But she *was* an airhead, and airheads could go all emotional. Especially when he became a star. Lucy obviously thought, deep down, that *she* should have been a star, or at the very least married to a celebrity. When his series took off, she might think it was worth her while to ditch Nigel. She might ring him constantly. If he didn't return her rampant affections, she might be stupid enough to tell Christina. She might even be stupid enough to tell Christina tomorrow, for that matter. Who knew with women like her? They had power they weren't intelligent enough to know how to harness, so they played with it carelessly. Telling Christina might give Lucy a kick. Lucy wasn't an evil step-sister. Toby guessed she had never had sex with Richard or even considered having sex with him, not the way she talked about him. However, she was not entirely benign, either. If she had been, she would have gone after Christina when she ran out. Instead she'd stayed put. Why? Toby was positive he knew the answer.

Although he was also positive now that he wasn't going to marry Chris, he wasn't quite as certain that he was prepared for a final break with her, and that would be the inevitable result if Lucy spilled the beans. What if he didn't get the part? Where would he live? Besides, he genuinely liked Christina when she wasn't being an emotional wreck and he reckoned she'd pull herself together again soon.

He was pleased with himself for forcing this meeting between Lucy and Chris. Although she might be upset at the moment, in the long run she'd thank him for making her face her fears. For God's sake, he had to face his own fear every time he went for an audition. She'd get over this absurd inferiority complex she had, especially if he told her exactly what he thought of Lucy now.

I can fix her, he said to himself. And it won't take much energy at all. That doesn't mean I want to marry her, but I can do her some good. That will even the score. She's helped me out over the past year, when I was at my low ebb – I can help her out by pointing out that her Nemesis, the beautiful step-sister Lucy, is deeply, ineffably boring.

'Do you think you could arrange it so that some of my friends might meet her too?'

'What's that?' Toby struggled to bring his attention back to Lucy.

'Could my friends meet Lisa Thomas as well?'

'I'm sure. Listen, Lucy. You're going to be back very late at this rate. Nigel will be worried about you.'

'He won't be. I could stay here, if I like,' she smiled. 'He wouldn't mind if I spent the night at Chris' flat. I can get up early and be back in time to take the children to school.'

'Nigel would miss you,' Toby said quickly. 'He'd miss you dreadfully. You really must go back to him.'

The disappointment was almost invisible, but not quite. Toby could see a slight lowering of the eyes, a tiny clenching of the face muscles.

She's one of those women so used to being attractive, she can't quite believe I've turned down her offer, so she'll now convince herself she never made it. That makes life easier for me. She won't turn sulky and pout. She'll gather herself up and go back to Esher and boast to all her friends about the fact that I know Lisa Thomas. In not so very long a time, she'll boast even more when she sees me on television. 'He's a great friend of mine,' she'll say. 'We had lunch together only the other day.' She may even go so far, if she's had a few glasses of wine, to confide in one of her friends that I fancied the pants off her. And if she'd wanted to . . . but that, of course, she couldn't be unfaithful to Nigel. Thank God I never had to meet him or the kids. Christina was right to keep me away from them, as it turns out. A day in Esher would be a gruesome, depressing experience. Like going by ferry across the North Sea.

'You're right,' Lucy said, standing up and handing him her wine glass. 'Poor Nigel does get lonely without me. I'll be off, then.'

'It was terribly nice of you to come,' Toby said, putting his arm around her delicious waist and giving her a squeeze. He could allow himself that much, he thought. Now that he'd been such a good, forward-thinking boy.

'I hope Chris will be all right.'

'She'll be fine.'

'Tell her to ring me, will you? I can make her see how silly she's been about Richard.'

'I will.' He squeezed her waist again.

Wait a minute, he thought. Why am I backing off? She wouldn't tell Christina. There's still time. I could still . . .

'And promise me you'll introduce me to Lisa Thomas?'

Forget it, Toby said to himself, letting go of her. Trek back to Esher and Nigel and the kiddies.

'I promise,' he smiled. 'As her husband Skip would say, it's a done deal.'

'You know him too?'

'I do indeed,' he nodded, placing his hand firmly on the small of her back and guiding her to the door. 'He's a prince among men.'

'Is this all right by you?' Skip asked, outside the entrance of the hotel on Sloane Street.'

'Fine,' Alison replied.

This is supremely tacky of you, Skip. Taking her to a hotel and paying for it with Lisa's money. The Visa card has my name on it, but Lisa pays the bills. What else can I do, though? No way am I going back to her and Declan's house. I'm stuck. I just hope Lisa hasn't called and cancelled the card.

'Are you sure about this, Skip?'

'Sure about what?' he asked as he opened the door for her.

'Sure about me. Are you sure you don't want to go back and try to patch things up with Lisa?'

'No. Come on, let's register. We'll look suspicious without any luggage but I'm sure they're used to that.'

'Third-rate romance, low rent rendezvous.'

'What?'

'That's the title of a song one of the bands I worked with once did a cover version of.' Alison frowned. 'I'm not sure who did the original. So many of the songs are covers – you wouldn't believe it.'

'No creativity,' Skip nodded. 'No originality. Stay here and I'll take care of this.'

After he'd checked in and they'd gone to the second floor where their room was, Skip found himself struggling to open the door with the plastic card.

'Here, let me do that,' Alison said, taking it out of his hand. 'There – it's simple.'

'*Nothing's* simple,' Skip groaned. He went in, sat down on the bed, and patted the space beside him. 'Come join me,' he said.

'I feel a little odd.' Alison looked around the room. 'As if I shouldn't be here. It's strange. When she didn't know, I didn't feel guilty; now that it's out in the open, I do.' She reached up and rubbed her neck. 'She kept talking about guilt, you know. The guilt bug. As if it were an insect. I understood what she was saying – more or less. She was talking about Adam and Eve.'

'Oh yeah?' *Could you please stop talking and get over here and let me take your clothes off?*

'Yes. She was saying how because Eve bit the apple, all women have guilt and that's why they sabotage themselves.'

You're sabotaging my sexual urge when you keep on talking about Lisa, he thought.

'Let's forget about Lisa, please, Alison. Come over here, beside me.'

'I didn't tell you before. My idea for infomercials. Do you want to hear it?'

'Of course I do.' *What the fuck? Infomercials – now?*

'I think there should be a twenty-four-hour infomercial.'

'Mmhmm.' Skip bit the inside of his cheeks.

'A day in the life, you know. One man or one couple. You follow them through their day. So, for example, they wake up and the woman says, "I'd love some coffee, some of that special coffee you brought back from Italy that makes my day start with a bang." And the man says, "I'll get it for you. Just let me put on these amazing slippers you gave me for Christmas." You see? As they go about their day, they talk about product after product;

at the end I suppose they could discuss the best non-prescription sleeping pill. Do you see how limitless the possibilities are?'

'Umm, I think I do. But wouldn't people get bored?'

'They don't get bored with thirty-minute ones advertising one product. Why would they get bored with twenty-four-hour ones advertising tons of products to help them with their lives?'

'Exactly how do you sell these products at the end? If someone wanted every single product mentioned, you'd have to ship it to them in trucks.'

'I'll have to think about that. But I'm sure we could work something out. We could do it together, Skip. You and I. We'd make a great team, don't you think?'

'Sure,' Skip said quietly. The overwhelming exhaustion had returned and instantly extinguished what had been an equally overwhelming desire to have sex with Alison. He was too tired to move or think, or even to sleep. He wanted to turn on the television and watch a detective story or CNN or, God help him, cricket. Instead he closed his eyes and whispered: 'We sure would. Tell me more about it.'

Chapter 13

I know what you're thinking. You're thinking: I'm on the last page of this book now. What is she going to say to sum everything up?'

What can I say? That if you haven't gotten it by now, you never will?

No – that's unfair. First of all, I'm sure you've understood what I'm saying. Why am I sure? Because it's simple. It's common sense. I'm not throwing fancy words or technical terms at you. None of this is scientific mumbo-jumbo. It's all about human nature. And how human beings work when they fall in love.

They see something in each other which makes them happy and blissful and confident. Over the years, as I've said, that vision can blur. But that's nobody's fault, folks. That's human nature too. It happens to all of us. What I'm saying is that we can get our sight back. We can see what we first saw in our loved one and from that point on, we can make sure we get our eyes checked all the time so we don't lose that vision again.

All you have to do is use a little imagination and make a little effort. There's nothing I've suggested in these pages which is radical. It doesn't cost money. It doesn't take up all your time. My exercises are simple, my philosophy is simple.

Find that person you fell in love with. He or she is still there. You two can conquer the world together. You're on the same team.

Don't let yourself down by giving up. Don't throw that love away. Rediscover it! And when you do, you'll find you've come upon that pot of gold at the end of your very own rainbow!!!

And my very last word to you, my very last suggestion? ENJOY!!!

I Saw You First, Chapter Fifteen, p. 302

As Declan made himself a piece of toast, he wondered whether he should worry about Alison, but decided that she'd either spent the night with Skip or gone to her mother's in Essex. The latter was the better bet – for how could she get away with Skip when Lisa was ensconced in Pimlico? Alison hadn't wanted to see him, that much was perfectly clear, and he couldn't say he was too upset by this fact. They could discuss the mechanics of their split later. By not turning up last night, by not even ringing to tell him where she was, she had signalled that he was no longer a part of her life.

So be it, Declan thought. Alison isn't my problem. Christina is.

As he was dressing for work, he realized that the office was the last place he wanted to be. He wasn't in the mood to be cheerful or friendly, and he couldn't imagine having the energy to make the telephone calls he had to make or do the paperwork which sat waiting on his desk. He'd call in sick, he decided. This wasn't something he often did, so no one would question him. A summer cold was a legitimate excuse. Or he could say he'd had a mild case of food poisoning.

And then what would he do all day? He hadn't a clue. It hardly mattered. The point was not to have to work.

Susan answered the phone when he rang and he used the food poisoning story. She was sympathetic and told him Coca Cola was always a help for upset stomachs. Declan thanked her and was about to ring off when she said: 'Oh, if you're ill in bed, you should watch Lisa Thomas on *This Morning*.'

'I will,' he replied. 'I'll watch her and drink some Coke and recuperate. See you tomorrow.'

Taking off his suit and putting on a pair of shorts, he began to go from room to room in the house deciding what possessions he could do without. The televisions in the kitchen and bedroom were first on his list; from there he moved on to the portable sound system in the bathroom, one of the two radios in the bedroom, a spare old computer he kept in the hall closet and a portable CD player he never used. And as for the wine he had stocked – that was a complete waste of time. He would never be a connoisseur – the bottles were there for snob appeal only. Declan smiled, imagining himself swirling it around in his glass, sniffing and tasting it.

It's not me, he thought, looking at the bottles lying in wait. I don't want to give flash dinner parties and decant it and later on pass the port to the left or the right or whichever direction it has to be passed in. When it comes down to it, I prefer beer.

By the time he'd finished mentally clearing the house of extraneous goods, he reckoned a burglar might still find a few items, but not half what he would have before. Looking at his watch, he turned on the kicthen television for what he hoped would be the last time, and settled down to watch Lisa on *This Morning*. He sat patiently through various items before Lisa was introduced. She sat in a chair between Richard and Judy, wearing a blue dress and looking uncharacteristically nervous.

Why is she waving her foot up and down like that? he wondered. And her mouth is twitching. This isn't the Lisa I know. What's happened? She must be used to television – she's a pro. She's been on countless shows in the States. Is it the English bit that's disconcerting her?

Declan leaned forward as the interview began and concentrated on Lisa. The beginning was fine and he relaxed a little. Lisa was talking about why she wrote *I Saw You First* – how seeing an old couple bickering in the park had prompted her to think of what they must have been like at the beginning of their relationship. Lisa then explained why she'd called the book *I Saw You First* and did her little riff on how the emphasis should be on the *you*. Richard and Judy both looked interested.

It will all be fine, Declan thought. Except her foot is still bobbing and there's something definitely odd about her mouth. Calm down, Lisa. You've got them in the palm of your hand. Chill out.

'And you convinced your husband to leave work altogether to save your marriage – is that right, Lisa?' Richard asked. 'How did he feel about that?'

'He was fine,' Lisa replied. 'Just fine and dandy. But it wasn't as if I stopped him from doing what he liked doing or sabotaged him in any way, the way men sabotage women or women sabotage themselves because of guilt, because of Adam and Eve and the Bible.'

Richard looked over at Judy and raised his eyebrows. Judy smiled at Lisa and said: 'You've written a lot of exercises people can do to help them get back to the beginning, haven't you? When I was reading *I Saw You First*, I picked out one exercise in particular which – '

'It's probably all right for you two,' Lisa cut in, addressing Judy. 'You're doing the same thing so you're on the same level and so guilt isn't a factor although I wonder if he – ' she pointed at Richard ' – gives you a hard time about children, for example.'

What the hell? Declan wanted to reach out and grab Lisa and muzzle her. What was she doing? What point was she making?

'But take, for example,' Lisa continued, oblivious to Richard and Judy's discomfiture, 'that show you have here, that one called *Countdown*. I happened to watch it the other afternoon. It's wonderful, isn't it? Making all those words out of all those letters and then doing math problems as well, and there was that man hosting it who was wearing a really snazzy suit and that incredibly bright woman who does those math problems. Are those two married? Because if they are, you have to wonder whether they're happy. You have to ask yourself whether he's cheated on her. He might not like it that she's so good at math when he doesn't seem to be so hot at it himself. He might want to get back at her by finding some other woman, some woman who will say: "You're the best thing since sliced bread. Don't worry if you can't add two and two, I can't either."'

'Richard Whiteley and Carol Vorderman aren't married,' Richard smiled. 'Let's get back to what people see in each other at the beginning of relationships?'

'They're not married? Well, that's lucky. Marriage can be a huge mistake, you know. Marriage can be hell.'

'We have to take a break now, but Lisa Thomas will be back to take phone-ins from viewers with relationship problems, won't you, Lisa?'

'Yes,' she nodded, looking distracted.

She's lost it, Declan thought. On national television. She's found out about about Skip and Alison, and she has gone into meltdown. Poor Lisa. Will they hustle her out of the studio? Say she's been taken ill suddenly? Or will they let her pull herself together again and answer the phone-ins? This is awful. I should have been there. I should at least have checked on her last night or telephoned her early this morning. I wasn't thinking about Lisa in all this – only myself.

I suppose a one-minute loss of sanity might pass unnoticed. Maybe viewers will be intrigued by all the talk about Richard Whiteley and Carol Vorderman. Doesn't Carol Vorderman present a show on unsolved mysteries? Lisa's performance this morning could be one of them.

When *This Morning* returned after the break, Lisa was still sitting there, but this time, Declan was relieved to see, she was looking far more composed. Not only did she appear to be more relaxed, she also handled the phone-ins brilliantly, never deviating from the *I Saw You First* philosophy.

She's come back from 5-0 down, Declan said to himself, cheering her on. She's back on form and she's the old Lisa again. Thank Christ.

'We have time for one more call,' Judy announced. 'This one's from Roger in Hove. Roger's married and is worried that his wife has lost interest in him. She seems to be spending less and less time at home. Roger – is there anything in particular you'd like to ask Lisa?'

'Yes, there is. Lisa, I'm mad about my wife. I love every single thing about her. I want to know how I can make her see the real me. I think she thinks I'm weak. But that's only because I love her so much she makes me *feel* weak. I'm not a weak person. Not deep down. Only whenever she walks in the room.'

'Roger,' Lisa frowned. 'This sounds like a familiar story.'

'What would you advise Roger to do, Lisa?' Judy asked.

'I think he should try one of my exercises,' Lisa replied. 'Perhaps he and his wife could recreate their first date.'

'She didn't like me much on our first date,' Roger said. 'She was pregnant by some other bloke and she wasn't feeling very well, and she wasn't paying much attention to me.'

'Roger.' Lisa's voice was angry. 'Now I remember. You're the same Roger, aren't you? We've had this discussion before. I don't know why you've called me again. It's ridiculous. Remember what I said before? I said, "Get over it," all right? Got the picture? *She doesn't love you.* End of story. Move on. You're obsessed. It's not healthy.'

'Lisa, I don't think—'

'No, Richard. You don't understand. I've spoken to Roger before. His wife is using him and has been from day one. The situation is hopeless. He shouldn't sit around and wallow in his misery.'

'Well, Roger, I hope this has helped—' Judy began.

'She's a fake,' Roger said. 'I am crying out for help here and what do I get? Lisa Thomas is a—' He was cut off then and Richard and Judy managed to reassert control and end the show without seeming to be flustered in the least by their guest's erratic behaviour.

Lisa, Lisa, Declan said to himself. What are you going to do next?

'Your next appointment is here,' the receptionist announced

over the intercom. 'I think you'll be pleased to see who it is.'

Christina wondered whether it could be Declan again and if so how the receptionist would know that he was the one person she'd be pleased to see. No, that was wishful thinking. It was probably one of her old clients whom she hadn't seen in a while. Still, she hoped it was Declan and found herself irritated, disappointed and frightened all at the same time when Toby walked in.

'Hello, there,' he said, combing his rain-soaked hair with his fingers. 'It's filthy out there. You're lucky not to have to brave the elements today.'

Christina wished he would sit down rather than stand there looking at her expectantly. What did he think would happen? Did he believe she'd rush into his arms?

'Why did you come?' she asked, standing her ground as well. He wasn't going to bully her – not any more.

'I thought you might like to know what I think of Lucy.'

'I don't care what you think of Lucy.'

'No? I think you do.'

He was still attractive, she couldn't deny that; especially attractive with that windswept, wet look. She'd always preferred it when the elements messed his hair, and now that he was literally dripping on the floor, she felt vulnerable. If he moved closer to her now, she wasn't sure what she'd do.

'Fine. Don't ask me. Pretend you don't care. But I'm going to tell you anyway. Lucy is unremittingly boring, Christina. She is beautiful, technically, yes. But she's bourgeois and silly and boring. You have nothing to worry about there and you should have realized that ages ago. You're above this petty jealousy.'

'I seem to remember you being jealous of Richard not so long ago,' she countered.

'That's different. I didn't know Richard. Richard might have been God's gift to the female species for all I knew.'

'Do you believe me now? Do you believe that he was in love with her?'

'Anything's possible, of course, Christina. As a matter of fact, she practically threw herself at me last night, but I wasn't interested. Maybe she did the same with Richard and he *was* interested. I don't know. I don't care. All that matters is your reaction, how you let it rule your life when you shouldn't have.'

'She threw herself at you?'

'More or less. Let me put it this way: I certainly could have had her if I had wanted to. But I didn't.'

'Why not?'

'I told you – she was boring. She was going on and on about Lisa Thomas' book, if you can believe that. I would wager a million quid she'll be having Nigel do those exercises with her. All her neighbours in Esher will be doing those exercises. Everyone will be seeing everyone for the first time again.' Toby snorted. 'It would be depressing if it weren't funny.'

'That's true,' Christina said quietly.

'There – you see, we still agree about things. Important things. We may have jumped the gun vis à vis marriage, but we get along well, Chris. As the great Lisa herself would say, we shouldn't throw the baby out with the bathwater.'

'Skip is having an affair with Alison, by the way.'

'Really?' Toby moved to the massage table and sat down on it. 'Did Declan ring here and blub down the phone to you?'

'No – '

'Not that I'd mind if he did. I'm not always unreasonably jealous, Christina. I'm sure, for example, that Declan's not your type. Too weedy. He doesn't appreciate his father, he's not exactly Tom Cruise, and he has to kowtow to people like Lisa. Anyway, isn't life interesting? I suppose I should feel sorry for Declan, but I don't. And I don't feel sorry for Lisa, either. The way she led Skip around like a puppy dog must have been humiliating. The poor man was on a very public leash.'

'Mmm,' was all Christina said.

'So – I'll see you later, then. I'm off now to visit my old housemaster at Harrow. I looked him up in the directory and he's living in Ealing. So I gave him a ring and he remembered who I was straight off – that's the way they are, these poor sods. What a sad life. I can pick up a few of his mannerisms I've forgotten, although I have to be careful – I'm going to be a young, trendy housemaster, not an old fart.'

'Toby.' Christina remained standing as she had throughout their talk. 'Are you going to pay for this hour?'

'Excuse me?' Toby jumped off the table. 'Why would I do that? You haven't touched me, I'm sorry to say.'

'But you must have rung and booked the hour.'

'Yes. I wanted to be sure to see you and the receptionist said it looked from the appointment book as if you were working through lunch. This was the only time you had free.'

'That's an hour of my time, then.'

Toby cocked his head. 'You're serious? Come off it, Christina. We live together, remember? I'll buy some food for dinner, how's that? Anyway, in a short time I'll be able to afford all sorts of treats. You'll be living with a star.'

'No, I won't.'

'I *am* going to get that part, you know. You should believe in me.'

'I'm sure you'll get the part. But we won't be living together and we won't be seeing each other.'

'I thought we'd cleared all this up.'

'We have. Our relationship is over.'

'Oh Christ,' Toby sighed. 'Am I supposed to grovel in some way? I don't even know what I should grovel about. I've tried to help you get over a problem. That's all I've done – help you. If it's because I said we jumped the gun on the marriage idea – '

'No, that's not it. I'll tell you exactly why it is. You didn't come after me last night when I was so upset and you knew I was. You didn't try to find me, you didn't ask me where I've been or why, exactly, I was so upset, and you didn't have sex with Lucy – '

'What? Was I *supposed* to have sex with Lucy? You're crazy, you're – '

316

'Let me finish my sentence. You didn't have sex with Lucy because she was boring. Not because you felt loyal to me or happy enough with me that you didn't want to have sex with her. The point is you *would* have had sex with her if she hadn't been boring. Am I right?'

'Of course not.'

'And you're a good liar and I'm a bad one. It's over, Toby. You'll have to find somewhere else to stay. Maybe you can bed down with your old housemaster.'

'Christina, you're not being logical. You're hysterical.'

'I don't expect you to have moved everything out by the time I get back, but I think you should have made a start.'

'Fine. I'm not going to take any abuse from someone who needs psychological help. This is a waste of my time. Ring me if your sanity returns. This is a stupid threat, Christina. You'll never find anyone like me again, you know that, don't you?'

'God,' Christina shook her head. 'I hope I don't.'

She waited until he left before she cried, but this time the tears weren't as fierce or as long-running as they had been the night before. By the time her next client came in, she was in a reasonable state to work. Mrs Lavell had a terrible sunburn, but then Mrs Lavell had terrrible sunburns once every few months – either from the English sun in summer or the West Indian sun in winter. Christina knew from experience how difficult it would be to work on her without causing pain, but as Mrs Lavell got undressed, she took out her lavender oil and mixed it with water in a spray bottle.

'You're a genius at this,' Mrs Lavell said as soon as Christina sprayed her back with a fine mist. 'I know I should stay away from the sun, but I just can't help myself. It's too wonderful, the sun . . .'

And I couldn't help myself either by staying away from Toby at the beginning, Christina thought. He was too beautiful. He was a male version of Lucy, in a way. He was beautiful and he seemed to care for me and I wanted so badly for him to love me as well.

But he never did. And Lucy never did and never will. She was kind in a patronizing way, she and Chloë both. They all felt sorry for me, but they didn't actually love me or even truly care about me. I have to accept that now. I have to bite the bullet. But this time I won't choke on it.

'Declan. It's Lisa. Your office said you were sick at home, but I thought you might be sick for the same reason I'm sick.'

'Oh, Lisa.' Declan had never heard her sound so frail. 'I'm sorry. I should have rung you before to see how you're doing, but I didn't know you knew.'

'I didn't know. Not until last night. You knew before.'

'Only the night before last. Are you going to be all right?'

'I don't know, Declan. I was on television this morning and I didn't do so well, I'm afraid. I couldn't concentrate. Everything's going wrong.'

Lisa Thomas *crying*? He couldn't imagine what her face would look like with tears running down it. Some people's faces didn't change when they cried, but Declan reckoned Lisa's definitely would. It was too used to smiling.

'What can I do to help?' he asked quickly.

'Aren't you furious too? Couldn't you kill them both?'

'Lisa – Alison and I weren't married. We'd been together almost two years but it's not the same as a long marriage. I'm upset but I can understand that you'd be even more upset.'

Was that the right thing to say? How would I know? I don't have much experience in situations like this. In fact, I don't have any.

'I thought I was OK. I made all these plans last night, but then I called my editor in New York and she didn't understand my ideas and then this morning I wasn't myself and I wasn't concentrating and then that awful man called me *again*. He's harassing me, Declan, this man Roger who keeps calling in to phone-ins I do. If you could have heard him, you'd know how terrible he is. He's *hounding* me.'

Declan didn't say that he *had* heard Roger. When you're suffering from embarrassment, you don't want to find out how many other people were witness to it.

'Is there anything I can do to help?' he repeated, at a loss.

'I don't know.' Lisa caught her breath in a little gasp. 'I don't know anything any more, that's the problem. Last night I was so angry I felt OK. Now I just want to go back to America. Except home would remind me of Skip and I never want to think about him again.'

'Are you sure your marriage is finished?' Declan wound the phone cord around his wrist.

'Oh, please. You know, I might have lived with his infidelity – maybe. We might have been able to talk things out. I'm not an unforgiving person.' Lisa sniffed. 'Things like this happen, I know. But he said my book was crap, Declan. And I know that's what he thinks. That's the same as saying *I'm* crap.'

'I'm sure Skip doesn't think that.'

'I'm sure he does. He's kept quiet about it because it has made money, but he thinks it is crap. Oh Declan, I'm a mess. I can't think straight. I came back from that show and I crawled into bed, and right now I'm in bed with the covers over my head. I want to run away. I want to hide.'

'Lisa,' Declan said firmly. 'You're having lunch with me.'

'I am?' she whimpered.

'Yes.'

'Oh.' She was silent for a second and then said: 'This morning, in the studio, I overheard someone talking about some restaurant called Harvey something. Do you know where that is?'

'It could be the fifth floor of the Harvey Nichols store on Sloane Street. There's a restaurant there. It's supposed to be very good.'

'Great – then you make a reservation and I'll meet you there at one.' Lisa paused. 'We'll show them, won't we, Declan? You're so right to think we should go out and face the world. We can't let them beat us. We have our pride, after all. Don't we?'

'We do, Lisa.'

'And you can tell me what you think of my next book proposal. It's a title you haven't heard before. I know it will be even bigger than *I Saw You First*.'

Declan frowned and rubbed his forehead. 'I can't wait to hear about it, he said.

I wonder if my face is as much of a giveaway as Christina's, he said to himself. I hope not.

Alison was sipping orange juice and nibbling at a croissant. Skip was staring out of the hotel window, watching the rain.

'It's pouring with rain, isn't it?' Alison commented.

'Pouring with rain?'

'Yes.'

'Is that an English expression?'

'I don't know. Is it?'

'Well, it must be. I mean, what do people here think? That it might be pouring with concrete? Do you say it's flurrying with snow? Beaming with sunshine?'

'No.' Alison stared at Skip. 'It's just an expression, Skip. There's no need to get so worked up about it.'

'I know.' He continued to stare out of the window. 'We're going to have to think about money,' he said bleakly. 'It isn't exactly pouring down on me at the moment.'

'Right,' Alison nodded. 'That's why I was telling you about my infomercial plans last night. I have other plans too, Skip. For other infomercials.'

'What kind of plans?' He turned to look at her.

'Well, as far as I can make out, no upmarket company has done infomercials yet.'

'It's not an upmarket niche. The target audience isn't upmarket.'

'Exactly. So there's a gap in the market – the sort of gap you were talking about that first night. I was walking down Bond Street the other day and I thought: Look, DKNY, Tiffany's, Chanel – all these expensive shops. Why don't *they* make infomercials?

Products from those shops change people's lives for the better as well, you know. The right diamond from Tiffany's can make much more of an impact on a woman than the right diet. Or the right designer dress can. Look at Liz Hurley and that safety-pin dress she wore that literally changed her life for ever. That's perfect material for an infomercial: "You can be Liz Hurley, all you have to do is buy this dress." That sort of thing.'

'You have a point there.'

'The concept is the same; the prices are higher, that's all. Imagine a testimonial from a woman who has been given a piece of jewellery designed by Paloma Picasso. It makes her feel more confident at parties; she feels more valuable because she's wearing something valuable. It shines, she shines. You see what I'm getting at?'

'But could people afford these things? The kind of people who watch infomercials?' Skip moved away from the window and sat down at the end of the bed, at Alison's feet.

She's a wonder, he thought. I was tired last night, that's why I didn't want to listen. I wasn't ready to listen then. Too much had happened too quickly. But she's right. We could make a fantastic team. When we finally did have sex last night it was well worth the wait. We could be dynamite together, in bed and in the boardroom.

'They *make* themselves afford those things. Do you know how many women buy dresses which they know they can't really afford? Hundreds of thousands. Millions. They go into debt for a dress they love. It's psychological, you know. And it works. You *do* feel better if you're wearing something beautiful. Or exclusive. Designers wouldn't exist if that weren't the case.'

'Would a company like Tiffany's lower itself to an infomercial, though? They have a reputation to uphold.'

'They have a company to run, don't they? In the end the men in suits look at profits. Besides, what do they have to lose? We produce an infomercial for them and screen it for a test audience and see the reaction. If it works, if people are signing up to buy, how can they resist? Once one upmarket company does it, the rest will follow. It's not as if Mick Jagger doesn't do videos, you know. He doesn't think he's above all that – he knows they work and they're necessary.' Alison put the plate with the croissant on the bedside table. 'Take me, for example. I surf the satellite channels and if I come to the Shopping Channel, I keep going. I don't stop. Why? Because they're selling what I consider to be naff products, things the typical Essex Girl would buy. Now if I came to an infomercial which had some woman who looked enough like me for me to identify with her talking about a necklace that changed her life, I'd watch.'

'Wouldn't the thought that everyone else might be wearing the same necklace spoil it?'

'Has it spoiled Armani shirts or Versace trousers or Chanel bags?'

'You're a smart woman, Alison. And a sexy one, too.' Skip leaned over and sucked her toe.

'Skip, we're talking business.'

He stopped what he was doing and looked up at her. 'Not now, we're not.'

Declan was pleased to see that Lisa had a healthy appetite. She'd wolfed down a plate of smoked salmon and was digging into her duck with relish. Between mouthfuls, she'd explained her idea for *You Can Do Anything I Can Do Better*. Declan had tried his hardest to look enthusiastic, but he thought she was verging on madness. A philosophical essay on the nature of guilt was not, he thought, the self-help book readers were looking for. They wanted problems solved rather than explained. However, he was relieved that she hadn't gone into a diatribe about Skip and Alison. The book was a distraction which he welcomed and would have liked to help her with. When he finally had the chance to speak, he phrased his objections very carefully.

'I wonder about the title, Lisa. It's catchy, but then you're a star. How will ordinary women think they can do better than you? Isn't that setting too high expectations?'

She was off again, answering his question in paragraphs. The torrent of words was making Declan dizzy. The Bible, self-sabotage, guilt – he'd heard it all during the first course and now she was repeating it, almost verbatim.

Will this manic energy ever subside? Declan asked himself. And if it does, will she collapse? He didn't get the chance to find out. Just as Lisa was saying, 'Why do people worship the Virgin Mary? All she did was have a baby. They should worship Eve. She's the one who *did* something on her own . . .' Declan caught sight of Skip and Alison entering the restaurant.

'Lisa – ' he interrupted her. 'I have some bad news.'

'What?' she asked. 'Do you have a problem with Eve?'

'No. *We* have a problem. Skip and Alison are over there, getting seated at that corner table.'

'No.' Lisa shrank back in her chair. 'Go tell them to leave, Declan. I don't want to see either of them. They can't flaunt themselves like this – it's obscene.'

'They haven't seen us. We could pay our bill and leave now, without any trouble.'

'I'm not going anywhere.' Lisa suddenly sat up straight and threw her shoulders back. 'Why should we leave? We haven't done anything wrong. *They* have.'

'Well, I don't want to make a scene. I don't want to go over and force them out.'

'What are they doing now?' Lisa's back was to their table.

'They're looking at menus.'

'And who is paying for this, I ask? *I* am. I should have cancelled Skip's credit card. He's having an affair and paying for it with my money, money I earned from a book he thinks is crap. That's it.' Lisa stood up and threw her napkin on the table. 'I've had enough.'

Toby would appreciate this scene, Declan found himself thinking. This is high drama. Why aren't I more involved? Why would I prefer to leave them in peace? Because I don't think it's going to work out between them, not in the end? Because I believe they'll both suffer enough without Lisa or I saying a word? Is that it?

When she turned around and spotted where they were sitting, she immediately got up and began to stride toward them. Declan followed her. For a moment, he thought of restraining her and taking her away from the restaurant, but he couldn't fathom how he'd do it, short of throwing her over his shoulder and carrying her out while she thumped his back and screamed bloody murder.

The second Skip noticed Lisa, he sprang up, upsetting his empty wine glass.

'What are you doing here?' he asked, terror in his voice.

'I'm having lunch with Declan,' she answered. Declan was surprised by how calm she sounded. It was a lethal calm, though; the sort of dead calm that leaves ships stranded for months.

'And may I ask who is paying for this lunch you're having?'

'I am,' Alison said.

Her voice matched Lisa's. Declan thought of the Gladiators and almost smiled.

'I'm contacting my lawyer as soon as I get back to the house,' Lisa said, ignoring Alison. 'And if you think you'll get any of the money I worked so hard for, you're wrong, both of you.' She glared briefly at Alison, then swung her gaze back to Skip. 'I will also be cancelling your Visa card, Skip. I'll give you enough money to get a plane back to New York and that's it. You're dead meat. I hope you have a wonderful time living in poverty.'

'The idealistic, caring, sharing Lisa Thomas,' Alison spat out.

'Alison – ' Declan started.

'Lisa – ' Skip interrupted. 'I didn't mean to hurt you. It just happened. I'm sorry, really I am. I don't know what to say.'

'Then shut up,' Lisa said, her tone heating up. 'I wouldn't believe

324

a word you said anyway. I want you out of here on the next plane. I'll give you two hours to use your Visa and fix a ticket and then I'm cancelling the card. If you don't leave immediately I'll give an·interview to *People Magazine* telling them what you've done – how you've lived off me and cheated on me and behaved like a – like a lying, cheating bastard. *And*' Lisa took a deep breath, 'I'll find your mother and I'll do the talk-show circuit with her and she can tell the world how you abandoned her and left her to rot in a trailer park while you lived the Life of Riley.'

'You wouldn't,' Skip whispered.

'Want to bet?'

'Lisa – this isn't like you. Don't do this to yourself.'

'I'm not doing anything to myself, Skip. I'm doing it to you. So if I were you, I'd be on the afternoon flight to New York. I'm sure there is one. And I don't care who you take with you. It might be easier for a couple to beg than a single person – you might get more sympathy.'

Lisa turned her back and walked off.

'What a bitch,' Alison said, grabbing Skip's hand.

'That wasn't Lisa,' Skip mumbled.

'It looked like Lisa to me,' she replied.

'I don't think you should have told her her book is crap,' Declan said.

'Well, it is,' Skip sighed. 'Can I help that? I mean – those Exercises. You know I'm in favour of anything that works commercially, but that doesn't mean I have to like it, does it? All that back to the beginning stuff . . . I mean, that's impossible – we all know that. You can't go back.'

Declan looked at Alison. 'No,' he said quietly. 'You can't.'

Christina didn't know why she was doing it, but she went ahead anyway. She called Directory Enquiries and found Owen and Jessica's number. Without stopping to think, she dialled it and found herself listening to Jessica saying, 'Hello.'

'Hello, Jessica, it's Christina Billings.'

'Christina – hello again. How nice to hear from you. How are you?'

'I'm all right,' she answered. 'It's a little complicated to explain, but Toby and I have split up and I was wondering if it would be possible to me to take the train this afternoon after work and come and stay with you for the night. I don't mean to impose and I know this is unusual, but I need to get out of London and clear my head. Just say if it's a problem – please be honest.'

'It's not a problem, honestly,' Jessica said. 'We'd love to see you again. I'm sorry about you and Toby. Owen would love to see you, too. Please come.'

'Are you sure?'

'I'm positive.'

'I'll find out the times of trains and ring you back, then.'

'Wonderful. I'm looking forward to it. The station isn't far. I'll come and meet you, whatever time.'

'Thank you, Jessica. You're a lifesaver.'

'That's usually Owen's job,' Jessica said lightly. 'It's nice that I get that title too once in a while.'

After Christina had rung off, she went back to her treatment room and prepared it for the next client.

I can't wait, she thought. I can't wait to get out of London and go to a place where I know I can relax. I won't burden Owen and Jessica with my story. I want to sit at that table and talk about anything but myself and my problems. I want to go on a long walk with the dog. I need the atmosphere in that cottage, the warmth. Tonight is a night I don't want to feel lonely.

'Christina.' The receptionist's voice startled her. 'I'm afraid your next appointment has just rung and cancelled.'

'Oh.' Christina was surprised how disappointed she was. She needed to work. She needed to keep her mind occupied. 'Mary, is there any beauty therapist available this hour?'

'Let me look – hang on. Yes, Gina is free.'

'Could you book me in with her? She can do massage as well, can't she?'

'Of course she can. All the beauty therapists can do relaxing massages.'

'That's what I need,' Christina said. 'A relaxing massage. I'll pay for it, of course.'

'Or you could swap, if you wanted to. She does an hour's massage for you and you do an hour's aromatherapy some other time for her.'

'That's a good idea.'

'You'd lose a little money, though. Aromatherapy is more expensive.'

'I know,' Christina nodded. 'But I don't care. I'll come out and go to Gina's room now.'

'Fine,' Mary said. 'I hope you enjoy it. You were looking a little worse for wear this morning. Hangover?'

'Something like that,' Christina said. 'Not too much to drink, but too much to digest.'

'You're not going to do it, are you?'

'What choice do I have?' Skip scratched the back of his neck. 'I can't stay here and live off you, Alison. I have to get back to New York as soon as possible. At least I have some friends there and I can crash with one of them for a while until I get back on my feet.'

'I can come with you. I have a passport.'

'What about your job?'

'I'll leave it. I've wanted out for ages anyway. Do you know how bitchy they were when I called in sick today? I hate them. I want to go to New York.'

'It doesn't make sense, Alison. As much as I'd love it if you did come, I have to get my shit together. Two people out of work in New York is worse than one. And Lisa might go even more ballistic, whatever she says about not caring who I take with me. The thought of my mother on television . . .' Skip shuddered. 'Look – I'll call you as soon as I get there. The minute I get my act together, you can fly over and join me. It won't be long.'

'I suppose that makes sense.' Alison squeezed Skip's hand. 'I have to sort out my life as well. We'll have to put the house on the market. Once that's sold, I'll have some money. That should help.'

'I'm not taking your money.'

'Skip – we're partners. We're equals. We're going to work together. We should share.'

'As long as it stays equal,' Skip muttered.

'Pardon?'

'Nothing. Listen, I better get going. I have to buy a ticket, I have to get organized.' Skip's face reddened. 'Did you mean it when you said you'd pay for this lunch?'

'Of course,' Alison replied.

'She's gone crazy.' He shook his head. 'I can't believe she said those things. She's gone nuts.'

'She's jealous,' Alison shrugged. 'Jealous of us. Who wouldn't be?'

'I didn't think she had it in her.' Skip stared at his plate. 'I didn't think she loved me that much.'

'What? You're mumbling, Skip. I can't hear you.'

'I didn't say anything important.'

'Everything you say is important to me.'

'That's a nice compliment,' Skip remarked dully. 'Let's get the bill.'

By the time Declan got back to Henning Street he actually did feel ill. It served him right, he thought, for lying that morning. Lisa's transformation from a cheerful bouncy optimist into a quite vicious angry and vengeful scorned woman depressed him. Was that all Skip's fault, or had the darker side of her character always lurked there, waiting for a trigger to start it running its race in public? Was betrayal a legitimate reason for the sort of behaviour he'd seen at lunch and afterwards when he'd accompanied her home? She was manic, baying for Skip's blood, revelling in the thought of him penniless and destitute, dragging Alison down with him.

That's what happens when you think you own someone, he thought. What would Owen have done if Mum had had an affair? Would he have turned into a male version of Lisa this afternoon? No. Declan flopped on to the bed. No, he would have talked and talked and talked. By the time he finished talking to Mum, he would have analysed it into the ground and Mum would have been too exhausted to even contemplate doing it again. Alison – what will Alison do if Skip does go back to New York? Will she throw caution to the wind and go with him? Will she want to stay here? Or sell the house? Alison is tough, but is she a match for Lisa when Lisa's in a mood like this?

What was all that about Skip's mother? And what will happen if Lisa's next book fails? Will *she* fall apart and end up destitute herself?

There is too much to think about, too much going on here. I need some distance from it all. I need to talk to Christina. Which I can't do because Christina has her own life to get on with. She doesn't need me barging into her Club or driving up and down her street like some demented teenager with a crush.

Declan made himself get up from the bed, go downstairs and make a cup of coffee. When the telephone rang, he prayed it wasn't Lisa Thomas.

'Declan,' Owen said. 'Your office said you were ill. Are you OK?'

'More or less,' Declan answered, feeling immense relief. A sane person. I've thought he was mad for so long, but he's one of the few sane people I know. How wonderful it is to hear the voice of a sane person.

'Actually I called in sick and I'm not. I wanted a day off.'

'Good for you,' Owen said. 'You need a break – you work too hard. I was ringing to tell you something I thought might amuse you. I'm at the university now and I've been talking about *Plots in a Box* and *Plato on a Plate* to various colleagues of mine. They're all intrigued. They've come up with some wonderful ideas. One of them was *Hegel in a Hammock* – you see, you can swing back and forth as you listen to an explanation of the dialectical imperative. Swing to the left for the thesis, to the right for the antithesis and when the hammock comes to rest you've reached synthesis.' Owen giggled.

'That's nice.'

'Declan – you sound miserable. What's going on?'

'Do you have a few years to listen?'

'I have all the time in the world.'

Chapter 14

I want to dedicate I Saw You First to my wonderful husband, Skip Thomas. He has made this book possible and has supported me in my work every step of the way. What can I say, Skip? You are the light of my life and I know that light will never grow dim. Whatever happens in our lives, remember, honey, I saw you first. And I will love you for ever.

After Declan had dropped her off in the taxi, Lisa sat in the kitchen trying to work out what she should do next.

What are you supposed to do when your husband has cheated on you? Do you scream in rage or do you call a lawyer or do you cry? Maybe you do all three. The sight of Skip and Alison sitting together was too much. It's not something I can forget, ever. They made a fool of me and that's something I can't ever forgive, either.

Sooner or later she'd have to go back home and build a new life for herself. But not yet. First she had to put some distance between the past and the future. She had to expunge Skip from her heart and her brain, cut him out and throw him away. She'd done everything she possibly could to keep the marriage going happily and he had turned around and destroyed all her efforts.

Skip. Skip and Alison. How had it started? What were they

like in bed together? Why had he done this? Were they laughing at her – dumb little Lisa, the only one who didn't know what was going on?

Well, she would be the one to have the last laugh. They might be able to wound Lisa Thomas the woman, but they couldn't harm Lisa Thomas the Author. Or could they?

How could she say another word about *I Saw You First* when her own husband was seeing someone else? He'd put her in the worst possible spot imaginable. Skip had not only betrayed her, he'd endangered her career. Who would buy any book she wrote, knowing the first one was a sham? That her own marriage had failed miserably? A sensible author in Lisa's position would stay with Skip whatever he did, in order to keep her credibility intact.

But I'm not like that, Lisa said to herself. I can't pretend. I can't be a hypocrite and live one way in private and another in public. I don't want to live with a man who doesn't love me and who thinks I'm crap. I won't do it.

When the doorbell rang, Lisa rose wearily to answer it, wondering whether Skip was now so frightened of her, he didn't dare use his key and come in without permission. If that was the case, it was fine by her. She wasn't going to let him know how upset she was. Angry, yes. She *wanted* him to see her rage, but not her tears.

'Lisa Thomas?' A middle-aged woman in what Lisa tagged as a Donna Karan cream pantsuit stood on her doorstep. She had a very short haircut and an ingratiating smile. She looked like a caterer Lisa had once hired for a particularly important dinner party.

'Yes?' Lisa tried to return the smile. It was a major effort.

'I'm Jane Swallow, from the *Mail*.'

Did the people who delivered the mail always identify themselves like this? And was the pantsuit some kind of uniform? If so, the British postal workers did a hell of a lot better than Americans. Maybe this welfare state business had its advantages.

'Yes?' Lisa held out her hand, expecting some letters to be put in it. Instead Jane shook it and made her way past Lisa into the house.

'I'm sorry I'm a little late,' she said. 'I hope you don't mind.'

'Of course not.' What a strange system. Did mail people expect tea and crumpets every time they delivered? In that case, it's a good thing we haven't had any letters before today. It would be exhausting having to cater for this woman every day.

'I don't know if there's anything I can offer you,' Lisa said politely. 'It must be a difficult job. All that walking. And those dogs.'

'Dogs?' Jane turned around. 'I know foreigners think the English are mad about animals, but I don't tend to interview too many dogs.'

'No.' Lisa wiped her brow, flustered. How could she have forgotten? Jane was a journalist, not a mailman or mailwoman. Harriet had told her she had an interview with a woman from the *Daily Mail* that afternoon and Lisa had blanked it. Seeing Skip and Alison at lunch had shortcircuited her brain. Luckily, Jane Swallow didn't appear to have noticed.

'Why don't you come into the kitchen,' Lisa suggested. 'It's cosier there. We can do the interview and I'll get you some ice tea. Or whatever you'd like.'

'Has Milo come yet?'

'Milo?'

'The photographer.'

'No, no.' Lisa shook her head. This was all she needed. A photographer. On a day when she knew trying to produce a smile would be like asking a mugger to have a heart and please not take the diamond engagement ring.

'Is your husband here?' Jane queried. Her voice was worryingly assertive. Lisa knew she couldn't pretend she hadn't heard the question.

'Skip? No, not at the moment. He's due back soon, though.' *He's coming back to pick up his things and get out. I think. Please God, don't let him show up with Alison. I'm not ready to come out of the closet as the cheated-on wife, not yet. Not until the book has had time to sell here.*

'So,' Jane started, sitting down in a chair while Lisa went to the fridge and got out a pitcher of ice tea. 'How do you do it? Manage to have this perfect marriage *and* a career? Does your husband – Skip, did you say?'

Lisa nodded. Jane's voice had turned the assertive corner and was heading straight for aggressive.

'Does *Skip* mind? Does it put pressure on your marriage – your success, that is?'

Let me get the goddamn tea out before you bombard me with these questions, Lisa thought. You haven't been here for longer than a minute and you're asking about my personal life and saying my husband's name as if it were an old piece of chewing gum you can't wait to get out of your mouth. Where are your manners?

'No. Skip is very supportive.'

'You don't mind if I tape this interview, do you?' Jane brought out a Sony and placed it on the kitchen table. How old is she? Lisa asked herself. Is she married? Should I try out my Guilt Bug theory on her or not? No. She's a journalist. She's one of the few women who doesn't believe in guilt. She didn't look guilty at all when she brought out that tape-recorder before I had a chance to say 'yes' or no'. I have to get her out of here before Skip comes back. And hope that photographer can't find the place or gets run over on his way here.

It was too late. Lisa heard the front door open and the sound of Skip's feet on the marble floor, trudging toward the kitchen. Why didn't he go straight upstairs to pack? Why did he have to come in now?

'Oh, there you are, honey,' Lisa said in a rush. 'Jane here, who is interviewing me for a newspaper piece, was just asking where you were. She was also asking whether my success has put pressure on our marriage and I told her it hadn't, because it hasn't, has it?' She looked up at him with begging eyes. Not now, please, she was trying to convey. I've done enough for you in your life. I won't get your mother on TV. I didn't mean some of those things I said at lunch. Don't spill the beans now. I can't take it.

Skip put out his hand and shook Jane's. He stood, shoulders hunched, his mouth slightly twisted. It was hard for Lisa to know whether he was about to smile or frown.

'I'm sorry to interrupt,' he said. 'I have to catch a plane to New York. I'd love to stay and talk but I need to pack my things quickly.'

'A business trip?' Jane asked.

'No. Personal.' He paused, looked at Lisa. 'A funeral,' he added. 'Otherwise I'd stay and tell you how great our marriage is. But you don't really need me, do you, hon?' He turned to Lisa.

'No, sweetheart. Of course not. You have to catch that plane.'

'Nice to meet you.' He held out his hand to Jane and shook it again. 'I hope you get a great interview. I'm sure you will. Lisa's a pro.'

'Nice to have met you too, Skip. I'm sorry we couldn't get a picture of the two of you together. I hope it's not a family member.'

'What's not?' Skip raised his eyebrows.

'The person whose funeral you're going to.'

Skip put his hands on Lisa's shoulders. 'No,' he said. 'An old friend. Someone I met while I was at Harvard Business School. Someone I seem to have lost touch with over the years.'

Skip squeezed Lisa's shoulders, reached down and gave her a kiss on the head, then walked out of the kitchen.

'Can you wait for a minute while I say goodbye to him?' Lisa asked Jane. 'It won't take long.'

'Don't worry. It's nice to see such a happy couple. I don't mind waiting.'

Yes, that's what we are, Lisa thought as she went after Skip. Even that nasty journalist can see it. We're a happy couple, despite everything that's happened. I *can* forgive him. We can forget about Alison. We can leave England and go back to America and start again. Anything is possible. I do love him still. The way he stood there, that face of his, his voice – I still love it all. And he loves me. He *must* love me. Why else would he lie for me like that?

'Skip,' she cried, running up the stairs. 'Wait a second. I need to talk to you.' She caught up with him in the bedroom. He'd just dragged a suitcase out of the closet. 'Skip, I'm sorry about what I said at lunch. You don't have to go. I was mad and hurt. I didn't mean it about your mother or the money or anything. I don't want you to leave. I want us to leave together, go back and start again.'

'Go back to the beginning?' Skip threw the suitcase on the bed. 'I don't think so, Lisa.'

'Why not? I know you don't like the Exercises in my book, but there are ways to start fresh again, I'm sure there are. And I'm sure I can think of them. Different Exercises.'

'No Exercise you think up will give me an undergraduate degree from Harvard.'

'That's not fair. You're taking all those things I said when I was so angry and throwing them back at me. I bet if you'd found out I'd cheated on you, you would have said a lot worse things to me. We can't leave each other, Skip. You know we can't. We love each other – we always have.'

'Lisa.' He sat down on the bed. 'You know what I thought when I first saw you?'

'It doesn't matter.'

'Oh yes, it does. That's the one part of that book I'm beginning to agree with. When I first saw you, I saw a cute girl with wide eyes. One who looked so goddamn straight and un-fucked up I couldn't resist.'

'What's wrong with that?'

'Nothing. But it's not enough, Lisa. Because there's more to you – a lot more. You're sharp and ambitious and you have a lot to prove to the world. I saw a cute, sweet, uncomplicated girl. I saw the wrong Lisa.'

'You mean I can't be cute and sweet and also successful – is that it?' Lisa put her hands on her hips.

'The Lisa I first saw wouldn't have lied to a journalist like that to help book sales. She wouldn't have wanted me to lie, either.

You know, back at that restaurant, I thought you might really love me. You were so jealous and angry – it was pure emotion, Lisa. Coming straight from the heart. And then you turn around again as soon as I get back, and all you want is the goddamn book to succeed. That's all you care about. You'll lie or do whatever you need to do to keep that fucking book selling.'

Lisa stared at her husband, wondering how she could have so many wildly shifting mood swings in such a short time. She wanted him out of her life, she wanted him back in her life and now – now she looked at the man sitting on the bed, the man she had loved since she was twenty-two years old. The man waiting for her when she took that long walk down the aisle. She could do it now. She could give in to him and tell him how right he was, and – how had she put it in the book? – pace him. Go along with his criticism of her, thereby stalling the brewing argument, an argument she guessed neither of them had a chance of winning if, that is, they wanted to keep the marriage going. But this wasn't about their marriage any more, it was about her. Who Lisa Thomas really was and what she wanted. She was fighting for her *self* and when you're in that kind of position you don't pace. As soon as you pace, you get trampled on.

'Nice try, Skip,' she said, 'You're a real spin doctor. You're the one who has the affair and I somehow turn out to be the one who lies, right? "Cute", "sweet", "uncomplicated" – those are terrific adjectives, aren't they? You'd just love to be described that way, wouldn't you? If that's all you saw in me, then you're absolutely right, you saw the wrong Lisa. There *is* more to me, and if you can't handle that, then go off with your new little friend, and I hope she feeds your ego every second of the day.' She turned around then and made to leave the room. At the door to the bedroom she stopped.

'You better figure out right now what you first saw in Alison, you know. Because I doubt whether she's a cute little uncomplicated thing either. Have a nice flight. It's your funeral.'

*　　*　　*

Toby Goodyear gathered as many of his belongings as he could and shoved them into suitcases. Christina kicking him out now was nothing if not bad timing – he wanted to be relaxed and confident when he went for his audition on Friday. She could have had the decency to let him stay until then, at the very least. All this shit about Lucy and why he didn't sleep with her was stupid – and irritating as well. You get screwed for *not* screwing someone because you didn't screw them for the wrong reasons? That was typical female logic for you. Christina was, underneath her calm exterior, a raving psycho. If he woke up one day and read that a family of four had been murdered in Esher, Toby would know straight off who was responsible. Christina was probably hormonally imbalanced, being as tall as she was. Who was that actress? Janet McTeer – that's who – she was tall as well, and dark-haired like Christina. She could play the part perfectly and someone – a younger version of Greta Scaatchi – could be Lucy. Call the play *The Sexy Step-Sister* or *Sibling Slaughter* – that would be good.

David Hare wouldn't write it, neither would Tom Stoppard; it probably wouldn't get to the West End, but it had a lot of potential anyway. If it was done right. That was the point: anything, if it was done right, was potentially art – even that silly *Plots in a Box*.

Which reminded him – Skip hadn't got back to him about that. Well, the bugger was probably having his own domestic problems now that he'd taken up with Alison. How would Lisa, the Happy Dwarf, the Doris Day refugee from the Fifties, cope with that? People didn't have affairs in the Fifties in America, did they? No, women baked apple pies and men went off to work and came back saying, 'Hi, honey, I'm home.' Unless they were in Tennessee Williams country. In which case they would come home saying: 'Hi, honey, I'm having a nervous breakdown.'

Toby lay down on the bed and lit a cigarette. He'd try ringing Skip tomorrow, just to check in. Skip owed him, for one. And if he didn't get the part on Friday, he'd not only need the money, he'd need a back-up job – *Plots in a Box*. Which might make him a household name in the States. He didn't want that opportunity to slip by just because Skip was getting it on with some bird outside the nest.

Christina should have been home by now. Scowling at him and telling him to hurry up and clear out. He was well out of it. That weekend in Amersham had temporarily unhinged him, and he'd gone soft for a few days. The fact that Owen and Jessica had seen his Hamlet had pushed all sorts of buttons in his psyche; some of which were best left untouched.

Talking to Owen about boarding-school days was fine – perfect, actually; he could plumb all that angst for his part, but he didn't need to envy Owen and Jessica's stability and happy coupledom. Who was ever interested in stories or plays or movies about happy couples? No one. Boring, boring, boring. Marrying Christina would have been a disaster. He would have been stuck, cooped up, reined in. Thank God he'd seen the light before the darkness closed in.

As break-ups went, this wasn't the worst he'd been involved in, not by a long shot. He'd been through tantrums, women actually punching him, others clinging on to him like parasites. Christina might be mad in her own way, but he reckoned she wouldn't make any scenes or try to hang on. She'd struggle on without him, miserable for a while, until she met some other tedious man like Richard. She'd keep him away from Lucy and he wouldn't, like Toby, be adventurous enough to find Lucy for himself. They'd marry and have lots of children and this other bloke would love the stink of those oils around the house. He'd probably be some sort of aromatherapist himself.

I'll miss those massages, Toby thought. That's true. But I won't miss the smell of some of those rank oils, and if I want a massage I'll have enough money to pay for it myself.

Toby reached over, put out his cigarette in the ashtray by the bed, lay back with his hands behind his head and fell asleep.

When Christina came in she thought of waking him up but decided against it. Instead, she tiptoed around the room, collected a few things for her trip to Amersham and left.

Like a burglar, she thought. Stealing into my own house and making a quick getaway. No more smoke-filled rooms. No more jumping with anxiety every time the phone rings, in case it might be his agent. No more little arguments about who gets to use the hair-dryer first. No more listening to soliloquies. Actually, I'll miss that bit. He'll probably find an actress next and they can play scenes with each other. If I want to listen to soliloquies, I'll just have to pay for a theatre ticket myself.

Alison sat staring at Declan as if he were a waxwork figure in Madame Tussaud's.

'You're going to buy me out? How exactly?'

'I'm borrowing some money from my parents.'

'And they have money? Please. They can't even afford furniture.'

'They choose not to have furniture. There's a huge difference. They don't spend money. It doesn't mean they don't have it.'

'What? They've stuffed pound notes under the mattress? I can't believe your father would use a bank.'

'I didn't ask where they kept the money. My father offered to loan me some and I accepted.'

'Oh, and I'm sure I've been painted as the bitch of the century, haven't I? They always hated me. Now they hate me more.'

'Al,' Declan protested. 'My parents don't hate anyone.'

'Which is why I always knew I couldn't trust them.'

'What?'

'Forget it.' Alison rolled her eyes

She looks the way I do when I'm exasperated, Declan said to himself. Did she take that expression from me by osmosis or was it one of the things we had in common?

'The point is, I can buy you out of your share of the house. Isn't that better for you? Putting it on the market would take time. And I assume you're joining Skip in New York as soon as possible.'

'I'm going as soon as he gets settled in again.'

'And meanwhile? Where will you stay?'

'I don't know. With my mother, I suppose. I can't stay here, can I?'

She wants me to say yes, of course she can, but there is a limit and I've reached it.

'Fine. I take it from your silence that I can't stay here. But tell me something, Declan. Now that your father is your new best friend, are you going to turn into another Michael?'

Declan didn't respond. She was angry and so was he, but their anger was useless now; it was the dregs of a relationship being pushed and prodded and stirred around the bottom of a cup. They were both proving how wise a decison it was to leave each other, trying to forget what had worked between them before. Declan was busy not thinking about sex, and Alison – well, she was probably trying to forget the times he'd been able to make her laugh or the moments when she'd curled up against his chest and talked babytalk. Neither wanted to think about the exchanged vulnerability at the core of any even semi-successful relationship. Both were thinking about new people and different exchanges.

But it is always the same vulnerability, Declan thought. You carry it on to the next person and hope she or he will know how to handle it, never taking advantage of it, never betraying it, never letting it drop and shatter. That's the result you want – one person who treats your heart with more care than you give it yourself.

'Skip and I are going to work on infomercials together,' Alison said after a moment of silence. 'We've got a few very good ideas to start with.'

'That's good,' Declan picked up a spoon and stirred his coffee. 'What about *Plots in a Box*, by the way? Is he going to go ahead with that idea?'

'Maybe.' Her eyes turned cagey. The way she shifted in her seat made Declan wonder what was coming next. 'It's a possibility. He told me as we were on our way to that disastrous lunch where Oprah went mad, that he thought you and Toby had produced a decent script.'

'Decent?'

'That was his word. Decent. If he goes ahead with it he'll use some of what you've done, but he'll take it from there on his own. *We'll* take it from there. He owes you some money for your contribution and I'm sure he'll get that to you soon. Not that you need it badly seeing as how you're being funded by the bank of Amersham now.'

'But after that I'm out of the picture, is that it?'

'Declan. Excuse me, but since when did you want to be involved in infomercials?'

'It *was* my idea, Alison. Remember?'

'You'd never even heard of an infomercial. You can hardly take credit. You were drunk, you were joking. You can't expect Skip to include you in the process. You don't have a clue.'

What happens? You sleep with another man and your loyalties switch immediately, as if you'd crossed the floor of the House of Commons. It is truly amazing, Declan thought, how new love erases old love and memories of that old love instantaneously. It is terrifying.

How would Alison describe me now? As some bloke she lived with for a while, nice but nothing special? A stopgap until she met Mr Right? If Skip is, indeed, Mr Right. Somehow I still can't picture it. Alison and Skip don't scan, as they say. Is it physical, or is it a business merger which has melded their minds and bodies, two identical dreams of infomercial success? Was that what led to their first kiss – talk of gaps in the marketplace?

'My father has some other ideas for infomercials,' he told Alison. 'Should I advise him to patent them? Should we hire someone who is an expert at industrial espionage to keep Skip and Company from stealing them?'

'You're impossible.' Alison stood up.

She was preparing for her exit, Declan could see. Getting set to deliver the final words.

'You were always a baby, Declan. You haven't changed. You've regressed, actually.'

'What you're saying is that we never would have worked.' Declan found himself, unaccountably, smiling. 'The merger was never viable.'

'What's so amusing? Why are you smiling like an idiot?'

'Because you are so straightforward, Al. So clearcut. So tidy. The package is wrapped and sent. Now it's time to unwrap the next. Did you spend hours wrapping presents when you were a child?'

'Yes,' she sighed. 'What does that prove?'

'Nothing,' Declan shrugged. 'I did too, as it happens. I still do.'

Alison's eyes showed sudden fear, Declan was startled to see. Why? What had he said to make her so nervous?

'Did you have a yo-yo?' she asked, her voice carrying the same fear. 'Did you play with a yo-yo when you were a boy?'

She wanted him to say no, he could tell, although he had no idea why this might be so important to her. She was clutching the top of the kitchen chair, leaning forward as if her fate depended on his answer, as if he were a gypsy about to inform her how long her lifeline was.

'No.'

'Of course you didn't.' She let go of the chair and stood up straight. 'You and I,' she picked up her handbag from the table, 'we're completely different types. We have almost nothing in common. I'll pick up my things over the weekend, if that's all right with you.'

'It's fine,' he replied, finding himself speaking to her back. She was out of the room and out of the house with phenomenal speed. Declan poured the rest of his coffee down the sink and took out a bottle of wine from the fridge.

What was that all about? Why yo-yos? As his brain struggled to replay the conversation and make some sense of it, he found it drifting elsewhere instead, as if a wind had come up in his mind, blowing his thoughts inexorably toward Christina.

When did I fall in love with her? At which precise moment? he asked himself, going through every meeting with her in as much detail as he could recollect. Was it the first time I saw her, her eyes closed, sitting next to Toby on that sofa? Or was it later on in the evening, when she suggested a romantic self-help book to accompany the *Plots in a Box* tape? That phrase she used about a Heathcliff in every woman's life – did that set my heart into orbit without my recognizing it at the time? I can remember almost every word she said that night, but I'm not sure when exactly every word she spoke became so important. I liked her from the beginning and my response has never changed, it has simply grown with each encounter. Does that mean I've loved her from the beginning?

It didn't matter, he knew, but Declan was still driven to replay all the time they had spent together, which wasn't much, but which was evidently more than enough to have him pining for her at this very moment. He wanted her hand on his wrist again, feeling his pulse. He was desperate to sit at the end of her bed and listen to her talk. And, like some obsessed man in a Bryan Adams lyric, he'd do anything to see her smile the way she'd smiled when she told the man in Windsor she'd been that tall since birth.

Putting his glass of wine down, Declan stood up, searched his pockets, found the keys at the bottom of his left one, and made for the door, almost as quickly as Alison had moments before. He didn't set the alarm when he left, he closed the door behind him without a thought and headed for his car. This time he didn't take the M25, but went via the A40. Halfway to Amersham he beat his fist on the dashboard.

It wasn't the first time he saw her, no. It didn't happen at that dinner, but later. Yes, the process was already in motion, but it took something else to shift gears from like to love, something incredibly simple. All it took was one declarative sentence: Christina saying she hated The Carpenters. *That's* when he'd fallen head over heels, outrageously, hopelessly in love.

Skip hadn't dared to buy a first-class or business ticket, so he sat in the back with the rest of sweltering humanity, squeezed in a seat between a priest and a woman who looked as if she needed a priest. She had a racking cough and seemed to be feverish as well. Although he tried his best to lean away from her, he couldn't go very far without undue intimacy with the priest. Skip knew with a terrible certainty that he would be coughing her same cough within days of landing. The priest was reading a John Grisham novel; the woman, in her mid-thirties, he guessed, had a copy of *Vogue* on her lap but each time she picked it up, she struggled with it as if it were a two-hundred-pound barbell, eventually giving up the fight, laying it back down and wiping her forehead with a Hermès scarf.

I should have gone Business Class, he thought. What difference will it make to Lisa? She won't congratulate me on saving her some money, all she is interested in is getting rid of me. Skip Thomas, the man who let her down. The guy who cheated on her, the guy who had the bad judgment to think she was 'cute' and 'uncomplicated' when in fact she is a goddamn shark.

How was I supposed to know there was so much more to her? She never showed any signs of wanting a brilliant career or star status on an international scale. She seemed happy to hang out with her friends in Connecticut and do her shopping and give her dinner parties. And when she said she wasn't happy, I paid attention. I quit my job, I made a major sacrifice for the marriage and then she turns around and becomes a fucking tycoon. Not only that, I get a new job. I get to be her personal assistant. Now when did I ever apply for that one? I don't remember the interview. I don't think my degree from Harvard Business School naturally leads on to giving a woman pep talks before television interviews. Life is complicated enough as it is. Competing with your wife doesn't make it any easier.

Marriage is supposed to be a partnership but I got the junior partner slot. The chances of me ever making full partner were negligible at best. I would have always been the one in the background. Look how antsy she got when I mentioned my idea for bringing infomercials to England. No, I'm the one who tells the journalist how happily married we are. That's my role. That's all I'm good for.

Skip tried not to breathe as the woman let out another round of tubercular coughs.

What will Lisa say when the split does become public – that I wanted to keep her pregnant and barefoot in the kitchen? Well, OK, maybe I wanted her pregnant but what's so wrong with that? Most married couples have babies, don't they? Isn't that supposed to be part of the programme? It's not as if I were suggesting some unnatural practice. I didn't tie her to bedposts or make her wear leather. I don't think wanting a baby qualifies me as male chauvinist of the century. And I have nothing against women working. Look at Alison. I liked her from the start because she was sharp and ambitious. And now, if it all goes well, we'll be working together. That's the key word – together.

No, Lisa is the one who wanted *me* barefoot and in the back room, supporting, supporting, supporting. On certain occasions I was allowed out to support her even more. But she didn't want me to be the man she claims she first saw – the Harvard guy. Any Harvard man would laugh at every damn page of that book. He'd respect the fact that it made so much money, just like I did. But he wouldn't *believe* in all that junk. No way!

What was it with people who bought that book? What were they looking for? Was it like mass voodoo? You believe in it, so it works? If Lisa had said the way to save a marriage was to wear a paper bag over your head and eat shellfish every day, would they have bought that too? Probably.

'Would you mind covering your mouth when you cough?' he barked at the woman beside him. She answered by coughing again and, to cap his day off perfectly, bursting into tears.

Skip closed his eyes and tried to conjure up images of Alison in bed. What floated in front of him instead was a picture of him deliberately spilling red wine over Lisa's pink dress.

All right. OK, I'm a bastard. Cough in my face some more. Throw me out of the plane. And shoot me on the way down. Make the world a kinder, more caring place. Do everyone, including me, a favour.

After dinner, Christina, Jessica and Owen sat on the pillows in the front room, talking. Hercules the dog was in Christina's lap and she was patting his head as she spoke. She wasn't entirely surprised that she was telling them everything about her break-up with Toby; a part of her had known the minute she called Jessica to invite herself for the night, that she'd end up recounting bits of the story over the last few days no matter how sincerely she'd wished not to burden them with it, but she was amazed by how *much* of it she recounted, going back to her childhood and teenage days at home. If they had sat there without speaking themselves, she knew she would have felt guilty, but both Jessica and Owen asked questions and joined in with recollections of their own past and families.

Jessica's mother, as it happened, had died when she was thirteen – the same age Christina had been when her father had the accident, and she also had a step-family. Although her father hadn't re-married immediately – in fact had spent five years on his own with Jessica before finding his second wife, Jessica had found it hard to come to terms with her step-mother and older step-brother. Everything was fine now, Jessica explained, but there had been a few difficult years of adjustment. She and Christina discussed how large a part timing had played in Christina's reactions, and whether it would have been easier or more difficult if Lucy and Chloë had come into her life later on.

As she told them about Toby bringing Lucy to the house for a confrontation, she was very careful to try to be fair. Toby was doing what he thought was helpful, she said, he wasn't purposefully trying to humiliate her; he had misjudged Christina's feelings, that was all. He hadn't really understood the history – how could he when he hadn't been a part of it? Toby was looking from the outside in and trying to sort a problem out. Perhaps he'd been right to do what he did. Perhaps she *had* overreacted.

'Then you and Toby might be able to sort things out?' Owen had asked, his face earnest and concerned.

'No.' Christina thought of telling them about Toby almost sleeping with Lucy, but couldn't bring herself to. It would sound too self-righteous, somehow. It would cast Toby in the part of the evil bastard, and it wasn't, the more she pondered it, the real cause of the break-up. She had seized on it when Toby came to her treatment room as the reason to get him out of her life – a reason he would understand, at least partially. When she said it to him, she had believed herself that his reaction to Lucy was the cause of her need to be free of him, but now she thought differently. She knew that if he ever had to explain to his next lover why he and Christina had split up, he could do it in one quick sentence: 'She thought I fancied her step-sister.' The real problem between them was more complicated and, she thought, not one Toby would be able to take on board.

'He makes me nervous,' she said. 'I'm not comfortable with him. I feel as if I have to watch what I say the entire time, that I have to regulate myself. Often, when I talked to him about work or almost any subject, I felt as if he had an invisible stopwatch and was timing me, that I only had a certain amount of time to talk before he got bored with what I was saying. I don't think he was particularly interested in me. My neck always ached when I was with him. And that should have told me something important a long time ago. Does that make sense?'

'It makes sense – absolutely,' Jessica said. She glanced at Owen with a look Christina wasn't able to interpret. There was a tiny smile on her face, which seemed as though it was desperate to turn into a full-fledged one. Owen smiled back at her, with the same restraint. Christina couldn't fathom why they would both seem semi-pleased with what she'd just said.

'It helps, in a way – the fact that Lucy isn't really involved in the equation. I suppose she was a catalyst for the split, but she wasn't, this time, the real cause.'

'Perhaps she wasn't the cause before, either, with Richard.'

Christina stopped patting the dog. She looked at Owen with what she knew must be an expression of incredulity. It was as if he'd dropped a rock into the middle of a lake: she could feel his words rushing from her mind downwards, falling until they hit bottom with a thud. Was it possible? Had she left Richard for another reason, or other reasons she hadn't recognized? If she had loved him as much as she thought she did, wouldn't she have at least tried to talk to him about his feelings for Lucy, instead of running away? Was Lucy a convenient excuse, someone she could hang her anxieties on whenever she chose to?

'You might be right,' she replied at last. 'Have you ever considered becoming an analyst?'

'No way,' Owen laughed. 'Psychiatrists have to be analysed themselves first, before they can begin on other people. I hate to think how long it would take to work through my neuroses.'

'I don't believe that.'

'Oh, you should,' Jessica laughed as well. 'I deal with those neuroses every day. They number in the thousands – at the very least.'

Car lights flashed through the window at the same time as they heard the tyres scrunch on the drive.

'Who's that?' Owen leapt up and went to the front door.

'It could be anyone,' Jessica said to Christina. 'That's one of the nice bits of Owen's neuroses; he needs people in the way other people need food. He invites everyone he meets to visit us here, and you can never be sure who is going to take him up on it. Sometimes I feel as if I am managing a hotel. A good hotel, though. Most of the droppers-by are people we enjoy having. Although sometimes . . .' she stopped and Christina watched her face turn from amused into joyful. 'Declan!' She sprang from the pillow and rushed to the door. 'You didn't tell us. How wonderful.'

'Spur of the moment,' he said, smiling. 'I needed some country air and – ' He saw Christina then and his smile vanished. 'I should have rung,' he said quickly. 'You have guests.'

'Declan – hello.' She pushed herself off the floor and stood awkwardly. 'It's nice to see you again.'

It must have been close to eighty degrees outside, but Christina thought Declan looked as if he'd just come in from a raging blizzard. He kept running his hand through his hair as if to get all the wet snow out. Owen was glancing back and forth from Declan to her with that same strange, hesitant smile he'd worn earlier.

'Come join us,' he said to his son, 'if you can bear sitting in the ping-pong room. Or would you like to move to the kitchen? Do you want something to drink?'

'No, I'm fine thanks, Dad.' He didn't move but his eyes were all over the place, searching.

'So,' he said as Jessica took his arm and led him past the ping-pong table to a floor-cushion. 'Where's Toby?'

Christina found herself concentrating on the dog at her side.

'Christina came on her own,' Jessica said.

'Oh.' Declan dropped on to the pillow. He rubbed his forehead. 'I hope I haven't interrupted something important?'

'No.' Christina sat back down, across from him. 'No, we were just talking.'

'Right,' he nodded. 'That's nice.'

There was a silence, an unusual silence. Christina desperately wanted to break it by asking a silly question about the traffic on Declan's trip, but she was stymied by how heavy and dense the silence was. It seemed as though the only way to begin talking again would be to start off with a profound observation on politics or philosophy.

'Declan.' Owen was the one, finally, to speak. His voice sounded portentous, so full of ominous feeling Christina wondered what could possibly be coming next. 'You wouldn't want a game of ping pong, would you?'

Declan didn't hesitate. 'Absolutely,' he replied.

'Careful, Owen. He'll beat you, you know,' Jessica said.

'Not a chance,' her husband retorted.

Jessica and Christina retired to the kitchen to spectate as Owen found the bats and table-tennis ball.

'They haven't done this for ages,' Jessica whispered. 'Years. Decades.' She put her hand on Christina's briefly.

'Does it matter who wins?'

'No,' Jessica smiled. 'Not in the least. But neither of them knows that. You'll be surprised by how competitive Owen is. You'll think it's out of character, but it's not.'

Christina was surprised; she was stunned, in fact. Owen, even while they were warming up, patting the ball back and forth across the net easily, had a determined, fierce face and his body was all concentration.

'All right,' he said after five or so minutes. 'Rally for serve.'

What followed was an epic battle. Christina and Jessica leaned against the kitchen counter and watched the unfolding drama, both men intensely involved, spinning the ball, smashing the ball, placing deft little shots just over the net. By the time the score had reached ten apiece, they were visibly sweating. Neither of them talked, except for an occasional, grudging, 'Nice shot,' and the announcement of the score before each serve. Declan fell behind, 19-12, but miraculously caught up and evened the game again. It was his turn to serve and he produced a shot with an angle so wide, Owen missed the ball completely.

'Bastard,' Owen swore.

'Are you referring to me or yourself?' Declan looked over at his father, the ball poised against his bat. 'Do you want me to serve another one just like it?'

'Go ahead,' Owen panted. 'I'm ready.'

Declan did exactly what he'd said he was going to do, serving into the far right-hand corner yet again. This time Owen managed to get his bat on the ball, but it shot wildly to the ceiling and then fell to the floor.

'I do not, I refuse to believe you won!' Owen almost shouted, but Christina could hear the affection behind the protest. 'Do you play every day?'

'I haven't touched a bat since the last time I played here against Michael. What was I – fourteen years old?'

'Impossible. How did you get that serve? You must be practising secretly at work. I don't think you actually do work for Green & Wilson. I think you've been lying to us. I think all you do is play ping pong every day.'

'Sorry.' Declan shrugged and placed his bat on the table. 'The best man won. What can I say?'

Jessica nudged Christina with her elbow and whispered, 'Boys – they're all boys, every last one of them.'

'Another game?' Owen pressed.

'Maybe later. I need a drink now.'

'Well done. You have a vicious spin,' Christina commented as he came to the kitchen.

'I was showing off.'

'At my expense,' Owen added, coming up behind Declan. 'Sons are supposed to respect their fathers.'

'Oh, I do, Dad. Up to a point.'

I should leave them alone, Christina thought. They need time together and I'm intruding. Declan wasn't expecting me and Jessica and Owen weren't expecting Declan. It's time to take myself out of the family picture.

'I think I'll go upstairs now,' she said. 'I have the day off tomorrow but I should get back to London in the morning.'

'Why?' Owen asked. 'Why not stay for the day? Relax. Chill out, as my students would say. Sit out in the garden. Do whatever you want, but stay.'

'You must stay,' Jessica pressed. 'It's ridiculous to go back and swelter in the city. It's bad for your health.'

Christina smiled and looked over to Declan who had taken a seat at the kitchen table with a glass of water in his hand. He shrugged and smiled back. 'They're very persuasive,' he said. 'You shouldn't say no to my parents. It's politically incorrect.'

'And you too, Declan.' Owen turned to him. 'I have students to see in the morning but I'll be back after lunch. We

352

need a long ping-pong match. Call in sick again. Go on, be a truant.'

'You see what they're like?' Declan addressed this question to Christina. 'They encourage their children to rebel, they *want* me to lose my job. He – ' Declan pointed at Owen ' – would probably love to have a son in jail, in fact. I can see him at visiting hours. Talking to all the other inmates, discussing their childhoods. We let you down, didn't we, Dad, Michael and I? We weren't the revolutionary subversives you wanted us to be. We never broke a law. What a disappointment.'

If he'd said this in the same tone he was using that first night we came here, the whole situation would have been tense and fraught and awful, Christina mused, but he's relaxed now. He's playing with Owen. He even put himself and Michael into the same category. Christina looked at Declan with wonder. Could I do that now, with Lucy; with Chloë, with my mother? Relax and tease them and feel at ease? No. Not in the same way, they're not teasable people. People break down into two categories – the ones who can be teased and the ones who can't. I want to be one of the ones who can. I wish Declan would tease *me*. I wouldn't mind if *he* called me a giant. Why not, I wonder? Why is it fine for him but not for Toby?

'There's still time, I suppose,' Declan continued. 'And loads of laws I can break. Maybe I should rob this house tonight.'

What was in his voice that made her stare at him the way she was staring? Christina knew she must have that look on her face – the same one Alison had had at the Thomases' house when she couldn't take her eyes off Skip. Declan could have said anything, he could be talking about the weather and she would have listened, watching his face, how he held the glass of water with those thin fingers of his. He made her want to pay attention.

What does it mean? What do I want from him? I want – I want to get him into bed and tease the life out of him. I want to have sex with him on the rope-swing. I want to make love on the ping-pong table, I want to grab his wrists, both of them and . . . Christina shook her head abruptly, and then shook it again.

'Are you all right, dear?' Jessica asked.

'I'm fine.' I want to kiss your son. One of those kisses that makes you wonder if it will ever stop, and forget when it ever began. 'I think I had a fly in my ear.'

'A fly in your ear?' Owen looked at her with interest. 'Did you hear it or feel it fly in?'

'Um, I felt it,' she lied, afraid to look at Declan any more in case the wild fantasies started again. 'It's gone now. I should get to bed.' Before I jump on him. Before I tackle him and pin him to the ground. Before you drag me off him kicking and screaming.

She felt like running upstairs, she felt as if they could all see what was happening in her brain. They were looking at her oddly and she thought that she must be blushing so deeply the colour would never fade – she'd still be blushing in the morning; she would have been blushing in her sleep.

But all Declan said was: 'Sleep well,' and Jessica and Owen repeated those words or similar ones – she couldn't quite grasp what they were saying and she walked as slowly as she could up the wooden staircase, careful not to trip. She knew that she didn't have a prayer of sleeping, but after she'd been to the bathroom and brushed her teeth, she went to her room, undressed, put on her pyjamas and lay down anyway, stretching out under the window; one corner of the moonlight coming through illuminating the little mound her feet made underneath the sheet.

Calm down, she told herself. Do breathing exercises. Try to remember that mantra the acupuncturist gave you years ago. Was it 'um so' or 'so um'?

Don't ask yourself what's going on because you won't find an answer. Declan walked into your heart and now he won't leave. That's not an answer, it's only a fact. You don't know why or when it happened, how he sneaked in or how you're going to get him to leave.

Perhaps when you wake up tomorrow he will have walked

out again. Maybe you can dream him away. He has just gone through what must have been an emotional crisis with Alison, and for all you know they might be back together again, and you broke up your relationship with Toby when? Approximately ten hours ago.

Say 'um so' and don't ask yourself what he feels for you or why he was driving down your street yesterday. Don't think about how easy it feels to be with him. Clear your mind of all thought and say the mantra, whether it's the right one or not, and stop imagining how it would feel to have him hugging you.

Get a grip, Christina! You can't rid your mind of thoughts? All right, then think of something practical. Think up infomercials. How would you do an infomercial for aromatherapy? Would you have someone being massaged on camera? Is someone walking upstairs or are you imagining it? You're imagining it. Yes, you'd have a person being masssaged on camera, absolutely. And this person could be giving one of those testimonials while she was being massaged. 'My life was miserable until I discovered . . .'

'Goodnight, John Boy.'

The figure was standing on the threshold of her room. The voice was Declan's.

'Goodnight, John Boy,' she echoed. 'It's awful. I can't remember any of the other names.'

'Wasn't there a Mary Lou?'

'There might have been. That sounds right.'

'It might have been Mary Ellen.'

'That sounds right too,' she smiled. He wouldn't be able to see her smile. Could he hear it in her voice? His hand, she could see, was on the frame of what should have been the door. His head was at an angle and she thought he was going to say something else, but he turned around and left. She could hear his feet going back downstairs.

Well, that's done it, she thought. Now I won't be able to get him out of my heart for months. For years. For another ten millennia. And sleep? No chance.

Declan has murdered sleep.

Lisa paced. She had a whole house to pace in and she used it all. A whole, empty house. No Skip. Skip was somewhere over the Atlantic by now. Had he flown first class? Was he drinking champagne with Alison, toasting their future together? Well, he wouldn't drink much – that was a little comfort. Skip wouldn't get blotto. He had sex with another woman but he didn't drink, beyond a few sips here and there. Maybe if he had drunk more he wouldn't have had this fling. He'd be here now, sitting in the living room watching television. Life would be fine. Normal. Not empty.

It was all his mother's fault. Lisa had stuck up for his mother, she'd tried to effect a reconciliation between them and it had failed miserably. Was that why he had gone off with Alison? Because of that trip Lisa had made him take, all those years ago?

What did it matter? Skip was gone. The difference between the thought of Skip leaving and the actuality was what was making Lisa pace. At first she'd felt victorious. She'd won a major battle and vanquished the enemy – Skip – from the field. But once that journalist was through, as soon as the photographer, who had finally showed up and who chainsmoked like some lunatic Marlboro Man, had finished posing her for pictures and the two had taken off, Lisa had been attacked from a different front. Loneliness assaulted her, tearing away at her like a vulture. She'd tried to stave it off by telephoning her editor in New York again, but Deborah had been so downbeat about the new book idea, Lisa had felt like taking a plane to Manhattan herself and setting fire to her publisher's headquarters. What did they know? Nothing. They were idiots who didn't understand what she was trying to say. Deborah went on and on about the nature of self-help books, as if Lisa didn't know. As if Lisa was some *dumb* idiot who hadn't sold enough books to keep those jerks having lunch at the Four Seasons for the next twenty-five years.

The problem was, though, that Deborah made a little sense. Not much, but enough to make Lisa pause while she paced. *You Can Do Anything I Can Do Better* wasn't like *I Saw You First*. Of course the main problem was that it wouldn't appeal to men, not even gay men, she suspected. Plus, the concept was complex and maybe a little too philosophical. Also, Lisa wasn't really sure how she could spin it out beyond a few chapters. *I Saw You First* had flown out of the computer and on to the page. Each chapter led naturally into the next. The Exercises were creative and fun to put together. It would be hard to make any little jokes in *You Can Do Anything I Can Do Better*. The subject was serious. How could she make light of the Bible? People wouldn't like it. But people did like humour in self-help books. Enough of her fans had told her how much they'd enjoyed the lighter moments for Lisa to know the wisdom of occasional levity.

So now she wasn't so sure about her brilliant idea and she couldn't talk to Skip about it and she couldn't talk to anyone, really. Except herself. The abandoned, not-good-enough-to-make-a-husband-stay-faithful Lisa Thomas.

Lisa paced some more. She did another circuit of the house and she cried while she did it. There were moments when she felt good about crying. Times when she enjoyed feeling sorry for herself, but she'd catch herself in these and tell herself this misery wasn't something she should get off on in any way. It was *serious*. It was *devastating*. It was *divorce*. She shouldn't be picturing herself shedding tears on *Oprah* while the audience made loud, sympathetic noises and shouted, 'Kill that bastard Skip!' at the end.

Still – it was kind of impossible not to imagine it. Oprah hugging her, maybe saying something like, 'He's not worth your tears, girlfriend,' hundreds of thousands of consoling letters from women who had been cheated on all over the world. The loneliness might abate with that kind of response.

But – Lisa stopped on her fifth tour of the kitchen, shook her head and reached for the bottle of wine on the counter – she didn't want to be seen as pathetic. Sure, she wanted people to feel sorry for her, but she wanted them to see how strong she was, too. Oprah wouldn't have her on just to moan and cry. She had to have something else to say, a book to present, an idea to convey to the masses. What would her brothers say if she went on television and sobbed? Dumb – that's what. They'd say she was dumb to have chosen Skip in the first place and dumb not to have been able to hang on to him in the second.

I need respect, Lisa said to herself, pouring the wine into a tumbler. I need to be Lisa Thomas the author again, not some sad housewife in the divorce courts. Although they might televise the divorce on *Court TV* if I could make it go to trial. That would fix Skip.

A voice came to her at that moment; one she didn't recognize at first. It murmured in her ear. She looked at her wine, wondering if Alison or Skip had spiked it with an hallucinogenic drug. But she hadn't even tasted the wine yet and the voice kept talking. 'You've got a problem? He doesn't go down on you? Move on. Find someone who does. *Get over it!*'

Lisa sat down with her wine. She drank it as she listened to the voice and she kept drinking until she'd finished the bottle. The voice became louder, it said some funny things. It started to make a lot of sense. *Get over it!* was the refrain. Always those three words, after every couple of sentences. Lisa stumbled a little, but eventually found a pen and a piece of paper. Then she sat back down again and started taking notes.

Two hours must have gone by before she heard the steps again. During all that time she'd alternated between thinking of every moment she'd spent with Declan and thinking about anything and everything that had nothing to do with Declan. This time Declan didn't stop at her doorway, he went straight down the landing to the bathroom and then, a few minutes later, she could hear him padding softly into the room across from hers.

I could go in there, Christina thought. And I could sit at the end of his bed the way he sat at the end of mine and talk to him. But I'm too shy. I've always been shy.

She remembered moments of supreme, paralysing shyness in her youth. Times when she'd hide in her room when she knew visitors were coming to the house; times when she'd be expected to go downstairs and shake hands and talk about how school was going. On one of these occasions, after her father had called for her and finally come upstairs and found her underneath her bed, he'd pulled her out gently and sat her down on the bed beside him.

'You don't have to come downstairs,' he said quietly. 'You don't have to meet anyone you don't want to. Mr and Mrs Downey are friends of ours and they'd like to see you, but if you want to hide up here, you can.'

'I want to stay here,' she'd said, hanging her head.

'You know what I've discovered?' Her father posed this question, but he wasn't looking at her. He seemed to be talking to the wall. 'I've found out over the years that every person I've ever met is shy. Even the ones who talk and parade themselves and tell jokes and make speeches. Each and every one of them, male or female, says that they were shy when they were children. Or they're shy now, but they're very adept at hiding it. I think Mr and Mrs Downey are shy too. They want to meet you, but they won't mind if they don't because they're shy about meeting new people as well. Everyone is shy, even the people who grow out of it.'

She'd gone downstairs with him after that, shyly. And she'd shaken hands with Mr and Mrs Downey who didn't *seem* shy, but as she'd sat and listened to the grown-ups talk, she'd thought that her father might be right. Mr Downey kept wagging his foot as if it were a dog's tail. Mrs Downey had a nervous giggle. Even her outgoing, extrovert mother sometimes seemed at a loss for words when the conversation stalled. At some point during the visit, Christina looked over at her father and he tilted his head and raised his eyebrows and smiled a 'you see?' smile. Christina had smiled back.

Getting up from the bed, Christina stretched. She was wearing ivory silk pyjamas she'd bought on a salary-defying whim from an expensive store called Night Owls on the Fulham Road. Having seen them in the window, she'd assumed they'd be too short to fit her so had gone in expecting to be disappointed, but also relieved not to have to decide whether she could afford them. When the salesgirl almost immediately found a pair her size, she found she couldn't resist.

He's shy too, she thought. Remember that. Everyone is shy.

'Declan?' She stood at the entrance to his room.

'Christina? You're supposed to be asleep.' He sat up. 'Come and sit down.' She could see that he was motioning to the end of his bed. 'This is our official position for chatting. One or the other of us at the end of a bed. Is it too hot for you to sleep?'

'Well, it *is* hot.'

'Yes. It's hot.'

Christina went and sat tentatively on the bed, wishing she hadn't had the courage to come in the first place, now that she was here and actually had to think of something to say. Declan looked at ease, as far as she could make out in the dark. He was leaning back against the headboard, his arms crossed over his chest.

'I'm glad you came in,' he said. 'I wanted to ask you something. I was thinking about it when I was lying here. In the heat,' he added. 'Because it *is* hot.'

'It *is*,' she laughed. 'What do you want to ask me?'

'Well, I was wondering. You've told me about the people you hate and I've told you. I was wondering who you love.'

Unfair, Christina wanted to say. Ref! Unfair. Show him a red card.

'I loved my father,' she said instead. 'And I love my mother, even though sometimes I think we're from a different family and I was switched in the hospital at birth. And . . .' she paused.

'Yes?'

360

'And I have two female friends, one I was at university with and another I met a few years ago. I'd say I love them, but not in a – you know . . .'

'Not in a sexual way.'

'Right. It depends on how you define love, I suppose. I think I'd do almost anything for them. If one of them was in trouble, I'd do everything I could do to help. It's difficult, though, because both of them are away at the moment, in different countries, one is in Spain and the other is in the States. In California.' Why am I banging on like this? He couldn't possibly care.

'What are their names?'

'Georgia and Francesca.'

'Nice names. What do they do?'

'Georgia is an artist. She paints. Francesca is a nurse.'

'What do they look like?'

'Declan?' Christina tried to make out the expression on his face. 'Do you really want to know all this?'

'Yes.'

Christina stretched out and leaned on her elbow. She told Declan all she could about Georgia and Francesca, what they looked like, how they had met, in what way they differed from each other and why she loved them both.

When is he going to interrupt? she kept wondering as she talked. Or is he asleep?

'I miss them,' she said finally, waiting to hear his snores.

'You should think about getting online,' he said. His voice wasn't tired or bored. Christina was amazed. 'You could e-mail them every day. It's cheap. It's a fantastic way to communicate.'

'So . . .' Her hand had fallen asleep; she shifted position and shook the tingling out. 'Who do *you* love?'

'Ah,' he said, shifting as well, so that his hands were now locked behind his head. 'I think you already know the answer to that question.'

'Oh, I know you love your parents. And Michael. I meant other people as well. Friends.'

361

'Friends,' he repeated.

'Yes.'

'It's hot in here, isn't it?'

'It is,' she laughed. 'You're not answering my question.'

'My parents told me that you and Toby are no longer a couple.'

'That's right,' she said softly.

'Do you mind that they told me?'

'No. It's not a secret, Declan.'

'I think they told me for a reason. I think – no, I *know* – they'd like it if you and I turned into a couple. Which is a very distressing prospect.'

Christina shut her eyes. Why? Had he been setting her up for this all along? Did he take pleasure in humiliating her like this? Why? What had she done? It wasn't fair. It wasn't right. All that John Boy business. The rope-swing. Driving down her street. Coming to see her at work. What was he trying to prove? And why did he have to use her to prove it?

'It's distressing – ' he had moved, he was no longer sitting at his end of the bed but was suddenly two inches away from her, his hand on her wrist – 'because you know I want it too – us to be together as a couple, that is – and I'm so used to *not* doing what I think my father wants me to do that it all seems too much. It's too neat. Do you understand? I spent years distancing myself from them and now I don't need to do that any more but I'm not sure I can be *too* close, either. And of course Michael adores you too, I know. I could see it last weekend. They all adore you. *Everyone* adores you, it's impossible *not* to adore you. All of which has absolutely nothing to do with anything in your life because as far as I know, you don't give a toss what they think or what I think or how I feel about you.'

He stopped and Christina could hear him take a deep breath. 'It is *unbelievably* fucking hot in here, Christina. Help me out, will you? It's over with Alison – all over. I don't love her. I'm in love with you and I'm making no sense and talking about my family like a madman because I'm not sure how I can tell you how I feel without using other people to say it and I feel as if I were locked in a sauna and some perverse person keeps turning up the temperature when what I want is to be cool and dashing. Debonair. Nonchalant. Witty.'

He sighed and let go of her wrist. 'Let's forget I said any of this. Let's start back at the beginning. Let's talk some more about Georgia and Francesca. I liked hearing about them. We can pretend I never said anything, can't we? We can keep chatting. We're friends, after all. Aren't we?'

Christina was silent. Declan retreated back to his end of the bed and folded his arms across his chest.

'You don't have to stay,' he said. 'You must be tired.'

'Sometimes I ring Francesca.' Christina finally spoke. 'Not often, because it's too expensive, but occasionally, to catch up on her life. She's out a lot and has an answering-machine. She always puts songs on the answering machine tape. She'll say the number and ask you to leave a message at the beep and then she plays a bit of a song.' Christina stood up. 'You'd love the last message she left – the last song.' She approached Declan, motioned for him to move over in the bed. When he did, she sat down beside him. 'She left her message and then the song played and it was a woman singing.'

'And?' Declan stared at her.

'Shut up and kiss me.'

'What?'

'That's the name of the song,' Christina laughed and began to tickle Declan. *Shut up and kiss me.*

Toby Goodyear woke up, rolled over, looked at the bedside clock and saw the time: 1:30 a.m. Christina hadn't come back, which was fine by him. He needed his sleep. He could make some calls and clear out his things tomorrow. One of his friends would put him up. Maybe one of his old girlfriends – one of those who didn't bear a grudge, that is. Just as he was lighting a cigarette, he remembered his dream.

Lisa Thomas was teaching a class at Harrow. She was pointing at the blackboard, saying: 'When you first saw long division, did you fall in love with it or was it just a one-night stand?' Lisa had on a white leather micro skirt and pink polka-dot bikini top. The boys around Toby were whispering lewd remarks. Toby had told them to be quiet. 'Lisa Thomas is a woman beyond reproach,' he'd lectured. 'She's brilliant. Be quiet and listen.' All the boys had laughed and jeered. Lisa cartwheeled over to Toby and proceeded to shove her tongue halfway down his throat. He could hear Skip Thomas shouting, 'Go for it, Tobe!'

Thank God, Toby thought, inhaling. Thank God I woke up.

To sleep, perchance to dream.

If Shakespeare had spent any time with Americans he would have changed the line to: '*To sleep, perfuckingcertain to have nightmares.*'

Alison Austin didn't need to hear this lecture from her mother. It had gone on endlessly, and had started almost from the moment Alison had walked into the house in Chelmsford.

'That's enough,' she finally said. 'I'm going to bed now. You've been at me for four hours, you know. Yes, he's a married man. Yes, he's American. Yes, I'm probably mad to leave Declan. But it's a done deal.' Alison yawned.

'A done deal?' Her mother looked as if she were going to cry. 'Is that one of *his* clever expressions?'

'I'm going to bed now.'

'Does he drink?'

'No.'

'But he doesn't have a job.'

'We've been over this before. I'm going to bed.'

'You're going to your ruin, Alison. He won't ring, you know. He won't leave his wife. Your youth will be wasted. I'm sure he does drink.'

'Goodnight.'

'We'll talk about this tomorrow, Alison.'

'There's nothing more to say.'

'Oh yes, there is. There's plenty more to say. He's an alcoholic, I know he is. All Americans are. They're all in clinics. That's where Elizabeth Taylor met her last husband – that construction worker. In a clinic.'

'So?' Alison stood up.

'So – look what happened to that marriage.'

'Mum, Skip Thomas is not Larry Fortensky. And I'm not Elizabeth Taylor.'

'Not yet. But years of waiting for a married alcoholic to divorce his wife and you'll be in a clinic too.'

'Maybe I'll meet Larry Fortensky there.'

'Is he back in? You see? They're all in clinics. They might leave for a little while but they all go back eventually. That Presley girl who married Michael Jackson – isn't she in a clinic? And that man from *Friends*, the one who plays Chandler. He was in a clinic too.'

'I'm going to bed now, Mum. Goodnight.'

'Alison – '

'I need my beauty sleep,' she kissed her mother on the cheek, 'if I'm going to meet all these movie stars in the clinic.'

Skip was grateful to leave the plane, finally, and put some space between himself and the woman who he was now convinced had TB. He went through passport control, waited what seemed a phenomenally long time for his bag, and made his way past Customs and into the arrival hall at JFK. As he was working out if he had enough cash to take a taxi into Midtown and how irritated his friend Bob would be at having to put him up for a while, he noticed the people walking in front of him stop, stare, point and laugh at someone standing in the crowd waiting for incoming passengers. He stopped himself, to see what was so funny – doubtless, he thought, some crazed New Yorker doing a little street theatre in the airport.

What he saw was a man in a chauffeur's uniform standing holding a sign. Skip couldn't work out why this was so hilarious, but other people had gathered to look as well. They were laughing and pointing too. Walking a few steps further and stopping again, Skip finally saw what was so funny. The sign the chauffeur was holding had SKIP THOMAS written on the top in big black letters, and underneath, in even bigger letters were the words: YOUR WIFE IS DIVORCING YOU.

'Whaddya think?' a man in front of him said to another man pushing a trolley. 'Do you think the Skip Thomas guy, when he sees this sign, he bursts into tears? Or does he punch his fist in the air and yell: "YES!!"?'

Skip lowered his head and kept on walking.

Chapter 15

'It's a pleasure to have you here, Lisa.'

'It's my pleasure to be here, Mike.'

'Since we last talked, you've written another bestselling book. You just don't stop, do you?'

'I like to keep going,' Lisa smiled. 'I like to harness the energy.'

'This one is different from the last one, though. Can you tell us a little bit about it? What inspired you to write it?'

'Well, it's always personal experience, isn't it, Mike? I couldn't write about nuclear physics, for example, much as I might like to. I'm sure people are fascinated by neutrons or whatever they're called – atomic particles and whatnot – I'm fascinated myself, but I don't really know much about it. I like to write about something which fascinates me *and* something I know about. And that's people. People and their relationships. They're endlessly interesting, don't you think?'

'They certainly are,' Mike nodded. 'In your last book, *I Saw You First*, you explained how to keep relationships going. Now in this one, *Get Over It!*, you're telling people how to *end* relationships. You've changed your tune, haven't you?'

'Mike, what goes on between men and women doesn't change, not fundamentally. It's the same old song, as they say. I haven't changed the tune, I've changed the words of the tune to fit the occasion.'

'I'm not sure I understand, Lisa. Could you delve into that some more?'

'It's quite straightforward, really. My point is this: if you're in a relationship worth saving, one you think you can save, one you want to save and hope to save, then *I Saw You First* can help you do that. If I say so myself, it has helped hundreds and thousands of people to get back to the beginning of a relationship and rediscover their partner. The issue I'm addressing in *Get Over It!* is a whole different ballgame. I'm talking about relationships that *can't* be saved. You know and I know, we all know, it happens. We'd like every partnership to last for ever and we do everything in our power to make those relationships last, but sometimes it's beyond us, Mike. We have to face facts. The relationship is a dead duck. Try as you might to revive it, it's over. Now, that's when *Get Over It!* kicks in. That's when you have to look at life straight in the eye and say: "All right, this isn't working, this is dead in the water, what do I do? Do I sit around and moan and cry and live a miserable existence for the rest of my life, or do I face the future and walk boldly, head held high and move on. Get over it?"'

'I don't want to get *too* personal, Lisa. But this is what you've done yourself, isn't it? Your own marriage ended in divorce.'

'That's right. It did. And that was a terrible, sad thing, Mike. I was devastated. You wouldn't believe how many tears I cried. I think I could have filled the Atlantic Ocean, twice over. I was heartbroken. And I thought about going into a corner and hiding for ever. Giving up and giving in, as I put it in my book. It's a common response, you know. So many readers have told me that. You feel as though an earthquake has hit, or a tidal wave, or a typhoon . . .'

'More, Lisa,' Declan said. 'We need more natural disasters.'
'Shh!' Christina hit him on the head. 'I'm listening to this.'
'You can't be.'
'I am. I might have to get over you some day.'
'Impossible. It's completely impossible to get over me.'

'*Would you two please be quiet?*' Lucy glared at Christina and Declan. '*I want to hear what she's saying.*'

'You feel powerless, Mike. That's what affects you the most, this total sense of disempowerment. So what do you do? How *do* you get your life back together? *That's* what I talk about in my book: reclaiming your life. I believe almost every man and woman in the world knows what I'm talking about. OK, maybe there are some lucky people out there who have never gone through the trauma of a break-up or been left by the person they love, but I haven't met many of them, I can tell you.'

'How did you cope yourself, Lisa?'

'When my husband Skip – sorry, Mike, *ex*-husband. You see how old habits die hard? Anyway, when Skip left me, I was a mess, I admit it. I had to go through a period of grieving, of anger, all the stages I describe in my book. And then, when I thought I'd hit just about rock bottom, I picked myself up. I began to see that I had to think of the future, not the past. I began to rediscover the person I was before I was so hurt and betrayed. I thought to myself: so Skip isn't here any more, Lisa? Get over it! You're feeling like a piece of discarded garbage? Get over it! You don't need to depend on someone else for your own definition – that's the key. You existed before this person came into your life. You can exist after she or he has left it. You're yourself, Mike. It's as simple as that.'

'*No!*' Declan clapped his hand to his head. '*Tell me that's not true, Lisa. Tell me I'm not myself.*'

'Of course, taking all this in and finding yourself again is easier said than done, I know – believe me, I know. It's a gradual process. And that's where the Exercises come in. In *Get Over It!* I've included twenty Exercises to help people find themselves again so they can face the future and move forward instead of wallowing in the past.'

'Could you give us an example? Tell us about one of the Exercises?'

'*No!' Declan covered his ears. 'Not the Exercises. Please God, not the Exercises.*'

'*Yes!' Christina grabbed his hands away and held them. 'You must listen to the Exercises. Life without them is meaningless.*'

'*You two. You're worse than the children.*'

'*Sorry, Lucy,' Christina giggled.*

'*Sorry, Lucy.' Declan hung his head. 'Does this mean you won't give us any sweets?*'

'All twenty of the Exercises are important, Mike, but I have to admit, I have my personal favourite. Why? Because I was amazed by how powerful it was myself, when I tried it. I couldn't believe how it shifted my perspective. I hadn't planned it as an Exercise, I hadn't even thought of writing the book when I did it. It happened naturally, spontaneously – and that's always the best way, isn't it? Spontaneity.'

'You bet,' Mike nodded.

'I was on a plane, travelling back from London to New York, when things with Skip – well, let's just say they were tough. I was at my lowest point. I was sitting beside a businessman on the plane and he didn't recognize me, which was fine and dandy by me because sometimes you just want to be you instead of a famous author. The man was very polite and he asked me, after we'd arranged our luggage in the compartment above – you know, that little hold above the seats that's never big enough and other people always put their stuff in so there's no room for your own – anywho, he asked me what I was doing on this flight. Where I was from, why I was travelling from London to New York. The usual questions nice strangers ask. And the thing of it is, I did something wild and crazy. I made up a story about myself.

'Now, I know it's a bad idea to lie and I'm not suggesting people do it in their day-to-day lives – lying is not a good way of handling problems, but this was different, Mike. I didn't know this man, I wasn't hurting him, I was just having a little fun, telling him a story. I told him I was a hairdresser who had moved from New York to Britain and was going back to the States for a visit. I talked about what it's like to cut hair and what it was like to live in a foreign country; I had a whale of a time making up a whole new life for myself. And all the time I was also thinking: Lisa, you don't *have* to talk about Skip and your heartbreak, you don't *have* to be that poor sad woman crying into your pillow at night. You can be someone else. OK, you can't be this hairdresser you've made up, not for long. But you *can* be the person you were before all this misery. You can find your pride, because you have your pride – it's still there, it hasn't run away – and you can find your true self again. You're the person you think you are; you have to see yourself through your own eyes, not someone else's.

'So that's my Exercise. Go out there, somewhere, anywhere, it doesn't matter, a supermarket, a baseball game, wherever – and turn yourself into someone different for a while. Tell the girl at the checkout counter you're a fighter pilot or a museum curator, I don't care, just be someone *different* for a few minutes or a few hours. And then you can get back to being *yourself*. The self you were before all this heartache happened. And then you can get over it. And *then* you can go forward.'

'Those are truly inspirational words, Lisa. And you know why? Because you've been through it, you've lived the pain. And you've come out the other side.'

'I certainly have,' Lisa smiled. 'And I want to help other people to do the same.'

'Testimonial time?' Declan asked.
'Testimonial time.' Christina nodded.

'And now it's time for some testimonials from people who've been helped by the words of wisdom in Lisa Thomas' book *Get Over It!*. We have four people, two men and two women, who want to tell us how *Get Over It!* changed their lives and pulled them out of depression after their relationships had broken up . . .'

'*Mummy!*'

'Sophie. You're supposed to be in bed.' Lucy pushed the pause button on the video.

'I know. But I came down to find out if Chris and Declan are staying here for the night. Are you?'

'No, Soph,' Declan said. 'We have to get back to London. We just came for a visit and to show your mum this tape she wanted to see.'

'You said you'd show me how to do that trick with the yo-yo.'

'I know,' Declan nodded. 'And I will, I promise. The next time we come.'

'When is Daddy coming home?'

'Soon,' Lucy said. 'But it's bedtime, Sophie. Go back upstairs.'

'Do I have to?'

'Yes.'

'Children,' Lucy sighed, watching Sophie leave the room with evident reluctance. 'You think it's going to get easier as they grow older, but it doesn't.'

'Wait till she's a teenager,' Declan smiled.

'She's besotted by you two. Today, at breakfast, she announced that she wants to be an aromatherapist. She even pronounced it right. Nigel told her she should be thinking of doing something a little more important – oh, I'm sorry, Chris.'

'Don't worry. I'm not offended.'

'I'm just going to check on her and make sure she's in bed. Then I'll come down and we can finish watching this tape. It's fascinating.'

'Are you all right?' Declan turned to Christina when Lucy had left the room. 'She can come out with some hurtful comments, can't she?'

'I'm fine,' Christina took his hand. 'I'm used to Lucy now.

Having you here helps. It's still a little awkward when we're alone together, but I relax when you're with me. And I am glad we came. The more often we visit, the less anxious I am around her. I'm beginning to see her as a human being, not a goddess. And Sophie is adorable.'

'What do you think of this book of Lisa's?'

'I think she has another bestseller.'

'So do I. It's strange, you know.'

'What?'

'This is how we first met. This was when I first saw you. Watching Lisa's video. Almost two years ago.'

'When I closed my eyes.'

'When you closed your eyes. Would you mind closing them again for a second?'

Christina leaned back and closed her eyes.

'All right. OK. Hold on. I know this isn't the time or the place, Christina. But I'm not sure I can wait for the right time or the right place and so I'm just going to say it now. I love you and I want to be with you for the rest of my life and I want to marry you. And I wish I had set this up properly and we were in some nice restaurant or somewhere romantic, not a drawing room in your step-sister's house, but I can't help it. I've waited too long as it is. I felt like asking you that first night we kissed, but I thought I'd be rushing things. Now two years is not rushing things, is it? What do you think? Could you bear to live with me and all my quirks? Is that possible?'

'Put that yo-yo away NOW!' They heard Lucy scream.

'Oh, I should tell you something.' Declan squeezed Christina's hand. 'You should know something about me before you answer. I lied once. I mean, I've lied more than once in my life, but I lied to someone about yo-yos. I said I never played with yo-yos as a child, and I did. So there. I thought you should know that. It may be important. It may change the way you feel about me.'

Christina opened her eyes and smiled. 'I can live with that, Declan. I mean, it's shocking, absolutely appalling, – lying about yo-yos. But I can live with it. In fact, I'd *love* to live with it.'

'That's a real smile, isn't it?'

'You know it is.'

'Snogging again?' Lucy walked into the room and picked up the remote-control device. 'Honestly, you two are worse than Nigel and I used to be. I wish you'd just get on with it and get married. Then you might behave like a normal couple. Now – ' she clicked on the play button ' – let's get back to Lisa Thomas. She's amazing, isn't she? I was thinking, though. It can't be all that difficult to write one of those books. I wouldn't mind trying to do one myself. What do you think, Declan?'

'I think it's a brilliant idea, Lucy,' Declan beamed. 'Absolutely perfecto.'

'There's a conference call going on at the moment. You can go in when it's finished,' the secretary said.

Skip took a seat and picked up a copy of *Forbes Magazine*, pretending to read it.

This was humiliating. This was *so* embarrassing. How had it happened? How could he be told to wait like some little minion who delivered the mail? The whole thing had gone haywire and he'd allowed it to happen. He'd let it spin out of control and now he had to sit in the outer office like some sap and wait for the damn conference call to end. A conference call he should have been in on, except he didn't even know what the hell it was about. It was too much. Way, way too much.

'All right, Mr Thomas. The call is over. You can go in now.'

'Thanks a bunch,' he said under his breath as he walked past her. 'You're a real babe.'

'Hi,' Alison said, looking up from her desk. 'What's happening?'

'What was the call all about?'

'The conference call? Oh, you'll love it. It's brilliant. I thought of it when I woke up this morning and I got to work on it straight away.'

'You thought of *what*? What is *it* exactly?'

'A new infomercial. There's a gap in the market, Skip. No one has done an infomercial for clinics yet.'

'Clinics?'

'Yeah. Alcohol and drug rehabilitation clinics, you know. Perfect material for an infomercial. First I had to find the right clinic, of course. There are so many of them here. Find the right one which has catered to the stars, taken care of their little problems, and then do an infomercial, with some of those stars giving testimonials: "This place changed my life blah blah blah". You know the deal. There are thousands, millions of people out there in television land who would want to go to a clinic just to be in the same clinic Elizabeth Taylor or someone was in, you know. Maybe Elizabeth Taylor is a little old hat now, but you get my drift.'

'Isn't there a privacy issue here?'

'No way. You know how fashionable it is to crack up or overdose or become dependent on some kind of foreign substance. It's part of the American way of life. Who wants to be private about it? I got the idea from my mother, actually. That night ages ago when you flew off here and I had to go home and stay with her. She kept banging on about you being an alcoholic and ending up in a clinic. I should have thought of this before, definitely.'

'Are you going to give a free introductory offer? A money-back guarantee? If you're not cured within five days, we'll what? Give you a refund and a drink?'

'I think we do have to offer something along with it, yes. Maybe a book of recipes.'

'Recipes – for what? "How to make crack cocaine in the privacy of your back yard. No need to go to inner cities and score any more – we'll show you how to do it at home, with your loved ones".'

'Don't be silly, Skip. Recipes for alcohol-free cocktails, something along those lines.'

'Hash-free brownies? I think Betty Crocker has already done that.'

'Why are you being so negative?'

'I don't see this supposed gap in the market, Alison. I don't think people are sitting there watching TV, wondering what clinic they should check themselves into.'

'I do. Think of all those housewives on tranquillizers or sleeping pills; men watching ESPN with bottles of whisky beside them. They see an infomercial for a clinic and some movie stars telling them how fantastic the clinic is, and they're hooked.'

'Oh, great. Now they're hooked on advertising instead of booze or drugs.'

Alison picked up the telephone. 'If you don't want to help on this,' she waved the receiver in the air, 'that's not a problem. I'm busy. Go back and do whatever it is you were doing. We'll talk later.'

Yeah, right, Skip thought, staring at her set jaw. We'll talk later by which time the deal will be so far down the road it will have left me in its dust. And you will have pulled off another little coup. No, a *big* coup. You're on a roll. Ever since you took infomercials upmarket, you can do no wrong. And I don't know how it all happened. There we were struggling along with these ideas of ours, working together to try and break into the market, and suddenly you're schmoozing with the bigwigs in the fashion and jewellery world and having meetings with Tiffany's and Whatshername Karan and Ralph fucking Lauren and the whole idea hits paydirt. Like an oil well coming in – they go for it, the infomercials take off and we're in offices on Madison Avenue. Meanwhile little Skip here has his success too. *Plots in a Box* is also a winner and the two of us are a team – the King and Queen of Infomercials. Only your ideas made more money than mine did and you aren't so willing to share the credit equally. You suddenly have a bigger office than I do because, let's face it, you're taking a meeting with Ralph while I'm taking a meeting with the guys who manufacture china on the cheap.

Skip turned and left Alison's office. He tried to walk down the corridor to his own office with a degree of authority, but he felt his shoulders slouching and his feet shuffle.

I'm selling culture, he said to himself. And you're selling clinics. At least I'm working with intelligent, respected people. Owen Lewis and his gang at Reading University are gifted. Thank God I ate humble pie and got in touch with Declan after *Plots in a Box* took off. Now there is a decent human being. Not pissed off with me for stealing his girlfriend, not to mention his ideas. Happy to take a tiny percentage of the profit, amazed even that I offered it to him. I'm feeling guilty as shit for cutting him out of it to begin with and dealing only with Toby, and he's actually laughing on the telephone, telling me he never expected to be cut in. 'I wrote a script and you paid me for it, Skip,' he said. 'I'm pleased it has worked for you but frankly I'm surprised you rang. Alison led me to believe that I wasn't going to be involved.' 'Yeah, well Alison didn't think ahead,' was what he didn't say to Declan. He didn't say: 'This one worked and we need the next, Declan.' No, he played it cool and told Declan that of course he was always going to give him part of the profits and was Declan maybe interested in thinking about another?

The English spin was key. As soon as Declan told him his father and some of Owen's fellow professors had come up with a few ideas for further infomercials along the *Plots in a Box* line, he knew he was on a winner. Of course it would have been better if these professors were from Oxford or Cambridge, but hell, any English university sounded good. You put their names and titles on the cassette. People buy it and feel as if they've trodden on the playing-fields of Eton. It was a question of class, and superior tone. He could have contacted people at Harvard or Yale, he knew. But you can't beat the Brits at culture. They have it sewn up.

Skip reached his office and sat down at his desk. He unlocked the top drawer and took a photograph out. It was a picture of Lisa. She was sitting on a rock, dressed in shorts and a bikini top, with a picnic spread out before her; smiling at the camera, at him.

Lisa knew. She'd always said he was idealistic and he'd thought she was nuts. But she was right. He *did* care about helping people. He wanted these infomercials to educate people and make them learn things they never normally would. She'd seen something in him that was buried, but definitely there. Why hadn't he listened to her? She knew him better than he knew himself. And now she was over him. And now he was with Alison. Who was, he had to admit, dynamite in bed, but who also made him feel . . . made him feel what, exactly? Dumb, that's what. At least Lisa had been a success in a different field. He'd never wanted to write self-help books. He had, however, wanted to be the top dog in the infomercial world. And he would have shared that status with Alison. Now she had elbowed him aside and he had to wait in the outer office while she took conference calls. She thought his connection with Owen Lewis and his colleagues was laughable, he knew. 'This series won't continue to sell, Skip. It has a shelf-life. People will get bored with culture. It's too much like homework even though you've tried to make it easy for them. It's too daunting. You should think of something else now. Be careful or you'll end up hugging the anchor.'

Hugging the anchor? That was an expression his co-workers had used at AT&T. It meant you were embracing a concept which was doomed and sinking fast. Where had Alison picked that up? She was talking like a corporate executive these days. Oh, sure, she still knew what to do with his toes, but she did it less and less frequently.

She thinks *I'm* the anchor, Skip said, addressing the photograph. And she's going to let go soon, I can feel it. All right. But she's not going to jettison me entirely. This is our business. She can kick me out of bed but she can't kick me out of my office.

I don't even know how she managed to get her Green Card. I don't know anything. What does that make me? Dumb.

Reaching further back in the drawer, Skip grabbed the book and brought it out, careful to make sure no one was around to see him. He then went to close the door to his office and told his secretary that he didn't want to be disturbed. Still, he didn't feel entirely safe, so he picked up a large volume from his bookshelf, *War and Peace*, opened it up and used it as a front for what he really wanted to read.

You feel awful, don't you? Your confidence is low, your self-esteem is flagging. How can you feel good about yourself when someone you once loved and maybe love still is leaving you? What happened? you ask yourself. What did I do wrong?

You didn't do a damn thing wrong! Excuse my language, but sometimes it's necessary to swear to make a point. But what you have done which is not wrong, but mistaken, is to see yourself through someone else's eyes. Your partner doesn't love you any more? Right. So what? Get over it. There are people out there who will love you. Go find one. You don't think that's easy? Come off it. You're a special person with a lot to give and all you have to do is have faith in yourself. Your partner said some mean things to you? Forget it! Who is he to tell you anything about yourself? You're the person who knows you. You have a PhD in yourself. No one else is qualified to teach you as a course. They haven't lived your life, have they? So why are you listening to what they say?

Your partner prefers someone else?

Skip winced.

Hey. That's life. That's his problem. How much do you want to bet that he moves on from that relationship too? People who keep looking for new adventures never stop looking, you know. Wait a while and that new relationship of his will crumble. And meanwhile you will have found someone worthwhile, someone solid. Someone who appreciates you for who you are.

You know that old saying – there are plenty of other fish in the sea? Well, OK, in these days of pollution we might have a problem with the toxic qualities of those fish, but what's a little food poisoning when you're having fun? (Jokey, jokey!)

No, seriously, folks, there are plenty of other fish in the sea. Don't be shy. Go out there and hook one . . .

Skip sighed and scratched his head. 'Who have you found, Lisa?' he murmured. 'Who have you hooked? I envy the guy, I really do.'

He turned the page and kept reading.

Lisa arrived at Broadcasting House fifteen minutes early. She decided to sit on one of the seats in Reception and go over some notes she had made before signing in and going to the studio. As she looked for an unoccupied chair, she saw a man come through the front doors, jacket slung over his shoulder.

'Toby!' she shrieked. 'Oh my God.' She rushed over to him. 'What are you doing here?'

'Lisa. Lisa Thomas. Oh *my* God. I've come to do a radio play, actually. I'm a few minutes early and—'

'So am I. Come sit down with me. Tell me everything.' She took his arm and led him to seats she'd spotted in the far corner of the reception area. 'I can't believe this! You never run into people you know in New York. Well, sometimes you do. But I never thought I'd meet up with you again. God! You look terrific. But then you always did.'

'Thank you, Lisa.' Toby placed his jacket on his lap. 'It's always nice to get a compliment. And you're looking wonderful too. You look – well, taller. You can't have grown, can you?'

'It's the high heels,' Lisa blushed. 'I've started to wear them.'

'They suit you. And your hair – that's different as well.'

'Oh,' she said, reaching up to her head self-consciously. 'Do you think it's too short?'

'No. No. You look very chic indeed. Very Nineties. Now, why are *you* here? Promoting a new book?'

'Yes. I have some interviews. I wish I could come listen to you record the play, though. That would be much more fun. You know, I watch *Away Days* on PBS faithfully. Never miss an episode. I *love* it, Toby. You are amazing, fantastic. Incredible.'

'Enough!' Toby put up his hands. 'This will go straight to my head, Lisa and I won't be able to concentrate on the play.'

She's not as dreadful as I remember. In fact, she *does* look well. Doris Day turns into who? Goldie Hawn? Yes. Cute, bubbly, surprisingly sexy Goldie Hawn. What a fortunate transformation.

'I always knew how talented you are. From that first moment I saw you in *Northanger Abbey*, I just knew. And now you've had this success with your show and with *Plots in a Box*, too, of course.' Lisa frowned.

'I was sorry to hear about you and Skip,' Toby said quickly. 'I hope you don't hold it against me – working for him. It was my first and last infomercial.'

'Of course I don't hold it against you. I would never – no. I'm pleased for you, Toby. Really.'

'Well, I'd best be going.' Toby stood up. 'It was lovely to see you again, Lisa.' He bent over and kissed her on both cheeks. 'Good luck with the interviews, although I'm sure you don't need luck.'

'Toby – ' Lisa stood as well and grabbed his forearm. 'I know this is forward of me, but I was wondering . . . I mean, I don't know that many people here. Declan and Christina – that's about it as far as friends are concerned – and you know three's a crowd. Oh, I'm sorry. Maybe I shouldn't have brought them up.'

'No worries,' Toby cut in. 'That's ancient history. I wish them the best, actually.'

'Now that's sweet of you. Anywho, I thought maybe you wouldn't mind joining me for dinner some night this week. I'm off around the country next Monday, but do you have a free evening between now and then? If you don't, I understand. You must be so busy these days.'

'Lisa, say no more.' He put his hand on her shoulder. 'I'd love to join you. I'm free tomorrow night, as it happens. I was supposed to go to a dinner party, but the hostess rang today to say she's down with the flu. I'd very much enjoy having dinner with you. Where shall we meet, or shall I give you my number?' Toby glanced at his watch.

'No, no. You're in a rush. Let's say we'll meet at San Lorenzo's at eight tomorrow. If there's any problem, just leave a message there.'

'Wonderful.' Toby kissed her again. 'See you then.'

'Oh, and it's my treat.'

'Even more wonderful,' Toby said as he began to walk away. 'I'm looking forward to it.'

'So am I,' Lisa said, staring at his back. 'So am I.'

'Declan!' Christina called upstairs. 'You have to come down here. You have to see this.'

'Hold on,' he yelled back. 'I'm putting my socks on.'

'You're not going to believe this.'

'OK – I'm here.' He thumped down the stairs. 'Has a meteorite landed in the kitchen?'

'More amazing than that. *Much* more amazing.'

'What? Tell me.'

'Come here.' She took his hand and led him into the kitchen. 'Look.' She pointed to the *Daily Mail*.

'*Impossible.*' Declan stepped back, then forward again, crouching over the newspaper. 'Is there some coffee? Is there some vodka? I'm seeing things.'

'Then we both are.'

'Mass delusion?'

'It can't be true.'

'No.' He shook his head. 'It can't be. We're both imagining it.'

'I suppose . . .' Christina went and poured a mug of coffee, put some milk into it and handed it to him as he stood staring at the paper. 'I suppose it *is* possible. It's not wholly out of the bounds of probability.'

'Close, though.' He took a gulp.

'Close,' she agreed.

'Christina. He has his arm around her. You don't think . . . ?'

'I have no idea.'

'No. That's a standard luvvie pose. All actors hug people. Like polar bears.'

'What?'

'I don't know – I've always pictured polar bears hugging each other.'

'Outside San Lorenzo's?'

He laughed, reached over and put his arm around her. 'They met up somehow. And they went to dinner together. That's all there is to it.'

'But how did they meet up?'

'Don't have a clue. But he's a rising star, she's a famous author of self-help books. Famous people hang out with famous people. That's how the world works.'

'He always thought Lisa was a figure of fun. On our way back from that first dinner he said she reminded him of one of the Seven Dwarfs – no, *two* of the seven dwarfs, actually. Happy and Doc.'

'They're nice dwarfs. She could have reminded him of Grumpy. Or Sneezy. Maybe he had a crush on her and he didn't want to tell you about it.'

'Oh no,' Christina smiled. 'Toby would have told me. He always told me when he fancied someone.'

'Do you ever miss him? Even the slightest bit? Be honest.'

'Are you jealous?'

'Of course.'

'Good. No, I don't miss him, but I am glad he's doing well. Look at that dress Lisa is wearing. It's so *short* and so fashionable.'

'You'd look terrific in it.'

'It would come up to my navel, Declan.'

'Exactly. That's why you'd look terrific in it.'

'Do you see the expression on her face? I think she's in love.'

'In love with the fact photographers are taking her picture outside a restaurant, or in love with Toby?'

Christina took the mug out of Declan's hand and drank some of his coffee. 'You know Lisa better than I do. What do you think?'

'Well, she loves being famous and successful, but . . .'

'But?'

'She's gazing up at him with utter – '

'Adoration,' Christina finished.

'I think she's in trouble, then.'

'I *know* she is.'

'Should we invite them to the wedding?'

'We should invite Lisa. She's the reason we met. I'm not sure about Toby. What do you think?' Christina slipped her arm around his waist.

'I don't know. He might corner my father again. Perhaps we should leave exes out of it.'

'I think that would be better. I'm not too keen on having Alison there.'

'If we had Alison we'd have to have Skip and then Lisa might object. God,' Declan shook his head. 'These things are complicated, aren't they? Maybe we should sneak off to Gretna Green or Las Vegas.'

'Is that what you'd really prefer?'

'No. I want to see you walk down the aisle.'

'You don't think I'll look ridiculous?'

'Christina,' Declan reached out and took her chin in his hand. 'There is not one single ridiculous thing about you. You know, sometimes I think we're so sickeningly happy that if I were someone else watching us, I'd be nauseated.'

'No, you wouldn't. You're forgetting something. The whole world loves a lover,' Christina said in an American accent.

'How right you are, Lisa,' Declan laughed. 'As always. Any more clichés before I go to work? Something to help me through the day?'

'How about: Thank God it's Friday?'

'That's a clichéd restaurant chain, not a cliché. Listen, I was thinking. Would you like to go to Milton Keynes tomorrow? I've always wanted to see that Japanese Peace Pagoda and the Concrete Cow and the house that's painted to look like someone's face.'

'I thought you wanted to go to Bognor Regis.'

'We can do that next Saturday.'

'I'm not sure I can stand all the excitement.'

'It's a hectic life, living with a jet-setter like me, but I know you can take the pace.' He kissed her and headed back upstairs.

Christina could hear him humming *Whistle While You Work* as he went. Why do *we* work so well together? she wondered. Because I genuinely like him so much? Or because he has magic? Because he's a voodoo doctor who knows the spells to cast to make me happy?

'I'm not sure how to describe him,' she'd told Francesca when she and Declan had first become a couple. 'It sounds soppy but he's my best friend as well as my lover. I can tell him anything, talk to him about everything. We – '

'Yes?' Francesca pressed.

'In my experience – which granted, isn't vast – men tend to fall asleep or turn on the television or get up and do something after sex. Declan and I – well – '

'Yes? Come on, Christina, you can't start a sentence like that and not finish it.'

'We have incredible, wonderful sex and then we talk afterwards. We have incredible, wonderful conversations. And we laugh a lot. I'm not sure how to put it, except to say he has a genius for intimacy.'

'I think I get the gist. That will do it for me,' Francesca sighed.

Me too, Christina thought. She looked at the photo of Toby and Lisa again.

Lisa, be careful. Toby has a genius for acting.

Here we go again, Skip thought. Another argument on the same topic. We say the same things over and over again. It's like watching someone trying to waterski who can never make it to the standing position. The boat takes off, he struggles to get up, he falls. The boat circles, someone throws him the line again, the boat takes off. He struggles to get up, he falls.

A lot of fun to watch from the sidelines. No fun at all if you're a participant.

'You're deliberately setting out to make me feel guilty, you know,' Alison was saying. Skip couldn't decide whether to keep on going with this fight or abandon it totally. If he abandoned it, would she think she had won? Or would she understand that he was just plain sick and tired of repeating himself? She was staring at him now, with that challenging, aggressive expression of hers, waiting for him to say something so she could interrupt him again and point out how wrong and stupid he was.

'I'll say it once more, Alison. I am *not* trying to make you feel guilty. All I am doing is asking you where I fit into your plans these days. You've got – '

'That's my point. See? You ask me where you "fit in" as if I'm supposed to be responsible for you. And if I'm not responsible for you, I'm a nightmare woman who has attacked your masculinity.'

'Al – '

'I've told you, you should work on other infomercials. You bring me some ideas and we'll do them together, the way we were supposed to. Is it my fault you got sidetracked on this *Plots in a Box* series?'

'I like that series,' Skip said.

'And now you're sulking. You look approximately two years old.'

'Alison,' Skip sighed. 'What has happened to us?'

'I don't know,' she bristled. '*I* haven't changed.'

'We have to . . .' Skip stopped speaking and felt himself blush. 'We have to what?'

We have to get back to the beginning, I was about to say. But then you'd ridicule me for sounding like Lisa.

'Would you like to go out to dinner tonight?' Skip looked past her, at the sun setting over her left shoulder. She seemed so unapproachable behind that huge mahogany desk of hers. He could barely remember the woman who had sat across the table from him at Zafferano's, telling him the story of her life. Alison fitted into New York City; she belonged here. For a second Skip forgot himself and chuckled at the image of Alison as an Essex girl, dancing around her handbag.

'What's so amusing?'

'I was thinking of that time in London – when you told me about Essex Girls.'

'That's an odd thought to have.'

'Let's go out to dinner. Let's talk about anything except work. I don't know – let's go dancing, Al. Why not? We might have fun. All we do is work these days.'

Do I still love him? Alison asked herself, focusing on Skip's face. Yes, I do, funnily enough. But does he still love *me*? That's the question. I'm not trying to be more successful than he is – it just worked out that way. And he takes some kind of pleasure in feeling put-upon. Perhaps he thinks all women are out to humiliate him like his mother did and he's made it a self-fulfilling prophecy. He could have joined in on the infomercials I was setting up at the beginning, but he insisted on staying with the *Plots in a Box* series. Now he's blaming me for his own mistakes.

I wish we could start all over again. If we went out tonight and tried to have a decent conversation, we might click again. I miss the way we used to be together. We *did* have fun. I've spent so much energy adjusting to a new city, a new country, a new career, I haven't spent enough time with Skip, doing the things couples do. He's trying, now, I can see that. I should try as well.

'That's a good idea, you know. Where would we go?'

'Well . . . how about the Rainbow Room?'

Alison narrowed her eyes. She crossed her legs, one foot tightly behind the other ankle. Here we go again, she thought. I'm sick of it. He won't let go. They've been divorced almost two years now and he still won't let go.

'You don't remember, do you?' she said heavily.

'Remember what?'

'You told me – at the beginning – our second dinner together, in London, the night we first kissed. You told me Lisa loved to go to the Rainbow Room and how tired you were of that place. And now you want to go again? Are you going to close your eyes and pretend I'm Lisa as we dance, is that it? You still love her, don't you?'

'You have a jealousy mania. It's obsessive. How many times have you asked me that question in two years? It's getting tired, Alison. *I'm* getting tired of this unfounded jealousy.'

'Is that right?'

'Yes.'

'I see. I have a jealousy mania and you have a photograph of Lisa in your desk.'

'What is this? Did you used to work for Richard Nixon?'

'Skip.' Alison turned around and looked out of the window. 'You really piss me off, you know.'

'Ditto.'

'Good news!' Lisa said, jumping back into bed.

'What's that?'

'I don't have to go out tonight.' She snuggled up against Toby's chest.

'Mmm,' he said, reaching for his pack of cigarettes on the bedside table. 'That's nice.'

'They didn't mind when I cancelled. I hardly know them, anyway. Some friends of friends from Connecticut who are here for a few weeks.'

'Sounds tedious.'

'It would have been. I mean, they're nice people, but I'd much rather be here with you.'

'I should take that as a compliment?'

'Of course!' She thumped him on the chest. 'What else would it be? I *love* being here with you. I *adore* it.'

'Don't say it, Lisa. Don't tell me you're my biggest fan again. Or I'll think you're Kathy Bates in *Misery* and you'll tie me to the bed and take a sledgehammer to my legs.'

'You're so funny.'

'I try.'

'Toby?' Lisa said after he'd lit his cigarette and taken a drag.

'Yes?'

'I was thinking.'

'Yes?'

'I was thinking that it's fate.'

'What's fate?'

'Us. Our meeting each other. It's fate.'

'That's comforting.'

'Yes, it is. Exactly. You see, there we all were, the six of us that first evening. And then everything went crazy and Skip went off with Alison and Declan and Christina ended up together.'

Toby pulled the ashtray from the table and placed it beside him.

'Anywho, you see what I'm getting at?'

'No.'

'Well, we've all switched partners now. All six of us. That's fate. It's amazing.'

'Mmm.'

'I know you and I – we haven't been together long. Not even forty-eight hours, but sometimes you don't need time.'

'I'm sorry?'

'You don't need time to know what the future holds – you just know it. The way I knew from the very beginning what a great actor you are and how sweet you are, too. I just *knew*. I saw all that in you the first time we met. Fate brought us together. We were destined to meet again.'

'Have you ever thought about writing lyrics for Julio Iglesias?'

'What?' Lisa drew back, looked at Toby, then resumed her original position. 'Oh, jokey, jokey. I get it. Toby, I'm being serious here. I've never experienced anything like this.'

'Like what?'

'You know.' She nuzzled him. 'What we've been doing for the past two days. When we haven't been out. You know what I'm talking about. I've never, I mean, you do incredible things. You drive me crazy. It's as if you've released something in me. I've gone wild.'

'I've noticed.'

'And I was thinking – well, I'm supposed to go on tour around the country soon, but I don't *have* to. I could stay here.'

'You have commitments, Lisa.'

'Nothing I can't get out of. The thing is, you know, Skip used to talk about things . . .' Lisa paused and buried her head in Toby's chest.

'That's nice. I'm glad Skip used to talk. It would have been a difficult marriage if he'd been mute throughout.'

'Toby – stop teasing me.'

'What? I can't hear you.'

Lisa sat up. 'I said, stop teasing me. I'm trying to say something serious.'

'Right. Sorry. Go ahead.'

'Skip used to talk about having children and I always put it off. I was too committed to my career. But now, well, I'm older. You know that whole biological time clock business. I'm starting to think about it. And I realize we haven't known each other for long, but we are so perfect together. And I was thinking that maybe I put off the idea of having children with Skip because deep down I knew he wasn't the person I should be having children with. That there was someone else out there who would be absolutely, completely perfect. And now I think, you know . . . maybe I've met that person. Maybe fate has brought that person to me.'

'Lisa.' Toby put his left arm around her and folded her back into his body. He kissed her on top of her head.

'Yes?'

'I have three words to say to you.'

'Three little words?'

Summer camp is a place that hums with crickets and is so green it sometimes hurts my eyes to look.

I'm afraid to be here, because it is outside, and because outside there are bees. Bees make my stomach feel like a fist, even seeing one makes me want to run and hide. In my nightmares I picture them sucking my blood like it is honey.

My mother tells the camp counselors I'm afraid of bees. They say that in all the years of camp, not a single child has been stung.

I think, Someone has to be first.

One morning, my counselor – a girl with a macramé necklace that she wears even during swim time – takes us into the woods on a hike. It's time for a circle, she says. She moves one log, to make a bench. She moves a second log, and there are all the yellow jackets.

I freeze. The bees cover the counselor's face and arms and belly. She tries to bat them away while she's screaming. I throw myself at her. I slap my hands on her skin. I save her, even while I am being stung and stung.

At the end of camp that summer, the counselors give out awards. They are blue ribbons, each one, printed with fat black letters. Mine says Bravest Boy.

I still have it.

4

In the moments after, Patrick wonders how he could know that Nina's favorite number is 13, that the scar on her chin came from a sledding crash, that she wished for a pet alligator for three Christmases straight – yet not know that inside her, all this time, was a grenade waiting to explode. 'I did what I had to,' she murmurs, all the way across the slick and bloodied court.

In his arms, she trembles. She feels light as a cloud. Patrick's head whirls. Nina still smells of apples, her shampoo; she still can't walk a straight line – but she is babbling incoherently, not at all in control the way Patrick is accustomed to seeing her. As they cross the threshold into the holding cell, Patrick looks behind him into the courtroom. *Pandemonium*. He's always thought that word sounds like a circus, but here it is now. Brain matter covers the front of the defense attorney's suit. A litter of paper and pocketbooks covers the gallery, as some reporters sob, and others direct their cameramen to film. Caleb stands still as a statue. Bobby, one of the bailiffs, is talking into the radio at his shoulder: 'Yeah, shots were fired, and we need an ambulance.' Roanoke, the other bailiff, hustles a white-faced Judge Bartlett into chambers. 'Clear the court!' the judge yells, and Roanoke answers: 'But we can't, Your Honor. They're all witnesses.'

On the floor, being completely ignored, is the body of Father Szyszynski.

Killing him was the right thing, Patrick thinks before he can stop himself. And then immediately afterward: *Oh, God, what has she done?*

'Patrick,' Nina murmurs.

He cannot look at her. 'Don't speak to me.' He will be a witness at – *Christ* – Nina's murder trial. Whatever she tells him, he will have to tell a court.

As an aggressive photographer makes her way toward the holding cell, Patrick moves slightly to block the camera's view of Nina. His job, right now, is to protect her. He just wishes there were someone to protect *him*.

He jostles her in his arms so that he can shut the door. It will be easier to wait out the arrival of the Biddeford Police Department that way. As it swings closed, he sees the paramedics arriving, leaning down over the body.

'Is he dead?' Nina asks. 'I just need you to tell me, Patrick. I killed him, right? How many shots did I get off? I had to do it, you know I had to do it. He's dead, isn't he? The paramedics can't revive him, can they? Tell me they won't. Please, just tell me he's dead. I promise, I'll sit right here and not move if you just go look and see if he's dead.'

'He's dead, Nina,' Patrick says quietly.

She closes her eyes, sways a little. 'Thank God. Oh, God, God, thank God.' She sinks down onto the metal bunk in the small cell.

Patrick turns his back on her. In the courtroom, his colleagues have arrived. Evan Chao, another detective-lieutenant in the department, supervises the securing of the crime scene, yelling over the crescendo of shrieks and sobs. Policemen crouch, dusting for fingerprints, taking photos of the spreading pool of blood and the broken railing where Patrick tackled Nina to get the gun out of her hand. The Maine state police SWAT team arrives, thundering down the center aisle like a tornado. One woman, a reporter sequestered for questioning, glances at what is left of the priest and vomits. It is a grim, chaotic scene; it is the stuff of nightmares, and yet Patrick stares fixedly, far more willing to face this reality than the one crying quietly behind him.

*   *   *

What Nathaniel hates about this particular board game is that all you have to do is spin the spinner the wrong way, and that's it, your little game piece is coasting down that big long slide in the middle. It's true that if you spin the *right* way, you can climb that extra tall ladder . . . but it doesn't always work like that, and before you know it, you've lost.

Monica lets him win, but Nathaniel doesn't like that as much as he thought he would. It makes him feel the way he did when he fell off his bike and had this totally gross cut all across his chin. People looked at him and pretended that there was nothing wrong with him but you could see in their eyes that they really wanted to turn away.

'Are you going to spin, or do I have to wait until you turn six?' Monica teases.

Nathaniel flicks the spinner. *Four.* He moves his little man the right number of spaces and, it figures, winds up on one of those slides. He pauses at the top, knowing that if he only moves three instead, Monica won't say a word.

But before he can decide whether or not to cheat, something catches his attention behind her shoulder. Through the wide glass window of the playroom, he sees one policeman . . . no, two . . . five . . . racing through the hallway. They don't look like Patrick does when he works – all rumply, in a regular shirt and tie. They are wearing shiny boots and silver badges, and their hands are on their guns, just like Nathaniel sees late at night on TV when he comes downstairs to get a drink and his parents don't change the channel fast enough.

'Shoot,' he says softly.

Monica smiles at him. 'That's right, a chute. But you'll have better luck next time, Nathaniel.'

'No . . . shoot.' He curves his fingers into a gun, the sign for the letter *G*. 'You know. Bang.'

He realizes the moment Monica understands him. She looks behind her at the sound of all those running feet, and her eyes go wide. But she turns back to Nathaniel with a smile glued over the question that shivers on her lips. 'It's your spin, right?' Monica says, although they both know his turn has come and gone.

When feeling returns to Caleb's fingers and feet, it comes slowly, an emotional frostbite that leaves his extremities swollen and unfamiliar. He stumbles forward, past the spot where Nina has just shot a man in cold blood, past the people jostling for position so that they can do the jobs they were trained to do. Caleb gives the body of Father Szyszynski a wide berth. His body jerks toward the door where he last saw Nina, being shoved forward into a cell.

Jesus, a *cell*.

A detective who does not recognize him grabs his arm. 'Where do you think you're going?' Silent, Caleb pushes past the man, and then he sees Patrick's face in the small window of the door. Caleb knocks, but Patrick seems to be deciding whether or not to open the door.

At that point, Caleb realizes that all these people, all these detectives, think he might be Nina's accomplice.

His mouth goes dry as sand, so that when Patrick finally does open the door a crack, he can't even request to see his wife. 'Get Nathaniel and go home,' Patrick suggests quietly. 'I'll call you, Caleb.'

Yes, Nathaniel. *Nathaniel*. The very thought of his son, a floor below while all this has been going on, makes Caleb's stomach cramp. He moves with a speed and grace unlikely for someone his size, barreling past people until he reaches the far end of the courtroom, the door at the rear of the aisle. A bailiff stands guard, watching Caleb approach. 'My son, he's downstairs. Please. You have to let me get to him.'

Maybe it is the pain carved into Caleb's face; maybe it is the way his words come out in the color of grief – for whatever reason, the bailiff wavers. 'I swear I'll come right back. But I have to make sure he's all right.'

A nod, one that Caleb isn't meant to see. When the bailiff

looks away, Caleb slips out the door behind him. He takes the stairs two at a time and runs down the hall to the playroom.

For a moment, he stands outside the plate-glass window, watching his son play and letting it bring him back to center. Then Nathaniel sees him and beams, jumping up to open the door and throw himself into Caleb's arms.

Monica's tight face swims into the sea of his vision. 'What happened up there?' she mouths silently.

But Caleb only buries his face against his son's neck, as silent as Nathaniel had been when something happened that he could not explain.

Nina once told Patrick that she used to stand at the side of Nathaniel's crib and watch him sleep. *It's amazing,* she'd said. *Innocence in a blanket.* He understands, now. Watching Nina sleep, you'd never know what had happened just two hours before. You'd never know from that smooth brow what thoughts lay underneath the surface.

Patrick, on the other hand, is absolutely ill. He cannot seem to catch his breath; his stomach knots with each step. And every time he looks at Nina's face, he cannot decide what he'd rather find out: that this morning, she simply went crazy . . . or that she didn't.

As soon as the door opens, I'm wide-awake. I jackknife to a sitting position on the bunk, my hand smoothing the jacket Patrick gave me as a makeshift pillow. It is wool, scratchy; it has left lines pressed into my cheek.

A policeman I don't know sticks his head inside. 'Lieutenant,' he says formally, 'we need you to come give a statement.'

Of course. Patrick's seen it too.

The policeman's eyes are insects on my skin. As Patrick moves toward the door I stand, grab onto the bars of the cell. 'Can you find out if he's dead? Please? I have to know. I have to. I just have to know if he's dead.' My words hit Patrick between the shoulder blades, slow him down. But he doesn't look at me, not as he walks away from the holding cell, past the other policeman, and opens the door.

In the slice of room revealed, I see the activity that Patrick's kept hidden from me for the past few hours. The Murder Winnebago must have arrived – a state police mobile unit that contains everything the cops need to investigate a homicide and the key personnel to do it. Now they cover the courtroom like a mass of maggots, dusting for fingerprints and taking down the names and statements of eyewitnesses. A person shifts, revealing a crimson smear that outlines a splayed, graying hand. As I watch, a photographer leans down, captures the spatter pattern of the blood. My heart trips tight. And I think: *I did this; I did this.*

It is a God's honest fact that Quentin Brown does not fancy driving anywhere, especially long distances, particularly from Augusta to York County. By the time he's in Brunswick he's certain that another moment and his six-foot-five frame will be permanently stunted into the position demanded by this ridiculously tiny Ford Probe. By the time he reaches Portland, he needs to be put into traction. But as an assistant attorney general on the murder team, he has to go where he is summoned. And if someone offs a priest in Biddeford, then Biddeford is where he has to go.

Still, by the time he reaches the district court, he is in a formidable mood, and that's saying something. By normal standards, Quentin Brown is overpowering – add together his shaved head, his unusual height, and his more unusual skin color, given this lily-white state, and most people assume he is either a felon or a vacationing NBA draft pick. But a lawyer? A *black* lawyer? *Not heah,* as the locals say.

In fact, the University of Maine law school heavily recruits students of color, to make up for their rainbow deficiency. Like Quentin, many come; unlike Quentin, they all leave. He's spent twenty years walking into provincial courts and surprising the hell out of the defense attorneys who come expecting someone – or some*thing* – different. And truth be told, Quentin likes it that way.

As always, a path parts for him when he strides into the Biddeford District Court, as people fall back to gape. He walks into the courtroom with the police tape crossing the doors, and continues up the aisle, past the bar. Fully aware that movement has slowed and conversation has stopped, Quentin leans down and examines the dead man. 'For a crazy woman,' he murmurs, appraising, 'she was a damn good shot.' Then Quentin eyeballs the cop who is staring at him as if he's arrived from Mars. 'What's the matter?' he deadpans. 'You never seen someone six-foot-five before?'

A detective walks up to him, swaggering with authority. 'Can Ihelp you?'

'Quentin Brown. From the AG's office.' He extends a hand.

'Evan Chao,' the detective says, working his damnedest not to do a double-take. God, how Quentin loves this moment.

'How many witnesses do we have to the shooting?'

Chao does some arithmetic on a pad. 'We're up to thirty-six, but we've got about fifty people in the back room who haven't given us statements yet. They're all saying the same thing, though. And we have the whole shooting on tape; WCSH was filming the arraignment for the five o'clock news.'

'Where's the gun?'

'Bobby grabbed it, bagged it.'

Quentin nods. 'And the perp?'

'In the holding cell.'

'Good. Let's draft up a complaint for murder.' He glances around, assessing the state of the investigation. 'Where's her husband?'

'With all the other people, waiting to be questioned, I suppose.'

'Do we have any evidence linking him to the crime? Did he participate in any way?'

Chao exchanges a glance with a few police officers, who

murmur among themselves and shrug. 'He hasn't been questioned yet, apparently.'

'Then get him in here,' Quentin says. 'Let's ask him.'

Chao turns to one of the bailiffs. 'Roanoke, find Caleb Frost, will you?'

The older man looks at Quentin and quails. 'He, uh, ain't in there.'

'You know this for a fact,' Quentin says slowly.

'Ayuh. He, well, he asked me if he could go get his kid, but he told me he'd come back.'

'He said *what?*' This is little more than a whisper, but coming from Quentin's great height, it is threatening. 'You let him walk out the door after his wife murdered the man who's charged with molesting his son? What is this, the Keystone Kops?'

'No, sir,' the bailiff replies solemnly. 'It's the Biddeford District Court.'

A muscle jumps in Quentin's jaw. 'Get someone to go find this guy and interview him,' he tells Chao. 'I don't know what he knows; I don't know whether he's involved, but if he needs to be arrested, do it.'

Chao bristles. 'Don't pin this on the police force; it was the bailiff's mistake. Nobody even told me he was in the courtroom.'

And where else would he be, if his son's abuser was being arraigned? But Quentin only takes a deep breath. 'Well, we need to deal with the shooter, anyway. Is the judge still here? Maybe we can get him to arraign her.'

'The judge is . . . indisposed.'

'Indisposed,' Quentin repeats.

'Took three Valium after the shots flew, and hasn't woken up yet.'

There is a possibility of getting another judge in, but it is late in the day. And the last thing Quentin wants is to have this woman released because of some stupid bail commissioner. 'Charge her. We'll hold her overnight and arraign her in the morning.'

'Overnight?' Chao asks.

'Yes. Last time I checked, there was still a York County Jail in Alfred.'

The detective looks down at his shoes for a moment. 'Yeah, but . . . well, you know she's a DA?'

Of course he knows, he's known since the moment his office was called to investigate. 'What I know,' Quentin answers, 'is that she's a murderer.'

Evan Chao knows Nina Frost; every detective in Biddeford has worked with her at some time or another. And like every other guy on the force, he doesn't even blame her for what she's done. Hell, half of them wish they'd have the guts to do the same thing, were they in her position.

He doesn't want to be the one to do this, but then again, better him than that asshole Brown. At least he can make sure the next step is as painless as possible for her.

He relieves the officer guarding her and takes up the position himself outside the holding cell. In a more ideal situation, he would take her to a conference room, offer her a cup of coffee, make her comfortable so that she'd be more likely to talk. But the court doesn't have a secure conference room, so this interview will have to be conducted on opposite sides of the bars.

Nina's hair is wild around her face; her eyes are so green they glow. On her arm are deep scratches; it looks as though she's done that to herself. Evan shakes his head. 'Nina, I'm really sorry . . . but I have to charge you with the murder of Glen Szyszynski.'

'I killed him?' she whispers.

'Yes.'

She is transformed by the smile that unwinds across her face. 'Can I see him, please?' she asks politely. 'I promise I won't touch anything, but please, I have to see him.'

'He's gone already, Nina. You can't see him.'

'But I killed him?'

Evan exhales heavily. The last time he'd seen Nina Frost,

she'd been arguing one of his own cases in court – a date rape. She had gotten up in front of the perp and wrung him dry on the witness stand. She had made him look the way she looks, right now. 'Will you give me a statement, Nina?'

'No, I can't. I can't. I did what I had to do, I can't do any more.'

He pulls out a Miranda form. 'I need to read you your rights.'

'I did what I had to do.'

Evan has to raise his voice over hers. 'You have the right to remain silent. Anything you say can be used against you in a court of law. You have the right . . .'

'I can't do any more. I did what I had to do,' Nina babbles.

Finally Evan finishes reading. Through the bars he hands her a pen to sign the paper, but it drops from her fingers. She whispers, 'I can't do any more.'

'Come on, Nina,' Evan says softly. He unlocks the holding cell, leads her through the hallways of the sheriff's office, and outside to a police cruiser. He opens the door for her and helps her inside. 'We can't arraign you till tomorrow, so I've got to take you down to the jail overnight. You're gonna get your own cell, and I'll make sure they take care of you. Okay?'

But Nina Frost has curled up in a fetal position on the back-seat of the cruiser and doesn't seem to hear him at all.

The correctional officer at the booking desk of the jail sucks on a Halls Mentho-Lyptus cough drop while he asks me to narrow my life down to the only things they need to know in a jail: *name, date of birth, height, weight. Eye color, allergies, medications, regular physician.* I answer softly, fascinated by the questions. I usually enter this play in the second act; to see it at its beginning is new for me.

A blast of medicinal mint comes my way, as the sergeant taps his pencil again. 'Distinguishing characteristics?' he asks.

He means birthmarks, moles, tattoos. *I have a scar,* I think silently, *on my heart.*

But before I can answer, another correctional officer unzips my black purse and empties its contents on the desk. Chewing gum, three furry Life Savers, a checkbook, my wallet. The detritus of motherhood: photographs of Nathaniel from last year, a long-forgotten teething ring, a four-pack of crayons pinched from a Chili's restaurant. Two more rounds of ammunition for the handgun.

I grab my arms, suddenly shivering. 'I can't do it. I can't do any more,' I whisper, and try to curl into a ball.

'Well, we're not done yet,' the correctional officer says. He rolls my fingers across an ink pad and makes three sets of prints. He props me up against a wall, hands me a placard. I follow his directions like a zombie; I do not meet his eyes. He doesn't tell me when the flash is going to go off; now I know why in every mug shot a criminal seems to have been caught unaware.

When my vision adjusts after the burst of light, a female guard is standing in front of me. She has one long eyebrow across her forehead and the build of a linebacker. I stumble in her wake into a room not much bigger than a closet, which holds shelves full of neatly folded hazard-orange jail scrubs. The Connecticut prisons had to sell all their brand-new forest-green jumpsuits, I suddenly remember, because the convicts kept escaping into the woods.

The guard hands me a pair of scrubs. 'Get undressed,' she orders.

I have to do this, I think, as I hear her snap on the rubber gloves. *I have to do whatever it takes to get out of here.* So I force my mind to go blank, like a screen at the close of a movie. I feel the guard's fingers probe my mouth and my ears, my nostrils, my vagina, my anus. With a jolt, I think of my son.

When it is over, the guard takes my clothes, still damp with the blood of the priest, and bags them. I slowly put on the scrubs, tying them so tight at the waist that I find myself gasping for breath. My eyes dart back and forth as we walk back down the hall. The walls, they're watching me.

In the booking room at the front of the jail again, the female guard leaves me standing in front of a phone. 'Go ahead,' she instructs. 'Make your call.'

I have a constitutional right to a private phone call, but I can feel the weight of their stares. I pick up the receiver and play with it, stroking its long neck. I stare at it as if I have never seen a telephone before.

Whatever they hear, they won't admit to hearing. I have tried to pressure enough correctional officers to come testify, and they never will, because they have to go back and guard these prisoners every day.

For the first time, this works to my advantage.

I meet the gaze of the nearest correctional officer, then slowly shake off the act. Dialing, I wait to be connected to something outside of here. 'Hello?' Caleb says, the most beautiful word in the English language.

'How's Nathaniel?'

'*Nina.* Jesus Christ, what were you doing?'

'How's Nathaniel?' I repeat.

'How the hell do you *think* he is? His mother's been arrested for killing someone!'

I close my eyes. 'Caleb, you need to listen to me. I'll explain everything when I see you. Have you talked to the police?'

'No –'

'Don't. Right now, I'm at the jail. They're holding me here overnight, and I'm going to be arraigned tomorrow.' There are tears coming. 'I need you to call Fisher Carrington.'

'Who?'

'He's a defense attorney. And he's the only person who can get me out of this. I don't care what you have to do, but get him to represent me.'

'What am I supposed to tell Nathaniel?'

I take a deep breath. 'That I'm okay, and that I'll be home tomorrow.'

Caleb is angry; I can hear it in his pause. 'Why should I do this for you, after what you just did to us?'

'If you want there to be an *us*,' I say, 'you'd better do it.'

After Caleb hangs up on me, I hold the phone to my ear, pretending he is still on the other end of the line. Then I replace the receiver, turn around, and look at the correctional officer who is waiting to take me to a cell. 'I had to do it,' I explain. 'He doesn't understand. I can't make him understand. You would have done it, wouldn't you? If it was your kid, wouldn't you have done it?' I make my eyes flicker from left to right, lighting on nothing. I chew my fingernail till the cuticle bleeds.

I make myself crazy, because this is what I want them to see.

It is no surprise when I am led to the solitary cells. In the first place, new prisoners are often put on a suicide watch; in the second place, I put half the women in this jail. The correctional officer slams the door shut behind me, and this becomes my new world: six feet by eight feet, a metal bunk, a stained mattress, a toilet.

The guard moves off, and for the first time this day, I let myself unravel. I have killed a man. I have walked right up to his lying face and shot four bullets into it. The recollection comes in bits and pieces – the click of the trigger past the point of no return; the thunder of the gun; the backward leap of my hand as the gun recoiled, as if it were trying, too late, to stop itself.

His blood was warm where it struck my shirt.

Oh, my God, I have killed a man. I did it for all the right reasons; I did it for Nathaniel; but *I did it*.

My body starts shaking uncontrollably, and this time, it is no act. It is one thing to seem insane for the sake of the witnesses that will be called to testify against me; it is another thing entirely to sift through my own mind and realize what I have been capable of all along. Father Szyszynski will not preside over Mass on Sunday. He will not have his nightly cup of tea or say an evening prayer. I have killed a priest who was not given Last Rites; and I will follow him straight to Hell.

My knees draw up, my chin tucks tight. In the overheated belly of this jail, I am freezing.

'Are you all right, girlfriend?'

The voice floats from across the hall, the second solitary confinement cell. Whoever has been in there watching me has been doing it from the shadows. I feel heat rise to my face and look up to see a tall black woman, her scrubs knotted above her bellybutton, her toenails painted to orange to match her jail uniform.

'My name's Adrienne, and I'm a real good listener. I don't get to talk to many people.'

Does she think I'm going to fall for that setup? Stoolpigeons are as common in here as professions of innocence, and I should know – I have listened to both. I open my mouth to tell her this, but at second glance, realize I've been mistaken. The long feet, the rippled abdomen, the veins on the backs of the hands – Adrienne isn't a woman at all.

'Your secret,' the transvestite says. 'It's safe with me.'

I stare right at her – his – considerable chest. 'Got a Kleenex?' I ask flatly.

For just a moment, there is a beat of silence. 'That's just a technicality,' Adrienne responds.

I turn away again. 'Yeah, well, I'm still not talking to you.'

Above us, there is the call for lights out. But it never gets dark in jail. It is eternally dusk, a time when creatures crawl from swamps and crickets take over the earth. In the shadows, I can see Adrienne's smooth skin, a lighter shade of night between the bars of her cell. 'What did you do?' Adrienne asks, and there is no mistaking her question.

'What did _you_ do?'

'It's the drugs, it's always the drugs, honey. But I'm trying to get off them, I truly am.'

'A drug conviction? Then why did they put you in solitary?'

Adrienne shrugs. 'Well, the boys, I don't belong with them; they just want to beat me up, you know? I'd like to be in with the girls, but they won't let me, because I haven't had the operation yet. I been taking my medicine regular, but they say it don't matter, so long as I've got the wrong kind of plumbing.' She sighs. 'Quite frankly, honey, they don't know what to do with me in here.'

I stare at the cinderblock walls, at the dim safety light on the ceiling, at my own lethal hands. 'They don't know what to do with me either,' I say.

The AG's office puts Quentin up at a Residence Inn that has a small efficiency kitchen, cable TV, and a carpet that smells like cats. 'Thank you,' he says dryly, handing the teenager who doubles as bellman a dollar. 'It's a palace.'

'Whatever,' the kid responds.

It amazes Quentin, the way adolescents are the only group that doesn't blink twice upon seeing him. Then again, he sometimes believes they wouldn't blink twice if a herd of mustangs tore past inches from their Skechered feet.

He doesn't understand them, either as a breed or individually.

Quentin opens the refrigerator, which gives off a dubious odor, and then sinks onto the spongy mattress. Well, it could be the Ritz-Carlton and he'd hate it. Biddeford, in general, makes him edgy.

Sighing, he picks up his car keys and leaves the hotel. Might as well get this over with. He drives without really thinking about where he's going. He knows she's there, of course. The address for the checks has stayed the same all this time.

There is a basketball hoop in the driveway; this surprises him. Somehow, he hasn't thought past last year's debacle to consider that Gideon might have a hobby less embarrassing to a prosecutor. A beat-up Isuzu Trooper with too many rust holes in the running board is parked in the garage. Quentin takes a deep breath, draws himself up to his full height, and knocks on the door.

When Tanya answers, it still hits him like a blow to the chest – her cognac skin; her chocolate eyes, as if this woman is a treat to be savored. But, Quentin reminds himself, even the most exquisite truffles can be bitter on the inside. He takes small comfort in the fact that she steps back when she sees him, too. 'Quentin Brown,' Tanya murmurs, shaking her head. 'To what do I owe this honor?'

'I'm here on a case,' he says. 'Indefinitely.' He's trying to peer behind her, to see what her home looks like inside. Without him in it. 'Thought I'd stop by, since you'd probably be hearing my name around town.'

'Along with other, four letter words,' Tanya mutters.

'Didn't catch that.'

She smiles at him, and he forgets what they were discussing. 'Gideon around?'

'No,' she says, too quickly.

'I don't believe you.'

'And I don't like you, so why don't you take your sorry self back to your little car and –'

'Ma?' The loping voice precedes Gideon, who suddenly appears behind his mother. He is nearly Quentin's height, although he's just turned sixteen. His dark face draws even more closed as he sees who's standing at the doorway. 'Gideon,' Quentin says. 'Hello again.'

'You come to haul my ass back to rehab?' He snorts. 'Don't do me any favors.'

Quentin feels his hands balling into fists. 'I did do you a favor. I pulled enough strings with a judge to keep you out of a juvenile detention facility, even though I took heat for it in my own department.'

'Am I supposed to thank you for that?' Gideon laughs. 'Just like I get down on my knees every night and thank you for being my daddy?'

'Gideon,' Tanya warns, but he shoves past her.

'Later.' He pushes Quentin hard, a threat, as he passes down the steps and gets into the Isuzu. Moments later, the car peels down the street.

'Is he still clean?' Quentin asks.

'Are you asking because you care, or because you don't want that stain on your career again?'

'That's not fair, Tanya –'

'Life never is, Quentin.' For the slightest moment, there is a sadness caught in the corners of her eyes, like the seeds of a dream. 'Go figure.'

She closes the door before he can respond. Moments later Quentin backs carefully out of the driveway. He drives for a full five minutes before he realizes that he has no idea where he is headed.

Lying on his side, Caleb can see the night sky. The moon is so slender it might not even be there the next time he blinks, but those stars, they're flung wide. One bright beacon catches his eye. It's fifty, maybe a hundred light-years away from here. Looking at it, Caleb is staring right into the past. An explosion that happened ages ago, but took this long to affect him.

He rolls onto his back. If only they were all like that.

All that day he's been thinking that Nina is sick; that she needs help, the way someone with a virus or a broken leg needs help. If something in her mind has snapped, Caleb will be the first to understand – he has come close to that himself, when thinking of what has been done to Nathaniel. But when Nina called, she was rational, calm, insistent. She meant to kill Father Szyszynski.

That, in and of itself, doesn't shock Caleb. People are able to hold the greatest scope of emotions inside them – love, joy, determination. It only stands to reason that negative feelings just as staggering can elbow their way in and take over. No, what surprises him is the way she did it. And the fact that she actually thinks this is something she did for Nathaniel.

This is about Nina, through and through.

Caleb closes his eyes to that star, but he still sees it etched on the backs of his eyelids. He tries to remember the moment that Nina told him she was pregnant. 'This wasn't supposed to happen,' she said to him. 'So we can't ever forget that it has.'

There is a rustle of blankets and sheets, and then Caleb

feels heat pressed along the length of his body. He turns, hopeful, praying that this has all been a bad dream and that he can wake up to find Nina safe and sleeping. But on her pillow lies Nathaniel, his eyes shining with tears. 'I want Mommy back,' he whispers.

Caleb thinks of Nina's face when she was carrying Nathaniel, how it was as bright as any star. Maybe that glory faded long ago, maybe it has taken all these light-years to only reach him now. He turns to his son and says, 'I want that too.'

Fisher Carrington stands with his back to the door of the conference room, looking out onto the exercise courtyard. When the correctional officer closes the door behind himself, leaving me there, he turns slowly. He looks just the way he did the last time I saw him, during Rachel's competency hearing: Armani suit, Bruno Magli shoes, thick head of white hair combed away from his sympathetic blue eyes. Those eyes take in my oversize jail scrubs, then immediately return to my face. 'Well,' he says gravely. 'I never imagined I'd talk to you here.'

I walk to one of the chairs in the room and throw myself into it. 'You know what, Fisher? Stranger things have happened.'

We stare at each other, trying to adjust to this role reversal. He is not the enemy anymore; he is my only hope. He is calling the shots; I am just along for the ride. And over this is a veneer of professional understanding: that he will not ask me what I've done, and that I will not have to tell him.

'You need to get me home, Fisher. I want to be back by the time my son sits down for lunch.'

Fisher just nods. He's heard this before. And it doesn't really matter what I want, when all is said and done. 'You know they're going to ask for a Harnish hearing,' he says.

Of course I know this; it is what I would do if I were prosecuting. In Maine, if the state can show probable cause that a capital crime was committed, then the defendant can be held without bail. In jail until the trial.

For months.

'Nina,' Fisher says, the first time he has called me anything other than *counselor*. 'Listen to me.'

But I don't want to listen to him. I want him to listen to me. With great self-control I raise a blank face to his. 'What's next, Fisher?'

He can see right through me, but Fisher Carrington is a gentleman. And so he pretends, just the way I am pretending. He smiles, as if we are old friends. 'Next,' he replies, 'we go to court.'

Patrick stands in the back, behind the throngs of reporters that have come to film the arraignment of the prosecutor who shot a priest in cold blood. This is the stuff of TV movies, of fiction. It is a story to debate at the water cooler with colleagues. In fact, Patrick has been listening to the commentary on more than one channel. Words like *retribution* and *reprisal* slide like snakes from these journalists' mouths. Sometimes, they don't even mention Nina's name.

They talk about the angle of the bullet, the number of paces it took to cross from her seat to the priest's. They give a history of child molestation convictions involving a priest. They do not say that Nina learned the difference between a front-end loader and a grader to satisfy the curiosity of her son. They do not mention that the contents of her pocketbook, catalogued at the jail, included a Matchbox car and a plastic glow-in-the-dark spider ring.

They don't know her, Patrick thinks. *And therefore, they don't know why.*

A reporter in front of him with a helmet of blond hair nods vigorously as her cameraman films her impromptu interview of a physiologist. 'The amygdala influences aggression via a pathway of neurons that leads to the hypothalamus,' he says. 'It sends bursts of electrical excitation down the stria terminalis, and that's the trigger of rage. Certainly, there are environmental factors, but without the preexisting pattern . . .'

Patrick tunes them out. A tangible awareness sweeps the gallery, and people begin to take their seats. Cyclopsian cameras blink. Hanging behind, Patrick tucks himself against the wall of the courtroom. He does not want to be recognized, and he isn't quite sure why. Is he ashamed of bearing witness at Nina's shame? Or is he afraid of what she might see in his face?

He should not have come. Patrick tells himself this as the door to the holding cell opens and two bailiffs appear, flanking Nina. She looks tiny and frightened, and he remembers how she shivered against him, her back to his front, as he pushed her from the fray yesterday afternoon.

Nina closes her eyes and then moves forward. On her face is the exact expression she wore at age eleven, a few feet up from the base on a ski lift, the moment before Patrick convinced the operator to let Nina off lest she pass out.

He should not have come, but Patrick also knows he could not have stayed away.

I am to be arraigned in the same courtroom where, yesterday, I murdered a man. The bailiff puts his hand on my shoulder and escorts me through the door. Hands cuffed behind my back, I walk where the priest walked. If I look hard enough, I can see his footsteps glowing.

We march past the prosecutor's table. Five times as many reporters are present today; there are even faces I recognize from *Dateline* and CNN. Did you know that television cameras running in unison sound like the song of cicadas? I turn to the gallery to find Caleb, but behind Fisher Carrington's table there is only a row of empty seats.

I am wearing my prison scrubs and low-heeled pumps. They cannot give you shoes in jail, so you wear whatever you were arrested in. And just yesterday, a lifetime ago, I was a professional woman. But as the heel of my shoe catches on the natty nap of a mat, I stumble and glance down.

We are at the spot where the priest lay dead, yesterday. Where, presumably, the cleaning people who scoured this courtroom could not completely remove the stain of blood from the floor, and covered it with an industrial carpet remnant.

Suddenly I cannot take a single step.

The bailiff grabs my arm more firmly and drags me across the mat to Fisher Carrington's side. There, I remember myself. I sit down in the same seat the priest was sitting in yesterday when I walked up and shot him. It's warm beneath my thighs – lights beating down on the wood from the courtroom ceiling, or maybe just an old soul that hasn't had the time to move on. The moment the bailiff steps away, I feel a rush of air at the nape of my neck, and I whip around, certain there will be someone waiting with a bullet for me.

But there is no bullet, no sudden death. There are only the eyes of everyone in that courtroom, burning like acid. For their viewing pleasure, I start to bite my nails, twitch in my seat. Nervousness can pass for crazy.

'Where is Caleb?' I whisper to Fisher.

'I have no idea, but he came to my office this morning with the retainer. Keep your head straight.' Before I can answer, the judge raps his gavel.

I do not know this judge. Presumably, they've brought him in from Lewiston. I do not know the AG either, sitting in my usual spot at the prosecution desk. He is enormous, bald, fearsome. He glances at me only once, and then his eyes move on – he has already dismissed me for crossing over to the dark side.

What I want to do at that moment is walk over to this prosecutor and tug on his sleeve. *Don't judge me,* I'd say, *until you've seen the view from here. You are only as invincible as your smallest weakness, and those are tiny indeed – the length of a sleeping baby's eyelash, the span of a child's hand. Life turns on a dime, and – it turns out – so does one's conscience.*

'Is the state ready to proceed?' the judge asks.

The assistant attorney general nods. 'Yes, Your Honor.'

'Is the defense attorney ready to proceed?'

'Yes, Your Honor,' Fisher says.

'Will the defendant please come forward?'

I don't stand, at first. It is not a conscious rebuff; I'm just not used to being the one who rises at this point in the arraignment. The bailiff hauls me out of my seat, wrenching my arm in the process.

Fisher Carrington remains in his chair, and my whole body grows cold. This is his chance to insult me. When a defendant stands and the attorney stays seated, it is a clear sign to insiders that he doesn't give a damn about the client. As I lift my chin and turn away, resolved, Fisher slowly unfolds from his chair. He is a solid presence along my right side, a fortifying wall. He turns to me and raises an eyebrow, questioning my faith.

'Please state your name?'

I take a deep breath. 'Nina Maurier Frost.'

'Will the clerk please read the charge?' the judge asks.

'The state of Maine hereby charges that on or about the thirtieth day of October, 2001, the defendant, Nina Maurier Frost, did slay and murder Glen Szyszynski in Biddeford, in the County of York, Maine. How do you plead?'

Fisher smooths a hand down his tie. 'We're going to enter a plea of not guilty, Your Honor. And I'm putting the court and state on notice that we may be entering a plea of not guilty by reason of insanity at a later date.'

None of this surprises the judge. It does not surprise me either, although Fisher and I have not discussed an insanity defense. 'Mr. Brown,' the judge says, 'when would you like to schedule a Harnish hearing?'

This is expected, too. In the past I have seen *State v. Harnish* as a godsend, keeping felons temporarily off the street while I'm working to permanently lock them up. After all, do you really want someone who's committed a capital crime walking free?

Then again, in the past, I have not been the criminal in question.

Quentin Brown looks at me, then turns to the judge. His eyes, obsidian, do not give anything away. 'Your Honor, at this time, due to the severity of the crime and the open nature in which it was committed in this very courtroom, the state is asking for bail in the amount of $500,000 with surety.'

The judge blinks at him. Stunned, Fisher turns to Brown. I want to stare at him, too, but I can't, because then he will know that I'm sane enough to understand this unexpected gift. 'Am I understanding, Mr. Brown, that the state is waiving its right for a Harnish hearing?' the judge clarifies. 'That you wish to *set* bail in this case, as opposed to *denying* it?'

Brown nods tightly. 'May we approach, please?'

He takes a step forward, and so does Fisher. Out of long habit, I take a step forward too, but the bailiffs standing behind me grab my arms.

The judge puts his hand over the microphone so that the cameras cannot hear the conversation, but I can, even from a few feet away. 'Mr. Brown, I understood that your evidence in this case was rather good.'

'Judge, to tell you the truth, I don't know whether she has a successful insanity plea or not . . . but I can't in good faith ask this court to hold her without bail. She's been a prosecutor for ten years. I don't think she's going to flee, and I don't think she's a risk to society. With all due respect, Your Honor, I've run that past my boss and her boss, and I'm asking the court to please do this without making it an issue for the press to devour.'

Fisher immediately turns with a gracious smile. 'Your Honor, I'd like to let Mr. Brown know that my client and I appreciate his sensitivity. This is a difficult case for everyone involved.'

Me, I feel like dancing. To have the Harnish hearing waived is a tiny miracle. 'The state is asking for bail in the amount of $500,000. What are the defendant's ties to this state, Mr. Carrington?' the judge asks.

'Your Honor, she's a lifelong resident of Maine. She has a small child here. The defendant would be happy to turn in her passport and agree to not leave the state.'

The judge nods. 'Given the fact that she's worked as a prosecutor for so long, as a condition of the defendant's bail I am also going to bar her from speaking with any employees currently working at the York County District Attorney's office until the completion of this case, to ensure that she doesn't have any access to information.'

'That's fine, Your Honor,' Fisher says on my behalf.

Quentin Brown jumps in. 'In addition to bail, Judge, we're asking for a special condition of a psychiatric evaluation.'

'We have no problem with that,' Fisher answers. 'We'd like one of our own, with a private psychiatrist.'

'Does it matter to the state whether a private or a state psychiatrist is used, Mr. Brown?' the judge asks.

'We want a state psychiatrist.'

'Fine. I'll make that a condition of bail, as well.' The judge writes something down in his file. 'But I don't believe $500,000 is necessary to keep this woman in the state. I'm setting bail at $100,000 with surety.'

What happens next is a whirlwind: hands on my arms, pushing me back in the direction of the holding cell; Fisher's face telling me he'll call Caleb about the bail; reporters stampeding up the aisles and into the hall to phone their affiliates. I am left in the company of a deputy sheriff so thin his belt is notched like a pegboard. He locks me into the cell and then buries his face in *Sports Illustrated*.

I'm going to get out. I'm going to be back home, having lunch with Nathaniel, just like I told Fisher Carrington yesterday.

Hugging my knees to my chest, I start to cry. And let myself believe I just might get away with this.

The day it first happened, they had been learning about the Ark. It was this huge boat, Mrs. Fiore told Nathaniel and the others. Big enough to fit all of them, their parents, and their pets. She gave everyone a crayon and a piece of paper to draw their favorite animal. 'Let's see what we come up with,' she had said, 'and we'll show them all to Father Glen before his story.'

Nathaniel sat next to Amelia Underwood that day, a girl who always smelled of spaghetti sauce and the stuff that gets caught in bathtub drains. 'Did elephants go on the boat?' she asked, and Mrs. Fiore nodded. 'Everything.'

'Raccoons?'

'Yes.'

'Narwhals?' That from Oren Whitford, who was already reading chapter books when Nathaniel wasn't even sure which way the loop went on a *b* and a *d*.

'Uh-huh.'

'Cockroaches?'

'Unfortunately,' Mrs. Fiore said.

Phil Filbert raised his hand. 'How about the holy goats?'

Mrs. Fiore frowned. 'That's the Holy Ghost, Philip, which is something totally different.' But then she reconsidered. 'I suppose it was there too, though.'

Nathaniel raised his hand. The teacher smiled at him. 'What animal are you thinking of?'

But he wasn't thinking of an animal at all. 'I need to go pee,' he said, and all the other kids laughed. Heat spread across his face, and he grabbed the block of wood that Mrs. Fiore gave him for a bathroom pass and darted out the door. The bathroom was at the end of the hall, and Nathaniel lingered in there, flushing the toilet a bunch of times just to hear the sound of it; washing his hands with so much soap bubbles rose in the sink like a mountain.

He was in no rush to get back to Sunday school. In the first place, everyone would still be laughing at him, and in the second place, Amelia Underwood stank worse than the little cakes inside the bathroom urinals. So he wandered down the hall a little farther, to Father Glen's office. The door was usually locked, but right now, there was a crack just big enough for someone like Nathaniel to slip through. Without hesitation, he crept inside.

The room smelled of lemons, just like the main part of the church. Nathaniel's mother said that was because a lot of ladies volunteered to scrub the pews until they were shining, so he figured they probably came into the office and scrubbed too.

There were no pews, though – only row after row of book-shelves. There were so many letters jammed onto the spines of the books that it made Nathaniel dizzy to try to sort them all out. He turned his attention instead to a picture hanging on the wall, of a man riding a white stallion, and spearing a dragon through its heart.

Maybe dragons hadn't fit onto the Ark, which was why no one ever saw them anymore.

'St. George was awfully brave,' a voice said behind him, and Nathaniel realized he was not alone. 'And you?' the priest asked with a slow smile. 'Are you brave too?'

If Nina had been his wife, Patrick would have sat in the front row of the gallery. He would have made eye contact with her the second she walked through the door of the courtroom, to let her know that no matter what, he was there for her. He wouldn't have needed someone to come to his house and spoon-feed him the outcome of the arraignment.

By the time Caleb answers the doorbell, Patrick is furious at him all over again.

'She's out on bail,' Patrick says without preamble. 'You'll have to get a check for ten thousand dollars to the courthouse.' He stares Caleb down, his hands jammed into the pockets of his jacket. 'I assume you can do that. Or were you planning to leave your wife high and dry twice in one day?'

'You mean the way she left *me?*' Caleb retorts. 'I couldn't go. I had no one to watch Nathaniel.'

'That's bullshit. You could have asked me. In fact, I'll watch him right now. You go ahead, get Nina. She's waiting.' He crosses his arms, calling Caleb's bluff.

'I'm not going,' Caleb says, and in less than a breath Patrick pins him against the doorframe.

'What the fuck is the matter with you?' he grits out. 'She needs you now.'

Caleb, bigger and stronger, pushes back. He balls a fist, sends Patrick flying into the hedge on the path. 'Don't you tell me what *my* wife needs.' In the background is the sound of a tiny voice, calling for his father. Caleb turns, walks inside, closes the door behind him.

Sprawled in the bushes, Patrick tries to catch his breath. He gets to his feet slowly, extricating leaves from his clothing. What is he supposed to do now? He cannot leave Nina in jail, and he doesn't have the cash to bail her out himself.

Suddenly the door opens again. Caleb stands there, a check in hand. Patrick takes it and Caleb nods in gratitude, neither one alluding to the fact that only minutes ago, they were willing to kill. This is the currency of apology; a deal transacted in the name of the woman who has unbalanced both of their lives.

I'm ready to give Caleb a piece of my mind for missing the arraignment, but it's going to have to wait until after I've held Nathaniel so close that he starts to melt into me. Fidgety, I wait for the deputy to unlock the holding cell and escort me into the anteroom of the sheriff's department. There is a familiar face there, but it's the wrong one.

'I posted bail,' Patrick says. 'Caleb gave me a check.'

'He . . .' I start to speak, and then remember who is standing in front of me. It may be Patrick, but still. I turn to him, wide-eyed, as he leads me out the service entrance of the court-house, to avoid the press. 'Is he really dead? Do you promise me he's really dead?'

Patrick grabs my arm and turns me toward him. 'Stop.' Pain pulls his features tight. 'Please, Nina. Just stop.'

He knows; of course he knows. This is Patrick. In a way it is a relief to no longer have to pretend with him; to have the opportunity to talk to someone who will understand. He leads me through the bowels of the building to a service entrance, and ducks me into his waiting Taurus. The parking lot is filled with news vans, satellite dishes mounted on top like strange birds. Patrick tosses something heavy in my lap, a thick edition of the *Boston Globe*.

ABOVE THE LAW, the headline reads. And a subtitle: *Priest*

Murdered in Maine; A District Attorney's Biblical Justice. There is a full-color photo of me being tackled by Patrick and the bailiffs. In the right-hand corner is Father Szyszynski, lying in a pool of his own blood. I trace Patrick's grainy profile. 'You're famous,' I say softly.

Patrick doesn't answer. He stares out at the road, focused on what lies ahead.

I used to be able to talk to him about anything. That cannot have changed, just because of what I've done. But as I look out the window I see it is a different world – two-legged cats prance down the street, Gypsies twirl up driveways, zombies knock on doors. Somehow I've forgotten about Halloween; today nobody is the person he was just a day ago. 'Patrick,' I begin.

He cuts me off with a slash of his hand. 'Nina, it's already bad enough. Every time I think about what you did, I remember the night before, at Tequila Mockingbird. What I said to you.'

People like that, they ought to be shot. I hadn't remembered his words until now. Or had I? I reach across the seat to touch his shoulder, to reassure him that this isn't his fault, but he recoils from me. 'Whatever you're thinking, you're wrong. I –'

Suddenly Patrick wrenches the car to the shoulder of the road. 'Please, don't tell me anything. I'm going to have to testify during your trial.'

But I have always confided in Patrick. To crawl back behind my shell of insanity seems even crazier; a costume two sizes too small. I turn with a question in my eyes, and as usual, he responds before I can even put it into words. 'Talk to Caleb instead,' he says, and he pulls back into the midday trickle of traffic.

Sometimes when you pick up your child you can feel the map of your own bones beneath your hands, or smell the scent of your skin in the nape of his neck. This is the most extraordinary thing about motherhood – finding a piece of yourself separate and apart that all the same you could not live without. It is the feeling you get when you place the last scrap of the thou-sand-piece jigsaw puzzle; it is the last footfall in a photo-finish race; exhilaration and homecoming and stunned wonder, caught between those stubby fingers and the spaces where baby teeth have given way. Nathaniel barrels into my arms with the force of a hurricane, and just as easily sweeps me off my feet. 'Mommy!'

Oh, I think, *this is why.*

Over my son's head, I notice Caleb. He stands at a distance, his face impassive. I say, 'Thank you for the check.'

'You're famous,' Nathaniel tells me. 'Your picture was in the paper.'

'Buddy,' Caleb asks, 'you want to pick out a video and watch it in my room?'

Nathaniel shakes his head. 'Can Mommy come?'

'In a little while. I have to talk to Daddy first.'

So we go through the motions of parenting; Caleb settling Nathaniel on the great ocean of our bedspread, while I push the buttons that set a Disney tape into motion. It seems natural that while he waits here, entranced by fantasy, Caleb and I go into his little boy's room to make sense of what's real. We sit on the narrow bed, surrounded by a bevy of appliquéd Amazon tree frogs, a rainbow of poisonous color. Overhead, a cater-pillar mobile drifts without a care in the world. 'What the hell were you doing, Nina?' Caleb says, the opening thrust. 'What were you *thinking?*'

'Have the police talked to you? Are you in trouble?'

'Why would I be?'

'Because the police don't know you weren't planning this with me.'

Caleb folds in on himself. 'Is that what you did? Plan it?'

'I planned to make it look unplanned,' I explain. 'Caleb, he hurt Nathaniel. He *hurt* him. And he was going to get away with it.'

'You don't know that –'

'I do. I see it every day. But this time, it was *my* baby. *Our* baby. How many years do you think Nathaniel will have nightmares about this? How many years will he be in therapy? Our son is never going to be the way he was. Szyszynski took away a piece of him that we'll never get back. So why shouldn't I have done the same to him?' *Do unto others,* I think, *as you would have them do unto you.*

'But Nina. You . . .' He cannot even say it.

'When you found out, when Nathaniel said his name, what was the first thought that ran through your mind?'

Caleb looks into his lap. 'I wanted to kill him.'

'*Yes.*'

He shakes his head. 'Szyszynski was headed to a trial. He would have been punished for what he did.'

'Not enough. There is no sentence a judge could pass down that would make up for this and you know it. I did what any parent would want to do. I just have to look crazy to get away with it.'

'What makes you think you *can?*'

'Because I know what it takes to be declared legally insane. I watch these defendants come in and I can tell you right away who's going to get convicted and who's going to walk. I know what you have to say, what you have to do.' I look Caleb right in the eye. 'I am an attorney. But I shot a man in front of a judge, in front of a whole court. Why would I do that, if I weren't crazy?'

Caleb is quiet for a moment, turning the truth over in his hands. 'Why are you telling me this?' he asks softly.

'Because you're my husband. You can't testify against me during my trial. You're the only one I *can* tell.'

'Then why didn't you tell me what you were going to do?'

'Because,' I reply, 'you would have stopped me.'

When Caleb gets up and walks to the window, I follow him. I place my hand gently on his back, in the hollow that seems so vulnerable, even in a man full-grown. 'Nathaniel deserves this,' I whisper.

Caleb shakes his head. 'No one deserves this.'

*   *   *

As it turns out, you can function while your heart is being torn to shreds. Blood pumps, breath flows, neurons fire. What goes missing is the affect; a curious flatness to voice and actions that, if noted, speak of a hole so deep inside there's no visible end to it. Caleb stares at this woman who just yesterday was his wife and sees a stranger in her place. He listens to her explanations and wonders when she took up this foreign language, this tongue that makes no sense.

Of course, it is what any parent would want to do to the devil who preys upon a child. But 99.9 percent of those parents don't act on it. Maybe Nina thinks she was avenging Nathaniel, but it was at the reckless expense of her own life. If Szyszynski had gone to jail, they would be patchwork and piecemeal, but they would still be a family. If Nina goes to jail, Caleb loses a wife. Nathaniel loses his mother.

Caleb feels fire pooling like acid in the muscles of his shoulders. He is furious and stunned and maybe a little bit awed. He has traveled every inch of this woman, he understands what makes her cry and what brings her to rapture; he recognizes every cut and curve of her body; but he doesn't know her at all.

Nina stands expectantly beside him, waiting for him to tell her she did the right thing. Funny, that she would flout the law, but still need his approval. For this reason, and all the others, the words she wants to hear from him will not come.

When Nathaniel walks into the room with the dining room tablecloth wrapped around his shoulders, Caleb latches onto him. In this storm of strangeness, Nathaniel is the one thing he can recognize. 'Hey!' Caleb cries with too much enthusiasm, and he tosses the boy into the air. 'That's some cape!'

Nina turns too, a smile placed on her face where the earnestness was a moment before. She reaches for Nathaniel, too, and out of pure spite, Caleb hefts the child high on his shoulders where she cannot reach.

'It's getting dark,' Nathaniel says. 'Can we go?'

'Go where?'

In answer, Nathaniel points out the window. On the street below is a battalion of tiny goblins, miniature monsters, fairy princesses. Caleb notices, for the first time, that the leaves have all fallen; that grinning pumpkins roost like lazy hens on the stone walls of his neighbor's home. How could he have missed the signs of Halloween?

He looks at Nina, but she has been just as preoccupied. As if on cue, the doorbell rings. Nathaniel wriggles on Caleb's shoulders. 'Get it! Get it!'

'We'll have to get it later.' Nina tosses him a helpless look; there is no candy in this house. There is nothing left that's sweet.

Worse, yet, there is no costume. Caleb and Nina realize this at the same moment, and it sews them close. They both recall Nathaniel's previous Halloweens in descending order: knight in shining armor, astronaut, pumpkin, crocodile, and, as an infant, caterpillar. 'What would you like to be?' Nina asks.

Nathaniel tosses his magical tablecloth over his shoulder. 'A superhero,' he says. 'A new one.'

Caleb is fairly sure they could muster up Superman on short notice. 'What's wrong with the old ones?'

Everything, it turns out. Nathaniel doesn't like Superman because he can be felled by Kryptonite. Green Lantern's ring doesn't work on anything yellow. The Incredible Hulk is too stupid. Even Captain Marvel runs the risk of being tricked into saying the word *Shazam!* and turning himself back into young Billy Batson.

'How about Ironman?' Caleb suggests.

Nathaniel shakes his head. 'He could rust.'

'Aquaman?'

'Needs water.'

'Nathaniel,' Nina says gently, 'nobody's perfect.'

'But they're *supposed* to be,' Nathaniel explains, and Caleb understands. Tonight, Nathaniel needs to be invincible. He needs to know that what happened to him could never, ever happen again.

'What we need,' Nina muses, 'is a superhero with no Achilles' heel.'

'A what?' Nathaniel says.

She takes his hand. 'Let's see.' From his closet, she extracts a pirate's bandanna, and wraps this rakishly around Nathaniel's head. She crisscrosses a spool of yellow crime-scene tape Patrick once brought around Nathaniel's chest. She gives him swimming goggles, tinted blue, for X-ray vision, and pulls a pair of red shorts over his sweatpants because this is Maine, after all, and she is not about to let him go out half-dressed in the cold. Then she surreptitiously motions to Caleb, so that he pulls off his red thermal shirt and hands it to her. This she ties around Nathaniel's neck, a second cape. 'Oh, my gosh, do you see who he looks like?'

Caleb has no idea, but he plays along. 'I can't believe it.'

'Who? Who!' Nathaniel is fairly dancing with excitement.

'Well, IncrediBoy, of course,' Nina answers. 'Didn't you ever see his comic book?'

'No . . .'

'Oh, he's the most super superhero. He's got these two capes, see, which allow him to fly farther and faster.'

'Cool!'

'And he can pull people's thoughts right out of their heads, before they even speak them. In fact, you look so much like him, I bet you've got that superpower already. Go ahead.' Nina squinches her eyes shut. 'Guess what I'm thinking.'

Nathaniel frowns, concentrating. 'Um . . . that I'm as good at this as IncrediBoy?'

She slaps her forehead. 'Oh my *gosh!* Nathaniel, how'd you *do* that!'

'I think I got his X-ray vision, too,' Nathaniel crows. 'I can see through houses and know what candy people are giving out!' He dashes forward, heading for the stairs. 'Hurry up, okay?'

With the buffer of their son gone, Caleb and Nina smile uncomfortably at each other again. 'What are you going to do when he can't see through doors?' Caleb asks.

'Tell him it's a glitch in his optical sensor that needs to be checked out.'

Nina walks out of the room, but Caleb stays upstairs a moment longer. From the window, he watches his ragtag son leap off the porch in a single bound – grace born of confidence. Even from up here, Caleb can see Nathaniel's smile, can hear the sharp start of his laugh. And he wonders if maybe Nina is right; if a superhero is nothing but an ordinary person who believes that she cannot fail.

She is holding the gun that's a blow-dryer up to her head, when I ask. 'What's the next thing after love?'

'What?'

The stuff I need to say is all tangled. 'You love Mason, right?'

The dog hears his name and smiles. 'Well, sure,' she says.

'And you love Daddy more than that?'

She looks down at me. 'Yes.'

'And you love me even higher?'

Her eyebrows fly. 'True.'

'So what comes after that?'

She lifts me and puts me on the edge of the sink. The countertop is warm where the blow-dryer has been sitting; it just might be alive. For a minute, she thinks hard. 'The next thing after love,' she tells me, 'is being a mom.'

5

At one point in my life, I had wanted to save the world. I'd listened, dewy-eyed, to law school professors and truly believed that as a prosecutor, I had a chance to rid the planet of evil. This was before I understood that when you have five hundred open cases, you make the conscious decision to plead as many as you can. It was before I realized that righteousness has less to do with a verdict than persuasion. Before I realized that I had not chosen a crusade, but only a job.

Still, it never entered my mind to be a defense attorney. I couldn't stomach the thought of standing up and lying on behalf of a morally depraved criminal, and as far as I was concerned most of them were guilty until proven innocent. But sitting in Fisher Carrington's sumptuous paneled office, being handed Jamaican coffee, $27.99 per pound, by his trim and efficient secretary, I start to understand the attraction.

Fisher comes out to meet me. His Newman-blue eyes twinkle, as if he couldn't be more delighted to find me sitting in his antechamber. And why shouldn't he be? He could charge me an arm and a leg and knows I will pay it. He has the chance to work on a high-profile murder that will net him a ton of new business. And finally, it's a departure from your run-of-the-mill case, the kind Fisher can do in his sleep.

'Nina,' he says. 'Good to see you.' As if, less than twenty-four hours ago, we hadn't met each other in the conference room of a jail. 'Come back to my office.'

It is heavily paneled, a man's room that conjures the smell of cigar smoke and snifters of brandy. He has the same books of statutes lining his shelves that I do, and somehow that is comforting. 'How's Nathaniel?'

'Fine.' I take a seat in an enormous leather wing chair and let my eyes wander.

'He must be happy to have his mother home.'

More than his father is, I think. My attention fixes on a small Picasso sketch on the wall. Not a lithograph – the real thing.

'What are you thinking?' Fisher asks, sitting down across from me.

'That the state doesn't pay me enough.' I turn to him. 'Thank you. For getting me out yesterday.'

'Much as I'd like to take the credit, that was a gift horse prancing in, and you know it. I didn't expect leniency from Brown.'

'I wouldn't expect it again.' I can feel his eyes on me, measuring. As compared to my behavior at yesterday's brief meeting, I'm under much greater control.

'Let's get down to business,' Fisher announces. 'Did you give the police a statement?'

'They asked. I repeated that I'd done all I could do. That I couldn't do any more.'

'You said this how many times?'

'Over and over.'

Fisher sets down his Waterman and folds his hands. His expression is a curious mix of morbid fascination, respect, and resignation. 'You know what you're doing,' he says, a statement.

I look at him over the rim of my coffee mug. 'You don't want to ask me that.'

Leaning back in his chair, Fisher grins. He has dimples, two in each cheek. 'Were you a drama major before you got to law school?'

'Sure,' I say. 'Weren't you?'

There are so many questions he wants to ask me; I can see them fighting inside of him like small soldiers desperate to join this fray. I can't blame him. By now, he knows I'm sane; he knows the game I have chosen to play. This is equivalent to having a Martian land in one's backyard. You can't possibly walk away without poking it once, to see what it's made of inside.

'How come you had your husband call me?'

'Because juries love you. People believe you.' I hesitate, then give him the truth. 'And because I hated going up against you.'

Fisher accepts this as his due. 'We need to prepare an insanity defense. Or go with extreme anger.'

There are no different degrees of murder in Maine, and the mandatory sentence is twenty-five years to life. Which means if I am to be acquitted, I have to be not guilty – (difficult to prove, given that the act is on film); not guilty by reason of insanity; or under the influence of extreme anger brought on by adequate provocation. That final defense reduces the crime to manslaughter, a lesser charge. It's somewhat amazing that in this state, it is legal to kill someone if they piss you off enough and if the jury agrees you had good reason to be pissed off, but there you have it.

'My advice is to argue both,' Fisher suggests. 'If –'

'No. If you argue both, it looks sleazy to the jury. Trust me. It seems like even *you* can't make up your mind why I'm not guilty.' I think about this for a minute. 'Besides, having twelve jurors agree on what justifies provocation is more of a long shot than having them recognize insanity when a prosecutor shoots a man right in front of a judge. And winning on extreme anger isn't an out-and-out win – it only lessens the conviction. If you get me off on an insanity charge, it's a complete acquittal.'

My defense is starting to form in my mind. 'Okay.' I lean forward, ready to let him in on my plan. 'We're going to get a call from Brown for the state psychiatric investigation. We can go to that shrink first, and based on that report, we can find someone to use as our own psychiatric expert.'

'Nina,' Fisher says patiently. 'You are the client. I am the attorney. Understand that now, or this isn't going to work.'

'Come on, Fisher. I know exactly what to do.'

'No, you don't. You're a prosecutor, and you don't know the first thing about running a defense.'

'It's all about putting on a good act, right? And haven't I already done that?' Fisher waits until I settle back in my chair with my arms crossed over my chest, defeated. 'All right, fine. Then what are we going to do?'

'Go to the state psychiatrist,' Fisher says dryly. 'And then find someone to use as our own psychiatric expert.' When I lift my brows, he ignores me. 'I'm going to ask for all the information Detective Ducharme put together on the investigation involving your son, because that was what led you to believe you needed to kill this man.'

Kill this man. The phrase sends a shiver down my spine. We toss these words about so easily, as if we are discussing the weather, or the Red Sox scores.

'Is there anything else you can think of that I need to ask for?'

'The underwear,' I tell him. 'My son's underwear had semen on it. It was sent out for DNA testing but hasn't come back yet.'

'Well, that doesn't really matter anymore –'

'I want to see it,' I announce, brooking no argument. 'I need to see that report.'

Fisher nods, makes a note. 'Fine, then. I'll request it. Anything else?' I shake my head. 'All right. When I get the discovery in, I'll call you. In the meantime, don't leave the state, don't talk to anyone in your office, don't screw up, because you're not going to get a second chance.' He stands, dismissing me.

I walk to the door, trailing my fingers over the polished wainscoting. With my hand on the knob, I pause, then look over my shoulder. He is making notes inside my file, just the way I do when I begin a case. 'Fisher?' He glances up. 'Do you have any children?'

'Two. One daughter's a sophomore at Dartmouth, the other is in high school.'

It is suddenly hard to swallow. 'Well,' I say softly. 'That's good to know.'

*   *   *

Lord have mercy. Christ have mercy.

None of the reporters or parishioners who have come to Father Szyszynski's funeral Mass at St. Anne's recognize the woman draped in black and sitting in the second-to-last row of the church, not responding to the Kyrie. I have been careful to hide my face with a veil; to keep my silence. I have not told Caleb where I am headed; he thinks I am coming home after my appointment with Fisher. But instead I sit in a state of mortal sin, listening to the archbishop extol the virtues of the man I killed.

He may have been accused, but he was never convicted. Ironically, I have turned him into a victim. The pews are crushed with his flock, coming to pay their last respects. Everything is silver and white – the vestments of the clergy that have come to send Szyszynski off to God, the lilies lining the aisle, the altar boys who led the procession with their tapers, the pall over the casket – and the church looks, I imagine, like Heaven does.

The archbishop prays over the gleaming coffin, two priests beside him waving the censer and the Holy Water. They seem familiar; I realize they are the ones that recently visited the parish. I wonder if one of them will take over, now that there is no priest.

I confess to Almighty God, and to you here present, that I have sinned through my own fault.

The sweet smoke of candles and flowers makes my head swim. The last funeral Mass I attended was my father's, one with far less pageantry than this, although the service bled by in the same stream of disbelief. I can remember the priest who had put his hands over mine and offered me the greatest condolence he could: 'He's with God, now.'

As the Gospel is read, I look around the congregation. Some of the older women are sobbing; most are staring at the archbishop with the solemnity he commands. If Szyszynski's body belongs to Christ, then who controlled his mind? Who placed in that brain the seed to hurt a child? What made him pick mine?

Words jump out at me: *commend his soul; with his Maker; Hosanna in the highest.*

The organ's notes throb, and then the archbishop stands to deliver the eulogy. 'Father Glen Szyszynski,' he begins, 'was well loved by his congregation.'

I cannot say why I came here; why I knew that I would swim an ocean, break through fetters, run cross-country if need be to witness Szyszynski's burial. Maybe it is closure for me; maybe it is the proof I still need.

This is My Body.

I picture his face in profile, the minute before I pulled the trigger.

This is the cup of My Blood.

His skull, shattered.

Into the silence I gasp, and the people sitting on either side of me turn, curious.

When we stand like automatons and file into the aisle to take Communion, I find my feet moving before I can remember to stop them. I open my mouth for the priest holding the Host. 'Body of Christ,' he says, and he looks me in the eye.

'Amen,' I answer.

When I turn my gaze falls on the front left pew, where a woman in black is bent over at the waist, sobbing so hard she cannot catch her breath. Her iron-gray curls wilt beneath her black cloche hat; her hands are knotted so tightly around the edge of the pew I think she may splinter the wood. The priest who has given me Communion whispers to another clergyman, who takes over as he goes to comfort her. And that is when it hits me:

Father Szyszynski was someone's son, too.

My chest fills with lead and my legs melt beneath me. I can tell myself that I have gotten retribution for Nathaniel; I can say that I was morally right – but I cannot take away the truth that another mother has lost her child because of me.

Is it right to close one cycle of pain if it only opens up another one?

The church starts to spin, and the flowers are reaching for my ankles. A face as wide as the moon looms in front of me, speaking words that I cannot hear. *If I faint, they will know who I am. They will crucify me.* I summon all the strength I have left to shove aside the people in my way, to lurch down the aisle, to push open the double doors of St. Anne's and break free.

Mason, the golden retriever, has been called Nathaniel's dog for as long as Nathaniel can remember, although he was part of the family for ten months before Nathaniel was even born. And the strange thing is, if it had been the other way around – if *Nathaniel* had gotten here first – he would have told his parents that he really wanted a cat. He likes the way you can drape a kitten over your arm, the same way you'd carry a coat if you got too hot. He likes the sound they make against his ear, how it makes his skin hum, too. He likes the way they don't take baths; he likes the fact that they can fall from a great height, but land on their feet.

He asked for a kitten one Christmas, and although Santa had brought him everything else, the cat didn't happen. It was Mason, he knew. The dog had a habit of bringing in gifts – the skull of a mouse he'd chewed clean, the body of a thrashed snake found at the end of the drive, a toad caught in the bowl of his mouth. *God knows,* Nathaniel's mother said, *what he'd do to a kitten.*

So that day when he wandered in the basement of the church, the day he'd been looking at the dragon painting in Father Glen's office, the first thing Nathaniel noticed was the cat. She was black, with three white paws, as if she'd stepped into paint and realized, partway through, that it wasn't such a good idea. Her tail twitched like a snake charmer's cobra. Her face was no bigger than Nathaniel's palm.

'Ah,' the priest said. 'You like Esme.' He reached down and scratched between the cat's ears. 'That's my girl.' Scooping the cat into his arms, he sat down on the couch beneath the painting of the dragon. Nathaniel thought he was very brave. Had it been him, he'd be worried about the monster coming to life, eating him whole. 'Would you like to pet her?'

Nathaniel nodded, his throat so full of his good fortune that he couldn't even speak. He came closer to the couch, to the small ball of fur in the priest's lap. He placed his hand on the kitten's back, feeling the heat and the bones and the heart of her. 'Hi,' he whispered. 'Hi, Esme.'

Her tail tickled Nathaniel under the chin, and he laughed. The priest laughed too, and put his hand on the back of Nathaniel's neck. It was the same spot where Nathaniel was petting the cat, and for a moment he saw something like the endless mirror in a carnival's fun house – him touching the cat, and the priest touching him, and maybe even the big invisible hand of God touching the priest. Nathaniel lifted his palm, took a step back.

'She likes you,' the priest said.

'For real?'

'Oh, yes. She doesn't act this way around most of the children.'

That made Nathaniel feel tall all over. He scratched the cat's ears again, and he would have sworn she smiled.

'That's it,' the priest encouraged. 'Don't stop.'

Quentin Brown sits at Nina's desk in the district attorney's office, wondering what's missing. For lack of space, he has been given her office as a base of operations, and the irony has not been lost on him that he will be planning the conviction of this woman from the very seat in which she once sat. What he has learned, from observation, is that Nina Frost is a neat-freak – her paper clips, for the love of God, are sorted by size in small dishes. Her files are alphabetized. There is not a clue to be found – no crumpled Post-it with the name of a gun dealer; not even a doodle of Father Szyszynski's face on the blotter. *This could be anyone's workspace,* Quentin thinks, *and therein lies the problem.*

What kind of woman doesn't keep a picture of her kid or her husband on her desk?

He mulls over what this might or might not mean for a moment, then takes out his wallet. From the folds he pulls a worn baby photo of Gideon. They'd had it taken at Sears. To get that smile on the boy's face, Quentin had pretended to hit Tanya on the head with a Nerf football, and he'd inadvertently knocked out her contact lens. He sets the photograph square, now, in the corner of Nina Frost's blotter, as the door opens.

Two Biddeford detectives enter – Evan Chao and Patrick Ducharme, if Quentin recalls correctly. 'Come in,' he says, gesturing to the seats across from him. 'Take a seat.'

They form a solid block, their shoulders nearly touching. Quentin lifts a remote control and turns on a television/VCR on the shelf behind them. He has already watched the tape a thousand times himself, and imagines that the two detectives have seen it as well. Hell, most of New England has seen it by now; it was run on all the CBS news affiliates. Chao and Ducharme turn, mesmerized by the sight of Nina Frost on the small screen, walking with a preternatural grace toward the railing of the gallery and lifting a handgun. In this version, the unedited one, you can see the right side of Glen Szyszynski's head exploding.

'Jesus,' Chao murmurs.

Quentin lets the tape run. This time, he isn't watching it – he's watching the reactions of the detectives. He doesn't know Chao or Ducharme from a hole in the wall, but he can tell you this – they've worked with Nina Frost for seven years; they've worked with Quentin for twenty-four hours. As the camera tilts wildly, coming to rest on the scuffle between Nina and the bailiffs, Chao looks into his lap. Ducharme stares resolutely at the screen, but there is no emotion on his face.

With one click, Quentin shuts off the TV. 'I've read the witness statements, all 124 of them. And, naturally, it doesn't hurt to have the entire fiasco in living color.' He leans forward, his elbows on Nina's desk. 'The evidence is solid here. The only question is whether she is or isn't guilty by reason of insanity. She'll either run with that, or extreme anger.' Turning to Chao, he asks, 'Did you go to the autopsy?'

'Yeah, I did.'

'And?'

'They already released the body to the funeral home, but they won't give me a report until the victim's medical records arrive.'

Quentin rolls his eyes. 'Like there's a question here about the cause of death?'

'It's not that,' Ducharme interrupts. 'They like to have all the medical records attached. It's the office protocol.'

'Well, tell them to hurry up,' Quentin says. 'I don't care if Szyszynski had full-blown AIDS . . . that isn't what he died of.' He opens a file on his desk and waves a paper at Patrick Ducharme. 'What the hell was this?'

He lets the detective read his own report about the interrogation of Caleb Frost, under suspicion for molesting his own son. 'The boy was mute,' Patrick explains. 'He was taught basic sign language, and when we pressed him to ID the perp, he kept making the sign for *father*.' Patrick hands back the paper. 'We went to Caleb Frost first.'

'What did she do?' Quentin asks. There is no need to spell out to whom he's referring.

Patrick rubs a hand over his face, muttering into his hand.

'I didn't quite catch that, Detective,' Quentin says.

'She got a restraining order against her husband.'

'Here?'

'In Biddeford.'

'I want a copy of that.'

Patrick shrugs. 'It was vacated.'

'I don't care. Nina Frost shot the man she was convinced molested her son. But just four days earlier, she was convinced it was a different man. Her lawyer's going to tell a jury that she killed the priest because he was the one who hurt her child . . . but how sure *was* she?'

'There was semen,' Patrick says. 'On her son's underwear.'

'Yes.' Quentin rifles through some more pages. 'Where's the DNA on that?'

'At the lab. It should be back this week.'

Quentin's head comes up slowly. 'She didn't even see the DNA results on the underwear before she shot the guy?'

A muscle jumps along Patrick's jaw. 'Nathaniel *told* me. Her son. He made a verbal ID.'

'My five-year-old nephew tells me the tooth fairy's the one who brought him a buck, but that doesn't mean I *believe* him, Lieutenant.'

Before he has even finished his sentence, Patrick is out of his chair, leaning across the desk toward Quentin. 'You don't know Nathaniel Frost,' he bites out. 'And you have no right to question my professional judgment.'

Quentin stands, towering over the detective. 'I have every right. Because reading your file on the investigation, it sure looks to me like you fucked up simply because you were giving a DA who jumped to conclusions special treatment. And I'll be damned if I'm going to let you do that again while we prosecute her.'

'She didn't jump to conclusions,' Patrick argues. 'She knew exactly what she was doing. Christ, if it were my kid, I would have done the same thing.'

'Both of you listen to me. Nina Frost is a murder suspect. She made the choice to commit a criminal act. She killed a man in cold blood in front of a courtroom of people. Your job is to uphold laws, and no one – *no one* – gets to bend those to their own advantage, not even a district attorney.' Quentin turns to the first policeman. 'Is that clear, Detective Chao?'

Chao nods tightly.

'Detective Ducharme?'

Patrick meets his eye, sinks into his chair. It is not until long after the detectives have left the office that Quentin realizes Ducharme never actually answered.

*   *   *

Getting ready for winter, in Caleb's opinion, is only wishful thinking. The best preparation in the world isn't going to keep a storm from catching you unaware. The thing about nor'easters is that you don't always see them coming. They head out to sea, then turn around and batter Maine hard. There have been times in recent years that Caleb has opened the front door to find a chest-high drift of snow; has dug his way free with a shovel kept in the front closet to find a world that looks nothing like it did the night before.

Today, he is readying the house. That means hiding Nathaniel's bike in the garage, and unearthing the Flexible Flyer and the cross-country skis instead. Caleb has covered the shrubs in the front of the house with triangular wooden horses, little hats to keep their fragile branches from the ice and snow that slide off the roof.

All that is left, now, is storing enough chopped wood to last through the winter. He's brought in three loads now, stacking them in crosshatches in the basement. Slivers of oak jab his thick gloves as he moves in rhythm, taking a pair of split logs from the pile dumped down the bulkhead and laying them neatly in place. Caleb feels a wistfulness press in on him, as if each growing inch of the woodpile is taking away something summerish – a bright flock of goldfinches, a raging stream, the steam of loam overturned by a tiller. All winter long, when he burns these stacks, Caleb imagines it like a puzzle. With each log he tosses on a fire, he is able to remember the song of a cricket, or the arc of stars in the July sky. And so on, until the basement is empty again, and springtime has flung itself, jubilant, over his property.

'Do you think we'll make it through the winter?'

At Nina's voice, Caleb startles. She has come down the basement stairs and stands at the bottom with her arms crossed, surveying the stacks of wood. 'Doesn't seem like much,' she adds.

'I've got plenty.' Caleb places two more logs. 'I just haven't brought it all in yet.'

He is aware of Nina's eyes on him as he turns and bends, lifts a large burl into his arms, and deposits it at the top of a tall stack. 'So.'

'Yes,' she answers.

'How was the lawyer's?'

She shrugs. 'He's a defense attorney.'

Caleb assumes this is meant as an insult. As always in legal matters, he doesn't know what to say in response. The basement is only half full, but Caleb is suddenly aware of how big he is, and how close he is to Nina, and how the room does not seem able to hold both of them. 'Are you going back out again? Because I need to go to the hardware store to get that tarp.'

He doesn't need a tarp; he has four of them stored in the garage. He does not even know why those words have flown from his mouth, like birds desperate to escape through a chimney flue. And yet, he keeps speaking: 'Can you watch Nathaniel?'

Nina goes still in front of his eyes. 'Of course I can watch Nathaniel. Or do you think I'm too unstable to take care of him?'

'I didn't mean it like that.'

'You did, Caleb. You may not want to admit it, but you did.' There are tears in her eyes. But because he cannot think of the words that might take them away, Caleb simply nods and walks past her, their shoulders brushing as he makes his way up the stairs.

He doesn't drive to the hardware store, naturally. Instead he finds himself meandering across the county on back roads, pulling into Tequila Mockingbird, the little bar that Nina talks about from time to time. He knows she meets Patrick there for lunch every week; he even knows that the ponytailed bartender is named Stuyvesant. But Caleb has never set foot in the place, and when he walks through the door into the nearly empty afternoon room, he feels like a secret is swelling beneath his ribs – he knows so much more about this place than it knows about him.

'Afternoon,' Stuyvesant says, as Caleb hovers at the bar. Which seat does Nina take? He stares at each of them, lined up like teeth, trying to divine the one. 'What can I get you?'

Caleb drinks beer. He's never been much for hard liquor. But he asks for a shot of Talisker, a bottle he can read across the bar whose name sounds just as soothing on the tongue as, he imagines, the whiskey it describes. Stuyvesant sets it down in front of him with a bowl of peanuts. There is a businessman sitting three stools away, and a woman trying not to cry as she writes a letter at a booth. Caleb lifts the glass to the bartender. *'Sláinte,'* he says, a toast he once heard in a movie.

'You Irish?' Stuyvesant asks, running a cloth around the polished hood of the bar.

'My father was.' In fact, Caleb's parents had both been born in America, and his ancestry was Swedish and British.

'No kidding.' This from the businessman, glancing over. 'My sister lives in County Cork. Gorgeous place.' He laughs. 'Why on earth did you come over here?'

Caleb takes a sip of his whiskey. 'Didn't have much choice,' he lies. 'I was two years old.'

'You live in Sanford?'

'No. Here on business. Sales.'

'Aren't we all?' The man lifts his beer. 'God bless the corporate expense account, right?' He signals to Stuyvesant. 'Another round for us,' he says, and then to Caleb: 'My treat. Or rather, my company's.'

They talk about the upcoming Bruins season, and the way it feels like snow already. They debate the merits of the Midwest, where the businessman lives, versus New England. Caleb doesn't know why he is not telling the businessman the truth – but prevarication comes so easily, and the knowledge that this man will buy anything he says right now is oddly liberating. So Caleb pretends he's from Rochester, New Hampshire, a place he has never actually been. He fabricates a company name, a product line of construction equipment, and a history of distinguished achievement. He lets the lies tumble from his lips, gathers them like marker chips at a casino, almost giddy to see how many he can stack before they come crashing down.

The man glances at his watch and swears. 'Gotta call home. If I'm late, my wife assumes I've wrapped my rental car around a tree. You know?'

'Never been married,' Caleb shrugs, and drinks the Talisker through the sieve of his teeth, like baleen.

'Smart move.' The businessman hops off the stool, headed toward the rear of the bar, a pay phone from which Nina has called Caleb once or twice when her own cell phone's battery died. As he passes, he holds out his hand. 'Name's Mike Johanssen, by the way.'

Caleb shakes. 'Glen,' he answers. 'Glen Szyszynski.'

He remembers too late that he is supposed to be Irish, not Polish. That Stuyvesant, who lives here, will surely pick up on the name. But neither of these things matters. By the time the businessman returns and Stuyvesant thinks twice, Caleb has left the bar, more comfortable wearing another man's unlikely identity than he feels these days in his own.

The state psychiatrist is so young that I have a profound urge to reach across the desk separating us and smooth his cowlick. But if I did that, Dr. Storrow would probably die of fright, certain I mean to strangle him with the strap of my purse. It is why he chose to meet me at the court in Alfred, and I can't say I blame him. All of this man's clients are either insane or homicidal, and the safest place to conduct his interview – in lieu of jail – is a public venue with plenty of bailiffs milling around.

I have dressed with great deliberation, not in my usual conservative suit, but in khaki pants and a cotton turtleneck and loafers. When Dr. Storrow looks at me, I don't want him to be thinking *lawyer*. I want him to remember his own mother, standing on the sidelines of his soccer game, cheering him to victory.

The first time he speaks, I expect his voice to crack. 'You were a prosecutor in York County, weren't you, Ms. Frost?'

I have to think before I answer. How crazy is crazy? Should

I seem to have trouble understanding him, should I start gnawing the collar of my shirt? It will be easy to deceive a shrink as inexperienced as Storrow . . . but that is no longer the issue. Now, I need to make sure that the insanity is temporary. That I get, as we call it, acquitted without being committed. So I smile at him. 'Call me Nina,' I offer. 'And yes.'

'Okay,' Dr. Storrow says. 'I have this questionnaire, um, to fill out, and give to the court.' He takes out a piece of paper I have seen a thousand times, fill-in-the-blanks, and begins to read. 'Did you take any medication before you came here today?'

'No.'

'Have you ever been charged with a crime before?'

'No.'

'Have you ever been to court before?'

'Every day,' I say. 'For the past ten years.'

'Oh . . .' Dr. Storrow blinks at me, as if he's just remembered who he is talking to. 'Oh, that's right. Well, I still need to ask you these questions, if that's okay.' He clears his throat. 'Do you understand what the role of the judge is in a trial?'

I raise one eyebrow.

'I'm going to take that as a yes,' Dr. Storrow scribbles on his form. 'Do you know what the role of the prosecutor is?'

'Oh, I think I have a pretty good idea.'

Do you know what the defense attorney does? Do you understand that the state is trying to prove you guilty beyond a reasonable doubt? The questions come, silly as cream pies thrown at the face of a clown. Fisher and I will use this ridiculous rubber stamp interview to our advantage. On paper, without the inflection of my voice, my answers will not look absurd – they will only seem a little evasive, a little strange. And Dr. Storrow is too inexperienced to communicate on the stand that all along I knew exactly what he was talking about.

'What should you do if something happens in court that you don't understand?'

I shrug. 'I'd have my attorney ask what legal precedent they were following, so that I could look it up.'

'Do you understand that anything you say to your lawyer, he can't repeat?'

'Really?'

Dr. Storrow puts down the form. With a perfectly straight face, he says, 'I think we can move on.' He looks at my purse, from which I once pulled a gun. 'Have you ever been diagnosed with a psychiatric illness?'

'No.'

'Have you ever been on any medication for psychiatric problems?'

'No.'

'Do you have a history of emotional breakdown triggered by stress?'

'No.'

'Have you ever owned a gun before?'

I shake my head.

'Have you ever been to counseling of any kind?'

That question gives me pause. 'Yes,' I admit, thinking back to the confessional at St. Anne's. 'It was the worst mistake of my life.'

'Why?'

'When I found out my son had been sexually abused, I went to confession at my church. I talked to my priest about it. And then I found out that he was the bastard who did it.'

My language makes a blush rise above the collar of his button-down shirt. 'Ms. Frost – Nina – I need to ask you some questions about the day that . . . that everything happened.'

I start to pull at the sleeves of my turtleneck. Not a lot, just so that fabric covers my hands. I look into my lap. 'I had to do it,' I whisper.

I am getting so good at this.

'How were you feeling that day?' Dr. Storrow asks. Doubt ices his voice; just moments ago, I was perfectly lucid.

'I had to do it . . . you understand. I've seen this happen too many times. I couldn't lose him to this.' I close my eyes, thinking of every successful insanity defense I've ever heard proposed to a court. 'I didn't have a choice. I couldn't have stopped myself . . . it was like I was watching someone else do it, someone else reacting.'

'But you knew what you were doing,' Dr. Storrow replies, and I have to catch myself before my head snaps up. 'You've prosecuted people who've done horrible things.'

'I didn't do a horrible thing. I saved my son. Isn't that what mothers are supposed to do?'

'What do *you* think mothers are supposed to do?' he asks.

Stay awake all night when an infant has a cold, as if she might be able to breathe for him. Learn how to speak Pig Latin, and make a pact to talk that way for an entire day. Bake at least one cake with every ingredient in the pantry, just to see how it will taste.

Fall in love with your son a little more every day.

'Nina?' Dr. Storrow says. 'Are you all right?'

I look up and nod through my tears. 'I'm sorry.'

'Are you?' He leans forward. 'Are you truly sorry?'

We are not talking about the same thing anymore. I imagine Father Szyszynski, on his way to Hell. I think of all the ways to interpret those words, and then I meet Dr. Storrow's gaze. 'Was he?'

Nina has always tasted better than any other woman, Caleb thinks, as his lips slip down the slope of one shoulder. Like honey and sun and caramel – from the roof of her mouth to the hollow behind her knee. There are times Caleb believes he could feast on his wife and never feel that he is getting enough.

Her hands come up to clutch his shoulder, and in the half dark her head falls back, making the line of her throat a landscape. Caleb buries his face there, and tries to navigate by touch. Here, in this bed, she is the woman he fell in love with a lifetime ago. He knows when she is going to touch him, and where. He can predict each of her moves.

Her legs fall open to either side of him, and Caleb presses himself against her. He arches his back. He imagines the moment he will be inside her, how the pressure will build and build and explode like a bullet.

At that moment Nina's hand slips between their bodies to cup him, and just like that, Caleb goes soft. He tries grinding against her. Nina's fingers play over him like a flutist's, but nothing happens.

Caleb feels her hand come up to his shoulder again, feels the cold air of its absence on his balls. 'Well,' Nina says, as he rolls to his back beside her. 'That's never happened before.'

He stares at the ceiling, at anything but this stranger beside him. *It's not the only thing,* he thinks.

On Friday afternoon, Nathaniel and I go grocery shopping. The P&C is a gastronomic fest for my son: I move from the deli counter, where Nathaniel gets a free slice of cheese; to the cookie aisle, where we pick up the box of Animal Crackers; to the breads, where Nathaniel works his way through a plain bagel. 'What do you think, Nathaniel?' I ask, handing him a few grapes from the bunch I've just put in the cart. 'Should I pay $4.99 for a honeydew?'

I pick up the melon and sniff at the bottom. In truth, I have never been a good judge of fruit. I know it's all about softness and scent, but in my opinion some with the sweetest insides have been hard as a rock on the surface.

Suddenly, the bagel Nathaniel's been eating falls into my hand. 'Peter!' he yells, waving from his harness in the shopping cart. 'Peter! Hey, Peter!'

I look up to find Peter Eberhardt walking down the produce aisle, holding a bag of chips and a bottle of Chardonnay. Peter, whom I have not seen since the day I had my restraining order against Caleb vacated. There is so much I want to say to him – to ask him, now that I am not in the office to find out myself – but the judge has specifically prohibited me from speaking to my own colleagues as a condition of bail.

Nathaniel, of course, doesn't know that. He just understands that Peter – a man who keeps Charms lollipops on his desk, who can do the best impression of a duck sneezing, whom he hasn't seen in weeks – is suddenly standing six feet away. 'Peter,' Nathaniel calls again, and holds out his arms.

Peter thinks twice. I can see it in his face. But then again, he adores Nathaniel. All the reason in the world cannot stand up to my son's smile. Peter lays his bag of chips and bottle of wine on top of a display of Red Delicious apples and gives Nathaniel a bear hug. 'Listen to you!' he crows. 'That voice is back to a hundred percent working order, isn't it?'

Nathaniel giggles when Peter opens up his mouth to check inside. 'Does the volume work too?' he asks, pretending to twist a knob on Nathaniel's belly, so that he laughs louder and louder.

Then Peter turns to me. 'He sounds great, Nina.' Four words, but I know what he is really saying: *You did the right thing.*

'Thanks.'

We look at each other, measuring what can and cannot be said. And because we are so busy making a commodity of our friendship, I never notice another grocery cart approaching. It pings against the rear of mine gently, just loud enough to make me look up, so that I can see Quentin Brown smiling beside a sea of navel oranges. 'Well, well,' he says. 'Aren't things ripe here?' He pulls a cell phone out of his breast pocket and dials. 'Get a squad car down here now. I'm making an arrest.'

'You don't understand,' I insist, as he puts away his phone.

'What's so difficult to grasp? You're in blatant violation of your bail agreement, Ms. Frost. Is this or is this not a colleague from the district attorney's office?'

'For Christ's sake, Quentin,' Peter interjects. 'I was talking to the kid. He called me over.'

Quentin grabs my arm. 'I took a chance on you, and you made me look like a fool.'

'Mommy?' Nathaniel's voice rises to me like steam.

'It's okay, sweetie.' I turn to the assistant attorney general and speak through my teeth. 'I will come with you,' I say in an undertone. 'But please have the decency to do this without traumatizing my child any more.'

'I didn't speak to her,' Peter yells. 'You can't do this.'

When Quentin turns, his eyes go as dark as plums. 'I believe, Mr. Eberhardt, that the exact words you *didn't* speak were:

"He sounds great, Nina." *Nina*. As in the name of the woman you weren't talking to. And frankly, even if you were stupid enough to approach Ms. Frost, it was her responsibility to take her cart and walk away from you.'

'Peter, it's all right.' I talk fast, because I can hear the sirens outside the store already. 'Get Nathaniel home to Caleb, will you?'

Then two policemen come running into the aisle, their hands on the butts of their guns. Nathaniel's eyes go wide at the show, until he realizes what they are doing. 'Mommy!' he screams, as Quentin orders me to be handcuffed.

I face Nathaniel, smiling so hard my face may break. 'It's fine. See? I'm fine.' My hair falls out of its clip as my hands are pulled behind me. 'Peter? Take him *now*.'

'Come on, bud,' Peter soothes, pulling Nathaniel out of the cart. His shoes get caught on the metal rungs, and Nathaniel starts fighting in earnest. His arms reach out to me and he starts crying so violently he begins to hiccup. *'Mommeeeee!'*

I am marched past the gaping shoppers, past the slack-jawed stockboys, past the cashiers who pause in midair with their electronic scanners. The whole way, I can hear my son. His shrieks follow me through the parking lot, to the squad car. The lights are spinning on its roof. Once, long before all this, Nathaniel pointed to a cruiser in pursuit, and called it a zooming holiday.

'I'm sorry, Nina,' one of the policemen says as he ducks me inside. Through the window I can see Quentin Brown, arms crossed. *Orange juice,* I think. *Roast beef and sliced American cheese. Asparagus, Ritz crackers, milk. Vanilla yogurt.* This is my litany the whole way back to jail: the contents of my abandoned shopping cart, slowly going bad, until some kind soul has the inclination to put them back where they belong.

Caleb opens the door to find his son sobbing in Peter Eberhardt's arms. 'What happened to Nina?' he immediately asks, and reaches for Nathaniel.

'The guy's an asshole,' Peter says desperately. 'He's doing this to leave his mark on the town. He's –'

'Peter, *where's my wife?*'

The other man winces. 'Back in jail. She violated her bail agreement, and the assistant attorney general had her arrested.'

For a moment, Nathaniel feels like a lead weight. Caleb staggers under the responsibility of bearing him, then finds his footing. Nathaniel is still crying, more quietly now, a river that runs down the back of his shirt. Caleb makes small circles on the child's spine. 'Back up. Tell me what happened.'

Caleb picks out select words: *grocery, produce, Quentin Brown.* But he can barely hear Peter over the roar in his own head, one single phrase: *Nina, what have you done now?* 'Nathaniel called me over,' Peter explains. 'I was so psyched to hear him talking again, I couldn't just ignore him.'

Caleb shakes his head. 'You . . . you were the one who approached her?'

Peter is a foot shorter than Caleb and feels every inch of it at that moment. He takes a step backward. 'I never would have gotten her in trouble, Caleb, you know that.'

Caleb pictures his son screaming, his wife being sandwiched between policemen, a barrage of fruit spilled on the floor in this fray. He knows it is not Peter's fault, not entirely. It takes two to have a conversation; Nina should have simply walked away.

But as Nina would tell him, she probably wasn't thinking at the time.

Peter places a hand on Nathaniel's calf and rubs gently. It only sets the child off again; screams ricochet around the porch and peal off the thick bare branches of trees. 'Jesus, Caleb, I'm sorry. It's ridiculous. We didn't do anything.'

Caleb turns so that Peter can see Nathaniel's back, heaving with the force of his fear. He touches the damp cap of his son's hair. 'You didn't do anything?' Caleb challenges, and leaves Peter standing outside.

*　　*　　*

I move stiffly as I'm led to the solitary cells again, but I cannot tell what's made me numb – my arrest, or the simple cold. The furnace at the jail has broken, and the correctional officers are all wearing heavy coats. Inmates usually clad in shorts or underwear have put on sweaters; having none, I sit shivering in my cell after the door is locked behind me.

'Honey.'

I close my eyes, turn in to the wall. Tonight, I don't feel like dealing with Adrienne. Tonight I have to find a way to understand that Quentin Brown has screwed me. Getting released on bail the first time was a miracle; good fortune rarely strikes twice in the same spot.

I wonder if Nathaniel is all right. I wonder if Fisher has spoken to Caleb. This time, being booked, I chose my attorney as my one phone call. It was the coward's way out.

Caleb will say this is my fault. That is, if he's still speaking to me.

'Honey, your teeth are chattering so hard you're gonna give yourself a root canal. Here.' Something swishes near the bars; I turn to see Adrienne tossing me a sweater. 'It's angora. Don't be stretching it out.'

With jerky movements, I tug on the sweater, which I couldn't stretch in my wildest imaginings, Adrienne being six inches and two cup sizes larger than me. I am still shaking, but at least now I know it has nothing to do with the cold.

As the guards call lights out, I try to think of heat. I remember how Mason, when he was a puppy, would lie on my feet with his soft belly hot against my bare toes. And the beach in St. Thomas, where Caleb buried me up to my neck in the hot sand on our honeymoon. Pajamas, pulled off Nathaniel's body in the early morning, still warm and smelling of sleep.

Across the corridor Adrienne chews Wintergreen Life Savers. They give off green sparks in the near dark, as if she has learned how to make her own lightning.

Even in the muffled silence of jail, I can hear Nathaniel screaming for me as I am being handcuffed. Nathaniel, who had been doing so well – edging toward normal – what will this do to him? Will he wait for me at a window, even when I don't come home? Will he sleep next to Caleb, to chase away nightmares?

I rerun my actions at the grocery store like the loop of a security camera's video – what I did, what I should have done. I might have appointed myself to be Nathaniel's protector, but today I did not do a crackerjack job of it. I assumed that talking to Peter was harmless . . . and instead that one action might have set Nathaniel back by leaps and bounds.

A few feet away, in Adrienne's cell, sparks dance like fireflies. Things aren't always what they seem.

For example, I have always believed I know what is best for Nathaniel.

But what if it turns out I've been wrong?

'I put in some hot chocolate to go with your whipped cream,' Caleb says, a lame joke, as he sets the mug down on Nathaniel's nightstand. Nathaniel doesn't even turn to him. He faces the wall, wrapped like a cocoon, his eyes so red from crying that he does not look like himself.

Caleb pulls off his shoes and gets right onto Nathaniel's bed, then wraps his arms tight around the boy. 'Nathaniel, it's okay.'

He feels that tiny head shake once. Coming up on an elbow, Caleb gently turns his son onto his back. He grins, trying so hard to pretend that this is entirely ordinary, that Nathaniel's whole world has not become a snow globe, waved intermittently every time things begin to settle. 'What do you say? You want some of this cocoa?'

Nathaniel sits up slowly. He brings his hands out from underneath the covers and curls them into his body. Then he raises his palm, fingers outstretched, and sets his thumb on his chin. *Want Mommy.*

Caleb's whole body goes still. Nathaniel hasn't been very forthcoming since Peter brought him home, except for the crying. He stopped sobbing sometime between when Caleb bathed him and got him into his pajamas. But surely he can talk, if he wants to. 'Nathaniel, can you tell me what you want?'

That hand sign, again. And a third time.

'Can you say it, buddy? I know you want Mommy. Say it for me.'

Nathaniel's eyes shine, and the tears spill over. Caleb grabs the boy's hand. 'Say it,' he begs. 'Please, Nathaniel.'

But Nathaniel doesn't utter a word.

'Okay,' Caleb murmurs, releasing Nathaniel's hand into his lap. 'It's okay.' He smiles as best he can, and gets off the bed. 'I'm going to be right back. In the meantime, you can start on that hot chocolate, all right?'

In his own bedroom, Caleb picks up the phone. Dials a number from a card in his wallet. Pages Dr. Robichaud, the child psychiatrist. Then he hangs up, balls his hand into a fist, and punches a hole in the wall.

Nathaniel knows this is all his fault. Peter said it wasn't, but he was lying, the way grown-ups do in the middle of the night to make you stop thinking about something awful living under the bed. They'd taken the bagel out of the store without letting the machine ring up its numbers; they'd driven to his house without his car seat; even just now, his dad had brought cocoa to the bedroom when no food was ever allowed upstairs. His mother was gone, all the rules were getting broken, and it was because of Nathaniel.

He had seen Peter and said hi, which turned out to be a bad thing. A very, very bad thing.

This is what Nathaniel knows: He talked, and the bad man grabbed his mother's arm. He talked, and the police came. He talked, and his mother got taken away.

So he will never talk again.

By Saturday morning, they have fixed the heat. They've fixed it so well that it is nearly eighty degrees inside the jail. When

I am brought to the conference room to meet Fisher, I'm wearing a camisole and scrub pants, and sweating. Fisher, of course, looks perfectly cool, even in his suit and tie. 'The earliest I can even get to a judge for a revocation hearing is Monday,' he says.

'I need to see my son.'

Fisher's face remains impassive. He is just as angry as I would be, in his shoes – I have just complicated my case irreparably. 'Visiting hours are from ten to twelve today.'

'Call Caleb. Please, Fisher. Please, do whatever you have to do to make him bring Nathaniel down here.' I sink into the chair across from him. 'He is five years old, and he saw me being taken away by the police. Now he has to see that I'm all right, even in here.'

Fisher promises nothing. 'I don't have to tell you that your bail is going to be revoked. Think about what you want me to say to the judge, Nina, because you don't have any chances left.'

I wait until he meets my eye. 'Will you call home for me?'

'Will you admit that I'm in charge?'

For a long moment, neither of us blinks, but I break first. I stare at my lap until I hear Fisher close the door behind him.

Adrienne knows I'm anxious as visiting hours come to an end – nearly noon, and still I have not been called to see anyone. She lies on her stomach, painting her nails fluorescent orange. In honor of hunting season, she said. As the correctional officer walks past for his quarter-hour check, I stand up. 'Are you sure no one's come yet?'

He shakes his head, moves on. Adrienne blows on her fingers to dry the polish. 'I got extra,' she says, holding up the bottle. 'You want me to roll it across?'

'I don't have any nails. I bite mine.'

'Now, that is a travesty. Some of us just don't have the sense to make the most of what God gives us.'

I laugh. 'You're one to talk.'

'In my case, honey, when it came to passing out the right stuff, God was having a senior moment.' She sits down on her lower bunk and takes off her tennis shoes. Last night, she did her toenails, tiny American flags. 'Well, fuck me,' Adrienne says. 'I smudged.'

The clock has not moved. Not even a second, I'd swear it.

'Tell me about your son,' Adrienne says when she sees me looking down the hallway again. 'I always wanted to have me one of them.'

'I would have figured you'd want a girl.'

'Honey, us ladies, we're high maintenance. A boy, you know exactly what you're getting.'

I try to think of the best way to describe Nathaniel. It is like trying to hold the ocean in a paper cup. How do I explain a boy who eats his food color by color; who wakes me in the middle of the night with a burning need to know why we breathe oxygen instead of water; who took apart a microcassette recorder to find his voice, trapped inside? I know my son so well, I surprise myself – there are too many words to choose from.

'Sometimes when I hold his hand,' I answer slowly, finally, 'it's like it doesn't fit anymore. I mean, he's only five, you know? But I can feel what's coming. Sometimes his palm's just a little too wide, or his fingers are too strong.' Glancing at Adrienne, I shrug. 'Each time I do it, I think this may be the last time I hold his hand. That next time, he may be holding mine.'

She smiles softly at me. 'Honey, he ain't coming today.'

It is 12:46 P.M., and I have to turn away, because Adrienne is right.

The CO wakes me up in the late afternoon. 'Come on,' he mutters, and slides open the door of my cell. I scramble upright, rubbing the sleep from my eyes. He leads me down a hallway to a part of the jail I have not yet visited. A row of small rooms, mini-prisons, are on my left. The guard opens one and guides me inside.

It is no bigger than a broom closet. Inside, a stool faces a Plexiglas window. A telephone receiver is mounted to the wall at its side. And on the other side of the glass, in a twin of a room, sits Caleb.

'Oh!' The word comes on a cry, and I lurch for the telephone, picking it up and holding it to my ear. 'Caleb,' I say, knowing he can see my face, read my words. 'Please, please, pick up the phone.' I pantomime over and over. But his face is chiseled and hard; his arms crossed tight on his chest. He will not give me this one thing.

Defeated, I sink onto the stool and rest my forehead against the Plexiglas. Caleb bends down to pick something up, and I realize that Nathaniel has been there all along, beneath the counter where I could not see him. He kneels on the stool, eyes wide and wary. He hesitantly touches the glass, as if he needs to know that I am not a trick of the light.

At the beach once, we found a hermit crab. I turned it over so that Nathaniel could see its jointed legs scrambling. *Put him on your palm,* I said, *and he'll crawl.* Nathaniel had held out his hand, but every time I went to set the crab on it, he jerked away. He wanted to touch it, and he was terrified to touch it, in equal proportions.

So I wave. I smile. I fill my little cubicle with the sound of his name.

As I did with Caleb, I pick up the telephone receiver. 'You too,' I mouth, and I do it again, so Nathaniel can see how. But he shakes his head, and instead raises his hand to his chin. *Mommy,* he signs.

The receiver falls out of my hand, a snake that strikes the wall beside it. I do not even need to look at Caleb for verification; just like that, I know.

So with tears running down my face, I hold up my right hand, the *I-L-Y* combination that means *I love you.* I catch my breath as Nathaniel raises one small fist, unfurls the fingers like signal flags to match mine. Then, a peace sign, the number two handshape. *I love you, too.*

By now, Nathaniel is crying. Caleb says something to him that I cannot hear, and he shakes his head. Behind them, the guard opens the door.

Oh, God, I am losing him.

I rap on the glass to get his attention. Push my face up against it, then point to Nathaniel and nod. He does what I've asked, turning his cheek so that it touches the transparent wall.

I lean close, kiss the barrier between us, and pretend it isn't there. Even after Caleb's carried him from the visiting room, I sit with my temple pressed to the glass, convincing myself I can still feel Nathaniel on the other side.

It didn't happen just that once. Two Sundays afterward, when Nathaniel's family went to Mass, the priest came into the little room where Miss Fiore was reading everyone a story about a guy with a slingshot who took down a giant. 'I need a volunteer,' he said, and even though all the hands went up, he looked right at Nathaniel.

'You know,' he said in the office, 'Esme missed you.'

'She did?'

'Oh, absolutely. She's been saying your name for days now.' Nathaniel laughed. 'She has not.'

'Listen.' He cupped his ear, leaned in to the cat on the couch. 'There you go.'

Nathaniel listened, but only heard a faint mew.

'Maybe you have to get closer,' the priest said. 'Climb up here.' For just a moment, Nathaniel hesitated, remembered. His mother had told him about going off alone with strangers. But this wasn't really a stranger, was it? He sat down in the priest's lap, and pressed his ear right against the belly of the cat. 'That's a good boy.'

The man shifted his legs, the way Nathaniel's father sometimes did when he was sitting on his knee and his foot fell asleep. 'I could move,' Nathaniel suggested.

'No, no.' The priest's hand slipped down Nathaniel's back, over his bottom, to rest in his own lap. 'This is fine.'

But then Nathaniel felt his shirt being untucked. Felt the long fingers of the priest, hot and damp, against his spine. Nathaniel did not know how to tell him no. His head was filled with a memory: a fly caught in the car one day when they were driving, which kept slamming itself into the windows in a desperate effort to get out. 'Father?' Nathaniel whispered.

'I'm just blessing you,' he replied. 'A special helper deserves that. I want God to know that every time He sees you.' His fingers stilled. 'You *do* want that, don't you?'

A blessing was a good thing, and for God to keep an extra eye on him – well, it was what his mother and father would want, Nathaniel was sure of it. He turned his attention back to the lazy cat, and that was when he heard it – just a puff of breath – Esme, or maybe not Esme, sighing his name.

The second time I am called out by a correctional officer is Sunday afternoon. He takes me upstairs to the conference rooms, where inmates meet privately with their attorneys. Maybe Fisher has come to see how I am holding up. Maybe he wants to discuss tomorrow's hearing.

But to my surprise, when the door is unlocked, Patrick is waiting inside. Spread out on the conference table are six containers of take-out Chinese food. 'I got everything you like,' he says. 'General Tso's chicken, vegetable lo mein, beef with broccoli, Lake Tung Ting shrimp, and steamed dumplings. Oh, and that crap that tastes like rubber.'

'Bean curd.' I lift my chin a notch, challenging him. 'I thought you didn't want to talk to me.'

'I don't. I want to eat with you.'

'Are you sure? Think of all the things I could say while your mouth is full, before you have a chance to –'

'Nina.' Patrick's blue eyes seem faded, weary. 'Shut up.'

But even as he scolds me, he holds out his hand. It rests on the table, extended, an offering more tantalizing than anything else before me.

I sit across from him and grab on. Immediately, Patrick

squeezes, and that's my undoing. I lay my cheek on the cold, scarred table, and Patrick strokes my hair. 'I rigged your fortune cookie,' he confesses. 'It says you'll be acquitted.'

'What does yours say?'

'That you'll be acquitted.' Patrick smiles. 'I didn't know which one you'd pick.'

My eyes drift shut as I let down my guard. 'It's okay,' Patrick tells me, and I believe him. I place his palm against my burning face, as if shame is something he might carry in the cup of his hand, fling someplace far away.

When you call someone on the prison pay phone, they know it. Every thirty seconds a voice gets on the line, informing the person on the other end that this transmission is taking place from the Alfred County Jail. I use the fifty cents Patrick gave me that afternoon, and make the call on my way to the shower. 'Listen,' I say, the minute I reach Fisher at his home number. 'You wanted me to tell you what to say on Monday morning.'

'Nina?' In the background I hear the laughter of a woman. The sound of glasses, or china, in a sink.

'I need to talk to you.'

'You've caught us in the middle of dinner.'

'Well, for God's sake, Fisher.' I turn my back as a line of men straggles in from the outside courtyard. 'Why don't I just call back then when it's more convenient for you, because I'm sure I'll have another opportunity, in, oh, three or four days.'

I hear the distant noise growing more faint; the click of a door. 'All right. What is it?'

'Nathaniel isn't speaking. You need to get me out of here, because he's falling apart.'

'He isn't speaking? Again?'

'Caleb brought him yesterday. And . . . he's signing.'

Fisher considers this. 'If we get Caleb down here to testify, and Nathaniel's psychiatrist –'

'You'll have to subpoena him.'

'The psychiatrist?'

'Caleb.'

If this surprises him, he doesn't admit it. 'Nina, the fact is, you messed up. I'm going to try to get you out. I still think it's unlikely. But if you want me to give it a shot, you're going to have to sit tight for a week.'

'A *week?*' My voice rises. 'Fisher, this is my son we're talking about. Do you know how much worse Nathaniel might get in a week?'

'I'm counting on it.'

A voice cuts in. *This call is being made from the Alfred County Jail. If you wish to continue, please deposit another twenty-five cents.*

By the time I tell Fisher to go screw himself, the line has already been disconnected.

Adrienne and I are given a half hour together outside in the exercise courtyard. We walk the perimeter, and then when we get cold, we stand with our backs to the wind beneath the high brick wall. When the CO goes inside, Adrienne smokes cigarettes that she makes by burning down orange peels she collects from the cafeteria trash, and rolling the ash in onion-skin pages torn from *Jane Eyre,* a book her Aunt Lu sent for her birthday. She has already ripped through page 298. I told her to ask for *Vanity Fair* next year.

I sit cross-legged on the dead grass. Adrienne kneels behind me, smoking, her hands in my hair. When she gets out, she wants to be a cosmetologist. Her nail makes a part from my temple to the nape of my neck. 'No pigtails,' I instruct.

'Don't insult me.' She makes another part, parallel to the first, and begins to braid in tight rows. 'You've got fine hair.'

'Thank you.'

'It wasn't a compliment, honey. Look at this . . . slips right out of my fingers.'

She pulls and tugs, and several times I have to wince. If only it were that easy to tighten up the tangles inside my head, too. Her glowing cigarette, smoked down to within an inch, sails over my shoulder and lands on the basketball court. 'There,' Adrienne says. 'Ain't you the bomb.'

Of course, I can't see. I touch my hands to the knobs and ridges the braids have made on my scalp, and then, just because I am feeling mean-spirited, begin to unravel all Adrienne's hard work. She shrugs, then sits down next to me. 'Did you always want to be a lawyer?'

'No.' Who does, after all? What kid considers being an attorney a glamorous vocation? 'I wanted to be the man at the circus who tames the lions.'

'Oh, don't I know it. Those sequined costumes were something.'

For me, it hadn't been about the outfits. I'd loved the way Gunther Gebel-Williams could walk into a cage full of beasts and make them think they were house cats. In this, I realize, my actual profession has not fallen that far off the mark. 'How about you?'

'My daddy wanted me to be the center for the Chicago Bulls. Me, I was angling for Vegas showgirl.'

'Ah.' I draw up my knees, wrap my arms around them. 'What does your daddy think now?'

'He ain't doing much thinking, I imagine, six feet under.'

'I'm sorry.'

Adrienne glances up. 'Don't be.'

But she has retreated somewhere else, and to my surprise, I find I want her back. The game that Peter Eberhardt and I used to play swims into my mind, and I turn to Adrienne. 'Best soap opera,' I challenge.

'What?'

'Just play along with me. Give your opinion.'

'*The Young and the Restless,*' Adrienne replies. 'Which, by the way, those fool boys in Minimum don't even have the good sense to listen to on their TV at one P.M.'

'Worst crayon color?'

'Burnt sienna. What is *up* with that, anyway? They might as well call it Vomit.' Adrienne grins, a flash of white in her face. 'Best jeans?'

'Levi's 501s. Ugliest CO?'

'Oh, the one who comes on after midnight that needs to bleach her moustache. You ever see the size of her ass? *Hello*, honey, let me introduce you to Miss Jenny Craig.'

Then we are both laughing, lying back on the cold ground and feeling winter seep into us by osmosis. When we finally catch our breath, there is a hollow in my chest, a sinking feeling that here, of all places, I should not be capable of joy. 'Best place to be?' Adrienne asks after a moment.

On the other side of this wall. In my bed, at home. Anywhere with Nathaniel.

'Before,' I answer, because I know she'll understand.

In one of Biddeford's coffee shops, Quentin sits on a stool too small for a gnome. One sip from his mug, and hot chocolate burns the roof of his mouth. 'Holy shit,' he mutters, holding a napkin to his mouth, just as Tanya walks in the door in her nurse's outfit – scrubs, printed with tiny teddy bears.

'Just shut up, Quentin,' she says, sliding onto the stool beside him. 'I'm not in the mood to hear you make fun of my uniform.'

'I wasn't.' He gestures to the mug, then just gives up the battle. 'What can I get you?'

He orders Tanya a decaf mochaccino. 'You like it, then?' he asks.

'Coffee?'

'Nursing.'

He had met Tanya at the University of Maine when she was a student, too. *What's this*, he'd asked at the end of their first date, trailing his fingers over her collarbone. *A clavicle*, she said. *And this?* His hand had run down the xylophone of her spine. *The coccyx*. He'd spread his fingers over the curve of her hip. *This is the part of you I like best*, he said. Her head had fallen back, her eyes drifting shut as he bared the skin and kissed her there. *Ilium*, she'd whispered.

Nine months later, there had been Gideon. They were married, a mistake, six days before he was born. They stayed married for less than a year. Since then Quentin had supported his son financially, if not emotionally.

'I must hate it, if I've stuck with it that long,' Tanya says, and it takes Quentin a moment to realize that she is only answering his question. Something must have crossed his face, because she touches her hand to his. 'I'm sorry, that was rude. And here you were just being polite.'

Her coffee arrives. She blows on it before taking a sip. 'Saw your name in the paper,' Tanya says. 'They got you down here for that priest's murder.'

Quentin shrugs. 'Pretty simple case, actually.'

'Well, sure, if you look at the news.' But Tanya shakes her head, all the same.

'What's that supposed to mean?'

'That the world isn't black and white, but you never did learn that.'

He raises his brows. 'I didn't learn it? Who threw whom out?'

'Who found whom screwing that girl who looked like a mouse?'

'There were mitigating circumstances,' Quentin says. 'I was drunk.' He hesitates, then adds, 'And she looked more like a rabbit, really.'

Tanya rolls her eyes. 'Quentin, it's been sixteen and a half years and you're still being a lawyer about it.'

'Well, what do you expect?'

'For you to be a man,' Tanya replies simply. 'For you to admit that even the Great and Powerful Brown is capable of making a mistake once or twice a century.' She pushes away her mug, although she isn't even half-finished. 'I've always wondered if you're so good at what you do because it takes the heat off you. You know, if making everyone else walk the straight and narrow makes you righteous by association.' She fishes in her purse and slaps five dollars on the counter. 'Think about that when you're prosecuting that poor woman.'

'What the hell is that supposed to mean?'

'Can you even imagine what she was feeling, Quentin?' Tanya asks, her head tipped to the side. 'Or is that kind of connection to a child beyond you?'

He stands when she does. 'Gideon wants nothing to do with me.'

Tanya buttons her coat, already halfway to the door. 'I always said he got your intelligence,' she says, and then, once again, she slips right through his grasp.

By Thursday, Caleb has established a routine. He gets Nathaniel up, feeds him breakfast, and takes him for a walk with the dog. They drive to whatever site Caleb might be working at that morning, and while he builds walls Nathaniel sits in the bed of the truck and plays with a shoebox full of Legos. They eat lunch together, peanut butter and banana sandwiches or Thermoses of chicken soup, and soda that he's packed in the cooler. And then they go to Dr. Robichaud's office, where the psychiatrist tries, unsuccessfully, to get Nathaniel to speak again.

It is a ballet, really – a story they are crafting without words, but comprehensible to anyone who sees Caleb and his silent son moving slowly through their days. To his surprise, this is even beginning to feel like normal. He likes the quiet, because when there are no words to be had, you can't tangle yourself up in the wrong ones. And if Nathaniel isn't talking, at least he isn't crying anymore.

Caleb keeps blinders on, moving from one task to the next, getting Nathaniel fed and clothed and tucked in, and therefore only has a few moments each day to let his mind wander. Usually, this is when he is lying in bed, with the space beside him where Nina used to be. And even when he tries to keep himself from thinking it, the truth fills his mouth, bitter as a lemon: Life is easier, without her here.

On Thursday, Fisher brings me the discovery to read. This consists of 124 eyewitness accounts that describe my murder of Father Szyszynski, Patrick's report on the molestation, my own incoherent statement to Evan Chao, and the autopsy report.

I read Patrick's file first, feeling like a beauty queen poring over her scrapbook. Here is the explanation for everything else that sits in a stack at my side. Next, I read the statements of all the people who were in the courtroom the day of the murder. Of course, I save the best for last – the autopsy report, which I hold as reverently as if it were the Dead Sea Scrolls.

First I look at the pictures. I stare at them so hard that when I close my eyes I can still see the ragged edge where the priest's face was simply gone now. I can envision the creamy color of his brain. His heart weighed 350 grams, or so says Dr. Vern Potter, coroner.

'Dissection of the coronary arteries,' I read aloud, 'reveals narrowing of the lumen by atherosclerotic plaque. The most significant narrowing is in the left anterior descending coronary, where the lumen is narrowed by about 80 percent of the cross-sectional area.'

Lumen. I repeat this word, and the others that are all that are left of this monster: *no evidence of thrombus; the gallbladder serosa is smooth and glistening; the bladder is slightly trabeculated.*

The stomach contains partly digested bacon and a cinnamon roll.

Powder burns from the gun form a corona around the small hole in the rear of his head, where the bullet entered. There is a zone of necrosis around the bullet tract. Only 816 grams of his brain were left intact. There were contusions of the cerebellar tonsils bilaterally. Cause of death: Gunshot wound to head. Manner of death: Homicide.

This language is foreign, and I am suddenly, miraculously fluent. I touch my fingers to the autopsy report. Then I remember the twisted face of his mother, at the funeral.

Attached to this file is another one, with the name of a local physician's office stamped on its side. This must be Father Szyszynski's medical history. It is a thick file, far more than fifty years of routine checkups, but I don't bother to crack it open. Why should I? I have done what all those ordinary flus and hacking coughs and aches and cramps could not.

I killed him.

'This is for you,' the paralegal says, handing Quentin a fax. He looks up, takes the pages, and then stares down at them, confused. The lab report has Szyszynski's name on it; but has nothing to do with his case. Then he realizes: It is from the previous case, the closed case – the one involving the defendant's son. He glances at it, shrugging at the results, which are no great surprise. 'It's not mine,' Quentin says.

The paralegal blinks at him. 'So what am I supposed to do with it?'

He starts to hand it back to the woman, then puts it on the edge of his desk instead. 'I'll take care of it,' he answers, and buries himself in his work again until she leaves his office.

There are a thousand places Caleb would rather be – in a prisoner-of-war's hovel, for example; or standing in an open field during a tornado. But he had to be present today, the subpoena said so. He stands in the courtroom cafeteria in his one jacket and threadbare tie, holding a cup of coffee so hot it is burning his palm, and tries to pretend that his hands aren't shaking with nerves.

Fisher Carrington is not such a bad guy, he thinks. At least, he's not nearly the demon that Nina has made him out to be. 'Relax, Caleb,' the attorney says. 'This will be over before you know it.' They make their way to the exit. Court will convene in five minutes; even now, they might be bringing Nina in.

'All you have to do is answer the questions we've already gone over, and then Mr. Brown will ask a few of his own. No one's expecting you to do anything but tell the truth. Okay?'

Caleb nods, tries to take a sip of the fire that is his coffee. He doesn't even like coffee. He wonders what Nathaniel is doing with Monica, downstairs in the playroom. He tries to distract himself by picturing an intricate brick pattern he created for a former insurance CEO's patio. But reality crouches like a tiger in the corner of his mind: In minutes, he is going to be a witness. In minutes, dozens of reporters and curious citizens and a judge will be hanging on the words of a man who much prefers silence. 'Fisher,' he begins, then takes a deep breath. 'They can't ask me anything, you know, that she told me . . . can they?'

'Anything Nina told you?'

'About . . . about what she did.'

Fisher stares at Caleb. 'She talked to you about it?'

'Yeah. Before she –'

'Caleb,' the lawyer interrupts smoothly, 'don't tell me, and I'll make sure you don't have to tell anyone else.'

He disappears through a doorway before Caleb can even measure the strength of his relief.

As Peter takes the stand for Quentin Brown at my bail revocation hearing, he shoots me a look of apology. He can't lie, but he doesn't want to be the one responsible for landing me in jail. To make this easier on him, I try not to catch his eye. I concentrate instead on Patrick, sitting somewhere behind me, so close I can smell the soap he uses. And on Brown, who seems too big to be pacing this tiny courtroom.

Fisher puts his hand on my leg, which has been jiggling nervously without my even noticing. 'Stop,' he mouths.

'Did you see Nina Frost that afternoon?' Quentin asks.

'No,' Peter says. 'I didn't see her.'

Quentin raises his brows in absolute disbelief. 'Did you walk up to her?'

'Well, I was coming down the produce aisle, and her cart happened to be placed along the path I was taking. Her son was sitting in it. He's the one I approached.'

'Did Ms. Frost walk up to the cart as well?'

'Yes, but she was moving closer to her son. Not to me.'

'Just answer the questions as I ask them.'

'Look, she was standing next to me, but she didn't speak to me,' Peter says.

'Did you speak to her, Mr. Eberhardt?'

'No.' Peter turns to the judge. 'I was talking to Nathaniel.'

Quentin touches a stack of papers on the prosecutor's table. 'You have access to the information in these files?'

'As you know, Mr. Brown, I'm not working on her case. *You* are.'

'But I'm working in her former office, the one right next to yours, aren't I?'

'Yes.'

'And,' Quentin says, 'there aren't any locks on those doors, are there?'

'No.'

'So I guess you think she approached you so that she could squeeze the Charmin?'

Peter narrows his eyes. 'She wasn't trying to get into trouble, and neither was I.'

'And now you're trying to help her out of all that trouble, aren't you?'

Before he can answer, Quentin turns over the witness to the defense. Fisher gets up, buttoning his jacket. I feel a line of sweat break out on my spine. 'Who spoke first, Mr. Eberhardt?' he asks.

'Nathaniel.'

'What did he say?'

Peter looks at the railing. He knows by now, too, that Nathaniel has gone mute again. 'My name.'

'If you didn't want Nina to get into trouble, why didn't you just turn around and walk away?'

'Because Nathaniel wanted me. And after . . . after the abuse, he stopped talking for a while. This was the first time I'd heard him speak since all that happened. I couldn't just do an about-face and walk away.'

'Was it at that exact moment that Mr. Brown rounded the corner and saw you?'

'Yes.'

Fisher clasps his hands behind his back. 'Did you ever speak to Nina about her case?'

'No.'

'Did you give her any inside information about her case?'

'No.'

'Did she ask you for any?'

'No.'

'Are you working on Nina's case at all?'

Peter shakes his head. 'I will always be her friend. But I understand my job, and my duties as an officer of this court. And the last thing I'd want to do is involve myself in this case.'

'Thank you, Mr. Eberhardt.'

Fisher settles into place beside me at the defense table, as Quentin Brown glances up at the judge. 'Your Honor, the state rests.'

That makes one of us, I think.

Caleb's gaze is drawn to her, and he is shocked. His wife, the one who always looks crisp and fresh and coordinated, sits in bright orange scrubs. Her hair is a cloud about her head; her eyes are shadowed with circles. There is a cut on the back of her hand and one of her shoelaces has come untied. Caleb has the unlikely urge to kneel before her, to double-knot it, to bury his head in her lap.

You can hate someone, he realizes, and be crazy about her at the same time.

Fisher catches his eye, pulling Caleb back to this responsibility. If he screws up, Nina may not be allowed to come home. Then again, Fisher has told him that even if he is flawless on the stand, she may still be locked up in jail pending trial. He clears his throat and imagines himself in an ocean of language, trying to keep his head above water.

'When did Nathaniel start speaking again, after you found out about the abuse?'

'About three weeks ago. The night Detective Ducharme came to talk to him.'

'Had his verbal ability increased since that night?'

'Yes,' Caleb answers. 'He was pretty much back to normal.'

'How much time was his mother spending with him?'

'More than usual.'

'How did Nathaniel seem to you?'

Caleb thinks for a moment. 'Happier,' he says.

Fisher moves, so that he is standing behind Nina. 'What changed after the incident at the grocery store?'

'He was hysterical. He was crying so hard he couldn't breathe, and he wouldn't talk at all.' Caleb looks into Nina's eyes, hands her this phrase like a gift. 'He kept making the sign for *Mommy.*'

She makes a small sound, like a kitten. It renders him speechless; he has to ask Fisher to repeat his next question. 'Has he spoken at all in the past week?'

'No,' Caleb replies.

'Have you taken Nathaniel to see his mother?'

'Once. It was very . . . hard on him.'

'How do you mean?'

'He didn't want to leave her,' Caleb admits. 'I had to physically drag him away when the time was up.'

'How is your son sleeping at night?'

'He won't, unless I take him into bed with me.'

Fisher nods gravely. 'Do you think, Mr. Frost, that he needs his mother back?'

Quentin Brown stands immediately. 'Objection!'

'This is a bail hearing, I'll allow it,' the judge replies. 'Mr. Frost?'

Caleb sees answers swimming in front of him. There are so many, which is the one he should choose? He opens his mouth, then closes it to start over.

At that moment he notices Nina. Her eyes are bright on his, feverish, and he tries to remember why this seems so familiar. Then it comes to him: this is the way she looked weeks ago when she was trying to convince a mute Nathaniel that all he had to do was speak from the heart; that any word was better than none. 'We both need her back,' Caleb says, the right thing after all.

Halfway through Dr. Robichaud's testimony, I realize that this is the trial we would have had to convict the priest, had I not killed him. The information being presented focuses on the molestation of Nathaniel, and the consequences. The psychiatrist walks the court through her introduction to Nathaniel, his sexual abuse evaluation, his therapy sessions, his use of sign language. 'Did Nathaniel ever reach a point where he could talk again?' Fisher asks.

'Yes, after he verbally disclosed the name of his abuser to Detective Ducharme.'

'Since then, as far as you know, has he been talking normally?'

The psychiatrist nods. 'More and more so.'

'Did you see him this past week, Doctor?'

'Yes. His father called me, very upset, on Friday night. Nathaniel had stopped speaking again. When I saw him on Monday morning, he'd regressed considerably. He's withdrawn and uncommunicative. I couldn't even get him to sign.'

'In your expert opinion, is the separation from his mother causing Nathaniel psychological damage?'

'No question,' Dr. Robichaud says. 'In fact, the longer it goes on, the more permanent the damage might be.'

As she gets down from the stand, Brown gets up to do his closing. He starts by pointing at me. 'This woman has a blatant disregard for rules, and clearly, this isn't the first time. What she should have done the moment she saw Peter Eberhardt was turn around and walk the other way. But the fact is, she didn't.' He turns to the judge. 'Your Honor, you were the one who imposed the condition that Nina Frost not have contact with members of the district attorney's office, because you were concerned about treating her differently than other defendants. But if you let her go without sanction, you'll be doing just that.'

Even on edge, as I am, I realize that Quentin's made a tactical mistake. You can make suggestions to a jury . . . but you never, *ever* tell the judge what to do.

Fisher rises. 'Your Honor, what Mr. Brown saw in the produce department was nothing more than sour grapes. The reality of the matter is that no information was exchanged. In fact, there's no evidence that information was even sought.'

He puts his hands on my shoulders. I have seen him do this with other clients; in my office, we used to call it his Grandfather Stance. 'This was an unfortunate misunderstanding,' Fisher continues, 'but that's all it is. Nothing more, nothing less. And if, as a result, you keep Nina Frost from her child, you may wind up sacrificing that child. Certainly after what everyone's been through, that's the last thing this court would like to see happen.'

The judge lifts his head and looks at me. 'I'm not going to keep her away from her son,' he rules. 'However, I'm also not going to give her the opportunity to violate the rules of this court again. I release Ms. Frost on the condition that she be on home confinement. She'll wear an electronic bracelet, and will be subject to all the rules of probation and parole with regards to electronic monitoring. Ms. Frost.' He waits for me to nod. 'You are not to leave the house, except to meet with your attorney or to come to court. For those times, and only those times, the bracelet will be reprogrammed accordingly. And God help me, if I have to patrol your street myself to make sure you're adhering to these provisions, I will.'

My new wrist cuff works through telephone lines. If I move 150 feet away from my house, the bracelet makes an alarm go off. A probation officer may visit me at any time, demand a sample of my blood or urine to make sure I have not had any drugs or alcohol. I opt to wear my scrubs home, and ask the deputy sheriff to instruct that my old clothes be given, a gift, to Adrienne. They'll be short and tight – in other words, a perfect fit for her.

'You have nine lives,' Fisher murmurs as we walk out of the parole office, where my cuff has been computer-programmed.

'Seven left,' I sigh.

'Let's hope we don't have to use them all.'

'Fisher.' I stop walking as we reach the staircase. 'I just wanted to tell you . . . I couldn't have done that any better.'

He laughs. 'Nina, I think you'd actually choke if you had to say the word *thanks*.'

We walk side by side upstairs, toward the lobby. Fisher, a gentleman to the last, pushes open the heavy fire door of the stairwell and holds it while I step through.

The immediate burst of light as the cameras explode renders me blind, and it takes a moment for the world to come back to me. When it does, I realize that in addition to the reporters, Patrick and Caleb and Monica are waiting. And then, emerging from a spot behind his father's big body, I see my son.

She is wearing funny orange pajamas and her hair looks like a swallow's nest Nathaniel once found behind the soda bottles in the garage, but her face is his mother's and her voice, when it says his name, is his mother's too. Her smile is a hook in him; he can feel the catch in his throat as he swallows it and lets himself be reeled across the space between them. *Mommy.* Nathaniel's arms rise up from his sides. He stumbles over a wire, and someone's foot, and then he is running.

She falls to her knees and that only makes the tug stronger. Nathaniel's so close that he can see she is crying, and this isn't even very clear because he is crying too. He feels the hook coming free, drawing out the silence that has swelled in his belly for a week now, and the moment before he reaches her embrace it bursts from his lips in a rusty, trebled joy. 'Mommy, Mommy, Mommy!' Nathaniel shouts, so loud that it drowns out everything but the drum of his mother's heart beneath his ear.

He's gotten bigger in a week. I heft Nathaniel into my arms, smiling like a fool, as the cameras capture every move. Fisher has corralled the reporters, is even now preaching to them. I bury my face in Nathaniel's sweet neck, matching my memory with what is real.

Suddenly Caleb stands beside us. His face is as inscrutable as it was the last time we were alone, on opposite sides of a glass visitation booth at jail. Although his testimony helped free me, I know my husband. He did what was expected, but it was not necessarily something he wanted to do. 'Caleb,' I begin, flustered. 'I . . . I don't know what to say.'

To my surprise, he offers an olive branch: a crooked smile. 'Well, that's a first. No wonder so many reporters are around.' Caleb's grin slides more firmly into place; and at the same time, he anchors his arm around my shoulders, guides me one step closer to home.

These are the jokes I know.
What's in the middle of a jellyfish?
A jellybutton.

Why didn't the skeleton cross the road?
It didn't have the guts.

Why did the cookie go to the hospital?
It felt crumby.

What do lizards put on their kitchen floors?
Reptiles.

What do you call a blind dinosaur?
An I-don't-think-he-saurus.

There is one more:
Knock knock.
Who's there?
Sadie.
Sadie who?
Sadie magic word, Nathaniel, and then you'll be allowed to go.
When he told it to me, I didn't laugh.

6

And just like that, I have fallen back into my former life. The three of us sit around the breakfast table, like any other family. With his finger, Nathaniel traces the letters in the headline of the morning paper. '*M*,' he says quietly. '*O, M . . .*' Over my coffee cup, I look at the photograph. There I am, holding Nathaniel, Caleb at my side. Fisher, somehow, has managed to get his face in the picture too. In the distance, a few steps behind, is Patrick; I recognize him only by his shoes. Across the top, in screaming black letters: MOMMY.

Caleb takes Nathaniel's empty cereal bowl away as he runs off into the playroom, where he has set up two armies of plastic dinosaurs for a Jurassic war. I glance at the paper. 'I'm the poster child for bad parenting,' I say.

'Beats being the local Maine murderess.' He nods to the table. 'What's in the envelope?'

The manila mailer is the interoffice kind, tied shut with red floss. I found it stuffed between the Local and Sports sections of the paper. I flip it over, but there is no return address, no marking of any kind.

Inside is a report from the state lab, the kind of chart I have seen before. A table with results in eight columns, each a different location on human DNA. And two rows of numbers that are identical at every single spot.

Conclusions: The DNA profile detected on the underpants is consistent with the DNA profile of Szyszynski. As a result, he cannot be eliminated as a possible contributor of the genetic material detected in this stain. The chances of randomly selecting an unrelated individual who matches the genetic material found in the underwear are greater than one in six billion, which is approximately the world population.

Or in English: Father Szyszynski's semen was found on my son's underwear.

Caleb peers over my shoulder. 'What's that?'

'Absolution,' I sigh.

Caleb takes the paper from my hands, and I point to the first row of numbers. 'This shows the DNA from Szyszynski's blood sample. And the line below it shows the DNA from the stain on the underpants.'

'The numbers are the same.'

'Right. DNA is the same all over your body. That's why, if the cops arrest a rapist, they draw blood – can you imagine how ridiculous it would be to ask the guy to give a semen sample? The idea is, if you can match the suspect's blood DNA to evidence, you're almost guaranteed a conviction.' I look up at him. 'It means that he did it, Caleb. He was the one. And . . .' My voice trails off.

'And what?'

'And I did the right thing,' I finish.

Caleb puts the paper facedown on the table and gets up.

'What?' I challenge.

He shakes his head slowly. 'Nina, you didn't do the right thing. You said it yourself. If you match the DNA in the suspect's blood to the evidence, you're guaranteed a conviction. So if you'd waited, he would have gotten his punishment.'

'And Nathaniel would still have had to sit in that courtroom, reliving every minute of what happened to him, because that lab report would mean nothing without his testimony.' To my embarrassment, tears rise in my eyes. 'I thought Nathaniel had been through enough without that.'

'I know what you thought,' Caleb says softly. 'That's the problem. What about the things Nathaniel's had to deal with *because* of what you did? I'm not saying you did the wrong thing. I'm not even saying it wasn't something I'd thought of doing, myself. But even if it was the just thing to do . . . or the fitting thing . . . Nina, it still wasn't the *right* thing.'

He puts on his boots and opens the kitchen door, leaving me alone with the lab results. I rest my head on my hand and take a deep breath. Caleb's wrong, he *has* to be wrong, because if he isn't, then –

My thoughts veer away from this as the manila envelope draws my eye. Who left this for me, cloak-and-dagger? Someone on the prosecution's side would have fielded it from the lab. Maybe Peter dropped it off, or a sympathetic paralegal who thought it might go to motive for an insanity defense. At any rate, it is a document I'm not supposed to have.

Something, therefore, I can't share with Fisher.

I pick up the phone and call him. 'Nina,' he says. 'Did you see the morning paper?'

'Hard to miss. Hey, Fisher, did you ever see the DNA results on the priest?'

'You mean the underwear sample? No.' He pauses. 'It's a closed case, now, of course. It's possible somebody told the lab not to bother.'

Not likely. The staff in the DA's office would have been far too busy to see to a detail like that. 'You know, I'd really like to see the report. If it did come back.'

'It doesn't really have any bearing on your case –'

'Fisher,' I say firmly, 'I'm asking you politely. Have your paralegal call Quentin Brown to fax the report over. I need to see it.'

He sighs. 'All right. I'll get back to you.'

I place the receiver back in its cradle, and sit down at the table. Outside, Caleb splits wood, relieving his frustration with each heavy blow of the ax. Last night, feeling his way under the covers with one warm hand, he'd brushed the plastic lip of my electronic monitoring bracelet. That was all, and then he'd rolled onto one side away from me.

Picking up my coffee, I read the twin lines on the lab report again. Caleb is mistaken, that's all there is to it. All these letters and numbers, they are proof, in black and white, that I am a hero.

* * *

Quentin gives the lab report another cursory glance and then puts it on a corner of his desk. No surprises there; everyone knows why she killed the priest. The point is, none of this matters anymore. The trial at hand isn't about sexual abuse, but murder.

The secretary, a harried, faded blonde named Rhonda or Wanda or something like that, sticks her head in the door. 'Does no one knock in this building?' Quentin mutters, scowling.

'You take the lab report on Szyszynski?' she asks.

'It's right here. Why?'

'Defense attorney just called; he wants a copy faxed over to his office yesterday.'

Quentin hands the papers to the secretary. 'What's the rush?'

'Who knows.'

It makes no sense to Quentin; Fisher Carrington must realize that the information will not make or break his case. But then again, it doesn't matter at all for the prosecution – Nina Frost is facing a conviction, he's certain, and no lab report about a dead man is going to change that. By the time the secretary has closed the door behind herself, Quentin has put Carrington's request out of his mind.

Marcella Wentworth hates snow. She had enough of it, growing up in Maine, and then working there for nearly a decade. She hates waking up and knowing you have to shovel your way to your car; she hates the sensation of skis beneath her feet; she hates the uncontrollable feel of wheels spinning out on black ice. The happiest day of Marcella's life, in fact, was the day she quit her job at the Maine State Lab, moved to Virginia, and threw her Sorrel boots into a public trash bin at a highway McDonald's.

She has worked for three years now at CellCore, a private lab. Marcella has a year-round tan and only one medium-weight winter coat. But at her workstation she keeps a postcard Nina Frost, a district attorney, sent her last Christmas –

a cartoon depicting the unmistakable mitten shape of her birth state, sporting googly eyes and a jester's hat. *Once a Mainiac, always a Mainiac,* it reads.

Marcella is looking at the postcard, and thinking that there may already be a dusting on the ground up there by now, when Nina Frost calls.

'You're not going to believe this,' Marcella says, 'but I was just thinking about you.'

'I need your help,' Nina answers. All business – but then, that has always been Nina. Once or twice since Marcella left the state lab, Nina called to consult on a case, just for the purpose of verification. 'I've got a DNA test I need checked.'

Marcella glances at the overwhelming stack of files piling her in-box. 'No problem. What's the story?'

'Child molestation. There's a known blood sample and then semen on a pair of underwear. I'm not an expert, but the results looks pretty cut and dried.'

'Ah. I'm guessing they don't jive, and you think the state lab screwed up?'

'Actually, they do jive. I just need to be absolutely certain.'

'Guess you really don't want this one to walk,' Marcella muses.

There is a hesitation. 'He's dead,' Nina says. 'I shot him.'

Caleb has always liked chopping wood. He likes the Herculean moment of hefting the ax, of swinging it down like a man measuring his strength at a carnival game. He likes the sound of a log being broken apart, a searing crack, and then the hollow *plink* of two halves falling to opposite sides. He likes the rhythm, which erases thought and memory.

Maybe by the time he has run out of wood to split, he will feel ready to go back inside and face his wife.

Nina's single-mindedness has always been attractive – especially to a man who, in so many matters, is naturally hesitant. But now the flaw has been magnified to the point of being grotesque. She simply cannot let go.

Once, Caleb had been hired to build a brick wall in a town park. As he'd worked, he'd gotten used to the homeless man who lived beneath the birthday pavilion. His name was Coalspot, or so Caleb had been told. He was schizophrenic but harmless. Sometimes, Coalspot would sit on the park bench next to Caleb as he worked. He spent hours unlacing his shoe, taking it off, scraping at his heel, and then putting his shoe back on. 'Can you see it?' the man asked Caleb. 'Can you see the hole where the poison's leaking?'

One day a social worker arrived to take Coalspot to a shelter, but he wouldn't go. He insisted he would infect everyone else; the poison was contagious. After three hours, the woman had reached the end of her rope. 'We try to help them,' she sighed to Caleb, 'and this is what we get.'

So Caleb sat down beside Coalspot. He took off his own work boot and sock, pointed to his heel. 'You see?' he said. 'Everyone already has one.'

After that, the homeless man went off, easy as a kitten. It didn't matter there was no poisonous hole – just at that moment, Coalspot truly believed there was one. And that for a second, Caleb had told the man he was right.

Nina is like that, now. She has redefined her actions so that they make sense to her, if not to anyone else. To say that she killed a man in order to protect Nathaniel? Well, whatever trauma he might suffer as a witness couldn't be nearly as bad as watching his mother get handcuffed and carted off to jail.

Caleb knows that Nina is looking for vindication, but he can't do what he did with Coalspot – look her in eye and tell her that yes, he understands. He can't look her in the eye, period.

He wonders if the reason he's putting up a wall between them is so that, when she is sentenced, it is easier to let her go.

Caleb takes another log and sets it on end on the chopping block. As the ax comes down, the wood cleaves into two neat pieces, and sitting in the center is the truth. What Nina has done doesn't make Caleb feel morally superior, by default. It

makes him a coward, because he wasn't the one brave enough
to cross the line from thought to deed.

There are parts of it Nathaniel can't remember – like what he
said when Nathaniel first shook his head no; or which one of
them unbuttoned his jeans. What he can still think of, sometimes even when he is trying his hardest not to, is how the air
felt cold when his pants came off, and how hot his hand was
after that. How it hurt, it hurt so bad, even though he had said
it wouldn't. How Nathaniel had held Esme so tight she cried;
how in the mirror of her gold eyes he saw a little boy who no
longer was him.

It will make Nina happy.

Those are Marcella's first thoughts when she reads the DNA
results, and sees that the semen stain and the priest's blood
are indistinguishable from each other. No scientist will ever
say it quite this way in testimony, but the numbers – and the
stats – speak for themselves: This is the perp, no question.

She picks up the phone to tell Nina so, tucking it under her
chin so that she can rubber-band the medical files that came
attached to the lab report. Marcella hasn't bothered to scan
these; it is pretty clear from what Nina said that the priest died
as a result of the gunshot wound. But still, Nina has asked
Marcella for a thorough review. She sighs, then puts back the
receiver and opens the thick folder.

Two hours later, she finishes reading. And realizes that in
spite of her best intentions to stay away, she'll be heading back
to Maine.

Here is what I have learned in a week: A prison, no matter
what shape and size, is still a prison. I find myself staring out
windows along with the dog, itching to be on the other side
of the glass. I would give a fortune to do the most mundane
of errands: run to the bank, take the car to Jiffy Lube, rake
leaves.

Nathaniel has gone back to school. This is Dr. Robichaud's suggestion, a step toward normalcy. Still, I can't help but wonder if Caleb had some small part in this; if he really doesn't like the thought of leaving me alone with my son.

One morning, before I could think twice, I walked halfway down the driveway to pick up the newspaper before I remembered the electronic bracelet. Caleb found me on the porch, sobbing, waiting for the sirens I was certain would come. But through some miracle, the alarm did not go off. I spent six seconds in the fresh air, and no one was the wiser.

To occupy myself, sometimes I cook. I have made *penne alla rigata,* coq au vin, potstickers. I choose dishes from foreign places, anywhere but here. Today, though, I am cleaning the house. I have already emptied the coat closet and the kitchen pantry, restocked their items in order of frequency of use. Up in the bedroom, I've tossed out shoes I forgot I ever bought, and have aligned my suits in a rainbow, from palest pink to deepest plum to chocolate.

I am just weeding through Caleb's dresser when he comes in, stripping off a filthy shirt. 'Do you know,' I say, 'that in the hall closet is a brand-new pair of cleats fives sizes bigger than Nathaniel's foot?'

'Got them at a garage sale. Nathaniel'll grow into them.'

After all this, doesn't he understand that the future doesn't necessarily follow in a straight, unbroken line?

'What are you doing?'

'Your drawers.'

'I like my drawers.' Caleb takes a torn shirt I've put aside and stuffs it back in all wrinkled. 'Why don't you take a nap? Read, or something?'

'That would be a waste of time.' I find three socks, all without mates.

'Why is just taking time a waste of it?' Caleb asks, shrugging into another shirt. He grabs the socks I've segregated and puts them into his underwear drawer again.

'Caleb. You're ruining it.'

'How? It was fine to start with!' He jams his shirt into the waist of his jeans, tightens his belt again. 'I like my socks the way they are,' Caleb says firmly. For a moment he looks as if he is going to add to that, but then shakes his head and runs down the stairs. Shortly afterward, I see him through the window, walking in the bright, cold sun.

I open the drawer and remove the orphan socks. Then the torn shirt. It will take him weeks to notice the changes, and one day he will thank me.

'Oh, my God,' I cry, glancing out the window at the unfamiliar car that pulls up to the curb. A woman gets out – pixie-small, with a dark cap of hair and her arms wrapped tight against the cold.

'What?' Caleb runs into the room at my exclamation. 'What's the matter?'

'Nothing. Absolutely nothing!' I throw open the door and smile widely at Marcella. 'I can't believe you're here!'

'Surprise,' she says, and hugs me. 'How are you doing?' She tries not to look, but I see it – the way her eyes dart down to try and find my electronic bracelet.

'I'm . . . well, I'm great right now. I certainly never expected you to bring me my report in person.'

Marcella shrugs. 'I figured you might enjoy the company. And I hadn't been back home for a while. I missed it.'

'Liar,' I laugh, pulling her into the house, where Caleb and Nathaniel are watching with curiosity. 'This is Marcella Wentworth. She used to work at the state lab, before she bailed on us to join the private sector.'

I'm positively beaming. It's not that Marcella and I are so very close; it's just that these days, I don't get to see that many people. Patrick comes, from time to time. And there's my family, of course. But most of my friends are colleagues, and after the revocation hearing, they're keeping their distance.

'You up here on business or pleasure?' Caleb asks.

Marcella glances at me, unsure of what she should say.

'I asked Marcella to take a look at the DNA test.'

Caleb's smile fades just the slightest bit, so that only if you know him as well as I do would you even catch the dimming. 'You know what? Why don't I take Nathaniel out, so that you two can catch up?'

After they leave, I lead Marcella into the kitchen. We talk about the temperature in Virginia at this time of year, and when we had our first frost. I make us iced tea. Then, when I can stand it no longer, I sit down across from her. 'It's good news, isn't it? The DNA, it's a match?'

'Nina, did you notice anything when you read the medical file?'

'I didn't bother, actually.'

Marcella draws a circle on the table with her finger. 'Father Szyszynski had chronic myeloid leukemia.'

'Good,' I say flatly. 'I hope he was suffering. I hope he puked his insides out every time he got chemotherapy.'

'He wasn't getting chemo. He had a bone marrow transplant about seven years ago. His leukemia was in remission. For all intents and purposes, he was cured.'

I stiffen a little. 'Is this your way of telling me I ought to feel guilty for killing a man who was a cancer survivor?'

'No. It's . . . well, there's something about the treatment of leukemia that factors into DNA analysis. Basically, to cure it, you need to get new blood. And the way that's done is via bone marrow transplant, since bone marrow is what makes blood. After a few months, your old bone marrow has been replaced completely by the donor's bone marrow. Your old blood is gone, and the leukemia with it.' Marcella looks up at me. 'You follow?'

'So far.'

'Your body can use this new blood, because it's healthy. But it's not your blood, and at the DNA level, it doesn't look like your blood used to. Your skin cells, your saliva, your semen – the DNA in those will be what you were born with, but the DNA in your new blood comes from your donor.' Marcella puts her hand on top of mine. 'Nina, the lab results were accurate. The DNA in Father Szyszynski's blood sample matched the semen in your son's underwear. But the DNA in Father Szyszynski's blood isn't really his.'

'No,' I say. 'No, this isn't the way it works. I was just explaining it the other day to Caleb. You can get DNA from any cell in your body. That's why you can use a blood sample to match a semen sample.'

'Ninety-nine point nine percent of the time, yes. But this is a very, very specific exception.' She shakes her head. 'I'm sorry, Nina.'

My head swings up. 'You mean . . . he's still alive?'

She doesn't have to answer.

I have killed the wrong man.

After Marcella leaves, I pace like a lion in a cage of my own making. My hands are shaking; I can't seem to get warm. What have I done? I killed a man who was innocent. A *priest*. A person who came to comfort me when my world cracked apart; who loved children, Nathaniel included. I killed a man who fought cancer and won, who deserved a long life. I committed murder and I can no longer even justify my actions to myself.

I have always believed there is a special place in Hell for the worst ones – the serial killers, the rapists who target kids, the sociopaths who would just as soon lie as cut your throat for the ten dollars in your wallet. And even when I have not secured convictions for them, I tell myself that eventually, they will get what's coming to them.

So will I.

And the reason I know this is because even though I cannot find the strength to stand up; even though I want to scratch at myself until this part of me has been cut away in ribbons, there is another part of me that is thinking: *He is still out there*.

I pick up the phone to call Fisher. But then I hang it up. He needs to hear this; he could very well find out by himself. But I don't know how it will play in my trial, yet. It could make the prosecution more sympathetic, since their victim is a true victim. Then again, an insanity defense is an insanity defense. It doesn't matter if I killed Father Szyszynski or the judge or every spectator in that courtroom – if I were insane at the time, I still wouldn't be guilty.

In fact, this might make me look crazier.

I sit down at the kitchen table and bury my face in my hands. The doorbell rings and suddenly Patrick is in the kitchen, too big for it, frantic from the message I've left on his beeper. 'What?' he demands, absorbing in a single glance my position, and the quiet of the household. 'Did something happen to Nathaniel?'

It is such a loaded question, that I can't help it – I start to laugh. I laugh until my stomach cramps, until I cannot catch my breath, until tears stream from my eyes and I realize I am sobbing. Patrick's hands are on my shoulders, my forearms, my waist, as if the thing that has broken inside me might be as simple as a bone. I wipe my nose on the back of my sleeve and force myself to meet his gaze. 'Patrick,' I whisper, 'I screwed up. Father Szyszynski . . . he didn't . . . he wasn't –'

He calms me down and makes me tell him everything. When I finish, he stares at me for a full thirty seconds before he speaks. 'You're kidding,' Patrick says. 'You shot the wrong guy?'

He doesn't wait for an answer, just gets up and starts to pace. 'Nina, wait a second. Things get screwed up in labs; it's happened before.'

I grab onto this lifeline. 'Maybe that's it. Some medical mistake.'

'But we had an ID before we ever had the semen evidence.' Patrick shakes his head. 'Why would Nathaniel have said his name?'

Time can stop, I know that now. It is possible to feel one's heart cease beating, to sense the blood hover in one's veins. And to have the awful, overwhelming sense that one is trapped in this moment, and there is just no way out of it. 'Tell me again.' My words spill like stones. 'Tell me what he told you.'

Patrick turns to me. 'Father Glen,' he replies. 'Right?'

*   *   *

Nathaniel remembers feeling dirty, so dirty that he thought he could take a thousand showers and still need to clean himself again. And the thing of it was, the dirty part of him was under his skin; he would have to rub himself raw before it was gone.

It burned down *there*, and even Esme wouldn't come near him. She purred and then hopped onto the big wooden desk, staring. *This is your fault,* she was saying. Nathaniel tried to get his pants, but his hands were like clubs, unable to pick up anything. His underwear, when he finally managed to grab it, was all wet, which made no sense because Nathaniel hadn't had an accident, he just knew it. But the priest had been looking at his underpants, holding them. He'd liked the baseball mitts.

Nathaniel didn't want to wear them again, ever.

'We can fix that,' the priest said, in a voice soft as a pillow, and he disappeared for a moment. Nathaniel counted to thirty-five, and then did it again, because that was as high as he could go. He wanted to leave. He wanted to hide under the desk or in the file cabinet. But he needed underpants. He couldn't get dressed without them, they came first. That was what his mom said when he forgot sometimes, and she made him go upstairs to put them on.

The priest came back with a baby pair, not like his dad's, which looked like shorts. He'd gotten these, Nathaniel was sure, from the big box that held all the greasy coats and smelly sneakers people had left behind in the church. *How could you leave without your sneakers, and never notice?* Nathaniel always had wanted to know. For that matter, how could you forget your underpants?

These were clean and had Spiderman on them. They were too tight, but Nathaniel didn't care. 'Let me take the other pair,' the priest said. 'I'll wash them and give them back.'

Nathaniel shook his head. He pulled on his sweatpants and tucked the boxers into the kangaroo part of his sweatshirt, turning the icky side so that he didn't have to touch it. He felt the priest pet his hair and he went perfectly still, like granite, with the same thick, straight feelings inside.

'Do you need me to walk you back?'

Nathaniel didn't answer. He waited until the priest had picked up Esme and left; then he walked down the hall to the boiler room. It was creepy inside – no light switch, and cobwebs, and once even the skeleton of a mouse that had died. No one ever went in there, which is why Nathaniel did, and stuffed the bad underwear way behind the big machine that hummed and belched heat.

When Nathaniel went back to his class, Father Glen was still reading the Bible story. Nathaniel sat down, tried to listen. He paid careful attention, even when he felt someone's eyes on him. When he looked up, the other priest was standing in the hallway, holding Esme and smiling. With his free hand he raised a finger to his lips. *Shh. Don't tell.*

That was the moment Nathaniel lost all his words.

The day my son stopped speaking, we had gone to church. Afterward, there was a fellowship coffee – what Caleb liked to call Bible Bribery, a promise of doughnuts in return for your presence at Mass. Nathaniel moved around me as if I were a maypole, turning this way and that as he waited for Father Szyszynski to call the children together to read.

This coffee was a celebration, of sorts – two priests who had come to study at St. Anne's for some sort of Catholic edification were going back to their own congregations. A banner blew from the base of the scarred table, wishing them well. Since we were not regular churchgoers, I had not really noticed the priests doing whatever it was they were supposed to be doing. Once or twice I'd seen one from behind and made the assumption it was Father Szyszynski, only to have the man turn around and prove me wrong.

My son was angry because they had run out of powdered sugar doughnuts. 'Nathaniel,' I said, 'stop pulling on me.'

I'd tugged him off my waist, smiling apologetically at the couple that Caleb was speaking to; acquaintances we had not seen in months. They had no children, although they were our ages, and I imagine that Caleb liked talking to them for the same reason I did – there was that amazing *What if* permeating the conversation, as if Todd and Margaret were a funhouse mirror in which Caleb and I could see who else we might have become, had I never conceived. Todd was talking about their upcoming trip to Greece; how they were chartering a boat to take them from island to island.

Nathaniel, for reasons I could not fathom, sank his teeth into my hand.

I jumped, more shocked than hurt, and grabbed Nathaniel by the wrist. I was caught in that awful limbo of public discipline – a moment when a child has done something truly punishable but escapes without penalty because it isn't politically correct to give him the quick smack on his behind that he deserves. 'Don't you ever do that again,' I said through my teeth, trying for a smile. 'Do you hear me?'

Then I noticed all the other kids hurrying down the stairs after Father Szyszynski, a Pied Piper. 'Go,' I urged. 'You don't want to miss the story.'

Nathaniel buried his face underneath my sweater, his head swelling my belly again, a mock pregnancy. 'Come on. All your friends are going.'

I had to peel his arms from around me, push him in the right direction. Twice he looked back, and twice I had to nod, encouraging him to get a move on. 'I'm sorry,' I said to Margaret, smiling. 'You were talking about Corsica?'

Until now, I did not remember that one of the other priests, the taller one who carried a cat as if it were part of his clerical attire, hurried down the steps after the children. That he caught up to Nathaniel and put his hand on his shoulder with the comfort of someone who had done it before.

Nathaniel said his name.

A memory bursts and stings my eyes: *What's the opposite of left?*

White.

What's the opposite of white?

Bwack.

I remember the priest at Father Szyszynski's funeral who had stared through my veil as he handed me the Host, as if my features were familiar. And I remember the sentences printed carefully on a banner beneath the coffee table on that last day, before Nathaniel stopped speaking. PEACE BE WITH YOU, FATHER O'TOOLE. PEACE BE WITH YOU, FATHER GWYNNE.

Tell me what he told you, I'd asked Patrick.

Father Glen.

Maybe that is what Patrick heard. But that isn't how Nathaniel would have said it.

'He wasn't saying Father *Glen*,' Nina murmurs to Patrick. 'He was saying Father *Gwynne*.'

'Yeah, but you know how Nathaniel talks. His *L*'s always come out wrong.'

'Not this time,' Nina sighs. 'This time he was saying it right. Gwen. Gwynne. They're so close.'

'Who the hell is Gwynne?'

Nina rises, her hands splayed through her hair. 'He's the one, Patrick. He's the one who hurt Nathaniel and he's still, he could still be doing this to a hundred other boys, and –' She wilts, stumbling against the wall. Patrick steadies her with one hand, and he is startled to feel her shaking so hard. His first instinct is to reach for her. His second, smarter response is to let her take a step away.

She slides down the side of the refrigerator until she is sitting on the floor. 'He's the bone marrow donor. He *has* to be.'

'Does Fisher know about this yet?' She shakes her head. 'Caleb?'

In that moment, he thinks of a story he read long ago in school, about the start of the Trojan War. Paris was given a choice to be the richest man in the world, the smartest man in the world, or the chance to love another man's wife. Patrick, fool that he is, would make the same mistake. For with her hair in knots, her eyes red and swollen, her sorrow cracked open in her lap, Nina is every bit as beautiful to him now as Helen was back then.

She lifts her face to his. 'Patrick . . . what am I going to do?'

It shocks him into a response. 'You,' Patrick says clearly, 'are not going to *do* anything. You are going to sit in this house because you're on trial for a man's murder.' When she opens her mouth to argue, Patrick holds up his hand. 'You've already been locked up once, and look what happened to Nathaniel. What do you think's going to happen to him if you walk out that door for more vigilante justice, Nina? The only way you can keep him safe is to stay with him. Let me . . .' He hesitates, knowing that on the edge of this cliff, the only way out is to retreat, or to jump. 'Let me take care of it.'

She knows exactly what he has just vowed. It means going against his department, going against his own code of ethics. It means turning his back on the system, like Nina has. And it means facing the consequences. Like Nina. He sees the wonder in her face, and the spark that lets him know how tempted she is to take him up on his offer. 'And risk losing your job? Going to jail?' she says. 'I can't let you do something that stupid.'

What makes you think I haven't already? Patrick doesn't say the words aloud, but he doesn't have to. He crouches down and puts his hand on Nina's knee. Her hand comes up to cover his. And he sees it in her eyes: She *knows* how he feels about her, she has always known. But this is the first time she has come close to admitting it.

'Patrick,' she says quietly, 'I think I've already ruined the lives of enough people I love.'

When the door bursts open and Nathaniel tumbles into the kitchen on a whirl of cold air, Patrick comes to his feet. The boy smells of popcorn and is carrying a stuffed frog inside his winter coat. 'Guess what,' he says. 'Daddy took me to the arcade.'

'You're a lucky guy,' Patrick answers, and even to his own ears, his voice sounds weak. Caleb comes in, then, and closes the door behind him. He looks from Patrick to Nina, and smiles uncomfortably. 'I thought you were visiting with Marcella.'

'She had to go. She was meeting someone else. As she was leaving, Patrick stopped by.'

'Oh.' Caleb rubs the back of his neck. 'So . . . what did she say?'

'Say?'

'About the DNA.'

Before Patrick's very eyes, Nina changes. She flashes a polished smile at her husband. 'It's a match,' she lies. 'A perfect match.'

From the moment I step outside, the world is magic. Air cold enough to make my nostrils stick together; a sun that trembles like a cold yolk; a sky so wide and blue that I cannot keep it all in my eyes. Inside smells different from outside, but you don't notice until one of them is taken away from you.

I am on my way to Fisher's office, so my electronic bracelet has been deactivated. Being outside is so glorious that it almost supersedes the secret I am hiding. As I slow for a stoplight I see the Salvation Army man swinging his bell, his bucket swaying gently. This is the season of charity; surely there will be some left for me.

Patrick's offer swims through my mind like smoke, making it difficult to see clearly. He is the most moral, upstanding man I know – he would not have offered lightly to become my one-man posse. Of course, I cannot let him do this. But I also can't stop hoping that maybe he will ignore me and do it anyway. And immediately, I hate myself for even thinking such a thing.

I tell myself, too, that I don't want Patrick to go after Gwynne for another reason, although it is one I will admit only in the darkest corners of the night: Because I want to be the one. Because this was *my* son, *my* grievance, *my* justice to mete out.

When did I become this person – a woman who has the capacity to commit murder, to want to murder again, to get what she wants without caring who she destroys in the process?

Was this always a part of me, buried, waiting? Maybe there is a seed of malfeasance even in the most honest of people – like Patrick – that requires a certain combination of circumstances to bloom. In most of us, then, it lies dormant forever. But for others, it blossoms. And once it does, it takes over like loosestrife, choking out rational thought, killing compassion.

So much for Christmas spirit.

Fisher's office is decorated for the holidays too. Swaths of garland drape the fireplace; there is mistletoe hanging square over the secretary's desk. Beside the coffee urn sits a jug of hot mulled cider. While I wait for my attorney to retrieve me, I run my hand over the leather cushion of the couch, simply for the novelty of touching something other than the old sage chenille sofa in my living room at home.

What Patrick said about labs making mistakes has stayed with me. I will not tell Fisher about the bone marrow tranpslant, not until I know for sure that Marcella's explanation is right. There is no reason to believe that Quentin Brown will dig up this obscure glitch about DNA; so there is no reason to trouble Fisher yet with information he might never need to know.

'Nina.' Fisher strides toward me, frowning. 'You're losing weight.'

'It's called prisoner-of-war chic.' I fall into step beside him, measuring the dimensions of this hall and that alcove, simply because they are unfamiliar to me. In his office, I stare out the window, where the fingers of bare branches rap a tattoo against the glass.

Fisher catches the direction of my gaze. 'Would you like to go outside?' he asks quietly.

It is freezing, nearly zero. But I am not in the habit of handing back gifts. 'I would love that.'

So we walk in the parking lot behind the law offices, the wind kicking up small tornadoes of brown leaves. Fisher holds a stack of papers in his gloved hands. 'We've gotten the state's psychiatric evaluation back. You didn't quite answer his questions directly, did you?'

'Oh, come on. *Do you know the role of a judge in the courtroom?* For God's sake.'

A small grin plays over Fisher's mouth. 'All the same, he found you competent and sane at the time of the offense.'

I stop walking. What about now? Is it crazy to want to finish the job once you've found out you didn't succeed the first time? Or is that the sanest thing in the world?

'Don't worry. I think we can chew this guy up and rip his report to shreds – but I also would like a forensic shrink to say you were insane then, and aren't now. The last thing I want is a jury thinking you're still a threat.'

But I am. I imagine shooting Father Gwynne, getting it right this time. Then I turn to Fisher, my face perfectly blank. 'Who do you want to use?'

'How about Sidwell Mackay?'

'We joke about him in the office,' I say. 'Any prosecutor can get through him in five minutes flat.'

'Peter Casanoff?'

I shake my head. 'Pompous windbag.'

Together we turn our backs to the wind, trying to make a very logical decision about whom we can find to call me insane. Maybe this will not be so difficult after all. What rational woman still sees the wrong man's blood on her hands every time she looks down, but spends an hour in the shower imagining how she might kill the *right* man?

'All right,' Fisher suggests. 'How about O'Brien, from Portland?'

'I've called him a couple of times. He seems all right, maybe a little squirmy.'

Fisher nods in agreement. 'He's going to come off like an academic, and I think that's what you need, Nina.'

I offer him my most complacent smile. 'Well, Fisher. You're the boss!'

He gives me a guarded look, then hands over the psychiatric report. 'This is the one the state sent. You need to remember what you told him before you go see O'Brien.'

So defense attorneys *do* ask their clients to memorize what they said to the state psychiatrist.

'We've got Judge Neal coming down, by the way.'

I cringe. 'Oh, you've got to be kidding.'

'Why?'

'He's supposed to be incredibly gullible.'

'How lucky for you, then, that you're a defendant,' Fisher says dryly. 'Speaking of which . . . I don't believe we're going to put you on the stand.'

'I wouldn't expect you to, after two psychiatrists testify.' But I am thinking, *I cannot take the stand now, not knowing what I know.*

Fisher stops walking and faces me. 'Before you start telling me how you think your defense ought to be handled, Nina, I want to remind you you're looking at insanity from a prosecutor's perspective, and I —'

'You know, Fisher,' I interrupt, glancing at my watch, 'I can't really talk about this today.'

'Is the coach turning into a pumpkin?'

'I'm sorry. I just can't.' My eyes slide away from his.

'You can't put it off forever. Your trial will start in January, and I'll be gone over the holidays with my family.'

'Let me get examined first,' I bargain. 'Then we can sit down.'

Fisher nods. I think of O'Brien, of whether I can convince him of my insanity. I wonder if, by then, it will be an act.

For the first time in a decade, Quentin takes a long lunch. No one will notice at the DA's office; they barely tolerate his presence, and in his absence, probably dance on the top of his desk. He checks the directions he's downloaded from the computer and swings his car into the parking lot of the high school. Teens sausaged into North Face jackets give him cursory glances as he passes. Quentin walks right through the middle of a hackeysack game without breaking stride, and continues around the back of the school.

There is a shoddy football stadium, an equally shoddy track, and a basketball court. Gideon is doing an admirable job of guarding some pansy-ass center six inches shorter than him. Quentin puts his hands into the pockets of his overcoat and watches his son steal the ball and shoot an effortless three-pointer.

The last time his son had picked up the phone to get in touch, he'd been calling from jail, busted for possession. And although it cost Quentin plenty of snide comments about nepotism, he'd gotten Gideon's sentence transmuted to a rehab facility. That hadn't been good enough for Gideon, though, who'd wanted to be released scot-free. 'You're no use as a father,' he'd told Quentin. 'I should have known you'd be no use as a lawyer, either.'

Now, a year later, Gideon high-fives another player and then turns around to see Quentin watching. 'Shit, man,' he mutters. 'Time.' The other kids fall to the sidelines, sucking on water bottles and shrugging off layers of clothes. Gideon approaches, arms crossed. 'You come here to make me piss in some cup?'

Shrugging, Quentin says, 'No, I came to see you. To talk.'

'I got nothing to say to you.'

'That's surprising,' Quentin responds, 'since I have sixteen years' worth.'

'Then what's another day?' Gideon turns back toward the game. 'I'm busy.'

'I'm sorry.'

The words make the boy pause. 'Yeah, right,' he murmurs. He storms back to the basketball court, grabbing the ball and spinning it in the air – to impress Quentin, maybe? 'Let's go, let's go!' he calls, and the others rally around him. Quentin walks off. 'Who was that, man?' he hears one of the boys ask Gideon. And Gideon's response, when he thinks Quentin is too far away to hear: 'Some guy who needed directions.'

From the window of the doctor's office at Dana-Farber, Patrick can see the ragtag edge of Boston. Olivia Bessette, the oncologist listed on Father Szyszynski's medical reports, has turned out to be considerably younger than Patrick expected – not much older than Patrick himself. She sits with her hands folded, her curly hair pulled into a sensible bun, one rubber-soled white clog tapping lightly on the floor. 'Leukemia only affects the blood cells,' she explains, 'and chronic myeloid leukemia tends to have an onset in patients in their forties and fifties – although I've had some cases with patients in their twenties.'

Patrick wonders how you sit on the edge of a hospital bed and tell someone they are not going to live. It is not that different, he imagines, from knocking on a door in the middle of the night and informing a parent that his son has been killed in a drunk driving accident. 'What happens to the blood cells?' he asks.

'Blood cells are all programmed to die, just like we are. They start out at a baby stage, then grow up to be a little more functional, and by the time they get spit out of the bone marrow they are adult cells. By then, white cells should be able to fight infection on your behalf, red blood cells should be able to carry oxygen, and platelets should be able to clot your blood. But if you have leukemia, your cells never mature . . . and they never die. So you wind up with a proliferation of white cells that don't work, and that overrun all your other cells.'

Patrick is not really going against Nina's wishes, being here. All he's doing is clarifying what they know – not taking it a step farther. He secured this appointment on a ruse, pretending that he is working on behalf of the assistant attorney general. Mr. Brown, Patrick explained, has the burden of proof. Which means they need to be a hundred percent sure that Father Szyszynski didn't drop dead of leukemia the moment that his assailant pulled out a gun. Could Dr. Bessette, his former oncologist, offer any opinions?

'What does a bone marrow transplant do?' Patrick asks.

'Wonders, if it works. There are six proteins on all of our cells, human leukocyte antigens, or HLA. They help our bodies recognize you as you, and me as me. When you're looking for a bone marrow donor, you're hoping for all six of these proteins to match yours. In most cases, this means siblings, half-siblings, maybe a cousin – relatives seem to have the lowest instance of rejection.'

'Rejection?' Patrick asks.

'Yes. In essence, you're trying to convince your body that the donor cells are actually yours, because you have the same six proteins on them. If you can't do that, your immune system will reject the bone marrow transplant, which leads to Graft Versus Host disease.'

'Like a heart transplant.'

'Exactly. Except this isn't an organ. Bone marrow is harvested from the pelvis, because it's the big bones in your body that make blood. Basically, we put the donor to sleep and then stick needles into his hips about 150 times on each side, suctioning out the early cells.'

He winces, and the doctor smiles a little. 'It *is* painful. Being a bone marrow donor is a very selfless thing.'

Yeah, this guy was a fucking altruist, Patrick thinks.

'Meanwhile, the patient with leukemia has been taking immunosuppressants. The week before the transplant, he's given enough chemotherapy to kill all the blood cells in his body. It's timed this way, so that his bone marrow is empty.'

'You can live like that?'

'You're at huge risk for infection. The patient still has his own living blood cells . . . he's just not making any new ones. Then he gets the donor marrow, through a simple IV. It takes about two hours, and we don't know how, but the cells manage to find their way to the bone marrow in his own body and start growing. After about a month, his bone marrow has been entirely replaced by his donor's.'

'And his blood cells would have the donor's six proteins, that HLA stuff?' Patrick asks.

'That's right.'

'How about the donor's DNA?'

Dr. Bessette nods. 'Yes. In all respects, his blood is really someone else's. He's just fooling his body into believing it's truly his.'

Patrick leans forward. 'But if it takes – if the cancer goes into remission – does the patient's body start making his own blood again?'

'No. If it did, we'd consider it a rejection of the graft, and the leukemia would return. We *want* the patient to keep producing his donor's blood forever.' She taps the file on her desk. 'In Glen Szyszynski's case, five years after the transplant, he was given a clean bill of health. His new bone marrow was working quite well, and the chance of a recurrence of leukemia was less than ten percent.' Dr. Bessette nods. 'I think the prosecution can safely say that however the priest died, it wasn't of leukemia.'

Patrick smiles at her. 'Guess it felt good to have a success story.'

'It always does. Father Szyszynski was lucky to have found a perfect match.'

'A perfect match?'

'That's what we call it when a donor's HLA corresponds to all six of the patient's HLA.'

Patrick takes a quick breath. 'Especially when they're not related.'

'Oh,' Dr. Bessette says. 'But that wasn't the case here. Father Szyszynski and his donor were half-brothers.'

Francesca Martine came to the Maine State Lab by way of New Hampshire, where she'd been working as a DNA scientist until something better came along. That something turned out *not* to be the ballistics expert who broke her heart. She moved north, nursing her wounds, and discovered what she'd always known – safety came in gels and Petri dishes, and numbers never hurt you.

That said, numbers also couldn't explain the visceral reaction she has the minute she first meets Quentin Brown. On the phone, she imagined him like all the other state drones – harried and underpaid, with skin a sickly shade of gray. But from the moment he walks into her lab, she cannot take her eyes off him. He is striking, certainly, with his excessive height and his mahogany complexion, but Frankie knows that isn't the attraction. She feels a pull between them, magnetism honed by the common experience of being different. She is not black, but she's often been the only woman in the room with an IQ of 220.

Unfortunately, if she wants Quentin Brown to study her closely, she'll have to assume the shape of a forensic lab report. 'What was it that made you look at this twice?' Frankie asks.

He narrows his eyes. 'How come you're asking?'

'Curiosity. It's pretty esoteric stuff for the prosecution.'

Quentin hesitates, as if wondering whether to confide in her. *Oh, come on,* Frankie thinks. *Loosen up.* 'The defense asked to take a look at it, specifically. Immediately. And it didn't seem to merit that kind of request. I don't see how the DNA results here make a difference for us *or* for them.'

Frankie crosses her arms. 'The reason they were interested isn't because of the lab report I issued. It's because of what's in the medical files.'

'I'm not following you.'

'You know the way the DNA report says that the chances of randomly selecting an unrelated individual who matches this genetic material are one in six billion?'

Quentin nods.

'Well,' Frankie explains, 'you just found the one.'

It costs approximately two thousand dollars of taxpayer money to exhume a body. 'No,' Ted Poulin says flatly. As the attorney general of Maine, and Quentin's boss, that ought to be that. But Quentin isn't going to give up without a fight, not this time.

He grips the receiver of the phone. 'The DNA scientist at the state lab says we can do the test on tooth pulp.'

'Quentin, it doesn't matter for the prosecution. She killed him. Period.'

'She killed a guy who molested her son. I have to change him from a sexual predator into a victim, Ted, and this is the way to do it.'

There is a long silence on the other end. Quentin runs his fingertips along the grain of wood on Nina Frost's desk. He does this over and over, as if he is rubbing an amulet.

'There's no family to fight it?'

'The mother gave consent already.'

Ted sighs. 'The publicity is going to be outrageous.'

Leaning back in his chair, Quentin grins. 'Let me take care of it,' he offers.

Fisher storms into the district attorney's office, uncharacteristically flustered. He has been there before, of course, but who knows where the hell they've ensconced Quentin Brown while he's prosecuting Nina's case. He has just opened up his mouth to ask the secretary when Brown himself walks out of the small kitchen area, carrying a cup of coffee. 'Mr. Carrington,' he says pleasantly. 'Looking for me?'

Fisher withdraws the paperwork he's received that morning from his breast pocket. The Motion to Exhume. 'What is this?'

Quentin shrugs. 'You must know. You're the one who asked for the DNA records to be rushed over, after all.'

Fisher has no idea why, in fact. The DNA records were rushed over at Nina's behest, but he'll be damned if he lets Brown know this. 'What are you trying to do, counselor?'

'A simple test that proves the priest your client killed wasn't the same guy who abused her kid.'

Fisher steels his gaze. 'I'll see you in court tomorrow morning,' he says, and by the time he gets into his car to drive to Nina's home, he has begun to understand how an ordinary human might become frustrated enough to kill.

'Fisher!' I say, and I'm actually delighted to see the man. This amazes me – either I have truly bedded down with the Enemy, or I've been under house arrest too long. I throw open the door to let him in, and realize that he is furious. 'You knew,' he says, his voice calm and that much more frightening for all its control. He hands me a motion filed by the assistant attorney general.

My insides begin to quiver; I feel absolutely sick. With tremendous effort I swallow and meet Fisher's eye – better to come clean eventually, than to not come clean at all. 'I didn't know if I should tell you. I didn't know if the information was going to be important to my case.'

'That's *my* job!' Fisher explodes. 'You are paying me for a reason, Nina, and it's because you know on some level, although apparently not a conscious one, that I am qualified to get you acquitted. In fact, I'm more qualified to do that than any other attorney in Maine . . . *including* you.'

I look away. At heart, I am a prosecutor, and prosecutors don't tell defense attorneys everything. They dance around each other, but the prosecutor is always the one who leads, leaving the other lawyer to find his footing.

Always.

'I don't trust you,' I say finally.

Fisher fields this like a blow. 'Well, then. We're even.'

We stare at each other, two great dogs with their teeth bared. Fisher turns away, angry, and in that moment I see my face in the reflection of the window. The truth is, I'm not a prosecutor anymore. I'm not capable of defending myself. I'm not sure I even want to.

'Fisher,' I call out when he is halfway out the door. 'How badly will this hurt me?'

'I don't know, Nina. It doesn't make you look any less crazy, but it's also going to strip you of public sympathy. You're not a hero anymore, killing a pedophile. You're a hothead who knocked off an innocent man – a *priest*, no-less.' He shakes his head. 'You're the prime example of why we have laws in the first place.'

In his eyes, I see what's coming – the fact that I am no longer a mother doing what she had to for her child, but simply a reckless woman who thought she knew better than anyone else. I wonder if camera flashes feel different on your skin when they capture you as a criminal, instead of a victim. I wonder if parents who once fathomed my actions – even if they disagreed with them – will look at me now and cross the street, just in case faulty judgment is contagious.

Fisher exhales heavily. 'I can't keep them from exhuming the body.'

'I know.'

'And if you keep hiding information from me, it *will* hurt you, because I won't know how to work with it.'

I duck my head. 'I understand.'

He raises his hand in farewell. I stand on the porch and watch him go, hugging myself against the wind. When his car heads down the street, its exhaust freezes, a sigh caught in the cold. With a deep breath I turn to find Caleb standing not three feet behind me. 'Nina,' he says, 'what was that?'

Pushing past him, I shake my head, but he grabs my arm and will not let me go. 'You lied to me. *Lied* to me!'

'Caleb, you don't understand –'

He grasps my shoulders and shakes me once, hard. 'What is it I don't understand? That you killed an innocent man? Jesus, Nina, when is it going to hit you?'

Once, Nathaniel asked me how the snow disappears. It is like that in Maine – instead of melting over time, it takes one warm day for drifts that are thigh-high in the morning to evaporate by the time the sun goes down. Together we went to the library to learn the answer – *sublimation*, the process by which something solid vanishes into thin air.

With Caleb's hands holding me up, I fall apart. I let out everything I have been afraid to set free for the past week. Father Szyszynski's voice fills my head; his face swims in front of me. 'I know,' I sob. 'Oh, Caleb, I know. I thought I could do this. I thought I could take care of it. But I made a mistake.' I fold myself into the wall of his chest, waiting for his arms to come around me.

They don't.

Caleb takes a step back, shoves his hands in his pockets. His eyes are red-rimmed, haunted. 'What's the mistake, Nina? That you killed a man?' he asks hoarsely. 'Or that you didn't?'

'It's a shame, is what it is,' the church secretary says. Myra Lester shakes her head, then hands Patrick the cup of tea she's made him. 'Christmas Mass just around the corner, and us without a chaplain.'

Patrick knows that the best road to information is not always the one that's paved and straightforward, but the one that cuts around back and is most often forgotten as an access route. He also knows, from his long-lapsed days of growing up Catholic, that the collective memory – and gossip mill – most often is the church secretary. So he offers his most concerned expression, the one that always got him a pinch on the cheek from his elderly aunts. 'The congregation must be devastated.'

'Between the rumors flying around about Father Szyszynski, and the way he was killed – well, it's most un-Christian, that's all I have to say about it.' She sniffs, then settles her considerable bottom on a wing chair in the rectory office.

He would like to have assumed a different persona, now – a newcomer to Biddeford, for example, checking out the parish – but he has already been seen in his capacity as a detective, during the sexual abuse investigation. 'Myra,' Patrick says, then looks up at her and smiles. 'I'm sorry. I meant Mrs. Lester, of course.'

Her cheeks flame, and she titters. 'Oh, no, you feel free to call me whatever you like, Detective.'

'Well, Myra, I've been trying to get in touch with the priests that were visiting St. Anne's shortly before Father Szyszynski's death.'

'Oh, yes, they were lovely. Just lovely! That Father O'Toole, he had the most scrumptious Southern accent. Like peach schnapps, that's what I thought of every time he spoke . . . Or was that Father Gwynne?'

'The prosecution's hounding me. I don't suppose you'd have any idea where I could find them?'

'They've gone back to their own congregations, of course.'

'Is there a record of that? A forwarding address, maybe?'

Myra frowns, and a small pattern of lines in the shape of a spider appears on her forehead. 'I'm sure there must be. Nothing in this church goes on without me knowing the details.' She walks toward all the ledgers and logs stacked behind her desk. Flipping through the pages of a leather-bound book, she finds an entry and smacks it with the flat of her hand. 'It's right here. Fathers Brendan O'Toole, from St. Dennis's, in Harwich, Massachusetts, and Arthur Gwynne, due to depart this afternoon as per the See of Portland.' Myra scratches her hair with the eraser of a pencil. 'I suppose the other priest could have come from Harwich, too, but that wouldn't explain the peach schnapps.'

'Maybe he moved as a child,' Patrick suggests. 'What's the Sea of Portland?'

'See, *S-E-E.* It's the governing diocese hereabouts in Maine, of course.' She lifts her face to Patrick's. 'They're the ones who sent the priests to us in the first place.'

Midnight, in a graveyard, with an unearthed casket – Patrick can think of a thousand places he'd rather be. But he stands beside the two sweating men who have hauled the coffin from the ground and set it beside Father Szyszynski's resting place, like an altar in the moonlight. He has promised to be Nina's eyes, Nina's legs. And if necessary, Nina's hands.

They are all wearing Hazmat suits – Patrick and Evan Chao, Fisher Carrington and Quentin Brown, Frankie Martine, and the medical examiner, Vern Potter. In the black circle beyond their flashlights, an owl screams.

Vern jumps a foot. 'Holy sweet Jesus. Any minute now I keep expecting the zombies to get up from behind the tombstones. Couldn't we have done this in broad daylight?'

'I'll take zombies over the press any day,' Evan Chao mutters. 'Get it over with, Vern.'

'Hokey-dokey.' The medical examiner takes a crowbar and pries open Father Szyszynski's casket. The foul air that puffs from its insides has Patrick gagging. Fisher Carrington turns away and holds a handkerchief to his face mask. Quentin walks off briskly to vomit behind a tree.

The priest does not look all that different. Half of his face is still missing. His arms lie at his sides. His skin, gray and wrinkled, has not yet decomposed. 'Open wide,' Vern murmurs, and he ratchets down the jaw, reaches inside, and pulls out a molar with a pair of tooth pliers.

'Get me a couple wisdom teeth, too,' Frankie says. 'And hair.'

Evan nods to Patrick, calling him aside. 'You believe this?' he asks.

'Nope.'

'Maybe the bastard's just getting what he deserves.'

Patrick is stunned for a moment, until he remembers: There is no reason to believe Evan would know what Patrick knows – that Father Szyszynski was innocent. 'Maybe,' he manages.

A few minutes later, Vern hands a jar and an envelope to Frankie. Quentin hurries away with her, Fisher close behind. The ME closes the casket and turns to the grave diggers. 'You can put him back now,' he instructs, then turns to Patrick. 'On your way out?'

'In a sec.' Patrick watches Vern go, then turns to the grave, where the two big men have dropped the coffin again and are starting to shovel dirt over it again. He waits until they are finished, because he thinks someone should.

By the time Patrick gets to the Biddeford District Court, he wonders whether Father Arthur Gwynne ever existed at all. He's driven from the graveyard, where the body was being exhumed, to the Catholic See in Portland . . . where he was told by the chancellor that their records only showed Father O'Toole coming to visit Biddeford. If Father Gwynne was at the church too, it might have been a personal connection to the Biddeford chaplain that brought him there. Which, of course, is exactly what Patrick needs to confirm.

The probate clerk hands him a copy of the priest's Last Will and Testament, which became a public record a month ago, when it was filed with the court. The document is simple to a fault. Father Szyszynski left fifty percent of his estate to his mother. And the rest to the executor of his will: Arthur Gwynne, of Belle Chasse, Louisiana.

Enamel is the strongest material naturally found in the human body, which makes it a bitch to crack open. To this end, Frankie soaks the extracted molar in liquid nitrogen for about five minutes, because frozen, it is more likely to shatter. 'Hey, Quentin,' she says, grinning at the attorney, waiting impatiently. 'Can you break a dollar?'

He fishes in his pockets, but shakes his head. 'Sorry.'

'No problem.' She takes a buck from her wallet and floats it in the liquid nitrogen, then pulls it out, smashes it on the counter, and laughs. 'I can.'

He sighs. 'Is this why it takes so long to get results from the state lab?'

'Hey, I'm letting you cut in line, aren't I?' Frankie removes the tooth from its bath and sets it in a sterile mortar and pestle. She grinds at it, pounding harder and harder, but the tooth will not crack.

'Mortar and pestle?' Quentin asks.

'We used to use the ME's skull saw, but we had to get a new blade every time. Plus, the cutting edge gets too hot, and denatures the DNA.' She glances at him over her protective goggles. 'You don't want me to screw up, do you?' Another whack, but the tooth remains intact. 'Oh, for God's sake.' Frankie plucks a second tooth out of the liquid nitrogen. 'Come with me. I want to get this over with.'

She double-bags the tooth in Ziplocs and leads Quentin to the stairwell, all the way to the basement garage of the laboratory. 'Stand back,' she says, and then squats, setting the bag on the floor. Taking a hammer out of the pocket of her lab coat, Frankie begins to pound, her own jaw aching in sympathy. The tooth shatters on the fourth try, its pieces splintering into the plastic bag.

'Now what?' Quentin asks.

The pulp is brownish, slight . . . but most definitely there. 'Now,' she says, 'you wait.'

Quentin, who is unused to staying up in graveyards all night and then driving to the lab in Augusta, falls asleep on a bank of chairs in the lobby. When he feels a cool hand on the back of his neck, he startles awake, sitting up so quickly he is momentarily dizzy. Frankie stands before him, holding out a report. 'And?' he asks.

'The tooth pulp was chimeric.'

'English?'

Frankie sits down beside him. 'The reason we test tooth pulp is because it has blood cells in it . . . but also tissue cells. For you and me and most people, the DNA in both of those cells will be the same. But if someone gets a bone marrow transplant, they're going to show a mixture of two DNA profiles in their tooth pulp. The first profile will be the DNA they were born with, and that'll be in the tissue cells. The second profile will be the DNA that came from their marrow donor, and will be in the blood cells. In this sample, the suspect's tooth pulp yielded a mixture.'

Quentin frowns at the numbers on the page. 'So –'

'So here's your proof,' Frankie says. 'Somebody else perved that kid.'

After Fisher calls me with the news, I go right into the bathroom and throw up. Again, and again, until there is nothing left in my stomach but the guilt. The truth is, a man was killed by my own hand, a man who deserved no punishment. What does this make me?

I want to shower until I don't feel dirty; I want to strip off my own skin. But the horror is at the heart of me. Cut a gut feeling, watch yourself bleed to death.

Like I watched him.

In the hallway, I brush past Caleb, who has not been speaking to me anyway. There are no more words between us, each one has a charge on it, an ion that might attach to either him or to me and push us farther apart. In my bedroom, I kick off my shoes and crawl fully dressed under the covers. I pull them up over my head; breathe in the same cocoon. If you pass out, and there's still no air, what will happen?

I can't get warm. This is where I will stay, because now any of my decisions may be suspect. Better to do nothing at all, than to take another risk that might change the world.

It's an instinct, Patrick realizes – to want to hurt someone as badly as they've hurt you. There were moments in his career in the military police that his arrests became violent, blood running over his hands that felt like a balm at the time. Now, he understands that the theory can go one step further: It's an instinct to want to hurt someone as badly as they've hurt someone you care about. This is the only explanation he can offer for sitting on a 757 en route from Dallas-Fort Worth to New Orleans.

The question isn't what he would do for Nina. 'Anything,' Patrick would answer, without hesitation. She had expressly warned him away from hunting down Arthur Gwynne, and all of Patrick's actions up to this point could be classified as information-seeking, but even he could not couch the truth, now: He had no reason to fly to Louisiana, if not to meet this man face-to-face.

Even now, he cannot tell himself what is going to happen. He has spent his life guided by principle and rules – in the Navy, as a cop, as an unrequited lover. But rules only work when everyone plays by them. What happens when someone doesn't, and the fallout bleeds right into his life? What's stronger – the need to uphold the law, or the motive to turn one's back on it?

It has been shattering for Patrick to realize that the criminal mind is not all that far away from that of a rational man. It comes down, really, to the power of a craving. Addicts will sell their own bodies for another gram of coke. Arsonists will put their own lives in danger to feel something go up in flames around them. Patrick has always believed, as an officer of the law, he is above this driving need. But what if your obsession has nothing to do with drugs or thrills or money? What if what you want most in the world is to recapture the way life was a week, a month, a year ago – and you are willing to do whatever it takes?

This was Nina's error; she wrongly equated stopping time with turning it backward. And he couldn't even blame her, because he'd made the same mistake, every time he was in her company.

The question Patrick knew he should be asking was not what he would do for Nina . . . but what he *wouldn't*.

The flight attendant pushes the beverage cart like a baby carriage, braking beside Patrick's row. 'What can I get for you?' she asks. Her smile reminds him of Nathaniel's Halloween mask from last year.

'Tomato juice. No ice.'

The man sitting beside Patrick folds his newspaper. 'Tomato juice and vodka,' he says, grinning through his thick Texan drawl. 'Yes, ice.'

They both take a sip of their drinks as the flight attendant moves on. The man glances down at his newspaper and shakes his head. 'Ought to fry the sumbitch,' he mutters.

'Excuse me?'

'Oh, it's this murder case. Y'all must have heard about it . . . there's some fool who wants an eleventh hour pardon from death row because she's found Jesus. Truth is, the governor's afraid to give her the cocktail because she's a woman.'

Patrick has always been in favor of capital punishment. But he hears himself say, 'Seems reasonable.'

'Guess you're one of those Yankee left-wingers,' the man

scoffs. 'Me, I think it don't matter if you've got a pecker or not. You shoot someone in the back of the head at a convenience store, you pay the price. You know?' He shrugs, then finishes his drink. 'You flying out on business or pleasure?'

'Business.'

'Me, too. I'm in sales. Hav-A-Heart traps,' he confides, as if this is privileged information.

'I'm a lawyer with the ACLU,' Patrick lies. 'I'm flying down to plead that woman's case to the governor.'

The salesman goes red in the face. 'Well. I didn't mean no disrespect —'

'Like hell you didn't.'

He folds his newspaper again, and stuffs it into the seat pocket in front of him. 'Even you bleeding hearts can't save them all.'

'One,' Patrick answers. 'That's all I'm hoping for.'

There is a woman wearing my clothes and my skin and my smell but it isn't me. Sin is like ink, it bleeds into a person, coloring, making you someone other than you used to be. And it's indelible. Try as much as you want, you cannot get yourself back.

Words can't pull me back from the edge. Neither can daylight. This isn't something to get over, it is an atmosphere I need to learn to breathe. Grow gills for transgression, take it into my lungs with every gasp.

It is a startling thing. I wonder who this person is, going through the motions of my life. I want to take her hand.

And then I want to push her, hard, off a cliff.

Patrick finds himself peeling off layers of clothing as he walks through the streets of Belle Chasse, Louisiana, past wrought-iron gates and ivy-trellised courtyards. Christmas looks wrong in this climate; the decorations seem to be sweating in the humid heat. He wonders how a Louisiana boy like Glen Szyszynski ever survived so far north.

But he already knows the answer. Growing up among Cajuns and the Creoles wasn't all that far a stretch from tending to the Acadians in his parish. The proof of that rests in his breast pocket, public records copied by a clerk at the Louisiana Vital Records Registry in New Orleans. Arthur Gwynne, born 10/23/43 to Cecilia Marquette Gwynne and her husband, Alexander Gwynne. Four years later, the marriage of Cecelia Marquette Gwynne, widowed, to Teodor Szyszynski. And in 1951, the birth of Glen.

Half-brothers.

Szyszynski's will was last revised in 1994; it is entirely possible that Arthur Gwynne is no longer a member of the Belle Chasse community. But it is a starting point. Priests don't go unnoticed in a predominantly Catholic town; if Gwynne had any contact at all with his neighbors, Patrick knows he can pick up a paper trail and track his whereabouts from there. To this end, there is another clue in his pocket, one ripped from the rear of a phone book. Churches. The largest one is Our Lady of Mercy.

He doesn't let himself think what he will do with the information, once he gets it.

Patrick turns the corner, and the cathedral comes into view. He jogs up the stone steps and enters the nave. Immediately in front of him is a pool of Holy Water. Flickering candles cast waves on the walls, and the reflection from a stained-glass window bleeds a brilliant puddle on the mosaic floor. Above the altar, a cypress carving of Jesus on the cross looms like an omen.

It smells of Catholicism: beeswax and starch and darkness and peace, all of which bring Patrick back to his youth. He finds himself unconsciously making the sign of the cross as he slides into a pew at the rear of the building.

Four women nod their heads in prayer, their faith settling softly around them, like the skirts of Confederate belles. Another sobs quietly into her hands while a priest comforts her in whispers. Patrick waits patiently, running his hands along the bright, polished wood and whistling under his breath.

Suddenly the hair stands up on the back of his neck. Walking along the lip of the pew behind him is a cat. Its tail strokes Patrick on the nape again, and he lets out his breath in a rush. 'You scared the hell out of me,' he murmurs, and then glances at the carving of Jesus. 'The *heck*,' he amends.

The cat blinks at him, then leaps with grace into the arms of the priest who has come up beside Patrick. 'You know better,' the priest scolds.

It takes Patrick a moment to realize the cleric is speaking to his kitten. 'Excuse me. I'm trying to locate a Father Arthur Gwynne.'

'Well.' The man smiles. 'You found me.'

Every time Nathaniel tries to see his mother, she's sleeping. Even when it's light outside; even when it's time for *Franklin* on Nickelodeon. *Leave her alone,* his father says. *It's what she wants.* But Nathaniel doesn't think that's what his mother wants at all. He thinks about how sometimes in the middle of the night he wakes up dreaming of spiders under his skin and screams that don't go away, and the only thing that keeps him from running out of the room is how dark it is and how far it seems from his bed to the door.

'We have to do something,' Nathaniel tells his father, after it has been three days, and his mother is still asleep.

But his father's face squeezes up at the top, like it does when Nathaniel is yelling too loud while he's having his hair washed and the sound bounces around the bathroom. 'There's nothing we *can* do,' he tells Nathaniel.

It's not true. Nathaniel knows this. So when his father goes outside to put the trash cans at the end of the driveway *(Two minutes, Nathaniel . . . you can sit here and be good for two minutes, can't you?)* Nathaniel waits until he can no longer hear the scratch-drag on the gravel and then bolts upstairs to his bedroom. He overturns his garbage can to use as a stool and takes what he needs from his dresser. He twists the knob to his parents' room quietly, tiptoes inside as if the floor is made of cotton.

It takes two tries to turn on the reading lamp near his mother's

side of the bed, and then Nathaniel crawls on top of the covers.
His mother isn't there at all, just the great swollen shape under
the blankets that doesn't even move when he calls her name.
He pokes at it, frowns. Then he pulls away the sheet.

The Thing That Isn't His Mother moans and squints in the
sudden light.

Her hair is wild and matted, like the brown sheep at the
petting zoo. Her eyes look like they've fallen too deep in her
face, and grooves run the length of her mouth. She smells of
sadness. She blinks once at Nathaniel, as if he might be something she remembers but can't quite fish to the front of her
mind. Then she pulls the blankets over her head again and
rolls away from him.

'Mommy?' Nathaniel whispers, because this place cries for
quiet. 'Mommy, I know what you need.'

Nathaniel has been thinking about it, and he remembers what
it felt like to be stuck in a dark, dark place and not be able to
explain it. And he also remembers what she did, back then, for
him. So he takes the sign-language binder he got from Dr.
Robichaud and slips it under the blankets, into his mother's hands.

He holds his breath while her hands trace the edges and
rifle through the pages. There is a sound Nathaniel has never
heard before – like the world opening up at the start of an
earthquake, or maybe a heart breaking – and the binder slips
from beneath the sheets, cracking open onto the floor. Suddenly
the comforter rises like the hinged jaw of a white whale and
he finds himself swallowed whole.

Then he is in the spot where he put the sign-language book,
smack in the middle of her arms. She holds him so tight there
is no room for words between them, spoken or signed. And it
doesn't matter one bit, because Nathaniel understands exactly
what his mother is telling him.

Christ, I think, wincing. *Turn off the lights.*

But Fisher starts laying out papers and briefs on the blankets,
as if it is every day that he conducts meetings with a client too

exhausted to leave her bedroom. Then again, what do I know? Maybe he does.

'Go away,' I moan.

'Bottom line: He had a bone marrow transplant,' Fisher says briskly. 'You shot the wrong priest. So we need to figure out how to use that to our best advantage and get you off.' Before he remembers to check himself, his eyes meet mine, and he cannot hide it: the shock and, yes, distaste of seeing me like this. Unwashed, undressed, uncaring.

Yes, look, Fisher, I think. *Now you don't have to* pretend *I'm crazy.*

I roll onto my side, and some of the papers flutter off the edge of the bed. 'You don't have to play this game with me, Nina,' Fisher sighs. 'You hired me so that you won't go to jail, and goddammit, you're not going to jail.' He pauses, as if he is about to tell me something important, but what he says doesn't matter at all. 'I've already filed the paperwork requesting a jury, but you know, we can waive it at the last minute.' His eyes take in my nightgown, my tangled hair. 'It might be easier to convince one person that . . . that you were insane.'

I pull the covers over my head.

'We got the report back from O'Brien. You did a nice job, Nina. I'll leave it for you to look over . . .'

In the dark under here, I begin to hum, so that I can't hear him.

'Well.'

I stick my fingers in my ears.

'I don't think there's anything else.' I feel a commotion to my left as he gathers his files. 'I'll be in touch after Christmas.' He begins to walk away from me, his expensive shoes striking the carpet like rumors.

I have killed a man; I have killed a man. This has become a part of me, like the color of my eyes or the birthmark on my right shoulder blade. I have killed a man, and nothing I do can take that away.

I pull the covers down from my face just as he reaches the door. 'Fisher,' I say, the first word I've spoken in days.

He turns, smiles.

'I'm taking the stand.'

That smile vanishes. 'No you're not.'

'I am.'

He approaches the bed again. 'If you take the stand, Brown is going to rip you to shreds. If you take the stand, even *I* can't help you.'

I stare at him, unblinking, for a lifetime. 'So?' I say.

'Someone wants to talk to you,' Caleb announces, and he drops the portable phone on the bed. When I don't bother to reach for it, Caleb seems to think twice. 'It's Patrick,' he adds.

Once, on a trip to the beach, I let Nathaniel bury me in the sand. It took so long that the hills enclosing my legs – the spot where he'd started – had dried and hardened. The weight of the beach pressed down on my chest, and I remember feeling claustrophobic as his small hands built a dune around me. When I finally *did* move, I was a Titan, rising from the earth with enough leashed power to topple gods.

Now, I watch my hand crawl across the covers toward the phone, and I cannot stop it. As it turns out, there is one thing strong enough to seduce me away from my careful paralysis and self-pity – the possibility of action. And even though I have looked the consequences right in their yellow-wolf eyes, it turns out I am still addicted. *Hello, my name is Nina, and I need to know where he is.*

'Patrick?' I press the receiver to my ear.

'I found him. Nina, he's in Louisiana. A town called Belle Chasse. He's a priest.'

All my breath leaves my lungs in a rush. 'You arrested him.'

There is a hesitation. 'No.'

As I sit up, the covers fall away. 'Did you . . .' I cannot finish. There is a part of me hoping so hard that he will tell me something horrible, something I desperately want to hear. And there is another part of me hoping that whatever I have turned into has not poisoned him too.

'I talked to the guy. But I couldn't let him know I was onto him, or that I was even from Maine. You remember going through this at the beginning, with Nathaniel – tip off a molester and he's going to run, and we'll never get a confession. Gwynne's even more cagey, because he knows his half-brother was killed due to an allegation of child sexual abuse that he committed himself.' Patrick hesitates. 'So instead I said I was getting married and looking for a church for the ceremony. It was the first thing that came to mind.'

Tears spring to my eyes. He was within Patrick's grasp, and still nothing has happened. 'Arrest him. For God's sake, Patrick, get off this phone and run back there –'

'Nina, stop. I'm not a cop in Louisiana. The crime didn't happen here. I need an arrest warrant in Maine before I can get a fugitive charge lodged against Gwynne in Louisiana, and even then, he might fight extradition.' He hesitates. 'And what do you imagine my boss will say when he finds out I'm using my shield to dig up information about a case that I haven't even been assigned to?'

'But Patrick . . . you *found* him.'

'I know. And he's going to be punished.' There is a silence. 'Just not today.'

He asks me if I am all right, and I lie to him. How can I be all right? I am back where I started. Except now, after I am tried for the murder of an innocent man, Nathaniel will be embroiled in another trial. While I sit in jail, he'll have to face his abuser, drag back the nightmare. Nathaniel will suffer; he will hurt.

Patrick says good-bye, and I hang up the phone. I stare at the receiver in my hand for a minute, rub the edge of the smooth plastic.

The first time, I had much more to lose.

'What are you doing?'

My head pops through the turtleneck to find Caleb standing in the bedroom. 'What does it look like I'm doing?' I button my jeans. Stuff my feet into my clogs.

'Patrick got you out of bed,' he says, and there is a note in his voice that strikes off-chord.

'Patrick gave me information that got me out of bed,' I correct. I try to move around Caleb, but he blocks my exit. 'Please. I have to go somewhere.'

'Nina, you're not going anywhere. The bracelet.'

I look at my husband's face. There are lines on his brow I cannot remember seeing; with no small shock I realize I have put them there.

I owe him this.

So I put my hand on his arm, lead him to the bed, have him sit beside me on the edge. 'Patrick found the name of the bone marrow donor. He's the priest that came to visit St. Anne's this October. The one with the cat. His name is Arthur Gwynne, and he works at a church in Belle Chasse, Louisiana.'

Caleb's face goes pale. 'Why . . . why are you telling me this?'

Because the first time, I acted alone, when I should have at least told you my plans. Because when they ask you in court, you will not have to testify. 'Because,' I say, 'it's not finished yet.'

He reels back. 'Nina. No.' I get up, but he catches my wrist, pulls me up close to his face. My arm, twisted, hurts. 'What are you gonna do? Break your house arrest to go kill another priest? One life sentence isn't enough for you?'

'They have the death penalty in Louisiana,' I shoot back.

My response is a guillotine, severing us. Caleb releases me so quickly I stumble and fall onto the floor. 'Is that what you want?' he asks quietly. 'Are you that selfish?'

'Selfish?' By now I am crying, hard. 'I'm doing this for our son.'

'You're doing this for *yourself*, Nina. If you were thinking of Nathaniel, even a little, you'd concentrate on being his mother. You'd get out of bed and get on with your life and let the legal system deal with Gwynne.'

'The legal system. You want me to wait for the courts to get around to charging this bastard? While he rapes ten, twenty other children? And then wait some more while the governors of our states fight over who gets the honor of holding his trial? And then wait again while Nathaniel testifies against the son of a bitch? And watch Gwynne get a sentence that ends before our son even stops having nightmares about what was done to him?' I draw in a long, shaky breath. 'There's your legal system, Caleb. Is it worth waiting for?'

When he doesn't answer, I get to my feet. 'I'm already going to prison for killing a man. I don't have a life anymore. But Nathaniel *can*.'

'You want your son to grow up without you?' Caleb's voice breaks. 'Let me save you the trouble.'

Standing abruptly, he leaves the bedroom, calling Nathaniel's name. 'Hey, buddy,' I hear him say. 'We're going on an adventure.'

My hands and feet go numb. But I manage to get to Nathaniel's bedroom, and find Caleb haphazardly stuffing clothes into a Batman knapsack. 'What . . . what are you doing?'

'What does it look like I'm doing?' Caleb replies, an echo of my own earlier words.

Nathaniel jumps up and down on his bed. His hair flies to the sides like silk. 'You can't take him away from me.'

Caleb zips shut the bag. 'Why not? You were willing to take yourself away from him.' He turns to Nathaniel, forces a smile. 'You ready?' he asks, and Nathaniel leaps into his outstretched arm.

'Bye, Mommy!' he crows. 'We're on an adventure!'

'I know.' Smiling is hard, with this knot in my throat. 'I heard.'

Caleb carries him past me. There is the thunder of footsteps on the stairs, and the definitive slam of a door. The engine of Caleb's truck, revving and reversing down the driveway. Then it is so quiet I can hear my own misgivings, small susurrations in the air around me.

I sink onto Nathaniel's bed, into sheets that smell of crayons and gingerbread. The fact of the matter is, I cannot leave this house. The moment I do, police cars will come screaming up behind me. I will be arrested before I ever board a plane.

Caleb has succeeded; he's stopped me from doing what I so badly want to.

Because he knows if I do walk out that door now, I won't go after Arthur Gwynne at all. I'll be searching for my son.

Three days later Caleb has not called me. I have tried every hotel and motel in the area, but if he is staying at one, it's not under his own name. It's Christmas Eve, though, and surely they will come back. Caleb is a big one for having holiday traditions, and to this end I have wrapped all of Nathaniel's Christmas presents – ones I've stored in the attic all year. From the dwindling supply of food in the refrigerator I have cooked a chicken and made celery soup; I have set the table with our fancy wedding china.

I have cleaned up, too, because I want Caleb to notice that the moment he walks through the door. Maybe if he sees a difference on the outside, he will understand that I'm different within, too. My hair is coiled into a French twist, and I'm wearing black velvet pants and a red blouse. In my ears are the present Nathaniel gave me last Christmas – little snowman earrings made from Sculpy clay.

And yet, this is all just a surface glaze. My eyes are ringed with circles – I have not slept since they left, as if this is some kind of cosmic punishment for dozing away the days when we were all together. I walk the halls at night, trying to find the spots in the carpet that have been worn down by Nathaniel's running feet. I stare at old photographs. I haunt my own home.

We have no tree, because I wasn't able to go out to chop one down. It's a tradition for us to walk our property the Saturday before Christmas and pick one out as a family. But then, we have not been much of a family this holiday season.

By four P.M. I've lit candles and put on a Christmas CD. I sit with my hands folded in my lap and wait.

It's something I'm working on.

At four-thirty, it begins to snow. I rearrange all of Nathaniel's presents in size order. I wonder if there will be enough of an accumulation for him to sled down the back hill on the Flexible Flyer that stands propped against the wall, festooned with a bow.

Ten minutes later, I hear the heavy chug of a truck coming down the driveway. I leap to my feet, take one last nervous look around, and throw open the door with a bright smile. The UPS man, weary and dusted with snowflakes, stands on my porch with a package. 'Nina Frost?' he asks in a monotone.

I take the parcel as he wishes me a Merry Christmas. Inside, on the couch, I tear it open. A leather-bound desk calendar for the year 2002, stamped on the inner cover with the name of Fisher's law office. HAPPY HOLIDAYS *from Carrington, Whitcomb, Horoby, and Platt, Esqs.* 'This will come in so handy,' I say aloud, 'after I'm sentenced.'

When the stars shyly push through the night sky, I turn off the stereo. I look out the window, watch the driveway get erased by snow.

Even before Patrick got his divorce, he'd sign up to work on Christmas. Sometimes, he even does double shifts. The calls most often bring him to the homes of the elderly, reporting a strange bump or a suspicious car that's disappeared by the time Patrick arrives. What these people want is the company on a night when no one else is alone.

'Merry Christmas,' he says, backing away from the home of Maisie Jenkins, eighty-two years old, a recent widow.

'God bless,' she calls back, and goes into a home as empty as the one that Patrick is about to return to.

He could go visit Nina, but surely Caleb has brought Nathaniel back for the night. No, Patrick wouldn't interrupt that. Instead he gets into his car and drives down the slick streets of Biddeford. Christmas lights glitter like jewels on porches, inside windows, as if the world has been strewn with an embarrassment of riches. Cruising slowly, he imagines children asleep. What the hell are sugar plums, anyway?

Suddenly, a bright blur barrels across the range of Patrick's headlights, and he brakes hard. He steers into the skid and avoids hitting the person who's run across the road. Getting out of the car, he rushes to the side of the fallen man. 'Sir,' Patrick asks, 'are you all right?'

The man rolls over. He is dressed in a Santa suit, and alcohol fumes rise from his phony cotton beard. 'St. Nick, to you, boyo. Get it straight.'

Patrick helps him sit up. 'Did you hurt anything?'

'Lay off.' Santa struggles away from him. 'I could sue you.'

'For *not* hitting you? I doubt it.'

'Reckless operation of a vehicle. You're probably drunk.'

At that, Patrick laughs. 'As opposed to you?'

'I haven't had a drop!'

'Okay, Santa.' Patrick hauls him to his feet. 'You got somewhere to call home?'

'I gotta get my sleigh.'

'Sure you do.' With a bracing arm, he steers the man toward his cruiser.

'The reindeer, they chew up the shingles if I leave them too long.'

'Of course.'

'I'm not getting in there. I'm not finished yet, you know.'

Patrick opens the rear door. 'I'll take the chance, Pop. Go on. I'll take you down to a nice warm bunk to sleep this off.'

Santa shakes his head. 'My old lady'll kill me.'

'Mrs. Claus will get over it.'

His smile fades as he looks at Patrick. 'C'mon, officer. Cut me a little slack. You know what it's like to go home to a woman you love, who just wishes you'd stay the hell away?'

Patrick ducks him into the car, with maybe a little too much force. No, he doesn't know what it's like. He can't get past the first part of that sentence: *You know what it's like to go home to a woman you love?*

By the time he gets to the station, Santa is unconscious, and has to be hauled into the building by Patrick and the desk officer. Patrick punches out on the clock, gets into his own truck. But instead of driving home, he heads in the opposite direction, past Nina's house. Just to make sure everything's all right. It is something he has not done with regularity since the year he returned to Biddeford, when Nina and Caleb were already married. He would drive by on the graveyard shift and see all the lights out, save the one in their bedroom. An extra dose of security, or so he told himself back then.

Years later, he still doesn't believe it.

It is supposed to be a big deal, Nathaniel knows. Not only does he get to stay up extra late on Christmas Eve, but he can open as many presents as he wants, which is all of them. And they're staying in a real live old castle, in a whole new country called Canada.

Their room at this castle-hotel has a fireplace in it, and a bird that looks real but is dead. Stuffed, that's what his father called it, and maybe it did look like it had eaten too much, although Nathaniel doesn't think you can die from that. There are two huge beds and the kinds of pillows that squinch when you lie on them, instead of popping right back.

Everyone talks a different language, one Nathaniel doesn't understand, and that makes him think of his mother.

He has opened a remote-control truck, a stuffed kangaroo, a helicopter. Matchbox cars in so many colors it makes him dizzy. Two computer games and a tiny pinball machine he can hold in his hand. The room is littered with wrapping paper, which his father is busy feeding into the mouth of the fire.

'That's some haul,' he muses, smiling at Nathaniel.

His father has been letting Nathaniel call the shots. To that end, they got to play at a fort the whole day, and ride up and down a cable car, the funsomething, Nathaniel forgets. They went to a restaurant with a big moose head mounted outside and Nathaniel got to order five desserts. They went back to the room and opened their presents, saving their stockings for tomorrow. They have done everything Nathaniel has asked, which never happens when he is at home.

'So,' his father says. 'What's next?'

But all Nathaniel wants to do is make it the way it used to be.

The doorbell rings at eleven, and it's a Christmas tree. Then Patrick's face pokes through the branches, from behind the enormous balsam. 'Hi,' he says.

My face feels rubbery, this smile strange upon it. 'Hi.'

'I brought you a tree.'

'I noticed.' Stepping back, I let him into the house. He props the tree against the wall, needles raining down around our feet. 'Caleb's truck isn't here.'

'Neither's Caleb. Or Nathaniel.'

Patrick's eyes darken. 'Oh, Nina. Christ, I'm sorry.'

'Don't be.' I give him my best grin. 'I have a tree now. And someone to help me eat Christmas Eve dinner.'

'Why, Miz Maurier, I'd be delighted.' At the same moment, we realize Patrick's mistake – calling me by my maiden name, the name by which he first knew me. But neither one of us bothers to make the correction.

'Come on in. I'll get the food out of the fridge.'

'In a second.' He runs out to his car, and returns with several Wal-Mart shopping bags. Some are tied with ribbons. 'Merry Christmas.' An afterthought, he leans forward and kisses me on the cheek.

'You smell like bourbon.'

'That would be Santa,' Patrick says. 'I had the unparalleled pleasure of sticking St. Nick in a cell to sleep off a good drunk.' As he talks, he starts unpacking the bags. Cracker Jacks, Cheetos, Chex Mix. Non-alcoholic champagne. 'There wasn't much open,' he apologizes.

Picking up the fake champagne, I turn it over in my hands. 'Not even gonna let me get trashed, huh?'

'Not if it gets you busted.' Patrick meets my gaze. 'You know the rules, Nina.'

And because he has always known what is right for me, I

follow him into the living room, where we set up the tree in the empty stand. We light a fire, and then hang ornaments from boxes I keep tucked in the attic. 'I remember this one,' Patrick says, pulling out a delicate glass teardrop with a figurine inside. 'There used to be two.'

'And then you sat on one.'

'I thought your mother was going to kill me.'

'I think she would have, but you were already bleeding —'

Patrick bursts out laughing. 'And you kept pointing at me, and saying, "He's cut on the butt."' He hangs the teardrop on the tree, at chest level. 'I'll have you know, there's still a scar.'

'Yeah, right.'

'Wanna see?'

He is joking, his eyes sparkling. But all the same, I have to pretend I am busy with something else.

When we are finished, we sit down on the couch and eat cold chicken and Chex Mix. Our shoulders brush, and I remember how we used to fall asleep on the floating dock in the town swimming pond, the sun beating down on our faces and chests and heating our skin to the same exact temperature. Patrick puts the other Wal-Mart bags beneath the tree. 'You have to promise me you'll wait till the morning to open them.'

It strikes me then; he is going.

'But the snow . . .'

He shrugs. 'Four-wheel drive. I'll be fine.'

I twirl my glass, so that the fake champagne swirls inside. 'Please,' I say, that's all. It was bad enough, before. Now that Patrick's been here, his voice filling the living room, his body spanning the space beside mine, it will seem that much emptier when he leaves.

'It's already tomorrow.' Patrick points to the clock: 12:14 A.M. 'Merry Christmas.' He pushes one of the plastic bags into my lap.

'But I haven't gotten you anything.' I do not say what I am thinking: that in all the years since Patrick has returned to

Biddeford, he has not given me a Christmas gift. He brings presents for Nathaniel, but there is an unspoken agreement between us – anything more would be tightrope-walking on a line of propriety.

'Just open it.'

Inside the first Wal-Mart bag is a pup tent. Inside the second, a flashlight and a brand-new game of Clue. A smile darts across Patrick's face. 'Now's your chance to beat me, not that you can.'

Delighted, I grin right back. 'I'm going to whip you.' We pull the tent out of its protective pouch and erect it in front of the Christmas tree. There is barely room enough for two, and yet we both crawl inside. 'Tents have gotten smaller, I think.'

'No, we've gotten bigger.' Patrick sets up the game board between our crossed legs. 'I'm even going to let you go first.'

'You're a prince among men,' I say, and we start to play. Each roll of the die reverses a year, until it is easy to imagine that the snow outside is a field of Queen Anne's lace; that this tournament is life-or-death; that the world is no larger than Patrick and me and a backyard campsite. Our knees bump hard and our laughter fills the tiny vinyl pyramid. The winking strand on the Christmas tree, out there, might be lightning bugs. The flames behind us, a bonfire. Patrick takes me back, and that is the best present I could ever receive.

He wins, by the way. It is Miss Scarlett, in the library, with the wrench.

'I demand a rematch,' I announce.

Patrick has to catch his breath; he's laughing that hard. 'How many years did you go to college?'

'Shut up, Patrick, and start over.'

'No way. I'm quitting while I'm ahead. By – what is it? – three hundred games?'

I grab for his game piece, but he holds it out of my reach. 'You're such a pain in the ass,' I say.

'And you're a sore loser.' He jerks his hand higher, and in

an effort to reach it, I knock the board sideways and overturn the tent as well. We go down in a tumble of vinyl and Clue cards and land on our sides, cramped and tangled. 'Next time I buy you a tent,' Patrick says, smiling, 'I'm springing for the next size up.'

My hand falls onto his cheek, and he goes absolutely still. His pale eyes fix on mine, a dare. 'Patrick,' I whisper. 'Merry Christmas.' And I kiss him.

Almost as quickly he jerks away from me. I can't even look at him, now. I cannot believe that I have done this. But then his hand curves around my jaw, and he kisses me back as if he is pouring his soul into me. We bump teeth and noses, we scratch and we scrape, and through this we do not break apart. The ASL sign for friends: two index fingers, locked at the first knuckles.

Somehow we fall out of the tent. The fire is hot on the right side of my face, and Patrick's fingers are wrapped in my hair. This is bad, I know this is bad, but there is a place in me for him. It feels like he was first, before anyone else. And I think, not for the first time, that what is immoral is not always wrong.

Drawing back on my elbows, I stare down at him. 'Why did you get divorced?'

'Why do you think?' he answers softly.

I unbutton my blouse and then, blushing, pull it together again. Patrick covers my hands with his own and slides the sheer sleeves down. Then he pulls off his shirt, and I touch my fingers lightly to his chest, traveling a landscape that is not Caleb.

'Don't let him in,' Patrick begs, because he has always been able to think my thoughts. I kiss across his nipples, down the arrow of black hair that disappears beneath his trousers. My hands work at the belt, until I am holding him in my hands. Shifting lower, I take him into my mouth.

In an instant he has yanked me up by the hair, crushed me to his chest. His heart is beating so fast, a summons. 'Sorry,' he breathes into my shoulder. 'Too much. All of you, it's too much.'

After a moment, he tastes his way down me. I try not to think of my soft belly, my stretch marks, my flaws. These are the things you do not have to worry about, in a marriage. 'I'm not . . . you know.'

'You're not what?' His words are a puff of breath between my legs.

'*Patrick.*' I yank at his hair. But his finger slides inside, and I am falling. He rises over me, holds me close, fits. We move as if we have been doing this forever. Then Patrick rears back, pulls out, and comes between us.

It binds us, skin to skin, a viscous guilt.

'I couldn't –'

'I know.' I touch my fingers to his lips.

'Nina.' His eyes drift shut. 'I love you.'

'I know that too.' That is all I can allow myself to say, now. I touch the slope of his shoulders, the line of his spine. I try to commit this to memory.

'Nina.' Patrick hides a grin in the hollow of my neck. 'I'm still better at Clue.'

He falls asleep in my embrace, and I watch him. That's when I tell him what I cannot manage to tell anyone else. I make a fist, the letter *S*, and move it in a circle over his heart. It is the truest way I know to say I'm sorry.

Patrick wakes up when the sun is a live wire at the line of the horizon. He touches his hand to Nina's shoulder, and then to his own chest, just to make sure this is real. He lies back, stares into the glowing coals of the fireplace, and tries to wish away morning.

But it will come, and with it, all the explanations. And in spite of the fact that he knows Nina better than she knows herself, he is not sure which excuse she will choose. She has made a living out of judging people's misdeeds. Yet no matter what argument she uses, it will all sound the same to him: *This should not have happened; this was a mistake.*

There is only one thing Patrick wants to hear on her lips, and that is his own name.

Anything else – well, it would just chip away at this, and Patrick wants to hold the night intact. So he gently slides his arm out from beneath the sweet weight of Nina's head. He kisses her temple, he breathes deeply of her. He lets go of her, before she has a chance to let go of him.

The tent, standing upright, is the first thing I see. The second is the absence of Patrick. Sometime during that incredible, deep sleep, he left me.

It is probably better this way.

By the time I've cleaned up our feast from the previous night and showered, I have nearly convinced myself that this is true. But I cannot imagine seeing Patrick again without picturing him leaning over me, his black hair brushing my face. And I don't think that the peace inside me, spread like honey in my blood, can be chalked up to Christmas.

Forgive me Father, for I have sinned.

But have I? Does Fate ever play by the rules? There is a gulf as wide as an ocean between *should* and *want,* and I am drowning in it.

The doorbell rings, and I jump up from the couch, hurriedly wiping my eyes. Patrick, maybe back with coffee, or bagels. If *he* makes the choice to return, I'm absolved of blame. Even if it was what I was wishing for all along.

But when I open the door, Caleb is standing on the porch, with Nathaniel in front of him. My son's smile is brighter than the dazzle of snow on the driveway, and for one panicked moment I peer over Caleb's shoulder to see whether the tracks made by Patrick's police cruiser have been covered over by the storm. Can you smell transgression, like a perfume deep in the skin? 'Mommy!' Nathaniel shouts.

I lift him high, revel in the straight weight of him. My heart beats like a hummingbird in my throat. 'Caleb.'

He will not look at me. 'I'm not staying.'

This is a mercy visit, then. In minutes, Nathaniel will be gone. I hug him closer.

'Merry Christmas, Nina,' Caleb says. 'I'll pick him up tomorrow.' He nods at me, then walks off the porch. Nathaniel chatters, his excitement wrapping us tighter as the truck pulls away. I study the footprints Caleb has left in the snowy driveway as if they are clues, the unlikely proof of a ghost that comes and goes.

III

Our virtues are most frequently but vices disguised.

– François, Duc de La Rochefoucauld

Today in school Miss Lydia gave us a special snack.

First, we had a piece of lettuce with a raisin on it. This was an egg.

Then we had a string cheese caterpillar.

Next came a chrysalis, a grape.

The last part was a piece of cinnamon bread, cookie-cuttered into the body of a butterfly.

After, we went outside and set free the monarchs that had been born in our classroom. One landed on my wrist. It looked different now, but I just knew this was the same caterpillar I found a week before and gave to Miss Lydia. Then it flew into the sun.

Sometimes things change so fast it makes my throat hurt from the inside out.

7

When I was four I found a caterpillar on my bedroom windowsill and decided to save its life. I made my mother take me to the library so that I could look it up in a Field guide. I punched pinholes in the top of a jar; I gave it grass and leaves and a tiny thimbleful of water. My mother said that if I didn't let the caterpillar go, it would die, but I was convinced I knew better. Out in the world, it could be run over by a truck. It could be scorched by the sun. My protection would stack the odds.

I changed its food and water religiously. I sang to it when the sun went down. And on the third day, in spite of my best intentions, that caterpillar died.

Years later, it is happening all over again.

'No,' I tell Fisher. We have stopped walking; the cold January air is a cobra charmed up the folds of my coat. I thrust the paper back at him, as if holding my son's name out of sight might keep it from being on the witness list at all.

'Nina, it's not your decision,' he says gently. 'Nathaniel's going to have to testify.'

'Quentin Brown's just doing this to get to me. He wants me to watch Nathaniel have a relapse in court so maybe I'll snap again, this time in front of a judge *and* a jury.' Tears freeze on the tips of my eyelashes. I want it over, *now*. It was why I had murdered a man – because I thought that would stop this boulder from rolling on and on; because if the defendant was gone then my son would not have to sit on a witness stand and recount the worst thing that had ever happened to him. I wanted Nathaniel to be able to close this godawful chapter – and so, ironically, I *didn't*.

But even this great sacrifice – of the priest's life, of my own future – has not done what it was supposed to.

Nathaniel and Caleb have kept their distance since Christmas, but every few days Caleb brings him to the house to spend a few hours with me. I don't know how Caleb has explained our living arrangements to Nathaniel. Maybe he says I am too sick to take care of a child, or too sad; and maybe either of these are true. One thing is certain – it is not in Nathaniel's best interests to watch me plan for my own punishment. There is already too much he's witnessed.

I know the name of the motel where they are staying, and sometimes, when I feel particularly courageous, I call. But Caleb always answers the phone, and either we have nothing to say to each other, or there are so many words clogging the wires between us that none of them fall forward.

Nathaniel, though, is doing well. When he comes to the house, he is smiling. He sings songs for me that Miss Lydia has taught the class. He no longer jumps when you come up behind him and touch his shoulder.

All of this progress, and it will be erased at a competency hearing.

In the park behind us, a toddler lies on his back making a snow angel. The problem with one of those is that you have to ruin it when you stand up. No matter what, there is always a footprint binding you to the ground. 'Fisher,' I say simply, 'I'm going to jail.'

'You don't –'

'Fisher. Please.' I touch his arm. 'I can handle that. I even believe that it's what I deserve, because of what I did. But I killed a man for one reason and one reason only – to keep Nathaniel from being hurt any more. I don't want him to think about what happened to him ever again. If Quentin wants to punish someone, he can punish me. But Nathaniel, he's off limits.'

He sighs. 'Nina, I'll do the best I can –'

'You don't understand,' I interrupt. 'That's not good enough.'

       ★   ★   ★

Because Judge Neal hails from Portland, he doesn't have chambers at the Alfred Superior Court, so he's been given another judge's lair to borrow for the duration of my trial. Judge McIntyre, however, spends his free time hunting. To this end, the small room is decorated with the heads of moose and ten-point bucks, prey that has lost the battle. *And me?* I think. *Will I be next?*

Fisher has filed a motion, and the resulting meeting is being held in private chambers to prevent the media from getting involved. 'Judge, this is so outrageous,' he says, 'that I can't begin to express my absolute chagrin. The state has Father Szyszynski's death on videotape. What possible need do they have for this child to testify to anything?'

'Mr. Brown?' the judge prompts.

'Your Honor, the alleged rationale for the murder was the boy's psychiatric condition at the time, and the fact that the defendant believed her son had been the victim of molestation at the hands of Father Szyszynski. The state has learned that, in fact, this is not the truth. It's important that the jury get to hear what Nathaniel actually told his mother before she went out and killed this man.'

The judge shakes his head. 'Mr. Carrington, it's going to be very difficult for me to quash a subpoena if the state alleges they can make it relevant. Now, once we're in trial, I may be able to rule that it's not relevant at all – but as it stands now, this witness's testimony goes to motive.'

Fisher tries once again. 'If the state will submit a written allegation of what they believe the child's testimony to be, maybe we can stipulate to it, so that Nathaniel doesn't have to take the stand.'

'Mr. Brown, that seems reasonable,' the judge says.

'I disagree. Having this witness, in the flesh, is critical to my case.'

There is a moment of surprised silence. 'Think twice, counselor,' Judge Neal urges.

'I have, Your Honor, believe me.'

Fisher looks at me, and I know exactly what he is about to do. His eyes are dark with sympathy, but he waits for me to nod before he turns to the judge again. 'Judge, if the state is going to be this inflexible, then we need a competency hearing. We're talking about a child who's been rendered mute twice in the past six weeks.'

The judge will leap at this compromise, I know. I also know that of all the defense attorneys I've seen in action, Fisher is one of the most compassionate toward children during competency hearings. But he won't be, not this time. Because the best-case scenario, now, is to get the judge to declare Nathaniel not competent, so that he will not have to suffer through a whole trial. And the only way Fisher can do that is to actively try to make Nathaniel fall to pieces.

Fisher has kept it to himself, but his personal opinion is that art is beginning to imitate life. That is, his insanity defense for Nina – a complete fabrication at first – is starting to hit quite close to the mark. To keep her from dissolving after the motions hearing this morning, he took her out to lunch in a swanky restaurant, a place where she was less likely to have a breakdown. He had her tell him all the questions the prosecutor would ask Nathaniel on the stand, questions she'd asked child witnesses a thousand times.

The courthouse is dark now, empty except for the custodial staff, Caleb, Nathaniel, and Fisher. They move down the hall quietly, Nathaniel clutched in his father's arms.

'He's a little nervous,' Caleb says, clearing his throat.

Fisher ignores the comment. He might as well be walking a tightrope ten thousand feet above the ground. The last thing he wants to do is deal harshly with the boy; but then again, if he's too solicitous, Nathaniel might feel comfortable enough at the hearing to be declared competent to stand trial. Either way, Nina will have his head.

Inside the court, Fisher switches on the overhead lights. They hiss, then flood the room with a garish brilliance. Nathaniel burrows closer to his father, his face pressed into the big man's shoulder. Where is a roll of Tums when you need it?

'Nathaniel,' Fisher says tersely, 'I need you to go sit in that chair. Your father is going to be in the back. He can't say anything to you, and you can't say anything to him. You just have to answer my questions. You understand?'

The boy's eyes are as wide as the night. He follows Fisher to the witness stand, then scrambles onto the stool that has been placed inside. 'Get down for a second.' Fisher reaches inside and takes out the stool, replacing it with a low chair. Now, Nathaniel's brow does not even clear the lip of the witness stand.

'I . . . I can't see anything,' Nathaniel whispers.

'You don't need to.'

Fisher is about to begin asking practice questions when a sound distracts him – Caleb, methodically gathering every high stool in the courtroom, corralling them near the double doors. 'I thought maybe these might be . . . better off somewhere else. So they're not around first thing in the morning.' He meets Fisher's gaze.

The attorney nods. 'The closet. One of the janitors can lock them up.'

When he turns back to the boy, he has to work to keep a smile off his face.

Now Nathaniel knows why Mason always tries to pull out of his collar – this thing called a tie that doesn't have a bow in it at all is choking his neck. He tugs at it again, only to have his father grab his hand. There are flutters in his stomach, and he'd rather be at school. Here, everyone is going to be staring at him. Here, everyone wants him to talk about things he doesn't like to say.

Nathaniel clutches Franklin, his stuffed turtle, more tightly. The closed doors of the courtroom sigh open, and a man who looks like a policeman but isn't one waves them inside. Nathaniel moves hesitantly down the rolled red tongue of carpet. The room is not as spooky as it was last night in the dark, but he still has the feeling that he is walking into the belly of a whale. His heart begins to tap as fast as rain on a windshield, and he holds his hand up to his chest to keep everyone else from hearing, too.

His mommy is sitting in the front row. Her eyes are puffy, and before she sees him standing there she wipes them with her fingers. It makes Nathaniel think of all the other times she's pretended she isn't crying, says it with a smile, even though there are tears right on her cheeks.

There is a big man in the front of the room too, with skin the color of chestnuts. It is the same man who was in the supermarket; who made his mother get taken away. His mouth looks like it has been sewn shut.

The Lawyer sitting next to his mother gets up and walks toward Nathaniel. He does not like the Lawyer. Every time the Lawyer comes to his house, his parents have yelled at each other. And last night, when Nathaniel had been brought here to practice, the Lawyer was downright mean.

Now, he puts his hand on Nathaniel's shoulder. 'Nathaniel, I know you're worried about your mommy. I am, too. I want her to be happy again, but there is someone here who doesn't like your mommy. His name is Mr. Brown. Do you see him over there? The tall man?' Nathaniel nods. 'He's going to ask you some questions. I can't stop him from doing that. But when you answer them, remember – I'm here to help your mommy. He isn't.'

Then he walks Nathaniel to the front of the courtroom. There are more people there than last night – a man wearing a black dress and holding a hammer; another person with hair that stands straight up on his head in little curls; a lady with a typewriter. His mom. And the big man who doesn't like her. They walk to the little fence-box where Nathaniel had to sit before. He crawls onto the chair that is too low, then folds his hands in his lap.

The man in the black dress speaks. 'Can we get a higher seat for this child?'

Everyone starts looking left and right. The almost-policeman says what everyone else can see: 'There don't seem to be any around.'

'What do you mean? We always have extra stools for child witnesses.'

'Well, I could go to Judge Shea's courtroom to see if he has any, but there won't be anybody here to watch the defendant, Your Honor.'

The man in the dress sighs, then hands Nathaniel a fat book. 'Why don't you sit on my Bible, Nathaniel?'

He does, wiggling a little, because his bum keeps sliding off. The curly man walks up to him with a smile. 'Hi, Nathaniel,' he says.

Nathaniel doesn't know if he is supposed to talk yet.

'I need you to put your hand on the Bible for me.'

'But I'm sitting on it.'

The man takes out another Bible, and holds it in front of Nathaniel like a table. 'Raise your right hand,' he says, and Nathaniel lifts one arm into the air. 'Your other right hand,' the man corrects. 'Do you swear to tell the truth, the whole truth, and nothing but the truth, so help you God?'

Nathaniel vehemently shakes his head.

'Is there a problem?' This from the man in the black dress.

'I'm not supposed to swear,' he whispers.

His mommy smiles, then, and hiccups out a laugh. Nathaniel thinks it is the prettiest sound he has ever heard.

'Nathaniel, I'm Judge Neal. I need you to answer some questions for me today. Do you think you can do that?'

He shrugs.

'Do you know what a promise is?' When Nathaniel nods, the judge points to the lady who is typing. 'I need you to speak out, because that woman is writing down everything we say, and she has to hear you. You think you can talk nice and loud for her?'

Nathaniel leans forward. And at the top of his lungs, yells, *'Yes!'*

'Do you know what a promise is?'

'Yes!'

'Do you think you can promise to answer some questions today?'

'Yes!'

The judge leans back, wincing a little. 'This is Mr. Brown, Nathaniel, and he's going to talk to you first.'

Nathaniel looks at the big man, who stands up and smiles. He has white, white teeth. Like a wolf. He is nearly as tall as the ceiling and Nathaniel takes one look at him coming closer and thinks of him hurting his mother and then turning around and biting Nathaniel himself in two.

He takes a deep breath, and bursts into tears.

The man stops in his tracks, like he's lost his balance. 'Go away!' Nathaniel shouts. He draws up his knees, and buries his face in them.

'Nathaniel.' Mr. Brown comes forward slowly, holding out his hand. 'I just need to ask you a couple of questions. Is that okay?'

Nathaniel shakes his head, but he won't look up. Maybe the big man has laser eyes too, like Cyclops from the X-Men. Maybe he can freeze them with one glance and with the next, make them burst into fire.

'What's your turtle's name?' the big man asks.

Nathaniel buries Franklin under his knees, so that he won't have to see the man either. He covers his face with his hands and peeks out, but the man has gotten even closer and this makes Nathaniel turn sideways in the chair, as if he might slip through the slats on the back side of it.

'Nathaniel,' the man tries again.

'No,' Nathaniel sobs. 'I don't want to!'

The man turns away. 'Judge. May we approach?'

Nathaniel peers over the lip of the box he is sitting in and sees his mother. She's crying too, but then that makes sense. The man wants to hurt her. She must be just as scared of him as Nathaniel is.

★   ★   ★

Fisher has told me not to cry, because I will get kicked out of the room. But I can't control myself – the tears come as naturally as a blush or a breath. Nathaniel burrows into the wooden chair, all but hidden by the frame of the witness stand. Fisher and Brown walk toward the bench, where the judge is angry enough to be spitting sparks. 'Mr. Brown,' he says. 'I can't believe you insisted on taking this so far. You know very well you didn't need this testimony, and I'm not going to allow psychological mind games to be played in my courtroom. Don't even think about making an argument to revisit this.'

'You're right, Judge,' answers that bastard. 'I asked to approach because clearly this child should not have to testify.'

The judge raps his gavel. 'This court rules that Nathaniel Frost is not competent to stand trial. The subpoena is quashed.' He turns to my son. 'Nathaniel, you can go on down to your dad.'

Nathaniel bolts out of the chair and down the steps. I think he is going to run to Caleb, in the back of the courtroom – but instead he rushes straight to me. The force of his body sends my chair scooting back a few inches. Nathaniel wraps his arms around my waist, squeezing free the breath I have not even noticed I am holding.

I wait until Nathaniel glances up, terrified by the faces in this foreign world – the clerk, the judge, the stenographer, and the prosecutor. 'Nathaniel,' I tell him fiercely, drawing his attention. 'You were the best witness I could have had.'

Over his head, I catch Quentin Brown's eye. And smile.

When Patrick met Nathaniel Frost, the child was six months old. Patrick's first thought was that he looked just like Nina. His second thought was that, right here, in his arms, was the reason they would never be together.

Patrick made an extra effort to get close to Nathaniel, even though sometimes it was painful enough to make him ache for days after a visit. He'd bring Weed little dolphins to float in the bathtub; Silly Putty; sparklers. For years Patrick had wanted to get under Nina's skin; Nathaniel, who'd grown below her heart, surely had something to teach him. So he tagged along on hikes, swapping off with Caleb to carry Nathaniel when his legs got tired. He let Nathaniel spin in his desk chair at the station. He even baby-sat for a whole weekend, when Caleb and Nina went away for a relative's wedding.

And somewhere along the way, Patrick – who'd loved Nina forever – fell just as hard for her son.

The clock hasn't moved in two hours, Patrick would swear to that. Right now, Nathaniel is undergoing his competency hearing – a procedure Patrick couldn't watch, even if he wanted to. And he doesn't. Because Nina will be there too, and he hasn't seen or spoken to her since Christmas Eve.

It's not that he doesn't want to. God, he can't seem to think of anything but Nina – the feel of her, the taste of her, the way her body relaxed against his in her sleep. But right now, the memory is crystallized for Patrick. Any words that come between them, aftershocks, are only going to take away from that. And it isn't what Nina would say to him that worries Patrick – it's what she *wouldn't* say. That she loves him, that she needs him, that this meant as much to her as it did to him.

He rests his head in his hands. Deep inside, there is a part of him that also knows this was a grave error. Patrick wants to get this off his chest, to confess his doubts to someone who would understand implicitly. But his confidante, his best friend, is Nina. If she cannot be that anymore . . . and she cannot be *his* . . . where does that leave them?

With a deep sigh he grabs the phone from his desk and dials an out-of-state number. He wants resolution, a present to give to Nina before he has to take the stand and testify against her. Farnsworth McGee, the police chief in Belle Chasse, Louisiana, answers on the third ring. 'Hello?' he drawls, extending the word an extra syllable.

'It's Detective-Lieutenant Ducharme, from Biddeford, Maine,' Patrick says. 'What's the latest on Gwynne?'

Patrick can easily envision the chief, with whom he'd met

before leaving Belle Chasse. Overweight by a good fifty pounds, with a shock of Elvis-black hair. A fishing rod propped up in the corner behind his desk; a bumper sticker tacked to the bulletin board: HELL, YES, MY NECK'S RED. 'Y'all got to understand that we move carefully in our jurisdiction. Don't want no hasty mishaps, if you understand my meaning.'

Patrick grits his teeth. 'Did you arrest him yet or not?'

'Your authorities are still talkin' to our authorities, Detective. Believe me, you'll be the first to know when something happens.'

He slams down the phone – angry at the idiot deputy, angry at Gwynne, angriest at himself for not taking matters into his own hands when he was in Louisiana. But he couldn't make himself forget that he was a law enforcement officer, that he was obligated to uphold certain rules. That Nina had said *no*, even if it was what she really wanted.

Patrick stares at the phone in its cradle. Then again, it is always possible to reinvent oneself. Particularly in the image of a hero.

He's seen Nina do it, after all.

After a moment, Patrick grabs his jacket and walks out of the station, intent on effecting change, rather than waiting for it to steamroll him.

It has turned out to be the best day of my life. First, Nathaniel was ruled not competent. Then Caleb asked me to watch Nathaniel after the hearing, and overnight, because he is scheduled to do a job up near the Canadian border. 'Do you mind?' he'd politely said, and I couldn't even form an answer, I was so delighted. I have visions of Nathaniel standing beside me in the kitchen while we cook his favorite dinner; I imagine watching his Shrek video twice in a row with a bowl of popcorn bridged between us.

But in the end, Nathaniel is exhausted from the events of the day. He falls asleep on the couch by six-thirty P.M. and doesn't wake when I carry him upstairs. In his bed, his hand unfurls on the pillow, as if he is offering me a hidden gift.

When Nathaniel was born, he waved tight fists in the air, as if he were angry at the world. They softened moment by moment, until I would nurse him and watch his fingers scrabble at my skin, clutching for purchase. I was mesmerized by that grasp, because of all its potential. Would Nathaniel grow up to wield a pencil or a gun? Would he heal with his touch? Create music? Would his palm be covered with calluses? Ink? Sometimes I would separate the tiny fingers and trace the lines of his palm, as if I could truly read his future.

If Nathaniel had been difficult to conceive in the wake of my cyst surgery, he'd been a positively horrendous delivery. Thirty-six hours of labor rendered me trancelike. Caleb sat on the edge of the bed watching a *Gilligan's Island* marathon on the hospital TV, something that seemed equally as painful as my contractions. 'We'll name her Ginger,' he vowed. 'MaryAnn.'

The vise inside me ratcheted tighter every hour, until agony became a black hole, each pain pulling in another. Over my head Gilligan voted for a chimp as beauty pageant queen, so that he wouldn't offend any of the stranded ladies. Caleb got behind me, propping up my back when I couldn't even find the energy to open my eyes. 'I can't,' I whispered. 'It's your turn.'

So he rubbed my spine and he sang. 'The weather started getting rough . . . the tiny ship was tossed . . . come *on*, Nina! If not for the courage of the fearless crew . . .'

'Remind me,' I said, 'to kill you later.'

But I forgot, because minutes afterward Nathaniel was born. Caleb held him up, a being so small he curled like an inch-worm in my husband's hands. Not a Ginger or a MaryAnn, but a Little Buddy. In fact, that was what we called him for three days, before we decided on a name. Caleb wanted me to choose, since he refused to take credit for work that was nearly all mine. So I picked Nathaniel Patrick Frost, to honor my deceased father, and my oldest friend.

Now, it is hard to believe that the boy sleeping in front of me was ever so tiny. I touch my hand to his hair, feel it slip through my fingers like time. *I suffered once before,* I think. *And look at what I got in return.*

Quentin, who will cross a black cat's path without blinking and walk beneath ladders without breaking a sweat, is strangely superstitious about trials. On mornings that he's set to go to court, he gets fully dressed, eats breakfast, and then takes off his shirt and tie to shave. It's inefficient, of course, but it all goes back to his very first case, when he was so nervous he nearly walked out the door with a night's beard.

Would have, too, if Tanya hadn't called him back in.

He rubs the shaving lather on his cheeks and jaw, then drags the razor the length of his face. He's not nervous today. In spite of the deluge of media that's sure to flood the court, Quentin knows he has a strong case. Hell, he's got the defendant committing the crime on videotape. Nothing she or Fisher Carrington do will be able to erase that action from the eyes of the jury.

His first trial was a traffic ticket, which Quentin argued as if it were a capital murder. Tanya had brought Gideon; had been bouncing him on her hip in the back of the courtroom. Once he'd seen that, well, he had to put on a show.

'Damn!' Quentin jumps as he nicks his jaw. The shaving cream burns in the cut, and he scowls and presses a tissue to the spot. He has to hold it there for a couple of seconds until it clots, blood welling between his fingers. It makes him think of Nina Frost.

He wads up the tissue and sends it shooting across the bathroom, into the trash can. Quentin doesn't bother to watch his perfect shot. Quite simply, when you think you're incapable of missing, you don't.

This is what I have tried on so far: my black prosecutor's suit, the one that makes me look like Marcia Clark on a tear; the pale rose suit I wore to my cousin's wedding; the corduroy jumper Caleb got me one Christmas that still has the tags on it. I've tried slacks, but that's too mannish, and besides, I can't

ever figure out whether you can wear loafers with slacks or if
that comes off as too casual. I am angry at Fisher for not
thinking of this – dressing me, the way defense attorneys dress
prostitutes – in oversize clothes with ugly floral prints, garments
handed down from the Salvation Army that never fail to make
the women look slightly lost and impossibly young.

I know what to wear so that a jury believes I'm in control.
I have no idea how to dress helpless.

The clock on the nightstand is suddenly fifteen minutes later
than it should be.

I pull on the jumper. It's nearly two sizes too big – have I
changed that much? Or did I never bother to try it on in the
first place? I hike it up to my waist and pull on a pair of stockings, only to notice that they have a run in the left leg. I grab
a second pair – but they are ripped too. 'Not today,' I say under
my breath, yanking open my underwear drawer, where I keep
a reserve pair of stockings for emergencies. Panties and bras
spill like foam over the sides of the bureau and onto my bare
feet while I search for the plastic packet.

But I used that spare pantyhose the day I killed Glen
Szyszynski, and since I haven't been working since then, never
thought to replace them.

'Goddammit!' I kick the leg of the dresser, but that only
hurts my toes and brings tears to my eyes. I toss out the
remaining contents of the drawer, yank the whole thing from
its slot in the bureau and throw it across the room.

When my legs give out, I find myself sitting on the soft
cloud of undergarments. I tuck my knees up under the skirt
of my jumper, bury my face in my arms, and cry.

'Mommy was on TV last night,' Nathaniel says as they are
driving to the courthouse in Caleb's truck. 'When you were in
the shower.'

Lost in his own thoughts, Caleb nearly drives off the side
of the road at this comment. 'You weren't supposed to be
watching TV.'

Nathaniel hunches his shoulders, and immediately Caleb is sorry. So quickly, these days, he thinks he has done something wrong. 'It's all right,' Caleb says. He forces his attention to the road. In ten minutes, he'll be at the superior court. He can give Nathaniel to Monica in the children's playroom; maybe she'll have some better answers.

Nathaniel, however, isn't finished yet. He chews the words in his mouth for a bit, then spits them out in one great rush. 'How come Mommy yells at me when I pretend a stick is a gun but she was playing with one for real?'

Caleb turns to find his son staring up at him, expecting explanations. He puts on his signal and pulls the truck onto the shoulder of the road. 'Remember when you asked me why the sky was blue? And how we went to go look it up on the computer and there was so much science stuff there that neither of us could really understand it? Well, this is kind of the same thing. There's an answer, but it's really complicated.'

'The man on TV said what she did was wrong.' Nathaniel worries his bottom lip. 'That's why today she's gonna get yelled at, right?'

Oh, Christ, if only it could be that easy. Caleb smiles sadly. 'Yeah. That's why.'

He waits for Nathaniel to speak again, and when he doesn't, Caleb pulls the truck back into the line of traffic. He drives three miles, and then Nathaniel turns to him. 'Daddy? What's a *martyr?*'

'Where did you hear that?'

'The man, last night, on TV.'

Caleb takes a deep breath. 'It means your mother loves you, more than anything. And that's why she did what she did.'

Nathaniel fingers the seam of his seat belt, considering. 'Then why is it wrong?' he asks.

The parking lot is a sea of people: cameramen trying to get their reporters in their sights, producers adjusting the line feeds from their satellites, a group of militant Catholic women demanding Nina's judgment at the hands of the Lord. Patrick shoulders his way through the throngs, stunned to see national newscasters he recognizes by virtue of their celebrity.

An audible buzz sweeps the line of onlookers hovering around the courthouse steps. Then a car door slams, and suddenly Nina is hurrying up the stairs with Fisher's avuncular arm around her shoulders. A cheer goes up from the waiting crowd, along with an equally loud catcall of disapproval.

Patrick pushes closer to the steps. 'Nina!' he yells. 'Nina!'

He yanks his badge out, but brandishing it doesn't get him where he needs to be. 'Nina!' Patrick shouts again.

She seems to stumble, to look around. But Fisher grabs her arm and directs her into the courthouse before Patrick has the chance to make himself heard.

'Ladies and gentlemen, my name is Quentin Brown, and I'm an assistant attorney general for the state of Maine.' He smiles at the jury. 'The reason you're all here today is because on October thirtieth, 2001, this woman, Nina Frost, got up and drove with her husband to the Biddeford District Court to watch a man being arraigned. But she left her husband waiting there while she went to Moe's Gun Shop in Sanford, Maine – where she paid four hundred dollars cash for a Beretta nine-millimeter semiautomatic handgun and twelve rounds of ammunition. She tucked these in her purse, got back in her car, and returned to the courthouse.'

Quentin approaches the jury as if he has all the time in the world. 'Now, you all know, from coming in here today, that you had to pass through a security-screening device. But on October thirtieth, Nina Frost didn't. Why? Because she'd worked as a prosecutor for the past seven years. She knew the bailiff posted at the screening device. She walked by him without a backward glance, and she took that gun and the bullets she'd loaded into it, into a courtroom just like this one.'

He moves toward the defense table, coming up behind Nina

to point a finger at the base of her skull. 'A few minutes later she put that gun up to Father Glen Szyszynski's head and fired four rounds directly into his brain, killing him.'

Quentin surveys the jury; they are all staring at the defendant now, just like he wants. 'Ladies and gentlemen, the facts in this case are crystal clear. In fact, WCSH News, which was covering that morning's arraignment, caught Ms. Frost's actions on tape. So the question for you will not be *if* she committed this crime. We *know* that she did. The question will be: Why should she be allowed to get away with it?'

He stares into the eyes of each juror in sequence. 'She would like you to believe that the reason she should be held exempt from the law is because Father Szyszynski, her parish priest, had been charged with sexually molesting her five-year-old son. Yet she didn't even bother to make sure that this allegation was true. The state will show you scientifically, forensically, *conclusively*, that Father Szyszynski was not the man who abused her child . . . and still the defendant murdered him.'

Quentin turns his back on Nina Frost. 'In Maine, if a person unlawfully kills someone with premeditation, she is guilty of murder. During this trial, the state will prove to you beyond a reasonable doubt that this is exactly what Nina Frost did. It doesn't matter if the person who is murdered was accused of a crime. It doesn't matter if the person who was murdered was murdered by mistake. If the person was murdered, period, there needs to be punishment exacted.' He looks to the jury box. 'And that, ladies and gentlemen, is where you come in.'

Fisher only has eyes for that jury. He walks toward the box and meets each man's or woman's gaze, making a personal connection before he even speaks a word. It's what used to drive me crazy about him, when I faced him in a courtroom. He has this amazing ability to become everyone's confidante, no matter if the juror is a twenty-year-old single welfare mother or an e-commerce king with a million tucked into the stock market.

'What Mr. Brown just told you all is absolutely true. On the morning of October thirtieth, Nina Frost did buy a gun. She did drive to the courthouse. She did stand up and fire four bullets into the head of Father Szyszynski. What Mr. Brown would like you to believe is that there's nothing to this case beyond those facts . . . but we don't live in a world of facts. We live in a world of feelings. And what he's left out of his version of the story is what had been going on in Nina's head and heart that would lead her to such a moment.'

Fisher walks behind me, like Quentin did while he graphically showed the jury how to sneak up on a defendant and shoot him. He puts his hands on my shoulders, and it is comforting. 'For weeks, Nina Frost had been living a hell that no parent should have to live. She'd found out that her five-year-old son had been sexually abused. Worse, the police had identified the abuser as her own priest – a man she had confided in. Betrayed, heartbroken, and aching for her son, she began to lose her grasp on what was right and what was wrong. The only thing in her mind by the time she went to court that morning to see the priest arraigned was that she needed to protect her child.

'Nina Frost, of all people, knows how the system of justice works for – and fails – children. She, of all people, understands what the rules are in an American court of law, because for the past seven years she has measured up to them on a daily basis. But on October thirtieth, ladies and gentlemen, she wasn't a prosecutor. She was just Nathaniel's mother.' He comes to stand beside me. 'Please listen to everything. And when you make your decision, don't make it only with your head. Make it with your heart.'

Moe Baedeker, proprietor of Moe's Gun Shop, does not know what to do with his baseball cap. The bailiffs made him take it off, but his hair is matted and messy. He puts the cap on his lap and finger-combs his hair. In doing so, he catches sight of his nails, with grease and gun blueing caught beneath the cuticles, and he quickly sticks his hands beneath his thighs. 'Ayuh, I recognize her,' he says, nodding at me. 'She came into my store once. Walked right up to the counter and told me she wanted a semiautomatic handgun.'

'Had you ever seen her before?'

'Nope.'

'Did she look around the store at all?' Quentin asks.

'Nope. She was waiting in the parking lot when I opened, and then she came right up to the counter.' He shrugs. 'I did an instant background check on her, and when she came out clean, I sold her what she wanted.'

'Did she ask for any bullets?'

'Twelve rounds.'

'Did you show the defendant how to use the gun?'

Moe shakes his head. 'She told me she knew how.'

His testimony breaks over me like a wave. I can remember the smell of that little shop, the raw wood on the walls, and the pictures of Rugers and Glocks behind the counter. The way the cash register was old-fashioned and actually made a *ching* sound. He gave me my change in new twenty-dollar bills, holding each one up to the light and pointing out how you could tell whether they were counterfeit or not.

By the time I focus again, Fisher is doing the cross-exam. 'What did she do while you were running the background check?'

'She kept looking at her watch. Pacing, like.'

'Was there anyone else in the store?'

'Nope.'

'Did she tell you why she needed a gun?'

'Ain't my place to ask,' Moe says.

One of the twenties he'd given me had been written on, a man's signature. 'I did that once,' Moe told me that morning. 'And, swear to God, got the same bill back six years later.' He'd handed me my gun, hot in my hand. 'What goes around comes around,' he'd said, and at the time, I was too self-absorbed to heed this as the warning it was.

*   *   *

The cameraman had been filming for WCSH and was set up in the corner, according to Quentin Brown's diagram of the Biddeford courtroom. As the videotape is slipped into a TV/VCR, I keep my eyes on the jury. I want to watch them watching me.

Once, maybe, I saw this segment. But it was months ago, when I believed I had done the right thing. The familiar voice of the judge draws my attention, and then I cannot help but stare at this small screen.

My hands shake when I hold up the gun. My eyes are wide and wild. But my motion is smooth and beautiful, a ballet. As I press the gun to the priest's head my own tilts backward, and for one stunning moment my face is split into masques of comedy and tragedy – half grief, half relief.

The shot is so loud that even on tape, it makes me jump in my seat.

Shouts. A cry. The cameraman's voice, saying, 'Holy fucking shit!' Then the camera tilts on its axis and there are my feet, flying over the bar, and the thud of the bailiffs' bodies pinning me, and Patrick.

'Fisher,' I whisper. 'I'm going to be sick.'

The viewpoint shifts again, spinning to rest on its side on the floor. The priest's head lies in a spreading pool of blood. Half of it is missing, and the spots and flecks on the film suggest the spray of brain matter on the camera lens. One eye stares dully at me from the screen. *'Did I get him?'* My own voice. *'Is he dead?'*

'Fisher . . .' The room revolves.

I feel him stand up beside me. 'Your Honor, if I could request a short recess . . .'

But there isn't time for that. I jump out of my seat and stumble through the gate at the bar, flying down the aisle of the courtroom with two bailiffs in pursuit. I make it through the double doors, then fall to my knees and vomit repeatedly, until the only thing left in my stomach is guilt.

*   *   *

'Frost Heaves,' I say minutes later, when I have cleaned myself up and Fisher has whisked me to a private conference room away from the eyes of the press. 'That'll be tomorrow's headline.'

He steeples his fingers. 'You know, I've got to tell you, that was good. Amazing, really.'

I glance at him. 'You think I threw up on *purpose?*'

'Didn't you?'

'My God.' Turning away, I stare out the window. If anything, the crowd outside has grown. 'Fisher, did you *see* that tape? How could any juror acquit me after that?'

Fisher is quiet for a moment. 'Nina, what were you thinking when you were watching it?'

'Thinking? Who had time to think, with all the visual cues? I mean, that's an unbelievable amount of blood. And the brains –'

'What were you thinking about yourself?'

I shake my head, close my eyes, but there are no words for what I've done.

Fisher pats my arm. 'That,' he says, 'is why they'll acquit you.'

In the lobby, where he is sequestered as an upcoming witness, Patrick tries to keep his mind off Nina and her trial. He's done a crossword puzzle in a paper left on the seat beside him; he's had enough cups of coffee to raise his pulse a few notches; he's talked to other cops coming in and out. But it's all pointless; Nina runs through his blood.

When she staggered from the courtroom, her hand clapped over her mouth, Patrick had risen out of his chair. He was already halfway across the lobby, trying to make sure she was all right, when Caleb burst out of the double doors on the heels of the bailiffs.

So Patrick sat back down.

On his hip, his beeper begins to vibrate. Patrick pulls it off his belt and glances at the number on the screen. *Finally,* he thinks, and he goes to find a pay phone.

*   *   *

When it is time for lunch, Caleb gets sandwiches from a nearby deli and brings them back to the conference room where I am ensconced. 'I can't eat,' I say, as he hands me one wrapped sub. I expect him to tell me that I have to, but instead Caleb just shrugs and lets the sandwich sit in front of me. From the corner of my eye I watch him chew his food in silence. He has already conceded this war; he no longer even cares enough to fight me.

There is a rattle of the locked door, followed by an insistent banging. Caleb scowls, then gets up to tell whoever it is to go away. But when he opens it a crack, Patrick is standing on the other side. The door falls open, and the two men stand uneasily facing each other, a seam of energy crackling between them that keeps them from getting too close.

I realize at that moment that although I have many photographs of Patrick and many photographs of Caleb, I haven't got a single one of all three of us – as if, in that combination, it is impossible to fit so much emotion in the frame of the camera.

'Nina,' he says, coming inside. 'I have to talk to you.'

Not now, I think, going cold. Surely Patrick has enough sense to not bring up what happened in front of my husband. Or maybe that is exactly what he wants to do.

'Father Gwynne's dead.' Patrick hands me a faxed Nexus article. 'I got a call from the Belle Chasse police chief. I got tired of working on Southern time a few days ago, and I put a little pressure on the authorities . . . anyway, it seems that by the time they went to arrest him, he'd died.'

My face is frozen. 'Who did it?' I whisper.

'No one. It was a stroke.'

Patrick keeps talking, his words falling like hailstones onto the paper I'm trying to read. '. . . took the damn chief two whole days to get around to calling me . . .'

Father Gwynne, a beloved local chaplain, was found dead in his living quarters by his housekeeper.

'. . . apparently, he had a family history of cardiovascular disease . . .'

'*He looked so peaceful, you know, in his easy chair,*' *said Margaret Mary Seurat, who had worked for the priest for the past five years. '*Like he'd just fallen asleep after finishing his cup of cocoa.*'

'*. . . and get this: They said his cat died of a broken heart . . .*'

*In a strange, connected twist, Gwynne's cherished pet, a cat well known to his parishioners, died shortly after authorities arrived. To those who knew the Father, this was no surprise: '*She loved him too much,*' Seurat suggested. '*We all did.*'

'It's over, Nina.'

Archbishop Schulte will lead a funeral Mass at Our Lady of Mercy, Wednesday morning at 9:00 A.M.

'He's dead.' I test the truth on my tongue. 'He's *dead.*' Maybe there is a God, then; maybe there are cosmic wheels of justice. Maybe this is what retribution is supposed to feel like. 'Caleb,' I say, turning. Everything else passes between us without a single word: that Nathaniel is safe, now; that there will be no sexual abuse trial for him to testify at; that the villain in this drama will never hurt someone else's little boy; that after my verdict, this nightmare will truly be finished.

His face has gone just as white as mine. 'I heard.'

In the middle of this tiny conference room, with two hours of damning testimony behind me, I feel an unmitigated joy. And in that instant it does not matter what has been missing between Caleb and myself. Much more important is this triumph of news, and it's something to share. I throw my arms around my husband.

Who does not embrace me in return.

Heat floods my cheeks. When I manage to lift my gaze with some shred of dignity, Caleb is staring at Patrick, who has turned his back. 'Well,' Patrick says, without looking at me. 'I thought you'd want to know.'

Bailiffs are human fire hydrants: They're placed in the court in case of an emergency but fade into the landscape otherwise and are rarely put to practical use. Like most bailiffs of my acquaintance, Bobby Ianucci isn't too athletic or too bright.

And like most bailiffs, Bobby understands he is lower on the feeding chain than the attorneys in the courtroom – which accounts for his absolute intimidation at the hands of Quentin Brown.

'Who was in the courtroom when you brought Father Szyszynski in from the holding cell?' the prosecutor asks, a few minutes into the testimony.

Bobby has to think about this, and the effort is visible on his doughy face. 'Uh, well, the judge, yeah. On the bench. And there was a clerk, and a stenographer, and the dead guy's lawyer, whose name I don't remember. And a DA from Portland.'

'Where were Mr. and Mrs. Frost sitting?' Quentin asks.

'In the front row with Detective Ducharme.'

'What happened next?'

Bobby straightens his shoulders. 'Me and Roanoke, that's the other bailiff, we walked the Father across the room to his lawyer. Then, you know, I stepped back, because he had to sit down, so I stood behind him.' He takes a deep breath. 'And then . . .'

'Yes, Mr. Ianucci?'

'Well, I don't know where she came from. I don't know how she did it. But the next thing, there's gunshots being fired and blood all over the place, and Father Szyszynski's falling out of his chair.'

'What happened after that?'

'I tackled her. And so did Roanoke, and a couple of other guys posted at the back of the courtroom, and Detective Ducharme, too. She dropped the gun and I grabbed it, and then Detective Ducharme, he hauled her up and took her off to the holding cell in cuffs.'

'Did you get shot, Mr. Ianucci?'

Bobby shakes his head, lost in his memories. 'No. But if I'd been, like, five inches to the right, she could have hit me.'

'So would you say the defendant was very careful with how she aimed that weapon at Father Szyszynski?'

Fisher stands beside me. 'Objection.'

'Sustained,' Judge Neal rules.

The prosecutor shrugs. 'Withdrawn. Your witness.'

As he returns to his seat, Fisher approaches the bailiff. 'Did you talk to Nina Frost the morning before the shooting?'

'No.'

'In fact, you were busy doing your job – maintaining the security of the courthouse, and dealing with prisoners – so you had no need to watch Mrs. Frost, did you?'

'No.'

'Did you see her pull the gun out?'

'No.'

'You said several bailiffs immediately jumped on her. Did you have to fight Mrs. Frost for the gun?'

'No.'

'And she didn't struggle with any of you when you tried to sub-due her?'

'She was trying to see around us. She kept asking if he was dead.'

Fisher dismisses this with a shrug. 'But she wasn't trying to get away from you. She wasn't trying to hurt you.'

'Oh, no.'

Fisher lets that answer hang for a moment. 'You knew Mrs. Frost before this, didn't you, Mr. Ianucci?'

'Sure.'

'What was your relationship with her like?'

Bobby glances at me; then his eyes skitter away. 'Well, she's a DA. She comes in all the time.' He pauses, then adds. 'She's one of the nice ones.'

'Had you ever considered her to be violent before?'

'No.'

'In fact, on that morning, she seemed nothing like the Nina Frost you knew, isn't that right?'

'Well, you know, she looked the same.'

'But her *actions*, Mr. Ianucci . . . had you ever seen Mrs. Frost act like this before?'

The bailiff shakes his head. 'I never saw her shoot nobody, if that's what you mean.'

'It is,' Fisher says, sitting down. 'Nothing further.'

That afternoon when court is adjourned, I don't go directly home. Risking an extra fifteen minutes' grace before my electronic bracelet is reactivated, I drive to St. Anne's and enter the church where this all began.

The nave is open to the public, although I don't think they've found a replacement chaplain yet. Inside, it's dark. My shoes strike the tile, announce my presence.

To my right is a table where white votives burn in tiers. Taking a stick, I light one for Glen Szyszynski. I light a second one for Arthur Gwynne.

Then I slip into a pew and get down on the kneeler. 'Hail Mary, full of grace,' I whisper, praying to a woman who stood by her son, too.

The lights in the motel room go out at eight, Nathaniel's bedtime. Beside his son, on a matching twin bed, Caleb lies with his hands folded behind his head, waiting for Nathaniel to fall asleep. Then, sometimes, Caleb will watch TV. Turn on one lamp and read the day's paper.

Today he wants to do neither. He is in no mood to hear local pundits guessing Nina's fate based on the first day of testimony. Hell, he doesn't want to guess, himself.

One thing is clear: The woman all those witnesses saw; the woman on that videotape – she isn't the woman Caleb married. And when your wife is not the same person you fell in love with eight years ago, where exactly does that leave you? Do you try to get to know who she has become, and hope for the best? Or do you keep deceiving yourself in the hope that she might wake up one morning and have gone back to the woman she used to be?

Maybe, Caleb thinks with a small shock, *he* isn't the same person he once was, either.

That brings him directly to the topic he didn't want to remember, especially not now in the dark with nothing to distract him. This afternoon, when Patrick had come to the conference room to bring them the news of Gwynne's death . . . well, Caleb must be reading into things. After all, Nina and Patrick have known each other a lifetime. And although the guy is something of an albatross, his relationship with Nina has never really bothered Caleb, because when push came to shove *he* was the one sleeping with Nina every night.

But Caleb has not been sleeping with Nina.

He squeezes his eyes shut, as if this might block out the memory of Patrick turning away abruptly when Nina put her arms around Caleb. That, in and of itself, wasn't disturbing – Caleb could list a hundred times that Nina touched him or smiled at him in the other man's presence that unsettled Patrick in some way . . . even if Nina never seemed to see. In fact, there have been times Caleb's even felt sorry for Patrick, for the blatant jealousy on his face the moment before he masks it.

Today, though, it wasn't envy in Patrick's eyes. It was grief. And that is why Caleb cannot pull away from the incident; cannot stop picking the moment apart like a carrion vulture going for the bone. Envy, after all, comes from wanting something that isn't yours.

But grief comes from losing something you've already had.

Nathaniel hates this stupid playroom with its stupid book corner and its stupid bald dolls and its stupid crayon box that doesn't even have a yellow. He hates the way the tables smell like a hospital and the floor is cold under his socks. He hates Monica, whose smile reminds Nathaniel of the time he took an orange wedge at the Chinese restaurant and stuffed it into his mouth, rind out, in a silly, fake grin. Most of all he hates knowing that his mom and dad are just twenty-two stairs up but Nathaniel isn't allowed to join them.

'Nathaniel,' Monica says, 'why don't we finish this tower?'

It is made of blocks; they built it all afternoon yesterday and put a special sign on overnight, asking the janitors to leave it until this morning.

'How high do you think we can go?'

It is already taller than Nathaniel; Monica has brought over a chair so that he can keep building. She has a small stack of blocks ready to go.

'Be careful,' she warns as he climbs onto the chair.

He places the first block at the top, and the whole structure wobbles. The second time, it seems certain to fall over – and then doesn't. 'That was close,' Monica says.

He imagines that this is New York City, and he is a giant. A *Tyrannosaurus rex*. Or King Kong. He eats buildings this big like they are carrot sticks. With a great swipe of his enormous paw, Nathaniel swings at the top of the tower.

It falls in a great, clattering heap.

Monica looks so sad that for just the slightest moment, Nathaniel feels awful. 'Oh,' she sighs. 'Why'd you do that?'

Satisfaction curls the corners of his mouth, blooming from a root inside. But Nathaniel doesn't tell her what he's thinking: *Because I could.*

Joseph Toro looks nervous to be in a courtroom, and I can't blame him. The last time I saw the man he was cowering beside the bench, covered with his own client's blood and brain matter.

'Had you met with Glen Szyszynski before you came to court that day?' Quentin asks.

'Yes,' the attorney says timidly. 'In jail, pending the arraignment.'

'What did he say about the alleged crime?'

'He categorically denied it.'

'Objection,' Fisher calls out. 'Relevance?'

'Sustained.'

Quentin reconsiders. 'What was Father Szyszynski's demeanor the morning of October thirtieth?'

'Objection.' Fisher stands this time. 'Same grounds.'

Judge Neal looks at the witness. 'I'd like to hear this.'

'He was scared to death,' Toro murmurs. 'He was resigned. Praying. He read to me aloud, from the book of Matthew. The part where Christ keeps saying '*My God, why hast thou forsaken me?*''

'What happened when they brought your client in?' Quentin asks.

'They walked him to the defense table where I was sitting.'

'And where was Mrs. Frost at the time?'

'Sitting behind us, and to the left.'

'Had you spoken with Mrs. Frost that morning?'

'No,' Toro answers. 'I'd never even met her.'

'Did you notice anything unusual about her?'

'Objection,' Fisher says. 'He didn't know her, so how could he judge what was and wasn't customary?'

'Overruled,' the judge answers.

Toro looks at me, a bird gathering courage to dart a glance at the cat sitting a few feet away. 'There *was* something unusual. I was waiting for her to come in . . . because she was the mother of the alleged victim, of course . . . but she was late. Her husband was there, waiting . . . but Mrs. Frost almost missed the beginning of the arraignment. I thought of all days, it seemed very strange that on this one, she wouldn't be on time.'

I listen to his testimony, but I am watching Quentin Brown. To a prosecutor, a defendant is nothing but a victory or a loss. They are not real people; they do not have lives that interest you beyond the crime that brought them into court. As I stare at him, Brown suddenly turns. His expression is cool, dispassionate – one I have cultivated in my repertoire as well. In fact I have had all the same training as him, but there is a gulf between us. This case is only his job, after all. But it is my future.

The Alfred courthouse is old, and the bathrooms are no exception. Caleb finishes up at the long trough of the urinal just as someone comes to stand beside him. He averts his eyes as the

other man unzips, then steps back to wash his hands, and realizes it is Patrick.

When Patrick turns, he does a double-take. 'Caleb?'

The bathroom is empty, save the two of them. Caleb folds
his arms, waits for Patrick to soap his hands and dry them
with a paper towel. He is waiting, and he doesn't know why.
He just understands that at this moment, he can't leave yet,
either.

'How is she today?' Patrick asks.

Caleb finds that he cannot answer, cannot force a single
word out.

'It must be hell for her, sitting in there.'

'I know.' Caleb forces himself to look directly at Patrick, to
make him understand this is not a casual reply, is not even a
sequitur. 'I *know*,' he repeats.

Patrick looks away, swallows. 'Did she . . . did she tell you?'

'She didn't have to.'

The only sound is the rush of water in the long urinal. 'You
want to hit me?' Patrick says after a moment. He splays his
arms wide. 'Go ahead. Hit me.'

Slowly, Caleb shakes his head. 'I want to. I don't think I've
ever wanted anything as much. But I'm not going to, because
it's too fucking sad.' He takes a step toward Patrick, pointing
his finger at the other man's chest. 'You moved back here to
be near Nina. You've lived your whole life for a woman who
doesn't live hers for you. You waited until she was skating over
a weak spot, and then you made sure you were the first thing
she could grab onto.' He turns away. 'I don't have to hit you,
Patrick. You're already pathetic.'

Caleb walks toward the bathroom door but is stopped by
Patrick's voice. 'Nina used to write me every other day. I was
overseas, in the service, and that was the only thing I looked
forward to.' He smiles faintly. 'She told me when she met you.
Told me where you took her on dates. But the time she told
me that she'd climbed some mountain with you . . . that was
when I knew I'd lost her.'

'Mount Katahdin? Nothing happened that day.'

'No. You just climbed it, and came down,' Patrick says. 'Thing is, Nina's terrified of heights. She gets so sick, sometimes, that she faints. But she loved you so much, she was willing to follow you anywhere. Even three thousand feet up.' He pushes away from the wall, approaching Caleb. 'You know what's pathetic? That you get to live with this . . . this goddess. That out of all the guys in the world, she picked *you*. You were handed this incredible gift, and you don't even know it's in front of you.'

Then Patrick pushes past Caleb, knocking him against the wall. He needs to get out of that bathroom, before he is foolish enough to reveal the whole of his heart.

Frankie Martine is a prosecutor's witness – that is to say, she answers questions clearly and concisely, making science accessible to even the high school dropout on a jury. Quentin spends nearly an hour walking her through the mechanics of bone marrow transplants, and she manages to keep the jury's interest. Then she segues into the mechanics of her day job – spinning out DNA. I once spent three days at the state lab with Frankie, in fact, getting her to show me how she does it. I wanted to know, so that I'd fully grasp the results that were sent to me.

Apparently, I didn't learn enough.

'Your DNA is the same in every cell in your body,' Frankie explains. 'That means if you take a blood sample from someone, the DNA in those blood cells will match the DNA in their skin cells, tissue cells, and bodily fluids like saliva and semen. That's why Mr. Brown asked me to take DNA from Father Szyszynski's blood sample and use it to see if it matched the DNA found in the semen on the underpants.'

'And did you do that?' Quentin asks.

'Yes, I did.'

He hands Frankie the lab report – the original one, which was left anonymously in my mailbox. 'What were your findings?'

Unlike some of the other witnesses the prosecutor's put on the stand, Frankie meets my eye. I don't read sympathy there, but I don't read disgust either. Then again, this is a woman who is faced daily with the forensic proof of what people are capable of doing to others in the name of love. 'I determined that the chance of randomly selecting an unrelated individual from the population other than the suspect, whose DNA matched the semen DNA at all the locations we tested, was one in six billion.'

Quentin looks at the jury. 'Six billion? Isn't that the approximate population of the whole earth?'

'I believe so.'

'Well, what does all this have to do with bone marrow?'

Frankie shifts on her seat. 'After I'd issued these results, the attorney general's office asked me to research the findings in light of Father Szyszynski's medical records. Seven years ago, he'd had a bone marrow transplant, which means, basically, that his blood was on long-term loan . . . borrowed from a donor. It also means that the DNA we got from that blood – the DNA that was typed to match the semen in the underwear – was not Father Szyszynski's DNA, but rather his donor's.' She looks at the jury, making sure they are nodding before she continues. 'If we'd taken saliva from Father Szyszynski, or semen, or even skin – anything but his blood – it would have excluded him as a donor to the semen stain in the child's underwear.'

Quentin lets this sink in. 'Wait a second. You're telling me that if someone has a bone marrow transplant, they've got two different types of DNA in their body?'

'Exactly. It's extremely rare, which is why it's the exception and not the rule, and why DNA testing is still the most accurate kind of evidentiary proof.' Frankie takes out another lab report, an updated one. 'As you can see here, it's possible to test someone who's had a bone marrow transplant to prove that they've got two different profiles of DNA. We extract tooth pulp, which contains both tissue and blood cells. If someone's had a bone marrow transplant, those tissue cells should show one profile of DNA, and the blood cells should show another.'

'Is that what you found when you extracted tooth pulp from Father Szyszynski?'

'Yes.'

Quentin shakes his head, feigning amazement. 'So I guess Father Szyszynski was the one person in six billion whose DNA might match the DNA found in the underwear . . . but who wouldn't have been the one to leave it there?'

Frankie folds the report and slips it into her case file. 'That's right,' she says.

'You've worked with Nina Frost on a few cases, haven't you?' Fisher asks moments later.

'Yes,' Frankie replies. 'I have.'

'She's pretty thorough, isn't she?'

'Yes. She's one of the DAs who calls all the time, checking up on the results we fax in. She's even come to the lab. A lot of the prosecutors don't bother, but Nina really wanted to make sure she understood. She likes to follow through from beginning to end.'

Fisher slants a look my way. *Tell me about it.* But he says, 'It's very important for her to make sure that she has the facts straight, isn't it?'

'Yes.'

'She isn't someone who'd jump to a conclusion, or rely on something she was told without double-checking it?'

'Not that I've seen,' Frankie admits.

'When you issue your lab reports, Ms. Martine, you expect them to be accurate, don't you?'

'Of course.'

'You issued a report, in fact, that said the chances of somebody other than Father Szyszynski contributing this semen to Nathaniel Frost's underwear were less than one in the population of the whole earth?'

'Yes.'

'You never put anything in that report qualifying your results in the case that the suspect was a bone marrow transplant recipient, did you? Because that's such a rare event that even you, as a scientist, would never assume it?'

'Statistics are statistics . . . an estimation.'

'But when you handed that initial report to the DA's office, you were prepared to ask the prosecutor to rely on it?'

'Yes.'

'You were prepared to ask a jury of twelve people to rely on it as evidence to convict Father Szyszynski?'

'Yes,' Frankie says.

'You were prepared to ask the judge to rely on it when he sentenced Father Szyszynski?'

'Yes.'

'And you were prepared to ask Nina Frost, the child's mother, to rely on it for closure and peace of mind?'

'Yes.'

Fisher turns to the witness. 'Then is it any wonder in your mind, Ms. Martine, that she *did?*'

'Of course Quentin objected,' Fisher says, his mouth full of pepperoni pizza. 'That's not the point. The point is that I didn't withdraw the question before I dismissed the witness. The jury's going to notice that nuance.'

'You are giving far too much credit to a jury,' I argue. 'I'm not saying the cross wasn't fantastic, Fisher, it was. But . . . watch it, you're going to get sauce on your tie.'

He looks down, then flips the tie over his shoulder and laughs. 'You're a riot, Nina. At what point during this trial do you think you might actually start to root for the defense?'

Never, I think. Maybe it is easier for Fisher, a defense attorney, to come up with rationalizations for why people do the things they do. After all, when you have to stand up next to felons on a daily basis and fight for their freedom, you either convince yourself they had some excuse for committing a crime . . . or you tell yourself this is nothing but a job, and if you lie on their behalf it's all in the name of billable hours. After seven years as a prosecutor, the world looks very black and white. Granted, it was easy enough to persuade myself that I was morally right-eous when I believed I'd killed a child molester. But to be absolved of murdering a man who was blameless – well, even Johnnie Cochran must have nightmares every now and then.

'Fisher?' I ask quietly. 'Do you think I ought to be punished?'

He wipes his hands on a napkin. 'Would I be here if I did?'

'For what you're making, you'd probably stand in the middle of a gladiator's ring.'

Smiling, he meets my eye. 'Nina, relax. I *will* get you acquitted.'

But I shouldn't be. The truth lies at the base of my stomach, even though I can't say it aloud. What good is the legal process if people can decide their motives are bigger than the law? If you remove one brick from the foundation, how long before the whole system tumbles down?

Maybe I can be pardoned for wanting to protect my child, but there are plenty of parents who shelter their children without committing felonies. I can tell myself that I was only thinking of my son that day; that I was only acting like a good mother . . . but the truth is, I wasn't. I was acting like a pros-ecutor, one who didn't trust the court process when it became personally relevant. One who knew better than to do what I did. Which is exactly why I deserve to be convicted.

'If I can't even forgive myself,' I say finally, 'how are twelve other people going to do it?'

The door opens and Caleb enters. Suddenly the atmosphere is plucked tight as a bowstring. Fisher glances at me – he knows that Caleb and I have been estranged, lately – and then balls his napkin up and tosses it into the box. 'Caleb! There's a couple slices left.' He stands up. 'I'm going to go take care . . . of that thing we were talking about,' Fisher says vacuously, and he gets out of the room while he can.

Caleb sits across from me. The clock on the wall, fast by five minutes, ticks as loud as my heart. 'Hungry?' I ask.

He traces the sharp corner of the pizza box. 'I'm starving,' Caleb answers.

But he makes no move to take one of the slices. Instead, we both watch as his fingers creep forward, as he clasps my hand between both of his. He scoots his chair closer and bows his head until it touches our joined fists. 'Let's start over,' he murmurs.

If I have gained anything over these months, it is the knowledge there is no starting over – only living with the mistakes you've made. But then, Caleb taught me long ago you can't build anything without some sort of foundation. Maybe we learn to live our lives by understanding, firsthand, how *not* to live them.

'Let's just pick up where we left off,' I reply, and I rest my cheek on the crown of Caleb's head.

How far can a person go . . . and still live with himself?

It's something that's been haunting Patrick. There are certain acts for which you easily make excuses – killing during wartime; stealing food if you're starving; lying to save your own life. But narrow the circumstances, bring them closer to home – and suddenly, the faith of a man who's dedicated his life to morality gets seriously shaken. Patrick doesn't blame Nina for shooting Glen Szyszynski, because at that moment she truly believed it was her only option. Likewise, he doesn't consider making love with her on Christmas Eve to be wrong. He'd waited for Nina for years; when she finally was his – even for a night – the fact of her marriage to another man was inconsequential. Who was to say that the bond between Patrick and Nina was any less strong because there was no piece of paper sanctifying it?

Justification is a remarkable thing – takes all those solid lines and blurs them, so that honor becomes as supple as a willow, and ethics burst like soap bubbles.

If Nina chose to leave Caleb, Patrick would be at her side in an instant, and he could come up with a multitude of reasons to defend his behavior. Truth be told, it's something he's let himself consider in the soft gray moments before sleep comes. Hope is his balm for reality; if Patrick spreads it thick enough, sometimes he can even envision a life with her.

But then, there's Nathaniel.

And that's the point Patrick cannot get past. He can rationalize falling in love with Nina; he can even rationalize her falling in love with him. There's nothing he would like more than to see Caleb gone from her life. But Caleb is not just Nina's husband . . . he is also the father of her son. And Patrick could not bear knowing that he was responsible for ruining Nathaniel's childhood. If Patrick did that after all that has happened, well . . . how could she ever love him?

Compared to a transgression of that size, what he is about to do seems insignificant.

He watches Quentin Brown from the witness box. The prosecutor is expecting this to go easily – just as easily as it did during the practice session. After all, Patrick is a law enforcement official, used to testifying. As far as Brown knows, despite his friendship with Nina, he's on the side of the prosecution. 'Were you assigned to work the Nathaniel Frost case?' Quentin asks.

'Yes.'

'How did the defendant react to your investigation of the case?'

Patrick can't look at Nina, not yet. He doesn't want to give himself away. 'She was an incredibly concerned parent.'

This is not the answer they have rehearsed. Patrick watches Quentin do a double-take, then feed him the response he was *supposed* to give. 'Did you ever see her lose her temper during the case?'

'At times she'd become distraught. Her child wasn't speaking. She didn't know what to do.' Patrick shrugs. 'Who wouldn't get frustrated in a situation like that?'

Quentin sends him a quelling glance. Commentary on the stand is not necessary, or desired. 'Who was your first suspect in the molestation case?'

'We didn't have a suspect until Glen Szyszynski.'

By now, Quentin looks ready to throttle him. 'Did you bring in another man for questioning?'

'Yes. Caleb Frost.'

'Why did you bring him in?'

Patrick shakes his head. 'The child was using sign language to communicate, and he ID'd his abuser with the sign for *father*. At the time, we didn't understand he meant *priest*, rather than *daddy*.' He looks directly at Caleb, in the front row behind Nina. 'That was my mistake,' Patrick says.

'What was the defendant's reaction to her son signing *father*?'

Fisher rises from his seat, poised to object, but Patrick speaks quickly. 'She took it very seriously. Her primary concern was always, *always*, protecting her child.' Confused, the attorney sits back down beside Nina.

'Detective Ducharme –' the prosecutor interrupts.

'I'm not quite done yet, Mr. Brown. I was going to say that I'm sure it tore her up inside, but she got a restraining order against her husband, because she thought it was the best way to keep Nathaniel safe.'

Quentin walks closer to Patrick, hisses through his teeth so that only his witness will hear. *'What the hell are you doing?'* Then he faces the jury. 'Detective, at what point did you make the decision to arrest Father Szyszynski?'

'After Nathaniel gave a verbal disclosure, I went down to talk to him.'

'Did you arrest him at that moment?'

'No. I was hoping he'd confess first. We always hope for that in molestation cases.'

'Did Father Szyszynski ever admit to sexually abusing Nathaniel Frost?'

Patrick has been a witness at enough trials to know that the question is blatantly unacceptable, because it calls for hearsay. The judge and the prosecutor both stare at Fisher Carrington, waiting for him to object. But by now, Nina's lawyer has caught on. He sits at the defense table with his hands steepled, watching this unfold. 'Child molesters almost never admit they've hurt a child,' Patrick says, filling the silence. 'They know jail's not going to be a pleasant place for them. And frankly, without a confession, a molestation trial is a roll of the dice. Nearly half the time, these guys get off because of insufficient evidence or because the child is too terrified to testify, or because they *do* testify and the jury doesn't believe the word of a kid . . .'

Quentin breaks in before Patrick can do any further damage. 'Your Honor, may we have a recess?'

The judge looks over his bifocals at him. 'We *are* in the middle of the direct.'

'Yes, Judge, I'm aware of that.'

Shrugging, Neal turns to Fisher. 'Does the defense object to stopping at this point?'

'I don't believe so, Your Honor. But I would ask the Court to remind all counsel that the witnesses have been sequestered and can't be approached during the break.'

'Fine,' Quentin grits out. He storms from the courtroom so quickly he doesn't see Patrick finally make eye contact with Nina, smile gently at her, and wink.

'Why is this cop working for us?' Fisher demands, as soon as he's bustled me into a private conference room upstairs.

'Because he's my friend. He's always been there for me.' At least, that is the only explanation I can give. I knew, of course, that Patrick would have to testify against me, and I didn't take it to heart. Part of what makes Patrick Patrick is his absolute devotion to the clear line dividing right and wrong. It is why he would not let me talk to him about the murder; it is why he has wrestled so hard to stand by my side while I was awaiting trial. It is why his offer to find Father Gwynne on my behalf meant so very much to me, and was so difficult for him.

It is why, when I think back to Christmas Eve, I cannot believe it ever happened.

Fisher seems to be considering this odd gift that has dropped into his lap. 'Is there anything I should watch out for? Anything he *won't* do to protect you?'

The reason we slept together isn't because Patrick tossed

morality to the wind that night. It's because he was too damn honest to convince himself the feelings weren't there.

'He won't lie,' I answer.

Quentin returns on the attack. Whatever game this detective's playing, it's going to stop right now. 'Why were you in court the morning of October thirtieth?'

'It was my case,' Ducharme answers coolly.

'Did you speak to the defendant that morning?'

'Yes. I spoke with both Mr. and Mrs. Frost. They were both very nervous. We discussed who they could leave Nathaniel with during the proceedings, because naturally, they were very wary of putting him into anyone's care at that point.'

'What did you do when the defendant shot Father Szyszynski?'

Ducharme meets the prosecutor's gaze head on. 'I saw a gun, and I went for it.'

'Did you know Mrs. Frost had a gun before that point?'

'No.'

'How many officers did it take to wrestle her to the ground?'

'She dropped to the ground,' the detective corrects. 'Four bailiffs dropped on top of her.'

'Then what did you do?'

'I asked for cuffs. Deputy Ianucci gave me a pair. I secured Mrs. Frost's hands behind her back and took her into the holding cell.'

'How long were you in there with her?'

'Four hours.'

'Did she say anything to you?'

In the practice session, Ducharme had told Quentin that the defendant confessed to him that she'd committed a crime. But now, he puts on a choirboy's expression and looks at the jury. 'She kept repeating over and over, "I did everything I could; I can't do any more." She sounded crazy.'

Crazy? 'Objection,' Quentin roars.

'Your Honor, it's his own witness!' Fisher says.

'Overruled, Mr. Brown.'

'Approach!' Quentin storms up to the bench. 'Judge, I'm going to ask to have this witness declared hostile, so that I can ask leading questions.'

Judge Neal looks at Ducharme, then back at the prosecutor. 'Counselor, he *is* answering your questions.'

'Not the way he's supposed to be!'

'I'm sorry, Mr. Brown. But that's your problem.'

Quentin takes a deep breath, turning away. The real issue here isn't that Patrick Ducharme is single-handedly destroying this case. The issue is *why*.

Either Ducharme is holding a grudge against Quentin, whom he does not even really know . . . or he's trying to help Nina Frost for some reason. He glances up, and notices the detective and the defendant staring at each other, a bond so charged that Quentin imagines walking through it might give him a shock.

Well.

'How long have you known the defendant?' he asks evenly.

'Thirty years.'

'That long?'

'Yes.'

'Can you describe your relationship with her?'

'We work together.'

My ass, Quentin thinks. *I'd bet my retirement pension you play together, too.* 'Do you ever see her outside the office in a nonprofessional capacity?'

It might not be noticeable to someone watching less closely than Quentin . . . but Patrick Ducharme's jaw tightens. 'I know her family. We have lunch together every now and then.'

'How did you feel when you heard this had happened to Nathaniel?'

'Objection,' Carrington calls out.

The judge rubs a finger over his upper lip. 'I'll allow it.'

'I was concerned for the boy,' the detective answers.

'How about Nina Frost? Were you concerned for her?'

'Of course. She's a colleague.'

'Is that all?' Quentin accuses.

He is prepared for Ducharme's reaction – a face bleached completely of color. An added bonus: the way Nina Frost looks as if she's been molded of stone. *Bingo,* Quentin thinks.

'Objection!'

'Overruled,' the judge says, narrowing his eyes at the detective.

'We've been friends for a long time.' Ducharme picks through a minefield of words. 'I knew Nina was upset, and I did what I could to make it easier.'

'Such as . . . help her kill the priest?'

Nina Frost shoots out of her seat at the defense table. *'Objection!'*

Her attorney shoves her back down. Patrick Ducharme looks ready to kill Quentin, which is fine by him, now that the jury thinks it's possible the detective could have been an accessory to one murder already. 'How long have you been a policeman?'

'Three years.'

'And before that, you were a detective in the military police?'

'Yes, for five years.'

Quentin nods. 'As an investigator and a detective and a police officer in both the United States military and the Biddeford Police Department, how often have you testified?'

'Dozens of times.'

'You are aware that as a witness, you're under oath, Detective.'

'Of course.'

'You've told the court today that during the four hours you spent in a holding cell with the defendant, she sounded crazy.'

'That's right.'

Quentin looks at him. 'The day after Father Szyszynski was murdered, you and Detective Chao came in to talk to me at the district attorney's office. Do you remember what you told me then about the defendant's state of mind?'

There is a long stalemate. Finally Ducharme turns away. 'I said she knew exactly what she was doing, and that if it was my son, I'd have done the same thing.'

'So . . . your opinion the day after the shooting was that Nina Frost was perfectly sane. And your opinion today is that she was crazy. Which one is it, Detective . . . and what on earth did she do between then and now to make you change your mind?' Quentin asks, and he sinks into his chair and smiles.

Fisher is playing the insider with the jury, but I can barely even follow his words. Watching Patrick on the stand has turned me inside out. 'You know,' Fisher begins, 'I think Mr. Brown was trying to imply something about your relationship with Mrs. Frost that isn't accurate, and I'd like to have a chance to make clear to the jury what *is* true. You and Nina were close friends as children, isn't that right?'

'Yes.'

'And like all children, you probably told a fib every now and then?'

'I suppose so,' Patrick says.

'But that's a far cry from perjury, isn't it?'

'Yes.'

'Like all children, you two hatched plots and schemes and maybe even carried through with them?'

'Sure.'

Fisher spreads his hands. 'But that's a far cry from planning a murder, right?'

'Absolutely.'

'And as children, you two were particularly close. Even now, you're particularly close. But that's all you two are – *friends*. Correct?'

Patrick looks directly at me. 'Of course,' he says.

The state rests. Me, I'm too keyed up for that. I pace the confines of the small conference room where I have been left alone – Caleb is checking on Nathaniel, and Fisher has left to call his office. I am standing by the window – something Fisher's told me not to do, because photographers down there have some super telephoto lenses they're using – when the door cracks and the sound from the hallway oozes inside. 'How is he?' I ask without turning around, assuming Caleb has returned.

'Tired,' Patrick answers, 'but I figure I'll bounce back.'

I whirl around and walk to him, but now there is a wall between us, one only he and I can see. Patrick's eyes, that beautiful blue, are swimming with shadows.

I state the obvious. 'You lied about us. On the stand.'

'Did I?' He comes closer, and it hurts. To have so little space between us, and to know I cannot erase it entirely.

We *are* only friends. It's all we're ever going to be. We can wonder, we can pretend otherwise for a single evening, but that is not the measure of a life together. There is no way to know what might have happened if I hadn't met Caleb; if Patrick hadn't gone overseas. But I've made a world with Caleb. I can't cut out that piece of myself, any more than I can carve away the part of my heart that belongs to Patrick.

I love them both; I always will. But this isn't about me.

'I didn't lie, Nina. I did the right thing.' Patrick's hand comes up to my face, and I turn my cheek into his palm.

I will be leaving him. I will be leaving everyone.

'The right thing,' I repeat, 'is thinking before I act, so that I stop hurting the people I love.'

'Your family,' he murmurs.

I shake my head. 'No,' I say, my good-bye. 'I meant you.'

After court is dismissed, Quentin goes to a bar. But he doesn't particularly feel like drinking, so he gets into his car and drives aimlessly. He goes to a Wal-Mart and buys $104.35 of items he does not need; he stops at a McDonald's for dinner. It isn't until two hours later that he realizes he has somewhere he needs to be.

It is dark by the time he pulls up to Tanya's house, and he has trouble getting the passenger out of the car. It wasn't as difficult as you'd imagine to find a plastic skeleton; the Halloween merchandise at the costume store was discounted sixty percent, heaped into an untidy corner.

He hauls the skeleton up the driveway like a buddy who's drunk too much, phalanges dragging on the gravel, and he uses one long bony finger to push in the doorbell. A few moments later, Tanya answers the door.

She's still wearing her scrubs, and her braids are pulled back into a ponytail. 'Okay,' she says, looking at Quentin and the skeleton. 'I've got to hear this.'

He shifts position, so that he can hold the skull and let the rest dangle, freeing up one hand. Quentin points to the shoulder. 'Scapula,' he recites. 'Ischium, ilium. Maxilla, mandible, fibula, cuboid.' He has labeled each of these on the appropriate bone, with a black permanent marker.

Tanya starts to close the door. 'You've lost it, Quentin.'

'No!' He wedges the wrist of the skeleton inside. 'Don't.' Taking a deep breath, Quentin says, 'I bought this for you. I wanted to show you . . . that I didn't forget what you taught me.'

She tilts her head. God, he used to love the way she did that. And how she'd massage her own neck when the muscles got sore. He looks at this woman, who he does not know at all any longer, and thinks she looks just the way *home* should.

Tanya's fingers slip over the bones he could not recall, wide white ribs and parts of the knee and ankle. Then she reaches for Quentin's arm, and smiles. 'You got a lot left to learn,' she replies, and she tugs him inside.

That night I dream that I am in court, sitting next to Fisher, when the hair stands up on the back of my neck. The air gets heavier, harder to breathe, and behind me whispers run like mice on the hardscrabble floor. 'All rise,' the clerk says, and I'm about to, but then there is the cold click of a gun against my scalp, the surge and stream of a bullet in my brain, and I am falling; I am falling.

The sound wakes me. Unmistakable, a celebration of clangs and clatter in ringing tin. Raccoons, but in January?

In my flannel pajamas I tiptoe downstairs. Stuff my bare feet into boots, my arms into a parka. Just in case, I grab the fireplace poker, and then I slip outside.

The cover of snow masks my footsteps as I walk the few feet to the garage. As I get closer, the huddled black shape is too large to be a raccoon. The head is bent into the trash. It isn't until I smack the poker against the can like a gong that the man even lifts his head, dizzy and ringing.

He is dressed like a cat burglar, and my first, too-charitable thought is that he must be freezing. His hands, covered in rubber gloves, are slick with the contents of my refuse. Like condoms, I think – he does not want to catch any dread disease, and who knows what you can contract by looking at the detritus of someone's life?

'What the hell are you doing?' I ask.

A war plays across his face. Then he takes a tape recorder out of his pocket. 'Would you be willing to give me a state-ment?'

'You're a *reporter?* You're going through my trash, and you're a reporter?' I advance on him. 'What did you think you would find? What else could you possibly need to say about my life?'

Now I notice how young he is: Nathaniel, give or take fifteen years. He is shaking, and I don't know if it is the temperature out here, or the fact that he has come face-to-face with someone as evil as me. 'Do your readers want to know that I had my period last week? That I finished a box of Honey Nut Cheerios? That I get too much junk mail?'

I grab the tape recorder and punch the record button. 'You want a statement? I'll give you a statement. You ask your readers if they can account for every minute of their lives, every thought in their heads, and be proud of it. You ask them if they've never jaywalked . . . never gone thirty-one miles per hour in a thirty-mile zone . . . if they've never sped up when they saw that yellow light. And when you find that single, sorry person who hasn't taken a misstep, that one person with the right to judge me, you tell him he's just as human as I am. That tomorrow, his world could turn upside down and he might find himself capable of actions he'd never believed possible.' I turn away, my voice breaking. 'You tell him . . . he could have been me.'

Then I take the tape recorder and throw it as hard and far as I can, into a high drift of snow. I walk inside and lock the door behind me, lean against it, and catch my breath.

Nothing I do will bring back Father Szyszynski. But nothing I do will ever wipe from my mind the error I've made. No jail sentence can punish me more than I will punish myself, or turn back time, or keep me from thinking that Arthur Gwynne deserved to die as much as his half-brother didn't.

I have been moving in slow motion, waiting for an inevitable ax to fall, listening to testimony as if these witnesses are discussing the destiny of a stranger. But now, I feel myself waking. The future may unfold in indelible strokes, but it doesn't mean we have to read the same line over and over. That's exactly the fate I *didn't* want for Nathaniel . . . so why should I want it for *me?*

Snow starts to fall, like a blessing.

I want my life back.

The bird looked like a tiny dinosaur, too small to have feathers or know how to open its eyes. It was on the ground next to a stick shaped like a V, and a yellow-hatted acorn. Its mouth folded back, a hinge, and one stub of a wing flopped. I could see the outline of its heart.

'It's okay.' I got down on the ground so I wouldn't be so scary. But it just lay there on its side, its belly swelled like a balloon.

When I looked up, I could see its brothers and sisters in the nest. With one finger I pushed it onto my hand. 'Mom!'

'What's the matter? Oh, Nathaniel!' She made that click with her tongue and grabbed my wrist, pushing it back to the ground. 'Don't pick it up!'

'But . . . but . . .' Anyone could see how sick it was. You were supposed to help people who were too sick or sad to take care of themselves; Father Glen said so all the time. So why not birds, too?

'Once a human touches the baby, its mother doesn't want it anymore.' And just like she said, the big robin came out of the sky and hopped right past the baby. 'Now you know better,' she said.

I kept staring at the bird. I wondered if it would stay there next to the V stick and the acorn until it died. I covered it with a big leaf, so that it would stay warm. 'If I was a bird and someone touched me, would I die?'

'If you were a bird,' she said, 'I never would have let you fall out of the nest.'

8

These are the things he takes: his Yomega Brain yo-yo; the starfish arm he found on a beach. His Bravest Boy ribbon, a flashlight, a Batman trading card. Seventy-six pennies, two dimes, and a Canadian quarter. A granola bar and a bag of jellybeans left over from Easter. They are treasures he brought with him when he moved to the motel with his father; he cannot leave them behind now. Everything fits in the white pillowcase and thumps lightly against Nathaniel's stomach when he zips it up inside his coat.

'You all set?' his father asks, the words lobbed like a stick into a field and forgotten. Nathaniel wonders why he's even bothered to try to keep this a secret, when his dad is too busy to notice him anyway. He climbs into the passenger seat of the truck and fastens the seat belt – then on second thought, unlatches it.

If he's going to be really bad, he might as well start now.

Once, the man at the cleaner's offered to take Nathaniel to see where the big moving millipede of pressed clothes began. His dad had lifted him over the counter and he'd followed Mr. Sarni into the way back, where the clothes were being cleaned. The air was so heavy and wet that Nathaniel wheezed as he pushed the big red button; started the conveyor of hangers chugging in its loop again. The air in the courthouse, it reminds Nathaniel of that. Maybe it's not as hot here, or as sticky, but it is hard to breathe all the same.

When his dad brings him to the playroom downstairs with Monica, they speak in marshmallow bites of words that they think Nathaniel cannot hear. He does not know what a hostile

witness is, or juror bias. But when his father talks the lines on
his face appear on Monica's, like it is a mirror.

'Nathaniel,' she says, fake-bright, as soon as his dad goes
upstairs. 'Let's take off that coat.'

'I'm cold,' he lies, and he hugs his pack against his middle.

She is careful to never touch Nathaniel, and he wonders if
that's because Monica has the X-ray vision to see how dirty he
is on the inside. She looks at him when she thinks he doesn't see,
and her eyes are as deep as a pond. His mom stares at him with
the same expression. It is all because of Father Gwynne; Nathaniel
wishes just once someone would come up to him and think of
him as some kid, instead of The One This Happened To.

What Father Gwynne did was wrong – Nathaniel knew it
then, from the way his skin shivered; and he knows it now,
from talking to Dr. Robichaud and Monica. They have said
over and over that it isn't Nathaniel's fault. But that doesn't
keep him from turning around sometimes, really fast, sure that
he's felt someone's breath on his neck. And it doesn't keep him
from wondering if he cut himself open at the belly, like his
father does when he catches a trout, would he find that black
knot that hurts all the time?

'So, how are we doing this morning?' Fisher asks, as soon as
I sit down beside him.

'Shouldn't *you* know that?' I watch the clerk set a stack of
files on the judge's bench. The jury box, without its members,
looks cavernous.

Fisher pats my shoulder. 'It's our turn,' he assures me. 'I'm
going to spend the whole day making the jurors forget what
Brown told them.'

I turn to him. 'The witnesses –'

'– will do a good job. Trust me, Nina. By lunchtime, everyone
in this court is going to think you were crazy.'

As the side door opens and the jury files in, I look away
and wonder how to tell Fisher that's not what I want, after all.

*　　　*　　　*

'I have to pee,' Nathaniel announces.

'Okay.' Monica puts down the book she has been reading to him and stands up, waiting for Nathaniel to follow her to the door. They walk down the hall together to the restrooms. Nathaniel's mother doesn't let him in the boy's room by himself, but it's okay here, because there's only one potty and Monica can check before he goes inside. 'Wash your hands,' she reminds him, and she pushes open the door so Nathaniel can go inside.

Nathaniel sits on the cold seat of the toilet to muddle it all out. He let Father Gwynne do all those things – and it was bad. *He* was bad; but he didn't get punished. In fact, ever since he was so bad, everyone's been paying extra attention to Nathaniel, and being extra nice.

His mother did something really bad, too – because, she said, it was the best way to fix what happened.

Nathaniel tries to make sense of all this, but the truths are too tangled in his head. All he knows is that for whatever reason, the world is upside-down. People are breaking rules like crazy – and instead of getting into trouble, it's the only way to make things right again.

He pulls up his pants, cinches the bottom of his jacket, and flushes. Then he closes the lid and climbs from the tank to the toilet tissue holder to the little ledge up high. The window there is tiny, only for fancy, because this is a basement floor. But Nathaniel can open it and he's small enough to slip through.

He finds himself behind the courthouse, in one of the window wells. Nobody notices a kid his size. Nathaniel skirts the trucks and vans in the parking lot, crosses the frozen lawn. He starts walking aimlessly down the highway, not holding an adult's hand, intent on running away. *Three bad things,* he thinks, *all at once.*

'Dr. O'Brien,' Fisher asks, 'when did Mrs. Frost first come to your office?'

'On December twelfth.' At ease on the stand – as he should be, for all the testimony he's given in his career – the psychiatrist relaxes in the witness chair. With the silver hair at his temples and his casual pose, he looks like he could be Fisher's brother.

'What materials had you received before you met with her?'

'An introductory letter from you, a copy of the police report, the videotape taken by WCSH-TV, and the psychiatric report prepared by Dr. Storrow, the state's psychiatrist, who had examined her two weeks earlier.'

'How long did you meet with Mrs. Frost that first day?'

'An hour.'

'What was her state of mind when you met?'

'The focus of the conversation was on her son. She was very concerned about his safety,' O'Brien says. 'Her child had been rendered mute; she was frantic with worry; she was feeling guilt as a working mother who hadn't been around enough to see what had been going on. Moreover, her specialized knowledge of the court system made her aware of the effects of molestation on children . . . and more anxious about her son's ability to survive the legal process without significant trauma. After considering the circumstances that led Mrs. Frost to my office, as well as meeting with her in person, I concluded that she was a classic example of someone suffering from post-traumatic stress disorder.'

'How might that have affected her mental stability on the morning of October thirtieth?'

O'Brien leans forward to address the jury. 'Mrs. Frost knew she was heading to court to face her son's abuser. She believed wholeheartedly that her son was permanently scarred by the event. She believed that testifying – as a witness, or even at a competency hearing – would be devastating to the child. Finally, she believed that the abuser would eventually be acquitted. All this was going through her mind, and as she drove to the courthouse, she became more and more agitated – and less and less herself – until she finally snapped. By the moment she put the gun to Father Szyszynski's head, she could not consciously stop herself from shooting him – it was an involuntary reflex.'

The jury was listening, at least; some of them were brave

enough to sneak glances at me. I tried for an expression that fell somewhere between Contrite and Shattered.

'Doctor, when was the last time you saw Mrs. Frost?'

'A week ago.' O'Brien smiles kindly at me. 'She feels more capable of protecting her son now, and she understands that her means of doing it was not right. In fact, she is filled with remorse for her previous actions.'

'Does Mrs. Frost still suffer from post-traumatic stress disorder?'

'PTSD isn't like chicken pox, which can be cured forever. In my opinion, however, Mrs. Frost is at a point where she understands her own feelings and thoughts and can keep herself from letting them overwhelm her. With subsequent outpatient therapy, I believe she will function quite normally.'

This lie cost Fisher, and therefore me, two thousand dollars. But it is worth it: Several members of the jury are nodding. Maybe honesty is overvalued. What's truly priceless is picking out from a stream of falsehoods the ones you most need to hear.

Nathaniel's feet hurt, and his toes are frozen in his boots. His mittens are in the playroom, so the tips of his fingers have turned pink, even buried in the pockets of his jacket. When he counts out loud, just to have something to do, the numbers hang in front of him, curled in the cold.

Because he knows better, he climbs over the guardrail and runs into the middle of the highway. A bus zooms by, its horn flaring as it swerves into the distance.

Nathaniel spreads his arms for balance, and begins to walk the tight-rope of the dotted line.

'Dr. O'Brien,' Quentin Brown says. 'You believe Mrs. Frost feels capable of protecting her son now?'

'Yes, I do.'

'So who's she going to pull a gun on next?'

The psychiatrist shifts in the chair. 'I don't believe she'll go to that extreme.'

The prosecutor purses his lips, considering. 'Maybe not now. But what about in two months . . . two years? Some kid on the playground threatens her son. Or a teacher looks at him the wrong way. Is she going to spend the rest of her life playing Dirty Harry?'

O'Brien raises a brow. 'Mr. Brown, this wasn't a situation where someone looked at her son the wrong way. He had been sexually molested. She believed that she knew beyond a reasonable doubt who'd done it. I also understand that the individual who was eventually identified as the real perpetrator has since died of natural causes, so she certainly no longer has an alleged vendetta to fulfill.'

'Doctor, you reviewed the state psychiatrist's report. Isn't it true that you reached the exact opposite conclusion that he did, regarding Mrs. Frost's mental state? That he not only deemed her competent to stand trial but also believed she was sane at the time of the offense?'

'Yes, Dr. Storrow did indicate that. But this is the first evaluation he's done for a court. On the other hand, I've been a forensic psychiatrist for over forty years.'

'And you don't come cheap, do you?' Brown says. 'Isn't the defense paying you for your testimony today?'

'My fee is two thousand dollars per day, plus expenses,' O'Brien answers, shrugging.

There is a stir in the back of the courtroom. 'Doctor, I believe you used the words "she finally snapped." Is that correct?'

'That's not the clinical term, of course, but it's the way I would describe it in conversation.'

'Did she snap before or after she drove to the gun store?' Brown asks.

'Clearly, that was part of her continuing mental decline . . .'

'Did she snap before or after she loaded six rounds into a nine millimeter semiautomatic handgun?'

'As I said earlier, that would be part –'

'Did she snap before or after she slipped past the metal detector, knowing the bailiff wouldn't stop her?'

'Mr. Brown –'

'And, Doctor, did she snap before or after she very carefully aimed at one person and only one person's head in a crowded courtroom?'

O'Brien's mouth flattens. 'As I told the court before, at that point Mrs. Frost had no control over her actions. She could no more stop herself from shooting the priest than she could stop herself from breathing.'

'She sure managed to stop someone else from breathing, though, didn't she?' Brown crosses toward the jury box. 'You're an expert on post-traumatic stress disorder, aren't you?'

'I'm considered to be rather knowledgeable in the field, yes.'

'And PTSD is triggered by a traumatic event?'

'That's correct.'

'You first met Mrs. Frost after Father Szyszynski's death?'

'Yes.'

'And,' Brown says, 'you believe that it was the molestation of Mrs. Frost's son that triggered her PTSD?'

'Yes.'

'How do you know it wasn't shooting the priest?'

'It's possible,' O'Brien concedes. 'It's just that the other trauma came first.'

'Isn't it true that Vietnam veterans can be plagued by PTSD their whole lives? That thirty years later these men still wake up with nightmares?'

'Yes.'

'Then you can't, with any degree of scientific certainty, tell this jury that the defendant is over the illness that – in your words – caused her to snap?'

More raised voices from the rear of the courtroom. I focus my attention forward.

'I doubt that Mrs. Frost will ever completely forget the events of the past few months,' O'Brien says diplomatically. 'However, in my personal opinion, she is not dangerous now . . . nor will she be dangerous in the future.'

'Then again, Doctor,' Brown says, 'you're not wearing a white collar.'

'Please,' a familiar voice shouts, and then Monica shoves

away from the bailiff restraining her and runs up the central aisle of the courtroom. Alone. She crouches down beside Caleb. 'It's Nathaniel,' she sobs. 'He's gone missing.'

The judge grants a recess, and the bailiffs in the courtroom are sent to look for Nathaniel. Patrick calls in the county sheriff and the state police. Fisher volunteers to appease the frenzy of media that's caught wind of a new problem.

I can't go, because I am still wearing that fucking electronic bracelet.

I think of Nathaniel, kidnapped. Of him wandering into the boxcar of an old train and freezing to death. Of the ship where he might stow away when no one is looking. He could travel the world, and I would still be imprisoned by these four walls.

'He told me he had to go to the bathroom,' Monica says tearfully. We wait in the lobby, which has been emptied of reporters. I know she wants absolution, but I'll be damned if I am going to give it to her. 'I thought maybe he was feeling sick, because it was taking so long. But when I went in, that window was open.' She grabs my sleeve. 'I don't think he was taken by anyone, Nina. I think he just did this for the attention.'

'Monica.' I am holding onto the thinnest filament of control. I remind myself that she could not have known what Nathaniel would do. That nobody is perfect; and that I had not protected him any better, apparently, than she could. But still.

Irony: I will be acquitted, and my son will be gone.

Out of a crowd of cries, I have always been able to hear Nathaniel's. As an infant; on a playground full of children; even with my eyes closed, playing Marco Polo in the shallow end of a pool. Maybe if I cry loud enough, now, Nathaniel will be able to hear me.

Two bright circles of color have appeared on Monica's cheeks. 'What can I do?' she whispers.

'Bring him back.' Then I walk away, because guilt is not only contagious but also deadly.

*   *   *

Caleb watches the police speed away in their cruisers, the lights flashing. Maybe they'll attract Nathaniel; maybe not. He knows one thing – these officers have forgotten what it is like to be five. To this end, he puts his back up against the window that leads into the basement bathroom. He kneels, until he is Nathaniel's height. Then he squints, taking into account everything that might capture his attention.

A clump of matted bushes, bare and shaking. An umbrella, turned inside out by the wind and discarded. A handicapped ramp painted with yellow zigzagged lines.

'Mr. Frost.' The deep voice startles Caleb. He gets to his feet and turns to find the prosecutor standing there, shoulders hunched against the cold.

When Monica ran into the courtroom to deliver the bad news, Fisher Carrington took one look at Nina's face and requested a recess. Brown, on the other hand, stood up and asked the judge if this might not be a ploy for sympathy. 'For all we know,' he said, 'the boy is safe and sound in a conference room upstairs.'

It didn't take him long to realize his tactical error, as the jury watched Nina become hysterical. But all the same, he is the last person Caleb expects to see out here.

'I just wanted to tell you,' Brown says now, 'if there's anything I can do . . .'

He lets his sentence trail off. 'You can do something, all right,' Caleb replies. Both men know what it is; know it has nothing to do with Nathaniel.

The prosecutor nods and walks inside. Caleb gets down on his knees again. He begins to move in a spiral around the court building, like the way he lays stone in a round patio – widening his circles so that he leaves out no space and maintains the arc of the ring. He does this as he does everything – slowly and tenaciously – until he is certain that he's seeing the world through the eyes of his son.

On the other side of the highway is a steep hill that Nathaniel slides down on his bottom. His pants snag on a branch and rip and it doesn't matter, because *no one will punish him*. He steps in melting puddles of icy water and through the ragged seam of the treeline, where he walks until he stumbles over a piece of the forest that has been left out by mistake.

It is the size of his bed at home and has been flattened by the tracks of animals. Nathaniel sits down on a log at the edge and pulls his pillowcase out from inside his coat. He takes out his granola bar and eats halfway, then decides to save the rest. He turns on his flashlight and holds it up to his palm so that the back of his hand glows red.

When the deer come, Nathaniel holds his breath. He remembers what his father told him – they are more afraid of us than we are afraid of them. The big one, a doe, has a coat the color of caramels and tiny high-heeled hoofs. Her baby looks the same, with white spots on her back, as if she has not been colored in the whole way. They bend their long throats to the ground, pushing through the snow with their noses.

It is the mother deer who finds the grass. Just a tuft, hardly a bite. But instead of eating it she shoves the fawn closer. She watches the baby eat, although it means she herself will get nothing.

It makes Nathaniel want to give her the other half of his granola bar.

But the minute he reaches into his pillowcase the heads of the deer jerk up, and they leap from all four feet, their tails white sails as they disappear farther into the woods.

Nathaniel examines the rip on the back of his pants; the muddy tops of his boots. He places the half of the granola bar on the log, in case the deer come back. Then he gets up and slowly heads back toward the road.

Patrick has canvassed a one-mile square around the courthouse, certain that Nathaniel left of his own free will, and even more certain that the kid couldn't have gotten much farther. He picks up his radio to place a call to the Alfred dispatch, asking if anyone's found anything yet, when a movement at the side of the road strikes his eye. As he watches, a quarter mile up the road, Nathaniel crawls over the iron horse of the guardrail and starts walking along the shoulder of the highway.

'I'll be damned,' Patrick breathes, pulling his truck forward slightly. It looks like Nathaniel knows exactly where he is going; from this spot, even someone as small as Weed would be able to see the high roof of the courthouse. But the boy can't see what Patrick can, from the high cab of his truck – Caleb, coming closer on the opposite side of the road.

He watches Nathaniel look right and then left, and Patrick realizes what he is planning to do. Sticking his flashing magnetic light on the roof of the truck, Patrick hurriedly swerves to block traffic. He gets out and clears the way, so that by the time Nathaniel sees his father waiting, he can run across the highway and into Caleb's arms safely.

'Don't do that again,' I say into Nathaniel's soft neck, holding him close to me. 'Ever. Do you hear me?'

He pulls back, puts his palms on my cheeks. 'Are you mad at me?'

'No. Yes. I will be, anyway, when I'm done being so happy.' I hug him tighter. 'What were you thinking?'

'That I'm bad,' he says flatly.

Over Nathaniel's head, I meet Caleb's eyes. 'No you're not, sweetheart. Running away, that wasn't good. You could have been hurt; and you worried me and Daddy like you can't believe.' I hesitate, picking my words. 'But you can do a bad thing and not be a bad person.'

'Like Father Gwynne?'

I freeze. 'Actually, no. He did a bad thing, and he *was* a bad person.'

Nathaniel looks up at me. 'What about you?'

Shortly after Dr. Robichaud, Nathaniel's psychiatrist, takes the stand, Quentin Brown is on his feet to object. 'Your Honor, what does this witness have to offer?'

'Judge, this goes to my client's state of mind,' Fisher argues. 'The information she received from Dr. Robichaud regarding her son's declining condition was highly relevant to her mental status on October thirtieth.'

'I'll allow it,' Judge Neal rules.

'Doctor, have you treated other children who were rendered mute after sexual abuse?' Fisher asks.

'Yes, unfortunately.'

'In some of these cases, do children never regain their voices?'

'It can take years.'

'Did you have any way of knowing whether this would be a long-term condition for Nathaniel Frost?'

'No,' Dr. Robichaud says. 'In fact, that was why I began to teach him rudimentary sign language. He was becoming frustrated with his inability to communicate.'

'Did it help?'

'For a while,' the psychiatrist admits. 'Then he began talking again.'

'Was the progress steady?'

'No. It broke down when Nathaniel lost contact with Mrs. Frost for a week.'

'Do you know why?'

'I understood she was charged with violating her bail conditions and was imprisoned.'

'Did you see Nathaniel during the week that his mother was in jail?'

'Yes, I did. Mr. Frost brought him in, quite upset that the child was no longer speaking. He'd regressed to the point where all he would sign for was his mother.'

'In your opinion, what caused that regression?'

'Clearly, it was the sudden and prolonged separation from Mrs. Frost,' Dr. Robichaud says.

'How did Nathaniel's condition change when his mother was released again?'

'He cried out for her.' The psychiatrist smiles. 'A joyful noise.'

'And, Doctor, were he to undergo a sudden and prolonged separation from his mother again . . . what do you think the likely outcome would be for Nathaniel?'

'Objection!' Quentin calls.

'Withdrawn.'

Moments later, the prosecutor stands up to cross-examine. 'In dealing with five-year-olds, Doctor, don't you find that they often become confused about events?'

'Absolutely. That's why courts have competency hearings, Mr. Brown.'

At the very mention, Judge Neal gives him a warning glance. 'Dr. Robichaud, in your experience, court cases of this type take several months to several years to come to trial, don't they?'

'Yes.'

'And the developmental difference between a five-year-old and a seven-year-old is significant, isn't it?'

'Definitely.'

'In fact, haven't you treated children who seemed like they might have trouble testifying when they first came to you . . . yet a year or two later – after therapy and time had healed them a bit – they were able to take the stand without a setback?'

'Yes.'

'Isn't it true that you have no way of predicting whether Nathaniel would have been able to testify a few years from now without it causing significant psychological harm?'

'No, there's no way to say what might have happened in the future.'

Quentin turns toward me. 'As a prosecutor, Mrs. Frost would certainly be aware of this time lag for court appearances, don't you think?'

'Yes.'

'And as the mother of a child this age, she would be aware of the development changes possible over the next few years?'

'Yes. In fact, I tried to tell Mrs. Frost that in a year or so, Nathaniel might be doing far better than she expected. That he might even be capable of testifying on his own behalf.'

The prosecutor nods. 'Unfortunately, though, the defendant killed Father Szyszynski before we could find out.'

Quentin withdraws the statement before Fisher can even object. I tug on the edge of his jacket. 'I have to talk to you.' He stares at me as if I have lost my mind. 'Yes,' I say. 'Now.'

I know what Quentin Brown is thinking, because I have seen a case through his eyes. *I proved she murdered him. I did my job.* And maybe I have learned not to interfere in the lives of others, but surely it's my responsibility to save myself. 'It's up to me,' I tell Fisher in the conference room. 'I need to give them a reason to say it doesn't matter.'

Fisher shakes his head. 'You know what happens when defense attorneys overtry a case. The prosecution has the burden of proof, and all I can do is pick holes in it. But if I pick too hard, the whole thing deflates. Put on one too many witnesses, and the defense loses.'

'I understand what you're saying. But Fisher, the prosecution *did* prove that I murdered Szyszynski. And I'm not your average witness.' I take a deep breath. 'Sure, there are cases where the defense loses because they put on one witness too many. But there are other cases where the prosecution loses because the jury hears from the defendant. They know horrible things have been done – and they want to hear why, right from the horse's mouth.'

'Nina, you can barely sit still when I'm doing cross-exams, you want to object so badly. I can't put you on the stand as a witness when you're such a goddamned prosecutor.' Fisher sits down across from me, splaying his hands on the table. 'You think in facts. But just because you're telling the jury something doesn't mean they're going to accept it as reality. After all the groundwork I've laid, they like me; they believe me. If I tell them you were so overcome with emotion you were beyond rational thought, they'll buy it. On the other hand, no matter *what* you say to them, they're predisposed to think you're a liar.'

'Not if I tell them the truth.'

'That you really meant to shoot the other guy?'

'That I wasn't crazy.'

'Nina,' Fisher says softly, 'that'll undo your whole defense. You can't tell them that.'

'Why not, Fisher? Why can't I make twelve lousy people understand that somewhere between a good deed and a bad deed are a thousand shades of gray? Right now, Quentin's got me convicted, because he's told them what I was thinking that day. If I take the stand, I can give them an alternative version. I can explain what I did, why it was wrong, and why I couldn't see that, then. Either they'll send me to jail . . . or they'll send me home with my son. How can I not take that chance?'

Fisher stares down at the table. 'You keep this up,' he says after a moment, 'and I may have to hire you when we're through.' He holds out a hand, counting off on his fingers. 'You answer only the questions I ask. The minute you start trying to educate the jury I'm yanking you off. If I mention temporary insanity, you damn well find a way to support it without perjuring yourself. And if you show any temper what-soever, get ready for a nice long stay in prison.'

'Okay.' I leap to my feet, ready to go.

But Fisher doesn't move. 'Nina. Just so you know . . . even if you can't convince that jury, you've convinced me.'

Three months ago, if I'd heard that from a defense attorney, I'd have laughed. But now I smile at Fisher, wait for him to come up beside me at the door. We walk into that courtroom as a team.

My office, for the past seven years, has been a courtroom. It's a space that is intimidating for many people, but not for me. I know what the rules are there: when to approach the clerk, when to talk to the jury, how to lean back and whisper to someone in the gallery without calling attention to myself. But now I am sitting in a part of that office I've never been in before. I am not allowed to move. I am not allowed to do the work I usually do.

I'm starting to see why so many people fear this.

The witness box is so small my knees bump up against the front. The stares of a couple hundred people poke at me, tiny needles. I think of what I have told thousands of witnesses during my career: *Your job is to do three things: Listen to the question, answer the question, and stop talking.* I remember something my boss used to say all the time – that the best witnesses were truck drivers and assembly line workers because they were far less likely to run off at the mouth than, for example, overeducated lawyers.

Fisher hands me the restraining order I took out against Caleb. 'Why did you procure this, Nina?'

'I thought at the time that Nathaniel had identified my husband as the person who'd sexually abused him.'

'What did your husband do to make you believe this?'

I find Caleb in the gallery, shake my head. 'Absolutely nothing.'

'Yet you took the extraordinary step of getting a restraining order to prevent him from seeing his own child?'

'I was focused on protecting my son. If Nathaniel said this was the person who hurt him . . . well, I did the only thing I could to keep him safe.'

'When did you decide to terminate the restraining order?' Fisher asks.

'When I realized that my son had been signing the word *father* not to identify Caleb, but to identify a priest.'

'Is that the point where you believed Father Szyszynski was the abuser?'

'It was a lot of things. First, a doctor told me that anal penetration had occurred. Then came Nathaniel's hand sign. Then he whispered a name to Detective Ducharme that sounded like "Father Glen." And finally, Detective Ducharme told me he'd found my son's underwear at St. Anne's.' I swallow hard. 'I've spent seven years putting together pieces to make cases that will stand up in court. I was just doing what seemed absolutely logical to me.'

Fisher glares at me. *Absolutely logical*. Oh, damn.

'Nina, *listen carefully* to my next question, please,' Fisher warns. 'When you started to believe that Father Szyszynski was your son's abuser, how did you feel?'

'I was a mess. This was a man I'd trusted with my own beliefs and my family's beliefs. With my son. I was angry with myself because I'd been working so hard – if I'd been home more, I might have seen this coming. And I was frustrated because now that Nathaniel had identified a suspect, I knew the next step would be –'

'Nina,' Fisher interrupts. *Answer the question,* I remind myself with a mental kick. *Then shut up.*

Brown smiles. 'Your Honor, let her finish answering.'

'Yes, Mr. Carrington,' the judge agrees. 'I don't believe Mrs. Frost is done.'

'Actually I am,' I say quickly.

'Did you discuss the best plan of action for your son with his psychiatrist?'

I shake my head. 'There was no best plan of action. I've tried hundreds of cases involving child victims. Even if Nathaniel started speaking normally again, and got stronger . . . even if there were a year or two before the case went to trial . . . well, the priest never admitted to what he did. That means it all hinged on my son.'

'What do you mean?'

'Without a confession, the only thing a prosecutor's got against the defendant is the child's testimony. That means Nathaniel would have had to go through a competency hearing. He'd get up, in a room full of people like this, and say what that man had done to him. That man, of course, would be sitting six feet away, watching – and you can be sure that he's told the child, more than once, not to tell. But no one would be sitting next to Nathaniel and nobody would be holding him, nobody would be telling him it's okay to talk now.

'Either Nathaniel would be terrified and fall apart during this hearing, and the judge would rule him not competent to stand trial – which means that the abuser would never get punished . . . or Nathaniel would be told he was able to stand trial – which means he'd have to go through it all over again in court, with the stakes cranked up a notch and a whole new set of people watching. Including twelve jurors predisposed to not believe him, because he's only a child.' I turn to the jury. 'I'm not all too comfortable here, now, and I've been in a court-room every day for the past seven years. It's scary to be trapped in this box. It's scarring for any witness. But we were not talking about *any* witness. We were talking about Nathaniel.'

'What about the best-case scenario?' Fisher asks gently. 'What if, after all that, the abuser was put in jail?'

'The priest would have been in prison for ten years, only ten years, because that's what people with no criminal record get for destroying a child's life. He would have most likely been paroled before Nathaniel even hit puberty.' I shake my head. 'How can anyone consider that a best-case scenario? How can any court say that would protect my son?'

Fisher takes one last look at me and requests a recess.

In the conference room upstairs, Fisher crouches down in front of my chair. 'Repeat after me,' he says.

'Oh, come on.'

'Repeat after me: *I am a witness. I am not an attorney.*'

Rolling my eyes, I recite, 'I am a witness. I am not an attorney.'

'*I will listen to the question, answer the question, and shut up,*' Fisher continues.

If I were in Fisher's shoes, I would want the same promise from my witness. But I am not in Fisher's shoes. And by the same token, he isn't in mine. 'Fisher. Look at me. I am the woman who crossed the line. The one who actually did what any parent would want to do in this horrible situation. Every single person on that jury is looking at me and trying to figure out whether that makes me a monster or a hero.' I look down, feeling the sudden prick of tears. 'It's something *I'm* still trying to figure out. I can't tell them why I did it. But I *can* explain that when Nathaniel's life changes, mine changes. That if Nathaniel never gets over this, then neither will I. And when you look at it that way, sticking to the testimony doesn't seem quite as important, does it?' When Fisher doesn't answer, I reach as far down inside me as I can for whatever confidence has been left behind. 'I know what I'm doing,' I tell Fisher. 'I'm completely in control.'

He shakes his head. 'Nina,' he sighs, 'why do you think I'm so worried?'

'What were you thinking when you woke up the morning of October thirtieth?' Fisher asks me, minutes later.

'That this would be the worst day of my life.'

Fisher turns, surprised. After all, we have not rehearsed this. 'Why? Father Szyszynski was about to be arraigned.'

'Yes. But once he was charged, that speedy trial clock would start ticking. Either they'd bring him to trial or let him go. And that meant Nathaniel would have to get involved again.'

'When you arrived at the courthouse, what happened?'

'Thomas LaCroix, the prosecutor, said they were going to try to clear the courtroom because this was such a high-profile case. It meant the arraignment would be delayed.'

'What did you do?'

'I told my husband I had to go to the office.'

'Did you?'

I shake my head. 'I wound up at a gun shop, in the parking lot. I didn't really know how I'd gotten there, but I knew it was a place I was supposed to be.'

'What did you do?'

'I went in when the store opened, and I bought a gun.'

'And then?'

'I put the gun in my purse and went back to court for the arraignment.'

'Did you plan what you were going to do with the gun during the drive?' Fisher asks.

'No. The only thing on my mind was Nathaniel.'

Fisher lets this lie for a moment. 'What did you do when you arrived at the courthouse?'

'I walked in.'

'Did you think about the metal detectors?'

'No, I never do. I just walk around them because I'm a prosecutor. I do it twenty times a day.'

'Did you purposefully go around the metal detectors because you were carrying a gun in your purse?'

'At that moment,' I answer, 'I was not thinking at all.'

I am watching the door, just watching the door, and the priest is going to come out of it at any moment. My head, it's pounding past the words that Caleb says. I have to see him. I can't hear anything but my blood, that buzzing. He will come through that door.

When the knob turns, I hold my breath. When the door swings open, and the bailiff appears first, time stops. And then the whole room falls away and it is me and him, with Nathaniel bound between us like glue. I cannot look at him, and then I cannot look away.

The priest turns his head and, unerringly, his eyes find mine.

Without saying a word, he speaks: I forgive you.

It is the thought of him *pardoning* me *that breaks something loose inside. My hand slides into my purse and with almost casual indifference I let it happen.*

Do you know how sometimes you know you are dreaming, even while it occurs? The gun is tugged forward like a magnet, until it comes within inches of his head. At the moment I pull the trigger I am not thinking of Szyszynski; I am not thinking of Nathaniel; I am not even thinking of revenge.

Just one word, clamped between the vise of my teeth:

No.

'Nina!' Fisher hisses, close to my face. 'Are you all right?'

I blink at him, then at the jury staring at me. 'Yes. I'm . . . sorry.'

But in my head I'm still there. I hadn't expected the recoil of the gun. For every action, there is an equal and opposite reaction. Kill a man, and you will be punished.

'Did you struggle when the guards fell on top of you?'

'No,' I murmur. 'I just wanted to know he was dead.'

'Is that when Detective Ducharme took you into the holding cell?'

'Yes.'

'Did you say anything to him back there?'

'That I didn't have any choice. I had to do it.'

Which, it turns out, was true. I had said it, at the time, to deliberately sound crazy. But what those psychiatrists have testi-fied to is technically accurate – I had no conscious control of my actions. They are only wrong in thinking that this means I was insane. What I did was no mental illness, no psychotic break. It was instinct.

Fisher pauses. 'You found out some time later that, in fact, Father Szyszynski was not the man who sexually abused your son. How did that make you feel?'

'I wanted to be put in jail.'

'Do you still feel that way?' Fisher asks.

'No.'

'Why not?'

In that instant, my eye falls on the defense table, where neither Fisher nor I are sitting. It is already a ghost town, I think. 'I did what I did to keep my son safe. But how can I keep him safe when I'm not with him?'

Fisher catches my eye meaningfully. 'Will you ever take the law into your own hands again?'

Oh, I know what he wants me to say. I know, because it is what I would try to draw from a witness at this moment too. But I have told myself enough lies. I'm not going to hand-feed them to this jury, too.

'I wish I could tell you I never would . . . but that wouldn't be true. I thought I knew this world. I thought I could control it. But just when you think you've got your life by the reins, that's when it's most likely to run away with you.

'I killed someone.' The words burn on my tongue. 'No, not just someone, but a wonderful man. An *innocent* man. That's something I'm going to carry with me, forever. And like any burden, it is going to get heavier and heavier . . . except I'll never be able to put it down, because now it's a part of who I am.' Turning to the jury, I repeat, 'I would like to tell you that I'd never do anything like this again, but then, I never thought I was capable of doing anything like this in the first place. And as it turned out, I was wrong.'

Fisher, I think, is going to kill me. It is hard to see him through the tears. But my heart isn't hammering, and my soul is still. *An equal and opposite reaction.* After all this time, it turns out that the best way to atone for doing something blatantly wrong is to do something else blatantly right.

But for the grace of God, Quentin thinks, and it could be him sitting in that box. After all, there is not that much difference between himself and Nina Frost. Maybe he wouldn't have killed for his son, but he certainly greased wheels to make Gideon's conviction for drug possession go down much easier than it might have. Quentin can even remember that visceral pang that came when he found out about Gideon – not because he'd broken the law, like Tanya thought, but because his boy must have been scared shitless by the system. Yes, under different circumstances, Quentin might have liked Nina; might even have had something to talk to her about over a beer. Still, you make a bed, you've got to lie in it . . . which has landed Nina on the other side of the witness box, and Quentin six feet away and determined to take her down.

He raises one eyebrow. 'You're telling us that in spite of everything you know about the court system and child abuse cases, on the morning of October thirtieth you woke up with no intention of killing Father Szyszynski?'

'That's right.'

'And that as you drove to the courthouse for this man's arraignment, which – as you said – would start the clock ticking . . . at that point, you had no plans to kill Father Szyszynski?'

'No, I didn't.'

'Ah.' Quentin paces past the front of the witness stand. 'I guess it came to you in a flash of inspiration when you were driving to the gun store.'

'Actually, no.'

'Was it when you asked Moe to load the semiautomatic weapon for you?'

'No.'

'So I suppose when you skirted the metal detector, back at the courthouse, killing Father Szyszynski was still not part of your plan?'

'It wasn't.'

'When you walked into the courtroom, Mrs. Frost, and took up a position that would give you the best vantage point to kill Glen Szyszynski without harming anyone else in the room . . . even that, at that moment, you had no plans to kill the man?'

Her nostrils flare. 'No, Mr. Brown, I didn't.'

'What about at the moment you pulled the gun out of your pocketbook and shoved it up to Glen Szyszynski's temple? Did you still have no plans to kill him then?'

Nina's lips draw tight as a purse. 'You need to give an answer,' Judge Neal says.

'I told the court earlier I wasn't thinking at all at that moment.'

Quentin's drawn first blood, he knows it. 'Mrs. Frost, isn't it true that you've handled over two hundred child molestation cases in your seven years with the district attorney's office?'

'Yes.'

'Of those two hundred cases, twenty went to trial?'

'Yes.'

'And of those, twelve were convictions.'

'That's true.'

'In those twelve cases,' Quentin asks, 'were the children able to testify?'

'Yes.'

'In fact, in several of those cases, there was no corroborating physical evidence, as there was in the case of your son, isn't that right?'

'Yes.'

'As a prosecutor, as someone with access to child psychiatrists and social workers and an intimate knowledge of the legal process, don't you think you would have been able to prepare Nathaniel to come to court better than just about any other mother?'

She narrows her eyes. 'You can have every resource in the world at your fingertips, and still never be able to prepare a child for that. The reality, as you know, is that the rules in court are not written to protect children, but to protect defendants.'

'How fortunate for you, Mrs. Frost,' Quentin says dryly. 'Would you say you were a dedicated prosecutor?'

She hesitates. 'I would say . . . I was *too* dedicated a prosecutor.'

'Would you say you worked hard with the children you put on the stand to testify?'

'Yes.'

'In light of those twelve convictions, wouldn't you consider the work you did with those children to be successful?'

'No, I wouldn't,' she bluntly replies.

'But didn't all those perpetrators go to jail?'

'Not long enough.'

'Still, Mrs. Frost,' Quentin presses. 'You made the justice system work for those twelve children.'

'You don't understand,' she says, her eyes blazing. 'This was *my* child. As a prosecutor, my responsibility was completely different. I was supposed to take justice as far as I could for each of them, and I did. Anything else that happened outside the bounds of that courtroom was up to the parents, not me. If a mother decided to go into hiding to keep an abusive father away from her child – that was *her* decision to make. If a mother walked away from a verdict and shot an abuser, it had nothing to do with me. But then one day I wasn't just the prosecutor anymore. I was the parent. And it was up to me to take every step to make sure my son was safe, no matter what.'

It is the moment Quentin's waited for. Finely tuned to her anger, he steps closer to her. 'Are you saying that your child is entitled to more justice than another child?'

'Those kids were my job. Nathaniel is my *life*.'

Immediately, Fisher Carrington bobs out of his seat. 'Your Honor, may we take a short break –'

'No,' Quentin and the judge say simultaneously. 'That child was your life?' Quentin repeats.

'Yes.'

'Were you willing to exchange your freedom, then, to save Nathaniel?'

'Absolutely.'

'Were you thinking about that when you held the gun up to Father Szyszynski's head?'

'Of course I was,' she answers fiercely.

'Were you thinking that the only way to protect your son was to empty those bullets into Father Szyszynski's head –'

'Yes!'

'– and to make sure he never left that courtroom alive?'

'*Yes*.'

Quentin falls back. 'But you told us you weren't thinking at all at that moment, Mrs. Frost,' he says, and stares at her until she has to turn away.

When Fisher stands up to redirect, I am still shaking. How could I, who knew better, let that get away from me? I frantically scan the faces of the jury, but I can't tell a thing; you can never tell a thing. One woman looks near tears. Another is doing a crossword puzzle in the corner.

'Nina,' Fisher says, 'when you were in the courtroom that morning, were you thinking that you would be willing to exchange your freedom to save Nathaniel?'

'Yes,' I whisper.

'When you were in the courtroom that morning, were you thinking that the only way to stop that clock from ticking was to stop Father Szyszynski?'

'Yes.'

He meets my gaze. 'When you were in the courtroom that morning, were you planning to kill him?'

'Of course not,' I reply.

'Your Honor,' Fisher announces, 'the defense rests.'

Quentin lies on the godawful bed in the efficiency suite, wondering why the heat hasn't kicked in, when he's cranked it up to eighty degrees. He yanks the covers over himself, then flips through the channels on the television again. An entertainment program, *Wheel of Fortune*, and an infomercial for balding men. With a small grin, Quentin touches his shaved head.

He gets up and pads to the refrigerator, but the only thing inside it is a six-pack of Pepsi and a rotting mango he cannot recall buying. If he's going to eat dinner, he's going to have to get dinner. With a sigh, he sinks down on the bed to put on his boots and accidentally sits on the remote.

The channel switches again, this time to CNN. A woman with a smooth space helmet of red hair is speaking in front of a small graphic of Nina Frost's face. 'Testimony in the DA Murder Trial finished this afternoon,' the anchor says. 'Closing arguments are scheduled for tomorrow morning.'

Quentin turns off the TV. He ties his boots and then his gaze falls on the telephone beside the bed.

After three rings, he starts debating with himself about whether or not to leave a message. Then suddenly music explodes into his ear, a deafening backfire of rap. 'Yeah?' a voice says, and then the sound is turned down.

'Gideon,' Quentin says. 'It's me.'

There is a pause. 'Me who?' the boy replies, and it makes Quentin smile; he knows damn well who this is. 'If you're looking for my mom, she's not here. Maybe I'll tell her to call you back and then again maybe I'll just forget to give her the message.'

'Gideon, wait!' Quentin can almost hear the phone, halfway to its cradle, being brought back to his son's ear.

'*What.*'

'I didn't call to talk to Tanya. I called to talk to you.'

For a long moment, neither of them speaks. Then Gideon says, 'If you called to talk, you're doing a lousy job of it.'

'You're right.' Quentin rubs his temples. 'I just wanted to say I'm sorry. About the whole rehabilitation sentence, all of it. At the time I really believed that I was doing what was best for you.' He takes a deep breath. 'I had no right to start telling you how to live your life when I voluntarily walked out of it years before.' When his son stays silent, Quentin begins to get nervous. Did he get disconnected, without knowing it? 'Gideon?'

'Is that what you wanted to talk to me about?' he says finally.

'No. I called to see if you wanted to meet me for some pizza.' Quentin tosses the remote control on the bed, watches it bounce. The moment he waits for Gideon's response stretches to an eternity.

'Where?' Gideon asks.

Funny thing about a jury: no matter how scattered they seem during testimony; no matter who falls asleep in the back row and who paints their nails right during your cross-examinations, the minute it's time to get down to business, they suddenly rise to the challenge. The jurors stare at Quentin now, their attention focused on his closing argument. 'Ladies and gentlemen,' he begins, 'this is a very difficult case for me. Even though I do not know the defendant personally, I would have called her my colleague. But Nina Frost is not on the side of the law anymore. You all saw with your own eyes what she did on the morning of October thirtieth, 2001. She walked into a courtroom, put a gun up to an innocent man's head, and she shot him four times.

'The ironic thing is that Nina Frost claims she committed this crime in order to protect her son. Yet as she found out later . . . as we all would have found out later, had the court system been allowed to work the way it is supposed to work in a civilized society . . . that in killing Father Szyszynski, she did not protect her son at all.' Quentin looks soberly at the jury. 'There are reasons we have courts – because it's very easy to accuse a man. Courts hold up the facts, so that a rational judgment can be made. But Mrs. Frost acted without facts. Mrs. Frost not only accused this man, she tried him, convicted him, and executed him all by herself on that morning.'

He walks toward the jury box, trailing his hand along the railing. 'Mr. Carrington will tell you that the reason the defendant committed this crime is because she knew the justice system, and she truly believed it would not protect her son. Yes, Nina Frost knew the justice system. But she used it to stack the odds. She knew what her rights would be as a defendant. She knew how to act to make a jury believe she was temporarily insane. She knew exactly what she was doing the moment she stood up and shot Father Szyszynski in cold blood.'

Quentin addresses each juror in turn. 'To find Mrs. Frost guilty, you must first believe that the state of Maine has proved beyond a reasonable doubt that Father Szyszynski was unlawfully killed.' He spreads his hands. 'Well, you all saw it happen on videotape. Second, you must believe that the defendant was the one who killed Father Szyszynski. Again, there's no doubt in this case that this is true. And finally, you must believe that Mrs. Frost killed Father Szyszynski with premeditation. It's a big word, a legal word, but you all know what it is.'

He hesitates. 'This morning, as you were driving to court, at least one of you came upon a four-way intersection with a traffic light that was turning yellow. You needed to make a decision about whether or not to take your foot off the gas and stop . . . or whether you should speed through it. I don't know what choice you made; I don't need to. All I need to know – all *you* need to know – is that the split second when you made the decision to stop or to go was premeditation. That's all it takes. And when Mrs. Frost told you yesterday that at the moment she held the gun to Father Szyszynski's head, she was thinking that she needed to keep him from leaving the courtroom alive in order to protect her son – that, too, was premeditation.'

Quentin walks back toward the defense table and points at Nina. 'This is not a case about emotions; this is a case about facts. And the facts in this case are that an innocent man is dead, that this woman killed him, and that she believed her son deserved special treatment that only she could give.' He turns toward the jury one last time. 'Don't give her any special treatment for breaking the law.'

'I have two daughters,' Fisher says, standing up beside me. 'One's a high school junior; the other goes to Dartmouth.' He smiles at the jury. 'I'm crazy about them. I'm sure many of you feel the same about your kids. And that's the way Nina Frost feels about her son, Nathaniel.' He puts his hand on my shoulder. 'However, one completely ordinary morning, Nina found herself facing a horrible truth no parent ever wants to face: Someone had anally raped her little boy. And Nina had to face a second horrible truth – she knew what a molestation trial would do to her son's fragile emotional balance.'

He walks toward the jury. 'How did she know? Because she'd made other parents' children go through it. Because she had witnessed, time after time, children coming to court and dissolving into tears on the witness stand. Because she had seen abusers walk free even as these children were trying to fathom why they had to relive this nightmare all over again in front of a room full of strangers.' Fisher shakes his head. 'This was a tragedy. Adding to it is the fact that Father Szyszynski was not the man who had hurt this little boy, after all. But on October thirtieth, the police believed that he was the abuser. The prosecutor's office believed it. Nina Frost believed it. And on that morning, she also believed that she had run out of options. What happened in court that morning was not a premeditated, malicious act but a desperate one. The woman you saw shooting that man might have looked like Nina Frost, might have moved like Nina Frost – but ladies and gentlemen, that woman on the videotape was someone different. Someone not mentally capable of stopping herself at that moment.'

As Fisher takes another breath to launch into the definition of not guilty by reason of insanity, I get to my feet. 'Excuse me, but I'd like to finish.'

He turns around, the wind gone from his sails. 'You *what?*'

I wait until he is close enough for me to speak privately. 'Fisher, I think I can handle a closing argument.'

'You are not representing yourself!'

'Well, I'm not misrepresenting myself either.' I glance at the judge, and at Quentin Brown, who is absolutely gaping. 'May I approach, Your Honor?'

'Oh, by all means, go right ahead,' Judge Neal says.

We all go up to the bench, Fisher and Quentin sandwiching me. 'Your Honor, I don't believe this is the wisest course of action for my client,' Fisher says.

'Seems to me that's an issue she needs to work on,' Quentin murmurs.

The judge rubs his brow. 'I think Mrs. Frost knows the risks here better than other defendants. You may proceed.'

Fisher and I do-si-do for an awkward moment. 'It's your funeral,' he mutters, and then he steps around me and sits down. I walk up to the jury, finding my footing again, like a long-ago sailor stepping back on the deck of a clipper. 'Hello,' I begin softly. 'I think you all know who I am by now. You've certainly heard a lot of explanations for what brought me here. But what you haven't heard, straight out, is the truth.'

I gesture toward Quentin. 'I know this, because like Mr. Brown, I was a prosecutor. And truth isn't something that makes its way into a trial very often. You've got the state, tossing facts at you. And the defense, lobbing feelings. Nobody likes the truth because it's subject to personal interpretation, and both Mr. Brown and Mr. Carrington are afraid you might read it the wrong way. But today, I want to tell it to you.

'The truth is, I made a horrible mistake. The truth is, on that morning, I was not the vigilante Mr. Brown wants you to believe I was, and I wasn't a woman having a nervous break-down, like Mr. Carrington wants you to believe. The truth is I was Nathaniel's mother, and that took precedence over every-thing else.'

I walk up to one juror, a young kid wearing a backward baseball cap. 'What if your best friend was being held at gunpoint, and you had a revolver in your own hand? What would you do?' Turning to an older gentleman, I ask, 'What if you came home and found your wife being raped?' I step back. 'Where is the line? We're taught to stand up for ourselves; we're taught to stand up for others we care about. But all of a sudden, there's a new line drawn by the law. *You sit back,* it says, *and let us deal with this.* And you know that the law won't even do a very good job – it will traumatize your child, it will set free a convict in only a few years. In the eyes of this law that's *dealing* with your problem, what's morally right is considered wrong . . . and what's morally wrong, you can get away with.'

I level my gaze at the jury. 'Maybe I knew that the judicial system would not work for my son. Maybe I even knew, on some level, that I could convince a jury I looked crazy even though I wasn't. I wish I could tell you for sure – but if I've learned anything, it's that we don't know half of what we think we do. And we know ourselves least of all.'

I turn toward the gallery and look, in turn, at Caleb and Patrick. 'For each of you sitting there, condemning me for my actions: How can you know that you wouldn't have done the same thing, if put to the test? Every day, we do little things to keep the people we love from being hurt – tell a white lie, buckle a seat belt, take away car keys from a buddy who's had one drink too many. But I've also heard of mothers who find the strength to lift cars off trapped toddlers; I've read of men who jump in front of bullets to save women they can't live without. Does that make them insane . . . or is that the moment when they are painfully, 100 percent lucid?' I raise my brows. 'It's not for me to say. But in that courtroom, the morning I shot Father Szyszynski, I knew exactly what I was doing. And at the same time, I was crazy.' I spread my hands, a supplicant. 'Love will do that to you.'

Quentin stands up to rebut. 'Unfortunately for Mrs. Frost, there are not two systems of justice in this country – one for people who think they know everything, and one for everyone else.' He glances at the jury. 'You heard her – she's not sorry that she killed a man . . . she's sorry she killed the *wrong* man.

'Enough mistakes have been made lately,' the prosecutor says wearily. 'Please don't make another one.'

When the doorbell rings, I think it might be Fisher. He hasn't spoken to me since we left court, and the three hours the jury deliberated after closing arguments does tend to support his belief that I shouldn't have gotten up to speak my mind. But when I open it, ready to defend myself – *again* – Nathaniel pitches into me. 'Mom!' he yells, squeezing me so tightly I stumble back. 'Mom, we checkered out!'

'Did you?' I say, and then repeat it over his head to Caleb. 'Did you?'

He sets down his small duffel bag, and Nathaniel's. 'I thought it might be a good time to come home,' he says quietly. 'If that's okay?'

By now Nathaniel has his arms around the barrel of our golden retriever's stomach; while Mason, wriggling, licks every spare inch of skin he can find. His thick tail thumps on the tile, a joyous tattoo. I know how that dog feels. Only now – in the presence of company – do I realize how lonely I have been.

So I lean against Caleb, my head tucked beneath his chin, where I cannot fail to listen to his heart. 'Perfect,' I reply.

The dog was a pillow breathing underneath me. 'What happened to Mason's mom?'

My mother looked up from the couch, where she was reading papers with big words printed so tiny it made my head hurt just thinking about them. 'She's . . . somewhere.'

'How come she doesn't live with us?'

'Mason's mother belonged to a breeder in Massachusetts. She had twelve puppies, and Mason was the one we took home.'

'Do you think he misses her?'

'I guess he used to, at first,' she answered. 'But it's been a long time, and he's happy with us. I bet he doesn't remember her anymore.'

I slid my finger past Mason's licorice gums, over his teeth. He blinked at me.

I bet she was wrong.

9

'Did you want the milk?' Nathaniel's mother asks.

'I already had a bowl of cereal,' his father replies.

'Oh.' She starts to put it back in the refrigerator, but his father takes it out of her hand. 'Maybe I'll have a little more.'

They look at each other, and then his mother steps back with a funny too-tight smile. 'All right,' she says.

Nathaniel watches this the way he would watch a cartoon – knowing in the back of his head that something is not quite real or right, but attracted to the show all the same.

Last summer when he was outside with his father he'd chased an electric green dragonfly all the way across the garden and the pumpkin patch and into the birdbath. There it found a bright blue dragonfly, and for a while they'd watched the two of them nip and thrust at each other, their bodies swords. 'Are they fighting?' Nathaniel had asked.

'No, they're mating.' Before Nathaniel could even ask, his father explained: It was the way animals and bugs and things made babies.

'But it looks like they're trying to kill each other,' Nathaniel pointed out.

Almost as soon as he said it, the two dragonflies hitched together like a shimmering space station, their wings beating like a quartet of hearts and their long tails quivering.

'Sometimes it's like that,' his father had answered.

Quentin had spent the night tossing on that godawful mattress, wondering what the hell was keeping the jury. No case was a sure thing, but for God's sake, they had this murder on tape.

It should have been pretty simple. Yet the jury had been deliberating since yesterday afternoon; and here it was nearly twenty-four hours later with no verdict.

He has walked past the jury room at least twenty times, trying ESP to will them toward a conviction. The bailiff posted outside the door is an older man with the ability to sleep on his feet. He snorts his way back to a deadpan position of authority as the prosecutor passes. 'Anything?' Quentin asks.

'Lot of yelling. They just ordered lunch. Eleven turkey sandwiches and one roast beef.'

Frustrated, Quentin turns on his heel and heads down the hall again, only to crash into his son coming around the corner. 'Gideon?'

'What's up.'

Gideon, in court. For a moment Quentin's heart stops, like it did a year ago. 'What are you doing here?'

The boy shrugs, as if he can't figure it out himself. 'I didn't have basketball practice today, and I figured I'd just come over and chill out.' He drags his sneaker on the floor to make it squeak. 'See what it looks like from the other side, and all.'

A slow smile itches its way across Quentin's face as he claps his son on the shoulder. And for the first time in the ten years that Quentin Brown has been in a courthouse, he is rendered speechless.

Twenty-six hours; 1,560 minutes; 93,600 seconds. Call it what you like; waiting in any denomination takes a lifetime. I have memorized every inch of this conference room. I have counted the linoleum tiles on the floor, marked the scars on the ceiling, measured off the width of the windows. What are they doing in there?

When the door opens, I realize that the only thing worse than waiting is the moment that you realize a decision has been made.

A white handkerchief appears in the doorway, followed by Fisher.

'The verdict.' The words cut up my tongue. 'It's in?'

'Not yet.'

Boneless, I sink back in the chair as Fisher tosses the handkerchief at me. 'Is this in preparation for their finding?'

'No, it's me, surrendering. I'm sorry about yesterday.' He glances at me. 'Although a little advance notice that you wanted to do the closing would have been nice.'

'I know.' I look up at him. 'Do you think that's why the jury didn't come back fast with an acquittal?'

Fisher shrugs. 'Maybe it's why they didn't come back fast with a conviction.'

'Yeah, well. I've always been best at closings.'

He smiles at me. 'I'm a cross-examination man, myself.'

We look at each other for a moment, in complete accord. 'What's the part you hate most about a trial?'

'Now. Waiting for the jury to come back.' Fisher exhales deeply. 'I always have to calm down the client, who only wants a prediction about the outcome, and no one can predict that. You prosecutors are lucky; you just win or lose, and you don't have to reassure someone that he's not going to go to prison for the rest of his life when you know perfectly well that he . . .' He breaks off, because all the color has drained from my face. 'Well. Anyway. You know that no one can guess a jury's outcome.'

When I don't look particularly encouraged, he asks, 'What's the hardest part for you?'

'Right before the state rests, because that's the last chance I have to make sure I got all the evidence in and that I did it right. Once I say those three words . . . I know I'm going to find out whether or not I screwed up.'

Fisher meets my eye. 'Nina,' he says gently, 'the state rests.'

I lay on my side on an alphabet rug on the playroom floor, jamming the foot of a penguin into its wooden slot. 'If I do this penguin puzzle one more time,' I say, 'I will save the jury some trouble and hang myself.'

Caleb looks up from where he is sitting with Nathaniel, sorting multicolored plastic teddy bears. 'I want to go outside,' Nathaniel whines.

'We can't, buddy. We're waiting for some important news for Mommy.'

'But I want to!' Nathaniel kicks the table, hard.

'Maybe in a little while.' Caleb hands him a batch of bears. 'Here, take some more.'

'*No!*' With one arm, Nathaniel swipes the entire tray off the table. The sorting containers bounce and roll into the block area; the plastic bears scatter to all four corners of the room. The resulting clatter rings inside my head, in the empty spot where I am trying so hard to think of absolutely nothing.

I get to my feet, grab my son by the shoulders, and shake him. 'You do *not* throw toys! You will pick up every last one of these, Nathaniel, and I mean it!'

Nathaniel, now, is sobbing at the top of his lungs. Caleb, tight-faced, turns on me too. 'Just because you're at the end of your rope, Nina, doesn't mean that you –'

'*'Scuse me.*'

The voice at the door makes all three of us turn. A bailiff leans in, nods at us. 'The jury's coming in,' he says.

'It's not a verdict,' Fisher whispers to me minutes later.

'How do you know?'

'Because the bailiff would have said so . . . not just that the jury was back.'

I draw back, dubious. 'Bailiffs never tell *me* anything.'

'Trust me.'

I wet my lips. 'Then why are we here?'

'I don't know,' Fisher admits, and we both turn our attention to the judge.

He sits at the bench, looking overjoyed to have finally reached the end of this debacle. 'Mr. Foreperson,' Judge Neal asks, 'has the jury reached a verdict?'

A man in the front row of the jury box stands up. He takes

off his baseball cap and tucks it under his arm, then clears his throat. 'Your Honor, we've been trying, but we can't seem to get together on this. There's some of us that –'

'Hold on, Mr. Foreperson, don't say any more. Have you deliberated about this case and have you taken a vote to see what every juror's position is on the issue of guilt or innocence?'

'We've done it a bunch of times, but it keeps coming back to a few that won't change their minds.'

The judge looks at Fisher, and then at Quentin. 'Counsel, approach.'

I stand up, too, and the judge sighs. 'All right, Mrs. Frost, you too.' At the bench, he murmurs, 'I'm going to give them an Allen charge. Any objections?'

'No objection,' Quentin says, and Fisher agrees. As we walk back to the defense table, I meet Caleb's eye, and silently mouth, 'They're hung.'

The judge begins to speak. 'Ladies and gentlemen, you've heard all the facts, and you've heard all the evidence. I am aware it's been a long haul, and that you have a difficult decision to make. But I also know that you *can* reach closure . . . and that you're the best jury to do it. If the case has to be tried again, another group of jurors will not necessarily do a better job than you are doing.' He glances soberly at the group. 'I urge you to go back to the jury room, to respectfully consider each other's opinions, and to see if some progress can't be made. At the end of the afternoon, I'm going to ask you to come back and let me know how you're doing.'

'Now what?' Caleb whispers, from behind me.

I watch the newly energized jury file out again. Now we wait.

Watching someone tie themselves in a knot makes you squirm in your own seat, or so Caleb discovers after spending two and a half more hours with Nina while the jury is deliberating. She sits hunched forward on a tiny chair in the playroom, completely ignorant of Nathaniel making airplane sounds as he zooms around with his arms extended. Her eyes stare intensely at absolutely nothing; her chin rests on her fist.

'Hey,' Caleb says softly.

She blinks, comes back to him. 'Oh . . . hey.'

'You okay?'

'Yes.' A smile stretches her lips thin. *'Yes!'* she repeats.

It reminds Caleb of the time years ago that he attempted to teach her to water-ski: She is trying too hard, instead of just letting it happen. 'Why don't we all go down to the vending machines?' he suggests. 'Nathaniel can get some hot chocolate, and I'll treat you to the dishwater that passes for soup.'

'Sounds great.'

Caleb turns to Nathaniel and tells him they are going to get a snack. He runs to the door, and Caleb walks up behind him. 'Come on,' he says to Nina. 'We're ready.'

She stares at him as if they have never had a conversation, much less one thirty seconds ago. 'To do what?' she asks.

Patrick sits on a bench behind the courthouse, freezing his ass off, and watching Nathaniel whoop his way across a field. Why this child has so much energy at four-thirty in the afternoon is beyond him, but then he can remember back to when he and Nina used to spend entire days playing pond hockey without tiring or getting frostbite. Maybe time is only something you notice when you get old and have less of it at your disposal.

The boy collapses beside Patrick, his cheeks a fiery red, his nose running. 'Got a tissue, Patrick?'

He shakes his head. 'Sorry, Weed. Use your sleeve.'

Nathaniel laughs, and then does just that. He ducks his head beneath Patrick's arm, and it makes Patrick want to shout. If only Nina could see this, her son seeking out someone's touch – oh, God, what it would do for her morale right now. He hugs Nathaniel close, drops a kiss on the top of his head.

'I like playing with you,' Nathaniel says.

'Well, I like playing with you too.'

'You don't yell.'

Patrick glances down at him. 'Your mom been doing that?'

Nathaniel shrugs, then nods. 'It's like she got stolen and they left someone mean in her place who looks just like her. Someone who can't sit still and who doesn't hear me when I talk and when I do talk it's always giving her a headache.' He looks into his lap. 'I want my old mom back.'

'She wants that too, Weed.' Patrick looks to the west, where the sun has begun to draw blood from the horizon. 'Truth is, she's pretty nervous right now. She isn't sure what kind of news she's going to hear.' When Nathaniel shrugs, he adds, 'You know she loves you.'

'Well,' the boy says defensively. 'I love her too.'

Patrick nods. *You're not the only one,* he thinks.

'A mistrial?' I say, shaking my head. 'No. Fisher, I can't go through this again. You know trials don't get any better with age.'

'You're thinking like a prosecutor,' Fisher admonishes, 'except this time, you're right.' He turns around from the window where he is standing. 'I want you to chew on something tonight.'

'What?'

'Waiving the jury. I'll talk to Quentin in the morning, if you agree, and see if he's willing to let the judge decide the verdict.'

I stare at him. 'You know that we were trying this case on the emotion, not the law. A jury *might* acquit based on emotion. But a judge is *always* going to rule based on the law. Are you crazy?'

'No, Nina,' Fisher answers soberly. 'But neither were you.'

We lie in bed that night with the weight of a full moon pressing down on us. I have told Caleb about my conversation with Fisher, and now we both stare at the ceiling, as if the answer might appear, skywritten with stars. I want Caleb to take my hand across the great expanse of this bed. I need that, to believe we are not miles apart.

'What do you think?' he asks.

I turn to him. In the moonlight his profile is edged in gold, the color of courage. 'I'm not making decisions by myself anymore,' I answer.

He comes up on an elbow, turning to me. 'What would happen?'

I swallow, and try to keep my voice from shaking. 'Well, a judge is going to convict me, because legally, I committed murder. But the upside is . . . I probably won't be sentenced as long as I would have been with a jury verdict.'

Suddenly Caleb's face looms over mine. 'Nina . . . you can't go to jail.'

I turn away, so that the tear slips down the side of my face he cannot see. 'I knew I was taking this chance when I did it.'

His hands tighten on my shoulders. 'You can't. You just can't.'

'I'll be back.'

'When?'

'I don't know.'

Caleb buries his face in my neck, drawing in great draughts of air. And then suddenly I am clutching at him, too, as if there cannot be any distance between us today, because tomorrow there will be so much. I feel the rough pads of his hands mark my back; and the heat of his grief is searing. When he comes inside me I dig my nails into his shoulders, trying to leave behind a trace of myself. We make love with near violence, with so much emotion that the atmosphere around us hums. And then, like all things, it is over.

'But I love you,' Caleb says, his voice breaking, because in a perfect world, this should be all the excuse one needs.

That night I dream I am walking into an ocean, the waves soaking the hem of my cotton nightgown. The water is cold, but not nearly as cold as it usually is in Maine, and the beach beneath is a smooth lip of sand. I keep walking, even when the water reaches my knees, even when it brushes my hips and my nightgown sticks to my body like a second skin. I keep walking, and the water comes up to my neck, my chin. By the time I go under I realize I am going to drown.

At first I fight, trying to ration the air I have in my lungs. Then they start to burn, a circle of fire beneath my ribs. My wide eyes burst black, and my feet start to thrash, but I am getting nowhere. *This is it,* I think. *Finally.*

With that realization I let my arms go still, and my legs go limp. I feel my body sinking and the water filling me, until I am curled on the sand at the base of the sea.

The sun is a quivering yellow eye. I get to my feet, and to my great surprise, begin to walk with ease on the bottom of the ocean floor.

Nathaniel doesn't move the hour I sit on his bed, watching him sleep. But when I touch his hair, unable to hold back any longer, he rolls over and blinks at me. 'It's still dark,' he whispers.

'I know. It's not morning.'

I watch him trying to puzzle this out: What could have brought me, then, to wake him in the middle of the night? How am I supposed to explain to him that the next time I have the opportunity to do this, his body might reach the whole length of the bed? That by the time I come back, the boy I left behind will no longer exist?

'Nathaniel,' I say, with a shuddering breath, 'I might be going away.'

He sits up. 'You can't, Mommy.' Smiling, he even finds a reason. 'We just got back.'

'I know . . . but this isn't my choice.'

Nathaniel pulls the covers up to his chest, suddenly looking very small. 'What did I do this time?'

With a sob I pull him onto my lap and bury my face against his hair. He rubs his nose against my neck, and it reminds me so much of him as an infant that I cannot breathe. I would trade everything, now, to have those minutes back, tucked into a miser's lockbox. Even the ordinary moments – driving in the car, cleaning up the playroom, cooking dinner with Nathaniel. They are no less miraculous simply because they are something we did as a matter of routine. It is not *what* you do with a child that brings you together . . . it is the fact that you are lucky enough to do it at *all*.

I draw away to look at his face. That bow of a mouth, the slope of his nose. His eyes, preserving memories like the amber they resemble. *Keep them,* I think. *Watch over them for me.*

By now, I am crying hard. 'I promise, it won't be forever. I promise that you can come see me. And I want you to know every minute of every day that I'm away from you . . . I'm thinking of how long it'll be before I come back.'

Nathaniel wraps his arms around my neck and holds on for dear life. 'I don't want you to go.'

'I know.' I draw back, holding his wrists loosely.

'I'll come with you.'

'I wish you could. But I need someone here to take care of your father.'

Nathaniel shakes his head. 'But I'll miss you.'

'And I'll miss you,' I say softly. 'Hey, how about if we make a pact?'

'What's that?'

'A decision two people make together.' I try for a smile. 'Let's agree *not* to miss each other. Is that a deal?'

Nathaniel looks at me for a long moment. 'I don't think I can do it,' he confesses.

I pull him close again. 'Oh, Nathaniel,' I whisper. 'Me neither.'

Nathaniel is glued to my side the next morning when we walk into the courthouse. The reporters that I have almost become accustomed to seem like a cruel torture, their questions and their blinding video cameras a modern gauntlet I have to survive. These will be my Before and After pictures; DA-cum-convict. *Print your headlines now,* I think, *since I am going to jail.*

As soon as I reach the barrier of the double doors, I hand Nathaniel to Caleb and make a dead run for the restroom, where I dry heave into a toilet and splash water on my face and wrists. 'You can get through this,' I say to the mirror. 'You can at least end it with dignity.'

Taking a deep breath I push my way out the swinging door to where my family is waiting, and see Adrienne, the trans-sexual, wearing a red dress two sizes too small and a grin as large as Texas. 'Nina!' she cries, and comes running to hug me. 'Last place I ever thought I'd want to be is in a courtroom again, but honey, I'm here for you.'

'You're out?'

'Since yesterday. Didn't know if I'd make it in time, but that jury deliberation's taking longer than my sex change operation.'

Suddenly Nathaniel has wormed his way between us, and is doing his best to climb me like a tree. I heft him into my arms. 'Nathaniel, this is Adrienne.'

Her eyes light up. 'I have heard so much about you.'

It is a toss-up as to who is more stunned by Adrienne's presence – Nathaniel or Caleb. But before I can offer any explanations, Fisher hurries toward us.

I meet his gaze. 'Do it,' I say.

Quentin finds Fisher waiting for him in the courtroom. 'We have to speak to Judge Neal,' he says quietly.

'I'm not offering her a plea,' Quentin answers.

'And I'm not asking for one.' He turns, heading for the judge's chambers without waiting to see if the prosecutor will follow.

Ten minutes later, they are standing in front of Judge Neal, the angry heads of safari animals bearing witness. 'Your Honor,' Fisher begins, 'we've been here so long; it's clear that the jury is going to hang. I've talked to my client . . . and if Mr. Brown is willing, we'd like to submit this case to Your Honor and have you decide the facts and the verdict.'

Well, if Quentin was expecting anything it wasn't this. He looks at the defense attorney as if the man has lost his mind. Granted, nobody likes a mistrial, but to let the judge rule is to adhere, strictly, to the letter of the law – something far more beneficial to the prosecution, in this case, than the defense. Fisher Carrington has just handed Quentin a conviction on a silver platter.

The judge stares at him. 'Mr. Brown? What would the state like to do?'

He clears his throat. 'The state finds this perfectly acceptable, Your Honor.'

'Fine. I'm going to let the jury go then. I need an hour to review the evidence, and then I'll make my ruling.' With a nod, the judge dismisses the two lawyers, and begins the process of deciding Nina Frost's future.

Adrienne, it turns out, is a godsend. She gets Nathaniel out of my arms by making herself into a jungle gym when Caleb and I are wrung too dry to play. Nathaniel crawls over her back and then down the long slide of her shins. 'If he's tiring you out,' Caleb says, 'just tell him to stop.'

'Oh, honey, I've been waiting my whole life for this.' She flips Nathaniel upside down, so that he giggles.

I am torn between watching them and joining in. My biggest fear is that if I let myself touch my son again, nothing they will do will be able to drag me away.

When there is a knock at the playroom door, we all turn. Patrick stands uncomfortably at the threshold. I know what he wants, and I also know that he will not ask for it with my family here.

To my surprise, Caleb takes the decision out of everyone's hands. He nods toward Patrick, and then to me. 'Go on,' he says.

So Patrick and I find ourselves walking down twisted basement corridors, a foot of space separating us. We travel so far in silence that I realize I have no idea where we now are. 'How could you?' he finally bursts out. 'If you'd gone with another jury trial, at least, you'd have a shot at an acquittal.'

'And I would have dragged Nathaniel and Caleb and you and everyone else along through it again. Patrick, this has to stop. It has to be over. No matter what.'

He stops walking, leans against a heating duct. 'I never really thought you'd go to jail.'

'There are a lot of places,' I reply, 'that I thought I'd never go.' I smile faintly. 'Will you bring me Chinese food every now and then?'

'No.' Patrick looks down at the floor between his shoes. 'I won't be here, Nina.'

'You . . . what?'

'I'm moving. There are some job openings out in the Pacific Northwest I might take a look at.' He takes a deep breath. 'I always wanted to see what it was like out there. I just didn't want to do it without you.'

'Patrick –'

With great tenderness, he kisses my forehead. 'You will be fine,' he murmurs. 'You've done it before.' He offers me a crooked smile to slip into my breast pocket. And then he walks down the hall, leaving me to find my own way back.

The bathroom door at the base of the staircase flies open, and suddenly Quentin Brown is no more than four feet away from me. 'Mrs. Frost,' he sputters.

'After all this, I would think you could call me Nina.' It is an ethical violation for him to speak to me without Fisher present, and we both know it. Yet somehow, bending that rule doesn't seem quite so horrific, after all this. When he doesn't respond, I realize he doesn't feel the same way and I try to step around him. 'If you'll excuse me, my family's waiting in the playroom.'

'I have to admit,' Quentin says as I am walking away, 'I was surprised by your decision.'

I turn. 'To let the judge rule?'

'Yes. I don't know if I'd do the same thing, if I were a defendant.'

I shake my head. 'Somehow, Quentin, I can't picture you as a defendant.'

'Could you picture me as a parent?'

It surprises me. 'No. I never heard that you had a family.'

'A boy. Sixteen.' He stuffs his hands in his pockets. 'I know, I know. You've done such a good job imagining me as a ruthless villain that it's hard to give me a vein of compassion.'

'Well.' I shrug. 'Maybe not a ruthless villain.'

'An asshole then?'

'Your words, counselor,' I reply, and we both grin.

'Then again, people can surprise you all the time,' he muses. 'For example, a district attorney who commits murder. Or an assistant attorney general that drives past a defendant's home at night just to make sure she's okay.'

I snort. 'If you drove by at all, it was to make sure I was still *there*.'

'Nina, didn't you ever wonder who in your office left you the lab report from the underwear?'

My jaw drops open. 'My son's name,' Quentin says. 'It's Gideon.'

Whistling, he nods to me, and jogs up the staircase.

The courtroom is so quiet that I can hear Caleb breathing behind me. What he said the moment before we walked in to hear the judge's verdict echoes too, in the silence: *I am proud of you.*

Judge Neal clears his throat and begins to speak. 'The evidence in this case clearly shows that on October thirtieth, 2001, the defendant Nina Frost went out, purchased a handgun, concealed it, and brought it into a Biddeford district courtroom. The evidence also shows that she positioned herself near Father Szyszynski, and intentionally and knowingly shot him four times in the head, thereby causing his death. The evidence is also clear that at the time she did these things, Nina Frost was under the mistaken impression that Father Szyszynski had sexually molested her five-year-old son.'

I bow my head, each word a blow. 'So what does the evidence not support?' the judge asks rhetorically. 'Specifically, the defendant's contention that she was legally insane at the time of the shooting. Witnesses testified that she acted deliberately and methodically to exterminate the man who she thought had harmed her child. And at the time, the defendant was a trained, practicing assistant district attorney who knew very well that every person charged with a crime – Father Szyszynski included – was innocent until proven guilty in a court of law. Basically, this court believes Nina Frost to be a prosecutor through and through . . . so much so, that to break a law, she would have had to give the act careful consideration.'

He raises his head and pushes his glasses up on his nose. 'And so I reject the defendant's insanity defense.'

A shuffling to my left, from Quentin Brown.

'However –'

Quentin stills.

'– in this state there is another reason to justify the act of murder – namely, if a defendant was under the influence of a reasonable fear or anger brought about by reasonable provocation. As a prosecutor, Nina Frost didn't have reason to be fearful or angry the morning of October thirtieth . . . yet as Nathaniel's mother, she did. Her son's attempt to identify the victim, the wild card of the DNA evidence, and the defendant's intimate knowledge of the treatment of a witness in the criminal justice system all add up, in this court's opinion, to reasonable provocation under the law.'

I have stopped breathing. This cannot be true.

'Will the defendant please rise?'

It is not until Fisher grabs my arm and hauls me to my feet that I remember the judge means me. 'Nina Frost, I find you Not Guilty of Murder. I do find you Guilty of Manslaughter pursuant to 17-A M.R.S.A. Section 203 (1)(B). Does the defendant wish to waive a presentence report and be sentenced today?'

'Yes, Your Honor,' Fisher murmurs.

The judge looks at me for the first time this morning. 'I sentence you to twenty years in the Maine State Prison, with credit for the time you have already served.' He pauses. 'The remainder of the twenty years will be suspended, and you'll be on probation for that time. You need to check in with your probation officer before you leave court today, and then, Mrs. Frost, you are free to go.'

The courtroom erupts in a frenzy of flashbulbs and confusion. Fisher embraces me as I burst into tears, and Caleb leaps over the bar. 'Nina?' he demands. 'In English?'

'It's . . . good.' I laugh up at him. 'It's *great,* Caleb.' The judge, in essence, has absolved me. I will never have to serve out my prison term, as long as I manage not to kill anyone again. Caleb grabs me and swings me around; over his shoulder I see Adrienne pump her fist in the air. Behind her is Patrick. He sits with his eyes closed, smiling. Even as I watch, they blink open to focus on me. *Only you,* Patrick mouths silently; words I will wonder about for years.

When the reporters run off to call their affiliates with the verdict and the crowd in the gallery thins, I notice one other man. Quentin Brown has gathered his files and his briefcase. He walks to the gate between our tables, stops, and turns to me. He inclines his head, and I nod back. Suddenly my arm is wrenched behind me, and I instinctively pull away, certain that someone who has not understood the judge's verdict is about to put handcuffs on me again. 'No,' I say, turning. 'You don't understand . . .' But then the bailiff unlocks the electronic bracelet on my wrist. It falls to the floor, ringing out my release.

When I look up again, Quentin is gone.

After a few weeks, the interviews stop. The eagle eye of the news refocuses on some other sordid story. A caravan of media vehicles snakes its way south, and we go back to what we used to be.

Well, most of us do.

Nathaniel is stronger every day; and Caleb has picked up a few new jobs. Patrick called me from Chicago, his halfway point to the West Coast. So far, he is the only one who has been brave enough to ask me how I will fill my days now that I am not a prosecutor.

It has been such a big part of me for so long that there's no easy answer. Maybe I'll write the book everyone seems to want me to write. Maybe I'll give free legal advice to senior citizens at the town recreation hall. Maybe I will just stay at home and watch my son grow up.

I tap the envelope in my hand. It is from the Bar Disciplinary Committee, and it has been on the kitchen counter, unopened, for nearly two months. There's no point in opening it now, either. I know what it will say.

Sitting down at the computer, I type a very concise note. *I am voluntarily turning in my license; I no longer wish to practice law. Sincerely, Nina Frost.*

I print it, and an envelope to match. Fold, lick, seal, stamp. Then I put on my boots and walk down the driveway to the mailbox.

'Okay,' I say out loud, after I put it inside and raise the red flag. 'Okay,' I repeat, when what I really mean is, *What do I do now?*

There's always one week in January that's a thaw. Without warning, the temperature climbs to fifty degrees; the snow melts in puddles wide as a lake; people take to sitting on Adirondack chairs in their shorts, watching it all happen.

This year, however, the thaw's gone on for a record number of days. It started the day of Nina's release. That very afternoon, the town skating pond was closed due to spotty ice; by the end of the week teenagers were skateboarding down sidewalks; there was even word of a few crocuses pushing their way up through the inevitable mud. It has been good for business, that's for sure – construction that couldn't get done in the dead of winter has suddenly been given a reprieve. And it has also, for the first time Caleb can recall, made the sap run in the maple trees this early in the year.

Yesterday Caleb set up his taps and buckets; today, he is walking the perimeter of his property, collecting the sap. The sky seems crisp as a lancet, and Caleb has his shirtsleeves rolled up to the elbow. The mud is a succubus, grabbing for his boots, but even that can't slow him. Days like this, they just don't come around often enough.

He pours the sap into huge vats. Forty gallons of this sweet juice will boil down to a single gallon of maple syrup. Caleb makes it right on the kitchen stove, in a spaghetti pot, straining each batch through a sieve before it thickens. For Nina and Nathaniel, it's all about the end product – pouring it on pancakes and waffles. But to Caleb, the beauty is in the way you get there. The blood of a tree, a spout, and a bucket. Steam rising, the scent filling every corner of the house. There is nothing quite like it: knowing every breath you take is bound to be sweet.

Nathaniel is building a bridge, although it might turn out to be a tunnel. The cool thing about Legos is that you can change them right in the middle. Sometimes when he builds he pretends he is his father, and he does it with the same careful planning. And sometimes when he builds he pretends he is his mother, and takes a tower as high as it can go before it falls to the ground.

He has to work around the dog's tail, because Mason happens to be sleeping right on the middle of his bedroom floor, but that's all right too, because this could be a village with a monstrous beast. In fact, he might be creating the wicked awesome getaway boat.

But where will they all go? Nathaniel thinks for a minute, then lays down four greens and four reds, begins to build. He makes sturdy walls and wide windows. A level of a house, his father has told him, is called a *story*.

Nathaniel likes that. It makes him feel like maybe he is living between the covers of a book himself. Like maybe everyone in every home is sure to get a happy ending.

Laundry is always a good, mindless start. Ours seems to reproduce at the dank bottom of its bin, so that regardless of how careful we are with our clothes, there is always a full basket every other day. I fold the clean wash and carry it upstairs, putting Nathaniel's items away before I tackle my own.

It is when I go to fold a pair of my jeans over a hanger that I see the duffel bag. Has it really been sitting here, shoved into the back of the closet, for two weeks? Caleb probably never even noticed; he has enough clothes in his drawers to have overlooked unpacking the bag he took with him to the motel. But seeing it is an eyesore; it reminds me of the moment he moved out.

I pull out a few long-sleeved shirts, some boxers. It is not until I toss them into the laundry bin that I realize my hand is sticky. I rub my fingers together, frown, pick up one shirt again and shake it out.

There is a big, green stain on one corner.

There are stains on some socks too. It looks as if something has spilled all over, but when I look in the bag, there's no open bottle of shampoo.

Then, it doesn't smell like shampoo either. It is a scent I cannot place, exactly. Something industrial.

The last item in the bag is a pair of jeans. Out of habit, I reach into the pockets to make sure Caleb hasn't left money or receipts inside.

In the left rear pocket is a five-dollar bill. And in the right rear pocket are boarding passes for two US Air flights: one from Boston to New Orleans, one from New Orleans to Boston, both dated January 3, 2002. The day after Nathaniel's competency hearing.

Caleb's voice comes from a few feet behind me. 'I did what I had to do.'

Caleb is yelling at Nathaniel to stop playing with the antifreeze.

'How many times do I have to tell you . . . It's poison.' Mason, lapping at the puddle because it tastes so sweet; he does not know any better.

'The cat,' I whisper, turning to him. 'The cat died too.'

'I know. I figure it got at the rest of the cocoa. Ethylene glycol is toxic . . . but it's sweet enough.' He reaches for me, but I back away. 'You told me his name. You said it wasn't over yet. All I did,' Caleb says softly, 'is finish what you started.'

'Don't.' I hold up my hand. 'Caleb, don't tell me this.'

'You're the only one I *can* tell.'

He is right, of course. As his wife, I am not obligated to testify against him. Not even if Gwynne is autopsied, and there are traces of poison in the tissues. Not even if evidence leads right to Caleb.

But then, I have spent three months learning the repercussions of taking the law into one's own hands. I have watched my husband walk out the door – not because he was judging me, it turns out, but because he was trying himself. I have come so close to losing everything I ever wanted – a life I was too foolish to value until it was nearly taken away.

I stare at Caleb, waiting for an explanation.

Yet there are some feelings so far-flung and wide that words cannot cover them. As language fails Caleb, his eyes lock onto mine, and he spells out what he cannot speak. His hands come up to clasp each other tightly. To someone who does not know how to listen in a different way, it looks like he is praying for the best. But me, I know the sign for *marriage*.

It is all he needs to say to make me understand.

Suddenly Nathaniel bursts into our bedroom. 'Mom, Dad!' he yells. 'I made the coolest castle in the world. You have to see it.' He spins before he has even come to a complete stop, and runs back, expecting us to follow.

Caleb watches me. He cannot take the first step. After all, the only way to communicate is to find someone who can comprehend; the only way to be forgiven is to find someone who is willing to forgive. So I start for the door, turning back at the threshold. 'Come on,' I say to Caleb. 'He needs us.'

It happens when I am trying to come down the stairs superfast, my feet ahead of the rest of me. One of the steps just isn't where it is supposed to be, and I fall really hard onto the railing where hands go. I hit the part of my arm that makes a corner, the part with the name that sounds just like what it is. L-bow.

The hurt feels like a shot, a needle going in right there and spreading out like fire under the rest of my arm. I can't feel my fingers, and my hand goes wide. It hurts more than when I fell on the ice last year and my ankle got as fat as the rest of my leg. It hurts more than when I went over the handlebars of my bike and scraped up the whole front of my face and needed two stitches. It hurts so much that I have to get past the ouch of it before I can remember to cry.

'Moooooooooooom!'

When I yell like that, she can come quick as a ghost, the air empty one minute and full of her the next. 'What hurts?' she cries. She touches all the places I am holding close to myself.

'I think I broke my funny bone,' I say.

'Hmm.' She moves that arm up and down. Again. Then she puts her hands on my shoulders and looks up at me. 'Tell a joke.'

'Mom!'

'How else are we going to know for sure if it's broken?'

I shake my head. 'It doesn't work that way.'

She picks me up and carries me into the kitchen. 'Says who?' She laughs, and before I know it I am laughing back, which must mean I'm going to be okay after all.

JODI PICOULT

Perfect Match

A Readers Club Guide

A Conversation with Jodi Picoult

Q: Your ability to tell a story from so many varying points of view in an engaging and believable manner is impressive. How do you crawl into the minds of so many different characters, with different motivations, insecurities, views on life, etc.? Are there exercises you do to help yourself understand where your characters are coming from?

A: Crawling into the minds of characters is actually one of the best parts of writing for me. After all, I'm never going to get to be a five-year-old boy, so it's a challenge to be able to pull it off. It's a little like trying on a costume – and getting to shrug it off my shoulders when I'm finished. When I write in multiple points of view, I'm very careful to make sure they all sound different, even to me – so that Patrick, for example, doesn't think like Nina, who doesn't think like Caleb. I will even deliberately change the syntax of their sentences, sometimes, to keep everyone separate and equal. As for exercises – the closest I come to this is knowing my characters all very well before I ever start writing for them. For example, we may never see Nina eat breakfast, but I can tell you that she grabs coffee and whatever's left on Nathaniel's plate. Patrick, however, has the same cereal – something healthy – every morning. And so on. If I don't know my characters well enough to provide details like this in a snap, I'm not ready to write in their minds yet.

Q: The scenes where Nathaniel is abused are striking and disturbing. Was it difficult for you, especially as a mother, to imagine yourself into that scenario? Did you know that you were going to include these scenes from the beginning? Were you dreading writing them?

A: You have NO idea! Most of my other books are totally unrelated to my real life, but while writing this one I would go to the breakfast table every morning and talk to my kids, and take their comments and filter them through Nathaniel's sad affect and into his narrative. In addition, many of Nathaniel's ways of looking at the world – poetically, and somehow startling and focused – came from actual experiences I had with my middle son, Jake. You know that 'slice of sky' Nathaniel describes lying on the ground in the first interchapter? Jake said that to me. Putting any piece of my children into Nathaniel was painful – but it also allowed for me to write Nina with heart. Because the more uncomfortable and upset I felt even marginally imagining my children as Nathaniel, she would be feeling a thousand times worse.

I knew that I would put the scenes of abuse in, because I really wanted to explain how and why a child might wind up in that situation – and how a child might feel responsible afterward. So much of the writing that's been done on child sexual abuse focuses on the perpetrators that we sometimes forget to listen to the voices of the victims. So yes, those segments were intentional and necessary and awful and revelatory all at once.

Q: It is interesting, and a bit shocking, that Nina gets away with the murder of Father Szyszynski. Why did you choose to let her go free? Did you have any alternate endings at any point in the process?

A: Actually, the DA I've worked with as a research consultant for several books was the reason I tipped the verdict the way I did. For years now, she's been complaining because I never convict anyone . . . so finally I decided I'd convict a DA. Naturally, she balked. I thought about it some more and realized that on a purely emotional level, the last thing I wanted was for Nathaniel to suffer any more trauma. I wanted the Frosts intact at the end of the book – not left with Mom in jail. So, legally, I chose to go with that freaky clause on the Maine books – the one that says, basically, if you have just cause to be angry enough to kill someone, it's okay. There is never any question that Nina has committed a crime – the question is really whether it's permissible, in certain circumstances, to commit a, crime. (And no, I'm not gonna answer that!) In my opinion, her verdict is an honest one for much the same reason that I felt it was okay to let Chris Harte free at the end of *The Pact:* I don't think Nina is going to go around blowing away people who upset her son. I think this is a one-time act she was driven to, and I think that at the end of the book she has acquired the forethought to reason through the consequences of her actions in a way she isn't capable of doing at the beginning of the book.

Q: The attention to detail regarding DNA analysis, police and court procedures, and medical matters in your novels is flawless. How do you get all your information? For instance, how did you come up with the idea that the priest's semen would match the semen found on Nathaniel's shorts, but would not actually be his?

A: I'm so glad you noticed! I love doing research, and research often drives story ideas for me. When necessary, I will go down to State Forensics labs to work with detectives, I will ride with policemen, I will visit labs. In fact, the reason I wrote this book, in part, came from DNA research I did while writing *Salem Falls:* the researcher mentioned that DNA is damning evidence, because it is accurate in 99.9% of the cases. And being me, I asked, 'What's the other one percent?' Well, the answer lies in the science that I included in *Perfect Match:* a bone marrow recipient doesn't have his own blood anymore. Hence, his bodily fluids will have a DNA different from that of a blood sample taken from his arm . . . which of course would render innacurate any semen evidence that's left behind and matched up via a traditional blood stick.

Q: You must have written this manuscript long before the recent priest scandal broke, but was there a particular news story that inspired this novel?

A: No. However, when I decided to make it a priest who was the perp, I interviewed four priests – all of whom said they knew someone who had been accused or transferred on allegations of sexual abuse. That told me I wasn't pulling this problem out of thin air . . . and that I had a legitimate reason to write the book with that particular plot twist. But then, when real life began to imitate my fiction, it was a little bizarre. I had one interviewer ask me if for my next book I could write about Mideast peace!

Q: Is there some over-arching message that you would like readers to take from this novel?

A: That we never know anyone as well as we think we do – least of all ourselves. And that we shouldn't rush to judgment until we've walked a mile in someone else's shoes. I can't tell you I would do what Nina did in her situation . . . but I can't tell you I wouldn't, either.

Q: What kind of unique challenges did writing *Perfect Match* present to you?

A: One of the most difficult things about *Perfect Match* was that it required me to write with a first-person narrator who was very hard to like! Nina is opinionated, single-minded, and thinks she knows all the right answers, even when she doesn't – there were times I wanted to knock her head against a wall, and I was the AUTHOR! But I had such fun trying on her voice, because she may be wrong, but she's impassioned, and it's very entertaining to write a character who fights you every step of the way. My other first-person narrator – Nathaniel – was equally difficult. I needed him to sound like a five-year-old, which limited my vocabulary and choice of phrase – and yet Nathaniel is much wiser than normal kids his age, because of what happened. That was a fine literary line to walk, too. And yet, I felt both first-person narratives were crucial, because to me, this is really a story about a mother and her child, and I wanted the reader to hear them both.

Q: The following quote near the end of the novel is quite striking: 'Remembering that although the future may unfold in indelible strokes, it doesn't mean we have to read the same line over and over.' Is this line a plea for self-efficacy, or just hope for the future? Do you believe that people can easily shake off the past and start fresh?

A: I'm laughing, because I think I keep changing my mind on this one with every subsequent book! In *Perfect Match*, I definitely come down on the side of free will rather than fate. But in other books, like *Salem Falls*, I've gone the other way. I guess I'm still deciding for myself! I will admit, though, that people who think they can shake off the past are usually wrong. You can build on your past, you can even whitewash over it, but it doesn't ever really go away.

Q: You have been quoted as saying, 'I'm a better mother because I have my writing and I'm a better writer because of the experiences of motherhood that have shaped me.' Discuss your experience of writing this book as a mother. Were there moments when you had to step back from the characters and observe them, not as a mother, but objectively, as an author? If so, was that difficult?

A: This is a hard read for parents of young children. I do believe that sometimes when you're a mother or father, it's just too painful to 'go' somewhere fictionally that you're terrified of in real life. Me, I zoom off in the other direction. I pretend that if I attack a topic that scares me to death, fictionally, it's like a good-luck charm – and I've got immunity from it in real life. (Which means, if you've read my other books, you realize that clearly my children are well protected from all sorts of horrors!) So yes, I had to definitely step back and think of the book from an overseer's perspective . . . but only sometimes. When I started thinking like a mom, I became too sympathetic to Nina. When I stopped thinking like a mom, I wanted to lock her up for life. I think readers will veer between the two extremes, and book clubs will come to blows over them. But actually, that's okay with me. Because the question I am asking is not an easy question, and it shouldn't have an easy answer.

Reading Group Guide for *Perfect Match*

1) Jodi Picoult subtly draws the reader into the delicate emotional lives of these characters through altering points of view. In what ways do the different narrators add to your understanding of individual character motivation as well as overall plot? Did you find that there was extra emotional weight in a novel that so effectively pulls the reader into the thoughts, feelings, and philosophies of such an array of characters?

2) Do you think there are unreliable narrators in this story, characters who either consciously or subconsciously misled you as the reader or even themselves? How do you think the story would have been different had Nina narrated it entirely? How would our view of the main characters differ? Do you think it would have been easier or harder to decipher things like plot and/or character motivation?

3) In what ways did the quotes found at the beginning of each section help inform your read? How did the stories, which seem to be told by Nathaniel, do the same?

4) Motherhood is a central theme in this novel; most of Nina's motivation, at least according to her, comes from her desire to keep her son safe, happy, and away from harm. But were there instances when you questioned Nina's reasons for doing things? Is she as selfless as she claims, or are there other forces at work? When ruminating on Nina's crime, Caleb thinks that 'this is about Nina.' What does he mean by this?

5) Before the rape, it is clear that Nina, although sometimes torn about her decisions, maintains a pretty even 50/50 split regarding her focus on work and her focus on family. She obviously loves her son and would do anything for him, but she keeps her career high on her list of priorities; so much so that when Nathaniel is sick, she ushers him off to school so she can spend the morning at work. Did you find yourself judging Nina for her choices? Do you think she judges herself? Could this have anything to do with her compulsive need to get revenge for Nathaniel? Would you judge her in the same way if she were a man?

6) Quentin Brown is a fascinating character, one who, in some ways, seems to share traits with Nina – at least traits that she had before her life was turned upside down. Discuss Brown's significance in this story. Although he could have been a peripheral character, Picoult really focuses on him, especially in the latter half of the novel, and obviously draws parallels between his character and that of Nina. Why do you think Picoult does this? Does Nina become more self-aware because of her observations of Quentin? What should we make of the fact that Quentin seems to have a breakthrough with his son, at least to some extent, due to Nina's case?

7) Caleb, who in many ways embodies the physical characteristics traditionally assigned men (the wood-chopping mountain man), often acts as a mothering figure in this novel. While Nina haphazardly seeks revenge for her son, Caleb quietly gives Nathaniel support and refuses to pressure the boy, opting instead for a surprising brand of motherly patience and love to get the boy through. What did you make of the fact that Nina takes on the bloodthirsty and angry attitude that one might expect from a father? Even when Caleb kills Father Gwynne, he does so by poisoning him – a mode of killing that is usually associated with women. Do you think Picoult is playing with gender dynamics in this story? Were you surprised when Caleb discloses his secret at the end?

8) Why do you think Nina followed through on her decision to kill the priest? Most mothers want to protect their children from danger, and many feel they could kill for their children if necessary. What, though, is different about Nina, who actually followed through with murdering her son's abuser when 99 percent of mothers don't?

9) Truth is a rather illusive concept in this story. The novel is littered with instances in which characters lie about who they are, what they know, and how they feel when they don't really need to (think about the scenes where Patrick and Caleb lie about what they do to complete strangers for absolutely no reason). Why is there so much dishonesty or withholding of the truth in this story? Is truth completely unattainable? In Nina's case, is it enough that she *believes* that she is doing the right thing when she lies, tells half-truths, or gives misleading statements, or is there a larger, unerring sense of justice that permeates this story?

10) On page 277, Nina admits, 'And I think, not for the first time, that what is immoral is not always wrong.' What kind of distinction do you think she is trying to make between morality and justice? Do you agree with her? Were you surprised when Nina slept with Patrick? Did you think it was 'wrong'? Is Nina acknowledging the subjective nature of truth here, or is she simply lying to herself to avoid guilt? What do you think Caleb would say?

11) In what ways does the setting work with the story to highlight, call attention to, or make more important the emotional lives of the characters? How central do you consider location to the story itself? Would this have been the same story if it had been set, for instance, in Los Angeles? How does this close-knit community in Maine help to establish the boundaries and inflexible moral world that the characters live in?

12) Near the end of the novel, Nina says, in a conversation with Patrick, 'The right thing, is thinking before I act, so that I stop hurting the people I love.' Do you think that, by the end of the story, Nina has learned something about herself and the way that she looks at/handles life that will serve her well in the future?

13) While on the stand, Nina says, 'The reality, as you know, is that the rules in court are not written to protect children, but to protect defendants.' Ideally, in our legal system, everyone is supposed to be protected. Do you agree with Nina that the system as it currently operates protects perpetrators more often than victims? Do you think the legal system should be changed? Has this book altered your opinion? Did you feel that justice was served when Nina, literally, got away with murder?

Once you've read one, you'll want ot read them all . . .

Plain Truth

£6.99 Paperback
OUT NOW

My Sister's Keeper

£6.99 Paperback
OUT NOW

Vanishing Acts

£12.99 Hardback
OUT NOW

The Pact

£6.99 Paperback
OUT NOW

Salem Falls

£6.99 Paperback
Publishing November 2005

Keeping Faith

£12.99 Hardback
Publishing January 2006

Tenth Circle

£12.99 Hardback
Publishing April 2006